ENTER THE WOLF

WAY OF THE WOLF   Copyright © 2003 by Eric E. Frisch
   Publication History: Roc mass market, September 2003
CHOICE OF THE CAT   Copyright © 2004 by Eric Frisch
   Publication History: Roc mass market, May 2004
TALE OF THE THUNDERBOLT   Copyright © 2005 by Eric Frisch
   Publication History: Roc mass market, March 2005

First Science Fiction Book Club Printing: February 2013

Selected by Rome Quezada, SFBC Senior Editor

Published by arrangement with
The Penguin Group (USA), Inc./ The Berkley Publishing Group, Ace
375 Hudson Street
New York, NY 10014

Visit The SFBC online at http://www.sfbc.com

ISBN # 978-1-62490-012-9

Printed in the United States of America.

ENTER THE WOLF

VAMPIRE EARTH VOLUME 1:
*Way of the Wolf, Choice of the Cat,
and Tale of the Thunderbolt*

E. E. Knight

**SFBC
SCIENCE
FICTION**

Contents

Foreword

I owe a good deal of happiness to the dark little journey you are about
to undertake, reader. When *Way of the Wolf* first appeared on the
shelves nationwide ten years ago in 2003, a decades-old dream came
true.

Ironic that it was a nightmare that started it all off.

During my boyhood, we lived on a suburban cul-de-sac on the outskirts of town, woods and lakes dark and deep beyond our houselights.
A single street light, centered in our front yard, illuminated the circle of
homes. One fall night, and I'm still not sure if this is dream or fantasy,
my early-teen self was looking out my bedroom window and I saw a
long cloaked figure standing up against the lamp-post, still as a tomb-
stone. It was featureless, arms lost in the sleeves of its coat and face invisible, save for the glowing Nazgûl-eyes, eyes that winked on and off
like synchronized fireflies as it watched our house. Or maybe me.

I'd just seen, or maybe imagined, my first Reaper.

I was too scared to yell, or do much other than remain frozen there,
hoping it didn't see me. Next thing I knew it was morning, and I convinced myself, more or less, that it had been an unusually vivid dream
(I've never been much of a dreamer, and when I do remember details,
it's mundane day-to-day stuff, like brushing my teeth or walking along
the side of the road).

That Thing watching the house had to be let out of my mind, so I
worked it into a role-playing game world for a post-apocalyptic game
called "Aftermath." We played post-apocalypse when we wanted a
break from the fantasy of Advanced Dungeons and Dragons or the SF
games in our repertoire. Out of that nightmare image, I created scenar-
ios about a world dominated by rival vampire cults. It proved popular

with the gaming group, as I recall, because more than just surviving, the players were trying to get rid of the vampires, which made for a great continuing storyline.

The gaming group broke up and we went off to our different colleges and I forgot about that world until I had an early-midlife crisis, the result of a liberal arts major's series of disappointing post-collegiate jobs. I seemed to be just spinning my wheels in life and one night, some mix of bad relationship, boring job, alcohol, and conversation with the mirror led to a resolve to accomplish a few of the goals I'd outlined for my life back when I was examining options for life after high school. I'd long dabbled in fiction and had placed "write a novel" on the list, probably as a one-shot goal like *climb Mt. Rainier*. So I read a few how-to books, took a couple of writing classes at the local community college, and set down to write a genre novel.

What resulted was maybe the worst cyberthriller ever written, a desperately bad first effort called *Pipeline*. I knew it was too awful to submit anywhere, and in my despair talked to the closest writer I knew, my aunt, an author of children's books. She asked me why I wrote a cyberthriller, and I answered that they were very popular at the moment – it was the mid-90s and *Johnny Mnemonic* was on the big screen.

"There's your mistake," she said. "You're writing what you think the audience wants. Write a story you want to read. It's the only way you'll really enjoy what you're doing, whether you ever get published or not."

At that, the proverbial light-bulb went off over my head. To be honest, I didn't really like cyberthrillers. I liked slam-bang action, John W. Campbell-esque capable-type heroes, Lovecraftian monstrosities and grim landscapes. I dusted off the old vampire cult world and set about creating a hero to blaze a trail through it.

I changed a few things. Rather than setting it a couple years after the vamps took over, I set in two generations after, deciding I wanted my hero to mimic Orwell's Winston Smith from *1984*, who was trying in dribs and drabs to get an idea of what life was like before the Party and the Ministry of Truth. I made the vampires a little more remote and alien and had them operate mostly through their Reapers and the human Quislings aiding them. I also decided I wanted to try and do a Hornblower type long series, save I'd shake up the usual pattern of "young, capable officer rises" by having David Valentine fail now and again and practically become an outcast. You'll note that I quote Churchill in the novel. "Success is not final, failure is not fatal: it is the courage to continue that counts" is another quote of his, very much to-the-point where Val is concerned.

By the time I finished what became *Way of the Wolf*, I had a new outlook on life. This grim little world served as something of a reboot, personally and professionally (I wound up working for a major consulting firm while putting together *Choice of the Cat*). By the time I was drafting *Tale of the Thunderbolt*, I was engaged to my wife Stephanie. We have three children now.

Even so, it was a rocky path to publication, and Vampire Earth might never have seen the Reaper-chasing light of day save for an experimental e-book imprint called iPublish. The editor there, Paul Witcover, shaped it into a much better story both in structure and prose style. The imprint disappeared in the aftermath of the dot-com meltdown in 2001, but it had done well enough that Laura Anne Gilman at Roc was willing to take a gamble on a three-book deal.

That's how that scary cloaked figure against the lamppost ended up in your hands. There are a lot of dreams, and nightmares, bound up in these pages. I hope you enjoy them.

E.E. Knight
February 2013

WAY OF
THE WOLF

To Mom and Dad, who believed

Have you ever dealt with people who have lost everything in just an hour? In the morning you leave the house where your wife, your children, your parents live. You return and you find a smoking pit. Then something happens to you—to a certain extent you stop being human. You do not need any glory, money anymore; revenge becomes your only joy. And because you no longer cling to life, death avoids you, the bullets fly past. You become a wolf.

—Russian General Aleksander Lebed,
veteran of Afghanistan

One

Northern Louisiana, March, the forty-third year of the Kurian Order: The green expanse once known as the Kisatchie Forest slowly digests the works of man. A forest in name only, it is a jungle of wet heat and dead air, a fetid overflowing of swamps, bayous, and backwaters. The canopy of interwoven cypress branches shrouded in Spanish moss creates a gloom so thick that twilight rules even at midday. In the muted light, collapsing houses subside every which way as roadside stops decay in vine-choked isolation, waiting for traffic that will not return.

A long file of people is moving among moss-covered trunks to the piping cries of startled birds. At the front and rear of the column are men and women in buckskin, their faces tanned to the same weather-beaten color as their leather garments. They carry sheathed rifles, and all are ready to use their weapons at the first hint of danger. The guns are for the defense of five clusters of families clad in ill-fitting lemon-colored overalls at the center of the file. Patches of brighter color under the arms and along the inner thighs suggest the garments once glowed a vivid optic yellow and are now faded from heavy use. A string of five pack mules follows behind them under the guidance of teenage versions of the older warriors.

At the head of the column, well behind a pair of silent scouts, a young man scans the trail. He still has some of the awkward gangliness of youth, but his dark eyes hold a canny depth. His shoulder-length black hair, tightly tied at the back of his head, shines like a raven's feathers even in the half-light. With his dusky skin and buckskin garb, he could be mistaken for a native resident of this area three centuries before: perhaps the son of some wandering French trapper and a Choctaw maiden. His long-fingered hands wander across his

heavy belt, from holstered pistol to binoculars, touching the haft of his
broad-bladed parang before moving on to the canteens at his waist.
A scratched and battered compass case dangles from a black nylon cord
around his neck, and a stout leather map tube bumps his back from its
slung position. Unlike his men, he is hatless. He turns now and again to
check the positions of his soldiers and to examine the faces of his
yellow-clad dependents as if gauging how much distance is left in their
weary bodies. But his restless eyes do not remain off the trail for long.

If they come, they'll come tonight. Lt. David Valentine returned to
that thought again as the sun vanished below the horizon. He had
hoped to get his charges farther north of the old interstate before nightfall, but progress had slowed on this, their fourth day out from Red
River Crossing. He and his Wolves shielded twenty-seven men, women,
and children who had hazarded the run to freedom. The families were
now adapted to the rigors of the trail, and followed orders well. But
they came from a world where disobedience meant death, so that trait
was understandable.

If they had been traveling by themselves, the detachment of Wolves
would already be in the Free Territory. But Valentine was responsible
for seeing the Red River farmhands brought safely north. Four hours
ago, the yellow-clad group had crossed the final barrier: the road and
rail line connecting Dallas with the Mississippi at Vicksburg. Then
Valentine had driven them another two miles. Now they had little left
to give.

It was hard to quiet his mind, with so much to think about on his
first independent command in the Kurian Zone. And quieting his mind,
keeping lifesign down, was literally a question of life and death with
night coming on. Being a Wolf was as much a matter of mental as
physical discipline, for the Reapers sensed the activity of human minds,
especially when fearful and tense. Every Wolf had a method of subsum-
ing consciousness into a simpler, almost feral form. But burdened with
new responsibilities and with night swallowing the forest, Valentine
struggled against the worries that shot up like poisonous weeds in his
mind. The Reapers read lifesign better at night. His charges were giving off enough to be read for miles even in the depths of the Kisatchie.
If his Wolves' minds were added to the total, the Reapers would home
on it like moths drawn to a bonfire.

A trilling call from ahead broke into his anxieties. Valentine raised
his arm, halting the column. Garnett, one of his scouts, gestured to him.

"Water, sir, in that little holler," the scout reported as Valentine came
up. "Looks safe enough."

"Good. We'll rest there for an hour," Valentine said, loudly enough for the column to hear. "No more. We're still too close to the road to camp."

The faces of the farm families brightened in contrast to the deepening night as they drank from the spring trickling down the side of a shallow ravine. Some removed shoes and rubbed aching feet. Valentine unscrewed the cap on his plastic canteen, waiting until the families and his men had a chance to drink.

A faint yelping echoed from the south. Wolves dived for cover behind trees and fallen logs. The yellow-clad families, who lacked the ability to hear the baying, shrank together in alarm at the sudden movement.

Sergeant Patel, Valentine's senior noncommissioned officer, appeared at his elbow. "Dogs? Very bad luck, sir. Or . . ."

Valentine, careering along in his runaway train of thought, only half heard Patel's words. The families broke out in noisy consternation.

"Silence," Valentine rasped at the civilians, his voice cracking with unaccustomed harshness. "Sergeant, who knows this area best?"

Patel's eyes did not leave the woods to the south. "Maybe Lugger, sir. Or the scouts. Lugger pulled a lot of patrols in this area; I think her people lived westaways."

"Would you get her, please?"

Patel pointed to and brought up Lugger, a seasoned veteran whose limber, sparse frame belied her name. She held her rifle in hands with alabaster knuckles.

"Sir?" she breathed.

"Lugger, we may have to do some shooting soon," Valentine said in an undertone, trying not to alarm the unsettled civilians. "Where's a good spot for it?"

Her eyes wandered skyward in thought. "There's an old barn we used to use on patrol. West of here, more like northwest, I reckon. Concrete foundation, and the loft's in good shape."

"How long to get there?"

"Under an hour, sir, even with them," she said, jerking her chin toward the huddled families. Their yellow overalls now looked bluish in the darkness. Valentine nodded encouragement.

"Solid foundation," she repeated. "And a big water trough. We used to keep it filled with a rain catcher."

Make a decision.

"No help in that direction. Mallow's more to the east, but it will have to do," Valentine said. Mallow, the senior lieutenant of Zulu Company, had remained in the borderlands with a cache of supplies to help them make it the rest of the way to the Ozark Free Territory. He considered something else. "Think you could find the rendezvous at night?"

"God willing, sir," she responded after a moment's cogitation.

"Take a spare canteen and run. Ask Mallow to come with everything he can."

"Yes, sir. But I don't need my gun to keep me company. I think you'll need every bullet you got before morning," she said, unslinging her rifle.

Valentine nodded. "Let's not waste time. Tell Patel where to go; then run for our lives."

Lugger handed her rifle to the senior aspirant, spoke briefly to Patel and the scouts, then disappeared into the darkness. Valentine listened with hard ears to her fading footfalls, as fast as his beating heart, and thought, *Please, Mallow, for God's sake forget about the supplies and come quick.*

As his men dusted the area around the spring with crushed red pepper, Valentine approached the frightened families.

"They found us?" asked Fred Brugen, the patriarch of the group. Valentine smiled into their dirty, tired faces.

"We heard something behind us. Could be they cut our trail—could be a dog got the wrong end of a skunk. But as I said, we have to play it safe and move to a better place to sleep. Sorry to cut the halt short."

The refugees winced and tightened their mouths at the news, but did not complain. Complainers disappeared in the night in the Kurian Zone.

"The good news is that we're really close to a place we can rest and get a hot meal or two. Personally, I'm getting sick of corn bread and jerky." He squatted down to the kids' level and forced some extra enthusiasm into his voice. "Who wants hot-cakes for breakfast tomorrow morning?"

The kids lit up like fireflies, nodding with renewed energy.

"Okay, then," he finished as he filled his canteen, forcing himself to go through the motions nonchalantly. "Everybody take one more drink of water, and let's go."

The aspirants somehow got the pack mules moving, and the column trudged forward into the darkness. With curses matching the number of stumbles brought on by confusion and fatigue in the night, the column continued north. Valentine led the way. A rope around his waist stretched back to Sergeant Patel at the tail end of the file. He bade the families to hold on to it to keep everyone together in the dark.

One scout guided him, and a second brought up the rear, in close contact with two fire teams shepherding the column's tail, their phosphorous candles ready. If the enemy was close enough for their dogs to be heard, the Reapers could be upon them at any moment. Valentine resigned himself to the orders he would give if they were set upon in the open: he would abandon his charges and flee north. Even a few Wolves were more valuable to the Free Territory than a couple of dozen farmers.

Valentine, continuing on that grim line of thought, decided that if he were a battle-hardened veteran from the campfire stories, he would stake the farmers out like goats to a prowling tiger, then ambush whatever took the bait. The death of the defenseless goat was worth getting the tiger. Those win-at-all-costs leaders from the Old World history books would never be swayed by sleepy voices repeatedly asking, "Is it much farther, Momma?"

"Close up and move on. Close up and move on," Valentine said over his shoulder, hurrying the column. Wolves picked up tired children, carrying them as easily as they bore their weapons.

They found the farm exactly as Lugger had described. Her Wolf's eye for terrain and detailed memory of places and paths would astound anyone who did not know the caste.

The barn was a little bigger than Valentine would have liked with only twenty-two guns. *No time to be picky, not with the Reapers on our trail,* he thought. Anyplace with the trees cleared away and walls would have to do.

Garnett entered with blade unsheathed, covered by his comrades' hunting bows and rifles. The parang—a shortened machete used by the Wolves—gleamed in the mist-shrouded moonlight. A few bats fluttered out, disturbed from their pursuit of insects among the rafters. The scout appeared at the loft door and waved the rest in. Valentine led the others inside, fighting a disquieting feeling that something was wrong. Perhaps his Indian blood perceived something tickling below his conscious threshold. He had spent enough time on the borders of the Kurian Zone to know that his sixth sense was worth paying attention to, though hard to qualify. The danger was too near somehow, but ill defined. He finally dismissed it as the product of overwrought nerves.

Valentine inspected the sturdy old barn. The water trough was full, which was good, and there were shaded lanterns and oil, which was better.

Patel posted the men to the doors and windows. Cracks in the walls of the time-ravaged structure made handy loopholes. The exhausted families threw themselves down in a high-walled inner corner. Valentine trotted to the hayloft ladder and began to climb. Someone had repaired a few of the rungs, he noticed as he went up squeaking wood. The barn's upper level smelled like bat urine. From the loft he watched his second scout, Gonzalez, backing into the barn, rifle pointed into the darkness.

"Gonzo's got wind of 'em, sir," Garnett reported from his perch at the upper door. "He always gets bug-eyed when *they're* around."

Three Wolves from downstairs joined them in the loft and took positions on each side of the barn. Valentine glanced down through a gap in the loft floor to the lower level, where Patel talked quietly to Gonzalez in the dim light of a screened lantern. Both glanced up into the loft. Gonzalez nodded and climbed the ladder.

"Sir, the sarge wanted me to show you this," he reported, extending a filthy and stinking piece of cloth drawn from his pocket.

Valentine reached out to take the rag, when a chorus of shrieks sounded from down the hill in the direction of the old road. He spun and ran to the wide loft door.

Garnett cursed. "Ravies, goddamn Ravies!"

The banshee wailing out of the midnight mists turned the back of his neck into a bristle-brush. *They're here!* He bent to the gap in the floor and called out to the Wolves. "Keep to your posts, look to your fronts! The Ravies might be a ruse. They could be on top of the hill already."

He ran to the ladder and clambered down the rungs two at a time, driving a splinter into the flesh opposite his thumb in his haste. Wincing, he unsnapped the leather strap of his parang sheath and drew his revolver.

"Uncle, the flares!" he shouted, but Patel knew better than to wait for an order. The veteran sergeant already stood at the gaping southern door, lighting one. A Wolf opened a lantern door so he could thrust it in. The high-pitched shrieking grew louder, until it filled the night.

The firework burst into flame, illuminating the barn with blue-white light and sharp black shadows. Patel wound up and threw the burning flare down the slope they had just traversed. Before it landed, he lit another and hurled it into the darkness, as well. Other Wolves copied him, tossing phosphorus candles in each direction.

Valentine stared down the hill, transfixed by a mob emerging into the glare. Running figures with arms thrashing as if trying to swim through the air swept up toward the barn. Seemingly endless supplies of wind powered their screams. Their siren wail was paralyzing. They were human, or what amounted to human, considering their minds burned with madness, but with the wasted look of corpses and sparse streams of unkempt hair. Few wore more than tatters of clothing; most ran naked, their skin pale in the light of burning phosphorus.

"Don't let 'em in close enough to bite. Drop 'em, goddammit!" Patel bellowed.

Shots rang out in the enclosed lower level of the barn. Ravies fell, one rising again with blood pouring from his neck, to stagger a few paces and fall once more, this time for good. Another had a bullet tear through her shoulder, spinning her around like a puppet with tangled strings. She regained her balance and came on, screaming all the while. What looked like a scrawny ten-year-old boy stepped on one of the flaring candles without a glance.

Valentine watched as the human wave approached, dribbling bodies as the Wolves' bullets struck. He knew the Ravies served as a distraction for something else lurking in the night. He felt the Reaper stalking his mind, approaching from the darkness, even if he could not see its body.

The Reaper came, full of awful speed and power. A cloaked figure charged into the light, seeming to fly over the ground in a blur of motion.

"Hood!" a Wolf shouted, squeezing off a shot and working the bolt on his rifle. The caped and cowled figure, still twenty feet from the barn, made a leap and crashed bodily through the old planks and beams as if they were papier-mâché.

The Reaper landed on all fours, arms and legs splayed like a spider. Before a gun could be turned in its direction, it sprang at the nearest Wolf, a shovel-bearded wedge of a man named Selbey. It was upon him before he could bring up his gun. The Hood's satchel-size mouth opened to display pointed ebony teeth. Large, inhuman jaws sank into Selbey's arm, thrown up in defense. The Wolf's scream matched those from outside as the thing opened its mouth to bite again.

Chaos reigned as the refugees began running. Wolves at the exits had to restrain them, taking up precious seconds when they should have been employing their guns. One Wolf pumped shot after shot, working the lever-action rifle from his hip, into the Reaper pressing Selbey to the detritus-covered floor. The Reaper fed, immune to the bullets hitting its heavy robes.

Valentine grabbed a candle flare from Patel's two remaining at the south door. He thrust the candle into the lantern, waiting for it to sputter into life. It caught after an eternity, and he ran toward the Hood.

The thing raised its blood-smeared face from its twitching victim to receive the burning end in its eye. It howled out its fury and pain and slapped the candle out of Valentine's hand with the speed of a cougar's paw. The flaming wand fell to the ground as the thing rose. Behind it, the Reaper's menacing black shadow filled the wall of the barn. Death reached for Valentine, who struggled to draw his blade from its sheath in time.

A bullet caught the Reaper in the armpit, staggering it. A heavier leather-clad missile hurled itself onto the Hood's back. Patel's body blow brought it down, and using every ounce of his formidable strength, the sergeant managed to keep it on the floor until Valentine brought his machete onto the back of its neck. The blade bit deep into flesh and bone, but failed to sever the head. Oily, ink-black ichor poured from the wound, but still the thing rose, rolling Patel off with a heave. The sergeant fought on and bore down on one arm, ignoring the deadly teeth opening for him. Valentine lashed out again with his machete, catching it under the jaw. The Reaper's head arced off to land with a thud next to Selbey's lifeless body.

"Jesus, they're in, they're in!" someone shouted.

A few Ravies, ghoulishly white in the glare of the candle, clambered through the gap in the wall created by the decapitated Reaper. Valentine shifted his parang to his left hand and reached for his pistol. The empty holster turned the movement into comic mime as he realized he had dropped the gun while getting the candle. But other Wolves drew their pistols, snapping off a shot at the shrieking forms.

The screaming grew into a chorus: a Ravie plunged in among the families. Valentine rushed to the corner to find the howling lunatic pinned against the wall by a man who'd had the presence of mind to grab an old pitchfork when the fight started. The Ravie had both hands on the haft of the weapon, trying to wrench the tines out of her belly, when Valentine came in, swinging his parang to strike and strike and strike again until she sank lifeless to the floor, at long last silent.

The screaming outside had ceased. The Wolves opened ammunition pouches and took bullets from belts and bandoliers. A final bullet or two ended the spasms of the few crawling, crippled targets still living and therefore still dangerous. The men in the loft called downstairs, in anxiety over their comrades. Valentine ignored the chatter and saw with a kind of weary grief that one of the wives had been bitten by the impaled Ravie. He went to check on Patel. The husky sergeant was on his feet, one arm hanging limp and useless, Valentine's pistol in his working hand.

Patel handed the pistol back to the lieutenant. "Quiet, up there! And keep your eyes peeled," the sergeant shouted at the uncomprehending floorboards above. He held his hurt arm closer to his body, grimacing.

"Broken collarbone, I think," he explained. "Could be my shoulder is out, as well. Are you okay, sir?"

"Hell, Patel, enough is enough. Next it'll be 'I hope you liked your drink.' Let's get that arm in a sling, for a start." Valentine motioned an idle Wolf over to help his sergeant. He saw another of his men bandaging the Ravie bite on the woman as her anxious family crowded around. "We've got a widower there who doesn't know it yet," he said, sotto voce. His sergeant nodded with sad understanding, and Valentine thought of Patel's family. They had been taken by the Raving Madness five years ago.

The lieutenant walked through his shaken command, checking on his men, and came into the corner sheltering the escapees. He shot a significant glance at his Wolf attending to the woman; the man caught the hint and nodded. "The bleeding's stopped already, sir."

"Quick action, Mosley. Grab someone and get that"—he pointed at the lifeless Ravie—"out of here."

The candles outside were sputtering out. Valentine walked over to the ladder, intending to check with Gonzalez upstairs . . .

. . . when the floor suddenly tilted beneath his feet. Thrown to the floor, he saw an albino-white arm open a heavy trapdoor in an explosion of dirt, dried leaves, and twigs.

The barn had a cellar.

The Reaper got halfway out the trapdoor as the bullets zipped over Valentine's head. His Wolves, still keyed up from the fight, aimed their guns with lethal accuracy and pumped bullet after bullet into the yellow-eyed creature. Under the point-blank cross fire from five directions, the black-robed shape jerked wildly and fell back into the basement.

"Grenades," Valentine bellowed. Three of his men gathered at the trapdoor, now shooting down with pistols.

Striking matches or using the lanterns, two Wolves lit fuses on the bombs and hurled them down the square hole. Valentine grabbed the trapdoor and flung it shut. The rusty hinges squealed their complaints.

The first explosion threw the door forever off its aged fastenings, and the second boomed with an earsplitting roar. Smoke mushroomed from the square hole.

A Reaper sprang from the gap like something a magician had conjured from the smoke, arms nothing but two tarry stumps, and head a bony mask of horror. Even with its face blown off, the Reaper was on its feet and running, seeming to favor them with a splay-toothed grin. The guns rang out again, but the creature fled through the exit, knocking Patel aside like a bowling pin in the path of a cannonball as the sergeant attempted another body blow. A tattered and smoldering cape streaming out behind it as it ran, the Reaper disappeared into the darkness.

Some of the children had hands over their ears, screaming in pain. Valentine tried to shake the drunken sensation that had come over him, but it was no use. The acrid air of the barn was too thick to breathe. He staggered to the doorjamb and vomited.

*   *   *

An hour later, with the barn cleared of bodies except for the unfortunate Selbey, who lay in his poncho in the empty blackness of the blasted cellar, Gonzalez again shared his discovery with Valentine. His scout, after asking for permission to speak privately in the loft, presented him with a filthy strip of cloth.

Valentine examined the excrement-stained yellow rag with tired eyes.

"Uncle smelled something, sir, you know? He told me to check the area where we heard the bloodhounds real careful after everyone pulled out. I found this in the bushes where the Red River people . . . er, relieved themselves, sir," Gonzalez elaborated, half whispering.

He read the semiliterate scrawl by lantern light: "N + W, barn, about twenty gun, yrs trly."

Betrayal. That explains a thing or two. But which one is "yrs trly"? Valentine wondered. He remembered a couple of the farmhands had hurried to the bushes as they assembled for the flight to the barn. He hadn't thought anything of it at the time: the fear in the night had turned his own bowels to water, as well.

He gathered three Wolves from downstairs and explained what he wanted to do when the sun came up.

Mallow and his reserve platoon trotted up to the barn, just beating the sun. He suppressed the urge to hug the panting Lugger, who looked as tired as Valentine felt.

The senior lieutenant responded to Valentine's report with a low whistle. "One in the basement, huh? You had some bad luck, rookie. But it could have been worse. Good thing the Kurian pulling the strings wasn't good enough to work more than one at a time." Mallow shook Valentine's hand, then offered the junior lieutenant a congratulatory swig of busthead from a silver flask.

Valentine tippled gratefully, remembering his mother's warning about men who drank before noon. Well, the sun wasn't up yet, so it didn't quite constitute morning.

"The Kurian had a little help, sir. Someone was sending the Hoods love notes. They knew we'd make for that barn; they brought up the Ravies and had everything ready."

"Aw, Christ," Mallow groaned. "Some clodhopper thought he'd be up for a brass ring, huh?"

"Seems like."

"What a welcome to Free Territory. One of their own dangling from a tree. No, I'll let them handle it back at the fort."

"I lost a Wolf, sir. They'll want quick justice." Valentine had hoped they would settle for a formal trial later, but the looks on his detail's faces when he told them why he wanted the farmers searched made him doubtful.

Mallow's face clouded over. "They'll obey orders, Valentine, or they'll see some quick justice. Tell 'em that, if you must."

"Yessir."

Mallow stepped inside the barn. The sky to the east was pinkening, ending the longest night of Valentine's young life. He nodded to his waiting Wolves, and they roused the sleepy farmers and began checking pockets and packs.

They had barely begun when the guilty party revealed himself. A sixteen-year-old boy, the one whose mother had been bitten the previous night, bolted for the gaping south doors. Two of Mallow's Wolves interposed and restrained him. Valentine found a charcoal pencil wrapped in more rags of cloth, as well as a small compass.

"A kid, whaddaya know," one of the men sighed. A couple of others swore.

The boy broke down, alternating threats and curses in between sobs. His ashen-faced father held his distraught wife. She already trembled with the weakness of the first stage of the disease that would claim her life within two or three more days, when she would have to be shot like a rabid dog. Mallow and Patel ignored the grieving parents and questioned the boy in time-honored good cop–bad cop fashion.

"Who put you up to this, boy?" Mallow asked, leaning to put his face below the boy's downcast eyes. "What did they promise you? If it were up to this guy here, he'd snap your neck with his good arm. I can't help you unless you talk to me. Tell you what, you leave another note, only write on it what we tell you, and you won't get hanged. Can't promise anything else, but you won't hang."

The boy's fear exploded into anger. "You don't get it, do you? They're in charge, not you. They make the laws. They run the show. An' when they get tired of you, you'll be emptied an' the Grogs'll have the leftovers! Them that don't want to die gotta go along with orders."

Valentine, sick with fatigue, stepped outside to watch the dawn. As the yellow-orange sun burned through the morning haze, he wondered what doom of fate had selected him to be born into such a fucked-up time.

Two

Northern Minnesota, the thirty-ninth year of the Kurian Order: He grew up in a pastoral setting among the lakes of upper Minnesota. David Stuart Valentine was born during one of the interminable winters in a sturdy brick house on Lake Carver. The scattered settlements of that area owed their survival not so much to resistance as to inaccessibility. The Kurians dislike cold weather, leaving the periodic sweeps and patrols of this area to their Quislings. The Reapers come only in the summer in a macabre imitation of the fishermen and campers who once visited the lakes between May and September.

In the first few years after the Overthrow, myriad refugees supported themselves amid the abundant lakes and woods of what had been known as the Boundary Waters. They exterminated the remaining disease-infested Ravies hotzones, but the settlers refused aid to would-be guerrilla bands, as most of them had already tasted Reaper reprisals elsewhere. They wished nothing more than to be left alone. The Boundary Waters people were ruled only by the weather. A frantic period of food storage marked each fall, and when snow came, the families settled in for winter, ice-fishing for survival, not sport. In summer they retreated into the deep woods far from the roads, returning to their houses after the Reapers were again driven south by the cold.

Young David's family reflected the diaspora that found refuge in the region. He had a collection of Scandinavian, American Indian, and even Asian ancestors in a family tree whose roots stretched from Québec to San Francisco. His mother was a beautiful and athletic Sioux from Manitoba, his father a former navy pilot.

His father's stories made the world a bigger place for David than it was for most of the children his age. He dreamed of flying across the

Pacific Ocean the way some boys dream of being a pirate or building a raft and drifting down the Mississippi.

His early life came to an abrupt stop at the age of eleven, on a cool September day that saw the first frost of the northern fall. The family had just returned from summer retreat to their home, but a Quisling patrol or two still lingered. Judging from the tire tracks that David found later, two trucks—probably the slow, alcohol-burning kind favored by rural patrols—had pulled up to the house. Perhaps the occupants were also liquor fueled. The patrol emptied the larder and then decided to spend the rest of the afternoon raping David's mother. Attracted by the sound of the vehicles, his father had died in a hail of gunfire as he came up from the lakeshore. David heard the shots while gathering wild corn. He hurried home, accompanied by a growing fear that the shots had come from his house.

David explored the too-silent house. The smell of tomatoes, which his mother had been stewing, filled the four-room cabin. He found his mother first, her body violated, her throat slit. Out of spite or habit, the intruders had also killed his little brother, who had just learned to write his own name, and then his baby sister. He did not cry—eleven-year-old men don't cry, his dad said. He circled the house to find his father lying dead in the backyard. A crow was perched on the former pilot's shoulder, pecking at the brains exposed by a baseball-size hole blown out of the back of his skull.

He walked to the Padre's. Putting one foot in front of the other came hard; for some reason he just wanted to lie down and sleep. Then the Padre's familiar lane appeared. The priest's home served as school, church, and public library for the locals. David appeared out of the chilly night air and told the cleric what he had heard and seen, and then offered to walk with the Padre all the way back to his house. The saddened priest put the boy to bed in his basement. The room became David's home for the remainder of his adolescence.

A common grave received the four victims of old sins loosed by the New Order. David threw the first soil onto the burial shrouds that masked the violence of their deaths. After the funeral, as little groups of neighbors broke up, David walked away with the Padre's hand resting comfortingly on his shoulder. David looked up at the priest and decided to ask the question that had been troubling him.

"Father Max, did anyone eat their souls?"

Every day at school they had to memorize a Bible verse, proverb, or saying. Often there was a lot of writing down and not much memorizing. Sometimes the lines had something to do with the day's lesson, sometimes not. The quotation prescribed for the rainy last day of classes had an extra significance to the older students who stayed on for a week after the grade-schoolers escaped the humid classroom for the summer. Their special lessons might have been called the "Facts of Death." The Padre hoped to correct some of the misinformation born of rumor and legend, then fill in the gaps about what had happened since the Overthrow, when *Homo sapiens* lost its position at the top of the food chain. The material was too grim for some of the younger students, and the parents of others objected, so this final week of class was sparsely attended.

The Padre pointed to the quotation again as he began the afternoon's discussion. Father Maximillian Argent was made to point, with his long graceful arms and still-muscular shoulders. Sixty-three years and many long miles from the place of his birth in Puerto Rico, the Padre's hair was only now beginning to reflect the salt-and-pepper coloring of age. He was the sort of pillar a community could rest on, and when he spoke at meetings, the residents listened to his rich, melodious, and impeccably enunciated voice as attentively as his students did.

The classroom blackboard that day had fourteen words written on it. In Father Max's neat, scripted handwriting, the words THE FARTHER BACKWARD YOU CAN LOOK, THE FARTHER FORWARD YOU CAN SEE.— WINSTON CHURCHILL were written with Euclidean levelness on the chalkboard. Normally Valentine would have been interested in the lecture, as he liked history. But his eye was drawn out the window, where the rain still showed no sign of letting up. He had even used the leaky roof as an excuse to shift his desk to the left so that it pressed right against the wall under the window, and the chipped white basin where his desk usually sat was now full enough with rainwater falling from the ceiling to add a plop every now and then as punctuation to the Padre's lesson. Valentine searched the sky for a lessening of the drizzle. Today was the final day of the Field Games, and that meant the Cross-Country Run. If the Councilmen canceled the games because of weather, he would finish where he now stood in the ranking: third.

The youths came from all over the Central Boundary Waters to compete against others in their age group each spring as part of the general festivities that ended the winter and began the great Hideout. This year Valentine had a shot at winning first prize. Second and third place got you a hearty handshake and an up-close look at the trophy as whoever came in first received it. The prize for boys aged sixteen to eighteen was a real over-under shotgun, not a hunting musket, and fifty bird-shot shells. A good gun meant a bountiful hunting season. The Padre and David needed all the help they could get. The Padre taught more or less for free, and Valentine didn't earn much at his job chopping endless cords of firewood for the neighbors. If Valentine won, he and Father Max would be dining on goose, duck, and pheasant until well after the snow flew.

"Mr. Valentine," Father Max said, interrupting David's mental meal. "Please rejoin the class. We're talking about a very important subject . . . your heritage."

"Funny," whispered Doyle from a desk behind. "I don't remember him saying anything about what a stupid son of a bitch you are."

Plop, added the basin to his right.

The Padre cracked his knuckles in a callused fist; profane jokes out of Doyle were as natural as water dripping into the classroom when it rained. He evidently chose to ignore both, keeping his eyes fixed on David.

"Sorry, Father," Valentine said with as much contrition as a seventeen-year-old boy could summon.

"You can apologize to the class by reviewing what you know about the Pre-entities."

Another whisper from behind: "This'll be short."

The Padre shifted his gaze. "Thank you for volunteering two hours of your free time to school maintenance, Mr. Doyle. The roof and I are grateful. Your summary, Mr. Valentine?"

Plop.

Valentine could hear Doyle slump in his seat. "They go back to before the dinosaurs, Father. They made the Gates, those doorways that connect different planets. The Interworld Tree. It's how the Kurians got here, right?"

Father Max held up his hand, palm outward. The thumb was missing from his right hand, and his remaining fingers were misshapen. They always reminded Valentine of tree roots that could not decide which way to grow. "You are getting ahead of yourself, Mr. Valentine. Just by sixty-five million years or so."

The Padre sat down on his desk, facing the eight older students. The classroom should have contained forty or so, had all the teenagers within a long walk attended. But education, like survival, depended on initiative in the disorganized Boundary Waters.

Valentine settled in for a good listen, as he always did when the Padre parked himself on the desk in that fashion. The rest of the class, not having the qualified joys of living with the Padre, did not know as he did that when the Padre perched there, he was imitating another teacher from his own youth, a determined San José nun who had woken a hunger for learning in the ganja-smoking teen he still had trouble imagining the Padre had been. His mind insisted on wandering off to the games.

"We know so very little about these beings, the Pre-entities, except that they predate everything else we do know about life on Earth," the Padre began. "I was telling you about the Doors yesterday. No, Mr. Doyle, not the Old World rock-and-roll band. I know we think of these Doors as a terrible curse, the cause of our trouble. Everything we know would be different if they had never been opened. But long ago they were marvelous things, connecting planet after planet in the Milky Way as easily as that door over there connects us with the library. We call the builders of this Interworld Tree the Pre-entities, because we are not even sure if they had bodies—in the sense that you and I have bodies, that is. They probably didn't need our little chemical engines to keep going. But if they did have bodies, they were big. Some of the Doors are said to be as big as a barn.

"We know they existed because they left the Interworld Tree and the Touchstones. A Touchstone is like a book that you can read just by laying your hand on it. They don't always work correctly on our human minds, however; there are always a few who touch them and go insane from the experience, which I find easy to believe. But a person with the right kind of mind who touches one has what we might call a revelation. Like the downloads I was telling you about when we were talking about the Old World's computer technology."

The Padre looked down and shook his head. Valentine knew the Padre had a love-hate relationship with the past; when he was in his cups, he would sometimes rave about the injustices in the Old World, which had the ability to feed and clothe all of its children but had chosen not to. This might lead to tears over missing something called McDonald's fries dipped into a chocolate shake, or overpriced souvenir T-shirts.

"The Pre-entities existed by absorbing energy; a very special kind of energy, produced by living things. Plants make it at a very low level. All animals, us included, possess it to a greater extent. This energy, which we call a 'vital aura' for lack of a better term, is determined by two factors in an organism: size and intelligence. The latter predominates. A cow, despite its size, gives off a smaller vital aura than a monkey. A monkey being the 'brighter' of the two in more ways than one, if you understand."

A student held up her hand, and the Padre stopped.

"You talked about this before, but I never got if the aura was your soul or not. Is it, I mean?" Elaine Cowell was a thirteen-year-old, but so bright she stayed for all the lessons with the older teens.

The Padre smiled at her. "Good question, Miss Cowell. I wish I had an absolute answer. My gut feeling is that a vital aura is not your soul. I think your soul is something that belongs to you and God, and no one else can interfere with it. I know some people say it is your soul that gets fed on, but there is no way we can ever know that. I think of the vital aura as being another special kind of energy you give off, just as you give off heat and an electromagnetic field."

Elaine fixed her gaze at an invisible point sixteen inches in front of her face, and Valentine sympathized. She was also an orphan; the Reapers had taken her parents five years ago in Wisconsin. She now lived with an aunt who scratched out a living weaving blankets and repairing coats. The others sat in silence. Whenever the Padre discussed the Facts of Death with the older students, their normal restlessness vanished.

"So why aren't they still around? I thought that energy stuff was what made the Kurians immortal?" another student asked.

"Evidently our Creator decided that no race can live forever, no matter how advanced their science. When they started to die, we think it caused a terrible panic. I wonder if beings who are nearly immortal are more afraid of death, or less? They needed more and more vital aura to keep going, and they cleaned out whole planets in their final years, trying to stave off the inevitable. They probably absorbed all the dinosaurs; the two events seem to have happened at the same time. In their last extremity, they ate each other, but it was all for nothing. They still died. With no one to maintain their portals, the doorways began to shut down over the thousands and thousands of years that followed. But pieces of their knowledge, and the Interworld Tree itself, survived for a new intelligence to find later on."

Thunder rumbled outside, and the rattling of the rain increased.

"So we call the Pre-entities Kurians now?" a young woman asked.

"No. The Kurians come from a race called the Lifeweavers. They found the remnants of the Pre-entity civilization. They pieced some of their history and technology back together and made use of what they could understand, like the barbarians who moved into Rome. We get the word *Lifeweaver* from their own language; it refers to those of the race who visit other worlds and interpopulate them. Just as man takes his livestock, crops, and orchards with him when he migrates, but is willing to adapt if something better is found, so did the Lifeweavers in their colonization of the Interworld Tree. Lifeweavers live a long, long time . . . many thousands of years. Some believe they were created by the Pre-entities as builders, but it seems strange that beings with a vital aura as strong as theirs would have survived the extinction throes of the Pre-entities.

"These Lifeweavers reopened the portals to our Earth about the time we were discovering that food tasted better if it was cooked first. Our ancestors worshiped them. Most of them were content to be teachers, but it seems a few wanted to be more. A Lifeweaver can appear to us as a man or woman, or an elephant or a turtle if it wants, so they must have seemed as gods to our poor forefathers. They can put on a new shape as easily as we can change clothes. Maybe they threw thunderbolts for good measure. I think they inspired many of our oldest myths and legends.

"They adopted us in a way. As we grew more and more advanced, they took a few of us to other worlds. I've been told humans are living on other planets even now. If so, I pray their fortune has been better than ours. The Lifeweavers could do anything they wanted with DNA. They could make useful creatures to suit themselves, or modify a species as they required. We know they liked making beautiful birds and fish to decorate their homes; some of these still live on our planet today."

The Padre smiled at them. "Ever seen a picture of a parrot? I think they tinkered with them a little bit." He paused in thought.

Valentine had seen pictures of parrots. Right now the only birds in his mind were pheasants, tender young pheasants rising in a flutter of wings. He could see them in his newly won shotgun sight. He'd heard the Kolchuks' lab-pointer pair had had another litter; maybe he could still get a puppy.

The Padre droned on.

Doyle held up his hand, serious for once. "Sir, why tell us all this now? We've known about vampirism and so on since we were kids. Okay, maybe some of the hows and whys were wrong. What difference does it make how any of it got started? We still have to hike out every summer—and every fall, a couple of families don't come back."

The Padre's face crumbled. He looked ten years older to Valentine.

"No difference, no difference at all. I wish every day of my life something could make a difference. Mr. Doyle, class, you are young, you've lived with it your whole lives, and it is not such a weight for you. But I remember a different world. People complained a lot about it, but in hindsight it was something like Eden. Why talk about this now? Look at the quotation on the board. Churchill was right. By looking back, we may often see the future. I tell you this because nothing lasts forever, not even those who will do anything to become immortal. They're not. The Kurians will eventually die, just like the Pre-entities. Once an old king paid to have a piece of knowledge carved deep in the side of a monument, something that would always be true. The wisest man of the age told him to carve the words 'This, too, shall pass.' But who shall pass first, us or them?

"We will not live to see it, but one day the Kurians will be gone, and the Earth will be clean again. If nothing else, I want you to take that certain knowledge from me and carry it with you wherever you go."

The rain left shortly after the rest of Valentine's schoolmates did. He hurried to empty the various bowls, basins, and pails brimming with rainwater from the leaky roof, then headed for the kitchen. Father Max sat at the battered table, staring at the bottom of an empty glass. He was already recorking the jug.

"David, telling that story always makes me need a drink. But the drink I have always wants another to keep it company, and I should not do that. At least not too often." He replaced the jug in its familiar spot on the shelf.

"That stuff's poison, Father. I wouldn't use it to kill rats; it'd be too cruel."

The old man looked up at David, who poured himself the last of the cow's vintage from the morning milking. "Isn't the race today?"

Valentine, now dressed in faded denim shorts and a leather vest, bolted a piece of bread and washed it down with mouthfuls of milk. "Yeah, at four or thereabouts. I'm glad the rain stopped. In fact, I better get moving if I'm going to walk the trail before the race."

"You've been running that trail since April. I'd think you'd know it by now."

"All the rain is going to make the footing different. Might be muddy going up the big hill."

Father Max nodded sagely. "David, did I ever tell you that your parents would have been proud of you?"

Valentine paused for a second as he laced his high moccasins. "Yes. Mostly after you've had a drink. It always makes you soft."

"You're a bit of the best of both of them. You've got his quick thinking and dedication, and enough of your mother's looks and humor and heart to soften his edges. I wish he—they—could see you today. We used to call the last day of school *graduation,* you know that?"

"Yup. I've seen pictures and everything. A funny hat and a piece of paper that says you know stuff. That would be great, but I want to get us that gun." He moved to the door. "You going to be in the public tent?"

"Yes, blessing the food and watching you collect first prize. Good luck, David."

He opened the patched, squeaky screen door and saw two bearded men coming up the path from the road. They were strangers to him.

They looked as though they had spent every moment of their adult years in the elements. They wore buckskin top to bottom, except for battered, broad-brimmed felt hats on their heads. They bore rifles in leather sheaths, but they did not have the shifty, bullying air that the soldiers of the patrols did. Unlike the soldiers charged by the Kurians with keeping order in the Boundary Waters, these men moved with a cautious, quiet manner. There was something to their eyes that suggested wary wild animals.

"Father Max," Valentine called into the house without taking his eyes off the men. "Strangers coming."

The men paused, smiling with tobacco-stained teeth. The taller of the two spoke: "Don't let the guns scare you, boy. I know your people."

Father Max emerged from the house and stepped out into the rain-soaked yard with arms outstretched. "Paul Samuels," he half shouted, walking out to embrace the tall man in his gangly arms. "You haven't come this way in years! Who is this with you?"

"My name's Jess Finner, sir. I've sure heard about you, sir."

The Padre smiled. "That could be good or bad, Mr. Finner. I'd like you both to meet my ward, David. He's the son of Lee Valentine and Helen Saint Croix."

"I knew your father, David," said the one named Samuels. Valentine saw memories lurking in the brown pools beneath his wrinkled brow. "Bad business, that day at his place. I saw you after the funeral. Took us four months, but we got the men that—"

"Let's not dredge up old history," the Padre interrupted.

Valentine caught the looks exchanged between the men and suddenly lost interest in the race and the shotgun.

The Padre patted his shoulder. "We'll talk later, David—that's a promise. Get going! But give my regrets to the Council at the public tent, and get back here as soon as you can. We're going to crack the seal on one of the bottles from the woodpile, and then you may have to put me to bed."

"Not likely," Samuels guffawed.

The Padre gave David his "I mean it, now" look, and Valentine headed off down the road. He still had time to look over the two-mile course if he hurried. Behind him, the three men watched him go, then turned and walked into the house.

The smell of cooking food greeted him at the campgrounds. The public tent, a behemoth, six-pole structure that saw weddings, baptisms, auctions, and meetings at the start of every summer, was hidden in a little glade surrounded by lakes and hills, miles from the nearest road and out of sight from any patrol in vehicles. The Hideout Festival featured sports and contests for the children and teenagers. A wedding or two always added to the celebratory atmosphere. The adults learned crafts; held riding, shooting, and archery competitions; and then feasted on barbecue each evening. Families brought their special dishes for all to share, for in a region of dreadful, cold winters and summers spent in hiding, there were few chances for large gatherings. With the festival's conclusion, the people would scatter into the woods and lakes to wait out the summer heat, hoping that the Reapers would comb some other portion of the Boundary Waters in search of prey.

The race felt less a sport and more of a chore to Valentine by the time he reached the crowd. The people, horses, wagons, and traders' stalls normally fascinated him, but the arrival of the two strangers held his thoughts in a grip that startled him. His desire for a ribbon and a shotgun in front of an applauding crowd seemed meaningless when compared with meeting a man who had known his father.

He resigned himself to running the race anyway. The course looped out in a horseshoe shape around Birch Lake. Usually a mud-rimmed half-swamp by mid-May, Birch Lake had swollen with the heavy rains until its fingers reached up almost to the public tent.

Valentine greeted Doyle and a few other acquaintances from school. He had many acquaintances but no close friends. As the Padre's live-in student, responsibilities in keeping the house and school running prevented him from forming attachments, and if that weren't enough, his bookish habits made him a natural outsider on the occasions when he did mix with the boisterous teenagers. He wandered off into the woods along the two-mile trail. He wanted time to be alone and to think. He had guessed right; the ground on the big hill to the west of Birch Lake was slick with clay-colored mud. He stood on the hill and looked out across the rippled surface of the lake toward the public tent. A thought sprang from the mysterious garden in his mind where his best ideas grew.

Fifteen boys participated in the race, though only a handful had enough points from the other Field Game events to have a chance at the prize. They were dressed in everything from overalls to leather loincloths, all tan and thin, tangle haired and wire muscled.

"One to be steady," invoked Councilman Gaffley to the rocking assortment of racers. "Two to be ready, and you're off!"

A few of the boys almost stopped a hundred yards into the race when Valentine made a sharp right turn off the trail, heading for Birch Lake. He sprinted out onto a long spit of land and thrashed his way into the water.

Valentine swam with lusty, powerful strokes, sighting on a tall oak on the other side. This neck of the lake was 150 yards or so across, and he figured he would be back on the trail about the time the rest of the boys skidded down the muddy hill.

And he was right, lunging dripping wet from the lake and pounding up the trail before the lead boy, Bobby Royce, could be seen emerging from the woods. David broke the string at the finish line with a muddy chest to a mixture of cheers and boos. Most of the boos came from families who had their boys in the race. A frowning Councilman grabbed it off him as if it were a sacred icon being defiled and not a piece of ratty twine.

The other boys hit the finish line two minutes later, and the debate began. A few maintained that the important thing was to race from point A to point B as quickly as possible, and the exact route, land or water, didn't matter. The majority argued that the purpose of the race was a two-mile run cross-country, not a swim, which would be a different sport altogether. Each side increased its volume under the assumption that whoever made the most noise would win the argument. Two old men found the whole fracas hilarious, and they pressed a bottle of beer into David's palm, slapping him on the back and pronouncing him a first-rate sport for getting Councilman Gaffley so huffy he looked like a hen with her feathers up.

A hasty, three-councilmen panel pronounced Valentine disqualified from the race, but the winner of a special award in recognition for his "initiative and originality." Valentine watched Bobby Royce receive the shotgun and shells and wandered out of the tent. The barbecue smell made him hungry all over again. He grabbed a tin tray and loaded it from the ample spread outside. The homemade beer tasted vile. *Had beer been this bad in the Old World?* he wondered. But somehow it complemented the smoky-tasting meat. He found a dry patch of ground under a nearby tree and went to work on the food.

One of the backslapping oldsters approached him, cradling a varnished wooden case and dangling two more bottles of beer from experienced fingers.

"Hey there, kid. Mind if I sit with you a bit?"

Valentine smiled and shrugged.

Almost seventy years of creaky bones eased themselves up against the trunk of the tree. "Don't have much of an appetite anymore, kid. When I was your age, give or take, I could put away half that steer. Beer tastes just as good, though," he said, taking a pull from one of the open bottles and handing the other to Valentine.

"Listen, son, don't let 'em get you down. Gaffley and the rest are good men, in their way; they just don't like the unexpected. We've seen too much unexpected in our days to want any more."

Valentine nodded to the old man, mouth working on the food, and took a companionable pull from the fresh beer.

"My name's Quincy. We were neighbors, once. You were a squirt then. Your ma used to visit, especially when my Dawn was in her last illness."

Valentine's tenacious memory, jogged, came to his rescue. "I remember you, Mr. Quincy. You had that bicycle. You used to let me ride it."

"Yeah, and you did good, considering it didn't have any tires. I gave it away with everything else when she passed on. Moved in with my son-in-law. But I remember your mother; she used to sit with her. Talk with her. Tell jokes. Get her to eat up. You know, I don't think I ever thanked her, even the day we put my wife in the ground. . . ."

The old man took a long pull at the beer.

"But that's water under the bridge, we used to say. Ever seen a real bridge, boy? Oh, of course you have, the one on old Highway Two is still up, isn't it. Anyhow, I'm here to give you something. Seeing you with your hair all wet and shiny made me think of your mom, and since those old dorks won't award you the prize you deserve, I thought I'd give you one."

He fumbled with the greenish latch on the case and raised the lid. Inside, nestled on formed blue velvet, rested a gleaming pistol.

Valentine gasped. "Wow! Are you kidding? That gun would be worth something at the wagons."

The old man shook his head. "It was mine. Your daddy probably had one just like it at some time or other. It's an automatic pistol, an old United States gun. I've kept it clean and oiled. No bullets, though, but it's a nine millimeter, which ain't too hard to find ammo for. I was going to give it to my son-in-law, but he's a putz. He'd just swap it for liquor, most likely. So I brought it here, figuring I'd trade it for some books or something. All at once I wanted to give it to you, where maybe it would do the most good. It's not too handy for hunting, but plenty comforting on a lonely road."

"What do you mean, Mr. Quincy?"

"Look, kid, er—David, right? I'm old, but not particularly wise. But I got old by being able to read people. You've got that look in you; I can tell you're hungry for something besides your food. Your dad was that way, too. You know he used to be in what we called the navy, and they went all over the world, which just suited him. After that, after all the shit came down, he did other things. He fought for the Cause just like the Padre. Did things he maybe even didn't tell your mother. You are a rolling stone, too, and all you need is a little push. What that push is gonna be, I can't say."

Valentine wondered if he had been pushed already. He wanted to talk to Paul Samuels, wanted to talk to him alone. He might as well admit it to himself, he had been thinking about asking to go with the men when they left the Padre's.

"This world is so cocked up I sometimes can't believe I'm still in it. You can do two things when something's wrong: fix it or live with it. All of us here in the Boundary Waters, we're trying to live with it, or hide from it, more like. We've gotten good at it. Maybe we should never have gotten used to it, I don't know, but there were always hungry kids to feed and clothe. Seemed better to hide, not rock the boat. But that's me, not you. You're a smart kid; that little stunt at the lake proved it. You know that the ones really in charge don't bother with us because we're not worth the trouble. Living with the Padre, you probably know that more than most. It's only a matter of time before they get around to us, no matter how deep in the woods we go. It's them or us. *Us* meaning human beings. Getting rid of them is work for the Cause."

David swallowed his food, but swallowing his mixed emotions was a much tougher proposition. Could he just take off? His vague plans for living in a lakeshore cabin in the company of books and fishing poles no longer applied or appealed, ever since Samuels and Finner had mentioned killing the patrollers who had turned the only world he'd known into piles of butchered meat. Odd that this old neighbor spoke as though he were privy to secret, half-formed thoughts. "Are you saying I should leave, join the resistance, take up the Cause?"

"A few of the boys your age are. It happens every year. Folks are quiet about it. If word of a son or daughter leaving got to the patrols, there'd be trouble. So it's usually 'Joe got married and is living with his wife's folks near Brainerd,' or some such. The councilmen discourage it, but Gaffley's own daughter ran away two years ago. Letters arrive every year, but he won't show them to anyone."

In a fit of contrariness, perhaps to show Quincy that he wasn't as astute a judge of human nature as the old man credited himself for being, David shrugged. "I can't say what I'll do, Mr. Quincy. I was thinking of going up to Lake of the Woods, building a boat . . . I love fishing, and they say next to no one lives there."

"Sure, son. And maybe twenty years from now, a patrol will come through, just like—"

"Hey," Valentine flashed, "that's not . . . fair."

"But it keeps happening. Just this spring, out by Grand Rapids. Eight people, that one. The way I hear it, it's a lot worse down south. Especially in the cities, where there's nowhere to hide."

Valentine was about to say, "That's not my problem," but held his tongue. An orphaned eleven-year-old had not been the Padre's problem that September afternoon so long ago, either. The Padre had faced the problem, took responsibility, because that is what decent people do.

It was an anxious young man who hurried to the Padre's that evening along familiar paths, carrying a burlap bag full of leftovers, an old empty pistol, and a head full of choices. The faces and animals at the public tent, the shores, hills, and trees—all pulled at him with promises of safety and security. *The woods are lovely, dark and deep . . .* He went into the backyard, checked on the animals, and began to chop wood. Turning cordwood into kindling always cleared his mind, even if it left his body wet and rubbery. He had been doing this chore for the Padre, and for a number of the neighbors in trade for sugar or flour, since his arrival five years ago. The solid feel of the ax in his hands, the *thwock* as the blade sank into the dried wood, absorbed the things that bubbled up from the dark corners of his mind.

He stacked the splintered results of his labor and went inside the house. He found the three men sprawled in the smoke-filled library around an empty bottle and a mostly empty jug. A small bag full of letters, including a couple from a young lady named Gaffley, sat on the Padre's nicked-up table, and a much larger bundle of letters lay tucked in one of the men's satchels, ready for the long return trip south. The one called Finner paged raptly through a battered volume titled *Classic Nudes through the Photographer's Lens.*

"David, you missed some boring catching up. And some even more boring drinking," Father Max said, not bothering to rise from his barely upholstered chair. "Did you win the race?"

"Sort of. It doesn't matter." He told the story. When he got to the part about being disqualified, Finner blew a raspberry. "I'd like to hear how you knew my father, Mr. Samuels."

Samuels looked at the Padre. "It's always Paul when I'm off my feet, son. When I was a kid about your age, give or take, your dad and I used to come up together from down south, just like me and Jess do now. We liked to keep in touch with the folks up here, and this old fraud. Well-lubricated philosophy sessions, you might say."

Valentine began distributing the bounty from the public tent. The men dug in with the enthusiasm of days spent on the road eating only what the wilderness provided.

"You fight them, right? The Kurians, the Reapers, the things they make? And the patrols, right?"

"Patrols are what we call the Quislings up here nowadays," the Padre interjected.

"Well, not all at once, son," Samuels answered. "In fact, we spend more time running scared from them than we do standing and fighting. We can hit them here and there, where we don't stand too much chance of getting hit back. When we're not doing that, we're trying to keep from starving. Ever drunk water out of a hoof print to wash down a couple handfuls of ground-up ants? Slept outside in the rain without even a tent? Worn the same shirt for a month straight? It really stinks, son. And I don't just mean the shirt."

Valentine stood as tall as he could, trying to add a couple of inches to his six feet one. "I'd like to join up, sir."

Father Max broke loose with a whiskey-fumed laugh. "I knew you could talk him into it!"

A week later, Father Max saw the party off on a warm, sun-dappled morning. He gave David an old musty-smelling hammock. It had uses other than rest; the Padre showed him how to roll his spare clothing up in it, then tie it across his back. By the time that was finished, other recruits who had collected over the past days began to shoulder their own burdens. Most carried backpacks bulging with preserved food. Valentine found that there were mouthfuls of words to be said, and no time or privacy to say them.

"God be with you, David," the graying old man finally said, tears wetting his eyes.

"I'll write. Don't worry about me. Jacob Christensen said he'd help out around here. He wants to teach the younger kids, too, so you don't have—"

The Padre held out his gnarled hand for a handshake. "Yes, David. I'll be fine. Soon you'll have more important things to worry about than getting the cow milked and the chickens fed. But the day I quit teaching the kids their ABC's is the day I'll be resting in the ground."

Samuels and Finner also shook hands with the Padre. How the men looked so alert was beyond Valentine; they seemed to be up every night drinking and talking, then visiting the trading wagons and surrounding homes in the day. David guided them, leading them on backwoods paths to the households that matched the names on the mail. One visit stood out, when Samuels had called on an old woman to deliver a few personal effects from her dead son, who had been a friend of Samuels's. Some intuition must have revealed her son's fate; she seemed neither surprised or grief stricken, and wasn't even preparing to leave her home for the summer. That night there had been more drinking and less laughter in the library.

Valentine began to learn on the first day of the journey south. He learned just how sore his legs could get. Though he had walked all day many times in his life, he had never done so with better than forty pounds of food, water, and possessions on his back at a pace set by a demanding sergeant. Other volunteers joined the group as they walked, one whom he knew. Gabriella Cho had gone to the Padre's school for a number of years; her rich black hair had fascinated him as he struggled through the awkward rites of puberty. Necessities at home kept her out of school past the age of fifteen. She had blossomed into a woman since Valentine had last seen her two years ago.

"Gabby, so you're coming, too," Valentine said, relieved to be finally taller than the doe-eyed young woman.

She looked at him once, twice. "Davy? Yeah, I'm taking the big trip."

"We missed you. Father Max had to start asking the rest of us the tough questions. It wasn't the same since you left."

"No, nothing's been the same since then," Cho responded. When she replied to further questions with one-word answers and downcast eyes, Valentine ended the conversation.

They spent the first evening at an overgrown crossroads more than a dozen miles south of the Padre's. They made camp and spent the next day talking, waiting, and nursing sore muscles. Another soldier showed up, escorting four more recruits. Two of the men were twin brothers, six-foot-six-inch blond giants. Valentine was surprised to learn their names were Kyle and Pete rather than Thor and Odin.

They repeated the process as they hiked south and west in easy stages—*easy*, that was, in the estimation of the men who bore the title *Wolves*. To Valentine, each day proved more exhausting than the last. By the time they reached the outskirts of Minneapolis, the group had swelled to thirty soldiers and over a hundred young men and women.

Lieutenant Skellen met them at a boat they used to cross the Mississippi. The lieutenant wore an eye patch so wide, it could have just as well been labeled an eye scarf, which mostly covered a crescent-shaped scar on the left side of his face. He had a dozens more recruits with him. Like the sergeant's they were in their teens or barely out of them, wide-eyed and homesick among new landscapes and unfamiliar faces. The travelers made a wide loop west around the Twin Cities, into empty lands teeming with prairie plants. One day they skirted a hundred-head herd of mountains of hair and hide, and the Wolves informed Valentine he was looking at his first buffalo.

"Ain't no weather can kill those big shaggies," Finner explained to his charges from the Boundary Waters. "The cows and wild horses gotta find low wooded spots when the snow is blowing out here, but them buffalo just form a big circle and wait it out."

Valentine picked up much more on that journey south. He learned he could make a compass by stropping an old double-edged razor blade against the back of his hand. Charged with static electricity, he suspended it from a string in a preserve jar to shield it from the wind. The little piece of metal found north after wavering indecisively like a bird dog sniffing the breeze. The recruits learned how and where to build a fire, using reflectors made of piled logs to hide the flame and direct the heat back toward the camper. He was taught about trench fires in high wind, and to always roast game skewered on a spit beside a fire, not over it, with a pan underneath to catch every drop of valuable fat. They learned how to make flour not only from wheat, but also with the flower-heads at the end of cattails and even with bark. Valentine pounded masses of bark in a pan of water, removed the fibers, and allowed it to settle, then poured off the water and toasted the pulpy starch on a stick. Even with salt it did not taste like much, but he found himself able to eat just about anything as the long weeks of walking wore on. Even more incredibly, he gained weight—though he was hungry from dawn to dusk.

When their packs emptied, they didn't always have to live off the land. They stopped at isolated farmhouses and tiny, hidden enclaves where the residents fed them. "I can't fight them, no sir, but I can feed them that does the fightin'," one goat-whiskered farmer explained, passing out bags of beans and corn flour to the hundred-odd campers on the banks of his stream.

He practiced with his pistol. The Wolves passed a hat around and collected two dozen bullets from the men with handguns that used the same ammunition as his. Some of the Wolves carried up to three side-arms in order to have a better chance at using bullets acquired from scavenging the deceased after a fight. He plinked away at old paint cans and weathered, paint-stripped road signs. It was during one of these marksmanship sessions in an old barn near camp that Valentine made an effort to talk to Sergeant Samuels. He had just knocked down a row of three aluminum cans, their colored labels illegible with the passage of years, and he was feeling pretty full of himself.

"You should try it with your left hand," the veteran suggested.

That cleaned the self-satisfied smile from Valentine's face in a hurry. "Why, Sergeant?"

"What if your right arm's busted, kid? What if someone just blew your hand off? I know, most instructors say it's a waste of time. Me, I think it's good to use your off hand. Makes your brain and body work different than it's used to."

Valentine set one of the cans back up, the sharp cordite smell tickling his nostrils. Feeling awkward, he raised the gun to eye level, feet shoulder-width apart. He sent the can flying with the second shot.

"May I?" Samuels asked.

Valentine passed him the gun. The sergeant examined it professionally.

"This was your dad's?"

"No, Sergeant. A—I suppose he's a neighbor—he gave it to me."

Samuels whistled. "A gun like this? It's in great shape. He must have thought a lot of you." He handed the gun back to Valentine.

"More like he thought a lot of my parents," Valentine mused. He paused for a moment, not sure how to phrase the question. "You seemed to think a lot of my father, too. I never knew about his life before he met my mother. He just said he traveled."

Samuels glanced out the missing barn doors. The campsite was nearly empty; a heavy patrol was out under the lieutenant, and most of the recruits were taking advantage of the afternoon off to wash clothes and bathe in the nearby river.

"Yeah, David. I knew him. Not from way back, from before the skies filled with ash, that is. We met in Michigan, soon after all this shit started. I was younger than you then, maybe fifteen. Your dad and I were in this outfit; we called ourselves the Band. Fighting sometimes, hiding mostly. Cops, army guys; we had some coast guard sailors from Lake Michigan, even. The uniform was a hat with a piece of camouflage material sewn on it somewhere. God, what a hungry, sorry-looking bunch we were."

He shook his head and continued. "Even when we were blasting away at the Grogs, we couldn't really believe it. It was like something out of a sci-fi movie. No one knew shit about what was going on. I used to cry every damn night, it seemed to me. My parents were in Detroit when the nuke went off, you see. I learned one thing: tears make you feel better, but they don't change anything. You'll still be hungry when they dry up. Still be lonely."

The two men, one mature and weathered, the other a few years past puberty, wandered out of the barn and watched the sun descend into the western haze. Samuels nodded to a couple of the Wolves carrying out camp duties, and sat down on the corpse of an old green tractor. The space where the engine once sat gaped, an open wound with wires dangling.

"So you were both Wolves then?" Valentine omitted the *sir,* since they were both sitting.

"That came later. God, we didn't know what to think. The rumors we heard. Stuff about government experiments. That the Apocalypse was here and Satan walked the earth. People getting rounded up into camps like in the Nazi movies. Creatures from outer space. Turned out the truth was even weirder than the rumors, of course.

"Seems to me we were trying to make for this Mount Omega—there was talk that the vice president was there with what was left of the government and the joint chiefs. Only problem with it was no one knew where Mount Omega was. And then we came across the Padre.

"The Padre was working for someone named Rho. Not that he'd given up on Holy Mother Church, of course. He said this Rho was very special and was advising us on how to fight these things. We weren't interested. He said Rho was holed up in a safe place with food, liquor, women—I can't remember what all he promised us. None of us were interested in that, either. We'd been almost trapped and killed by those kind of promises before; the Quislings were already running us down. Then the Padre said this Rho knew what was going on. That got us. Especially your father. Some of the guys said that it was another trap, but I went with your dad, because he'd done a good job looking after me.

"It turned out this Rho was a Lifeweaver. He looked like a doctor from TV, really distinguished and everything. Guess you know who the Lifeweavers are, living with the Padre as you did. He gave us this speech about doors to other planets and vampires and vital auras and how the Grogs were things cooked up in a lab. We didn't buy any of it. I remember some of the guys started singing 'Row, Row, Row Your Boat,' sort of having fun with him. We thought he and the Padre were a couple of fuckin' nuts, you know? He said something to the Padre, and then, I swear to Jesus, he turns into this big gold eagle, with flames for wings. Circled over us like the *Hindenburg* going up. None of us knew whether to shit or shoot, I can tell you. Your dad told us to quiet down, and it turned back into a man again, or the image of one.

"Believe me, after that we listened. He told us about a group of Lifeweavers on a planet called Kur. They'd learned from some Touch-stones the secret of how to live off vital auras. To beings with a life span of thousands of years, the chance to have a life span of millions must have been temptation, too much temptation. They violated the Lifeweaver law, their moral code, and started absorbing aura. They were trying to become immortal. In the interest of science, of progress. According to Rho, what they accomplished instead was to turn their world into a nightmare. They became what we call vampires, beings that are, to us, immortal. They do this through taking the lives of others. These rogue Lifeweavers, the Kurians, became the mortal enemies of the rest of their race.

"The Kurians smashed Lifeweaver society. They'd been transformed from researchers and scientists into something else. Cold. Ruthless. They used their skills to destroy all opposition. Overwhelmed, all the Lifeweavers could do was shut the portals to Kur. I guess it was in an attempt to keep the infection from spreading. But it was too late. A few Kurians had already escaped and were using the Interworld Tree to attack the whole Lifeweaver order. More doors were shut, but that only cut the Lifeweavers off, stopping them from organizing an effective resistance. It was like a houseful of people each hiding from a pack of killers in separate locked rooms instead of banding together to fight."

The sound of galloping hooves interrupted the story. A rider on one of the three horses in the group pulled up in the yard.

"Sarge," the rider said, walking his horse in a circle, "the lieutenant says there's a Grog column out east of here, heading this way. Mounted on legworms. Four legworms, twenty Grogs altogether. Not coming right for us, but definitely looking. You're supposed to gather everyone up and get to the Highway Forty-one bridge. If the lieutenant hasn't shown up by tomorrow, you're supposed to get everyone to Round Spring Cave."

"Got it, Vought. Now ride on down to the river and get the kids in gear. Slowly, don't scare them out of a year's life like you did me." The courier moved his roan off at a more sedate pace. "Damn, but the Grogs are far out from Omaha. Maybe someone saw us outside Des Moines. Lot of Quislings live in this area nowadays."

The sergeant gathered up the six Wolves remaining at the camp and issued orders. He motioned Valentine over.

"Sarge?"

Samuels pulled at the beard sprouting on his chin. "Valentine, we're going to be marching tonight. We're going to stick to an old road because I want to get some miles south of the Grogs, but that means I've got to have scouts and a rear guard. I'm shorthanded, what with the lieutenant and his group out. That means you're getting what's called a battlefield promotion. I'm going to put you in charge of the ass end of the recruit column. Make sure everyone keeps up. It's going to be six kinds of dark tonight with these clouds, so it won't be easy. Lucky for us, we've been slacking all afternoon. Can you handle that?"

Valentine threw out his chest. "Yes, Sergeant!" But nervous sweat was running down his back.

Already a few recruits were returning to the area around the old barn, some with wet clothes plastered to their bodies. They broke camp. Usually the shouts and curses of the Wolves trying to get their green levy to move faster came from simple habit, but this time the words were in earnest.

They moved off into the deepening night. Before, they had done only night marches when arcing around Des Moines. The Grogs out of eastern Nebraska patrolled this area. They could follow a trail in day or night by sight, by ear, or by smell.

They moved at a forced march with Valentine bringing up the rear. They walked, and walked fast, for fifty minutes, then rested for ten. The sergeant kept up a punishing pace.

Complaints started after the fourth rest. By the sixth, there was trouble. A recruit named Winslow couldn't get to her feet.

"My legs, Val," she groaned, face contorted in pain. "They've cramped up."

"More water, less hooch, Winslow. The sarge warned you. Don't come crying to me."

The column began to move. Gabby Cho, who had been keeping Valentine company at the rear, looked at him wonderingly. Valentine waved her off. "Get going, we'll catch up."

Valentine began massaging Winslow's quadriceps and calves. He tried to stretch one leg, but she moaned and cried something unintelligible into the dirt.

Insects chirped and buzzed all around in the night air.

"Just leave me, Val. When it wears off, I'll jog and catch up."

"Can't do it, Winslow."

He heard the three Wolves of the rear guard approach. It was now or never.

"Up, Winslow. If you can't walk, you can hobble. I'll help you. That's an . . . order." He reached out a hand, grabbed hers, and tried to pull her up. "But I'm not gonna carry you; you've got to move along as best you can."

The Wolves, rifles out of sheaths, looked at Valentine with raised eyebrows. They thought the situation humorous: a cramp-stricken recruit and would-be noncom trying to get her up by issuing orders with a voice that kept cracking.

"What's going on?" asked Finner, who was in the rear guard. "You two picked a helluva time to hold hands in the moonlight."

"She wants us to leave her," he explained.

"No, she doesn't," one of the Wolves demurred.

"Okay, Winslow," Valentine said, drawing his gun. "I've given you an order." *The word still sounds odd,* he thought. "And you're not obeying it. I'm not leaving you to get found and . . . made to talk about us or where we're going." *Do people really talk like this?* "So I guess I'll have to shoot you." He worked the gun's action and chambered a bullet.

"Val, you've got to be joking."

He looked at Finner, who shrugged.

Laboriously, she got to all fours. "See, Finner, I can barely crawl!" Valentine's bullet struck the dirt a foot to the left of her ear, sending pebbles flying up into her face.

She ran and he followed, leaving the three Wolves chuckling in the darkness.

Samuels met them at the rear of the column. "Christ, Sarge, he tried to kill me," Winslow said, telling her end of the story. The sergeant planted a boot in her scrawny behind.

"Keep up next time, Winslow. Valentine," he barked, fist and palm crashing together.

The two men waited while the file drew away. "Don't ever use your gun, except as a last resort on the enemy. Not out of consideration to that non-hacker, but 'cause the Grogs can hear like bats. You get me?"

"Sorry, Sergeant. Only thing I could think of to get her moving. Her legs were cramped up, she said."

"Next time, kick 'em in the ass, and if that doesn't work, you come get me."

"I thought you said I was responsible for keeping them moving, sir."

Sergeant Samuels considered this, then fell back on old reliable. "Shut up, smart-ass. I didn't give you permission to pull a gun on anyone. Get back in line. Keep 'em moving."

Finner, drawing near with the rear guard, had a few words with the sergeant. Samuels doubled the column, returning to the front.

"Hey, Valentine," Finner said, jogging up to him. "Don't worry about it. You tried to get her on her feet, when most guys in your spot would've turned to us. Don't let the sarge BS you about the gunshot; a single shot is tough to locate unless you're next to it. Plus, that thing doesn't make all that much noise. I told the sarge that if I thought there was a problem, I wouldn't have let you do it."

"What did he say?"

"He said I shouldn't think too much, it was dangerous for a guy like me. He added a few comments about my mother, too."

A cloud, shaped like a snail with an oversize shell on its back, began to cover the rising moon.

"I think he'd take a bullet for you though, Jess."

"Damn straight."

The lieutenant was not at the rendezvous. The tired recruits and tireless Wolves rested for four hours. At dawn, the sergeant sent Vought on his horse with three Wolves to scout the other side of the two-lane metal bridge spanning the Missouri. The land sloped upward as the wooded hills began beyond. Safety.

One of the rear guard, at a copse of trees half a mile up the highway, waved a yellow bandanna.

Samuels clapped Valentine on the back. "C'mon, son, you deserve to see this after last night. Everyone else, get across the bridge."

He jogged off northward along the edge of what was left of the road, and Valentine followed.

They reached the stand of trees. One of the Wolves had a spotting scope resting in the crotch of a young oak, pointed down the highway. Valentine could make out figures in the distance, but he was unwilling to believe what he saw.

Samuels looked through the scope. "They must have got wind of us last night. Not sure how many of us there are, so they're going back to report. Take a look at this freak show, Valentine."

He put his eye to the scope.

The Enemy.

They were apish figures sitting astride a long pencil of flesh. The mount was like a shiny, slug-skinned millipede. Hundreds of tiny legs moved too fast for the eye to follow, reminding him of a finger running across a piano keyboard. The riders, five in all, had armorlike gray skin that reminded Valentine of a rhinoceros's hide. Their shoulders were wide—almost two ax-handles across. They carried guns that looked like old Kentucky long rifles held pointed into the air like five waving antennae. Valentine wondered if he could even aim one of the six-foot weapons.

"They're even uglier from the front. Those are fifty-caliber single-shot breechloaders, Valentine, and they're handy with them," Finner elaborated. "They can blow your head off at a thousand yards if you're fool enough to be visible and not moving."

"Those are Grogs?" Valentine couldn't tear himself away from the eyepiece.

The sergeant retrieved the scope. "Those legworms are fun to stop, too. Brain is at the tail end, kind of like Finner here. Nothing up front but a mouth and some taste buds, I guess. Also like Finner here, come to think of it. Nothing short of a cannon will keep a legworm from coming at you. Good thing they're kinda slow."

"We try to pick off the riders, but the lead one always has a big riot shield, thick as tank armor," another Wolf said. "We have to get them from the side. One thing you do not want to ever see is about fifty of them coming at you in line abreast."

"That happened at the Battle of Cedar Hill," the sergeant put in. "We lost."

They made it across the Missouri on a Sunday. The sergeant led them in a prayer of thankfulness that their long journey was almost complete.

The next few days had briefer, harder runs mixed with walks and ten-minute breaks. They stayed away from the roads, and the Grog patrols stayed out of the hills, as each side considered this border region bushwhack ground. Around the campfire one night, Samuels told Valentine a little more about his father, how the Lifeweaver Rho had created a special body of men to fight the Reapers and their allies: the Hunters.

"He told us that these things had come to Earth once before, and some of Rho's people had taught men how to fight them. We'd forgotten it, except maybe as legends and myths garbled over the years. They took certain men and made them a match for what they were up against. Rho said he could do the same now, if we were willing to accept the bargain. But it would change us forever; we'd never be the same people again. Your father was willing. Soon he had the rest of us convinced. That was the beginning of a lot of hard years, son. But when you get to the Ozarks, you'll see it was worth it."

The lieutenant was waiting for them at Round Spring Cave. It was a road-hardened group that was welcomed by the officers in charge of training new blood in the Ozark Free Territory.

A welcoming banquet was spread out under the trees. Six weeks' worth of traveling on foot made the feast even more welcome. There was fresh bread, watermelons the size of hogsheads, meat from the fatted calf, the fatted hog, and the fatted chickens under the summer sky. Valentine ate an entire cherry pie at one sitting for the first time in his life. Another little cluster of would-be soldiers had arrived the day before, youths gathered from the Missouri valley in the Dakotas. They swapped good stories and bad in the pseudo–hard-bitten fashion of youth.

Gabby Cho shared a picnic table with Valentine under a spread of pine trees. The fresh, clean scent reminded him of Christmases before the death of his family. Valentine was experimenting with iced dandelion tea sweetened almost to syrup. The tea, ice (in summer!), and apparently plentiful sugar were all novelties to him.

"We made it, Davy," Cho said. She looked a little older now to Valentine; she had chopped her long black locks after the second day of hot marching out of the Boundary Waters. "I wonder what's next. You're in with these Wolf guys. Any idea what's up?"

"Not sure, Gab. I'd like to spend a few days sleeping."

Cho seemed unsure of herself. "Why'd you join up?"

Valentine shot her a questioning look. Cho had remained distant on the whole trip south whenever any personal topic arose. She politely rebuffed the other recruits' attempts to get to know her.

He rattled his ice in the pewter mug, enjoying the sound and the cool wet feel. "You probably think revenge, because of the whole family thing. You know about what happened, right?"

"Yes, David. From some of the guys at class. I asked the Padre about it once. He told me to ask you, but I didn't want to do that."

"Well, it's not that."

Are you sure? a voice in his head asked.

"I know now my dad was with these Wolves. Maybe he would have wanted me to do it, too. He must have thought it was worthwhile; he spent a lot of years at it." He paused at a rustle overhead. Squirrels, attracted by the masses of food, were chasing each other around in the tree branches, sending flecks of bark falling onto the pair below. They were cute, but they made a decent stew, too.

"I want to make a difference, Gab. It's obvious, something's not right about the way things are. You know the Jefferson stuff we used to read, about being endowed by our Creator with inalienable rights? It's like those rights of ours have been taken away, even the right to live. We have to do something about it."

"As simple as that?"

"As simple as that, Gabby." He finished off the iced tea. "What about you?"

"Did you know I had a baby?" she blurted.

Valentine absorbed the news in awkward silence, then cleared his throat. "No, you just disappeared from school. Went north with your family, I thought."

"We kept it quiet. The father was a patroller. . . ." She read Valentine's eyes. "No, it wasn't like that. I knew him. His name was Lars. Lars Jorgensen," she said, giving him the feeling that she had not said the name in a long time.

"He used to give me stuff. Nice clothes, shoes. I never thought to ask where it came from. Looted stores in Duluth, I figured. One day he gave me a watch, a real working watch. I could tell there had been engraving on it, even though he had tried to scratch it off. I told him not to give me any more presents. He disappeared when I told him about the baby coming."

"Who's got the kid? Your mom, or—?"

"Scarlet fever got her. Last winter. Remember the outbreak? It hit around where you were living, too. It took . . ." Her words began to fade.

"Jesus, Gabby, I'm so sorry."

She wiped her eyes. "I think about it too much. I talked to the Padre after it happened. I thought maybe I didn't take care of her right, not on purpose, but because of how I feel about the father. I just didn't know. The Padre put it down to a lack of qualified doctors. Or if they're good, they don't have the equipment or medicines."

She took a cleansing breath of the Ozark air. "The Padre said that lots of people he knew put this kind of thing behind them by helping others. He gave me a lecture about the need for strong bodies and good minds, got talking about the Cause. Well, you know him."

"I wonder if I do. He didn't talk like that to me."

"I think he knew you would go south when the time was right," she said, smiling her old "I've got the right answer" smile from school. "I wanted to tell you all this for some reason. I feel like someone has to know the real me here."

The recruits got the word from Capt. "Steam Engine" Fulton. He gathered them on a little slope in a ring of trees. In this natural amphitheater, he informed the mass of youths from Minnesota, the Dakotas, and a smattering of Great Plains outposts that they would form a reserve regiment for now. They would receive uniforms. They would be armed and taught how to use those weapons. They would be paid. But for now, their main duties would be as a disciplined labor force, to be moved about the Free Territory helping the residents at harvest, improving roads, and learning about how things were organized on the Ozark Plateau. The harder they worked, the more there would be to eat over the winter.

The bloody minded and the phony tough guys groaned at the news. But Valentine grinned at Cho. A gun, a uniform, and something he had heard about but never seen: a paycheck. He couldn't wait to get started.

Three

The Ozark Plateau, the fortieth year of the Kurian Order: An island of sanity in the eye of a hurricane of death, the scattered farms and towns of the Ozarks are a civilization under siege. The heartland of the region is bordered by the blasted ruins of Little Rock to the south; in the west by a line extending from the western Ouachitas and Fort Scott to Springfield, Missouri; in the north by the far-flung foothills of the Ozarks and the Mark Twain Forest; and to the east by the Saint Francis River. Known by some as the Ozark Free Territory, and by the more military-minded as the Southern Command, the region supports three quarters of a million survivors. They are mostly farmers and ranchers connected by a network of poor roads and unreliable rivers flowing through the worn-down remnants of America's oldest mountains. Heavy stands of oak, hickory, and pine give these hills a bluish tinge, fed by cool streams winding through limestone gorges. The small mountains have bare patches of exposed felsite and rhyolite, rocky scars that symbolize the flinty hardness beneath the exterior of the inhabitants.

New farming centers have sprung up to replace the old. Little clusters of homes huddle together like medieval villages, stone walls with narrow loopholes facing the world; doors, windows, and porches facing the neighbors. The squatty settlements, perhaps built by men whose motto is "Built for Safety, Not for Comfort," are linked by walls that do not divide home from home, but separate houses from the Outside. Corrugated aluminum barns and Quonset huts in the center of the ring of homes shelter livestock and machinery from the elements and thieves.

Some areas are electrified, and a substantial portion use natural gas. A ham radio network maintains communication. Telephones are back in action, but service is unreliable. The suspicious and tough-minded residents dislike strangers, and they sleep with rifles and shot-guns handy. Pack traders traverse the area with stock on muleback or in gaily painted wagons, bringing basic necessities and few luxuries. Both necessities and luxuries are paid with barter, sometimes with greenbacks. Perhaps a measure of the success and fortitude of the in-habitants of what used to be southern Missouri and much of Arkansas is their acceptance of paper currency as being worth something. But as gold coins can be changed at two thousand or more dollars to the ounce, perhaps paper money's value is not what it once was. A regu-lar judge advocate general, civilian relations (called the "Jagers" in a tone suggesting the word has an obscene connotation) Court rides circuit and brings some measure of order and law to the lives of the residents.

A few towns operate in the region, home to the artisans and tech-nicians that keep society together. There is still singing in Branson, and a riverboat casino is in operation on the White River, paying out prizes in a system of Byzantine complexity. A governor resides in Mountain Home, Arkansas, trying to keep the roads open and mail running on shoestring budgets.

The Soldiery, as the residents know them, are concentrated in the Ouachita Mountains to the south, and in the broken Ozark ridges to the north. Ceaseless long-range patrols circle the area, picking up in-formation and refugees from all points of the compass. Strong cavalry reserves train constantly in the center of the region, ready to go to the border to slow invasion or destroy a raid. Although the Ozark Free Territory is relatively safe, it is not impregnable, as small holders and settlements in the boundary areas learn the hard way.

The uniform combined the comfort of burlap with the durability of cheesecloth. How innocent cotton minding its own business could be turned into such a scratchy, sagging patchwork amazed Valentine. And the rifle! It was a single-shot breechloader, operated by a lever that flipped out the expended case of the bullet (woe to the recruit who failed to collect the hot brass thimble!) as it opened the chamber for the insertion of another round. At least, that was the theory. In practice, a few shots heated the action sufficiently to soften the thin brass encasing the heavy bullet, and Valentine became better at clearing jams than shooting the quickly fouled weapon. It kicked like a mule and aimed with the ease of a steel shovel. However, it had few moving parts and was within the manufacturing capacity of the Ozark Free Territory.

The pay was the biggest joke of all. The recruits received multicolored military scrip, usable at the scattered-to-the-point-of-inaccessibility Southern Command Trading Post commissaries and accepted by a few pack traders desperate enough to take it in return for merchandise that failed the caveat emptor test everywhere else.

Fulton pushed them through two months' worth of drill in an exhausting six weeks. A few recruits bristled at the discipline and gave it up after the first week, either trying the dangerous trip home or finding work on the farms and ranches of the Territory. The majority finished their training under the supervision of bellowing NCOs. They ran and memorized the simple Common Articles that governed them and the Territory. They ran and sat through lectures about recent United States history, about the other knots of the resistance in Oregon, Arizona, the Appalachians, and New England. They ran and practiced with their rifles, as well as the captured support weapons and the simple cannon produced in inadequate factories. They ran and learned about camp life: brain tanning, drying and smoking meat, planting, foraging, and where to find medicinal herbs. They ran and learned about running.

Labor-Private Valentine learned to recognize the divisions of Southern Command: Guards, Militia, and Hunters. The largest body of professional soldiery was the Guards. They provided a solid core for the defense of the Ozark Free Territory. Sometimes the NCOs and officers were veterans of the Lifeweaver-trained Hunters. The Guards reinforced the Militia, the first line of defense for most communities. Most able-bodied adults, especially in the border areas, belonged to the Militia. They drilled with the Guards one day a month and stood ready to assemble at the call of drum, whistle, or siren. The Hunters carried war into the Kurian Zone. Trained by the Lifeweavers, they were divided into the Wolf, Bear, and Cat castes, each with a unique duty to the Cause. At talks given by members of the castes, Valentine learned that the Wolves carried out long-range patrol duties and maintained communication between the other Commands across North America. The Cats, rarely seen in the Territory, served as spies and saboteurs across the country, often leading double lives deep in the Kurian Zone. The Bears fought as the shock troops of the Cause, the Reapers' most fearless and skilled enemies. A Hunter usually started as a Wolf, and some of the best stayed as Wolves rather than moving to a different caste. There were a few that knew all three of the Hunter's Arts, as they named the Lifeweavers' disciplines. But all fought and sacrificed together to bring mankind back to a place in the sun.

Valentine experienced the uneasy symbiotic relationship between the military and civilians when the labor regiment broke up into work squads and were dispersed to the surrounding farms for the harvest. The military could not understand why civilians seemed to begrudge every mouthful that went into the bodies of the men prepared to give their lives to protect them. The civilians failed to see why so much of what they produced, barely enough to feed the community in a good year, disappeared into a machine that often failed to keep them safe, and showed flashes of competence and efficiency only when gathering the agreed-upon 15 percent tithe.

The harvest came and went in a whirlwind of dawn-to-dusk labor. Valentine, in charge of Cho and eight other recruits between visits by an overworked officer, helped a dozen hardworking families in an enclave near the Arkansas–Missouri border. They built and repaired houses and barns, helped get in the crops, and then butchered and preserved the summer-fattened livestock. Most of the grain and corn filled a pair of silos at the center of the little defensive ring of homes called Weening, but they also hid a reserve in a series of clay-lined pits set between Weening's barns. They covered the pits with tarps and dirt, and hoped the village dog and cat population would protect the edible buried treasure from scavenging rodents.

Harvest Feast followed the weeks of frantic work. For three days the recruits participated in athletics while daylight lasted, then joined the farmers at long tables laden with roasts, hams, turkeys, chickens, side dishes, and desserts of every description at dinner. Valentine sat next to Cho and gorged himself, then retired distended to the Militia barracks above the town stable for the nightly farting contest.

With the food put away, literally and figuratively, a brief period of repair and maintenance ensured that the blockhouse homes and barns would keep their inhabitants in some measure of comfort for the winter. All the while, the oaks and hickories of the area turned red gold, until a period of dry, windy days whipped the leaves from their tethers and left the twigs dead and empty.

Rumor suggested that Valentine's team would soon pull back into winter camp in the Ouachitas. The labor crews in some of the neighboring villages had either left or were getting orders to do so. The farmers' generosity began to run out as soon as the last root cellar was filled and barrel of salted pork nailed shut. A family named Ross gave Valentine a padded overcoat stuffed with goose down and coated with a waxy waterproofing. Valentine had spent some of his few spare hours that fall raising the Ross children out of semiliteracy in well-remembered Father Max fashion, first reading to the kids from borrowed books and then having the children read the passages back to him.

Weening abutted Black River, a sandbar-clogged stream that flowed through a tunnel of black gum, oak, and river birch. Each night, even as the evenings grew cooler, Valentine waded out into one of the chilly, deeper pools for a bath. He had added another inch to his frame in the year since joining the Cause, and his long-limbed physique was leaving its boyish scrawniness behind. Lean muscle coiled up his arms and across work-widened shoulders brushed by his glossy black hair. His square-cut face was harder, and his bronze skin darker than he had ever seen before, but his eyes retained a youthful twinkle. Life in the Free Territory suited him: the work among the people of Weening was rewarding, and he had the memory of the Ross children swelling with pride as they sounded out compound words for him and their parents. He was happy.

One November evening, with a chill in the air promising an even cooler dawn, he waded into the scrotum-tightening current for his nightly bath. A few frogs started up their musical croaking, but it was far from the ear-filling chorus of the summer nights. A heron, standing sentinel on a snag in midstream, eyed him suspiciously as he plunged into his twilight revivification. He resurfaced with a "Cooeee!" torn from his lungs at the exquisite shock.

"Val, you're going to stop this nonsense by Christmas, I hope," Gabriella Cho called from beneath the tresses of a riverbank willow. "I'm all in favor of men that bathe. In fact, I wish you'd give lessons. But the river, in this temperature?"

He laughed, breathing hard in the cool water. "I can't pass up the chance for a swim in November. We couldn't do this in the Boundary Waters, not at this time of year. You should try it."

She stepped into the veiled moonlight, holding a wicker laundry basket. "I'll stick to dipping a piece of me at a time in a washbasin, thank you. It's slower, but I can do without the double pneumonia. Anyway, I brought you a treat, you nut."

Valentine waded up and out of the stream, toes pleasantly digging into the cool sand. He felt no embarrassment at being naked in front of Cho; they'd shared too many rough camps for him to worry about modesty. She knelt, unwrapping one of the bundles from her basket and then standing up again with the air of a magician performing a trick. The brick-heated towel she draped around his shoulders warmed him deliciously.

"Thanks, Gabby, this feels great! To what do I owe the royal treatment?" He began to dry himself off, goose-pimpled skin luxuriating in the welcome heat.

Cho retrieved the other towel, stepped behind him, and affectionately tousled his hair. "It's winter quarters for us soon. I hear they're going to split us up into apprenticeships or something in camp."

"That's the rumor," he agreed as she dried his back with a series of strong strokes. He found it easy to be agreeable with his skin tingling the way it was.

"You've filled out a little, Davy," Cho observed. "You used to be such a reed. Too much time cooped up in Father Max's library."

Valentine felt a spark. *Are you going where I think you're going?* he wondered, applying it equally to the direction of the conversation and her rubdown. Now aware of how close she stood behind him and drinking in her rich feminine scent, he thought with a little nervous thrill how easy it would be to turn around and embrace—

A shriek from the buildings on the other side of the belt of trees broke the moment like a thrown brick shattering a window.

"Fire!" echoed a second, more intelligible yell.

By the time Valentine pulled his pants on and stepped into his boots, a *ting-ting-ting-ting* sound rang from the metal tube in the gate watchtower that served as Weening's alarm gong.

"Flames, Val, and— *Jesus, what's that?*"

Something flapped across the night sky over the stream, bigger than a vulture, banking to make another pass over the ring of houses.

The two friends ran for the River Gap, a narrow alley between two homes that served as the smaller of the two entrances to the village. Cho ran three paces ahead of Valentine, who was still fumbling with his pants.

A shot flashed from one of the long rectangular windows just under the roof of the house overlooking the River Gap. Cho staggered as the whipcrack hit Valentine's ears, a leg yanked out from under her as if someone had pulled it with a trip wire.

Valentine waved his arms above his head. "Don't shoot, don't shoot, it's us!" A second shot whistled past his ear.

He dropped to the earth, crawling for Cho. He found her writhing in the undergrowth, clutching her injured left leg. Oath after oath spat from her contorted mouth.

"Val," she gasped. "Val, my leg's broken, I think. Help me—Oh Christ, it's bleeding bad."

"Don't shoot anymore!" Valentine shouted into the flame-lit night. He pulled off his belt and cinched it around her thigh as a tourniquet. "Send help out here, damn it, you shot her!"

More shots rang out from somewhere, not aimed at them, thankfully. Valentine tried picking Cho up, but an agonized scream dissuaded him.

A scared-witless voice called from the window: "That you, Mr. Valentine?"

He started to reply with profanity strong enough to blister paint, but cut it off. "I'm coming in, we need to get some help out here. Dorian Helm, right?"

"Yessir. I'm sorry, but when you came up so—"

"Never mind. C'mon out here, I want you to keep an eye on her. Get a good look at what happens when you shoot without knowing what you're shooting at."

"Tell him to bring some water," Cho groaned up at him. "David, the bleeding's slowed. Please, God, let them have chloroform or something."

"And water, Helm. A canteen, anything," he shouted at the house. No response. He turned back to Cho. "I hope he heard me. Just hold on for a little while; the two of you stay under these trees. Those flying things are busy lighting fires."

"Knock a couple down for me, Val. What a dumb way to get hit," she said from behind closed eyes. Her lip was bleeding; she must have bitten it in pain.

"Hang tough, Gab. Back in a few."

The Helm boy, sixteen at most and wide-eyed with fear, let him in the tall metal gate that barred entrance to the west gap.

"Mr. Valentine, I'd never . . . ," the Helm boy began, but Valentine had no time for him after seeing that the kid had recovered his wits enough to bring a blanket out for Cho.

He reached the center of Weening without further shots aimed at him. Smoke streamed from the top of one of the silos, where two men climbed an exterior ladder, laden with blankets wrapped around their shoulders. Flames licked at the side of the main barn, the largest building in the center of the ring of walled houses.

Two of his fellow reservists stood before the shed that contained their rifles. They were taking potshots at the bat shapes circling above. He ran for the shed, hunched over in expectation of claws digging into his head or shoulders any second. He retrieved his rifle and thrust a handful of cartridges into the pocket of his beltless pants, which threatened to drop to his ankles.

"They're throwing Molotov cocktails, I think, Val," Polluck, one of the would-be soldiers in Valentine's squad, warned. "You can see them burn as they come down."

"How many of them are there?" he asked, searching the skies. Thirty feet away, some of the residents worked the hose attached to the powered pump, directing a thin stream of water at the fire threatening the barn. At the other side of the village, a mountain of a farmer, gray-haired Tank Bourne, held his automatic rifle at the ready under his porch. The weapon looked like a toy pressed against his massive shoulder. Bourne aimed a shot at a shape arcing around the barn, diving at the firefighters, short leg-claws extended like an eagle after a fish. Valentine and his comrades' guns rang out at almost the same instant. The volley of shots brought the attacker crashing to earth.

Another flapper appeared on the slanted roof of the Bourne house, crawling down the shingles with leather-draped arms toward Bourne. Valentine chambered a fresh round, sighted, and fired. Bourne heard either creature or bullet, and came out from under the porch roof. Bourne pumped shells into the abomination. It turned over and rolled off the roof.

"That's two down," Valentine said, his heart pounding in his ears.

"The main hayloft's on fire!" someone shouted from the water pump.

Framed in the growing red-orange-yellow light of the burning hay, an ungainly shape waddled toward the upper doors from deep inside the loft. Tottering on short bowlegs, it pulled itself along with long arms like a webbed spider monkey. Two triangular ears jutted like sharp horns from its angular head.

Tank Bourne rested on one knee, feeding a fresh magazine into his rifle. Valentine and the reservists shot, apparently without effect as the bat-thing launched itself into the air. With a series of audible flaps, like clotheslined sheets whipped by the wind, the beast disappeared into the smoke above.

Bourne waved them toward the already burning barn. "We have to get the stock out of there!"

The hay, now well alight, threatened to take not only Weening's central structure, but much of its livestock, as well. Bourne, Valentine, and a handful of men dashed inside, throwing the lower doors all the way open. Rising heat whipped the wind inside. The men pulled, pushed, and cajoled the stupefied cattle, which stood frozen in their stalls, away from the flames. Weening's few horses needed little encouragement, but added to the Noah's Ark confusion in the great barn's lower level as they danced and collided in their rush for the door. Once they coaxed a few cows into moving, the rest took to the idea with a will and followed the horses, bellowing their panic into the night air.

The pair who dared climb the ladder, covered by every available gun, fought the fire on the roof of the silo. Valentine prayed there wouldn't be an explosion. Bullets felled two more bat-things as they tried to pluck the men from the heights. They extinguished the most immediate threat to the village. Layers of corrugated iron and shingles bought enough time for the coughing men to beat the fire into submission with water-soaked blankets.

As the gunfire died down, women and children emerged to help combat the blaze with bucket chains and another canvas hose. The main barn could not be saved, but the smaller buildings, coops, and pens that stood near it in the center of town stayed wet thanks to brave souls who dared the heat of the burning barn to douse them with buckets of water.

Bourne, rifle held ready at his chest, still watched the skies. "Those Harpies haven't been in these parts in years," he told Valentine. "When I was with the Bears, we caught a couple hundred of them in daylight. Burned them out of an old bank they were sleeping in. We shot them out of the sky in daylight easy. They're big, slow targets, compared to a duck on the wing."

"Slow?" Valentine asked.

"Yes, they're better gliders than they are fliers. Especially if they are loaded with grenades. They're pretty smart, at least enough to know when to attack and when to try to get away."

"Would they fly in the day?"

"I doubt it, too much chance of a patrol seeing them."

Valentine felt his pulse quicken. "They hit us within an hour of sunset. How far could they fly in that hour, Mr. Bourne?"

Tank looked at him, bushy eyebrow raised in interest. "I see where you're heading, young man. Hmmm, they'd be flying against the wind out of the east. I don't think they'd be more than fifteen miles away. Ten's more likely."

Valentine belatedly remembered Cho. "I've got a wounded man on the west gate. Can you help me get her in? After that, I want to find out which way they went when they flew off."

"There's a stretcher in the tack shed where you keep your gear. I'll help you bring her in, but we don't have a doctor anywhere hereabouts."

They found the young Helm boy propped up against a tree, eyes gaping and empty. His neck had a ragged hole in it just below the Adam's apple. The wound looked as if someone had probed his chest cavity with an oversize drill.

Cho was missing.

Whatever took place at the west gap had happened so fast that the boy couldn't even get off a shot with his carbine, which lay fully loaded and broken in half on either side of his body.

"There's a Hood nearby," Bourne observed coldly. "Poor kid, he was dead before he knew what was happening."

"Could Cho still be alive?"

"Maybe. It fed off Dorian here. Broke his neck then went for the blood. Chewed a hole in his neck and stuck its tongue right into his heart. Ever seen a Reaper tongue? Pointed at the end, like a big rubbery syringe."

Guilt hammered at Valentine with a string of precisely aimed blows. *You left Cho unprotected in the open, watched by a kid who shouldn't even have been responsible for covering the west gate from a loophole. You pulled him out of his house and left him in his own back-yard to get his heart pierced. Two people are dead because you couldn't stand hurting an injured buddy by moving her. Nice work, Valentine. The Kurians need a few more like you giving orders.*

All the more reason to make them wish they had tried someone else's friends, a stronger part of him countered.

At the watchtower over the main gate, three farmers gulped at the roasted hickory nut drink called *coffee* for lack of a more accurate term. Valentine asked them for their best guess about which direction the Harpies were last seen flying and got three slightly different answers. The consensus seemed to be a little north of east.

Most of the town still worked to keep the blaze from spreading. The exception was the Helm family; the father retrieved his son's body while Mrs. Helm sat on the steps of her porch with her arms around her other two children, dully watching the flames consume the great barn.

Valentine climbed down from the watchtower. Bourne and the other eight reservists waited by the Militia stable tack shed. Recently turned earth next to the little wooden shack exposed two stout cases. Bourne gingerly examined the contents of one of the open cases.

"How is it, Tank?" Valentine asked.

"Still usable. We turned it this summer when we blasted the new drainage ditch from town. Quickest way I know to get rid of tree stumps."

"If I promise not to ask where you got it, will you spare us some of that bang?" Valentine knew the dynamite had probably been lifted from a Southern Command supply cave, perhaps with the aid of a small bribe to the resident quartermaster.

"If it means paying the Harpies back in their own coin, I'll tie up a couple of five-stick bundles and have them fused before you can say *nitroglycerin*. Part that worries me though, kid, is you wanting to take off right now. Wandering around in the dark with a Hood around, looking for something you aren't sure where it is—well, it's like playing blindman's buff in a room full of buzz saws."

Valentine squatted down and looked at the dynamite. "I want to hit them while they think we're still busy with this fire."

"Yeah, I buy that. One thing you got going for you, anywhere these things are holed up, it's sure to smell like a well full of dead skunks. They shit as much as pigeons, and you up everything proportional. I know they eat like crazy and their handlers aren't too particular about what they feed them."

Valentine's entire team volunteered for the duty, but in the end he took two. He asked two others to borrow horses and ride for the nearest Command post. The rest would guard against further attack in case the Harpies came back to finish the job. He just prayed the Reaper didn't decide to come back.

Valentine took Gil DelVecchio and Steve Oran with him. Steve Oran, a brassy young man who enjoyed hunting, had ventured many times into the borderlands east of Weening in search of game. Oran had the best knowledge of the land and excellent eyes. He'd once explored as far as the Saint Francis River, which marked the belt of uninhabited land surrounding the Ozark Free Territory. Gil was a powerfully built farm boy from the Missouri Valley in the Dakotas. He exuded strength and could be relied on to keep his head in a fix. DelVecchio had been one of the two men to climb the silo: his sweaty skin was still stained with soot.

The three forced down a quick meal as they loaded up two days' supplies in rucksacks. With weapons, ammunition, dynamite, and almost no camp gear, they could move quickly even in rough terrain. Valentine brought his pistol, with six bullets left in the magazine, and the best compass and map Bourne could provide.

They hiked out the main gate a few minutes after midnight, turning down an offer by the other Helm boy to go along as guide. Valentine told him he would help his family more by fighting the fire that threatened their house. He mentally added that while the killing machine that took his brother was probably elsewhere by now, perhaps striking again in the confusion of another Harpy attack, there were too many other risks in the eastern dark for Valentine to chance losing both of a mother's sons the same night.

The Reaper was much on Valentine's mind as the three men moved east. Oran picked the trail; Valentine followed several paces behind, making sure he stayed on course; and DelVecchio walked just behind, rifle ready for instant use. The Hood obviously worked with the Harpies, but would it decide Cho was a valuable prize to be taken for questioning? Her nondescript uniform differed little from any other impoverished resident's, and she carried no weapon. She was grabbed as a weak target that could not put up much of a fight, to be consumed at a later time.

Valentine prayed Cho had lost consciousness from pain and shock. He could not bear the thought of his closest friend being carried east to a dreadful end, screaming out her pain the whole way.

By three in the morning the men reached the wide Saint Francis River. A few ruined buildings that had been reclaimed by the wilderness more or less stood on its hilly banks. Valentine looked into the skull-like emptiness of a brick house, the interior nothing but humps of collapsed roof and saplings, and thought of the world-that-was. Fifty years ago, little cabin cruisers and fishing boats must have floated up and down the river, its banks under control and sandbars dredged. But with man occupied elsewhere, Nature had reclaimed her own. At a rest halt, he began to despair of their hunt. The Harpies could be anywhere.

"Val, there's a light on the river," Oran reported.

The three climbed a little promontory and looked north at the distant speck of light. It was near the western bank of the hundred-yard-wide river, but whether it came from boat or shore could not be seen at this distance. Who would be fool enough to burn a light right at the border? *A guide for the returning fliers?* Valentine wondered, suddenly hopeful.

They decided to check it out. Valentine and Oran readied their rifles and picked their way north, keeping under cover. When they got close enough to see that the light in fact came from a boat, they rested for a few minutes before creeping forward again.

"It's a small barge and a towboat," said Oran, who had the best night vision of the three, and therefore used the binoculars. They lay in a little hollow, peeking at the river from behind a fallen tree. "Looks like five men visible on the towboat. One's got a gun. No one is on the barge. It's riding light, must be practically empty. The light is on the barge, electric, not a lantern."

The towboat was attached to a ruined concrete piling projecting out of the lake, perhaps the last remnant of a dock.

Oran leveled the binoculars at the barge. "They got it anchored at the front and back. If anyone's in it, they're staying hid."

A gust of wind off the river made the men wrinkle their noses. They exchanged glances.

"I think we've found the nest," said Valentine.

They hashed out a plan. Valentine would take a bundle of dynamite and swim to the ship from the north end of the barge. When he set it off, the other two men would start sniping at the tugboat, with hope that it would be lit by the burning barge, and use the other bundle of dynamite on it from the shore. Gil said he was sure he could throw the bundle the thirty feet from the shore to the boat.

"Here, Val," DelVecchio said, pulling a hand ax from his belt. "You might need this. Who knows what might be in that hull?"

The weapon was light and handy, more of a fighting tomahawk than a tool. "Thanks. We'll meet back here," Valentine ordered. "If you're being chased, just go west like hell, don't wait for me."

"Hope you don't puke easy, if you're going close up to that thing," Oran commented, tension written in boldfaced capital letters on his face.

"Let's not waste any time. I want to get this over before dawn. Maybe that Hood sleeps in the barge."

Valentine stole past the lounging figures on the tug. If five men were up and around at this hour, perhaps ten more might be crammed below. Or were they out, somehow helping the Harpies? Once he had the bulk of the barge between him and the towboat, he crawled through vegetation to the water. The dynamite, matches, and his pistol rested on his back, in a pack that might keep the water out for a moment or two, if he was lucky.

Valentine kicked off his shoes and crawled into the cold water. It reminded him of his bath, and how Cho had dried him off afterwards. He took the comforting wood handle of the tomahawk in his hand and half floated through the water toward the barge, moving like an alligator with just eyes and nostrils out of the water, the pack making a sea-monster hump on his back. He felt as alive and alert as if he had just finished a light breakfast after a long night's sleep, rather than having been awake for eighteen hours.

It was a good thing he hadn't eaten recently. When he slithered close enough to really smell the barge, a horrible musky odor mixed with a sharper turpentine-like smell assaulted his nostrils. The hazy moonlight revealed details of the ancient barge, a mass of rust and paint and makeshift welds with M-33 painted on its side in three-foot-high letters. He shifted the tomahawk to his mouth, holding it between his teeth with straining jaws, and breaststroked into the river. He made for the stern anchor line. The gentle current assisted him with its chilly flow. He reached the cable, grateful for its hand-filling thickness. He climbed it, still gripping the ax in his teeth like a dog with an oversize bone.

The deck of the barge was as beat-up as its sides. It had a single hatch open to the sky. The battery-powered lamp, a conglomeration of what looked like a car battery and a truck headlight, pointed up into the night but seemed to bathe the whole top of the barge with an intimidating, revealing light. Valentine wished he had told Oran and DelVecchio to start firing when they saw him reach the barge; he could use something to draw the men's attention to shore. Still dangling, he gently placed the hatchet on the deck of the barge. Now or never.

He hoisted himself up on deck and crawled for the hatch. Expecting a shout at any second, he peered into the reeking hold. He could make out little in the dark, but there seemed to be floor six feet or so down.

He rolled over the edge and landed barefoot in sticky filth, ax ready. The hold stank like a slaughterhouse, and he had to fight down his gorge as he stood up in a cramped little area. A gutter ran the length of the deck, filled with noisome excrement. The hollow interior was empty.

No. As his eyes adjusted, Valentine realized that a panting shape leaned against one wall. It was a Harpy, wrapped up in its own wings as though in a leathery cocoon. A trickle of blood pooled beneath its rump. Wounded, maybe dying. The debris on the floor included a mélange of bones. A cluster of human skulls decorated a metal pillar, part of the barge's rusting structure holding up the deck. The heads looked like a yellowish bunch of coconuts. There was a door forward out of the hold. A body lay at the bottom of stairs descending from the door: pale, naked, and headless. But it was nevertheless familiar.

Valentine had found Cho.

An awful kind of warmth filled his stomach. He no longer minded the reek. He padded toward the sleeping Harpy with slippery steps. He could make out slit nostrils and a toothy, pointed jaw decorated with bristling catlike whiskers protruding from the tent of folded wings. Wet drool dripped out with its rapid, shallow breathing. He raised the ax and buried it in the face with a bone-crushing blow. The thing never knew what happened, falling nervelessly sideways. Valentine leaped on top of it, bringing the blood-and-brain-soaked tomahawk down again and again with a series of wet smacks. Flecks of blood splattered his snarling features.

A familiar flapping sound came from the hatch, and the light reflected from the deck lamp was obscured by a winged shadow. Valentine crossed the hold to the forward stairs to the door, keeping clear of the hatch. He could sit there, light the dynamite, and blow a few Harpies to kingdom come.

Shots echoed from outside. DelVecchio and Oran must have panicked at the returning Harpies and tried to prevent them from reentering the barge. Valentine somehow ignored Cho's body, took his pistol, and tossed the backpack onto the stairs. A Harpy flopped into the hold, one wing injured.

"Welcome home, fucker," Valentine cursed, putting a bullet into its stomach. The spent cartridge case pinged off the metal interior.

The Harpy screamed out a horrible, burbling kind of call. Language or pain, it brought answering shrieks from outside. Valentine knew he was drawing all kinds of ugly from the skies as well as the tugboat, but he wanted Cho's body to have a lot of company feeding the crayfish and gars. He heard, for the first time in his life, the chatter of a machine gun fired in anger. The tugboat crew must have a support weapon mounted on deck. He prayed that DelVecchio and Oran were smart enough to pull out now and head west.

He pounded on the roof of the hold, dislodging a shower of grit. "Dinner, dinner, come and get it!" he shouted.

The wounded Harpy pulled itself toward him, gremlin mouth open in vicious anticipation. Other flappers dropped into the hold.

Valentine took two steps backwards toward the door and found the bundle of dynamite and tin of matches. Grabbing a bunch of matches, he struck them against the rough side of the stairwell. They flared into life, illuminating the dank little closet space. Valentine lit the fuse, dropped the matches to the floor, and picked up his pistol. He fired a shot into the vague shapes collected in the hold. He placed the hissing dynamite on the first stair and pushed at the hatch.

Locked.

He bashed at the hatch with his shoulder, closing his eyes to the expected oblivion that would blow him to bloody fragments, but the rusted lock gave way. He threw the door open and dashed onto the deck, then dived for the water on the river side of the barge. He felt a bullet pluck at him as it passed through his shirt at the armpit.

He was under water when the explosion hit. The *boom* sounded muted, but its force thumped at him even through the cushioning protection of the river, knocking the breath from his body. He surfaced, gasping for air.

The shattered rear half of the barge upended as pieces of its hull splashed into the river all around. The towboat was a mass of flame, the machine gun silent. The Harpies' incendiary bombs must have been on the towboats deck in readiness for another attack. Valentine got his bearings and submerged again, swimming for shore. No doubt a few very unhappy Harpies still circled above. His fingers struck the river bottom.

As his brain cleared, he realized that he was unarmed. His pistol was at the bottom of the Saint Francis, dropped when the concussion from the explosion racked him, and the tomahawk was probably landing somewhere in Mississippi. He gathered himself and ran out of the water and onto the riverbank.

Picking up a river-smoothed rock in each hand, Valentine hurried under the protective overhang of the trees. He felt defenseless as a rabbit with raptors circling above but made it to the little hollow without trouble. What was left of the tugboat was floating downstream in flames.

He crept to the place where he had left the other two and whistled softly.

An answering warble came out of the darkness. The pair joined him.

"Quite a show, Val," complimented Oran, returning Valentine's rifle. DelVecchio put the other bundle of dynamite back in his pack. Bourne could use it on more tree stumps or trade it for corrugated tin to build a new barn.

It felt good to have a rifle in his hands instead of rocks. "Oran, you need a break. I'll take point on the way back. You can keep us on course, and Gil, you cover."

"Sure thing, boss."

The light of the burning towboat faded as it sank behind them, and the three started for home. Not knowing how well the Harpies could see, hear, or smell, they stayed under the trees. Nothing dived at them or circled above. Later they sang softly as they walked through the shadowed woods, like young athletes returning home from a successful match. Beneath the bare-boughed canopy, Valentine felt safe from any of the surviving Harpies. But the trees made the Reaper's attack that much easier.

It stepped from behind a tree, plucking the gun from DelVecchio's hands and sending it spinning into the night. With its other hand, it picked him up by his backpack, holding the giant young man at arm's length like a filled diaper.

Valentine and Oran spun around, flicking the safeties on their rifles. The Reaper put the frantic DelVecchio between them like a shield.

"Drop him," was all Valentine could think to say.

"No! Wait! No!" DelVecchio was screaming. "Don't let him . . . don't shoot."

you might as well shoot, foodlings, the Reaper whispered, its voice all hissing air and menace. *you'll all three be dead as soon as i take you.*

"God, let me go," DelVecchio gibbered. "Val, get it off me!"

Valentine thought his heart was going to break out of his chest, it pounded so hard. His tongue felt dry, and his eyes seemed misted over. Only a burning sensation from the region of his kidneys prevented him from fainting dead away. He waved at Oran, motioning him to spread out. The Reaper couldn't hold DelVecchio in two directions at once. Oran, eyes fixed on the hypnotic yellow eyes of the pale, black-clad figure before them, did not respond. Valentine stepped backwards, rifle at his shoulder.

The thing turned its gaze to Valentine, bringing Oran out of his trance. Seeing Valentine stepping away, he turned and ran off into the night, discarding gun and pack.

run! i'll catch you, the Reaper breathed after him. *hide. i'll find you.* It turned to Valentine, shifting its gaze in a quick, lizardlike movement. *shoot, and i'll pull your legs apart, one joint at a time, as easily as you'd yank off a fly's wings.*

Valentine continued pacing backwards, lowering the gun barrel somewhat. He stepped behind a thick tree trunk, aiming his gun.

The Reaper laughed at the gesture, a sound indistinguishable from a cat's spitting fury: *pha pha pha!*

useless. It looked at Gil, the young man quivering in its grasp. *you got one thing right, foodling,* the predator said into DelVecchio's ear as it drew the thrashing figure close. *i am a god!*

DelVecchio screamed as it turned him around, pointed teeth tearing a hole in his neck. Gil pushed and flailed against the creature's grip, screaming the blubbery underwater screams of a man with a severed windpipe.

"Sorry, Gil. Hope you'd do the same for me," Valentine muttered, exhaling and squeezing the trigger.

The .45 shell found DelVecchio's backpack. The dynamite exploded in pinkish-orange light, throwing Valentine on his back with a warm, irresistible punch. Valentine's ears roared, and his head filled with light as he plunged into unconsciousness.

It was almost dinnertime when the exhausted residents of Weening heard a shout from the guard tower.

"Walker coming in." A moment's pause while the watchers in the tower employed an old telescopic sight. "It's Valentine. Alone."

The residents gathered, the still-smoldering barn behind them, to greet the strange apparition.

Barefoot, pants in tatters, shirt reduced to a few ribbons, and pale with fatigue, David Valentine walked into Weening. He held his rifle in one hand and bulging backpack in the other. He examined the crowd, looking for a face.

"Mr. Helm," he croaked, reaching into his backpack. "We killed the thing that got your son. And Gab. And Gil. Steve, I don't know about."

He pulled out a skull covered in sticky soot from the fire he'd used to burn off the flesh and hair. In everything but color it resembled a human skull, with an oversize forehead and an unusually long jawbone. The charred bone was bluish black and looked as if it had been carved from a block of onyx.

Randall Helm refused the offering and instead put his arms around the weary eighteen-year-old and walked him home.

That evening Bourne opened a jug of homemade whiskey and he, Valentine, and Helm took turns solemnly chiseling the names GILMAN DELVECCHIO, GABRIELLA CHO, and DORIAN HELM into the polished obsidian skull of the Reaper, still a little warm from its hours in the boiling pot. By the time the jug was recorked, the skull was mounted, slightly askew and off-center due to alcohol-impaired judgment, over the main gate of the village.

It stands there still.

Four

Ouachita Mountains, February of the forty-first year of the Kurian Order: The snow is retreating up the rugged, rocky hills of the Ouachitas, but an Arkansas winter still sits firmly in the saddle. In the narrow valley between two low mountain ranges pointing like cleft fingers at the blasted ruins of Little Rock, a little collection of cabins marks the temporary home of Fort Candela. It is a fort in name only; the soldiers are scattered across twelve square miles of the valley floor. There is electricity most of the time and fresh food some of the time, but warmth and companionship by the cabin hearths always.

The erratic war is blessedly far from the men and women quartered in this valley. They concentrate on making and repairing equipment, cutting and sewing new uniforms, eating, drinking, gambling, and trading. And most important, training. This winter, like every other for the past twenty-odd years, recruits get paired up with seasoned veterans, until the green soldiers can do what the vets do and know what the vets know. Specialists and artisans travel through, giving lessons and once in a while taking on permanent apprentices if a recruit shows unusual ability at veterinary work, perhaps, or in making quality leather goods.

The officers in charge of Fort Candela make decisions and act on them. One recruit has hopelessly bad vision, another drinks too much, and another cannot keep up on practice marches. The culls are offered support jobs—honorable service in paid labor outfits—or are returned to civilian life. Those who do not try for home are absorbed by the labor-hungry farms and towns of the Ozark Free Territory, but a few malcontents become "bummers" and inevitably a matter for the law.

For the rest, the question becomes Guards or Hunters. Seven out of ten go to the Guards, the military regiments that provide a defensive core for the Ozark Free Territory. Guard service is rewarding: The soldiers get the finest uniforms Southern Command can produce, ample ammunition for marksmanship training, and frequent parties and barbecues, games and riding contests. Many of them are mounted, adding to their dash and swagger. They also get plenty of opportunities to mix with civilians. No New Year's dance is complete without a handsome contingent of young Guards in polished boots and crisp charcoal-gray uniforms, kepis with regimental-colored neckerchiefs hanging to precisely the base of their tunic collars. The Guards are the well-ordered, well-disciplined, reassuring face of Southern Command, who can and do fight, giving their lives in defense of wives, children, and sweethearts.

The others—the men and women who will become cold-eyed Hunters ranging outside the friendly reaches of the Ozark Free Territory to slay the minions and Quislings of the Kurians—are brought before the Lifeweavers.

A glossy black house cat named Sailor Tom ruled the cabin with an iron paw. Six men shared the bunkhouse nestled in a hollow between two spurs of Fourche Mountain, but none disputed the feline's claim to the warmest chair by the stone fireplace or the best tidbit from the steer quarter hung in the cool room. The heavy cat looked like a witch's familiar with a lynx somewhere in the family tree. He strutted around the cabin on muscular rear legs, half-wild and all attitude. Sailor Tom asserted his authority with a rising corkscrew growl that blossomed into a biting, clawing fury aimed at anyone foolish enough to ignore that first and only warning. He gained his nickname when one Wolf declared, "If that tom spoke English, you just know he'd be cussing like a sailor." The men tolerated the bad-tempered cat and pointed him out to recruits as an example of tenacity to be imitated. The men depended on stored food to get them through the winter, and Sailor Tom exterminated trespassing mice, rats, squirrels, and even rabbits with samurai spirit.

The cat's realm encompassed a two-room, sooty kingdom full of beds and furniture as roughly finished as the men who occupied them. A fireplace of watercourse stones dominated one entire wall at the "sitting" part of the bunkhouse, and a two-hundred-years-old-and-still-going-strong potbellied stove warmed the "sleeping" part, a musky warren of bunk beds and old blankets hung for gloomy privacy.

Four veteran Wolves and two recruits shared the cabin. Pankow,

Gavineau, Big Seth, and Imai saw to it that neither David Valentine nor Marquez, the other Wolf Aspirant, enjoyed a moment's peace. Anytime they were not actually in the field or attending a lesson as part of their caste training, the four Senior Wolves dedicated themselves to seeing that the would-be Hunters idled as little as possible. Not just with training. Marquez found himself held responsible for the firewood supply and general cabin maintenance. The firewood might seem an easy task for a man in the middle of a forest, but the Wolves insisted he fell, and consequently haul, the timber from two miles away. If he so much as looked at one of the bushy pines surrounding the cabin, the trainers accused him of wanting to expose their temporary home to the enemy.

The Wolves assigned everything else to Valentine. "Everything else" included cooking, washing up, laundry, stocking the pantry, mending, disposing of Sailor Tom's half-eaten *corpus rodentia,* and the morning ersatz coffee. The men accepted a certain amount of slackness and inefficiency in all his responsibilities excepting the last. No matter that Valentine may have returned from a night orientation march exhausted at the first pink of dawn, if the coffee was not steaming and ready to be poured at the customary rising hour of 6 A.M., he was thoroughly cursed and punished. This required a fell run up Bald Knob, a forty-degree-grade hill bare of trees, under the disapproving eyes of the four coffeeless Wolves.

Valentine learned from all four, but his principal mentor was Evan Pankow. The child of a representative from Ohio, the then seven-year-old congressman's son had watched his privileged world disappear in a few insane weeks when the Raving Madness virus swept the United States. Young Evan was one of the few people immune to the virus. While this protected him from a death that claimed better than three quarters of the United States population, his genes were useless against the war and chaos that followed. He followed a stream of refugees into the tidewater of Virginia, where he got his first taste of the Kurian Order. He witnessed an albino man with yellowish eyes and a soft voice claiming to be a "crisis governor" kill an entire family in a hotel room. The boy, forever after avoiding the Reapers, was flown southwest by a woman who had also witnessed the "crisis governor" in action. Pankow had lost his parents, and she had lost a son, leading the two to form an increasingly real mother-son bond.

The pilot's name was Jamie Kostos, a former journalist who wrote some of the first pamphlets examining the Kurian Order. Her early writings, accurate in fact but mistaken in analysis, brought her to the attention of the Lifeweavers. Through her, Evan became a student of the Lifeweavers and a Wolf.

In his twenties, Pankow helped found Southern Command. Now fifty, with a seamed face and world-weary eyes that reminded Valentine of a Karsh portrait of Ernest Hemingway he had seen in one of the Padre's books, Pankow devoted himself to training a new generation of Wolves to carry on the struggle.

One late-February afternoon, with snow camouflaging the mud surrounding the little cabin, Pankow lectured his Aspirant about, of all things, tea.

"It's way too easy, when you're outdoors and on the move, to just eat rabbits and such," Pankow said, running his ungloved hand across the soft needles of a mountain spruce. "Especially in cold weather, you get hungry for meat and fat, and forget about everything else. But you've got to get your greens. You know what vitamins are?"

"Yes, I do, sir. It's those letters, *A, B, C,* and so on," David responded.

"Yeah, well, when I was a squirt we got them in stuff like breakfast cereal, little candy pills: damn near everything said 'vitamin fortified.' Now it's not so easy, it being winter. Take these spruce needles. In the spring, the little buds taste pretty good; you can just chew them. But if we pull some of these needles and boil them up into tea, you get as much vitamin C as from an orange, even. Ever had an orange?"

Valentine shook his head.

"Too bad. Sweet and juicy like a watermelon, but tart, too. Anyway, your greens aren't a problem in summer; any fool can pull up a dandelion, chew its leaves, and roast the root, but winter's a different story. You don't get your vitamins, you end up losing teeth, getting fevers. You'll catch some virus and die even if the scurvy doesn't take you. Trappers in Canada used to die of it; rabbit fever, it was called. They were starving their bodies to death while stuffing themselves with fresh meat every night. So never just eat meat, on the trail or at home. Add a lot of greens if you value your eyesight and your teeth."

"We should just raid more food off the Kurians," Valentine suggested.

Pankow scowled. "That's not so easy. But before you can fight, you have to be healthy in mind and body. I know it seems hard, what we've been having you do, but soon your body's going to be like a whole new machine. We're trying to get you as strong as possible so nothing quits on you once you start keeping the Way of the Wolf."

"When will that be?"

"Not for me to say. Not for you to say, not for the captain to say. It's up to the old Wizard. He might be watching you now, he might be advising the governor in Mountain Home. One thing is for sure, no one who meets him comes away the same as he was before."

Back at the cabin, like a demon invoked by mention of his name, word from the Lifeweaver waited in the form of a small printed list. The cabin was empty save for Seth and Sailor Tom, both napping in front of the Franklin stove.

"Amu's called an Invocation," Big Seth explained from his modified bunk. Reinforced wooden wings accommodated his six-foot-six-inch frame and supported an elongated mattress of his own making. "Starting Saturday and running for a week. One hundred fifteen fresh Wolves in this batch, thank God."

"Nice to see the roster growing this year. Many's the summer we had less than the year before. Let's see the list," Pankow said, reaching for the typed sheet of paper.

"Marquez made it. Bad news, Valentine," he said, watching Valentine's face fall. "You made it, Valentine. In fact, you're last on the list."

Valentine felt ambivalent at Pankow's joke, but a little pride still crept into his voice. "At least I made it, even if I'm dead last."

"Don't take it that way, son," Big Seth interjected. "It isn't good or bad, being last. Just means they may want to take more time."

"Doing what? Tattoos, a Vulcan mind-meld, what?"

Pankow laughed. "Hell, Valentine, where did you come up with that? Little before your time, and they haven't done reruns in over forty years."

"My dad liked to read science fiction. The man who brought me up after he died taught me to read my dad's books. But what is this *transformation* you all keep hinting about?"

Big Seth and Pankow exchanged a look. Pankow shook Valentine's hand.

"You'll just have to meet Father Wolf and see for yourself. Magic, son, is a little hard to explain."

The week dragged on, and Valentine made it pass more quickly by devouring the few books in the cabin. A heavy snowstorm came, and the Wolves relaxed the tough schedule shared by the two Aspirants. Valentine gratefully retreated to his bunk. Pankow gave him a pamphlet written by his foster mother. Printed in heavy, slightly smeared type and cumber-somely titled *Fallen Gods: The History, Theory, and Practice of the Kurian Order,* it was fifty pages relating the history of the Lifeweavers, their schism over the use of vital auras to attain immortality, and the Kurian takeover of Earth.

The Kurians failed in their first effort to take Earth because it was chaotic, badly planned, and they had not even consolidated their victory on Kur itself, where knots of Lifeweaver resistance slowed them. Humanity owes these brave lost souls a four-thousand-year debt of gratitude. Mankind in its primitive, isolated state was less vulnerable to the spread of the Ravies plague and quicker to accept the word and help of the Lifeweavers.

We hunted the horrors that came over from Kur, closed the doors, and having eradicated the threat promptly forgot about it two hundred years before Stonehenge was built. Vampires became rumor, then legend, and the Caste of the Bear trickled down into human legend as the berserkers of the Norse sagas.

Certainly a Kurian or two remained on Earth, lurking in untraveled corners of the globe. And Kurian-designed spawn, now known generically as *Grogs* and individually through slang and names out of mythology, no doubt survived to trouble humanity now and again as it pushed back the borders of the unknown.

But though the Gates of the Interworld Tree were closed, the Kurians in their red-clouded underground world learned in the long years of their exile how to open new ones. When and where the first of the new portals were opened is a matter of some dispute. Even the Lifeweavers are unable to say. It could have been as early as the Dark Ages in the Balkans, or as late as the eighteenth century. Opening the portals requires enormous sacrifices of vital auras to achieve, but after the first Kur came through the new Gate or Gates, humanity aided the Kurians in this all too frequently.

Humanity took the first step toward its own overthrow. Over the years, the Kurians recruited human allies, perhaps by striking Faustian bargains. The Kurian moles gained positions of trust and authority in society.

With the new millennium, the dragon's teeth sown in the last hundred or so years of man's history were ready to grow. In the first week of June 2022, they sprang the trapdoor on the vital auras of Earth's seven billion inhabitants.

The door to the cool room opened noisily, and Gavineau entered the cabin. He walked over to the hearth, apparently not seeing Valentine, and took the jug of busthead down from its place on the shelf. Gavineau collapsed in the leather-webbed camp chair by the empty fireplace, took a long pull, and stared at the cold ashes. Sailor Tom took advantage of the warm lap, and Gavineau scratched the cat between the ears without looking at it. Valentine considered greeting him, but didn't wish to be given something to do. He returned to his booklet.

THE OVERTHROW

The world was already a miserable place in the spring of that cursed year. The New Depression was at its height. Stocks fell, jobs were lost, and consumer consumption fell in a corporate death spiral as the aging technoczars were revealed to have feet of clay. Financial institutions underreacted, the government overreacted, and a society living on borrowed time paid for with borrowed dollars failed. Hard times and hunger came to the Western world, which was all the more of a shock because the generation that survived the last financial collapse had virtually died out.

Ancient hatreds smoldered and burst into flame. Europe saw its first real war in generations over food tariffs; China used America's preoccupation with its economy to overrun Taiwan. Russia and Japan, both backing different factions in Europe and the Pacific Rim, started a naval war that the United States, in its last great overseas commitment, stopped by cordoning off the two powers.

Civil unrest over the use of American wealth and resources abroad with so many suffering at home erupted into violence. Paramilitary groups took a hodgepodge of economic, political, and even racial grievances to the ultimate court of violence. A few polarizing and charismatic leaders further unraveled the tattered American social fabric.

The Earth itself added its cataclysmic voice to the dissonant chorus of human suffering. A worldwide string of earthquakes and volcanic eruptions leveled cities and made ash-covered wastelands of regions near the volcanoes. Particles in the atmosphere changed the climate more to the Kurians' liking. As if the tectonic damage was not enough, a plague added to the chaos. People called it *rabies,* but its twenty-four- to seventy-two-hour incubation cycle and mind-altering effects made the cure seem more like a job for exorcists than doctors. Wild mobs tore through the cities in a biting and clawing frenzy that shattered civic order.

Not even suspected at the time was that both events were

long planned. Kurian technology allowed the fallen Lifeweavers to use the Earth itself as a weapon, and the disease, which we know today as Raving Madness, had appeared on Earth in the first Kurian invasion. The pale, robed Reapers began to walk the night.

The Reapers strode into the maelstrom, alternately cowing and killing. They commanded legions of Grogs, genetically altered creatures designed to break up opposition. As fearless in battle as army ants, but far more cunning, the Grogs come in many shapes and sizes. The most common form is a large rhino-hided ape, with hands and brains capable of using weaponry from assault rifles to armored personnel carriers.

The military and civil forces of the United States, already unable to deal with the plague and widespread destruction, succumbed as spare parts, ammunition, and especially morale ran out. A few Kurian agents and collaborators in the command structure helped orchestrate defeat on a grand scale. In the final extreme, a scorched-earth policy destroyed military bases and their equipment to keep them out of the hands of the Kurians. A few nuclear and chemical weapons were used in the last gasp of the war, but this added to the suffering rather than slowing the Kurian takeover. The end came with a bang and a whimper. The president shot himself when he learned his family had caught the Raving Madness virus at a riot in Quantico, and the vice president fled with a few leading members of congress to Mount Omega after she read the president's final executive order. In it, the despairing president declared, like the captain of a sinking ship, that the situation was "every man for himself."

The United States, and as far as we can tell the rest of the world, belonged to the Kurians within a year.

Valentine could understand why Kostos ended her life a harddrinking woman. The facts of life of the New World Order came more easily to Valentine, who had been born well after the Kurian takeover. No memories of the vanished security and assorted technological delights of the past haunted him, just a wistful curiosity. He sometimes felt a schism between himself and Pankow's generation, including even the Padre. They cherished and fought for the past, a flag with stars and stripes, a way of living that would probably never return. Valentine wanted to win back his future.

A creaking from the sitting part of the room and a disgruntled *mi-*

aow from Sailor Tom made Valentine glance up from the old red pamphlet and look at Gavineau. The Wolf set the jug on the floor and shuffled over to his bed, a sad and sick look visiting his face with every intention of staying the night.

"You okay, Don?"

"Hey, Val," he slurred. "Didn't see you there. Pankow giving you some slack?"

"He rode up the Happy Trail today," Valentine explained. The Happy Trail Getaway was a saloon where the bartender was friendly to the Wolves and the girls were even friendlier, if the words were kind and the price was right, the price being anything from a new pair of shoes to an old song, depending on the charm of the man. "I think he's letting up on me with the Invocation a day away. All I had to do was draw him a hot bath and put an edge on the razor. He told me I couldn't eat anything, and just to take it easy. Wouldn't tell me why I couldn't eat, though."

"Valentine, Marquez is dead. Can't think of any other way to say it."

The Aspirant's thoughts about-faced and came to attention in a hurry. "What?"

Gavineau sat on his bed, a bunk away from Valentine's. A sheet of laundry hung between them.

"It just happens sometimes, boy," said Gavineau.

"He made it through the Invocation fine. It's not like you run an Indian gantlet or something," slurred Gavineau. "He got out of the cave and just lost it. It can affect you funny. I remember I got out of mine and all I could smell was wood smoke on everything. He looked around like he didn't know where he was and took off at a run. Jumped right off the damn cliff. I remember two years ago one kid quit eating after it. Wouldn't touch any food, always saying it was diseased or filthy or something. He starved himself to death, just threw up when we force-fed him. Usually the guys who come over funny are just jumpy for a couple of days, then they come round. Bad business with Marquez. A couple others volunteered to go down and get the body. I only saw it from three hundred feet up."

"My God, what made—?"

"Hey, David, don't let it get to you," he said. "He just wasn't wired right, and sometimes not even the Wizard can spot that. You'll be fine."

Gavineau's drunken prediction was something Valentine reminded himself of again and again as he climbed the mountainside with ten other Aspirants, the last set supposed to meet with the Lifeweaver known variously as Amu, the Wizard, and Father Wolf.

Named Winterhome Mountain, the 2,200-foot cap of rock and snow looked like a shark's tooth from some angles and a sagging tepee from others. The cave was a little more than halfway up, set back from Marquez's fatal cliff by a sloping meadow. Five goats grazed there, some stripping bark from the stunted mountain pine and others pawing at the lingering snow to expose dead bracken underneath.

Two totem poles flanked the crescent-shaped entrance to the cave. Carved wolf heads, ears erect and eyes alert, crowned the poles. Carved names covered the rest of the pole, some with dates written afterwards. Valentine decided these must be the tollpoles, mobile gravestones for Wolves who died in battle. *Not so bad,* Valentine thought, *a few hundred names for twenty years of fighting.*

Just inside the cave eleven more poles, filled with tightly packed names, formed an arch the recruits filed under like a wedding party passing under crossed swords. Valentine paused and ran a finger over the carved names on one of the poles. Would his name join the long list?

The tunnel widened into a teardrop-shaped cave with a curtain at one end. What might have been a tapestry decorated the curtain; Valentine couldn't make out much in the dim light trickling in from the entrance even after his eyes adjusted. The two Wolves guiding them motioned for them to sit.

"Just keep quiet, and let him work you one at a time," one of them warned. "After the ceremony, they'll be kinda twitchy, so keep still and quiet when they come out."

The curtain moved as a wet black nose appeared. A canine head the size of a champion pumpkin lifted the curtain, revealing blazing blue eyes that reminded Valentine of a husky from the Boundary Waters. A wolf that could be mistaken for a pony by its size strode into the ring of Aspirants sitting around the edges of a cave. It had striking white fur, with black tips visible only up close. It sniffed each man, stepping sideways on paws the size of horseshoes.

"Thank you all for earning your places in this cave," a rich, cultivated voice came from the wolf's mouth, which did not seem to be forming any words. The wolf quivered and blurred, to be replaced by a smiling old man. "Forgive the dramatic entrance; it's an illusion that impressed your ancestors. I continue it out of love of tradition. Ahem. I hope you all know who I am."

"Amu," said some of those present. "The Wizard," said a few others. Valentine just nodded. There was something noble and strong about the man, Valentine thought, but with just a hint of tired lunacy in his frosty blue eyes. Valentine for some reason thought of Cervantes's Don Quixote.

"My name is not as important as who I am, a matter entirely different from a simple name. For I am going to be your Father. You all have a biological father who started your life, and most of you believe in a spiritual father who will take you unto him after death. I am here to be a third Father. I will give you rebirth."

Eleven separate faces digested this.

"Yes, I am speaking in riddles. Riddles are simple, usually after you hear the answer. But I am a busy man and would prefer to deal with each of you individually. Michael Jeremy Wohlers," the Wizard said, standing in front of a husky, curly-haired youth. "I'll see you first."

The prospective Wolf shot to his feet, narrowly missing crashing his head against the ceiling. "How did—?"

"I didn't," interrupted the Wizard, opening the curtain and gracefully pointing with his chin to the inner cavern. "You did."

Valentine spent four increasingly sore hours waiting his turn. Hungry, anxious, cold, and confused seemed a strange way to go through this invocation ceremony. He watched each of the ten other recruits emerge one at a time from behind the tapestry and stare about at those remaining as if they had never seen them before. Pete, the Viking giant who came down from northern Minnesota with Valentine, looked around at the remaining Aspirants suspiciously, as if fifteen minutes ago he had not been shifting from one aching buttock to the other with the rest of them.

"Pete, how'd it go?" Valentine asked. The blond jumped away from Valentine like a horse startled by a firecracker. His head connected with the cavern roof with the audible *thump* of a dropped melon, and he crashed to the ground, unconscious.

"Told you to keep quiet. If he ain't up by the time you're done, you're carrying him out," one of the Wolves said.

Pete began to groan and rolled onto all fours. He retched, vomiting clear liquid across the floor of the cave.

"Oh, that's just fine," the second Wolf said. "Now the other three are sure to puke."

Pete staggered to his feet and lurched out of the cave, rubbing the back of his head.

And puke they did. As the last two returned to the cave, they each added their own puddles of bile to the floor of the cave before fleeing to the open air outside. Valentine wondered if this was the reason for the orders not to eat anything.

"You're up, kid," one said.

"Through the looking glass you go, Alice," added the other.

He pulled the tapestry aside and stepped through. Behind him, he heard one Wolf say to the other, "Glad this happens only twice a year."

The tunnel wound downward, illuminated by nearly guttered candles set into the irregular sides of the cave. Valentine counted twenty paces before a second heavy piece of cloth blocked his progress. He didn't know whether to just open it, say his name, or tap on the material. He cleared his throat.

"Come in, come in, Valentine the Younger."

He entered, bending beneath the low rock arch.

The cave was warm and well lit, with a clean, inviting smell, which Valentine identified as balsam. The warmth and light came from an apple-size glowing ball that floated a few inches below the cave's eight-foot ceiling. It was bright but somehow did not pain Valentine's eyes, even when he looked directly at it. The room reminded Valentine of the inside of an igloo, were the igloo constructed out of grayish ice.

Father Wolf sat cross-legged in the center of the room on a woven rug. The floor of the cave was a mass of pine needles and small branches, with more patterned rugs thrown over the boughs. Five four-legged wolves snored in a companionable heap near the door.

"My bodyguard, you might say," said Amu. "Long ago, in another part of your world, I traveled with twenty of them. It made more of an impression on those simple folk: they lived in fear of wolves. I have grown rather fond of them, and should our enemies discover me here, I would remask myself and slip out with them. Sit down, please."

Valentine sat, grateful for the cushioning needles and rug after the hard floor of the outer cave.

"What do you want me to do?" Valentine asked.

"The question would be better put as what do *you* want to do. Why did you leave Minnesota? You did not come south just for a change of geography."

"I want to do my part."

The Wizard smiled at this. "Simply put. I hear something a little different from each young man or woman. They want to defend hearth and home, liberate their enslaved fellow men, and kick the invaders back into their kennels.

"What is needed from you, and what you can give me if you are true to yourself, is an outlet for your hatred. Hatred makes for good killers. The word is anathema; your religions rightly discourage it because it makes poor mortar for a society. But, young Valentine, your race is being *eaten*. You should be consumed by hate; your every breath should be drawn to curse your enemies. It gives you energy and a purpose and a determination that only love matches. The more you love your fellow men, the more you should be aflame with hatred for your foe. Your culture is so full of the image of the reluctant warrior that it is an archetype. The man who kills regretfully, who goes into battle terrified but gets the job done and then shows mercy to his enemy afterwards. That kind of man will keep the Free Territory upright for a while. But he will not win the war. Not against this enemy.

"There is a beast in you that I'm going to help you release. If you agree, that is. I give fair warning, though. It means a vicious life and perhaps a hard end. You will live only to kill our enemies until you yourself are slain. Few of my warriors retire to marry as your father did. So if you want a role inside the human family, I'm giving you a chance to walk out of this cave and down the hill with your humanity intact. You can serve with honor in the Guards, living up to the image of noble crusader, or go back into hiding. There are many ways to do the right thing. Stay with us, though, and you will become the thing the enemy fears in the night. The prey will become the predator."

Valentine wondered how many refused the offer. How many men wanted to be killers? He had expected physical or mental tests, not a moral one. He thought of his father but could not make the connection between the Wizard's animalistic killers and the quiet man who was shot to death in his own backyard.

"Why don't the Lifeweavers fight? I would think that with your technology, magic I've heard it called, you'd be able to beat the Kurians."

The Wizard seemed a little surprised. "Usually I ask the questions, but I will do my best to answer yours: We are not any good at it. It would be like you defecating in your pants. You could do it if you put your mind to it, but you would not enjoy the experience, and until you had a chance to clean yourself, you would probably be preoccupied. We toilet-trained ourselves far too long ago, we are not numerous, and my ability to change into a wolf does not mean I could bite like one.

"You *Homo sapiens,* on the other hand, are almost perfect killing machines. You are flexible, aggressive, intelligent, and inventive. We examined life-forms on twelve worlds, and you half-savages revert to your terrible earlier selves with greater alacrity than any other. So we help you fight your battles, and in doing so you fight our war for us. Or am I speaking in riddles again?"

"No, I understand. It's your method I question. Instead of arming us with some kind of advanced technology, you turn us feral. That seems a strange way to help us win a war."

The Wizard abruptly disappeared, only to emerge from the dome-shaped cave's other exit, carrying what looked like a small mirror on a stand. "I am sorry," he said to the startled young man. "I had to get this, and I didn't want to interrupt, so I left you talking to an image. You said you understood, David. It is clear that you do not. I'm giving you the most powerful weapon on the planet: yourself at your full potential."

"I thought I was supposed to make up my mind."

"You did, David, you did," he said, sitting again opposite the young man. "The moment you thought of your father, and his death, and wondered if he was the kind of man I want you to become. You may not have felt it, but to me your fury was white hot. You can hide your rage from yourself, but not from me. It is so big, I wonder where you put it so you can sleep at night."

The item the Wizard placed between them looked like a plate-sized round mirror. It hovered at face level between them, held up by the same mysterious force that kept the light globe near the ceiling. Valentine saw in it only his own reflection, but fuzzy and out of focus, conforming to his general outline.

"What is this?" he asked.

Amu's face appeared in the mirror. The Lifeweaver's visage melted and shifted as though his skin were made of clouds boiling in the wind. "You could say it's the surgeon's scalpel, David. I will use it to operate on you. There is a cup in front of you. Drink up."

Valentine looked at the woven rug. A wooden cup, round like a hollowed-out coconut, sat before him. Had it been sitting there all the time? Valentine sniffed at it suspiciously.

"Just a little something to facilitate the ceremony. It is tasteless."

Valentine drank. Just before consciousness faded, he looked into the mirror-thing. First he saw his face, then the Wizard's, then a wolf's. The images flickered together: Wizard-Wolf-Self-Wizard-Wolf-Self-Wizard-Wolf-Self. Only the eyes were all the same. But they were not his. Not Amu's. The Wolf's. Valentine found himself fixing on the eyes of the three faces as they morphed from one manifestation to the next, all sharing the same ice-blue stare.

The young Wolf awoke to an overwhelming farrago of sounds and smells. The pine needles, musty rugs, dried lichen on the walls, and living wolves all vied to overthrow his brain. He could hear their heartbeats as with a stethoscope. Their breathing sounded like a gale. *Too much! Too much!* his brain shrieked at him. He leaped up and hurled himself away from the sleeping pack as if flung by a catapult, bruising himself with the force of the impact against the wall.

David, stay calm. Your senses are just sharpened up a little, that is all, Amu's voice in his head whispered in a soothing monotone. *I will help you through your first days; then you will learn on your own. You must learn to switch your senses between two levels, "hard" and "soft." You have to learn how to hear with soft ears and smell with soft nose first. You will use the hard ears and hard nose later, to sense over distance.*

"Where are you?" Valentine asked, hearing the echo of his voice in the outer cavern where he had waited before being called.

I have linked us. I cannot understand you very well. I am not as gifted as some in this type of communication with human thought-shapes. I just get impressions about your emotions. You need to take a deep breath, fill your lungs with air, and relax. Draw everything back into your center. Soften your eyes, let them go out of focus; soften your ears, let them relax and listen to the sound of the empty air in front of you; soften your nose and smell the heat of the light cube.

Valentine tried to relax, but the smell and sound of the slumbering wolves kept beating down the barriers. He felt dazed.

You are doing very well. I think you are a natural. Try to walk out of the cave the way you came in.

The musty old tapestry at the door reeked abominably, and he hurried past it. His legs were suddenly working too fast and he crashed into the cavern wall like a mechanized toy bouncing off an obstacle in its path. He steadied himself, but the flickering candles sounded like whip cracks in his ears.

Center! Center! the voice implored. *No, you still don't have it. Let me help you.*

Valentine felt himself steady, the cacophony of sensations fading into the background. He made it to the other curtain, but as he pushed through it, the acidic vomit smell overthrew him. His gorge rose and joined the slick mess on the floor.

"Serves you right," one of the Wolves thundered. Valentine leaped forward in alarm, but could not keep control of his spastic body and missed the exit. He ricocheted off the unforgiving stone and came away bleeding at the forehead. The coppery-smelling fluid infiltrated his nostrils, took over his sense of smell.

Breathe, breathe, bring it back to your center. Try crawling outside. You are fine.

The young Wolf did not feel fine.

"Hell, I think Father Wolf turned him all the way up," he heard one man whisper behind cupped palm.

On hands and knees, Valentine crawled through the cave, toward the light outside. He could smell the blood trail behind.

"The Wizard thought that Marquez was something special, too. Sent him right off the cliff," the other muttered back.

Valentine, remembering what had happened yesterday, brought himself back down with a determined effort. The world seemed almost normal. He climbed to his feet.

Good, good. Outdoors can be a little much; just keep breathing into your center and drawing everything back to that place inside you. You will learn in time. A good bloodhound controls his nose without even realizing it, the way you focus your eyes. You will be able to do the same soon.

Valentine made it into the daylight. Clear blue filled the sky overhead, a rarity on Kurian Earth. The snow seemed to gleam, and even across the valley, Valentine's visual acuity was such that he literally could not see the forest for the individual trees. It smelled as if he were standing in the center of the world's largest goat farm, despite the fact that the three goats stood a hundred yards away. Downwind.

He centered on his own. *David, try to find some goat droppings.* The voice in his head still made him uncomfortable. Although his nose told him he was in a sea of goat shit, he localized it with an effort and walked toward the still-warm source, pausing less and less frequently as he drew nearer. He found he could play with his ears as easily as his eyes. He located a creaking branch, and listened to one of the goats pull up fodder from beneath the snow.

There you are, he thought at the end of his pungent treasure hunt, standing over the rounded mass.

Now, David, you are doing excellently. Follow the trail the goats left. Not by using the tracks in the snow, but with your nose. Shut your eyes as much as possible. Hear and smell your way down the mountainside.

It occurred to him that none of the other Wolves had explored the field in this way. He would have known, since most of them had left within the last few hours and there were only a few irregular, staggering footprints in the field. He took a deep breath, closed his eyes, and began to smell for the trail left by the odiferous goats.

And fell flat on his face. A tree root hidden in the snow snagged his foot. Usually he was agile enough to catch himself if tripped, but his usual reflexes had gone AWOL. He had the disquieting sensation of being in a different body. The only memory he could compare it to was his rare all-day fishing expeditions in Minnesota: taking a small boat into a lake and then feeling a little unsteady on his feet when he returned to dry land.

He got up, closed his eyes again with an effort, and began walking with an unsteady tread like a drunk doing a Frankenstein's monster imitation. He found he could hear the location of trees by the sound of wind in the pine needles. He sensed a branch ahead and leaned back to avoid it, and fell flat on his back.

The goats showed a penchant for investigating clumps of thorny bramble. After a painful rake across his lips, he cursed and opened his eyes.

No peeking, Amu admonished.

Valentine sucked the blood from his punctured lip, took a deep breath, and tried again. He leaned forward and found the going easier with his hands placed ahead and his nose closer to the trail. Even when he bashed his head straight into a tree trunk, coming away with sticky pine bark tangled in his hair, he managed to keep his eyes closed. He found himself able to concentrate on the trail, letting the other senses fade into the background, like a reader absorbed in a book using just her eyes and her brain.

The odor became stronger, and he let out a yip like a foxhound. He began to lope, ignoring the bruises and scrapes as he bounced down the slope. He heard a panicked bleat from something ripe and warm, and he leaped. The goat collapsed under him, kicking.

The animal's struggles brought him out of his trance. He found himself with a mouthful of goat hair, feeling as if he had just woken from a vivid dream. He released the unfortunate herbivore.

"Sorry, Billy. I got carried away."

Terrible! the Wizard shouted into his brain. *Had you been following someone with a gun, they would have shot you like a frothing dog. You mustn't go feral. Do it again, but this time see if you can find one of your fellow Wolves as they disperse. Just follow him, don't let him see you. Open your eyes now and then if you must, but try to work with your former semi-dormant senses as much as possible. Practice, because when it's for real, there are no second chances, David.*

David Valentine, Wolf of the Southern Command, got his new, awkward, battered body to its feet, closed his eyes, and stalked on.

Five

The Yazoo Delta, summer of the forty-first year of the Kurian Order: The wet crescent between the Mississippi and Yazoo Rivers is one of the most uncomfortable pockets of the globe. The swamp-and-canebrake Delta, returned to its original waterlogged existence by the breaking of man's levees on the Father of Waters, is virtually empty of human habitation. The Yazoo's flow moves imperceptibly through the bayous, making it impossible to tell if a current exists at all among the soggy sloughs. The water is so choked by vegetation, it seems like earth, and the earth among the tangled roots of cypress, willow, and water oak is spongy and hard to separate from the water. From water beetle to cougar, the teeming wildlife lives an amphibian existence among the Spanish moss and cattail thickets. It is a patch of humid desolation, taking its name from an Indian word for "death."

This empty land is a fine training area for the young Wolves of the Ozark Free Territory. From the Yazoo Delta, they can keep an eye on Mississippi River traffic and explore outside its football-shape, 188-mile length into the burned-out shells of Memphis in the north and Jackson in the south. It is the most impenetrable and least guarded of all the empty borders of Southern Command, and the handful of Wolves in the Delta keep on the move, often going an entire season without supply or communication from the Territory.

David Valentine traveled here as a newly invoked Wolf and learned the Hunter's Arts under two unremitting teachers: Nature and a long-time Cat named Eveready. In nature, Valentine learned to apply the lessons of his winter on how to find food, water, shelter, and fire, what might be called the four primary elements of human existence. From Eveready, a man who accepted no rank in Southern Command because

it would mean an end to his one-man war against the Kurians as well
as his jealously guarded independence, he learned how to unify his
judgment, senses, skills, and tools into a single weapon. The young
Wolves under Eveready's tutelage practiced their art, improvising
weapons to hunt everything from submerged alligators to treed rac-
coons. They took not only nourishment from their kills, but also hide,
bone, and sinew for use in making clothing and tools. A few of the
more atavistic-minded fashioned lucky charms from their trophies.
Eveready, owner of perhaps the longest necklace of Reaper fangs in
the Old South, encouraged the practice.

What Eveready taught even better was the art of concealing life-
sign. His apprentices spent more time learning mental discipline than
they did physical, mastering a form of self-hypnosis that cloaked their
auras against the inhuman searching powers of the Reapers. Their
skill at this determined whether they would hunt the enemy or be
hunted like the game they brought home to camp.

The camp used a pair of ancient water oaks as its roof. The stump-
ier of the two oaks suffered a curious deformity; the main trunk ended
twelve feet up and branched into six limbs that curved out of the trunk
first sideways and then upward, resembling a cupped palm with too
many fingers. The Wolves had rigged a patchwork of tents into these
branches, making an area beneath that stayed dry as long as the wind
kept down.

Wind would have been welcome in the humid air of the swamp,
where runoff came to die. There was an air of death, decay, and corruption to the flooded Yazoo Delta that no graveyard could match.
Mists and fogs haunted the neophyte Wolves, and mysterious wildlife
voices croaked and hooted and gibbered from the bulrushes. Even their
camp resembled an abattoir, with their packs and water bottles hung
from the low branches like trophies on a gamekeeper's gibbet.

Valentine sweltered in his cocoon of mosquito netting in a shallow
sleep brought on by heat exhaustion. His usually pleasant hammock
had been transformed into a torture chamber by the temperature and
humidity. Naturally he preferred to keep himself, like his clothing and his
pack, off the ground and out of reach of the various multilegged crawlies
and snakes that might be attracted to a warm, motionless body on the
damp earth. Only the earliest hours of the morning brought a lessening
of the heat. He would give anything he owned for a swim in one of Minnesota's clear cool lakes in this Delta summer. But even if he had been
physically comfortable, he would still have passed a fitful night. The
old dream about his family home had come back.

Eveready's predawn return cut off his old nightmare. The Cat had walked off into the east within an hour of picking the spot for their camp days ago, leaving orders to wait and not to use guns while hunting. Eveready declined to explain whether this was because of nearby danger or just the parsimony brought on by visiting a supply station twice a year.

"Everybody up," Eveready announced, laboring into camp with a heavy sack across his shoulder. His ancient M-1 carbine was slung across his chest, stock glowing with its usual loving polish of well-oiled wood. Burton, who had the third watch, started to pour water into the coffeepot. "Forget that for now, Burt," the Cat rasped. "You boys aren't going to want breakfast when you see what I've brung home. Hand me that water, boy."

Valentine tried to rub the gum from his eyes as he watched Eveready drink. Though the black-skinned man was a Cat, one of the caste whose members operated alone deep in Kurian-conquered territory, there was nothing catlike about him. Eveready was a grizzled old warthog: all tough-minded determination on a thick body beneath a thicker hide. Barefoot, with ragged black trousers that ended at calves as wide as horse hooves, the rest of his body resembled a barrel with arms added as an afterthought. Chest muscles strained from an equally ragged vest cut from the heavy ablative cloth that the Reapers wore, and his neck was festooned with dangling teeth pulled from the Hoods he'd exterminated. The Wolves had never seen him eat anything but oversalted game stews and apples—Valentine believed Eveready knew the location of every single apple tree and grove within a three-hundred-mile arc of the Yazoo Delta—and this eccentric diet had left him with ageless vitality and shining white teeth. He was bald as the man in the moon but hid the fact with a battered baseball cap with a Saints logo. Eveready could climb like an ape, float like an alligator, and leap like a deer, all without making enough noise to cause a mouse to startle.

Easing himself out of the hammock, Valentine shook his head and took a pull from the water bottle he bedded down with to save a trip out of the mosquito netting. He pulled on his moccasins after eyeing the insides. Though they had hung from his hammock, the ingenuity of the Yazoo wildlife at curling up for a nap where least expected had been brought home to Valentine by a painful centipede bite earlier in the summer.

"What did you bring us, Santa?" Alistar, one of the Wolves, asked.

The Wolves gathered, and Eveready dumped the stained sack in the center of the campground. At first Valentine thought it was a trick of the rapidly growing light, but the sack seemed to writhe as it hit ground.

"Valentine, get your chopper," Eveready ordered. Valentine retrieved his parang, a fourteen-inch broad hunting knife swelled at the center like a pregnant machete. It had a heavy wood handle with the tang capped at the end, combining the sharpness of a skinning knife with the utility of a hatchet.

Eveready used his own smaller clasp knife to cut open the bag, which Valentine saw with a kind of cold horror really was squirming on its own in the center of the ring of five men. The big Cat dumped the sack's contents.

"Fuck me!" Burton said, and pulled at the beard he had been growing all summer.

Flopping in the dawn was a pale humanoid torso. Where arms and legs should have been, only tarry stumps remained. A second sack fixed by cording circled around the neck and hid the thing's face. Burton half laughed, half retched at the sweet corruptive odor that made the Wolves take a step back. Sixteen-year-old Hernandez, the youngest of the new Wolves, crossed himself.

"Never seen one this close, boys?" Eveready asked. The four shook their heads, disgusted and fascinated at the same time.

"There are these big hunting cats in a place on the other side of the world, boys. India, it was called. Big stripy orange things called tigers. You wouldn't think they could sneak up on anything, unless you saw them moving through tall grass on our televisions, that is. But a momma tiger would teach her baby to kill by swatting something so it was half-dead; then the cub would kill it. Now that ain't exactly what I'm doing with you cubs, but I want you to get a good look at a Hood up close, minus his robes, in such a way that you'll live through the seeing of it. Sort of a National Geographic, courtesy of old Eveready."

The thing rolled on its back and made an inarticulate glubbing sound.

"Bastard can't talk too good," Eveready continued, reaching into his forage pouch. "I yanked this out." The Cat handed over the Reaper's limp, sixteen-inch-long tongue, and the Wolves passed it around dubiously. It reminded Valentine of a snake, scaly with a beaklike point at the end. "That's the straw it sticks into you. See the scales? They come up in you like barbs, keep you from pulling away. Not that you have much chance if this honey's got you in his arms."

"How . . . how did you bag it?" Valentine asked.

"I was scouting a little railroad town southeast of Big M's ruins. Holly Springs. Sources told me this fella came into town about midnight, doing the usual checkup with a company of Quislings out of Corinth. Any time a Reaper comes through, a few folks try to leave town real quick, and this thing goes after them when it was getting on toward dawn. The Quislings were too busy in the henhouses and pigpens to notice much. A hungry Reaper is hard enough to keep up with and maybe they didn't want to be around when he fed. So these refugees are heading for tall timber on horseback, and the yellow eye here is after them. He got one just as the sun came up, fed, and I caught up with him when he got all dopey from the drinking. It was a pretty bright morning for a change, so his eyes weren't working too well, either. I emptied old Trudy into him from about ten feet," he said, patting his carbine affectionately. "Shot a leg more or less off where it was showing under the robe, and took the rest off with my cavalry saber before he knew what hit him. I hacked around at his throat and pulled his tongue out from beneath the jaw, Colombian-necktie style. Sacked him up, then caught up with the horse belonging to the poor bastard he caught. Then I about broke my ass getting west."

Eveready chuckled. "I wouldn't care to be that Quisling commander in Holly Springs. The Big Boss in Corinth will send some Hoods out to settle things, with me and them both."

"You covered some miles," Alistar said. "Where's the horse, rode to death? We could've traded it, at least."

Eveready shook his head. "There was some border trash camped out by a crick a few miles northeast of here. I gave the horse her head, just took the saddle and bridle off, and she scented the other horses and wandered off. I carried the saddle aways, but it was too much lugging the ghoul and all that leather, too. I didn't want to be too slow; this guy's friends might home in on him."

"Hard on the group by the crick, if the Reapers catch up with that horse," Valentine suggested.

"They ain't no friends of yours, son. That's why I've been warning you boys about these borderlands. No law and order. There's the bad order of the Kurian spaces, and the law of the Free Territory. In fact, you'd be surprised at how orderly some of those Kurian towns are. Everybody with identity cards and permission slips and papers just to go to the outhouse. But between 'em where we are is up for grabs, and these bastards will rob you and leave you for dead as soon as they'd say 'Good morning.' I figure any Hood pursuit is welcome to 'em.

"Now let's get down to business. Gimme your slaying blade, Valentine. Now watch this," Eveready lectured as if he were in a classroom with glossy black experiment tables instead of a patch of soggy ground forty miles from nowhere. He opened a vertical cut along the thing's stomach. "See how that black goo comes up when the air hits it? It's something in these things' blood that makes an instant suture. If you ever get any on your hands, get it off quick, and whatever you do, don't get it in your mouth. Put some of this stuff on a dog's tongue, and it'll kill the man holding the leash. It's not so bad though; even when you're hacking one up, the goo doesn't fly around that much. It's too sticky. Make sure you pull your blade out quickly, though; if you leave it in for a few seconds even, this stuff will sometimes glue it right in place. Take my word for it, you don't want that to happen."

The Reaper thrashed around in pain, and Valentine stuck his foot on its chest to hold it in place. The smell sickened him. He felt thankful for his empty stomach.

"The sumbitch is moving around too much," Eveready decided. "Let's finish him. But I want to look him in the eyes for a second," he stated, cutting the cords around the thing's neck with the sharp edge at the tip of Valentine's parang.

The Reaper's face was a mess. Two gummed-over bullet holes in the cheek and forehead stood out against the deathly pale skin. Black fangs snarled at them from above the butchered neck. Its eyes were not the pink of a true albino's but rather black, with slit pupils and yellowish reptilian irises. It hissed, glaring hatefully at the five humans around it. Valentine felt hard pressure against his foot as it tried to wiggle loose despite its injuries. Valentine looked into its eyes and felt lost in the black depths. Was there such a thing as blacker than black? He felt himself compelled to lift his foot off the thing's chest.

"Steady there, David. You look like you might keel over," a voice said from somewhere near the Gulf Coast.

Valentine tried to raise his eyes from the black slits, failed.

Don't give in to the darkness, a part of his consciousness urged. *It's only the black eyes of the crow, picking at your father's brains.* He raised his eyes up to the lightening sky and planted his foot even more firmly on the mutilated torso.

"That's better, David," Eveready said, patting Valentine's shoulder. "You got to watch those eyes. For a second there, you looked like a bird staring at a snake. You weren't seeing the Hood, it was the Kurian behind it."

Eveready leaned over its face, taking a small cylinder from his pocket with his left hand. It was a crusty old battery, of a type invented just before 2022 that had a very prolonged shelf life. A symbol of a black cat leaping through an electric hoop could be seen on the casing.

"Here I am again, hungry Prince," Eveready taunted at the snapping face. "Old Eveready got another of your drones, you murdering pig. I know it feels good when your little bloodsucker here takes a life. How do you like it when I do this?" He waved the battery label as close to the snarling face as he dared and brought the curved blade down on the thing's neck with a grunt of effort.

The body quit moving under Valentine's foot. He glanced down, afraid to meet those baleful eyes a second time. A fresh wave of moldy-crypt odor wafted from the corpse of the Reaper, causing Burton to empty the remains of last night's dinner from his stomach. Alistar sank to his knees, trying not to join him.

Eveready thrust the parang into the dirt and picked up the head, cautiously draining the black syrup from the neck. Holding it by the scraggly black hair, he displayed the trophy up for the Wolves to get a good look. "See how the teeth are black? We call that stuff carbonite. It's not a scientific name or anything; I think it's out of a movie. Stronger than steel, and Kur builds the Hoods so they use the stuff for their skeletons, teeth, and nails. Stops bullets pretty good. I saw one take a faceful of double-ought from about two feet one time. The eye and nose holes are baffled, not open like in a human skull, so the sumbitch was just blinded, and mebbe couldn't smell too good either. But it kept coming for us. And while I left this bastard's fingers behind, they have these pointed black carbonite fingernails that can claw through a safe door, peeling it back layer by layer."

The Cat wedged the old battery into the Reaper's mouth and stuck the head in the crotch of a nearby tree. Its eyes rolled around in their sockets. "It's dead, don't let that unsettle you. Just nerve impulses or something."

Returning to the body, Eveready continued the autopsy. He began to peel back layers of skin with parang and skinning knife, sticking small broken branches through the skin to keep the wounds open. The black tar had stopped flowing with the creature's death, but an abundance of oily clear liquid seeped out of the cadaver. Alistar was still on his knees and looked about to go to all fours, and Hernandez was wiping his mouth with the back of his hand. None of them would eat that day, Valentine suspected.

"Okay, a whole bunch of a human being is taken up by equipment to process different kinds of food into our blood. These monsters don't need all that; they have as simple a digestive system as can be. But they have this big bladder inside; see that thing that looks kind of like a honeycomb?" He opened up the spongelike organ, bigger than a bovine liver. "Those little sacks fill up with blood like a camel's hump, and pass through this thing, which is kind of like a big placenta, to its bloodstream. And see those two thick cables going down its sides? Those are nerve trunks; it's got more than one. Yours goes up the backbone; if that gets snapped, you're dead. You can break its back and maybe it'll just walk funny, 'cause it's got these other nerve trunks. All wired to a couple of balancing organs in the head, gives them ungodly reflexes and agility. Little clusters of nerve cells at pressure points help that. Their spines are much more flexible than yours, like a cat's, and their knees are hinged so they can bend backward, coiling just about every major muscle in their bodies for a jump.

"Everything's heavier than ours: bone, skin, muscle. Makes them crappy swimmers. They can move through water, but they really have to thrash, so you can hear them coming with all the splashing. I keep telling the jokers in the Free Territory to dig wide moats around everything they build, something they can't jump over, but they don't want to make the effort. If you ask me, if a hundred Kurians got organized, they could go through Southern Command like a bullet through a paper target."

Valentine raised his hand. Since Eveready was showing this unsuspected schoolmarm side, it seemed the appropriate thing to do.

"Why don't they?"

"Overrun us, you mean? One of the things we don't know. We do know that each Kurian boss or Prince or Master or whatever has grown his thirteen Reapers to feed him and run his show. We think it hurts them when one of their puppets gets killed. There's some kind of special link that allows the vital auras absorbed by the Reapers to feed the Kurian that controls them. Over the years, the stories about Kur got confused, that is if our ancestors ever had them right to begin with. We combined the two creatures, the Reaper and its Master, into one vampire legend. But 'that's got nuthin' to do with nuthin'" as my old man used to say. The Masters don't like to have all their Reapers together in one spot. We think if all of 'em buy it, so does the Kurian. Those Kurians are selfish pricks, too. They don't risk their Hoods helping out other Kurians. You see it in the different ways their little principalities are organized. Maybe they even fight among themselves, like Mafia gangs—if you know what those were. We can only hope. They're not too creative. They don't seem to invent anything. The Lifeweavers got a philosophical answer to that; they say that the Kurians have degenerated over the millennia, becoming like addicts who can't see beyond the next fix. Nothing matters to them but keeping the vital auras flowing. Even when they invaded, they laid the groundwork well, but once it started, it was like the Oklahoma land rush: they all grabbed a spot and started harvesting . . . well, us.

"But all that is for the thinkers and strategists and leaders. You boys have got to be the killers, so just remember this one thing: the only damage that puts a Hood permanently out of commission is a central nervous system disconnect. That means severing the head or blowing it to bits. And since they duck faster than most folks can swing, let alone pull a trigger, it ain't easy. You got to get them when they're dopey, after they've fed or in good daylight. You get them out in the sun without their robes, they get so sick you can slice them up easy as pie. Sometimes they get laid up in a trance, either daytime or nighttime, and that's a good time to hit 'em, too. My theory is that a Kurian Lord can't really control more than one Reaper at the same time, and the others either go on pure instinct, feeding off whatever's around until they're gorged and pass out, or they fall into this trance while the Kurian is controlling a different Hood."

"Sir," Hernandez piped up. "You said there would be others on this one's trail. Are we gonna jump 'em?"

A small smile broke out across Eveready's ebony features. "Son, you got more balls than brains. You ain't even blooded Wolves yet. For the last time, save the *sir* stuff for the ones that have to hear it to believe in themselves. I'm here to teach you how to keep hid so the Reapers don't find you. Fighting a Reaper's a job for a team of Wolves. Yassuh, about ten-to-one odds is what you need. And that's ten well-armed, experienced Wolves. Even I don't take on an up-and-running Reaper if I can avoid it. I got all these teeth by being patient," he said, fingering the rope of polished fangs across his hairy chest. "You need to hit the enemy when he ain't looking for you, not when he is. A stand-up fight is work for the Bears, and even they die faster than the Lifeweavers can replace 'em sometimes.

"Nope, it's been a fun summer, but I want to get you all back across the Saint Francis alive and well. Hopefully a little bit wiser, too. School's just about out, boys."

Getting to the Saint Francis meant they first had to cross the Mississippi. Wide, muddy, and sandbar-choked at this time of year, the Father of Waters was no easy obstacle to overcome. Quisling traders and river patrols frequented it in battered boats and bulky barges, pulled by diesel tugs.

The afternoon after the grim session with the Reaper's body, the party started a leisurely journey westward. The Cat encouraged them to concentrate on keeping lifesign down, but Valentine's doubts prodded and pulled him out of his sublimation with hard staves. What if he failed to keep himself centered, as the Cat liked to call it, and drew the hunting Reapers to his comrades like sharks to a blood trail? The others seemed so confident, talking about how they would take their first Hood, discussing ambushes and cross fires and carefully planned traps.

Valentine had barely survived his first encounter with a Hood, and heard again and again in his mind the terrible screaming of the steady, stolid DelVecchio as the Reaper's needle-tongue found his beating heart.

The plentiful wild rice and bullheads of the Delta fed the five men on their bayou-bridging journey to the river. The Wolves had grown so experienced in navigating the trackless morass that they hardly thought twice about wading or swimming a bayou in pairs and trios, one group always covering the other as they moved southwest. They reached the great river on a hazy afternoon two days later. Upon sighting it, Valentine forgot his doubts in the breadth and majesty of the current. Or perhaps it was just the change in the air after the miasma of the backwaters.

"Two choices, boys," Eveready announced from a team-huddle squat. "We build us a raft, or we go find the one we sunk after crossing over back in the spring. Might take a day or two to find the spot; we're just a little south of it now. If we build a raft, it means chopping wood, and that can be heard a long way off. Also, we won't stand a chance if we run into a patrol except to swim for it. If we go to the old boat and raise it, we'll have something a little more navigable. But I've got my doubts it'll even be there after all these months. The river men and patrols spend all their time along the banks, and chances are one of them already thumped it with a pole or a paddle even if it is still underwater."

The Wolves decided to vote, with Eveready as tiebreaker. Valentine was the lone vote for building a raft, as he saw little reward and a good deal of risk in blundering along the bank in search of the old aluminum fishing boat that had brought them across the first time. The others remembered a little too well the want-of-a-nail lecture they'd received before departing for the Delta. It concerned coming home with weapons and gear issued, under pain of having to spend the next year on stable and livestock duty.

So they turned north.

Traveling the banks of the Mississippi made even the bayous seem like afternoon picnicking. The flooded and unattended banks turned the great river into a twisting mass of horseshoe loops and tadpole floods. Eveready took what shortcuts he knew and always kept an eye to the river. Although they could spot a patrol boat long before the Quislings had a chance at seeing the Wolves, every appearance of one of the noisy, fiberglass cabin cruisers made them get under cover while it plodded back and forth across the river. The first day there were two such sightings, each one wasting over an hour.

Valentine was jumpy the whole march. The others noticed it and put his mood down to bitterness over the vote on how to get across the river.

"Ain't nothing here worth the bogeymen keeping an eye on," Hernandez asserted.

"C'mon, Val," Alistar added. "With that old gumbo stirrer up on point, we've never even been spotted, let alone walked into an ambush." The gumbo stirrer in question waved from the crest of a small hillock ahead. Eveready had spotted something, and the Wolves obediently waited as the Cat went in for a closer look at whatever it was.

The sun was at the final landing in its descent of the staircase at the horizon. Valentine wondered at the simplicity of the age Eveready and his own father had been born into, when a red sunset meant only a beautiful end to another day rather than the beginning of eight hours of shadowed threat.

Valentine tried listening with "hard" ears as Eveready moved up the crest of the little hill at a level so just the Cat's head could be seen from the reverse slope of the hill where the object of his attention lay. Eveready's sure footfalls snapped no branch or twig detectable to Valentine's senses, raised to atavistic acuity. Eveready stopped, having found the best vantage, and stood for a full quarter-hour, staring motionless into the lengthening shadows.

Burton, who had already acquired the veteran's knack of sleeping at any opportunity, was softly snoring by the time Eveready returned. Alistar jostled him into wakefulness with a push of his moccasined foot.

"Is it that dogleg pond where we sunk the boat?"

"It's a boat, all right," Eveready said. "But not ours. Big wooden canoe, pulled up and overturned. There weren't any leaves or twigs or anything on it, so I bet it's just been there a day or two. And I'd just about bet Trudy against one of your Free Territory buckchits there's oars sitting under it."

The Wolves exchanged grins, but Valentine's was forced, almost more of a grimace. Good boats didn't just get left on their own, even if they were wooden canoes. A canoe would be an impractical boat for a long patrol, and a tiring one for a trip upriver. And he knew, without knowing how he knew, that his uneasiness came from something having to do with the canoe in the same way that a plague-sheet hanging on the door of a house meant death inside. Something cold and fearful tickled at his mind.

"I say we move quick, before the owners come back," Alistar said, rubbing his palms against each other.

"It's a risk, but I'd like to be across tonight," Burton agreed. Hernandez just nodded, and the three turned to Valentine.

Eveready's eyes met his. "It's a gamble, David, but I think it's okay. You feeling all right? You look like something you ate doesn't agree with you."

Trust the Cat, who lived by and for his stomach, to chalk up Valentine's unease to indigestion.

"Just a feeling. Old Padre, the guy who raised me, used to call it a *vibe*. There were good ones and bad ones. I guess I'm getting a bad one. This place doesn't feel right."

Alistar made a sound that might be interpreted as clucking.

Eveready ignored it. "Son, when I used to have hair on my head, if it went up, I backed off. I wouldn't be alive today if I didn't pay attention to the part of me that was quivering like a bowl of Jell-O. Which reminds me. When the four of us are back at Newpost Arkansas, I'm going to do some trading at the butchers and make you all some apple Jell-O. My momma's own recipe, with custard crème on top."

"We'll hold you to it," Valentine said, steadiness returning to his voice. "Let's have a look at this boat of ours."

From Eveready's little hillock, it looked easy enough. The canoe was pulled up, well out of the river's reach, on a little backwater of the river. A long peninsula of land, probably an islet at some times of the year, pointed westward beyond the boat: rising and then falling away rapidly like the profile of a wooded sphinx.

Valentine, after a quick look at the overturned boat, gazed at the spur of land pointing into the river. Something about that ominous shape troubled him. But if Eveready, veteran of thirty years' guerrilla fighting against the Reapers, thought it was safe, why shouldn't he trust the wisdom that had not yet put them into danger?

Later, he castigated himself for his silence. The Wolves spaced themselves out and readied their weapons. Eveready unslung his carbine.

"I'm going to take a little look-see. You four relax, stay centered, keep your lifesign down, breathe deep. We got lucky. It'll be dark as we're trying to cross, and the moon won't be up for a while. But I want to make sure, just in case Val's radar is working better than my own."

Valentine nodded, struggling with an encouraging smile as he tried to put into practice what Eveready preached. He envisioned his body glowing with a warm red aura. As he centered himself, he envisioned that aura changing color to blue. Then he began to contract the blue, drawing it inward with each breath. As he inhaled, the blue glow shrank to a small, softly glowing ball in the center of his body. The world around him seemed to fade.

Eveready approached the boat in two great loops, moving to the low edge of the sphinx-peninsula and then back to the base of their own hill before scouting the boat more closely. He even pointed his rifle under it as he approached, but as the last of the daylight faded into twilight's gloaming, he waved the Wolves down.

The canoe was wider than most, well fashioned out of overlapping planks. Someone had put a great deal of time and effort into making it; the wood shone with a polished luster. Two men could sit abreast on its two fore-and-aft seats, and there was room for their packs under the thwarts. The canoe would have held twice their number. Four oars, matching the wood, lay underneath. They decided that the four young Wolves would row two to a side, and Eveready would sit in the center with rifle ready. Darkness grew as they inspected their prize.

"Let's get out into the current quick," Eveready ordered. "If someone starts shooting, the wood is thick enough to stop a bullet fired from anything but point-blank, so just dive into the bottom and let the river take us away. I'll row by myself if I have to. This old Reaper vest stopped a bullet in my back before. Southern Command, in its wisdom, saves this stuff for the Bears, when they can get our guys to turn in the spoils of war, that is. Many's the old Wolf that has one of these under his leathers where the officers don't see it. Not that I'm advising you young men to break regulations, now."

While Eveready stood guard, the four Wolves overturned the heavy canoe and slid it down the gentle gravelly slope. Hernandez pushed a driftwood log out of the way and hooked his hand on to the bow of the canoe as the team heaved their transportation into the Mississippi.

"Hey, did you see this?" Hernandez asked.

Valentine peered through the blue-black night at the bow of the canoe. An insigne had been branded into the wood, scarring the delicate grain with four black bent bars. Something about the spiderish design tickled Valentine's capacious memory. . . .

"That's a swash-sticker, I think. Only it's backwards," Alistar said, in a hushed tone.

"The Germans and Japanese had them on their planes and stuff in World War Two, right?" Burton added, uncertainty in his voice. His schooling, like that of his comrades with the exception of Valentine, had been sporadic.

"Just the Nazi Germans," Valentine said. "But Alistar is right, it's the wrong way around."

Eveready came down from his post. "Into the boat, boys. Try not to splash around when you row. I don't like being this close to the bank."

"Eveready, this mean anything?" Valentine asked, pointing at the palm-size design on the bow.

Eveready squinted his aging eyes at the swastika. Good as his distance vision was, he struggled with his "reading eyes." For the first time in the entire summer, the big Cat looked afraid. "It means trouble. Let's not waste time; we don't want the owners to find us." He clicked the safety off on his ancient gun. Another first, and far more unsettling.

They clambered into their allotted places and took up the oars. A few lusty strokes took them away from the bank. The canoe seemed to glide on a sea of oil.

"Breathe and row, breathe and row," Eveready half chanted, kneeling in the center of the canoe. Valentine glanced at him from the right forward seat. He and Burton, the most muscular of the Wolves, provided the power for Alistar and Hernandez at the back. Eveready searched the sphinx-shape to their right, rifle at his shoulder.

Valentine relaxed into his breathing and rowing. Reducing lifesign was a matter of falling into yourself, concentrating on a single tiny point in the center of your being, like a candle glimmering in the middle of an enormous lake.

The candle flickered.

He felt his hackles rise, a curious corkscrew electricity running up his backbone, as if Death had run a playful forefinger up his vertebrae. A cold, hard spot appeared in his mind, coming from the head of the sphinx. Unable to say what it was, he knew only that he feared it.

"Eveready," he said, voice low in his concentration. "The very top of the hill. Maybe by that big windfall trunk . . . I think something's up there."

The matchless night vision of the Cat searched the hilltop peak as the boat shot toward open river. Valentine dug his oar blade into the water as if trying to dig a hole for the boat to hide in.

"Val, I think you're right. It's up there, but not moving. A Reaper. Hard ears, boys. This is a sound you need to know."

Fingernails on the blackboard. The cry of a stricken hawk. Sheet metal squeezed in a compactor. Each would remember the banshee wail differently, loud and fresh and terrifying, to their dying day.

"*Madre de Dios,*" Hernandez gasped, missing a stroke. "Shit!" he added, "I'm sorry, I dropped my oar."

"Use your rifle butt!" barked Valentine.

Other, distant wails answered the ghostly cry.

"Five," counted Eveready. "One for each of us. Hope that's luck, not planning."

The clouds thickened and dropped, bringing the horizon to a few feet from their faces. Aghast, Valentine brought his palm to the sky, barely able to see its outline.

"How the hell . . . do they do that?" Burton asked, puffing between strokes.

"I'd rather know how they knew we were going to hit this stretch of the river," Valentine said as he paddled.

Even in their current perilous situation, Eveready had lessons to teach. "They're disrupting your minds, not the weather. This could even mean a Kurian himself is around or working us from his Seat of Power. I've heard they can make a city seem to go up in flames, or a building catch real fire, just by willing it.

"They're reading us somehow. One or more of you might be giving off lifesign. While the swamp is full of it, if one of them were close to us, they might have picked up on ours, kept their distance, and just plotted where we were going. We'll never know for sure. The good news is that while they can swim the river, it'll take 'em a while. We can be across and separate, and head for the New Arkansas Post like hell. They'll go after whoever they can pick up on, and with luck the rest of us will make it back."

"Jesus, that's cold," Burton gasped.

"Makes sense to me," Alistar said.

Valentine swallowed his fear. "Can't do it, Eveready. We're Wolves—"

"I was a Wolf before you were born, son, and—"

"Then you should know," Valentine interrupted right back. "We stay as a team, whether it's two or two hundred. Only the dead get left behind."

"Whoever's giving off lifesign is dead already, Val," Eveready argued, trying to pierce the black curtain behind them. "Maybe not tonight, but some other trip in the future."

"We don't know they're reading lifesign. Maybe they tracked us the old-fashioned way. There are sniffer-Grogs, I'm told."

"Sorry, kid. I've got experience, and you don't. Gotta be lifesign."

Valentine broke the glum silence. "I say we put it to a vote. Every man for himself, yea or nay. If we decide to stick together, we put you off on the west shore. Alone, the way you like it." Valentine feared he might have pushed the old Cat too far. Maybe the vote would go four to one against him again, but he needed to try.

"No, no votes. Not with five Reapers on your tail," rasped Eveready.

"This isn't about you anymore," said Burton. "It's for us to say."

"Have it your way. Idiots. You know, if one Reaper catches up with you four, *just one,* you'll all be dead in twenty seconds. Five seconds each."

"Okay, lets take a breather," Valentine ordered, turning himself around in the boat to face his fellow Wolves. "Tradition. Youngest first. Hernandez? Every man for himself: yea or nay."

Valentine expected the sixteen-year-old to glance around at the others, or at least Alistar, for approval. But he looked squarely into Eveready's eyes. His hero. The man he called *sir* despite Eveready's repeated commands to knock it off.

"Nay."

Valentine's heart leaped. He could have hugged the skinny youth. "Alistar?"

The tawny youth, who thought himself the leader of the Wolves through this summer, shook his head at Valentine, a half-sneer on his face. "Yea."

"Fuck you, Al," Burton spat. "Nay. And fuck you again, in case you didn't hear me the first time."

"Nay," added Valentine, trying not to grin in triumph. "Alistar, you can get off with Eveready, if you like."

"You bet your ass I like."

"Can we get moving, Valentine?" Eveready asked.

The four rowed with renewed vigor. Valentine, feeling the energy of vindication in his limbs, dug his paddle deep into the water. Burton poured out his fury on the other side, and the canoe sped through the night.

Within five minutes, the western shore loomed out of the darkness. Alistar buckled on his pack, and Eveready jumped out and held the canoe steady. Hernandez started to put on his pack.

"Wait, Hernandez. We're staying in the boat," Valentine ordered.

"What's that?" Eveready asked.

Valentine put his oar behind his back and stretched. "Burton, let's switch places so I can use some different muscles. Eveready, you said they don't swim too fast, right? We head downriver, with the current. We'll hear any patrol boat. Go all night if we have to, then start moving overland at dawn."

"Hell, kid, if you had a plan, you should have said so. You're still taking a risk that the Reapers don't have another boat."

"You said five. This boat fits five easy. Can you still draw one off?"

Eveready smiled, apple-whitened teeth the brightest thing Valentine had seen all night, like a beacon of hope. "If one is still following me by sunrise, it won't live to see another nightfall."

"Alistar, last chance," Valentine called to the receding figure.

"You'll be bled out before dawn, Valentine," Alistar said. He turned. "Hernandez, this is your last chance, too."

The teen shook his head. "Sorry, Al. The pack stays together."

Alistar tightened his straps, managing to put contempt in the gesture. "Hope you make it anyway. I'll wait for you at Arkansas Post."

Eveready stepped closer to Valentine. "David, give me your gun."

Valentine reached into the bottom of the boat and brought up the single-shot breechloader. "Why's that?"

"We're gonna swap. I don't know if you have more guts than brains, or more brains than guts, but Trudy can pump five shots into a Reaper faster than you can count. You shot her pretty good this summer. You may need her tonight."

"Aren't you worried you'll never see her again?"

"Just don't let some Quisling mother take her off your body. Bury her at sea when she's empty. You know what I mean?"

The men exchanged rifles and ammunition. "I know what you mean. See you in hell, Cat."

"I'll be waiting, Wolf." Eveready shook his hand, then gripped his fingers in a curious gesture. "David, if you make it, tell your CO about how you sensed that Hood. That's unique. They'll want to know more about it, and you."

"I'll worry about getting home first. Take care!"

Eveready, still standing in the water, turned the canoe and pushed them southward.

"Get running, Alistar, it's every man for himself," Eveready said. "You heading north or south?"

Valentine listened with hard ears.

"I thought we could make the run together," Alistar said, deflated.

"Not a chance. I have to move fast and alone if I'm gonna draw one of these off. Take off, boy. I hope you make it, but I can't have you around me."

As they drew away, Valentine heard a shout from the Cat's muscular throat, perhaps strong enough to be heard across the river by the Hoods' ears:

"Halloo! Hoods, come on over. Eveready's in the house, and he wants to par-tay. Bring it on, you balless bastards. I got forty-five sets of teeth around my neck, motherfuckers. I wanna make it an even fifty!"

The canoe glided southward, propelled by current and oars. Valentine realized he was achingly tired; they had marched all day on light food. Water was not a problem; the center of the big muddy gave them all they could desire, clear and cool.

"Hernandez, turn in. Just relax for a couple hours in the bottom of the boat. Burt, you'll be after him. Take the stern for now. I'll take the third shift."

Hernandez almost collapsed into the center of the boat, asleep in a few seconds with his head pillowed on his pack.

"Jeez, he didn't even put his blanket down," Burton observed, after gaining the stern.

Valentine paddled on. "Anyway, you give off less lifesign when you're asleep. Just in case it was him."

"I thought it was me," Burton said.

"Funny, I thought the same thing," Valentine admitted. Both men chuckled. The canoe shot southward.

Splashing . . . an overactive imagination at work?

"Did you hear that, Burt?" Valentine whispered.

"Hear what?"

"Hard ears, Wolf. To the left. Didn't he say they made a lot of noise swimming?"

Burton quit rowing as both men concentrated their ears to the left. Over the wind and noise of the river, a vigorous splashing could be heard.

"Oh, hell. Sorry, Burt. Looks like I guessed wrong,"

"Let's pump it, Val. We still got a chance. The fucker's a ways off, still. Hernandez," he said, knocking the sleeper with his foot. "Nap time's over, you got to do some rowing."

Hernandez yawned, pushing one arm into the sky and rubbing his eyes with the other. "Jeez, that felt great. How many hours did I sleep?"

"About two minutes. Get up here and row," Valentine ordered.

"What?"

Burton tossed the oar toward him. "Reaper is swimming for us. Don't drop your oar this time."

Propelled by terror, the three men pushed themselves to a stroke every two seconds. Valentine used his hard ears to locate the splashing, which began to fade first to the left, and then astern.

"We're leaving him behind. I think," Valentine said through gritted teeth.

A few minutes would tell the tale. Valentine counted strokes. At 214, he realized the ominous splashing was getting louder.

"Hell, a Hood," Burton swore, puffing. "How fast is it going?"

"Faster than us," Hernandez said.

Valentine could not resist looking over his left shoulder every few seconds. The moon was up, but high, thin clouds muted its three-quarter face. Their strokes began to slow as exhaustion set in. Valentine saw a pale figure, arms whirling like paddle wheels, splashing along behind them.

"I can see it now," Burton said, resigned.

A horrible image of the Reaper closing remorselessly on them flickered through Valentine's mind. It would swim underwater the last few feet, push up and turn over the boat, then tear each of them to bits in the water. He looked back at the steadily gaining swimmer, moving through the water at a speed no Olympian could match, pale back visible in the moonlight.

It had removed its robes to go faster through the water.

"Take a rest," Valentine ordered, picking up Trudy. The magazine held thirty rounds. Another magazine rested in a leather pouch on the offside of the stock.

"What do you mean, take a rest? We gonna shoot ourselves?" Hernandez asked.

"I'm going to take a crack at him with Trudy," Valentine explained. "It took off its robes to go faster through the water."

"Jesus help you shoot straight," Hernandez babbled.

Valentine carefully tucked himself against the stern. He sat down, bracing his back against Burton's seat. He brought the rifle to his cheek and set the sights for a hundred yards. The two other Wolves panted as Valentine tried to quiet his own respiration and steady his trembling muscles. *Exhaustion or fear?* he wondered.

Breathing out, he fired three times, pausing for a second between each shot. The thirty-caliber carbine shell had a fair kick, but braced as he was, knee against the side of the canoe and back braced by the bench mounted behind him, the recoil was negligible.

Machinelike, the Reaper swam on. At this distance, Valentine couldn't make out splashes to see if he was hitting. He let the distance close another twenty yards, then fired three more times.

The Reaper dived.

Valentine scanned the surface of the water. How far could it go without air?

The wooden stock felt comforting against his cheek. He lowered the barrel slightly.

The thing breached twenty yards closer, and Valentine shot five times, missing in his panic. It disappeared underwater again.

Calm, calm, his mind told his body, but the body refused to cooperate. He quivered, unable to control the nervous tremors.

Jesus, it's close. The fierce, pale face surfaced twenty yards away, gulping air. Valentine shot, splashes erupting within inches of the head. One shot tore a black gash in its cheek. The head disappeared.

"Now, row, row for your lives!" Valentine shouted. He braced himself for the expected upheaval, as the thing tried to make it under the boat.

The canoe gained speed. Barely an arm's length away, the Reaper breached, coming halfway out of the water like a porpoise. Its mouth was open. Black teeth gleamed in its hellish fury.

Trudy spat as fast as Valentine could pull the trigger. Black holes appeared in the Reaper's chest as the spent cartridges bounced off the wooden sides of the canoe and into the water. The thing fell backward, thrashing more feebly. It rolled over and floated, facedown.

Valentine looked wonderingly at the smoking weapon and said a silent prayer for Eveready's safety. Trudy had saved their lives.

Valentine angled the canoe toward the western shore with the earliest light. There was always the chance that a river patrol would stop them. From here on, getting back into the Ozark Free Territory was just a matter of bearing northwest for a couple of days.

Burton looked back into the river. "I don't believe it. He's still coming."

The Reaper swam on, using a sidestroke motion. So bullets were useless, after all. Valentine suppressed an urge to press the barrel of the rifle under his chin and blow his own brains out in defiance.

"Let's get ashore," he said, defeated.

The others carried their packs in one hand, rifles in the other. Valentine pushed the canoe off into the current and climbed up a short ledge to the riverbank proper. Burton was already heading toward a fallen tree.

The Wolves knelt down behind the log, too tired to run. *Two single-shot breechloaders and a full magazine in Trudy,* Valentine thought. *Plus our parangs. Enough?*

The Reaper paddled toward shore, leaving a wake that aimed at their tree like an arrow.

The haze dissipated into a cloudless morning. The sun shone yellow and bright, inching above the horizon.

Valentine looked at the sky in wonder. Only rarely, outside of winter, was it this clear overhead.

"We're saved. Saved by the sun," Valentine breathed.

The Reaper reached shallower water. It, too, raised its head to the sun, but in pain rather than praise. Thin black hair lay plastered over its chest and shoulders. Bullet holes formed a reverse question mark shape on its chest, and one arm hung askew.

Valentine stood up, copying Eveready's taunt. The Reaper cocked its head, shutting its eyes to squeeze out the daylight.

"Are you coming for us?" Valentine shouted.

The Reaper straightened. Its ears were working better than its eyes. It staggered, hammered by naked sunlight.

not today, it seems. but some night, in a lonely place, you'll be taken, it hissed.

"But not by you," Valentine said, raising his rifle.

The thing dived backwards, disappearing beneath the water.

In some ways, Valentine thought, *it's almost better than killing it. It ran. It was afraid.*

They made New Arkansas Post in four days. The little wooden fort on a bare hill overlooking the Black River was built like something out of an old-time western, right down to the sharpened logs serving as crenellated walls. More supply depot and stable than actual fort, it still contained the welcome sight of a cantina.

Eveready was waiting for them on the cantina's porch in a rocking chair, happily munching an apple, finishing everything but the stem. Two new fangs hung from his necklace. He chided Valentine about not finding the time to properly oil Trudy's stock after exposing her delicate wood to water.

Lewand Alistar was posted as missing a week later. His family received notification the following spring, during the recruiting swing through the Council Bluffs area of Iowa.

Six

Pine Bluff, Arkansas, fall of the forty-first year of the Kurian Order: At the beginnings of the fertile, flat corner of southeastern Arkansas, the crossroads town of Pine Bluff thrives. Strategically located on the chord of an inhabited arc covering the borderlands in that quarter, a permanent garrison regiment of Guards frequently offers its hospitality to Wolf patrols into Louisiana and Mississippi.

Independent farmers from as far away as Drew County come to barter with the Southern Command Commissioners. The town itself boasts eight churches, a high school, blacksmiths and boatwrights, teamsters and tailors. The Guards stable their horses at the old Livestock Showgrounds, and no less than a full regiment known as the Bluffs protects the Old Arsenal, the largest and arguably the best munitions plant in the Free Territory. The Old Arsenal produces everything from bullets to bombs, protected by the heaviest concentration of pre-Overthrow machine guns in Southern Command. In town, the Molever Industrial Wood Products plant has switched from making pallets to sturdy wagons and river barges, and numerous craftsmen exhibit their wares each weekend at the Sixth Avenue Street Market. On evenings each weekend, the Saenger Theater Players sing, dance, and act out famous scenes from old movies and plays. The aged theater's cool limestone and Florentine decor make an opulent break from the meanness of everyday life. Shakespeare makes an occasional appearance on the billboard, but more often a tear-streaked heroine shakes her fist at the sky against a fiery red backdrop, vowing never to be hungry again, or a pair of lovers affirm deathless devotion as they cling to wreckage behind billowing sheets meant to represent an icy sea.

There is a sense of stability, order, and permanence to the place that the settlements on the other borders lack. The tracts of relatively empty Louisiana and Mississippi wetlands protect it from quick forays, and the Guards are experienced at fighting river-borne incursions. Their clothes are a little better, the food is a little more varied, and the buckchits are more welcome here than in the remoter regions of the Free Territory. There is a regular newspaper and more regular mail, and even a social stratification of sorts has taken hold, for better or worse. The complacency here is a true achievement, one paid for in blood on the other borders.

David Valentine received orders to join Zulu Company at Pine Bluff shortly after making his report to the officers at New Arkansas Post. With the gift of an aged horse from the post commander, a haversack of food from the supply sergeant, and a parting bag of apples from Eveready, he rode west up the scenic, if broken-down, western highway. Once known as US Highway 65, now called the Arkansas River Trail, it is one of the better all-weather pikes of the Free Territory. Making easy stages out of respect for his slow-stepping mount, Valentine reached the shores of Lake Pine Bluff.

Valentine smelled the sentries before he saw them. The tobacco and wood-smoke odor meant there were men in the little earthen bunker even if nothing could be seen in the gloom beneath the head logs. A pair of horses stood side to side swishing flies in the morning breeze inside a little split-rail corral overlooking the broken road. Valentine sniffed again and suspected halfhearted enforcement of latrine discipline in what, to the Guards anyway, must seem wilderness.

Head bobbing and ears forward, his horse quickened its walk. The roan gelding was old and wise and knew the smell of horses on a good diet.

A slight figure in a charcoal-gray uniform, comfortably barefoot with riding boots off, appeared from the dugout and waved. Valentine turned his horse with a gentle nudge of his moccasined heel.

"Good morning, stranger," said the youth, teal blue kepi and neckerchief proclaiming his membership in the Bluff Regiment. "What's your business up in town?"

Valentine brought up his forearm, palm outward, in the old Indian greeting. Not quite a salute, but friendly enough.

"Good morning," responded Valentine, but as most of his mornings began at the first pink of dawn, it seemed a little late for the salutation. "I'm three days out of New Arkansas Post with orders to report to the Commanding Wolf. Whereabouts can I find Captain LeHavre?"

"I need to see your orders," the sentry said, holding out his hand.

"They're verbal. The Wolves don't use much paper, Bluff."

"Then I can't let you through. We can send a message to get one of your Wolves in for escort, but I don't have authority to let you through."

More like too much authority and too little brain, Valentine thought. A good empiricist, he decided to test the theory. "Is that so? What's up the road that a man with a single-shot rifle on an old horse might take out, anyway?"

The soldier patted his rifle stock.

"Maybe you're a spy, come to look at the arsenal. Count the machine-gun posts, map out the tanglefoot paths. Maybe you're going to set fire to a barge full of black powder and blow up everything on the dock—"

"Enough of that, Johnson," a stern female voice called from the bunker. "If he is a spy, he can turn around now. You just told him all he needs to know." A middle-aged, uniformed woman came out of the bunker and approached the road in the measured, confident stride of NCOs the world over. "We heard a Wolf was coming in from downriver. I figured you'd be on foot by now; any horse old Gregory would part with has got to be on its last trip. Is there news?"

"Not that I'm aware of. You're wrong about the horse, he's a nice ride, long as you don't ask more than he wants to give. Good thing, too, since I'm bareback," Valentine said.

"You'll find LeHavre up the road a few miles, just into town proper. The Wolves always camp at Old Harbor Woods, right at the north bend in the river. There's a brick entrance off the road, says it was a golf course. Still is, actually, on the sheep meadow. Don't have time for the game myself. You'll see your little tepees around the old clubhouse. Tell Captain LeHavre that Brit Manning says hi. We were at Webber's Falls together."

"You were a Wolf?" asked Valentine, not even knowing in what state to look for Webber's Falls on a map.

"No, but owing to your caste, we were ready for them when they tried to push into Fort Smith. Exactly ten years ago May. We bushwhacked them from the north while they were in the middle of ferrying across. So many Grogs ended up in the river, they say the Arkansas ran red. It didn't really, but it was still pretty hot there for a while. Two companies got caught on the wrong side of the river, and his Wolves saved our auras. You might say I thanked him personally afterwards," she reminisced, a sly smile crossing her weathered features.

"I'm sure he'll remember."

"You want some coffee, son? Just chicory, but it's hot. I'd offer you some lemonade, but my four boys here drank it all first two days we were here, and the rinds haven't soaked long enough to make another batch."

"No, thank you, Sergeant Manning. At my horse's pace, I'll be lucky to make the town by dinner." Valentine offered a true salute, crisply returned. "Thank you for the directions."

Captain LeHavre's steady green eyes evaluated Valentine from his pulled-back hair to his stained knee-high moccasins, fingers drumming against his thigh. The company commander wore the look of a busy man who accepted only efficiency.

The captain and Valentine both stood in the sole leak-free room in the old Harbor Clubhouse. Its dark paneling hinted at a previous existence as either an office or a small library. Two comfortable armchairs and a table, piled above and below with a honeycomb of plastic milk crates, almost filled the warm little room. Black-and-white photographs, most bearing the marks of poor film stock, hung in rough frames.

LeHavre flaunted the swarthy good looks and heavy mustache of a romance novel pirate or ruthless western outlaw. His athletic build, spoiled slightly by the hint of a paunch, set off his forest green buckskins, so dark they looked almost black in the dim light of the windowless office.

Offering Valentine a warm handshake in the worse-for-weather main entrance to the clubhouse, LeHavre invited his new Wolf to the "records room." Both men sank into the armchairs with the appreciation of the rarity of such comfort.

"You might call this our cave," LeHavre explained with a casual wave toward the laden table. "These papers are the closest thing we have to a headquarters. The milk crates just make moving easier. The rest I leave to the clerk. Coffee, tea, beer?"

"A beer would be very welcome, sir," Valentine responded gratefully. "It's been a long summer."

LeHavre rose from the chair without using his arms, almost a levitating trick. "I'll bring two cool ones from the basement," he said.

Valentine looked around at the pictures, wondering about a man who would treat a wet-behind-the-ears recruit like an honored guest. In less than a minute, a breathless brown-skinned girl, seven or eight years of rubber-band energy and frizzy hair, bounced into the room with a clasp-stoppered bottle. LeHavre followed the little dynamo. "Meet David, Jill. David hails all the way from the Land of Ten Thousand Lakes. Which state is that, tadpole?"

"Minnesota," she said, showing a proud smile as she handed over the bottled beer. "Hi, David. Did you swim in those lakes?"

"Er, some of them. Why, do you like swimming?"

"Does she like swimming!" LeHavre interjected. "I check her feet whenever I can to make sure they aren't growing flippers. Don't I, tadpole."

"Uncle Adam!" she squealed.

"David came on a horse. Can you take him to the corral? He looks like he needs a brushing."

"Can do!" Jill said. "Nice to have made your act-tense, David."

"Acquaintance," LeHavre corrected.

"Likewise, I'm sure," Valentine responded, shaking her hand.

"Acquaintance," the girl repeated, a furrow crossing her brow. She solemnly returned the handshake and stepped backwards out the door.

"That's Jill Poole. Her father was a lieutenant of mine. He died in a fight about three years ago. I look in on her mom whenever we're in the area. She runs a nice little boarding-house right by the river. Fine woman; she keeps a firm hand on the boatmen who stay. It's not quite a marriage, but I think of Jill as my daughter. She's fearless around the men. Most of them remember Poole, and they indulge her. She loves making beadwork. Most of the Wolves in Zulu Company have a bracelet or something of hers."

LeHavre opened his bottle. "To the people we're fighting for," he toasted.

"Prosit," Valentine responded, imitating a memory of his father. The cool froth flushed the dry road away.

"My apologies, Valentine. I'm sure you want to know about the outfit you've been ordered to join. Zulu Company is one of ten companies in the Arkansas Regiment, which makes up the smaller half of the Wolf Brigade. There's only three thousand or so Wolves in all of Southern Command, counting Aspirants and reserves, and we're the most numerous of the Hunters. We're in reserve now. But don't expect to spend a lot of time dancing at regimental balls. Maybe two thirds of the regiment is together when we're wintering in the Ouachitas. We don't often fight shoulder-to-shoulder; the last time was when we stopped a Grog incursion out of St. Louis. That's when Poole bought it.

"Zulu Company has four platoons of about thirty men each, as of this month. Fifteen support personnel, mostly older Wolves who aren't up to running fifty miles a day anymore, seven wives and two husbands who can keep up with the camp, and four transport teams of four men, making me responsible for a little over one hundred fifty lives. I have twelve senior NCOs, but I'm short a lieutenant out of the three I should have. You want the job?"

Valentine swallowed his mouthful of beer, which had turned into a grapefruit descending his throat. "Me, an officer? Sir, I'm not even twenty yet."

"Napoléon was a lieutenant of artillery at sixteen, David."

"And Alexander the Great was a king breaking up rebellions at twenty, sir," Valentine interjected. "But I'm not either. I've never read a book about tactics."

The captain set down his beer and crossed the room to the desk. "Valentine, I've got a folder here. In it is what we call your 'Q file.' Don't ask me what the Q means, because I don't know. It's got your reports, about what happened on that barge, and it's going to contain your report on the Mississippi crossing, once the copy works its way here. There are some words from Wolves like Pankow and Paul Samuels. I also knew your father, slightly. I was younger than you are now in those days, and I'd give my right nut to be half the man he was. I heard he was murdered when you were still a boy."

LeHavre returned to the chair. "David, I know from people I trust that you've got brains and guts. You also take responsibility; most people try to hide from it. You've shown some initiative in going after the enemy, and Eveready told me that you're smart about avoiding a fight, too. Which takes a certain kind of courage."

Valentine listened to LeHavre's summation of his record as a Wolf. But LeHavre didn't know about the fear and horror inside the Harpy barge that had unmanned him into lighting his bomb without thinking it through. Or the stupid theatrics with a gun (a valuable pistol now submerged in the muddy river bottom thanks to his forgetting to hang on to it in the water) to get a cramped recruit on her feet. Or the luck of a clear sunrise that saved them on the shores of the Mississippi.

"And one more thing, David. Our very own Wizard, Amu, recommended you to me. That counts for something; he reads people like a book. Don't misunderstand me, please. Being an officer is a tough tackle. You drink last, eat last, sleep last, and usually die first. No one notices your good decisions, and you have to bury your bad ones and then write home to somebody's parents that their son stopped a bullet carrying out your orders. Getting them to fight is the least of your worries; the Wolves know their business. But getting them ready for a fight, choosing where and when, and then getting them back safely takes a special kind of person."

"Why did you become one, sir? An officer, I mean."

LeHavre sighed and pulled down the last of his beer. "Long story, David. I wasn't even a sergeant, just a vet in charge of four kids younger than you. Our platoon went into the wrong town. Quislings had a hell of a fine ambush set up. They'd killed just about everyone in what had been a friendly stop and filled it up with their people. Somehow they scared a family we knew into greeting us and making everything seem normal. Everyone was tired and hungry, so we dispersed for dinner and sleep. That's when they hit us. The lieutenant and sergeants got it first—it seemed like the lead was flying from every direction but up. I made it out and got some other survivors together, dogs at our heels and Reapers screaming from the hills. I've never been so scared before or since—been pretty damn close a few times, though—but we made it back. I carried a wounded Wolf the whole way, but she didn't weigh much over one-fifteen. So they made me an officer. Funny thing to do for a guy who spent three solid days running from the enemy.

"But that was a good number of years back. The Free Territory's changed from a backwater cluster of hard-luck farms to a real patch of civilization. The Kurians haven't had any luck stomping us. We're not as big as some of the groups out east, even. I understand there's a band of Hunters ranging the Green Mountains of New England up to Canada and down through the Smokies about twice the size of us, and the freehold in the Pacific Northwest has more square miles. But out east, they're more of a wandering guerrilla army; they don't have a spot to really call home. And in the west, well, it's only a rough confederation out there. A couple of the strongmen paying lip service to the Constitution and Bill of Rights. A few even think the Hunters and the Lifeweavers are part of the same disease as the Kurians. You'd think the days of men fighting anything but the Kurians and their Quislings are over, but I'm sad to say it just isn't so."

The captain shook his head, eyes downcast. "Curse of Babel, I guess. We just won't work on the same team sometimes. But back to the here and now. Can I count on you, Valentine?"

Has anyone ever counted on me? Valentine wondered. He thought of the gangly little girl, Jill, and her unknown mother. *Can they count on me? Will I be able to prevent some black-fanged monster from making lifeless husks of them?* He remembered the little Poole girl's response to LeHavre's request. Maybe LeHavre liked to be answered that way.

"Can do, sir," Valentine said, hoping the enthusiasm did not sound too forced.

The captain walked him out into the pleasant afternoon. The worst of the summer's heat had faded, and the clouds were piling on and thickening overhead. Five-pole tepees filled what was probably once a lawn and putting green.

"Zulu Company is spending time in reserve, Valentine," LeHavre repeated. "Your last winter you stayed in true winter camp. Four com-

panies get to do that, another four are in reserve, leaving just two companies to stay in the Outlands. They'll be spread thin, patrolling and
relying on the Cats for notice of anything major outside the borders. If
something happens, or a good opportunity to hurt the Hoods comes
along, we go out of reserve. But that doesn't mean we'll be sitting on
our rears. As of today, you're Acting-Lieutenant Valentine on my authority. The colonel will confirm after your course work gets done.
We're not the Guards, the civilian government doesn't have to give its
rubber stamp. I'm not giving you a platoon yet, though you'll get your
bars right away. But back to your duties. You're going to be in charge of
the support staff, transport teams, and the Aspirants. When you aren't
doing that, you'll be running back and forth from the Officer's Training
College, which holds classes at the old UA Pine Bluff Campus on the
west side of the lake. If you want my advice, you'll memorize Sun-tzu
and study the nineteenth-century campaigns of the Apaches and Co-
manches, and some Civil War histories of Bedford Forrest and Stone-
wall Jackson. Just read enough about the rest to pass your tests. You'll
learn a lot about how to fight when you're outnumbered and outgunned.
When you're reading about the Chiricahua, try not to remember that
they were on the losing side. It'll be a hell of a schedule for you, but be
grateful for it. We've got officers all over the place who are just jumped-
up sergeants, and thought they're hell on wheels with the men, but
sometimes the lack of formal training leads to problems."

"When's this going to start, sir?"

"It started the minute you accepted your commission, Lieutenant.
The War College is always more or less in session. One more thing:
Eveready said you got some kind of premonition that there were Reapers around. Answer me straight, was it a lucky guess, or did you really
catch wind of something?"

Valentine thought for a moment before answering. "I can't account
for it, sir. It wasn't based on anything I actually sensed, more of a 'by
the pricking of my thumbs—'"

"'Something wicked this way comes'?" finished LeHavre. "That's
interesting. Reapers make horses and dogs nuts, too. Well, the nearest
thing we have to a center for study of the Kurians, by us humans anyway, is at the college here in Pine Bluff. They'll be interested in your
story. There's a half-dozen people researching the New Order; they like
to come out and talk to us after we've seen them up close. They always
want to know which Kurian sent which Reapers—as if we can tell.
Let's get you quartered, and you can go meet them tomorrow when you
enroll yourself at the OTC."

*   *   *

The following day, after a delicious cool night in a cot in the warmth of the junior officers' tepee, which he had to himself because his tent-mate was on a training patrol, Valentine rode through the bustling little town to the college campus. It was an uninspiring collection of solid little 1950s buildings dominated by a curious stunted tower: a clock that some tinkerer had restored to its function decorated it. Uniformed Guards sitting outside one brick building revealed the location of the War College. As he had business there, Valentine decided to make the OTC his first destination. Exchanging friendly nods with the lounging Guards outside, he followed an old black-and-white plastic sign with a red arrow. A chalkboard outside the open office door read:

THIS WEEK:
MAJ. JONAS BRATTLEBORO—MEDICINE IN THE FIELD
(TUES, WED, PM 114)
LT. P. HAYNES—BLACK POWDER TO THE STEEL-JACKETED BULLET
(FRI, AM 106 /PM RIFLE RANGE)

Valentine entered the office. A breeze came through the open windows, but it was still uncomfortably hot, and the room had the sour smell of old paper. A young female Guard in a white cotton uniform Valentine identified as a cadet's, her face as fresh as this morning's flowers, rose and smiled.

"You must be the new Wolf from Zulu Company, sir. Nice to meet you, Acting-Lieutenant Valentine," she said. "My name is Cadet Lambert, but the guys here call me Dots. Because I'm kind of a born picture-straightener. I dot all the i's and cross all the t's."

"You're well informed, Lambert. I didn't know you Guards paid that much attention to the Wolves."

"There's one other Wolf studying here right now, sir. She's from Tango Company over at Fort Smith. She stays at the Poole Boarding-house; she's a little older than you. Her name is Carol Pollisner. Usually the Wolves mustang up and don't have to do much formal classwork. Speaking of which, I have your packet all ready."

"Thank you, Lambert. How the hell old are you, if you don't mind me asking? You look about twelve." He took a heavy pack of paper wrapped up in a tied linen folder from her hand.

"I'm fifteen. But I passed the Guard physical, and I ran the table on the written test. I'm the Colonel Commanding's staff assistant until I turn eighteen. I actually prefer Dots, sir."

Valentine whistled, knowing the number of push-ups required to pass a Guard Cadet physical. He opened the linen folio.

"The OTC is mostly self-taught," Dots explained. "There's a reading list, and written test on each book. You have to do six months' worth of lectures unless you can pass out of the subject by taking an oral exam. The classwork is easier unless you're some kind of genius. Each week's lecture schedule is on the blackboard outside. Once you do that, and have your Certificates of Diligence, Responsibility, and Sobriety, you take the final oral exam. They hold those whenever there's three captains or above around. In fact, your Captain LeHavre is going to be serving on one a little later this month. I hear he's merciless on Grog Recognition. If you don't know where to shoot a Harpy to bring it down with one bullet, you're recycled."

"What's this thesis?" Valentine asked, looking at the graduation requirements.

"That's one of Colonel Jimenez's pet projects. Hope you can write. He wants a fifty-page paper on any subject, strictly nonmilitary. History's okay, as long as you keep off the wars and battles covered in the reading list. A week after you turn it in, you get questioned about it, so you better know whatever it is you're writing about. I did mine on the great mariners, Columbus and Cook and so on. A week later he was grilling me about how Columbus enticed his men to make the voyages, and how Captain Magellan might have avoided getting killed. I think Jimenez just does it to keep himself sharp."

"Thanks, Dots. I'll read this over. I'll start on the lectures this week, if LeHavre will spare me."

"The library's on the top floor. You can check out books if we have two or more copies available, but that covers almost everything on the reading list," she said, already making notes in her desk book.

"Which building is the student union, Dots?"

She looked up with a raised eyebrow. "Going to visit the Creeps, huh? There's a campus map in your packet, but it's just across the quad. It's a good place to learn about the Grogs, but I wouldn't let them talk you into trying for any bounty money."

"Bounty money?"

"For all sorts of stuff. Reaper clothes or artifacts. Written records stolen from the Kurian Zone. They offer big money for live prisoners, but if it's Quislings, they have to be officers. Their dream catch is a whole, live Reaper. They had one once, but it got out. LeHavre will look the other way if you grab a clipboard now and then, but don't ever try to throw a rope around a Reaper or he'll probably shoot you himself."

"Thanks for the tip, Dots. I have a feeling I'll be saluting you someday."

She looked pleased at the compliment. "If you need any help, I'm here every day. I live in the old dormitory."

Valentine exited past three Guards, who had quit skylarking and were talking over a broken-backed copy of *War and Society*. There were fewer than when he had entered; it seemed a couple of the number had duties elsewhere.

The stone on the student union read L. A. DAVIS STUDENT UNION and 1952, but someone had hung a carved wooden sign that read MISKATONIC UNIVERSITY over the door. Valentine entered the unlit building, which smelled of bad plumbing. A stairway leading up had a sign reading APPOINTMENTS ONLY, and a second notice board, which at one time had been behind glass, read BOUNTY INQUIRIES, PLEASE RING over a small hand bell. Valentine climbed the stairway.

The second floor was a warren of rooms, some with doors completely missing and others with darkened windows. A faint, Poe-esque tap-tap-tapping sounded from an inner chamber. Valentine hunted the source of the sound, which he eventually realized was a typewriter. It came from a central office with three overburdened desks, festooned with pin-filled maps and drawings of Grogs.

Under a bright electric desk lamp, a rotund and hairy man typed with two fingers and an occasional thumb. The mountain-man mass of hair on his head and face made his age hard to guess, but Valentine put the man in his late thirties, as his temples and chin were just beginning to be flecked with gray. He wore large, octagonal tortoiseshell glasses that had probably been originally worn by a woman. A bare chest that would have done a grizzly proud, fur-wise, bulged out of a sleeveless jeans jacket.

Valentine knocked on the doorjamb and broke the typist's concentration.

"Hi, can I help you?" the man asked in a friendly tone.

"I think I'm supposed to help you," Valentine said. "Are you one of the people who researches the Kurians?"

"Yeah. I sometimes think *research* isn't the right word, though. We're more like witch doctors trying to explain why a volcano erupts and throwing in the odd virgin to see if that helps. I think we used to put 'New Order Studies Institute' on our documents, mostly because it acronymed out as *NOSI*. But whoever we are, we're them."

Valentine entered the office, making his way around the desks and floor-filling mounds of binders to reach the scientist. As the latter stood up to shake hands, Valentine noticed that his pants were around his ankles.

"Oh, sorry," the man said. It was difficult to tell if he was blushing behind the beard. "Warm up here, you know. I swear that lightbulb puts out more calories than candlepower." He brought his trousers up to their conventional position.

"David Valentine, Wolf. Originally out of Minnesota. Pleased to meet you," Valentine said, taking the hairy-knuckled paw.

"David Walker O'Connor. From Indianapolis, myself. Ran away at the tender age of thirteen. I was brought here just because I knew about current conditions in Indiana, more or less, and stayed on. I read you took a Reaper outside of Weening about a year ago. What have you got for us now?"

"Do I talk to you? It's about a feeling I got when a Reaper was around. A couple weeks ago. A Cat named Eveready thought it was important enough that I should tell you."

O'Connor scratched himself under his shovel beard. "Let's go into the cellar. I need a break and a drink. You like root beer?"

"Yes, thank you. In fact, it'll be a treat. I've only had it once or twice."

The researcher grabbed a notebook and led the way out of the tangle of airless offices. The two descended into the cellar. At the base of the landing, a classic pawnshop barred door and window prevented further penetration. O'Connor pulled a ring of keys from his pocket and selected one. The door opened with a squeal from the hinges.

With the flick of a switch, O'Connor turned on a single bulb. Its pathetic forty watts did little to help the darkness and nothing at all to alleviate the musty smell coming from piles of clothing, trunks, and assorted boxes and crates heaped with artifacts.

"A lot of it is junk, but it all helps put together a story," his guide explained.

Something shuffled out of the shadows: slab skinned, inhuman, peering at them with a gargoyle face. Valentine startled, reaching for his absent weapons.

O'Connor put a comforting hand on his shoulder. "Easy, Valentine. This is Grishnak. As you can tell, he's a Grog. A couple of the Team found him after a battle, badly wounded. We patched him up, fed him. He's something of a mascot. He puts up with all our little experiments, don't you, Grish?" He thumped it affectionately on the arm.

The Grog cocked its head from side to side, half closing its eyes.

"Does it talk?" Valentine asked, touching its thick horn-skin.

"He gets by with a few meaningful grunts. He's a bit of a firebug; we can't let him have matches or a lantern or anything. Loves to watch things burn; they all do from what we can tell. He's a living table-scrap disposal. He thinks corncobs are a real treat. Potato peels, too. Would you like a root beer, Grish?"

Valentine looked at the half-dozen badly healed bullet wounds in the creature's leg and abdomen. A long knife scar also ran across its shoulder and down its armored chest. It unrolled its tongue.

"Grish loves root beer. Let's sit down."

Valentine listened to the small noises of the empty building. "There's more than just you to this Institute, I suppose?"

An icebox devoid of ice sat next to a slop sink, and a card table stood under the inadequate lightbulb. Shelves held a few dishes and cups. O'Connor drew three drafts from a scratched plastic barrel resting in the icebox. "There's one other scholarly fellow like myself around now, and he keeps even stranger hours. We have a couple of would-be students, but they have to scratch a living so they work in the day." The Grog held out both hands for its sweet drink and scuttled off into the shadows with its cup.

"Just as well. He's kind of messy when he drinks from a cup. I think Grishnak is pretty dumb even for a Grog. They have a language, but they don't use writing. They send little rune-stones in hollow bone tubes to communicate over distance. And the beads in their hair are kind of like military decorations, family totems, stuff like that. But back to the Institute. The rest of the team is in the field. Our elder sage is up around Mountain Home. I don't know if you heard, but five or six Reapers are on the loose up north, well within the Free Territory, and they're causing quite a problem. They're moving around faster than word of them travels, and every time it seems like they're cornered, they slip out. There's bad weather up north, and that's hurting things."

He solemnly opened his notebook and licked the end of his pencil. "Okay, Valentine, what's the story?"

Valentine relayed the events at the Mississippi crossing for the second time in as many days. O'Connor scribbled.

"And you can't link the hair-raising feeling to anything you heard, saw, or smelled. You're positive?"

"I guess I can compare it to . . . let me see . . . the feeling you get when you're next to a window on a very cold winter day. Like the heat is being pulled out of your body. I can't put it any better than that. Or a feeling I got once crossing under a high-voltage line in the dark; I knew something was above me, but I couldn't say what. How would you describe an itch to someone who has never had one?"

"I couldn't. You've smelled a Reaper, right? Since your invocation as a Wolf?"

Valentine nodded, relishing the smooth sweetness of the root beer. "Very up close. Eveready held an impromptu dissection of one before we pulled out of the Yazoo. Smelled like an offal heap."

O'Connor thought for a moment. He leaned back in the tube-steel chair, causing it to creak. "There've been a couple of incidents like yours. Not just Wolves, either. A few people have a sensitivity to Reapers. A lot of animals are the same way. We think it's because of smell, but we've seen too much weirdness in the last forty years to discount anything, including psychic powers. If it keeps happening, try to figure out at what range you sense them, if it makes a difference whether there are more than one, whether they can be distinguished as individuals, stuff like that."

"Can they tell who's who by our lifesign?"

"According to the Lifeweavers they can't, unless they're really close and it's a good read. Lifesign varies with mood, whether the person has just eaten, stuff like that. Of course you guys learn to disguise it. Distance seems to matter most of all. Like you can recognize movement from a long way away, tell a man from a woman at a certain distance, and then distinguish individuals up close. Of course it helps if you've run into the person a couple of times. But back to your question, I think they can tell who's who under certain circumstances. There've been incidents where the Reapers have gone after a specific person. I don't know if it was bullshit or not, but we had a report from New Mexico about Reapers gathering from miles off to hunt one of the Wolves out there. I guess his squad split up, and they all went after the one. Of course, lifesign reads better in the desert, there's less interference from plants and animals, and they might have just been chasing the best signal. Odd coincidence that it was someone who had done them a lot of damage, though."

"By the way," Valentine added, remembering. "There was a funny design on the boat. Kind of a bent *X*."

"That's good that you noticed it. Can you remember it well enough to draw it?"

Valentine reached for the pencil and beneath the researcher's notes traced out the design.

"You're sure it faced that way. Not like this?" He drew a Third Reich swastika.

"No, it was facing the other way. Is it important?" Valentine asked.

"Hard to say. It's been showing up lately, so I did some checking. That symbol can be found on temples in the Asian subcontinent, on Buddhist artifacts, as well as over here in American Indian cave paintings. It appears in the ruins of Troy, on Egyptian walls, even in China. I will say this: whoever used it in prehistoric times sure got around."

Seven

Arkansas, spring of the forty-second year of the Kurian Order: Valentine spent the winter months in diligent pursuit of his commission as lieutenant. While learning about interior lines and maneuver in the face of the enemy in the classroom, he became acquainted with the idiosyncrasies of oxen and pack mules in the field. He would wheedle six different calibers of ammunition out of the arsenal during the day and construe Clausewitz at night. He finished a thesis on the argument for objective reality, defending Socrates against Protagoras and Gorgias after earlier arguing about the quality of the latest barrel of flour with the demanding camp wives.

An astute observer with a detailed memory, Valentine molded his conduct after the officers he respected. He admired LeHavre's methodical planning of every company movement, each leader knowing his assignment so well the captain would often issue just two orders in a day of march: "strike the tents" at dawn and "make camp" at dusk. The company functioned as a well-tuned machine from the moment its commander hit the ON switch. He appreciated Lieutenant Mallow's role as senior in amplifying and following up on his commander's orders, and copied Brostoff's devotion to his men in supplying their every want. If he also avoided Mallow's indecisiveness in the absence of clear and specific orders from the captain and Brostoff's binge drinking, it showed that he could learn how not to behave, as well. His men liked him and, what was more, respected him for the simple reason that he showed them respect.

The Guards attending the Officer's Training College chided him for his drab deerskin clothing and his shyness. He avoided the boisterous weekend outings, a fixture of college life since education began, *and kept quiet in class unless called on. He remained silent about his experiences even with the other Wolves who dropped in occasionally as students and lecturers. He grew to know the scholars of Miskatonic Hall, read some of their raw files concerning the Kurians, and listened more than he talked. These traits, but especially the last, proved rare among the alternately bitching and bragging young Wolves.*

Still, he felt lonely and fell into the trap of pretending to prefer being alone, thus leading to further loneliness in a vicious circle of solitude that young men of a certain temperament build for themselves and then inhabit. But apart from the lack of companionship, he enjoyed his time as an acting-lieutenant more than anything else in his life up to that point. The constant challenges, physical and mental, stimulated him.

Zulu Company saw action twice that winter, but owing to his studies and lack of experience, Valentine remained back at the reserve camp with the sick and other dependents, commanding a squad of equally discouraged Wolves and being responsible for guarding the cumbersome wagons and baggage. Marksmanship contests for the non-combatants and rehearsing musical follies to welcome back the returning Wolves provided comic relief for the men's tensions, and every time one of his squad smuggled a woman into an isolated tepee, he pretended not to notice. By the first silent green explosion of spring, Zulu Company moved from Pine Bluff to the Ouachita River, returning to active duty.

"Sorry, Valentine, you're staying behind again." Captain LeHavre put down his piece of chalk. The slanted rays of the falling sun gave his features a warm golden cast.

Behind him, the blackboard (which was actually green) had a rough map of southeastern Arkansas and the Louisiana borderlands. Dotted circles traced locations the other two platoons would explore on the long-range patrol consuming the rest of the month. Next to the young Wolf, Brostoff and Mallow exchanged comments in an undertone.

"Questions, gentlemen?" the captain asked.

"What are you leaving Val, sir?" Brostoff asked.

"His whole platoon. Just because he's staying doesn't mean he'll be unoccupied. In a sense, while we're out, he's the first line of defense of Southern Command. Once the rivers fall a little more, a hard-riding column could raid this place without us cutting their trail, let alone sighting them. The river needs watching, too. He needs men for patrols, running supplies down from Regiment and out to our caches, mapping and surveying these border farms."

"Bartering for rice, too, Valentine," Mallow said. "We'll all be sick of the stuff by fall."

"Beats going hungry. Time was there wasn't much more than trappers out here," LeHavre added. "Now there are some farms—plantations more like—and if we can get them organized, we might count the land out to the Mississippi ours. It would take a couple thousand men to garrison it properly, though, and unless they provide some irregular forces, that's not going to happen. You're a good talker, Valentine. Sound out a few of these locals and see if they'll accept arms and ammunition for a patrol service."

Valentine and his platoon saw the other two thirds of Zulu Company off the following dawn.

"Give my regards to the gators," one of Valentine's platoon japed.

"Leastways we'll be doin' more with our blades than whittlin'," countered one of the men from the southbound files, spitting sunflower seed shells.

Valentine's platoon worked the lines of the ferry the company constructed for the river crossing. Within weeks, the river would be wadable at a number of drifts, but LeHavre wanted to start exploring the southern borders with the Kurian Zone now.

Blooming dogwoods decorated the slow-moving river. Valentine rode across the river with the supply mules and surveyed the campsite from the opposite bank. Zulu Company's tepees and tents were hidden, set well back from the river. Even if the Quislings sent armed patrol boats up the river, they wouldn't know the Wolves were there once the raft and lines were hidden.

"You might think you've got the easy duty, but it's a serious responsibility," a voice said from behind.

Valentine turned. LeHavre emerged from the foliage, weighed down by map cases, a telescope, and the company's only submachine gun. The clouds had thickened, and the forest was a canopy of shadow.

"This is a tricky corner you're in, Valentine. The Kurians could float up the Ouachita, raid in from Louisiana, or come across the Mississippi. They have a big garrison at Vicksburg and the barges to float them. Your first job is to protect Southern Command by looking out for that kind of thing. If they come in strength, send as much information back to Regiment double-quick. Cause trouble for 'em if you can, but your men are worth more than Quisling conscripts, so make sure you don't get cornered. I've left you here for a reason, not because you're the junior. Fact is, another time I'd stay myself."

"Yes, sir. Hopefully it'll be a quiet summer."

A third man joined them, the bulky senior NCO, Sergeant Patel. "Everything's across, sir. Scouts are out and the column is ready to go."

"Thank you, Sergeant. I'll be along in a moment." He turned back to Valentine.

"Count on us being gone six weeks. I'll send you on a short patrol when we get back, so you can get some experience. I'm going to leave Brostoff out all summer watching the rivers, but I'll be back with Mallow and his platoon."

"The chickens will be fat by then, and I'm sure I can find some good-size watermelon."

"So young, and you already know how old soldiers think. Take care, Mr. Valentine," LeHavre said, returning Valentine's salute with his usual grace. "Don't let anything happen to Southern Command while I'm gone."

Valentine forced a confident smile when LeHavre winked.

With the patrolling Wolves departing and the day fleeing, Valentine supervised the team dismantling the ferry. They floated the lines and stakes back to the camp-side and rolled the raft out of sight.

"There's a new occupied farm two miles north of here, Lieutenant Valentine," Sergeant Quist reported. "Will we be paying them a visit?"

"Keep the men out of the henhouse, if you value your rank, Quist. You know how the captain feels about that sort of thing," Valentine said, clouding over like the sky above.

"Didn't mean that, sir. They know better. I meant a social call. Get things off on the right foot. We'll be moving up and down the river, and we don't want a gut full of buckshot by accident. He might want to trade for some grub, too."

"I see. I'm sorry, Quist, wrong conclusion. I'll make it the first thing tomorrow morning. I'll take Bozich; having a woman along will seem less threatening. Michaels is the senior Aspirant now, right? I'll take him, as well. You'll have to handle things while I'm gone, Sergeant."

It began to rain, and Valentine walked the perimeter of the camp. He enjoyed a warm rain, the feeling of privacy it afforded. He smelled the sentries' tobacco smoke even in the wet before seeing them, considered issuing an order against smoking on duty, then rejected the idea. The veterans knew when it was safe to smoke, and the newbies could be taught. Shelter, food, firewood, and security occupied his mind as he wandered through the drizzle, an ear always cocked for sounds in the camp. He used his nose as much as his ears, smelling which way cooking smoke and latrine odors drifted in the prevailing winds. There were Grogs who could hear and smell better than the Wolves. He would have to set still-watches on the river, build some kind of redoubt in case of sudden attack, and arrange for safe storage of ammunition and food supplies. Some kind of netting in the overhead trees might be a good idea, he thought, remembering his encounter with the Harpies in Weening. That made him think of Gabby Cho, and his good mood vanished like a lump of sugar in the rain.

The farm Quist had spoken of consisted of a single well-built barn, still under repair. Only a foundation remained where there had once been a house. The barn stood above a wet inlet from the Ouachita, and rice paddies flourished in the cleared land.

Valentine led Bozich and Michaels up the path from the river. Bozich had a hard face but warm eyes; LeHavre was thinking of making her a sergeant. She was the most diminutive of the Valentine's Wolves, but had stamina in inverse proportion to her size and carried a carbine with a telescopic sight. Michaels still had pimples and wheezed sometimes, but a little asthma would not necessarily disqualify him from future service. More important, he took his duties as senior Aspirant seriously.

The Wolves smelled cows and goats in the barn, but no pigs. It appeared that the farmers, whoever they were, lived above their animals, and pigs were not ideal livestock for sharing accommodations.

Dogs barked, and a tousle-headed girl in the yard scrambled up a ladder at their approach, calling "Momma! Momma! Momma!" like a wailing siren. A hairy face appeared at one of the lower windows, and the Wolves stopped.

"It's sojers," somebody yelled. Valentine's ears picked up at the sound of a shotgun breech being closed.

Two men emerged, both bearded, one a little more grizzled than the other. The elder held the shotgun Valentine had heard. Both wore faded rags, patched and clean but obviously pre-Kur salvage.

"Y'all out upcountry? Command boys?" the younger asked, within jumping distance of the barn door.

"Course they is," the armed one said. "Wearin' skins an' deer-booties."

"We're camping a couple miles downstream. Thought we'd pay a call," Valentine said, hand well away from his holster.

One of the barking dogs decided nothing interesting was going to happen and flopped on its side with a sudden motion, almost as if it had been shot. Bozich and the Aspirant snickered, and the dog's owners exchanged a look.

"That dog beat all. Goes to sleep like he's droppin' deyad," the unarmed man said, showing a gap-toothed smile.

The ice was broken, and the men called out their families. Concrete Barn Farm, as the occupants styled it, consisted of two brothers, Rob and Cub Kelly. Their families and another unmarried young man worked the rice paddies, gardens, and fishing streams.

"We-uns think what's ours is ours," Rob Kelly, the younger of the brothers, said later, as the men and their wives sat with Valentine's team on the foundation of the house. Perhaps it had once been a front porch.

Cub nodded in agreement. "Couldn't take it up by y'all. Taxation, regulations. Law stopping by with empty bellies. Don't plant, don't pitch, but want it all the same. Paw took we-uns outer there."

Bozich opened her mouth, but Valentine shook his head.

"You're on your own down here, that's for sure. Lonely country, though, should the others come through."

Rob Kelly's wife tightened her mouth.

"Our boys keep good watch," the younger Kelly said. "We-uns too small fer them to bother with. We-uns jes' tell Steiner and his Beasts if'n anythin' dangerous shows up."

"Who's this Steiner?"

"His-uns got a few places in country. Half day's hard walk."

"I've got a box of shells for that twelve-gauge if one of your sons will take me to him. Looks like you could use some paint for that barn, too. I might be able to find some."

Cub Kelly looked suspicious. Of course Valentine had seen only two expressions on his face, suspicious and taciturn. He made up his mind and nodded to his brother.

"We-uns got a deal, sojer-man."

Cub Kelly's scarecrow-lean, half-naked son Patrick spoke as little as his father. All tan skin and searching eyes, he guided Valentine through a series of swamp trails. The boy carried a sling and a bag of rocks the whole way. Valentine watched the youth kill a watchful hawk atop an old utility pole. He retrieved the limp mass of talons and feathers, saying, "Sumpin' fer the boilin' pot."

Bozich whistled at the sight of the Steiner place. A cluster of buildings sat on a mound in the center of miles of rice paddies. The white-washed buildings were in good repair, with aluminum-covered roofs surrounded by walls, and the walls in turn surrounded by a wide moat.

The Wolves observed it from a little hummock of land marking the end of the trail and the beginning of the paddies. A small cemetery filled the hill, neat little crosses in rows, interspersed with rock cairns. Some of the graves were tiny, in clusters, telling the usual tale of high infant mortality in a rural region, lying next to cross after cross with DIED IN CHILDBED burned into the wood. After a moment's study of the community's dead, Valentine turned back to the living.

"Have you heard about this?" he asked Bozich.

"We knew there were some big plantations out here, but this beats all. These aren't border squatters—this is years of work, sir."

"Wonder how you get in? Drawbridge?" Valentine said.

"A boat on a line, sojer," Master Kelly said.

"Thanks, son. You can take your hawk home to the pot now. Tell your pa he needs anything, we're always ready to trade."

"Sure, sojer," the boy said, tying his sling around the legs of the hawk and trotting back into the brush.

"There's the boat," Michaels said. "Under where the wall goes down to the water."

Valentine surveyed the walls with his binoculars. The stone for them had been quarried; they were fitted together with no small skill. He saw another head, binoculars held to the eyes, staring back at him. "They've seen us, too. No use looking timid, let's go find the landing."

The three Wolves zigzagged across the earthen dikes separating the rice fields. It occurred to Valentine that anyone attacking the compound would have to take a circuitous route to rush the walls if they did not want to flounder through the mud.

"Think these folks'll feed us?" Bozich asked. "The Kellys weren't too hospitable."

"We'll learn soon enough," Valentine said. "Michaels, you stay outside of rifle range. There's a funny smell to this place."

Bozich sniffed the air. "Smells kinda like pigs . . . I hope, Mr. Valentine. Really clean ones?"

"Smells like Grogs to me. Doesn't look like there's been a fight. But be ready for anything. If night comes, Michaels, and you don't hear from us, you skedaddle. You hear shooting, you skedaddle. Understand?"

"Yes, sir. I'll bring help."

"You'll tell Quist to alert Southern Command is what you'll do."

Dogs barked as they approached, not just the yips of mongrels, but the deep baying of hounds. A man appeared at the wall. He looked at them from behind a firing slit.

"Hi-yi, strangers. Whatever you're selling, we don't need any."

"We're buyers, not sellers. We'd like to speak to Mr. Steiner. We don't have an appointment."

"You don't have a what?"

"Never mind, can we come in?"

There was a pause.

"He says he'll come out."

Steiner was a sizable man with a shock of red hair growing out of freckled skin. After a glance at the visitors, he rowed himself across in a small flat-bottomed boat.

Valentine guessed him to be about thirty-five. He wore rawhide sandals and a short wide-necked tunic that made Valentine think of pictures he had seen of Romans. It looked cool and comfortable.

"My guess is y'all are Wolves out of Southern Command. If you're looking to buy rice, I already sell mine up in Pine Bluff. I've got an agent there. And don't go quoting your Common Articles, this spread isn't part of Southern Command's ground. We built it, no help from you, and we hold it, no help from you. Last jumped-up bushwhacker that tried that ten percent routine walked up threatening and ran off yelping."

Valentine held the man's gaze. "You think you hold it, no help from us. How long you'd keep it if the Free Territory weren't still standing is another question. But I'll concede the point to save an argument."

"I'm done talking," said Steiner.

"Quite a spread you've got here. You must have room for fifty families or more. Is this a refuge if the Kur come through?"

"That's our business, Running Gun."

"We're a couple of tired Running Guns, Mr. Steiner. Hungry, too. Part of my unit is camped near the Ouachita, and I'm just trying to get to know the neighbors. I'm impressed. I've never seen a settlement quite like this in the borderlands. I'd like a better look."

"It took a lot of hard years, mister."

"Valentine, David. Lieutenant with the Arkansas Wolf Regiment."

Steiner considered. "Mr. Valentine, we don't take strangers in normally, but you seem a better sort than your usual Command type. I'll offer you a tour and a meal, but I don't want your men showing up weekly, making speeches about how totin' a gun for Southern Command entitles them to a fried chicken dinner. You'll see things not many in your outfit have seen, or want to see."

They took the little dinghy to the island. More corrugated aluminum covered the wooden gate. Valentine wondered if Steiner knew his aluminum wouldn't do him any good against white phosphorus bombs.

They passed through the gate—

And froze. A pair of Grogs stood inside, cradling their long rifles. They wore tunics similar to Steiner's and pulled back rubbery lips to reveal yellow teeth.

Bozich gasped, reaching for her carbine.

"Wait, Bozich, leave the gun," Valentine barked, putting his hand on her barrel to keep her from raising it. His heart pounded, but the Grogs kept their guns in a comfortable cradled position.

"Don't worry," Steiner said. "These aren't the usual Gray-backs. They're friendly."

"I've seen a tame Grog before."

"These ain't tame," Steiner said, flushing. "They're as free as you and me."

Valentine looked at the homes. The village resembled Weening in its circular shape, but there were no barns, just henhouses and goats. A water tower stood in the center of the village, and the community focal point appeared to be the troughs where the women did the laundry. A female Grog (with just two breasts; Valentine had heard they had four teats, like a cow) pressed the water out of her wash with a bellowslike tool. People and Grogs stopped to stare at the strangers.

Steiner invited them up onto a porch of a small house and bade them them to sit down on a comfortable-looking wooden bench.

"Mr. Valentine," Steiner began, "a long time ago I came out of Mississippi with a Grog named Big Joke. He helped me and my wife escape a labor camp, and we found the Free Territory. Some of your Wolves picked us up in the border region, took both of us prisoner. Prisoner! After weeks of trying to get to this 'bastion of freedom,' I had to go before a judge with the Grog who saved my life and beg for both of ours. I'm either convincing or she was liberal, and we were released as citizens of the Free Territory. Big Joke and I learned quick that there was no place for Grogs in your towns. The person—and he is a person, even if they think a little different than us—I owed my life to couldn't get a job, a bed, or a meal for love or money. Best he could do was 'work for food' on the docks. So my wife, Big Joke, and I headed south and found this land in the midst of these swamps. I'd spent years draining swamps and building paddies in Mississippi for *them*, so doing it a couple years for me came easy. A few others came down and joined us. That was the beginning of a lot of hard times, but we got this built."

"You lost your wife early on. I'm sorry."

Steiner's brows came together. "How—?"

"We came in past the cemetery. I saw a LaLee Steiner, who seemed about the right age. 'Evergreen' was a tribute to her?"

"No, it was her last name. I lost her to a fever, after she gave birth to my son. Two years after that some Southern Command Johnny shot Big Joke dead from ambush. He had been out hunting. I tried to understand. A Grog in the borderlands poking around with a crossbow. If I didn't know better, I'd shoot first and ask questions later myself. But y'all got to start knowing better."

"How's that?"

"Your Southern Command. Old thinking. Maybe it's because it was built by a bunch of military types. They're trying to preserve a past, not create a future. The Grogs are here, and they're here to stay. I'm sure there are hundreds of thousands, if not millions, by now. Seems a long way off, but if we ever do win, what'll we do with 'em? Kill 'em all? Not likely. Put 'em on reservations? Good luck."

"Southern Command is trying to stay alive," Valentine said. He silently agreed with Steiner about Southern Command, but he could not publicly criticize it, especially in front of Bozich. "They don't have the luxury of looking too far ahead."

"Not that living with Grogs is easy. They have a lot of fine qualities, but their brains work different. They're the most day-by-day thinkers you ever saw. If they plan three days ahead, it's an act of genius. How'd you like to wake up every morning surprised? That's what they do, in a way. Though they're smart enough at solving a problem once they understand it. You two hungry?"

"Yes, sir," Bozich said, turning from the sight of Grog children playing with a young dog. Valentine looked out; the Grogs were mimicking the dog's behavior, gamboling on all fours and interacting with it through body posture better than a human child could.

Steiner took them in to the dim house. The homemade furniture had a rough-and-ready look, though someone with some skill with a needle had added cushions.

"Sorry it's dark. We save kerosene, and anyway it just heats the place up." Steiner rekindled the fire and placed a pot from the coolroom on the stove.

"Hope you like gumbo. It's the staple here. The rice-flour buns are pretty good."

Steiner offered them a basin to wash in while the stew heated.

"I get the impression you're responsible for more than just this settlement."

The redhead laughed. "I'm still trying to figure out how that happened. Once this place got going, and we had wagons going up to Pine Bluff and back, some of the other smallholders started tailing along. With them and the Grogs guarding our wagons, it made quite a convoy. We have some great stonecutters and craftsmen here, and the locals just started trailing in, especially once we got the mill going. They started coming to me for advice, and the next thing I knew I was performing weddings and deciding whose lambs belonged to whom."

"King Steiner?"

"The thought's crossed my mind. Seems like the worry isn't worth it, but then when you get a baby or two named after you, it appears in a different light."

It occurred to Valentine that Steiner hadn't mentioned his son. He had already pressed the man on the sorrow involving his wife, and the grief in his eyes then made him hold his tongue now.

The food went into wooden bowls, and the Wolves scooped the spicy gumbo into their mouths using one rice-flour bun after another.

"Guess they call you Wolves 'cause of how y'all eat," Steiner said.

"Ain't the first time someone's said that," Bozich laughed, gumbo coating her lips.

Valentine finished his meal and helped his host clean off the dishes.

"Steiner, if you don't want to live under the Free Territory, how about you live with it?"

"With it?"

"Like an alliance."

Steiner shook his head. "What do I need Southern Command for? We do all right by ourselves."

"You might need guns and ammunition."

"We make our own shells and shot. Better than yours, mostly."

"Someday this swamp might find itself with a Kurian column in it. What then?"

"They'd lose more than they'd gain taking this place."

"We could give you a radio, and Southern Command would answer a call for help in this part of Arkansas. Anything coming through here is on its way to us."

The redhead looked doubtful, then shook his head. "Don't want a garrison, thanks."

"No garrison. We could build a hospital . . . well, health center anyway. A full-time, trained nurse and a doctor. Not just for here, but for all the farms in the area. Might mean a few less crosses in your cemetery. You could do even more for these people, if you'll just give the okay."

"Who are you, son? You have that kind of pull?"

"I'm an officer with Southern Command. I can offer whatever I think appropriate to the locals as long as it'll be used for us and not against us. Maybe I'm overstepping what they expected, but if they're going to grant me that authority, I'll use it. We put a health center up near the Saint Francis a year or so back. Why not here? Every gun you have means one more gun Southern Command can put on another border. You feed, clothe, and arm yourselves. That's a savings in money and organization. I'll put it all on paper, assuring your independence.

No ten percent tithe. You'd never have to defend anything but your own lands."

Steiner probed his teeth with his tongue and stared out the window at the wash troughs.

"Mr. Valentine, you have yourself an ally."

Lieutenant Mallow stared openmouthed as the sergeants quieted the excited comments of the men of First Platoon. Captain LeHavre shook his head, a wry smile on his face as the ferry pulled him and the weary men across.

LeHavre had sent a runner two days ago to let Valentine know the patrol was coming in, tired and hungry. The river was still deep enough to make refloating the ferry necessary. Valentine alerted his new ally at the swamp fortress to gather his militia for a meeting and review.

On one side of the landing Valentine had his platoon drawn up, at least the men who weren't working the lines and mules pulling the ferry across. On the other, Colonel Steiner stood at the head of three hundred men, women, and Grogs. Each wore a dark green bandanna tied around the neck, the only common item to the tatterdemalion Militia Steiner had christened the "Evergreen Rifles." To Valentine, the name had a certain amount of irony, as under half the group's members had firearms, mostly shotguns, and the rest carried spears, bows, pitchforks, and axes. A hundred more rifles were on their way from Southern Command, as Valentine had added several impassioned letters to the paperwork requesting heavier weapons, a health center, and a radio for the local residents. From the Wolf camp, smells of barbecue and cooking drifted out to the river. The first semiofficial gathering of the Evergreens would be celebrated with a feast.

LeHavre jumped off the ferry and splashed ashore.

"What's all this, Mr. Valentine? Grog prisoners, or a posse?"

Valentine saluted. "Welcome back, sir. Those are local Militia. Their commander and I are still going around to some other homesteads. We hope to get five hundred together before the summer is out. He's an influential man in this area."

"Leave it to you, Valentine. I leave you with a little over twenty men, and I come back to hundreds. What are you handing out, free beer?"

"Just free-*dom*, sir."

Eight

The battlefield, August of the forty-third year of the Kurian Order:
Burned-out motors and wagons fill the streets of Hazlett, Missouri.
Some of the brick buildings still stand, but of the wooden houses only
stone chimneys remain, standing as monuments to the homes that had
been.

A few soldiers still poke and rake among the sooty ruins, their
smoldering houses finally quenched by the morning's downpour. The
salvaged Grog weaponry and equipment lay in three heaps: destroyed,
repairable, and intact. Expert scroungers added to this mechanical
triage as they gleaned further material from the surrounding woods
and the road back to Cairo, Illinois.

The only bodies in evidence lay in neat, unshrouded rows lined up
outside a wooden barn a half-mile outside the town proper, conve-
niently close to a water spring. The maimed and wounded inside,
groaning their agony out on pallets, old doors, and even hay bales, en-
vied the corpses now past all suffering. Two-man teams of battlefield
surgeons, faces gray with fatigue and smocks brown with hundreds of
bloodstains, fought exhaustion and sepsis.

The gravediggers adhered to their own priorities. The first day after the battle, they put to rest the dead of Southern Command: Bears,
Wolves, Guards, and Militia. The second day, the dead Quislings were
buried in a long common grave, dug by the prisoners spared after the
fall of Hazlett. Finally on this day, the third after the battle, the gravediggers set alight a great pyre of Grogs, who shared the flame with
putrefying dead horses, oxen, and mules inside a ring of firewood.
Exhausted from the labor of dragging the bigger corpses out of sight
and smell, the officer in charge decided to rest his detail before attend-

ing to the row of this morning's bodies outside the field hospital. The doctors couldn't save everyone.

Thus the miasma of burned flesh introduced Lt. David Valentine to the tableau of a battlefield. Three companies of Wolves, including Zulu, marched up from reserve near the southern border. Sent to help deal with the incursion, they arrived too late to do anything but shake their heads at the destruction of the little town and join in the services held over the bodies of the slain.

Chuckwagon tales told by the survivors of the Battle of Hazlett described a push into the valuable mining towns of the area from the tip of Illinois. The Quislings and Grogs made a fortress of the little crossroads town, and only a concentration of every available Bear in eastern Missouri backed up by Wolves and a Guard regiment forced them out again. It might have been worse, but Valentine learned that a company of Wolves had ambushed reinforcements at the Mississippi, sacrificing themselves to keep the road to Hazlett closed. Out of a hundred Wolves, a bare sixteen now licked their wounds on the banks of the Whitewater River.

It was this destruction of Foxtrot Company that led Captain Le-Havre, the senior Wolf officer in the area, to call Valentine into his tepee one afternoon. Zulu Company was preparing to return below the state line again, as an incursion in the northeast might mean an even larger one in the southwest.

Valentine wondered, as he answered the summons that afternoon, what the news would be. LeHavre always hit his officers, whenever possible, with bitter medicine early in the morning and saved the sugar for evenings. So an afternoon conference might be a trail-mix assortment of sweet and sour.

He found LeHavre by a commissary wagon, sharing a cup of coffee with an unknown, clean-shaven Wolf.

"David Valentine, meet Randall Harper," the captain introduced. "Sergeant Harper here is part of the Command Staff. A courier, to be exact."

The young men shook hands. Harper seemed a little young to be a sergeant, particularly on the Command Staff, but then Valentine was even younger to be a lieutenant. The courier had a lazy eye, which made looking into his face unsettling, but he wore a cheerful smile that brightened his whole face to such a degree that Valentine liked him from first sight.

"Pleased to meet you, sir," Harper said.

"Valentine, you are going on a trip. I need some young legs to accompany Harper here on a four-hundred-mile jaunt. All the way up to Lake Michigan, as a matter of fact."

"I've got two bags of mail and one of dispatches, sir," Harper added.

"Why me, sir?" Valentine asked, risking a rebuke.

"Normally an officer from Foxtrot Company and another Wolf would go, but as of these last few days, Foxtrot doesn't exist anymore and probably won't for another year or so. There's only acting-lieutenants in the junior position in the other two Wolf companies, and I don't know enough about them to pick one. And you're from the Great White North, so I thought you'd like a trip back up. I was going to send you up with Paul Samuels anyway on one of his recruiting sweeps, but this'll be a better experience for you."

"Mounted or afoot, sir?"

"With a little luck, you'll be mounted all the way. Three horses plus a spare is what you have, right, Sergeant?"

"Yes, sir," Harper answered. "The fourth will carry the mail and some oats. Or if we lose one, it'll be a remount."

"So a third man is going, sir?" Valentine asked. "Who will that be?"

LeHavre patted Valentine on the shoulder. "Take who you want, Valentine. Except for Patel. I need him, and he's too old to cover forty miles a day for long stretches anymore."

Valentine mentally ran down the list of Wolves in Zulu Company.

"I'll take Gonzalez, sir. He has the best nose in the company, and he's first-rate with his hunting bow."

"Take him with my compliments, Lieutenant. Let me know your needs. I realize the company wagons haven't caught up with us yet, but I can probably scrounge you up about anything. Questions?"

The only questions that came to Valentine's mind implied evading responsibility, so he remained silent.

LeHavre finished his coffee. "You two get together with Gonzalez and talk it through. I know you've made the trip a couple of times, Harper, so tell as much about the route to the other two as you can, just in case. You leave at dawn."

Harper accepted the possibility of his death, suggested by the *just in case,* with the same sunny smile. "Gladly, sir."

That evening, Gonzalez joined them in an informal campfire conference.

"Seems like a lot of effort to deliver a few letters. How often do you do this?" Gonzo asked.

"Two or three times a year. Southern Command tries to stay in touch with the other Resistance pockets, at least the big ones. This is information we don't want to broadcast on the shortwave. That's why if it looks like we're going to be taken, you need to pour the fluid in the flasks onto the dispatches and burn 'em."

"If the Reapers are closing in, I'm going to be too busy to start any fires, Sarge."

Valentine mopped up his stew with a slab of bread. "How long are we going to be gone?"

"Depends on the horses, and then the sailors. If we can come up with feed now and then, about two weeks per leg. But there's no guarantee the ship will be in Whitefish Bay on time. The Lakes Fleet has troubles of its own. Luckily the Kurians don't pay much attention to the ships, unless they get too close to a city they care about. We'll just have to wait if they aren't there."

"Ever had any problems running the mail?" Valentine inquired.

Harper's smile returned. "A few close shaves. We should keep toward the Mississippi until the Wisconsin border or so. About all you have to worry about there is border trash, but they're mostly scared of everything. Wisconsin has the real Kurian lands we have to cross. Their pet humans farm that area pretty good, and of course the Reapers farm the humans. The shortest route would be up through central Illinois, but that's thickly settled, and unless you have a death wish, you'll want to keep away from Chicago."

Valentine and Gonzalez bade farewell to their company in the predawn gloom. LeHavre offered a final word of advice to his junior lieutenant.

"Keep your eyes open, Mr. Valentine," LeHavre said, solemnly shaking his protégé's hand. "We never know enough about what is happening in the Lost Lands. Try and pick up any information you can, even if it's just impressions."

"Thank you for the opportunity, sir."

LeHavre winced. *How many young men have you sent to their doom with those words on their lips?* Valentine wondered.

"You can thank me by coming back, David."

The three Wolves mounted their horses, the excited animals stamping and tossing their heads in their eagerness to be off, and rode into the misty dawn.

During the first leg of the journey, they kept to the rough terrain of the Mississippi Valley. They conserved the strength of horse and rider, walking their mounts and stopping often. On the second day, they crossed the Mississippi in a hollowed-out old houseboat, well camouflaged with dirt and plant growth on its battered sides. The trio of old Wolves who took them across laughed as they listened to the secondhand story of the Battle of Hazlett over the labored *putt*ing of the aged diesel engine.

"That'll learn 'em," one of them cackled as he brought the houseboat out of its hidden cove and into the current at the "all clear" signal from his observer. "Hank and I, we've been puttin' up signs all over the west bank for miles readin' 'Trespassers Will Be Prosecuted' and 'No Solicitors Invited,' but them Grogs don't read too good."

Once in no-man's-land, the Wolves traveled cautiously. They camped for the night when they found the right spot, not when the sun set. Daybreak never found them in the same location in which they bedded down. Each night Valentine ordered a camp change of at least a half-mile, and lost sleep was made up with a siesta each afternoon during the worst of the late summer heat. They set no watch, but relied on their senses to rouse them from their light slumber in the event of danger. They always cooked their meals before dark, knowing better than to call attention to themselves with the light of a campfire.

By the third night out, they were swapping life stories. Valentine had heard Gonzalez's before, but listened again to his scout's words as he lay in his hammock under a cloud-masked moon.

"I was born in Texas in 2041, out there in the western part. My parents were part of a guerrilla band called the Screaming Eagles, which my father told me was an old army unit and my *madre* said was a music group. They used to do a war cry. . . . I would do it, but it's too loud for these parts. Too loud for the Ozarks, too. I don't remember much fighting when I was young. I think the Eagles stole cattle off the Turncoats. That was what we called the Quislings out there. Sometimes in the summer we went as far north as Kansas and Colorado, and in the winter we would be in Mexico.

"I was about twelve when the Turncoats got us. It was in Mexico. We were in this kind of bowl-shaped valley, a few old buildings and tents, with the cattle all spread out. They got some cannon up in the hills somehow, and pretty soon there were explosions everywhere, with men on horseback pouring down from the mountains. My father fought them, but I'm sure he was killed with the rest. There were just two passes out of the valley, but they had hundreds of men with guns hidden in the rocks. I don't think anyone made it out that way. My *madre* got me and my baby brother out over the hills. One of the Turncoats caught up to us. He attacked her, but I picked up his gun and shot him in the foot. He grabbed the gun out of my hands and was going to shoot me, but my *madre* brought a boulder as big as a football down on his head and killed him. God knows how she found the strength to lift it; she was a small woman."

Gonzalez fingered a small silver crucifix around his neck.

"We walked for days and would have died, but a rainstorm saved us. We hid for a while in a Turncoat village. An old man who was kind to us arranged for my mother to move into eastern Texas where his son lived. My mother lived with his son and had a child with him, but she never loved him as she did my father, even though he was very good to us. She gave him two daughters, but when I turned sixteen, she said, 'Victor, you must leave this land, for the people here have forgotten themselves and God.' We heard rumors about a place in the mountains where the Hooded Ones could not go, and I found this place on my own, but I fear it went bad for my stepfather, who let me run away. But I know my *madre* still lives because I still live; her prayers protect me and keep me alive. With what I have seen, I cannot pray as she does, so when she dies, I will die, too."

Valentine told his story next, leaving out the fact that his father had been a Wolf. He described the cool beauty of the Boundary Waters' woods and lakes, and the challenge of living through a Minnesota winter.

"I hadn't seen much geography until I became a Wolf," Harper began. "I was born to a big family near Fort Scott. My pa was an officer in the Guards, and he tried to keep me in school, but I wouldn't have it. Everyone made fun of this eye of mine; you know how kids are. At nine, I tried to be an Aspirant, but they wouldn't let me. I hung out in Wolf camps whenever I could; my pa was away a lot, and my ma—Well, she had her hands full with the other children. They let me become an Aspirant at thirteen, finally. I was invoked when I was fifteen, and I was in the middle of it at Cedar Hill and then Big River. They made me a sergeant after all that. I was a champion distance runner, so I got put in the couriers. I made a trip to the Gulf in 'sixty-three, and did the run to Lake Michigan twice last year. I crossed Tennessee this spring going to the Appalachians, and that's the worst run I've ever been on. Took me forever to find resistance people in the Smokies. These trips should be run by just couriers, but we've lost so many out West over one thing and another that Command is short on messengers."

"I was wondering why you showed up with two empty saddles," Valentine said.

"Well, I'm grateful of your company. Mr. Valentine, you seem to be a right smart officer, afraid of all the right things, if you'll excuse me for saying so, sir. And Gonzalez—you, sir, have the most righteous set of ears in the Free Territory. I'm glad you're along to count the mouse farts, you know?"

Gonzalez proved just how good his hearing was somewhere east of Galena, Illinois. They had been traveling for a week when someone began trailing them.

"There are three or four riders coming up behind," Gonzo reported. "Haven't caught sight of them yet, but you can hear them. I don't know if they're right on our trail or just keeping with the old road."

The three Wolves rode parallel to an old road, now overgrown but still too far from tall timber for their purposes. Valentine debated the choices. An ambush would be easy enough to set up, but he balked at shooting down strangers in cold blood. Anyone close enough for the Wolves to hear would probably have cut their trail by now and would know someone was ahead. The idea of being trailed worried him.

"Do you know who lives around here?" he asked Harper.

"This far off the river? A few farmers scratch a living out here. On other trips we've crossed the trails of pretty big groups on horseback. I don't like thinking worst case, but this is just the kind of area a pair of Reapers might hunt."

"Yes, but they wouldn't be on horseback. And they wouldn't make enough noise for Gonzo to hear them," Valentine argued. As usual, someone else's opinion helped him form his own, for better or worse. "Let's go up the bluffs. If they're casual travelers, they won't follow. If they come up after us, we can get a good look at what we're taking on before we start shooting."

With that, the Wolves made a sharp turn east, moving into the wooded hills away from the overgrown road. Valentine removed his lever-action rifle from its sheath. Soon they were struggling up a steep slope, leaning far forward in their saddles to help the horses' balance.

As they ascended the hill, Valentine searched right and left. No rock pile or fallen trunk presented itself. Valentine cursed his luck at riding for the one uneroded hill covered with uniformly healthy timber in all of western Illinois.

Gaining the summit, the Wolves at last found a deadfall they could hide behind. The breeze blew fresh from the west hard enough to whip at the horses' manes and make the men clutch at their hats. They rode past the fallen log and looped back; tracks heading straight for an ambush spot would be investigated more cautiously. Valentine asked Harper to hold the four horses out of sight behind the crest of the hill.

Dismounted, with weapons in hand, Valentine and Gonzalez walked back to the fallen log. Gonzalez held an arrow to his bowstring. With luck, the trackers had a single scout out front who could be silently dispatched with a feathered shaft.

"Keep your bow ready, Gonzo," Valentine said in a low tone. "I'm going to get in that oak above our trail. If there's just two scouts, I'll drop on one. When you see me leap, try for the other with the bow. If it's three or four, I'll let them ride past, and I'll backshoot them."

"Let me go up the tree, sir."

"I'm not much with a bow, my friend. I doubt I could hit a horse at this distance, let alone a rider. Just stay cool and wait for my signal."

Valentine scrambled to his perch among the thick limbs of the grandfather oak. He hugged the tree limbs like a lizard, pulling a leafy branch toward his face for concealment. Whoever the trackers were, they had four scouts ahead on horseback. Valentine listened with hard ears past them, but his nose helped even more. A large group of horses and men were somewhere out of sight, upwind to the west. He smelled some tobacco, and cannabis, as well.

As the scouts walked their horses up the slope and into view, Valentine decided this was no Quisling patrol. The shabbiness of man and beast, from worn-out boots to collapsed felt hat brims, indicated either the worst kind of Quisling irregulars or simple bandits. They carried rifles, but some of the guns looked like black-powder muzzle-loaders.

Whatever their deficiencies in equipment, the four scouts knew their jobs. One concentrated on the trail, two a little behind him searched the terrain ahead, and the fourth stayed far back in case of trouble. One of the middle scouts didn't like the look of the hilltop, and they pulled up to a halt. Binoculars and small telescopes emerged from their patched overcoats.

One of the four Wolf horses, scenting those below, let out with a high, questioning neigh. The scouts spun their horses and plunged down the hill.

Valentine mouthed obscenities.

A good second line of defense, Valentine maintained, is running like hell. He jumped from the tree and, waving to Gonzalez, ran up toward the four horses.

"It's border trash, I think. A lot," he explained to Harper as they mounted.

Valentine led them at something less than a flat-out gallop along the ridgeline. Their horses had covered a lot of miles in the past week, but perhaps were of sterner stuff and in better health than the beasts of the ragamuffins below.

He reveled in the mad inconsequence of it all. Their pursuers might catch them; he and the two Wolves might die, and the world would change or care not a whit. But it felt glorious to pound through the woods on a running horse, his legs tight in the stirrups and hands far up the horse's neck. Clods of dirt kicked up by the horses' rhythmic gait flew up behind like birds startled at their passing.

Harper is having trouble with the spare horse, the sane part of his mind reminded him. Valentine spotted a clearing on a prominence ahead and turned his horse toward it, slowing the pace to a trot and then a walk. Reaching the bare spot, they saw a ruined house, roofless and empty.

"We covered some miles," Gonzalez gasped. "Where the hell is the road?"

"Somewhere down to the west of us," Valentine said, waving vaguely at the descending sun. Trees obscured the road's probable location. "Let's take a breather and see how our friends are doing."

The overlook gave them a good view of the hills to the south. Valentine and Harper listened to the steady drum of hooves in the distance.

"Aw, shit," Harper said. "I always figured a Reaper would get me, not some grubby thugs."

Valentine looked at the house. There were good walls there, and only two doors to cover. The horses would fit inside. "Okay, so their horses are fresher than ours. We've still got three guns and a good spot to shoot from."

He could now see distant riders galloping along the trail. He stopped counting after estimating fifty. "Let's get inside our new home and get ready to greet our guests."

Behind the house a pump stood on a concrete patio. "Oh, pretty please with sugar on it," Harper said, working the handle. It moved a little too easily; nothing came from the rusty metal spout but noise.

The main room of the house was filled with collapsed roof, but they were able to bring the horses through the back door into a room slightly lower than the larger one. The paneless windows were set so a man at the front could cover the main door, more or less, but the western exposure of rooms off the main one would have to go unguarded. Valentine posted himself at the front window, Harper at the side, and Gonzalez at the rear door. They manhandled an empty refrigerator into the doorway to the main room.

"We ought to be able to hold out for about two minutes now," Harper said.

"There's always the chance we'll make the price too steep for them," Valentine said, filling a pocket with cartridges.

"I was sick of riding anyway," Gonzalez said.

"That's the idea," Valentine responded. "If we can get them to wait until dark, we just might be able to slip out. Head for steep hills and thick woods. Maybe all they want is the horses. I know we can outrun them on foot, even carrying the mail. Whoever they are, they're not Wolves."

Their pursuers approached their refuge with caution. A thin man with a ragged straw hat bearing a single black feather in the brim trotted up toward the house, carbine at his hip. He turned his face suspiciously, first looking at the ruined dwelling with one eye, then the other. Valentine sighted on his dirty undershirt.

"That's far enough. What's on your mind?" Valentine shouted.

The thin man's long face split into a grin. "You boys want parley?"

"We're willing to let lead fly if you want it that way. Might be better for both if we talked first."

Straw Hat turned his horse and disappeared downslope. Valentine counted the minutes; every moment toward dusk helped their cause.

He heard horses moving through the woods below the hill. The pursuers were fanning out to surround the house. It sounded like a lot of riders.

Three heavy figures on tall quarterhorses approached the house. Even beneath beard and dirt, Valentine thought he saw a family resemblance. Their scruffy beards were black as coal, save for the center rider, who had two narrow streaks of gray running down his beard. Their hats also bore black feathers tucked in the left side of the hatband like that of the point man.

"Hello, the house," center rider called. "You wanted a parley, here it is."

"May I know to whom I'm speaking?" Valentine hollered back.

The man glanced at his younger associates. "Sure, stranger. My name's Mr. Mind Your Own Damn Business. This is my son Or I'll Tear Off Your Head and my nephew And I'll Shit Down Your Throat," he yelled. "That satisfy the rules of ettycute?"

A few guffaws broke out from below. "Charming," Harper said. "Why don't you plant him, Lieutenant?"

Valentine kept his concentration on the rider. "Thank you, Mr. Mind. Looks like you got us four in a box. Is there a way for us to get out of it without a bunch of you winding up dead?"

"Maybe there's four of you and maybe there's three. One of your horses is riding light, so maybe you got a woman or a kid in there to think about," the negotiator called back.

"All we're thinking about is how many of you we can take with us. The consensus is twenty. If you're smart enough to know what a claymore mine is, you'll agree that it's at least that."

"Son, we can smoke you out of there easy. You'll be better off to take my terms: leave us your rifles, and give us the horses and tack. You can keep all your food, all your water, and your handguns, if you got 'em. And your lives. Even your self-respect, knowing that you met the Black Feather Troop and lived to tell about it."

"You want the guns, you just try and get 'em," Valentine shouted back, trying to keep the calm assurance of Captain LeHavre in his voice. "You'll get plenty of the business end. How about this: We'll give you the horses and the tack, and walk out of here after you pull out."

"No bargaining! I'm giving you five minutes to talk it over. You're up a dry hill in a building you can't even cover all the sides of. Bring out your rifles, and we let you walk out and keep heading north," he demanded with the assurance of a man holding four aces.

Valentine knew he was beat on card strength, but he believed they wouldn't live to see the sunrise if they walked out of the house without their rifles. The men turned to him, having reached the same conclusions and wanting to go down shooting.

"Gonzo, Harper, get out your blades. There's something we have to do."

"Cut the horses' throats?" Harper asked.

Valentine decided there was still a chance at bluff. "No, we have to whittle."

Five minutes later, but with over an hour of daylight left, Valentine stepped out of the door with the three rifles in his arms. He inflated his lungs, threw out his chest, and let loose with a high-pitched shriek. The three Black Feathers startled at the cry, which didn't seem to echo off the hills so much as pass through them.

"Come and get your guns," Valentine called hoarsely, advancing a cautious pair of steps away from the door. His holster was empty; Harper covered him from behind with the revolver.

"You made the smart move, son," Mr. Mind said, trying to keep the satisfaction out of his voice. The three rode forward to claim the repeaters.

Valentine carefully placed them on the ground and stepped back.

The older man dismounted, covered by the guns of his younger relations. He knelt to pick up one of the guns. "So, there are only three of you. I thought so. These are mighty fine—"

He made a surprised choking sound and pulled his hands away from the rifle as if it were a rattlesnake shaking its tail.

Carved into the stock of each rifle was a small insigne, a reversed swastika identical to the one Valentine had seen on the canoe and discussed with the researcher at the Miskatonic.

He looked up at Valentine, lips trembling. "Where'd you get these?" he asked.

"Our Masters gave them to us. Their mark is on the saddles, as well. I even have a tattoo. We're scouting for them, you see. Eight of them moving west as we speak. So take them, but we'll have them back by morning. In good condition, too: They'll only be dropped once."

"Now, son, we had no knowing you had anything to do with the Twisted Cross. Hell, we're no enemies of yours. You might say we're on your side. Just this spring we caught a Cat out of the Ozarks. Real little spitfire; the boys ganged her, and we cut her throat, of course. You can ask Lord Melok-iz-Kur, in Rockford. We pay for what we take there with good silver, turned in runners even."

Valentine smiled. "It seems we've just had a misunderstanding here. No one was hurt, no one need know, Mr.—"

"It's Black Craig Lorraine, sir. At your service. If there's anything we can do to help you along, anything at all . . ." The Black Feather was almost groveling.

"Come to think of it . . . ," Valentine mused.

Valentine returned to the house, holding the rifles. "He folded." Harper handed the pistol back.

"Eh?" said Gonzalez.

"They're letting us go. In fact, they're giving us some supplies. Problem is, they're cannibals, so I had to promise them Gonzalez, since he's the plumpest of us."

"Bad joke, Val," Gonzalez said. "That was a joke, right?"

That night the Wolves rode north with guns, horses, and a new shoe on the spare horse. They were also weighed down by bags of corn, grain, and food from the supplies of the Black Feathers.

"Jesus, Lieutenant," Harper said, voice tinged with admiration. "When you did that Reaper scream, I about crapped my pants. You could have warned us."

One of the Black Feathers, part of the dispersing ring to the north, waved in a friendly fashion. Gonzalez eyed him warily.

"That was a joke, right, Lieutenant?"

Nine

Milwaukee, August of the forty-third year of the Kurian Order: The burned-out corpse of a city that once held nearly two million people rots across some eighty square miles on the shores of Lake Michigan. From the steep hills overlooking the great lake in the east to the Menominee and Root Rivers in the west, the city is nothing but hollow shells of buildings, the upper stories now housing bats, hawks, pigeons, and seagulls. The lower levels shelter everything from rats and coyotes to vagrant humans. Green has covered pavement throughout much of the city. Crickets chirp and grasshoppers leap along Locust Avenue, and Greenfield Avenue is precisely that: a green field where cattle are moved along to graze.

The new center of the city is the railway station, where the more favored soldiers and technicians house themselves in a ring around the Grand Avenue Mall. A hobo jungle of casual labor lives around and under the spaghetti-strand warren of overpasses that make up the old Interstate 94/43 juncture. Two Kurian Lords run the city, one from the Grog-guarded 1950 bomb shelter under the Federal Building, and the other from Tory Hill on the grounds of Marquette University. The Miller Brewing Company is still in business, producing but a trickle of the pilsner torrent it once did. Under new management, of course.

Lake Michigan awed Valentine with its quiet majesty. It had nothing of the crashing drama of the ocean shoreline he knew from books. The expanse of water covering 180 degrees of the horizon in almost a north-south line impressed him nonetheless.

He and Randall Harper camped together north of Whitefish Bay. They had left Gonzalez in a secluded barn far outside the city limits with the horses after a cautious but uneventful crossing of southern Wisconsin. The only difficulty had been from a pack of guard dogs at a lonely farming settlement who chased them out of a field where they were stealing corn for the horses. The dogs contented themselves with barking rather than biting, and the Wolves had hurried back to their mounts without injury to anything but their dignity.

Now each night they stood behind a four-foot-tall, decorative stone wall in an overgrown park overlooking the lake, waiting for a boat from the White Banner Fleet to show three lights, one flickering, which they would answer with two.

"What exactly is this Flotilla?" Valentine asked his companion.

Harper, comfortably seated with his back to the stone wall, took a puff of one of the noxious cigarettes he smoked. "They're sympathetic to the Cause, even if they don't fight the Kurians tooth and nail. They're smugglers, gunrunners, traders. When they fight the Quislings, it's more because somebody got double-crossed, or they asked for too big a payoff. The Hoods hate going out into blue water, I'm told, so they leave it to the Quislings and some amphibian Grogs. Naturally the Quislings take bribes whenever they can get away with it. But the Flotilla always fights the Grogs whenever they get the chance. It's a real blood feud. I guess these Grogs are more partial to human flesh than most."

"Oh, I think I've heard of these. Big Mouths, Snappers, or whatever. They have jaws that open right to left, instead of up and down, right? Kind of fish-frog things?"

"Yep, slimy skin, like an eel. They're a problem in summer. They go dormant in winter. The real danger's in the spring, when they lay their eggs, you gotta keep away from the shores of the places they inhabit. They forage miles inland for food. They like the water a little shallower though, so they're not such a problem here. Up by Green Bay it's another story, though. And Lake Erie is stiff with them, they tell me."

Valentine thought of all the times that he had taken a boat out into the lakes of the Boundary Waters, collecting fish for dinner. Strange to think of fish emerging and hunting ashore. "So why does the Fleet carry our mail for us?"

"The Hunters in upstate New York give them guns and ammo, that's why. Rope, lumber, paint, turpentine, engines, gasoline—all sorts of stuff. We're lucky. We're just delivery boys; we don't have to worry about payoffs. But I got a little grease for the wheels in my bag; it's sort of expected."

Valentine shrugged. "Whatever it takes. You'd think they'd be on our side."

"They are, they are. In fact, I guarantee that you'll like 'em. Those sailors got a million stories. Of course, most of it's lies and brag, but it's still fun to listen to."

"I'll bet," Valentine said.

The next night the boat arrived. Valentine almost missed it, having wolf-trotted back to Gonzalez's barn to check on things at the main camp. Both the horses and his scout looked better for a few days' rest. Gonzalez had explored the area, finding some apple trees and rhubarb growing nearby. The scout had collected a basket of green apples and an armful of rhubarb, and was sharing his findings with the horses. "I saw some tomatoes near there, too. I'll get 'em tomorrow, sir," he reported.

"Just make sure you're not raiding somebody's field. We might end up dealing with something worse than dogs. I don't want any locals to suspect we're here."

"No tracks, no sign, and best of all, no Reapers," Gonzalez reassured him.

"I hope not. Sleep light. I'll take some apples back, if you have no objections, Mr. Bountiful," Valentine said, filling his pockets.

"Of course, Lieutenant. Give a few to the sarge with my compliments."

It was a tired lieutenant who returned to the overlook that evening, having covered fifteen miles on foot in the course of the day. Two hours after sunset, the three lights appeared on the dark lake.

"Thar she blows," Harper quoted, choosing a curious allusion. Valentine was mentally reciting *two on the land and three in the sea, and I on the outskirts of Milwaukee will be.*

Harper poured his flammable liquid on two piles of wood, twelve feet apart on the lakeside of the overlook wall, and set them ablaze. One light on the boat began winking on and off, as somebody opened and closed a hooded lantern.

"Are you satisfied it's them?" Harper asked.

"Yes," answered Valentine, trying to make out the lines of the little ship.

"Then let's go down to the beach, sir, and deliver the mail," Harper said, kicking out his fires.

The ship bobbed in the small swell of the lake. The waters of Lake Michigan did not roar as they struck the shoreline, but instead gently slapped it. The lake almost seemed playful on this idyllic summer evening, and something about the cool water in the warm evening breeze made Valentine forget the dangers of the night. The men waded out, weighed down with their waterproofed message bags, moccasins tied around their necks.

A tiny dinghy met them, its sides a bare sixteen inches out of the water.

"Climb in sideways," a boy's voice said from the stern. "You'll capsize me if you try to vault in."

The Wolves threw their packs into the dink and rolled into the little boat. It settled in the water appreciably with their added weight.

Valentine looked into the stern, at the figure with the paddle. What he had thought was a young boy was in fact a young woman dressed in shapeless white canvas. She had a round face and merry eyes, looking at her passengers over freckled cheekbones.

"Nice night, eh, boys? Captain Doss sends her compliments to the representatives of the Ozark Free Territory and invites you aboard the yawl *White Lightning*," she said, flashing an impressive set of teeth.

"The what *White Lightning?*" Valentine asked.

"Yawl," she repeated. "You know nothing of ships, soldier?"

"Not much," Valentine admitted.

"It's a little thing, but seaworthy as a porpoise. A ship not very different from ours made it around the world with only a single man on board. Over a hundred years ago, that was."

"Good to see you again . . . Teri, is it?" Harper said, contemplating his soaked deerskin breeches.

"I thought you looked familiar. Aaron . . . no, Randall Harper. Met you twice before, I recall. But I didn't see you this spring."

"I had the overland route. I don't want it again," Harper explained.

"Well, the captain will be glad to see you. So who's this with you?"

"Lt. David Valentine. He hails from Minnesota."

She reached over to shake Valentine's hand. "Pleased to know you, Lieutenant. Teri Silvertongue, first mate of the *White Lightning*. Will it be possible for you gentlemen to be joining us as guests this lovely evening?"

"I can't think of anything I'd like more, Miss Silvertongue," Valentine said, imitating her courteous phraseology. He wondered if Silvertongue was a nickname.

"We go by *Mr.* in the flotilla, man or woman," Silvertongue corrected. "Just as you do in the Wolves. Will you take an oar, sir?"

"I beg your pardon, Mr. Silvertongue. Sergeant Harper here didn't tell me the ship had a female crew, let alone how you expected to be addressed. Likes to keep a good thing to himself, I guess," Valentine explained, shooting a glance at Harper. He paddled for the white blob outside the gentle surf.

"Oh, there's plenty of men in the Flotilla," Silvertongue explained. "The commodore of our fleet just has a soft spot in her heart for any woman with a sad tale. It's the only soft spot she has; the woman has steel in her backbone and flint in her heart in all other matters excepting her 'poor foundlings,' as she calls us. But yes, it's three women on the *Lightning*. But it beats life on land. The Capos just want us for breeding stock, and their gunbelt lackeys seem to think they have the right to get the job started on any girl who tickles their fancy."

"Capos?" Valentine asked.

"That's what we call the Reapers out east, handsome boy."

The dinghy reached the ship, and Valentine got a good look at the *White Lightning*. Her lines had kind of an off-balanced beauty, with an oversize central mast set well forward and a smaller, secondary mast projecting from far astern.

Captain Doss wore a smart white semi-uniform to greet her guests. The captain had beautiful, dusky skin and the angular features of a storybook pirate queen. Her short black hair matched even Valentine's own mane in its glossy sheen.

A third woman, who helped Valentine and Harper into the *White Lightning,* stood over six feet tall and had the long, graceful limbs of a ballerina. "Give me the bags up," she said perfunctorily, and Valentine realized he had heard a foreign accent for the first time in his life.

Once on board, the *White Lightning* seemed smaller than it had looked from the dinghy. It was wide-waisted; the top of what was obviously the cabin area filled the middle third of the ship. It had a wheel to steer it—someone had spent a lot of hours carving and polishing the spokes—placed in front of the rear mast. All the woodwork, save the planks of the deck and the decorative wheel, was painted a uniform light gray.

The captain introduced her crew. "You've met my first mate, Mr. Silvertongue. My second mate, who works so hard I don't need any more crew, is Eva Stepanicz. She crossed the Atlantic four round trips before ending up in the Lakes."

"It will be more times, once I have goods enough for my own ship," she said.

"You mean gold enough?" Harper asked

"No, sir. Goods. In Riga is agent of tradings, who pays most for paintings brought back from America. I am here collecting arts."

The captain smiled. "It's hard not to indulge someone so determined. And she's a hard bargainer. I don't know a Picasso from an espresso, but I think our Mr. Stepanicz has enough to start a gallery."

"But I'm forgetting my manners," Harper said, reaching into his haversack. "Captain, compliments of my last trip through Tennessee," he said, handing over a pair of elaborately wrapped and sealed bottles of liquor. In the muted light, Valentine couldn't read the black labels, but they looked authentic.

"Sergeant Harper, you just bought us a new coat of paint, and maybe some standing rigging. My thanks to you, sir."

Harper pointed to the three bags of correspondence. "You'll also find a box of cigars for each of you in those bags. If you don't smoke them yourselves, a little good tobacco helps grease the Quisling wheels, I believe."

"You southern gentlemen are too kind. I wish those Green Mountain Boys would show the same courtesy," Silvertongue said, with a curtsey involving her overbaggy trousers.

"Enough playacting," Captain Doss interrupted. "I'd like to be anchored off Adolph's Bunker by midnight. You Wolves want to pay a call on Milwaukee? Get a little taste of life in the KZ?"

"We're always interested in the Kurian Zone. But would that be wise, Captain?" Valentine asked.

"Well, Lieutenant, the pathfinder look would have to go. But we've got some extra whites in the slop chest. The Bunker's a rough spot, but I've never heard of the Reapers going in there. The owner never makes trouble; in fact, I've heard he turns troublemakers over to them. I'd like a little extra muscle showing for the deal we need to do. I'll make it worth your while."

Valentine thought for a moment. "Is this deal anything the New Order would object to?"

"If they knew about it, Lieutenant," Doss said, looking at the wind telltale. The tiny streamer fluttered east. "You might say we're fucking with the Quislings."

"Count us in, then."

An hour later, the yawl tacked into Milwaukee's harbor. A single decrepit police boat, piloted by a Quisling whose sole badge of rank was a grimy blue shirt, motored alongside and illuminated the *White Lightning* with a small spotlight.

Captain Doss held up a hand and flashed a series of hand signals that would have done a third-base coach proud. The Quisling nodded, satisfied.

"Just arranging what you might call the port charges," Doss explained to Valentine. The Wolves now wore white canvas shirts and trousers, as well. While more tattered than the mates' uniforms, they still found it a pleasant change from sweat-stained buckskins. During the run south, Valentine had questioned the captain about the Lakes Flotilla and its habits, and had learned a little about how the sails were balanced. Valentine sponged information off anyone he met, his mind always ready to learn something new.

They pulled up to the main civic pier, a cracked concrete affair that sloped toward Lake Michigan at a twenty-degree angle. Valentine noticed that the captain pivoted as she brought the ship in so that its bow pointed out to the lake.

"The Kurians aren't too big on infrastructure repairs," Silvertongue commented as she tied the *White Lightning* to the dock. A few boats, none of which matched Captain Doss's in lines or upkeep, bobbed along the pier.

"Stepanicz, you've got the first anchor watch. Don't give me that look; after the deal, I'll take over for you. If we're not back in two hours, or if anything goes down, you raise sail. There's a good wind for it tonight."

"Aye, aye, sir," she answered, drawing a sawed-off shotgun from the chart locker. She broke it open and inserted two loads of buckshot.

"And if our broad-shouldered young men would each grab one of the barrels lashed to the mast in the cabin—Silver, help Mr. Valentine with the knots, would you—we can be about the rest of this night's business."

Adolph's Bunker looked like a transplant from the Maginot Line. Whatever its original purpose, its builders had wanted it to last. They constructed it from heavy concrete, with narrow windows imitative of a castle's arrow slits. The bleached white of the concrete and the irregular rectangular slits gave it the countenance of a toothy skull. It lay on the lakeshore, set well away from the dead and empty buildings frowning behind.

"Why is it called Adolph's Bunker?" Valentine asked as they approached the squat, brick-shaped building. The ten-gallon cask grew heavier with each step.

"The guy who runs it is a dictator, for starts," Captain Doss said.

Silvertongue turned and looked at the men, each laboring with a cask on his shoulder. "There's a feeling about the place. It's a piece of sanity in an insane country. Or maybe a slightly different insanity within the insanity, take your pick. It's popular with the Quislings. When we found out we had to meet you this week, we contacted a Chicago big shot, so we could kill two birds with one stone this trip."

"As long as our bags get delivered," Valentine said, trying not to breathe too hard under his awkward burden.

"This trade will make getting your bags through a lot easier," Doss said.

The building seemed hollow and dead as a shucked oyster. Valentine surmised that the clientele liked to do their drinking in dark and quiet, when he realized that music, too loud to be the product of any instrument, was filtering up from somewhere beneath the building. He switched to hard ears and listened to the beat of ancient rock and roll and the gabble of voices echo up from a stairwell. Captain Doss turned to a set of narrow concrete steps that disappeared along the side of the building down into the earth. A knobless metal door opened out onto a small landing. Doss squatted down and said something into the hole. It swung open.

As he descended the stairs, Valentine plastered a drunken smile across his face, trying to live up to his role of eager sailor. The captain entered, nodding to someone. Valentine looked at Harper, and the two Wolves exchanged shrugs. Silvertongue turned to the men. "Don't worry, they're going to frisk you for weapons and smokes. Just put your hands on the wall and read the sign."

A Grog roughly the size of a Volkswagen Beetle barred their way. Over its yard-wide shoulder Valentine watched the captain and then her mate being frisked and sniffed by a dog-man right out of an H. G. Wells nightmare. When it finished with Silvertongue, the smelly roadblock at the door stepped aside and Valentine passed into the noise of the Bunker.

He mimicked Silvertongue's stance, placing his feet twice his shoulder width apart and putting his hands to either side of a sign, stenciled in paint onto another concrete wall just inside the door. To Valentine's left, a sumo-size man sat inside a wire cage, idly scratching his stubble with a Saturday night submachine gun.

As the dog-man gave him the once over, Valentine read the stenciled letters:

THE RULES
ADOLPH'S WORD IS LAW
NO SMOKING ANYTHING WE DIDN'T SELL YOU
NO DRINKING, UNLESS IT'S OURS
YOU'RE ONLY AS GOOD AS YOUR BARTER
YOU'RE ONLY AS BAD AS WE LET YOU BE
VISIT OUR GIFT SHOP
CONFUSED? SEE RULE 1

Valentine retrieved his keg and joined the women. He looked around the bar, trying to avoid staring like a corn-fed hick fresh off the back forty. Electric light and noise overwhelmed him. Prerecorded music played by machine was a rare treat to Valentine, and he gaped at the source. A box of neon and chrome against one cinderblock wall blared CD SELECTION & SOUND, as the reflective lettering on the glass proclaimed. A bar almost filled the wall opposite the jukebox, and a mismatched assortment of tables, booths, and benches stood about the sawdust-covered floor. The base of a flush toilet peeped from beneath a curtain in the corner farthest from the bar. A sour-smelling urinal next to it trickled water down the wall and into the soggy shavings beneath. An alcove, separated from the rest of the room by a layer of wire netting similar to the guard-cage at the door, advertised itself as CURRENCY EXCHANGE—GIFT SHOP—MANAGEMENT.

He was relieved to see the rest of the occupants of the Bunker were human, albeit a poor genetic cross section. Two bartenders stood only a hair shorter and slimmer than the Grog at the door, stuffed like a pair of pointy-headed sausages into red T-shirts with black lettering reading THE BUNKER. A desiccated weed of a man in a green visor sat behind a desk in the alcove-cage, smoking a cigarette from a long black holder. Gliding between the tables, laden tray miraculously balanced as she dodged and weaved, a nimble barhop waited on the customers. Clad only in a Bunker logoed baseball cap, bikini top, and a thong, she looked the happiest of anyone in the room. Valentine ran a quick estimate in his head and decided her hat contained more material, and covered a higher percentage of her body, than everything else she wore combined—high heels included. The patrons, dressed in ill-fitting black-and-tan fatigues or blue merchant marine overalls, drank, talked, and smoked in huddled groups.

The captain led her little party in single file to the Currency Exchange—Gift Shop—Management cage.

"Why, if it isn't the *White Lightning* herself come to pay me a visit," the gnome croaked, cigarette clenched between yellowed teeth. "And Teri Silvertongue! Ahhh, missy, what I wouldn't give to be young again! Any time you get sick of high seas and low wages, you just come see me."

"Thanks for the offer, Ade," Silvertongue said, exposing her rack of teeth in a forced smile. "But I catch cold kind of easy."

Captain Doss stepped up to the slot midway up the cage and placed a small leather pouch on the owner's desk. "Brought you some makings for your coffin nails, Ade. Do me a favor and die quick, would you?"

"I'll outlive you, Dossie. You got a couple new hands?" The owner ran his eyes quickly up and down Harper and Valentine, perhaps assessing their creditworthiness or potential as troublemakers.

"Just a little extra muscle for this run. Speaking of which, has the Duke arrived yet?"

"Take my advice, Cap. Slow down and enjoy life a little. But yeah, his party is in the card room. You buyin' for your crew, or are you gonna pull another Captain Bligh like last time?"

Doss shook her head. "After the deal, Ade, after the deal." She gestured to the other three, and they filed toward a door next to the long wooden bar. Valentine counted three casks and some thirty-odd bottles of assorted poison, all unlabeled. He watched one Quisling, crossed rifles of a captain on his epaulets, purchase a shot and a beer chaser by placing a pair of bullets on the bar. The Quisling tossed off the shot, face contorted as though he had poured an ounce of nitric acid down his throat.

Valentine tried not to think about the fact that he stood in a room with thirty people, each of whom could win a brass ring by turning him over alive to the Reapers.

Doss knocked on the door marked PRIVATE. It opened a crack, and half of an ebony face looked at her through a narrowed eye. The door shut again, but just for a moment.

The guard opened the door, and the crew entered a spacious, well-ventilated room. Three men and a woman sat around a felt-covered table. Cards and chips lay before three of the players; the fourth, a man, only watched. Valentine's eyes were drawn to him by his outlandish clothing if for no other reason.

The Duke of Rush wore a red uniform heavily trimmed with gold braid. Half high school marching band outfit and half toreador costume, it gaudily set off his pale skin and black hair. A brass ring, the first Valentine had ever seen, hung from a golden chain around his neck. Bored blue eyes stared up at the crew of the *White Lightning*.

The Duke's male henchmen wore the simple navy-blue battle dress of Chicago Quislings, and the card-playing woman an elegant blue cocktail dress glittering with real gemstones. No guns were evident, but the black man who opened the door toyed with a butterfly knife, opening and shutting it with quick flicks of the wrist.

"Captain, we expected you hours ago," the Duke said in an educated accent. "You know how I hate it when my own parties start late. What were you up to, running guns to insurgents?"

Doss let a simper mask her face. "No, trying to find something to wear. You always make such an entrance. I decided it would be better to let you enter first."

"You don't need to dress for this dive, Captain. The only reason I'm wearing my best is that the purported reason for this trip is social.

I spent the day calling on the Kur here and arranging beer trucks for Chicago. But our business is going to be much more lucrative. May we see the merchandise?"

The black man put aside his butterfly knife long enough to push a chair forward for Doss. She sat. "Put the bills on the table, and you'll see it," she said.

The Duke gestured to a lieutenant, who opened a leather satchel and drew out a sheaf of papers. Captain Doss pulled out a magnifying glass and went through the pages one at a time, examining the wax seals covering printed red-and-blue tape.

"Eight firearm permits, good," she counted to herself. "Five labor vouchers . . . twelve supply vouchers, sixteen . . . eighteen . . . twenty passports. Three dockyard releases . . . Hey, wait a second. The dock-yard releases aren't signed and sealed, my friend!"

The Duke smiled. "Sorry, Captain. An oversight on my part. I'll make it up to you next time, okay?"

"Afraid not. We're keeping a bag. You want it, get these filled out properly, and you can have it," she said firmly.

"Oh, very well. Have it your way, Captain. We'll take one bag less now, and I'll see if I can get the sign-offs for your next run. Though it breaks my heart that you don't trust me. Now bring out the snuff, and we'll see if your color is worth all this."

Valentine and Harper, on cue, placed their barrels in front of Silver-tongue, who popped the lids with a knife of her own. It was full of clumps of brown sugar. She upended the barrels one at a time and dumped the sugar on the floor. Glass test tubes filled with white powder soon emerged from the sugar. She gathered up two dozen tubes and placed them among the cards and chips on the table.

Captain Doss took two of the tubes and pocketed them.

The Duke wiped his mouth eagerly. "Test it, my dear."

The woman in the cocktail dress pulled a vial of clear liquid from her small handbag. She uncorked one of the tubes, licked a toothpick and coated it with the powder, then stirred it in the vial, which turned an azure blue.

"They don't call me the Duke of Rush for nothing," the Duke quipped. Valentine forced a laugh, but the captain and her mate ig-nored him.

"Can I take the bills now?" the captain asked.

"Of course, Captain. But I think this calls for a celebration. The drinks are on the Duke tonight, and your crew is invited, of course."

Doss rose from her chair. "Sorry, Duke. You know how I get when I'm away from my ship."

"I should be going, too. Maybe next time," Silvertongue said, bringing crestfallen expressions to the Quislings.

Harper patted Valentine on the shoulder. "Duty calls."

"It's not calling that loudly," Valentine demurred. "Captain, may I stay for a while?"

Captain Doss shot him a questioning glance. "Just be back by dawn. And I mean dawn, Tiny, because we sail with first light with or without you."

"Thank you, Captain. I'll be there."

"Finally one of your little flock shows some sense, Doss." The Duke laughed as the other sailors exited. "Ask anyone in Chicago, no one parties like the Duke. What's your name, son?"

"Dave, Mr. Duke. Dave Tiny."

The Duke clapped him on the back. "Glad to meet you, Tiny. I'm always making friends with traveling people, never know when they'll show up with something worth trading."

A knock sounded at the door.

"Duke, it's your other appointment," Butterfly Knife said.

"Oh, yeah. Tiny, you keep quiet; you might find this interesting. You'll see something you won't see sailing with Doss, that's for sure. I need to get a little dispute resolved."

The man with the butterfly knife opened the door, and two neatly dressed men and a woman entered.

"Thanks for the invite to the party, Duke," the tallest of the three said. Valentine noted he wore a wide brass ring similar to the Duke's, on his finger rather than on a chain.

"Good you could make it, Hoppy," the Duke said with a smile-snarl. "You seemed kind of preoccupied during my business call. Thought you might be tired of my company."

Valentine felt a shiver, but it had nothing to do with the nasty glint in the Duke's eye. There were Reapers outside. He thought of making up an excuse to leave, but decided to obey the Duke's order to remain silent.

"Glad you brought your assistant, but you didn't have to bring the muscle, Hoppy. This is just a friendly social gathering."

"Gail Allenby takes care of my professional life," Hoppy said. "Andersen here is responsible for the physical one. He uses a knife just as well in the kitchen as in an alley, by the way. I'll have you over for dinner tomorrow and prove it."

"I trust the cutlery will be well washed," the Duke responded. "Thanks for the offer, but I have to get back to Chicago. We need to get something straightened out, Hoppy. When it's done, you might not want to honor that invite anyway."

Someone screamed in the main part of the bar, and Valentine heard chairs tip over. Butterfly Knife opened the door again, and a Reaper entered the room, glancing around with wary yellow eyes. A muscular man in a sleeveless shirt followed. Then a female figure—at least, it appeared female to Valentine—slowly came in. She wore a black-and-gold woven robe and a heavy hood, her face hidden behind a shining mask. The mask was decorated only by a narrow eye slit; the rest was silvery, polished mirror-bright. She did not so much walk as float across the floor on legs unseen under the robe; Valentine heard no footsteps as she moved. A second Reaper remained at the open door, its back to the room, facing the rapidly emptying bar.

"Thank you for coming, Lord Yuse-Uth," the Duke said, his face calm and serious.

Valentine looked at Hoppy, who seemed to have lost three inches and twenty pounds since the Reaper and its Master Vampire had entered. He focused all his attention on the blanching man, hoping the Kurian would not probe his thoughts.

"Lord, what need brings You here?" Hoppy stammered.

"I asked Her to be present," the Duke said. "You've been cheating me, Hopps."

"Never!"

"Past couple months I've been noticing our beer running dry a lot. We opened up some kegs, found plastic balls inside. Not many, but enough to skim off ten percent or so. I had my men spill a keg after we made our purchase today: balls again."

Hoppy, who was apparently the factory manager, thought for a moment. "Maybe someone at the brewery is up to something. I had no knowledge of this, Duke. I'll make it up to you."

"I'm withholding payment. You've got ten percent less bodies coming north this shipment, and another ten percent less for the previous two." The Duke turned to Kurian. "With winter coming on, that's going to be fifty, sixty less auras for the Milwaukeee Families, my Lord."

The man in the sleeveless shirt spoke. "Lord Yuse-Uth says that the brewery will make it up next year. Her need is for the full allotment of auras."

"I don't like to say no to a Lord," the Duke said, "but my own Lords may have some say in the matter. Does She want a faction-war? That'd cost Her more. I'll split the difference, twenty-five fewer auras and you can make it up to me next year."

The mirrored face turned to look at the Duke. "Agreed. The ring is revoked." Valentine was not sure if the grating voice came from the mask or between his ears.

The Reaper grabbed Hoppy's arm and reached for the ring on the third finger of his right hand. It took the ring, pulling off the finger as well with a sickening snap of tearing cartilage. Hoppy screamed. His bodyguard stood frozen, staring in awe at the Reaper.

"He is no longer under Lord Yuse-Uth's protection," the Kurian's speaker said, watching Hoppy try to squeeze off the blood flowing from the pulpy mass where the digit had been. "Allenby, you are now the brewery manager. Lord Yuse-Uth trusts your deliveries will be complete. Perhaps in time you will wear this very ring."

The woman gulped, stepping away from her former supervisor. "Thank You, my Lord," she quavered. "Andersen, your contract with Mr. Hoppy is terminated. We will talk tomorrow about your future with the brewery. Think about it."

"Y-yes ma'am," Andersen said, his hands trembling.

"Dammit, I had nothing to do with shorting the shipments," Hoppy swore.

"Lord Yuse-Uth thanks you for bringing this matter to Her attention," the speaker said, turning to the Duke. "She looks forward to continued good relations and trade with Her Brethren in Chicago."

"I appreciate Her Lordship's time," the Duke said.

The Kurian, her speaker, and the Reapers departed, and Valentine found himself able to breathe again.

"Responsibility demands performance, Hoppy," the Duke said. "Personally, I think you were cheating me." The Duke looked at the man with the butterfly knife. "Make him shorter. Permanently."

Valentine watched, his face as passive as the Kurian's mask, as the man with the knife knocked Hoppy to the floor. He savagely hamstrung the screaming man, cutting the tendons at the back of his victim's knees.

"Guess they'll call you Crawly now," the Duke said. "Ms. Allenby, take that trash out with you as you leave. Dump him with the other garbage on the dock. I'll talk to you in the morning and see what kind of understanding we can come to."

None of the Duke's companions looked particularly upset as the brewery people dragged the bleeding, weeping wretch outside. The Duke's craggy face split into a smile.

"Party time. Go get a bottle of something decent, Palmers. And a couple cases of Miller, in sealed bottles. I'm going to get rolling on some of this white gold. Join me, Denise?"

She smiled and reached again into her purse for a mirror. "Tested high blue, Dukey? You bet your ring I am."

*   *   *

Twenty-odd beers, three bottles, and multiple toots later, the Quislings and Valentine were closing down the Bunker. Still behind the wire, Adolph counted out most of the contents of the Duke's purse. One bartender remained. A passed-out merchant marine was being dragged outside, and the waitress sat in the bodyguard's lap. Her bikini top rested on the closed eyes of Butterfly Knife, who had downed almost a whole bottle of the unlabeled house busthead. Behind the toilet curtain, Denise's shapely ankles with the blue dress around them twitched in time to the music. Valentine, who had drunk only a little booze while appearing to drink a lot, sat on the sawdust floor with his back to the jukebox, leaning up against the Duke.

Valentine had discovered a passion in the Duke for bad jokes and dirty songs. The ringholder had announced earlier in the evening, "This bar reminds me of what happens when you cross a German with an Irishman: you get someone too drunk to follow orders." After that the Wolf had dredged his brain for every mossy old chestnut he could remember from his early teens to barracks life. Finally, in keeping with his nautical disguise, he taught the Duke of Rush all the lines he could remember of "The Good Ship Venus."

"The cabin boy, the cabin boy, the dirty little nipper / Put ground glass inside his ass and circumcised the skipper," the Duke sang with him, giggling at the end of each verse.

Eva Stepanicz rested in the arms of the other Quisling, there more to keep an eye on Valentine per the captain's orders than to enjoy herself. A small tower of empties stood next to her, begun when she returned to the bar to find out what had transpired during the Kurian visit. She possessed an almost magical power over liquor, making her the choice for this particular assignment. She pushed the man's face away from her, directing his beer-fumed breath toward the floor.

The bartender returned from dumping the merchant marine, escorting First Mate Silvertongue.

"Okay, Tiny, on your feet. Day's breaking, and the captain wants you and Stepanicz back."

Stepanicz climbed to her feet with a relieved sigh.

Valentine looked up at the first mate from beneath his red Bunker T-shirt, worn pharaoh-style on his head. "C'mon, Silver. No reason she can't wait another hour or two. Shove off," he slurred, more from fatigue than alcohol.

"Stepanicz, let's get him up," Silvertongue ordered. The two women each took an arm and pulled Valentine to his feet. Valentine winked at Silvertongue.

"I said *shove off!*" he shouted, startling the Quislings from their slumber. Valentine grabbed a head of hair in each hand and seemingly knocked their heads together. He arranged it so his hands absorbed most of the impact.

And so began a semidrunken three-way brawl that brought even the passed-out Denise from her toilet-seat nap. The men roared approval every time Valentine knocked one of the women on her ass, and the two females ringside cheered whenever Stepanicz or Silvertongue landed a punch. The bare-breasted barhop had placed her pinkies in her mouth and produced a piercing whistle when Stepanicz brought the fight to a close with a powerful, accurate, and all-too-realistic kick in the proper place. Valentine folded like the Quisling's butterfly knife and dropped to the ground.

The Duke of Rush staggered to his feet, absently brushing sawdust from his garish uniform. He knelt next to Valentine and helped his groin-gripping drinking buddy sit up.

"Better get back to your ship, Tiny. Guess they weren't tiny enough, heh?"

Valentine managed a pained smile.

"Look, next time you port in Chicago, look me up. I'm pretty much in charge of R and R, that's rest and relaxation, you know, for those wise enough to join up with the Kurians. My place is above a group of bars called the Clubs Flush. On Rush Street, it's easy to find 'cause it's the part of the city lit up at night, unless you count the Zoo. I cater to the crème de la crème of Chicago society, you understand. Following orders from these bitches every day, I bet you and that other guy are about dying to get laid. I'll get you some on the house, okay?"

"Thanks, Duke," Valentine said, adjusting his trousers.

"You're my kind of people, Davy. And," he added, more softly in Valentine's ear, "if you can tie up to the big pier with another load of the white stuff as good as this, I'll see to it that even if you dock a swabbie, you'll sail out a captain, you know what I mean? Just stop in and see me first, at the Clubs Flush, like I said. I'll treat you right."

Valentine massaged his aching groin. "Thanks for the tip, sir."

With Silvertongue on one side and Stepanicz on the other, Valentine marched back to the ship, exhausted.

"What was all that about, Valentine?" Silvertongue asked as they climbed back on board. "Why were you toadying up to that ring-carrying clown?"

"He's a powerful man where he comes from. Sometimes just knowing the name of someone with that kind of influence can come in handy."

*　　*　　*

Later that morning, the *White Lightning* landed Harper and Valentine on a deserted stretch of beach north of where they first rendezvoused.

"Sorry for the kick," Stepanicz said, shaking Valentine's hand. "No hard feelings?"

"No, I don't think it'll be feeling hard for a while," Valentine answered. "But thanks for asking."

The captain presented them each with a fifth of rum brought all the way from Jamaica. "And the Lakes Flotilla is always willing to help you out," she said, handing them each a card with her name written on it in elegant calligraphy. "You can always tell a Flotilla ship because the word *white* is in the name somehow. Or a foreign version of white: *blanc, weiss*, something like that. Just give them this card, and tell them I owe you a favor."

"Thanks, Captain Doss," Harper said.

"Your servant, ma'am," Valentine added.

Each Wolf shouldered a bag of dispatches addressed to Southern Command. As they hopped out of the dinghy, again wetting their feet in the waters of Lake Michigan, the weight of their rifles brought home the seriousness of the journey back.

"Should we tell Gonzo about all this?" Harper asked.

"Why?" Valentine said, responding with a twinkle in his eye. "He just missed a boring evening with some sailors. And what he doesn't know won't piss him off. But I'll make it up to him. He can have my Bunker souvenir T-shirt."

Ten

Central Wisconsin, September of the forty-third year of the Kurian Order: North of the road and rail arc connecting Milwaukee with the Twin Cities, Wisconsin under the Kurians has lain fallow. Dense forests of pine and oak shelter deer, moose, and feral pigs. Four-legged wolves prey on both, and occasionally have to give up their kills to prowling bears and wolverines. A few logging camps dot the area around Oshkosh and Green Bay, taking oak and cedar for use in the south. Menominee trappers and hunters also traverse the woods and lakes, traveling down the Wisconsin River to the Dells Country to trade pelts.

The Kurian Order begins at the traveled belt linking Milwaukee, Madison, Eau Claire, and St. Paul, Minnesota. Rich corn and dairy farms still fill the southern half of the state. Three Kurian Lords, known as the Madison Triumvirate, control the farms, mines, and lines of communication from the outskirts of Milwaukee to LaCrosse. Within the gloom of their dominant hilltop dome in the old Wisconsin State Capitol building, they command Reapers from Fond du Lac to Platteville, Eau Claire to Beloit.

The humans under the teeth of the Kurians endure the New Order, living in the gray area between doing the minimum required for survival and full Quislinghood. Their family farms are self-controlled, very different from the brutal plantations of the south or the mechanized collectives of Nebraska, Kansas, and Oklahoma. But recently, a new shadow has fallen over the region. Rumors spread by milk-truck drivers and road crews tell of a new Kurian Lord turning the picturesque village of New Glarus into a hilltop fortress. To the fearful smallholders and townspeople of the area, this means thirteen more thirsty Reapers taking their human toll by night.

They camped on some hills above the Wisconsin River near Spring Green. The Wolves could see miles of river valley in either direction. A few electrified farms burned porch lights, but the prominence Valentine guessed to be Tower Hill seemed shunned by the residents, for no active farm lay at its feet, or indeed within miles.

They camped a little below the hill, in the ruins of what was apparently an outdoor stage in the middle of nowhere. Valentine had explored the warped and overgrown little wooden theater nestled in a kettle in the hillside. It reminded him of a fancy version of the simple outdoor platform at one end of the public tent in the Boundary Waters, where Bobby Royce had received a prize shotgun what felt like several lifetimes ago.

He paced the footboards in thought. Were the people in the Freeholds the ones who were crazy? All the loss, all the suffering caused by the never-ending battles. A life, of sorts, was possible under the Kurians. Perhaps they should weather the storm, turn it to their advantage by bargaining for some measure of independence, rather than fighting for it. He marveled at the adaptability of his race: the Lakes Flotilla, for example. They worked at the edges of the Kurian Order, sowing seeds of destruction while turning a profit. Then there was Steiner and his enclave, trying to build something new rather than keep alive the old. Or the determination of the outnumbered and outgunned Southern Command, standing in their hilly fastness and daring the Kurians to try to enter even as they carried the fight to the Lost Lands. Even the little clusters of hidden civilizations like the Boundary Waters contributed to the fight by simply surviving.

A tingle interrupted his ruminations upon the stage. With the frozen terror of a rabbit under an eagle's shadow, he sensed a Reaper. He stepped off the stage and padded downhill to the little cluster of cabins below. The Reaper seemed to be moving up Tower Hill, bringing silence to the nighted woods. Even the crickets ceased their chirping.

Valentine entered the Wolves' overnight home. It was a two-room house with small windows that made the absence of glass less of an inconvenience. The Wolves had stabled the horses in the larger room. He placed the fingers of one hand to his lips while making the pinkie-and-forefinger hand signal to his comrades that meant Reaper. Gonzalez and Harper unsheathed their rifles and checked their parangs.

All three concentrated on lowering lifesign, sitting back to back in a little cross-legged circle. The horses would give off no more lifesign than a group of deer; there was enough wildlife in the woods to confuse it even if it passed close, as long as they were able to mask their minds properly. As he quieted his mind and centered his breathing, Valentine found he could feel the Reaper atop the hill to the west. Minutes passed, then an hour, and the Reaper moved off to the west as clammy sweat trickled down Valentine's back.

"That was a little too close," Valentine said to his fellow Wolves. "Anyone want to move camp, just in case it circles around the hill?"

"Fine idea," Harper agreed. "I could walk all night anyway after that."

They decided to move south, treating the Reaper as a tornado that you can best dodge by moving at right angles to its path. As Harper readied the horses and Gonzalez hid evidence of their camp, Valentine cautiously walked up Tower Hill, rifle at the ready. He read the trail left by heavy bootprints. The Reaper had paused for an hour on the overlook. Valentine wondered why. After a word to Harper, he found an unobstructed knoll above the stage and scanned what parts of the horizon he could.

Two or three miles to the southeast, flame lit the clouded night. A pair of buildings seemed to be ablaze behind a screen of trees; he could make out a small grain silo lit by the red-yellow glow. Perhaps the Hood had a better view from the western crown of Tower Hill, but it was unlike a Reaper to just stand and watch a fire for the drama of it. And the blaze seemed unnaturally bright. Valentine wished the winds were favorable enough for him to smell the smoke.

He rejoined Gonzalez and Harper.

"There's a good-size fire," Valentine explained. "I think a barn or a house is going up. You want to check it out? It's on this side of the river, so we can get to it easy."

"Do we want to be there?" Harper asked. "If it's someone's house, neighbors will be coming from all over. It would be just like a Hood to pick someone off in the confusion."

"I thought we were headed south," Gonzalez said.

"Yes, eventually. But I think this Reaper watched what was going on there for a while, for whatever reason. It's not like them to just look at something for the sake of the view. I think it's worth checking out."

Harper shrugged. "It's your party. I don't mind watching a building burn. But I don't like the idea of making a decision 'cause of a prediction about a Reaper's behavior. Sounds like a good way to end up drained."

"It'll be okay, as long as the lieutenant's radar is working," Gonzalez suggested.

"Hope so," Harper said. "Let's get there before the patrols wake up."

*   *   *

They moved through the night, leading their horses. Gonzalez walked out ahead, picking the path, followed by Valentine and Harper, each taking two horses.

As they drew close to the fire, Valentine decided the burning buildings were just another abandoned farm in a region where two out of three homesteads were empty. New forests stood in fields that had once belonged to cows.

The Wolves tied up the horses near a shallow seasonal streambed, and the horses drank from runoff puddles scattered among the rocks. They could see the flames flickering through the thin-skinned trunks of scrub beech and young oaks. They crept up to within fifty feet of the dying fire. What was left of four buildings, one obviously a barn, had already collapsed into burning debris. Without the daily rains of the past week, the conflagration would have turned into a forest fire.

Harper spat cotton. "Okay, Lieutenant, here's your fire. What now?"

"No family, no neighbors," Valentine observed. "Must have been empty. These fields sure don't look used. I haven't seen anything but a few old fence posts around with the wire stripped off. So why's it burning?"

"Maybe a patrol came through, livened up a quiet night with a little arson," Harper mused. "That east-west road we crossed yesterday by the river's got to be up there somewhere."

"Could be," Valentine agreed. "If so, they used a lot of starter. You can smell it from here, kind of like gasoline."

Gonzalez and Harper sniffed. "Reminds me a little of napalm," Harper said. "The Grogs used it at Cedar Creek. They had an old fire truck filled with it. Doused some of the buildings our guys were holed up in and then lit it."

"I'd like to take another look around in daylight," Valentine said. "We can wait a few more hours before moving on. Let's get the horses and find a safe spot to sleep."

Valentine could tell from Harper's expression that he thought getting some rest was the first sensible plan out of his superior's mouth all evening.

Daylight inspection of the ruins told the end of the story but not the beginning. While Gonzalez squatted in cover along the road, ready to run like a jackrabbit back to the fire scene at the first sign of a patrol, only a livestock-laden tractor-trailer passed along the old highway, crawling east at a safe fifteen miles an hour along the potholed road.

"This makes no sense," Valentine said to a disinterested Harper.

"We've got four burning buildings, or three buildings and a shed, I guess. But what are those other three burned spots?"

Valentine indicated the blackened brush, circles of fire twelve to thirty feet in diameter, scattered around the buildings on what had once been lawn and garden.

"Weird thing number two. Look how the house is wrecked. The frame's been scattered all to hell, but only westward. Like a bunch of dynamite was set off on the east side of it."

Harper shrugged. "Maybe the Quislings were training with demolitions or something."

"Then where's the crater? And the foundation is in good shape; those cinder blocks would be gone if someone put a charge there. And look at those two saplings. They're both broken off three feet up, but the tops are lying *toward* the house. An explosion wouldn't do that. Weird thing number three. That hole dug in the ground by the barn."

The men walked over to the ruins of the old barn, next to the blackened column of the still-standing silo. A triangular furrow, three feet long and almost two feet deep, was gouged into the ground; a dug-up divot of earth and grass lay nine feet away, in the direction of the barn. "What did this?" asked Valentine. "The patrols brought out a backhoe? This was dug out in one clean scoop."

"You got me, Sherlock," Harper said with a shrug.

"And finally, there's no tracks. Unless that's why they burned out those patches of the scrub—to cover their tracks, or the marks of the weapons that did this."

Valentine kneeled and sniffed at the charred wood. It still retained a faint petroleum or medicinal smell, like camphor.

"Somebody's coming," Harper called, moving swiftly behind the silo, rifle already at his shoulder. Valentine threw himself to the ground, hearing footsteps from the forest. The person was not making any effort to keep quiet, whoever it was.

A middle-aged man in faded blue pants and a striped mattress-ticking shirt emerged from the forest. He surveyed the wreckage, not looking particularly surprised. He removed his baseball cap and wiped his face and neck with a yellow handkerchief. What was left of his hair, balding front and back, was a uniform gray.

"Whoever you are," the man called, "you're sure up early. Come out and show yourselves. I ain't armed."

Valentine hand-signaled Harper to stay concealed. Gonzalez had vanished, perhaps into the overgrown drainage ditch next to the road. He stood up, half fearing a sniper's bullet.

"Good morning to you, too," Valentine responded. "I'm just passing through."

"You mean 'we're passing through,' stranger," the unknown rustic chided. "I saw your buddy behind the silo. Since you're not from around here, I'll ask your name, son."

"David, sir. I'm down from Minnesota. Visiting friends, you might say."

The man smiled. "If that's the case, I'd keep that repeating rifle hid. I don't know how it is in Minnesota, but around here the vampires'll kill you for carrying a gun. Among other things."

"Thanks for the tip. We're trying to pass through without attracting attention. Do you live around here, sir?"

"All my life. My name's Gustafsen. I'm a widower now, and my kids are gone. I farm a little place up the road. Saw the sky lit up and figured it was the old Bauer farm. Don't have much business of my own to mind, so you might say I mind other people's, just to have something to do."

That could be good or bad for us, Valentine thought. "Did anyone live here?"

"No, not since they took over. The Bauers all died of the Raving Madness. No one's wanted to live here since: it's five miles from nowhere."

"I wonder what started the fire? There's been a lot of rain, but no lightning."

Gustafsen chuckled. "I wonder myself. I hear from some of the teamsters, there's been a few mysterious fires this summer. Started right around the time the new Big Boss showed up in Glarus. And things have gone from bad to worse for a lot of folks around here since then. There's been disappearances in almost every town, and I'm sure you know what that means."

"I'm surprised you ask questions, Mr. Gustafsen. Most places that's frowned upon."

"My curiosity is all I've got left, David." Gustafsen thrust his hands in his pockets, speaking to Valentine while standing side by side with him as was the custom in that part of the country. They looked over the wrecked barn and house. "I've lived a full life, considering the circumstances. After my Annie got took, I quit looking for anything else from this life, and I'm settin' my heart on the next."

Valentine liked the man on instinct. He thought for a moment about asking the man to come south with them. They had a spare horse, after all, and the Free Territory could always use another farmer or rancher.

Gustafsen said, "I didn't get much formal education. *They* don't like schools. But I'm smart enough to know that men in deerskins carrying guns and staying out of sight of the roads means trouble for them. So if you boys want to come to my place, I'll share what I got with you. Maybe you need to spend a couple nights in a bed. I've got some spares. I'd appreciate the company."

"We appreciate the offer, Mr. Gustafsen. Really. But we've got to move on east," Valentine lied, just in case. "If you could spare a bag of oats for the horses, we'd be in your debt, sir. I'd really like information about these fires, though. You seem to have your ear to the ground."

"It beats me as much as it does you, son. One old man saw some kind of airship over a fire. I don't know exactly where or when; it's a fourth-hand story. Like the old blimps you see in pictures. He said it moved around with sails. And I got a theory about where it's coming from: somewhere around Blue Mounds. They say it's death to go within five miles of there now. Whatever's happening, they got a lot of troops. The Commissary Patrols are culling stock all over this part of the state, taking good dairy stock and hogs, mostly. It's going to be a hard winter."

"Sounds like. You say this new Big Boss is in Glarus?"

"It's New Glarus on a map," Gustafsen corrected.

"We'd better avoid it," Valentine said, lying again. He had to account for the chance that Gustafsen might be going for a brass ring.

"Smart of you, son."

Two hours later, Valentine rode up to the other two Wolves, two bags of oats for the horses across the Morgan's broad back.

"It went well there?" Gonzalez asked.

"Sure. He gave me the feed, and I looked around his place. He seems a nice enough man. I didn't want him to get a look at either of you, just in case."

"Are we going to move on now?" Harper asked.

"Sort of. It seems like the Reapers have something big going on around Blue Mounds. It's about ten miles southeast of here. Good hilly country, plenty of cover. I want to ride over there and see if we can't get a look at what they're up to."

Harper nodded. "Not too much of a detour, then. Gotta ask you straight, though, Lieutenant, begging your pardon. Do you have something against getting back to the Ozarks? Got a woman in the family way, and you want to stay out of the Territory for a while or something? We could be halfway to the Mississippi by now. We're couriers, not Cats."

"If I knew a Cat in the area, I'd ask her to do it for us. But something that flies and drops firebombs is something Command will want to know about. Especially since whatever this is doesn't make noise.

You've seen the little prop jobs the Kurians use on us now and then. They're loud. We'd have heard it. And they can fly at night. Never heard of a plane or a helicopter doing that nowadays."

"Maybe they're trying to train Harpies to fly in teams or carry bombs together," Gonzalez thought out loud.

"Could be. Could be just about anything, Gonzo. The Kurians like dreaming up nasty surprises. But Southern Command is going to want facts. We're all this way anyway. When we get back, we might as well know what we're talking about."

"So what's next on the Lieutenant Valentine tour of southwestern Wisconsin?" Harper chuckled.

Valentine consulted his map and compass. "A short ride thataway. How's your nose this morning, Gonzalez?"

"Wishing it was smelling the masala in one of Patel's pepperpots right about now, sir. But it's working well enough."

"I hope so. We're going to need it."

You have to hand it to the Kurians, Valentine thought at midday, when they struck the line of fence posts. *They know how to send a message with easy-to-understand symbols.*

The Wolves sat their horses before the line of rust-colored pig iron posts. Atop each post, at ten-yard distances, a bleached human skull grinned at them. The warning line extended into the woods to either side of them, each skull facing outward in wordless warning to trespassers.

"Jesuchristo," Gonzalez whispered.

Grimly, Valentine performed some mental arithmetic. Gustafsen had said it was death to come within five miles of Blue Mounds. Thirty-odd miles of perimeter. That worked out to something like five thousand skulls. The one immediately in front of them was a child's.

Valentine dismounted, drawing his rifle from its leather sheath. "I'm going to have a look around. Sergeant Harper, I want you to stay with the animals. If you hear any shooting, try to break a record going west. Gonzalez, this is a one-man job, but I'd like to have your ears and nose along, so I'll leave it up to you."

Gonzalez removed his broad-brimmed hat and scratched the back of his neck. "Lieutenant, after I was invoked, I learned the Way from an old Wolf named Washington. Washington used to tell me, 'Victor, only idiots and heroes volunteer, and you're no hero.' But if I stay behind, it'll mean these skulls worked. I don't like to see anything the Reapers do work." He slid off his horse and began filling his pockets with .30-06 rifle shells from a box in his saddlebag.

"Lieutenant," Harper said, "watch your step now. I can see lot of tracks just behind this picket line of theirs. I'm going to take the horses down to that ravine we crossed and wait for you. Be careful; I'm going to make cold coffee for three, and I don't want any wasted."

"Thanks, Harper. No heroics, now. You hear anything, you just leave. I haven't looked at what's in those mail bags, but it's probably more important than we are."

Valentine and Gonzalez moved slowly through the heaviest woods they could find, zigzagging toward three hilltops they could occasionally glimpse through the trees. They moved in a twenty-yard game of leapfrog: first one would advance through the woods to cover; he would squat, and the other would move up past the first. They used their noses, and when Gonzalez picked up the scent of cattle, Valentine had them alter course to catch up.

It was a warm, partly cloudy day. Occasional peeks at the sun through the cumulus lightened their mood; it would inhibit any Reapers around. The cotton-fluff clouds were beginning to cluster and darken at their flat bases; more rain might be on the way. They found the cows, a herd of black-and-white Holsteins escaping the heat under a stand of trees bordering an open meadow.

"That's what we want," Valentine said. "I don't see a herdsman. Maybe they round them up at night."

"That's what we want?" Gonzalez whispered back. "What, you want cream for your coffee?"

"No. Let's get to the herd. Keep down in the brush."

They reached the cows, who gazed at the Wolves indifferently. The tail-swishing mass stood and lay in the shade, jaws working sideways in a steady cud-chewing rhythm. About a thousand flies per cow buzzed aimlessly back and forth.

"We need a little camouflage. The smelly kind," Valentine said, stepping into a fresh, fly-covered pile of manure. His moccasin almost disappeared into the brown mass. Gonzalez followed suit.

"Is this because of the tracks back at the fence?" Gonzalez asked.

"Yes. I saw dog prints by the hoofprints. Just in case we get tracked. The scent of the cows might confuse the dogs. Step in a few different piles, will you? Ah-ha," Valentine said, moving toward one of the standing milk factories.

The cow had raised its tail, sending forth a jet of semi-liquid feces. Valentine quickly wiped his foot in the body-temperature pool, then put each knee into it. "Keep an ear open, Gonzalez. It'd be great if one of them would take a leak for us."

Valentine's sharp ears picked up his scout muttering, "I don't even want to know, man, I don't even want to know."

Leaving the cows behind, but taking the smell with them, the Wolves began to move uphill, again keeping to the heaviest woods.

"So much for my nose, Val. I've heard of wolves in sheep's clothing, but this is above and beyond."

"Concentrate on your ears then," Valentine suggested.

They cut a trail at the base of the hills. Tire tracks informed him that vehicles passed through this area, circling the hills. Farther up the slope, they could see a metal platform projecting out of the trees, still well below the crown of the hill. It looked like a guard tower, but was missing walls and a roof.

"Maybe it's still under construction," Gonzalez theorized.

They moved up the gentle, tree-dotted meadow sideways, approaching the tower from a higher elevation. After completing the half-circle, listening all the way for telltale movement, they gained the tower base.

Concrete anchored the four metal struts supporting the thirty-foot platform. It was built out of heavy steel I-beams and was well riveted and braced. There was no ladder going up. It was new enough that scars in the earth from its construction were overgrown but not yet eroded away.

"What the hell kind of a lookout post is this?" Valentine wondered. "That's a lot of steel to hold up nothing."

Gonzalez knelt in the dirt beneath the structure. "Look here, sir. These tracks: small, narrow boots with heavy heels. Almost small enough for a woman."

"A Reaper?"

"That's my guess," Gonzalez said.

Valentine's spine bled electric tingles. *A Reaper stands on that platform?* he thought. *Watching what? Standing guard? What the hell is so valuable that the Kurians are using Reapers as sentries?*

He looked at the cross-braces. He might be able to climb it, if his fingers held out. Of course, a Hood would have no problem going up, but it presented quite a challenge to a human.

"I'm going to climb it. See if I can't get a look at the top. Maybe there's some sign of what it's used for up there."

"Sir," Gonzalez said. "I wouldn't advise that. Listen."

Valentine hardened his ears and heard thunderous hoof-beats echoing from somewhere over the hill. A lot of hoof-beats. Valentine suspected that these riders would not be scared off by the symbols carved into the butt of his rifle.

He looked at Gonzalez, meeting his scout's alarmed eyes, and nodded.

They ran.

Trained Wolves running though heavy wood, even downhill, have to be seen to be believed. They kept up a punishing pace through the thickest forest, a pace no horse and rider could match through this ground. They cleared fallen logs with the grace of springing deer. Their footfalls, like their breathing, sounded inhumanly light. The Wolves hunched their bodies atavistically forward, clearing low branches by fractions of an inch. The sound of the distant riders faded behind them, absorbed by hill and wood.

They reached the cow meadow, over a mile from the metal platform, in less than four minutes. Valentine altered the downhill course, and regained the wood. Still at a flat-out run, they were halfway to the line of skulls when Gonzalez was shot.

The bullet struck him in the left elbow as he brought his arm up while running. He spun, staggered, and continued running, gripping his shattered joint close to his body.

The sniper panicked at the sight of Gonzalez continuing straight for his hiding spot. He rose, a monstrous swamp-troll apparition trailing green threads like a living weeping willow. The sniper raised his rifle again with Gonzalez a scarce ten yards away.

The scout threw himself down at the shot. Valentine, a few yards behind Gonzalez, was breathing too hard to trust himself to shoot accurately. He shifted his grip to the barrel of the rifle and wound up as he dashed forward.

The long camouflage strips hanging from the Quisling's sleeves caught in his rifle's action. As he struggled with it, Valentine swung his gun baseball-bat style, using the momentum of his charge to add further force to the impact. He struck the sniper full in the stomach, emptying the man's lungs with the harsh cough of a cramping diaphragm. Valentine dropped his gun and drew his parang from its sheath on his belt. As the gasping Quisling writhed at his feet, Valentine stepped on the man's back and brought the blade down on the vulnerable back of his neck once, twice, three times. The blows felt good, sickeningly good: a release of fear and anger. The body, its head severed, twitched as the man's nervous system still reacted to the blow to the midriff.

Valentine moved to Gonzalez, who now sat up, shaking and swearing in Spanish.

"Vamos!" Gonzalez said through clenched teeth. "Get to the horses. I'll catch up."

"I need a breather, bud," Valentine said, and meant it. He listened to the distant horses. They were far off, maybe far enough.

"No, sir . . . I'll catch up."

"Let's get a tourniquet around your arm. I don't want you leaving a blood trail. I'm glad your legs are still working," he said, tearing a rag off the sniper's gillie suit, which served that purpose admirably. His hands flew into action with quick, precise movements, binding the wound. "Now hold this," he said, twisting a stick around the knot. "Does that arm feel as bad as it looks?"

"Worse. I think the bone's gone."

"Just hold it for now. We'll get you a sling once we get to the horses," Valentine said.

"Valentine, this is *loco. Loco,* sir. I can't get far like this. Maybe I can find an old basement or something, hole up for a few days."

"No more arguing, hero. Let's go. The posse is on its way. I'll take your rifle."

They walked, then jogged toward the fence line. *Each step must be agony for him,* Valentine thought. They made it past the skulls and to the ravine.

Two horses waited, reins tied to a fallen branch. Valentine's Morgan had a note tucked in the saddle. Valentine uncurled it and read the soft pencil letters: "Followed orders—good luck—God bless—R.H."

Same to you, Sarge, Valentine thought. He felt lonely and helpless. But it would not do to let Gonzalez see that.

"Harper's moving west. Let's go southwest. If they have to follow two sets of tracks, maybe it'll confuse them. I'm sorry, Gonzo, but we've got to ride hard. I'll help you into the saddle."

He tightened the girths on both horses and lifted Gonzalez into his seat.

"I'll take the reins, Gonzo, you just sit and enjoy the ride."

"Enjoy. Sure," he said with a hint of a smile, or perhaps an out-of-control grimace.

They rode up and out of the ravine, Gonzalez pale with pain.

Of all the strange *dei ex machinae,* Valentine least expected to be rescued by a livestock truck.

Valentine, after an initial mile-eating canter across the hills, slowed out of concern for his scout. Gonzalez could not last much longer at this rate. They spotted an ill-used road, in bad shape even for this far out in the country, and moved parallel, keeping it in sight.

The pair crested a hill, resting to take a good look ahead before proceeding farther. Gonzalez sat in his saddle like a limp scarecrow tied to the stirrups.

Valentine saw a little cluster of farms along a road running perpendicular to their path. Miles off to the west, a series of high bare downs marched southward. To his right, a small creek twisted and turned, moving south to where it crossed the road under a picturesque covered bridge. The bridge appeared to be in good repair, indicating the road might be in frequent use.

"Okay, Gonzo," Valentine said, turning his horse. "Not much farther now. We're going to walk the horses for a while in that stream. I want to pick us up an engine."

"Are we going to give up the horses?" Gonzalez croaked.

"Yes. You can't go on like this. By the way, do you know how to drive?"

"Maybe. I've worked a steering wheel a couple of times. You would have to shift, though. Can't you drive?"

Valentine shrugged. "I used to play in old wrecked cars, but I don't know what the pedals do."

"Sir, let's keep to the stream for a while. Get somewhere quiet and find an old house. Lay up for a while."

"They might know by now what direction we went. We have to assume they want us, even if we didn't see anything. Remember, we killed one of theirs. They won't brush that off. According to that old Gustafsen, they've got some manpower concentrated there, so they have the men to do a thorough search. We need to move faster than they can get organized, which won't be easy since they probably have radios. That means an engine. From the tracks Harper made, and ours, they're going to be looking for us west. If we turn east, we might get ahead of whatever containment they'll use."

Valentine hated the idea of giving up the sturdy Morgan. His horse had proved a sublime blend of speed and stamina. But the odds against them were also increasing, making a risk the only course of action giving them a chance to escape.

Gonzalez nodded tiredly, unable to argue. His scout believed in cautiousness in any maneuvers against the Reapers, discretion being the better part of survival. Gonzalez feared everything; otherwise he would not have lived so long.

The pair rode downhill. At the stream, its rock-strewn bed barely a foot deep in most places, Valentine dismounted and took both pairs of reins, leading the horses. He hoped none of the local farm children were whiling away the afternoon fishing.

They reached the covered bridge. After scouting the shaded tunnel to make sure it was unoccupied, Valentine tied the horses to a piece of driftwood and helped Gonzalez out of his saddle. The scout sank into the cool shade, asleep or unconscious within seconds of Valentine laying him down, head pillowed by his bedroll.

Valentine scrambled up the brush-covered riverbank. He found a position near one end of the covered bridge where he could see down the road a mile in either direction. The asphalt was patched into almost a checkerboard pattern, as if tar-footed giants had been playing hopscotch along the road. The bridge was a strange bastard construction, obviously a well-made iron-and-concrete span dating to before the coming of the Kurians but now covered with a wooden roof. The added-on planks were layered with peeling red paint, and the warped wood seemed to writhe and bend as if wishing to escape from the bridge frame.

The drone of insects and the muted trickling of the stream were soothing, and Valentine fought the urge to sleep. He counted potholes in the road, clouds, and bell-shaped white wildflowers to pass the time.

A truck appeared out of the east. It was a tractor-trailer, pulling a livestock rig. It plodded along at a gentle rate so as not to bounce its aged suspension too much over the uneven road. As it grew closer, Valentine saw that the door on the cab was either missing or removed, and the windshield on the passenger side was spider-webbed with cracks.

Valentine readied his rifle and ran to the edge of the covered bridge, keeping out of sight of the truck. He heard the truck slow as it approached the bridge, and the engine noise increased as it entered the echo chamber under the roof. Valentine sidestepped out and into the path of the creeping truck, rifle at his shoulder, and aimed at the driver.

Brakes squealed in worn-down protest, and the truck came to a stop. A head popped out of the doorless side, heavy sideburns flaring out from a ruddy face.

"Hey there, fella, don't shoot," the man called, as if people pointing rifles at him were an everyday irritation.

"Step out of there, and I won't. I don't want to hurt you; I just need the truck."

A pair of empty hands showed themselves. "Mister, you've got it backwards. We've been looking for you."

"What 'we' would that be?" Valentine asked, keeping the foresight in line with the bridge of the man's nose.

"Don't have time to go into it, mister. I know one of you's named David. You're three of those Werewolf fellows from down south, right? You went to take a look at Blue Mounds. The vampires' goons spotted you, and now there's a big net out trying to snare you. I heard it on the radio, except the David part. That came across over the Lodge's code through the telephone wires. I've been crawling up and down this road for the last hour looking for your tracks."

"Who are you?" Valentine asked, lowering his gun slightly.

"Ray Woods is my name. Wisconsin Lodge Eighteen. That guy you talked to earlier today, Owen Gustafsen, he's the Lodge leader here west of Madison. You might say we're like an underground railroad. We get orphaned kids and stuff out of the state."

Valentine wanted to believe him, badly. But Eveready had warned them time and again to look for traps. "Sorry, Ray, but I can't trust you. If you are who you say you are, you'll know why. We're going to take your truck, load our horses in it, and take off. If you are who you say you are, you won't tell anybody for a couple of hours. I could even knock you out so you have a convincing bump, if you want."

Woods plucked at his sideburns, twiddling the curly brown hair. "Maybe you can't trust me. But I'm going to have to ask you to take care of a friend of mine."

The truck driver jumped out of his cab and went to a little door mounted in the side of his truck. He opened it and extracted a toolbox. He then pulled out a metal panel and extracted an eight-year-old boy from the narrow slit like a magician pulling a rabbit from a hat. The boy clung to the driver's leg, watching Valentine with hollow eyes.

"This is Kurt," Woods explained. "He's out of Beloit. His father was taken by a Reaper a week ago, and his mother just up and disappeared. We're trying to get him over the Mississippi to a little town called La Crescent. Maybe you can trust him."

Valentine looked into the eyes of the little boy, and they were filled with the hurt confusion of a child whose world has vanished in an afternoon. Valentine wondered if he had looked that way to Father Max some ten-odd years ago. Woods stroked the boy's hair.

With Gonzalez hurt, Woods was their best chance of making it out of the Kurian Zone. More like their only chance.

"Okay, Mr. Woods. I hope you know what you're doing. Maybe you can talk your way out of getting caught bringing a child from point A to B. But we're armed and wanted. If you get caught with us, the least they'll do is kill you. If you have a family, you'd better think hard about them," Valentine said, looking at the driver's wedding ring.

"Ain't got no family no more, mister," Woods said. "I don't want to be parked out here arguing all day, so what's it going to be?"

"What do you want us to do?"

Ten minutes later, the semi was moving again. Valentine sat in a second secret compartment in the truck's cabin. Concealing himself would be a matter of lying down and closing a steel panel. Gonzalez lay next to the little boy somewhere beneath him behind the false-backed tool locker.

"Of course, if they make a thorough search, we're all dead," Woods said, speaking up over the clattering engine so Valentine could hear his voice. "But I'm on the regular livestock run into Blue Mounds now. Before that, I never caused a day's trouble—at least a day's trouble that they knew about—in sixteen years, except when the old diesel gives me problems, of course."

The horses rode in the trailer, hidden in plain sight next to two other crowbait nags. Valentine hoped the horses looked worn out enough to pass inspection as candidates for the slaughterhouse. Their saddles and bridles rested inside bags of feed. A few cows and pigs also rode in the trailer, adding to the camouflage and barnyard odor.

Woods listened to the Quislings' radio calls on a tiny CB hidden inside a much larger defunct one. He explained that the only place the Quislings never searched for guns or radios was inside the dysfunctional box, its dangling wiring and missing knobs mute testimony to its uselessness. Woods simply popped the cover and turned on the tiny functioning receiver inside. "Only problem is, it's just a scanner, so I can't send. I'm going to get you boys in with a family in LaGrange. Alan Carlson's part of the Lodge, and his wife's a nurse. She'll help your man there. Seems like most of the searchers lit off after your other guy. He dumped one of his horses in Ridgeway, and they seem to think one of you is hiding there. They're tearing the place apart. So hopefully he gave them the slip. Better get hid, we're coming up on some crossroads. They might have checkpoints."

For the next half hour, Valentine rode in darkness, lulled by the gentle, noisy motions of the truck. They stopped at one checkpoint, but all Valentine could hear was the exchange of quick greetings between Woods and a pair of unknown voices.

The Carlson farm was a nice-size spread. According to Woods, Carlson was in good with the local authorities. His wife's brother was some kind of Quisling big shot in Monroe, so he rarely had trouble finding supplies and tools to keep the place up. He even employed another family, the Breitlings, to help him farm the land. Under cover of picking up some livestock for the voracious appetites at Blue Mounds, Woods pulled the truck into the cluster of whitewashed buildings.

"Lieutenant, you can pop the box now," Woods said. "You're on Alan Carlson's place."

Valentine climbed into the passenger seat, an improvised upholstery job mummified in duct tape with a horse blanket tied over it. The door on the passenger side was missing, as well. ("The Quislings got a real bug about wanting to see all of you at checkpoints. Sucks to be me in the winter," Woods had explained.) The Wolf looked around. The truck had pulled around behind a little white house, between it and a well-maintained barn. The two-story frame house was screened from the road by trees and had the small, high-roofed look of a building trying to hide itself from the world. Three feet of foundation showed in the back, and the kitchen door could be reached only by ascending a series of concrete steps. The barn, on the other hand, looked like it wanted to take over the neighboring territory. It had grown smaller subbuildings like a primitive organism that reproduces itself by budding. An immobile mobile home stood beyond the barn, under the shadow of a tall silo. A garage with a horse wagon and an honest-to-goodness buggy parked side by side stood on the little gravel road that looped around the barn like a gigantic noose. Farther out, an obviously unused Quonset hut stood in an overgrown patch of brush, and a well-maintained shed completed the picture. Behind the house, cow-sprinkled fields ran to the base of a pair of tree-covered hills. Distant farms dotted the green Wisconsin hills.

The back door of the house opened, and a man in new-looking blue overalls and leather work boots stepped down the mini-staircase to the kitchen door. He fixed a nondescript red baseball cap over his sparse, sandy hair and turned to wave a boy out from the house. A young teen, in the midst of a growth spurt, judging from the look of his too-small clothes, emerged, as well. He had black skin and closely cropped hair and looked at the truck with interest. Carlson said a few quiet words to the boy, who scampered off to the road and made a great show of poking around in the ditch at the side of the road with a stick.

A golden-haired dog emerged from behind the barn and flopped down, panting in the shade with his body angled to observe the proceedings.

Woods jumped out of the truck and performed his trick with the tool locker again. At the sight of Gonzalez's wound, Carlson hollered back to the house. "Gwennie, one of them's hurt. I need you out here!"

"Mr. Carlson, I don't know what you've heard though this network of yours, but my name's David, and I want—," Valentine began.

"Introductions can wait, son. Let's get your man downstairs."

A red-haired woman came out of the house, moving with a quick, stocky grace. She wore a simple cotton shirt, jeans, and an apron that looked like it had been designed for a carpenter. She pressed two fingers expertly against Gonzalez's throat. Woods held the boy from Beloit in his arms. Valentine and Carlson each took an arm and helped Gonzalez. Gonzalez seemed groggy and drunk, and he mumbled something in Spanish.

They entered the house, skirting the tiny kitchen, and got Gonzalez into the basement. It was homey and wood paneled, with a little bed and some clothing that matched the kind the young teen watching the road was wearing. Mrs. Carslon put a finger into a pine knot on one of the wooden panels and pulled. The wall pivoted on a central axis near the knot. A small room with four cots, some wall pegs, and a washbasin was concealed on the other side.

"Sorry it's so dark," Mrs. Carlson said. "We're not electrified on this farm. Too far from Madison. But there's an air vent that comes down from the living room; you can hear pretty good what's going on above, as a matter of fact. Let's get the injured man down on the bed."

Carlson turned back to the stairs leading up to the main floor of the house. "Molly," he shouted, "bring a light down here!"

Mrs. Carlson extracted a short pair of scissors from her apron and began to cut away at Gonzalez's buckskins. "What's his name?" she asked.

"Injured man of average height," Valentine answered.

"Okay, Injured," she said insistently in his ear. "Can you move your fingers? Move your fingers for me. On your hurt arm."

Gonzalez came out of his trance, summoned by her words. A finger twitched, and sweat erupted on his brow.

"Maybe a break, maybe some nerve damage. I'm not a doctor, or even a nurse, you know," she said quietly to Valentine. "I'm a glorified midwife, but I do some work on livestock."

"We're grateful for anything," Valentine answered. "It looked to me like the bullet passed through."

"I think so. Seems like it just clipped the bone. There's a lot of ragged flesh for a bullet hole, though. Not that I've seen that many. I'm going to clean it out as best I can. I'll need some light, and some more water. Molly, finally!" she said, looking toward the open panel.

A lithe young woman of seventeen or eighteen, with the fine features of good genes fleshed out on a meat-and-dairy diet, stood at the entrance to the secret room. Her hair was a coppery blond and was drawn back from her face in a single braid dangling to her shoulder blades. She wore boyish blue overalls and a plain yellow shirt. The shapeless and oversize clothes made the curves they hid all the more tantalizing. She carried a lantern that produced a warm, oily scent.

"Dad, are you crazy?" she said, looking at the assembly suspiciously. "Men with guns? If someone finds out, even Uncle Mike can't help. How—?"

"Hush, Molly," her mother interrupted. "I need that lantern over here."

Valentine watched in admiration as Mrs. Carlson went about her business. Mr. Carlson held Gonzalez down as she searched and cleaned the wound. She then sprinkled it with something from a white paper packet. The scout moaned and breathed in short rasps as the powder went in.

"Doesn't sting quite like iodine, and does just as good a job," the woman said as she began bandaging. Valentine helped her hold the bandage in place as she tied it but found himself glancing up at the girl holding the lantern. Molly looked down at the procedure, lips tightly pursed, her skin pale even in the yellow light of the lantern.

Mrs. Carlson tied up the bandage, and Gonzalez seemed to sag even more deeply into the cot he lay on.

Ray Woods spoke up. "Hate to give you another mouth, but this boy Kurt here is on his way across the river. I'm not supposed to go out that far again for a few more days. D'ye think he could have a place here for a little while?"

"Of course, Ray," Mr. Carlson agreed. "Now you better be moving along."

He turned back to Valentine. "Now we can shake, son. Alan Carlson. This is my wife, Gwen. And you see there my eldest, Molly. We've got another daughter, Mary, but she's out exercising the horses. The lookout up the road is kind of adopted, as you might have guessed. His name is Frat, and he came up from Chicago about three years ago. On his own."

"Call me David. Or Lieutenant. Sorry to be so mysterious, but the less you know the better—for both of us."

"Well, Lieutenant, we have to get back to the upstairs. The other family who lives on the farm is the Breitlings. They don't know about this room. Same story: better for us and better for them to keep it that way. Their son is with Mary; he's just a squirt. Tom and Chloe are in LaGrange. I sent them there this morning when word came around about your little scrape. They're due back before dark. There's a chance, just a chance, that the house will be searched. If it happens, don't panic. So happens the local Boss is related to me, and we stay in their good graces in every way. Frat has a way of staring at our local goons; I think he makes them nervous. They never hang around long."

"Glad to hear it. You don't mind if we keep our guns, I hope?"

Carlson smiled. "I'd prefer if you did. And take 'em when you leave. Gun ownership is a one-way ticket to the Big Straw."

"Alan, I wish you wouldn't be so crude about it," Mrs. Carlson objected. "He means the Reapers get you."

Ray Woods put the little orphan, Kurt, down on a cot. "Now, Kurt," Ray said, "I've got to leave you here for a couple of days."

The little boy shook his head.

"Sorry, Kurt. That's the way it's got to be. You can't sleep with me in the cab again, and I can't take you to the place where I live. These people can take care of you better than I can, till we can get you up to the sisters across the Big Blue River. You said you'd never seen a river a mile wide, right?"

"Don't!" the boy finally said. Though whether he was objecting to Woods leaving or going to the river, he did not elaborate.

Woods looked away, almost ashamed, and left. The boy opened his mouth as if to scream, then closed it again, eyes glassing over into the wary stare that Valentine had first seen.

"We'll leave the lamp in here for you. We'll talk tonight if you want, after the Breitlings are in and the lights are out. Now I've got to get your horses hid in the hills. I'd give you something to read, but books are frowned on, too, so we don't have any," Carlson said. His wife and daughter stepped out the door, and Valentine caught the accusing look the young girl gave her mother.

As the door shut, Valentine realized the horrible danger their presence brought to the family. He admired Carlson's resolution. In a way, the courage of Mr. and Mrs. Carlson was greater than that of many of the soldiers of Southern Command. The Hunters risked their lives, armed with weapons and comrades all around, each of whom would risk anything to save his fellows. Here in the Lost Lands, this unarmed, isolated farm family defied the Kurians, putting their children in jeopardy, far from any help. Valentine wondered if even the Bears he had met had that kind of guts.

Hours later, Valentine heard Kurt whimpering in his sleep. He rose from his cot and crept through the darkness to the boy's bed. Valentine climbed in and cradled him until the boy gripped his hand and the sleepy keening stopped. Memories long suppressed awoke, tormenting Valentine. The smell of stewing tomatoes and the pictures in his mind appeared as awful and vivid as if he had seen them that afternoon. As he hugged the boy, silent tears ran down the side of his face and into the homemade pillow.

Eleven

LaGrange, Wisconsin: The town of LaGrange is nothing much to speak of. A crossroads with a feed store and an auxiliary dry goods shop marks the T-intersection of an old state road with a county highway. The irregular commerce that occurs there takes place with small green ration coupons, worthless outside the boundaries of the Madison Triumvirate. Across from the feed store is the house and ringing stable of the blacksmith. The blacksmith and his wife are old work-hard, play-hard bons vivants, and the breezeway between their house and garage is the nearest thing to the local watering hole. One or both seem always ready to sit down with a cup of tea, glass of beer, or shot of backyard hooch. The blacksmith's wife also gives haircuts, and longtime residents can tell how many drinks she's had by the irregular results.

The real LaGrange is in the surrounding farms, primarily corn or bean, hay, and dairy. The smallholds spread out beneath the high western downs that dominate the county. Their produce is transported to Monroe, and the thrice-a-week train to Chicago.

Survival here depends on having a productive farm and not drawing unwanted attention. During the day, the patrols drive their cars and ride their horses, looking for unfamiliar faces. Vagrants and troublemakers disappear to the Order building in Monroe and are seldom seen again. At night the residents stay indoors, never able to tell if a Reaper or two is passing through the area.

The residents live as a zebra herd surrounded by lions. There is safety in numbers and the daily routine, and sometimes years pass before when anyone other than the old, the sick, or the troublemakers gets taken. Their homes are modest, furnished and decorated with whatever

they can make or salvage. The Kurian Order provides little but the ra-
tion coupons in exchange for their labor, although a truly outstanding
year in production or community service will lead to a bond being is-
sued that protects the winner's family for a period of years. The Kuri-
ans provide only the barest of necessities in food, clothing, and
material to maintain shelter. But humanity being what it is, adaptable
to almost any conditions, the residents find a kind of fellowship in their
mutual deprivations and dangers. Barn raisings, roofing parties, quilt-
ing bees, and clothing swaps provide social interaction, and if they are
punctuated with "remembrances" for those lost to the Kurians, the
homesteaders at least have the opportunity to support each other in
their grief.

Valentine remembered little of his first few days with the Carlsons.
Gonzalez's condition worsened, and as his Wolf sank into a fever
brought on by the shock of his injury, Valentine found himself too busy
nursing to notice much outside the tiny basement room.

For three long, dark days Valentine remained at Gonzalez's bed-
side, able to do little but fret. The wound had seemed to be healing well
enough, though just before the fever set in, Gonzalez had complained
that he either could not feel his hand at all or that it itched madden-
ingly. Then, on the second evening after their arrival, Gonzalez had
complained of light-headedness, and later woke Valentine by thrashing
and moaning.

Kurt, the little boy from Beloit, had been sent on his way westward, and the Wolves had the basement room to themselves. Mrs. Carlson blamed herself for not properly cleaning the wound. "Or I should
have just amputated," she said reproachfully. "His blood's poisoned
now for sure. He needs antibiotics, but they're just not to be had anymore."

Valentine could do little except sponge his friend off and wait. It
seemed he had been in the darkness for years, but he could tell by the
growth on his chin that the true count was only days. Then on the third
night, Gonzalez sank into a deep sleep. His pulse became slow and
steady, and his breathing eased. At first Valentine feared that his scout
was slipping toward death, but by morning the Wolf was awake and
coherent, if weak as a baby.

He summoned Mrs. Carlson, who took one look at her patient and
pronounced him in the clear then hurried upstairs to heat some vegetable
broth. Rubber limbed, Valentine returned to his own cot and lost consciousness to the deep sleep of nervous and physical exhaustion. That
evening, with the rest of the house quiet and Gonzalez in a more

healthy slumber, Valentine sat in the darkened living room talking to Mr. Carlson.

"We owe our lives to you, sir. Can't say it any plainer than that," Valentine said from the comfort of feather-stuffed cushions in an old wood-framed chair.

"Lieutenant," the shadow that was Mr. Carlson replied, "we're glad to help. If things are ever going to change, for the better anyway, it'll be you boys that do the changing. We're rabbits in a warren run by foxes. Of course we're going to help anyone with a foxtail or two hanging from their belt."

"Still, you're risking everything to hide us."

"That's what I wanted to talk to you about, Lieutenant. A way to reduce the risk."

"Please call me David, sir."

"Okay, David. Then it'll be Alan to you, okay? What I wanted to say was with your buddy sick—"

"He's getting better."

"Glad to hear it. But I spoke to my wife, and she says he should stay for at least a couple of weeks. Between the wound and the fever, it'll be a month before you can do any hard riding, maybe. Your horses could use a little weight anyway."

Valentine gaped in the darkness. "A month? Mr. Carlson, we couldn't possibly stay—"

"David, I don't know you very well, but I like you. But please let a guy finish his train of thought once in a while."

Valentine heard the ancient springs in the sofa creak as Carlson shifted his weight forward.

"What I'm going to suggest might seem risky, David, but it'll make your stay here a lot safer if we can pull it off. It'll even get you papers to get out of here again. I mentioned to my brother-in-law that I might have some visitors in the near future, within the next week. I told him about a guy I met during summer labor camp up by Eau Claire. Summer labor is something we get to do now and then, keeping up the roads and clearing brush and such. While I was there I met some Menominee, and as a matter of fact you look a bit like them. Anyway, I told Mike that I met a hardworking, nice young man who was looking to move down here, marry, and get himself a spread. I hinted that I had in mind that this young guy would marry my Molly and told him that I invited him down to meet her. Of course, he's just made up to fit your description."

Valentine's mind leaped ahead, making plans. "And you think he'd get us some papers? Something official? It would make getting out of here again a lot easier if we had some identification."

"Well, it wouldn't cut no ice outside this end of Wisconsin. But it would get you to Illinois or Iowa at least. You'd have to lose the guns, or hide 'em well. You could keep to the roads until the hills begin; if questioned, you could say you're out scouting for a place with good water and lots of land, and that's only to be found around the borders. Also, I'd like to bring your horses down from the hill corral. I hate having them up there. Too much of a chance of their getting stolen. Or us getting the ax for withholding livestock from the Boss Man."

"If you think you can pull it off, I'm for it," Valentine decided.

"Give you a little chance for some light and air. Also you can get a taste of life here. Maybe someday a bunch of you Wolves will come up north and liberate us. Or just bring us the guns and bullets. We'll figure out how to use them."

Two days later, Valentine found himself standing outside the sprawling home of Maj. Mike Flanagan, Monroe Patrol Commissioner of the Madison Triumvirate. Valentine wore some oversize overalls and was barefoot. Carlson had driven him the twenty-three miles starting at daybreak in the family buggy.

"I don't know about the rest, but the *major* part fits him," Carlson explained at the sight of the little signboard on the driveway proclaiming the importance of the person residing within. "Major asshole, anyway."

Valentine did not have to feign being impressed with the major's home. It was opulent. Half French villa, half cattle-baron's ranch, it stretched across a well-tended lawn from a turret on the far right to an overwide garage on the left. Its slate-roofed, brick-covered expanse breathed self-importance. A few other similar homes looked out over Monroe from the north, from what had once been a housing development. Now the mature oaks and poplars shaded only grass-covered foundations like a cemetery of dead dreams.

"Listen to this," Carlson said, pressing a button by the door. Valentine heard bells chime within, awaking a raucous canine chorus.

The door opened, revealing two bristling black-and-tan dogs. Wide-bodied and big-mouthed, they stared at the visitors, nervously opening and shutting their mouths as if preparing to remove rottweiler-size chunks of flesh. The door opened wider to expose a mustachioed, uniformed man with polished boots and mirrored sunglasses. He wore a pistol in a low-slung, gunfighter-style holster tied to his leg with leather thongs displaying beadwork. Valentine wondered why the man needed sun protection in the interior of the house, as well as a gun.

"Hey, Virgil," Carlson said, nodding to the neatly uniformed man. "I've brought a friend to see the major."

Something between a smile and a sneer formed under the handle-bar mustache. "I guess he's in for you, Carlson. Normally he doesn't do business on a Saturday, you know."

"Well, this is more of a social call. Just want to introduce him to someone who might be a nephew someday. David Saint Croix, meet Virgil Ames."

Valentine shook hands, smiling and nodding.

Ames made a show of snapping the strap securing his automatic to its holster. "He's in the office."

"I know the way. C'mon, David. Virgil, be a pal and water the horses, would you?"

Carlson and Valentine passed a dining room and crossed a high-ceilinged, sunken living room, stepping soundlessly on elaborate oriental rugs. Valentine hoped he could remember the details of the story Carlson had told his brother-in-law.

The major sat in his office, copying notes into a ledger from a sheet on a clipboard. The desk had an air of a tycoon about it; carved wooden lions held up the top and gazed serenely outward at the visitors. The dogs padded after the visitors and collapsed into a heap by the desk.

Mike Flanagan wore a black uniform decorated with silver buttons and buckles on the epaulets. He exhibited a taste for things western, like a string tie with a turquoise clasp and snakeskin cowboy boots. He looked up from his work at his guests, drawing a long cheroot from a silver case and pressing a polished metal cylinder set in a stand on his desk. An electric cord ran down the front of the desk and plugged into a wall socket, which also powered a mock-antique desk lamp. Bushy eyebrows formed a curved umbrella over freckled, bull-dog features.

"Afternoon, Alan. You look well. How's Gwen?"

Carlson smiled. "Sends her best, along with a pair of blueberry pies. They're outside in the basket."

"Ahh, Gwen's pies. How I miss them. Siddown, Alan, you and your Indian friend."

The electric lighter on the desk popped up with an audible *ping*. Flanagan lit his cheroot and sent a smoke ring across his desk.

"How are things in Monroe, Mike?"

Flanagan waved at the neat little piles of paper on his desk. "The usual. Chicago's pissed because the Triumvirate is diverting so much food to that new fort up in the Blue Mounds. I'm trying to squeeze a little more out of everyone. I'm thinking about upping the reckoning on meat out of the farms. Think you can spare a few more head before winter, Alan?"

"Some of us can," Carlson asserted. "Some can't."

"Look at it this way: Your winter feed will go farther."

"Well, it's for you to say, Mike. But I don't know how it will go down. There's been some grumbling already."

"By whom?" Flanagan asked, piercing Carlson with his eyes.

"You know nobody tells me anything on account of us being close. Just rumor, Mike. But this visit isn't about the reckonings. I want you to meet a young friend of mine, David Saint Croix. I mentioned he'd be visiting and helping me with the harvest."

"Pleased to meet you, David." Flanagan did not look pleased. In fact, he looked perturbed. "Hell, Alan, first you take in Little Black Sambo, and now a mostways Indian?"

"He's a helluva hard worker, Mike. After I teach him a few things, he could run a fine farm."

"Let's see your work card, boy," Flanagan said.

Valentine's mind dropped out of gear for a second, but only a second. "Sorry, Major Flanagan. I traded it last winter. I was hungry, you know. It didn't have my real name on it anyway."

"Dumb thing to do, kid. You're lucky Alan here has connections," Flanagan said, putting down his thin cigar. He rummaged through his desk and came up with a simple form. "Fill this out for him, Alan. Just use your address. I'm giving him a temporary work card, six months. If he improves an old spread, I'll give him a permanent one."

"I need two, Mike. He brought a friend. There's a lot of guys in the north woods looking for something a little more permanent."

"Don't press me, Alan. Jeez, these guys are worse than Mexicans; another one is always popping up outta somewhere."

Carlson leaned forward, spreading his hands placatingly. "With two men helping me this fall, I can clear off an upper meadow I spotted. I was also thinking of building a pigpen across the road and raising some hogs, since meat is becoming such an issue. These men can help me, and I can be ready to go in the spring."

"Fine, Alan, two work permits. Your place is going to be a bit crowded."

"It's only temporary. Thanks a lot, Mike. Gwen and I really appreciate it. So does Molly, of course. Stop by anytime."

"Yeah," Flanagan mused, "you're a fortunate man, David. She's a real beauty. Some of my patrollers say she's kinda standoffish, so I wish you luck." The major pulled out a seal punch, filled out the expiration dates, signed both cards, and punched them with a resounding click. "You're lucky I take this with me. I don't trust my secretary with it; she'd probably sell documents. She can forge my signature pretty good."

"I'm in your debt, Michael," Carlson said, handing over the work cards.

"You've been in my debt since I let that little Fart or whatever his name is stay with you."

"Frat."

"Whatever. That big place and nothing to work it but women; I pity you. I'd offer you lunch, but I'm too busy to make it, and Virgil's hopeless. My girl is out at her parents' place this weekend."

"Thanks anyway, Michael, but it's going to be a long way back. The horses are tired, so they'll have to walk most of the way."

"Thank you, Major Flanagan," Valentine said, offering his hand. Flanagan ignored it.

"Thank my brother-in-law and his wife, not me. Guess they want a bunch of little half-breeds as grandchildren. Up to me, I'd take you to the Order building and let you wait for the next thirsty blacktooth, seeing as you don't have a work card and you're in Triumvirate lands."

Carlson made a flick of a motion with his chin. Valentine moved past the sleeping dogs and out the door, followed by his benefactor. Flanagan tossed away his cheroot and returned to the papers strewn across his desk.

Outside, the horses were very thirsty. Ames was poking in the picnic basket.

"Virgil, please take that in, will you? We'll water the horses ourselves. The pies are for Michael, and Gwen put in a jar of preserves for you. She remembers your sweet tooth."

The smile-sneer appeared again. "That was kind of her. You know where the trough is. I'll bring the basket back out to you."

As Carlson and Valentine brought the horses over to the trough, Alan spoke softly to Valentine. "See what I mean by Major Asshole?"

Valentine clucked his tongue against the roof of his mouth. "Seems like he's trying hard for a promotion to colonel."

That evening, after the long ride back, the Carlsons celebrated the "legitimate" arrival of their guests. Even the Breitlings attended, filling the dinner table past its capacity. As they made small talk, Valentine drew on his memories as a forester in the Boundary Waters to flesh out his David Saint Croix persona.

Valentine ate at Mrs. Carlson's end of the table, across from Molly, grateful for the room the corner chair gave his left elbow. Frat sat on his right, eating with the single-minded voracity of a teenager. The Breitlings were next to Mr. Carlson at the other end of the table, with the younger Carlson girl, Mary. Gonzalez stayed in his bunk in the basement, still too weak to socialize. Mrs. Carlson explained his absence to the Breitlings as being due to illness and a fall from his horse during the journey south.

During the dinner, Carlson told stories about his summer labor, mixed with fictitious ones about how he came to know "young Saint Croix here." Valentine played along as far as he dared but worried that the younger girl might say something about the Wolves or their horses that would blow the story. Mary kept her eleven-year-old mouth shut; her only comment during dinner was a request to ride Valentine's Morgan someday.

"Of course, once he's rested. Any time I'm not using him, that is. Of course I'm going to do some riding, looking for some nice land to get a farm going."

"Maybe Molly can show you around the county," Mr. Carlson suggested.

Molly focused her eyes on the plate in front of her. "Sure, Dad. Since you went to all this trouble to find me a husband, it's the least I can do. Glad you've given me so much say in the matter. Should I get pregnant now, or after the wedding?"

"Molly," Mrs. Carlson warned.

The Breitlings exchanged looks. Valentine figured that discord was rare in the Carlson house.

Molly stood and took up her plate. "I'm finished. May I be excused?" She went to the kitchen without waiting for an answer.

Valentine could not tell how much of the byplay was real, and how much was acting.

Two days later, he and Molly Carlson rode out on a fine, cool morning with a hint of fall in the air. Valentine's indomitable Morgan walked next to Molly's quarterhorse. She wore curious hybrid riding pants, leather on the inside and heavy denim elsewhere, tucked into tall rubber boots, and a sleeveless red flannel shirt. They chatted about their horses as they headed west toward the high, bare hills.

"Lucy here is great with the cows," Molly said, patting the horse on the neck affectionately. "They'll follow her anywhere. It's like she can talk to them."

"I've always wondered if animals talk to each other," Valentine ventured.

"I think they can, sort of. In a real simple way. Like if you and I had to communicate by just pointing at stuff. We couldn't write the Declaration of Independence, but we'd be able to find food and water and stuff. Warn each other about enemies. Hold it, Lucy's got to pee."

Molly stood up in her stirrups while the mare's stream of urine arced into the grass behind her.

"You know horses," Valentine observed. "Those are fine riding pants. Do you ride much?"

"No, too much to do at the farm. My sister's the horse nut. But I did make these breeches. I like working with leather especially. I used to have some nice riding boots, but some creep in the patrols took 'em off me. These rubber ones are hotter than hell, but they're good for working around the cows. I sewed a leather vest for Dad, and when Mom does her calving, she's got a big leather apron that I made."

They trotted for a while. Watching the up-and-down motion of Molly posting left him desperate to switch the conversation back on.

"I get the feeling you don't like us staying," he finally said when they slowed to cut through a copse of mixed oaks and pines. The sun had warmed the morning, but Valentine was flushed from more than the heat of the day.

"Oh, maybe at first. Still don't know what you're doing here—"

"Just passing through. I tried to find out what was going on up at Blue Mounds," Valentine explained.

"You probably wouldn't tell us the truth anyway. I don't know much about the insurgents, but I know you wouldn't tell what you were doing so they couldn't get it out of us, just in case. Or is it because I'm just a girl?"

"It's not that. We have plenty of women in the Wolves. And I hear over half of the Cats are women, too."

"We've heard about you. Werewolves, always coming in the dark, just like the Reapers. Don't you guys go into Kansas and Oklahoma and kill all the people there, so the Kurians have nothing to feed on?"

"No," Valentine said, somewhat taken aback. "Nothing . . . quite the opposite. Just this spring my company brought over a hundred people out of the Lost Lands. That's what we call places like this."

"Lost Lands," she said, rolling her eyes skyward. "I'll buy that. We're lost, all right. How would you like to spend your life knowing it's going to end with you being eaten? I've developed a lot of sympathy for our cows."

"Your uncle seems to be watching out for you all," Valentine said, trying to reassure her.

"My uncle. I should tell you about him. No, my uncle doesn't mean shit. A hungry vampire could still take us any night of the week, good record or no. Uncle Mike has done everything in his life exactly as the Kurians want, and he still doesn't have one of those brass rings. And even if you get it, any Kurian can still take it away if you screw up. And if I'm all testy over the husband thing, it's just because it makes me think about something I'd rather not think about. Let's go up this hill. The view's pretty nice from up top."

They walked their horses toward the grassy slope. They crossed a field with a herd of the ubiquitous Wisconsin Holsteins in it, and Molly waved to a man and a boy mending a fence.

"That's the Woolrich place. The poor woman who lives there is on her third husband. The first two got taken, one while doing the morning milking, and the second when a patrol came through just grabbing whoever they could get their hands on because a bunch of Reapers dropped in for a visit."

They rode to the top of the hill and dismounted, loosening the girths on their wet animals. The horses began to nose in the tall, dry grass at the top of the rolling series of hills. Farmland stretched below in all directions, crisscrossed with empty roads. A hundred yards away, an old highway running along the top of the hills had degenerated into a track cleared through the insistent plant life.

"Is that why you don't want to marry?" Valentine asked. "You're scared of becoming a widow?"

"Scared? I'm scared of a lot of things, but not that in particular. If you want to talk about what really scares me . . . But no, to answer your question, I don't want the life my mother has. She's brought two children into the world, and is taking care of another, and for what? We're all going to end up feeding one of those creatures. I don't want any children, or a man. It just means more fear. It's easy to talk about living your life, trying to get along with the system, but you try lying in bed at night when every little noise might mean something in boots and a cape is coming in your house to stick its tongue into your heart. The way I see it, the only way for us in the Madison Triumvirate to beat these vampires is to cut off their food supply. Quit pretending life is normal."

"I see."

"My grandmother on my mother's side, Gramma Katie Flanagan, she was a teacher or something in Madison before everything changed. When I was about eleven, we had a long talk. She was getting old, and I think she felt her time was coming. As soon as the old people slow down, the patrols show up, sometimes with some bullshit story about a retirement home. She told me about in ancient times there were these Jewish slaves of the Romans who rose up and fought them from a fortress on top of a mountain. The Romans finally built a road or something so their army could get up to the fortress, and all the Jews killed themselves rather than be slaves again. Gramma said if everyone were to do that, it would cut off their power, or whatever they get from us."

Valentine nodded. "I heard that story, too. It was a place called Masada. By the Dead Sea, I think. I always used to tell Father Max—he was my teacher—that I wouldn't have killed myself if I were up there. I would have taken a Roman or two with me."

"If it had just been another battle, would anyone have remembered it?" Molly asked.

"That's a good question. Maybe not. I think Gandhi, you know who he is, right? I think he suggested that the Jews should have done something like that when the Nazis were exterminating them. To me, that's just doing the enemy's job for them. Maybe some of you should try to sell your lives a little more expensively."

"That's easy for you to say. You have guns, friends, other soldiers to rely on. About all we have is a broken-down old phone system and a set of code words. 'John really needs a haircut' for 'We have a family at our place that is trying to go north.' Not much help when the vampires come knocking."

Strange how her thoughts mirror mine. I was thinking the same thing the night I got here, Valentine mused.

"Maybe we can't all commit suicide," she continued. "But for God's sake, we should quit helping them. We feed the patrols, work the railroads, keep the roads repaired. Then when we get old and sick, they gather us up like our cattle. They got it pretty good just because it's human nature to ask for another fifteen minutes when you're told you have an hour to live."

"Brave words," Valentine said.

"Brave? Me?" She sat down in the grass and plucked at the burrs clinging to her jeans. "I'm so scared at night I can barely breathe. I *dread* going to sleep. It's the dream."

"You have nightmares?"

"No, not nightmares. A nightmare. It's only one, but it's a doozy. Wait, I should tell this properly. We have to go back to Gramma Flanagan again. She told me a story about when the Triumvirate had first got things organized in Madison. I think it was in 2024, in the middle of summer. They had a group of men—well, some of them were Reapers, too—called the Committee for Public Safety. About two hundred people were working for this committee, in charge of everything from where you slept to where you went to the bathroom. The three vampires on the committee were kind of the eyes and ears of these Kurians who were dug into the State Capitol building. I don't know how much you know about the Kurian Lords, but they sure love to live in big empty monument-type buildings. I bet a bunch of them are in Washington. But back to the story my Gramma Katie told me. There was this woman, Sheila Something-or-other, who got caught with a big supply of guns: rifles, pistols, bullets, equipment for reloading, all kinds of stuff. I think even explosives. One of the vampires said her punishment was up to the people who worked for the Committee, and if it wasn't to their liking, they'd kill every last one of them and get a new bunch.

"So with that incentive, the whole committee goes over to where she's being held. And they tore her to bits. With their bare hands. They took the pieces and stuck them onto sticks. Gramma said the sticks looked like pool cues, or those little flagpoles from school classrooms, stuff like that. They put her head on one, her heart on another, her liver, her breasts, even her . . . you know . . . sex parts. They made streamers out of her intestines, and painted their faces with her blood. Then they paraded back to the basketball court at the university where the Committee met and showed what they did to her to the vampires. Some of them were drunk, I guess. The Reapers looked at it all and told them to *eat* the bits, or they'd be killed. Gramma said there were fistfights over her liver."

She sat silent for a moment. "Maybe I was too young to be told that story. It gave me a nightmare that night, and pretty often ever since. I'm always dreaming that I've done something wrong, and the crowd is coming for me. They're all around, and they grab me and start pulling me apart. That's when I wake up, cold and sweaty. Mary says I sometimes say 'no, no' in my sleep. She calls it the 'no-no' dream. It seems silly in the daylight, but try waking up from it at two in the morning on a windy night."

"I have a dream, or nightmare, I guess, that keeps coming back," Valentine began. "Never told anyone about it, not even Father Max. My mom and dad and little brother and sister got killed by a patrol when I was just a kid. I come into the house—I remember it smelled like tomatoes in the kitchen that day, but that's not in the dream—and there's my mother, lying in the living room, dead. Her legs were . . . Well, I guess they had raped her, or started to anyway. They shot my dad in the head. But in my dream, it's like they're still alive, and I can save them if I just could fix the bullet wounds. I press my hands against the blood that's coming out of my mom's throat, but it just keeps pulsing and pulsing out, while my little brother is crying and screaming. But I can't save them. Can't . . . ," he said, voice trailing off. He looked up at the clouds to try to get the tears to go away. High white cirrus clouds painted the blue sky with icy white brushstrokes.

"I guess everyone has their own set of nightmares," Molly said.

"Well, we're getting plenty of help. Whatever happened to your grandmother?"

Molly Carlson wiped tears from her own eyes with the back of her hand. "Oh, she injured her back and got taken away. The vampires got her in the end, I'm sure. She got driven away by my uncle Mike. Her son. Her own fucking son."

The following Saturday, Molly taught Valentine how to drive the four-wheeled topless buggy. The thicker reins felt funny in his left hand, the buggy whip held up in his right. Valentine was used to riding English-style with split reins, although he mostly used his legs to control the horse while riding. Driving was a completely different skill.

"You're doing great, David, really great," Molly said, beaming for a change. They were driving well ahead of the family cart, which held the rest of the Carlson clan as well as the Breitlings. "Of course, normally we drive the buggy tandem, which is tougher to manage, but they need the two horses for the big cart. And remember, if you ever have a load to carry in back, to place it evenly in the bed and secure it if you can. An unbalanced load will exhaust a horse faster than anything."

The combined families of the Carlson farm were on their way to Monroe. Mr. Carlson explained that there was a speaker in town, a visitor up from Chicago to give a lecture for the New Universal Church. A Kurian organization, the New Universal Church did not demand weekly assemblies but rather encouraged people in the Kurian Order to come to the occasional meeting to catch up on new laws and policies. But now and then a true "revival" took place, and attending them was a way of keeping in the Order's good graces.

The clouds piled up and darkened, threatening rain. Carlson opined that some would use it as an excuse not to attend, but this made him all the more determined to go. Showing up in spite of precipitation would just make their presence all the more notable, considering the long round trip to and from Monroe. "If we're going to play their game, we should really play it," he added, stowing tarps in the two horse-drawn vehicles and reminding everyone to bring rain slickers and hats.

Only Gonzalez—much improved but still not up to a long trip in the wet—and Frat stayed behind. The young man wanted to keep an eye on the stock and said he felt like he stuck out like a sore thumb in a sea of white faces.

So it turned out that Molly and Valentine ended up together in the buggy, bearing four baskets full of lunch, dinner, and gifts of food for Mrs. Carlson's brother, with the rest following in the larger wagon.

Valentine's Morgan trotted along behind the buggy, brought along as the equine equivalent of a spare tire.

At lunch, a few miles outside of Monroe, the first sprinkles of rain came. When they climbed back into the buggy, Valentine draped the tarp over himself and Molly and drove on, the heavy raindrops playing a tattoo on the musty-smelling oiled canvas. They used the buggy whip as an improvised tent pole and peered out from a cavelike opening, their faces wet with rain. Valentine felt the warmth of her body against his right side, her left arm in his right, helping him hold up the tarp. The rich, seductive smell of femininity filled his nostrils without his even using his hard senses. She also had a faint, flowery smell of lavender.

"You smell good today," Valentine said, then felt himself go red. "Not that you smell bad normally . . . I just mean the flowery stuff. What is that, toilet water?"

"No, just a soap. Mrs. Partridge, the blacksmith's wife, she's a wonder at making it. Puts herbs and stuff in some of them. I think she started doing it in self-defense; her husband picks up animals that have died of disease or whatever, turns them into pig and chicken feed. Dog meat, too. I guess he smelled so bad after working with the offal, she went into scented soaps as a last resort."

"It's nice. Hope I'm not too bad. This tarp kind of reeks."

"No. For a guy who traipses around in the hills, you're really clean. Some of the county men could take a lesson." Valentine felt a stab, remembering Cho's near-identical joke. "A lot of them are going to use this rainstorm as an excuse to skip their Saturday bath." She turned her face and pressed her nose to his chest. "You just smell kind of tanned and musky. Like the saddle from a lathered horse. I like it."

Valentine suddenly felt awkward. "So who exactly is this we're going to hear?"

"My dad says he's a speaker from Illinois, someone affiliated with their church. Kind of a bigwig. This church the Kurians run, it's not like you worship anything. The Triumvirate doesn't discourage the old churches, but they do listen to what gets said. As long as the ministers stick to the joys of the afterlife, and God's love in troubled times, they're fine. Anyone who speaks out against the Order is gone real fast. Most of them get the hint. No, this New Universal Church is more designed to get you to like the Kurian Order. They are always trying to recruit people into the patrols, or to come away and work their machinery, railroads, factories, and stuff. The real slick ones try to convince you that the Kurians came as the answer to man's problems. Some answer."

"So we just sit and listen, then go home?"

"That's about it. They try to recruit people right then and there. Take them up on stage, and everyone is supposed to applaud. Just clap when everyone else claps, and don't fall asleep. You'll be fine. I've got a feeling today's topic is going to be the importance of motherhood. They want more babies in Wisconsin."

The tent they eventually reached dwarfed the old public tent in the Boundary Waters. From a distance it resembled a sagging pastry. But as they grew closer, the mountain of canvas turned into an earthbound white cloud, complete with festive little flags atop the support poles that jutted through the material to either side of the center arch.

Horses, wagons, and vehicles of all description including cars and trucks were parked in the fields of the fairgrounds. Most of the people were already sheltering from the intermittent rain beneath the tent. The Carlson wagon pulled up, and the families all got out and released the horses from their harnesses. Tied to numerous posts in the field, the horses munched grain from their nosebags and stamped their unhappiness at being left in the weather. Carlson nodded to the uniformed patroller navigating the field, wearing a poncho that also covered much of his horse against the rain.

"Major Flanagan is inside. He's got some seats lined up for you, Carlson," the patroller called.

"Thanks, Lewis. Are you gonna get a chance to come in out of the rain?"

"Naw, we had our meeting this morning. All about how duty isn't the most important thing, it's the only thing. Your brother-in-law gave a pretty good speech. Be sure to tell him I said that."

"Deal. If you get real desperate out here, we got a thermos with some tea that might still be hot in the buggy. Help yourself."

"Thanks, Alan. Enjoy."

True to the patroller's word, Major Flanagan had some seats set off right up in front. There was a main stage, with a little elevated walkway going out into the crowd connecting it to a much smaller stage. The Carlsons, with the addition of Valentine and the subtraction of the three Breitlings, sat in a row of folding chairs lined up parallel to the walkway. A few hundred chairs formed a large U around the peninsular stage, and the rest of the spectators stood.

As part of the day's festivities, a comic hypnotist warmed up the crowd. His show was already in progress when Valentine sat at one end of the row. Molly sat to his right, then her sister, with Mr. Carlson next to her. Mrs. Carlson took the seat in between him and her brother, and they chatted as the hypnotist performed. He had a pair of newlyweds on stage; the young groom was hypnotized, and the wife was asking him to bark like a dog, peck like a chicken, and moo like a cow. The audience laughed out their appreciation for the act.

"I saw this guy in Rockford," Major Flanagan explained to his guests. "I recommended him to the Madison Bishop, and he got him up here for this meeting. Funny, eh?"

The young woman finished by having her husband lie down with his head and shoulders in one chair and his feet in another, four feet away from the first. The hypnotist then had her sit right on his stomach, which did not sag an inch. "Comfortable, yes?" the hypnotist asked.

"Very," she agreed, blushing.

The audience cheered for an encore, so she had her husband flap his arms and be a bird. As he flapped and hopped around the stage, the hypnotist finished off with a final joke, "Most women, it takes ten years till they can get their husbands to do this. How about that, ladies, after only two weeks of marriage?"

The audience laughed and applauded. "Let's hear it for Arthur and Tammy Sonderberg, all the way from Evansville, ladies and gentlemen."

After the befuddled Mr. Sonderberg came out of hypnosis, and his wife told him what he had been doing on stage, the hypnotist gave a good imitation of him to further laughter before they left the stage and returned to their seats.

A heavyset man in a brown suit that was simple to the point of shapelessness came onstage. He applauded the hypnotist as the latter backed off, bowing. Valentine marveled at the man's hair, brushed out at the temples and hairline until it looked like a lion's mane.

"Thank you, thank you to the Amazing Dr. Tick-Toc," he said in a high, airy voice.

"That's the bishop of the New Universal Church, David. From Madison," Mr. Carlson explained quietly across his two daughters.

The bishop stepped to the podium on the small stage at the end of the runway and picked up the microphone. "Thank you all for coming out in the rain, everyone," he said, looking at the speakers mounted high on the tent poles which broadcast his voice. "The Harvest Meeting is always a serious occasion. We have a lot more fun at Winterfest, and the Spring Outing. But I know everyone has all the coming work on their minds. Well, today we have an expert on hard work on loan to us from the flatlands in the south. Won't you please welcome Rural Production Senior Supervisor Jim 'Midas' Touchet, visiting us all the way from Bloomington."

A middle-aged, hollow-cheeked man strode out on stage, dressed in a red jumpsuit. He had thinning hair combed neatly back and held in place with an oily liquid, giving it a reddish tint. White canvas sneakers covered his feet. He took the microphone out of the bishop's hand with a flourish and a bow to the audience. He exuded the energy of a man younger than his years.

"Can you all see me?" he asked, turning a full 360 degrees. "I know it's hard to miss me with this on. You see, we're all color-coded in downstate Illinois. Red is for agricultural workers, yellow for labor, blue for administration and security, and so on. In Chicagoland, you can wear whatever you want. I mean, *anything* goes up there. Any of you guys been to the Zoo? You know what I mean, then."

A few hoots came from the audience, mostly from the patrollers, Valentine noticed.

"Oops," Touchet continued. "I forgot we have children present."

Valentine shot a questioning glance to Molly, who shrugged. He suddenly noticed how charming she looked with her wet blond hair combed back from her face. It accentuated her features and the tight, glowing skin of a vital young woman.

"Never mind about that. I bet you're out there wondering, 'Who is this guy? What does he have to show me, other than what not to wear, ever?' Anyone thinking that? C'mon, let's see your hands."

A few hands went up.

"I bet you're thinking, 'How long is he going to speak?' Let's see 'em!"

A lot of hands went up. Major Flanagan, smiling, raised his, and the Carlsons followed suit.

"Finally, some honesty. Okay, since you've been honest with me, I'll be honest with you. I'm nobody, and to prove to you what a big nobody I am, I'll tell you about myself.

"I'm from Nowhere, Illinois. Actually, more like South Nowhere. Just off the road from Podunk, and right next to Jerkwater. Typical small town, nothing much happened. I grew up quick and brawny. You wouldn't know it to look at me now, but I used to have a nice set of shoulders. So I ended up in the patrols. And the patrols in downstate Illinois, let me tell you, they're really something. I didn't have a car. I didn't even have a horse. I had a bicycle. It didn't even have rubber tires; I rode around on the rims. The highlight of most days was falling off my bike. It's a little better now down there, but back in the thirties, we were lean when it came to equipment. In the winter, I walked my route. We didn't get paid back then, just got rations, so there was no way I could even get a horse at my rank.

"I spent ten long, empty years riding that bike. Farm to farm, checking on things. I carried mail. I delivered pies and pot roasts to the neighbors. 'Since you're going that way, anyway,' they always used to say when they asked me. I was bored. I started reading a lot. I was curious about the Old World, the good old days, people called them. Do they call them that up here, too?"

A couple of "yeps," quietly voiced, came from the audience.

"It was lonely in the patrols, and when you're lonely, you need friends. So when I found a little hidden pigpen or chicken coop on someone's farm, and they said, 'Be a friend, forget you saw this, and we'll let you have a couple extra eggs when you come by,' I went along. Hey, everybody wants to be a friend. So I went along, got a friend and a few eggs in the bargain. On another farm, I had another friend and a ham now and then. On another farm, some fried chicken; down the road, a bottle of milk, a bagful of corn. I had tons of friends, and I was eating real good to boot. I had it made."

The red figure paced back and forth, microphone in one hand and cord in the other, first facing one part of the audience and then another.

"Eventually, I got caught. Like I told you, I'm nobody special. And I wasn't especially bright. One day my lieutenant noticed me wobbling down the road with a ham tied to my handlebars and a box of eggs in the basket in back. I think I had a turkey drumstick in my holster, I don't remember.

"Boy, it all came crashing down in a hurry. I think I died the death of a thousand cuts as my lieutenant walked up to me. I made the mistake of asking him to be a friend, and I'd give him everything I was collecting from the farms. He didn't have any of that.

"So within six hours of my lieutenant spotting me, I was sitting in the Bloomington train station, waiting for my last ride to Chicago. I was bound for the Loop. I was very, very alone. All those friends on all those farms, they didn't come get me, or turn themselves in and take their share of the blame. They weren't my friends after all.

"Well, it's a good thing for me I got caught in the spring of forty-six. I'm sure you remember the bad flu that went around that winter. It killed thousands in Illinois, and thousands more got so weakened by it, they caught pneumonia and died just the same. So we had a serious labor shortage in Illinois. I got put to work shoveling shit. I'm sure many of you know what that's like. But that's all I did, every single day. I worked at the Bloomington railroad livestock yards, taking care of the hogs and cows bound for Chicago's slaughterhouses. Of course, I was just on parole. Any time they felt like it, they could throw me on the next train to Chicago, and no more Jim Touchet.

"The first day shoveling, I was happy as a dog locked up overnight in a butcher shop. The second day, I was glad to be at work. The third day, I was happy to at least have a job. The fourth day, I began to look for ways to cut corners. By the fifth day, I was trying to find a nice spot to maybe take a nap where my boss couldn't find me.

"Of course, my boss noticed me slacking. He was a wise old man. His name was Vern Lundquist. Vern had worked at the railroad station in the olden days, and he still worked there. He didn't threaten me, not really. He just called me into his office and said that if I wanted to stay in his good graces, I'd better come in tomorrow and give an extra five percent effort.

"Even though he didn't threaten me, I got scared. That night I couldn't sleep. I was worried that I'd show up at work the next day, and the boys in blue would throw me on the first train to Chicago. I could be in the Loop in less than twenty-four hours."

He stood still, next to the lectern, wiping his sweating brow. His eyes passed over the Carlson family, and he smiled at Valentine. His face took on a scaly, cobralike cast when he smiled.

"That twenty-four hours changed my life. All that night, I thought about giving another five percent. How hard could that be? Vern wasn't asking me to work seven days a week, which is what most of you out there do on your farms.

"The next day, I gave the extra five percent. It was easy. I just did a little extra here and there. Did a job without being asked, fixed a loose gate. If old Vern noticed, he didn't say anything. I got worried; what if he wasn't noticing the extra five percent?

"So the next day, I did just a little bit more. Spent an extra fifteen minutes doing something I didn't have to do. Cleaned some old windows that hadn't been washed since Ronald Reagan was president. I found it was easy to give that extra five percent.

"It turned into a game. The next day, I gave another five percent. I was compounding my interest, to use an old phrase. In tiny little baby steps I was turning into a real dynamo. Jim Touchet, the guy who leaned his bike against a tree for a two-hour lunch, who always rode home on his route faster than he ever rode it while patrolling, was trying extra hard even when no one was looking.

"Vern was real happy with me. After a month, I took the job of his assistant. Within a year, I was old Vern's supervisor. I always gave that extra five percent no one else was giving. I always did more than my boss, and usually within two years I had his job.

"I said the same words to people under me. I asked for an extra five percent. That's all. An extra five percent, when you have a whole bunch of people doing it, can turn things around.

"Before I knew it, they were calling me 'Midas' Touchet. Everything I turned my hand to seemed to turn to gold. Me, the guy who never learned his multiplication tables as a kid, who couldn't stay upright on his bike, went from shitshoveler to production senior supervisor. I'm responsible for farms from Rockford to Mount Vernon, Illinois. I answer to the Illinois Eleven. You think you have tough quotas? What are they called up here, *reckonings?* I've seen the figures; the Illinois Eleven are a lot more demanding than your Triumvirate up in Madison. And last year, we were over production. I know what you're thinking; we broke quota by five percent, right? Wrong. We *doubled* the quota. That's right, doubled. The New Universal Church is handing out brass rings to my best people like lemon drops. See mine?" Touchet asked, holding up his hand. The coppery-gold ring glinted on his thick pinkie. He passed it through his oiled hair, removed it, and flicked it into the crowd before the platform. A woman caught it, screamed, and almost fainted into her husband's arms.

"Oh my God, oh my God," she blubbered, shoving it onto her thumb as the audience gaped.

"It's no big deal, that ring. I'll get another one this fall. Not that I need it. If I could have your attention back, I'll let you in on a secret. I've already given you one secret, the secret of the extra five percent. I'm a generous man. I'll give you a twofer.

"The secret is that you don't need a brass ring. That's the beauty of the New Universal Order," he said, lowering his voice.

Valentine looked around, trying to shake the feeling of being almost as hypnotized as the young Mr. Sonderberg.

"All the Order demands is production. Efficiency. Good old hard work. The things that made this country great before the social scientists and lawyers took over. I see some old-timers out in the audience. How was it when the lawyers ran the show? Did they make things more efficient, or less?"

"Are you kidding? Anytime lawyers got involved, things got cocked-up," one old man shouted.

Touchet nodded happily. "In the old Order, how far you went depended on going to the right school. Getting the right job. Having the right degree. Living on the right side of the tracks. Being the right color. Ten percent of the people owned ninety percent of the wealth. Anyone want to disagree?"

No one did.

"And not just the society was sick. The planet was sick too. Pollution, toxic waste, nuclear contamination. We were like fruit flies in a sealed jar with an apple core. Ever done that little experiment? Put a couple flies in with some food, knock some tiny holes in the lid, and watch what happens. They eat and breed, eat and breed. Pretty soon you'll have a jar filled with dead fruit flies. Mankind removed every form of natural selection. The weak, stupid, and useless were breeding just as fast as the successful. That isn't in nature's plan. And there's only one penalty for a species that breaks the laws of Mother Nature.

"Now you can drink out of any river, and you fishermen know the streams are full of fish again. The air is clean. It sounds crazy to say, but I'm one of the people who believes the Kurians were a godsend. The scale is back in balance. We're a better people for it. The Kurians have winnowed out the useless mouths. They don't play favorites; they don't make exceptions. They keep the strong and productive and take the slackers."

A few, perhaps surprisingly few, murmured disagreement.

"I'm not asking you to agree with me. Just hear me out and go home and think about it. And do one more thing. Think about how you can give that extra five percent. I know you all work hard. But I bet each of you can do what I did: figure out some way to do another five percent. You'll feel better about yourself, and your life will be more secure. Like me, you'll find you've got a brass ring in your pocket and not even need it because you're going the extra mile. How many of you slaughter your best milker for steaks? None, right? The Kurians are the same way. They're here, they're staying, and we've got to make the best of it.

"You've heard my story. You know I wasn't born special. No great brain, not much drive. Not even good-looking. But I've got a beautiful house—I've got pictures if any of you want to see it afterwards—a real gasoline car, and a nice house picked out down south for when I retire. So I guess that brass ring is worth something after all. Napoléon used to say that every private of his carried a marshal's baton in his knapsack. Each of you should carry a brass ring in your pocket. You can do it. Any of you out there spend ten hours a day shoveling shit? No? Then you've all got the jump on me. You're already way ahead of where I was when I decided to give that extra five percent. Whether you're sixteen or sixty, you can do what I did, believe me. Give the extra five, and it'll happen to you, too.

"Now, before I leave for the flatlands, as you call my home, I gotta do the usual recruitment drive. We're looking for young men and women, seventeen to thirty, who want to take some responsibility for public order and safety. I won't give the usual gung-ho speech or list all the perks: You know them better than I do. I will guarantee that you won't be mounted on a bicycle with no rubber on the tires. And don't forget, even if you go to boot camp and flunk out, you still get your one-year bond, no matter what. So who's going to be the first to come up on stage and get the bond? Okay, moms and dads, aunts and uncles, now's your chance to tell those kids to come up and get the bond."

Valentine listened to the forced applause as a few youths took to the main stage, then joined in. It seemed safest to do what everyone else was doing. He wondered how many in the audience believed the story, and how many were just going along to get along.

Touchet shook hands with the bishop who'd introduced him. The bishop patted his back and said something in his ear. Touchet returned to the microphone.

"Before you leave, I have a couple of announcements. The Triumvirate has changed your quotas, or reckoning, I mean. They'll be discussed individually with you by your local commissary officials."

The audience knew better than to groan at the news, but they did quiet down and stop filing out of the aisles.

"On the good news side, there's an exciting announcement from the New Universal Church and the Madison Triumvirate. Any couple that produces ten or more children in their lifetime automatically wins the brass ring."

Valentine and Molly Carlson exchanged a significant look, and she tweaked up the corner of her mouth at him.

"The New Order recognizes the importance of motherhood and family life," the snake oil salesman continued, "and wants to get the northern part of the state repopulated. Any children already born to the family count, so you big families with five or six children are already well on your way to the brass ring."

Some more applause broke out, probably from the bigger families.

"And finally, we've had some problems with insurgents and spies recently. The standard reward of a two-year bond has been upped to a ten-year bond in exchange for information leading to the capture of any undocumented trespassers in the Triumvirate's lands. Thank you for your cooperation."

"Thank you for your cooperation," Molly whispered. "Now go home and start making babies. God knows what you're going to feed them, since they are upping the reckoning."

"Now, Molly," Mr. Carlson said quietly. The tent was emptying fast, save for a few people with questions for either the bishop or Touchet. Valentine escorted Molly to the exit, following her parents, and paused to look back at the podium. Touchet was looking at him and speaking to the bishop. The Wolf smelled trouble at that look. He hurried out of the

tent, racking his brain as he tried to remember if he'd ever seen the Illinoisan's face before.

What was there about him that would draw the golden touch?

Back at the wagon and buggy, the Carlsons ate a quick dinner out
of their baskets. Flanagan joined them, helping himself to a choice
meat pie.

"He left a few things out, you know, Gwen," Flanagan said, treating them all to a view of half-chewed food. "In his lecture to the patrols, he elaborated a bit about how he got out of the jam after he was
caught helping those folks hide animals from the commissary. While
he was sitting in the depot, they offered him his life back if he would
turn in each and every farmer who withheld so much as an egg or a
stick of butter from the commissary. Turned out he had a real good
memory," Flanagan chuckled.

"It was all part of the talk he gave on duty this morning. Oh, and
the brass ring he threw out into the audience is a phony. But don't tell
anyone I told you. Don't hurt nothing to have those folks believing they
got it made, as long as they stay in our good graces."

"Duty, Mike?" Mrs. Carlson said. "I bet you could tell Mr. Midas
there a thing or two about devotion to duty. Like putting it before family.
You're an expert at that."

"Don't start, Gwen. That's in the past. I've done plenty for you
since, even a few things that would get me on the next train to Chicago. Oh, shit, it's starting to rain again," Major Flanagan grumbled,
looking at the sky. "Bye, kids. Stay out of trouble. Glad to see you
showed up for the meeting, Saint Croix. Maybe you're smarter than
you look."

On the ride back, Molly drove the buggy. Valentine was unsure of
himself on the rain-wet surface, and they decided a pair of experienced
hands on the reins would be best. Valentine and Molly sat together
under the tarp again, but he couldn't recapture the half-excited, half-
scared mood of the trip down when he first felt her close to him.

"You didn't fall for any of that baloney, did you?" Molly asked.

"No, but he did know how to tell a good story. He had me spellbound for a while."

"Yes, he's one of the best I can remember hearing. That's what
you'd expect right before they increase the reckoning." She paused for
a moment. "You seem a million miles away."

"I didn't like the way he looked at me. At the end, when he was talking to the bishop. Almost like he was asking about me. Funny, because I've never seen him before in my life."

"Well, according to Uncle Mike, he really is from Illinois. You ever been there?"

"I passed through it on the way here, but we stayed in the uninhabited part. Or mostly uninhabited, that is. Sorry if I seem preoccupied. You sure pegged the baby thing. How did you know?"

She smiled at him. "Just because I'm eighteen and hardly been more than twenty miles from home, you think I'm ignorant. There's a fresh batch of vampires up in New Glarus. Nobody knows when they came in with their Master exactly, but it seems like they're here to stay. That's more hungry mouths. How often do they need feeding, anyway?"

"That is one of the many things we don't know about the Reapers. According to the theories out of this group that studies them down in Arkansas, how much they need to eat depends on how active they and their Master are. We think a lot of times the Kurians have about half their Hoods shut down. This is just guesswork, but the fewer Reapers a Kurian has to control, the better he can control them. Sometimes when he's trying to work all thirteen at once, they just turn into eating machines and do stupid stuff like forget to get in out of the daylight. But the Kurian can't control too few, either. He takes a risk when he does that. If the link for feeding vital auras to the Kurian Lord gets shut down, like say if he's got only one Reaper left and it gets killed, we think the Kurian dies with it."

Molly rewrapped the thick reins in her hand. "That's interesting. It's funny to just be able to talk about them with somebody. Discussing the Kurians is a taboo subject here. Too easy to say the wrong thing. So a Reaper can be killed?"

"Yes," Valentine said, "but you need to put that at the top of your 'easier said than done' list. I've seen six trained men pump rifle bullets into one at a range of about ten feet, and all it did was slow it down. Of course, those robes they wear protect them a lot. If they're hurt, you can behead them. A lot of times we're satisfied just to blow them up or cripple them so they can't move around much and they're easier to finish off. But again, even catching one where you can gang up on it is hard. They're usually active only at night, and they see better than us, hear better than us, and so on."

"So how do you do it?"

"It's a long story. Kind of hard to believe, too, unless it's happened to you. Now I know I've told you there are also people like the Kurians, but they're on our side."

"Yes, the . . . Lifeweavers."

"Good, yes, you have it. Long time ago, I think we worshiped them, and made them out to be gods. But they have the ability to awaken latent . . . I don't know, I guess you'd call them powers . . . within a human. About four thousand years ago, they made it very totemistic so the people would accept what these gods or wizards or whatever were doing. 'The spirit of a wolf is in you.' "

"Can they do it with anyone?"

"I don't know. The Lifeweavers select you for it, I know that much. Down in the Ozark Free Territory, they have three kinds of warriors they create, each named for an animal. Maybe they use different animals elsewhere, like lions in Africa maybe. We're called the Hunters. We all carry a blade of some kind to finish off the Reapers. In the Wolves we just use a short, broad-bladed knife. It's a very handy tool in the woods, too. The Wolves are like the cavalry. We move fast from place to place, scout out the enemy troops, and fight guerrilla actions, mostly. There's lots of Wolves. Those Cats are spies, assassins, and saboteurs. I don't know about the Cat training, seems like they're just really, really good Wolves who prefer to work alone. I've known only one Cat. They go into the Kurian areas and mess with the Reapers. Maybe there's one around here somewhere. But if there is, he or she probably doesn't know I'm around. As I told you, I was just running the mail up to Lake Michigan. Then there are the Bears. They're the meanest bunch of bad-asses in the Southern Command, I can say for certain. I don't know what the Lifeweavers do to the Bears to make them the way they are, but I've heard of a single Bear taking on three Reapers and killing them all. They're like human tanks. We Wolves always make room for them at the bar when they come in."

They listened to the *clip-clop* of hoofbeats. Luckily it was an asphalt road, with only a few gravel stretches. The Morgan trotted steadily behind at the end of his lead, enjoying his exercise. Molly slowed the buggy to a walk and let the horse breathe, to give the rest of the family a chance to catch up a little in the plodding wagon.

"Do you win often?" Molly asked. "I mean, actually go out and beat the Reapers?"

"Sometimes. The Ozarks are still free, aren't they? But it costs people. Good people," Valentine said, remembering.

"Don't think about that too much," she suggested. "It makes you look all old and tired. You're what, twenty?"

"I feel older. Maybe it's all the miles."

Now it was Molly's turn to be lost in thought. "You beat them," she ruminated. "We've always been told you just hide out up in the mountains. Starving to death in winter, stuff like that. Even the lodges, our organization for getting people out of the Triumvirate's reach, discourage anyone from going down there."

"It's a long trip," Valentine agreed. "Long and dangerous."

"You must really trust us, David. I could turn you in and get a brass ring for sure. A Wolf, an officer even, they'd love that. Uncle Mike would shit himself to death if he knew. He even gave you a work card." She giggled.

"At first I didn't have much of a choice except to trust you. Seemed like we were going to get caught anyway. Gonzalez wanted me to leave him, but I couldn't do that. Now I'm glad I gambled."

She cocked her head and smiled. "Why?"

Valentine shook his head and averted his eyes. That smile was irresistible. "Father Max used to say, 'Women and six-year-olds never run out of questions.' "

"Only because men and four-year-olds never have the right answers," she countered.

"Listen to you," Valentine laughed.

"C'mon, I mean it, David, why are you glad? Do you like this little charade we're playing, the courtship thing?"

At the word *charade,* Valentine felt a glass splinter pierce his heart. He forcibly brightened his voice. "It's been fun, sure. I've enjoyed talking to you, being around your family. I haven't had a family since I was little."

Molly started the horse again at a slow walk. "I've had fun, too, David. Sometimes I can't tell if it's a role that I'm playing or not. I'm almost sorry it has to end. Not that I want to bring a baseball team of your kids into the world to win a brass ring, of course."

"Of course," Valentine agreed. *I'm sorry it has to end, too,* he added mentally.

Back at the Carlsons' home that night, Valentine and Gonzalez talked in the basement. Valentine told him about the pep talk that took place at the tent and the funny look he received from the speaker.

"I don't know, Val. All the more reason to get out of town soon. You don't think it's going to look suspicious if we just disappear?"

"No, I already talked about that with Mr. Carlson. He's going to say Molly and I didn't get along, and we took off for parts unknown after a big argument. How's that arm—can you ride yet?"

Gonzalez removed it from the sling. His fingers were curved, and the skin looked dry and unhealthy, like an octogenarian's arthritic hand. "It's bad, Lieutenant. I think the nerve is gone. It kind of burns and itches sometimes. I can still ride, but it'll be one-handed."

"You can't shoot one-handed. Looks like you're heading for a well-deserved retirement."

"I'll use a pistol."

"That's for Captain LeHavre to say. Speaking of which, I haven't had a good dressing-down in weeks. I'm ready to go home and get yelled at again. How about you?"

"Say the word."

"I want to wait another day or two. You still look kind of pale, Señor Gonzalez. I want to cook us some biscuits and see to the horses' shoes. Anyway, how was your day holding the fort with Frat?"

"He's a tough kid. We could use him in the Wolves."

Valentine was intrigued. He could not remember the last time Gonzalez had called anyone tough. "What do you mean?"

"We got talking while you were away. I told him where I come from, and he told me about Chicago. When he was little, he got put in the worst part of town with his mom and dad. In the center of the city, inside the river, there's this place called the Loop. It's got a river to the north and west, and the lake to the east. A bunch of those frog-Grogs live in the shallows. In the lake, you know? Then to the south, there's a big wall made out of an old expressway.

"According to Frat, trains still run people in, but no one can come out. The buildings are so tall, it's like being at the bottom of a canyon. No lights. The people there live on rats, birds, garbage that gets dumped in the river. He said they eat each other, too."

"You sure he wasn't just making it up?" Valentine said.

"If he is, he's good at it," Gonzalez argued. "The only people that go in are the Reapers. All the bridges are down, but they use a tunnel system under the city to get in and out. That whole Loop area is like the happy hunting ground for the Chicago Reapers. They just leave the bodies for the rats or those frog-Grogs."

"That's how the kid got out. Through the tunnels. Can you believe it, crawling in the dark through a tunnel the Hoods use? I couldn't do it, that's for sure."

Valentine shuddered at the thought. A pitch-black tunnel, Reapers maybe at either end. Of course, maybe the kid's bravado came from ignorance of how easily the Reapers could spot him.

Engine sounds from outside the house penetrated their refuge. Valentine's heightened hearing detected a vehicle slowing as it approached.

"Hey, sir . . . ," Gonzalez said, startled.

"Shh, I hear it, too." Valentine identified a car engine with a bad muffler. It pulled into the Carlsons' yard, and he heard two car doors open and shut. Muffled voices came from upstairs.

Valentine gestured toward the hidden room. Gonzalez kept watch at the stairs, and Valentine worked the pine knot that allowed him to pull open the door. The secret room was a little more spacious with their cots out in Frat's part of the basement. Their packs and weapons were still concealed within.

The ventilation duct let him hear the voices in the living room loud and clear. Mr. and Mrs. Carlson received Major Flanagan and his assistant Virgil in the main room. Even the squeaks of the old chairs could be heard through the air vent.

"What brings you out tonight, Major?" Carlson asked.

"It can't be a second helping of meat pie," Mrs. Carlson added. "I'm all out, and with the rain, there's no rabbits in the traps today. I can roast you a potato, if you want."

"It's a social call, Alan," Flanagan said. "Well, fifty-fifty. It's about the meeting at the tent today."

"What, did we miss an encore?" Mrs. Carlson asked. "Pull himself up by his bootstraps so hard he flew out of the tent?"

"Gwen, your sense of humor needs a good curb bit," Flanagan growled. "But it does have to do with Jim Touchet. He saw someone in your family who really intrigued him. Wants a personal interview, you might say."

Valentine reached for his rifle. It felt comforting in his hand.

"Who, Saint Croix? I'm not sure he's even going to be in the family yet, Mike."

"No, Alan," Flanagan said with a sardonic laugh. "It was Molly. He wants your daughter."

There was a silent pause in the room above. After a full ten seconds, Mr. Carlson's voice echoed forcefully down the vent. "Fuck you, Mike."

Valentine smiled with approval. He had never heard Mr. Carlson say anything stronger than *heck* before, but the occasion deserved it.

"Are you going to take—?" Virgil's voice demanded.

"Fuck you, too, Virgil."

"Now just wait—"

Flanagan interrupted his lieutenant. "Okay, before we get into a pissing contest, which you'd lose and you know it, Alan, just think this deal through. Listen to what I have to say. Not only would you be doing me a big favor, and I think you owe me one after all these years, but you'd be helping your family, too. They're offering the whole family a two-year bond. Actually it's a five-year bond; they said I could go up to five if I had to. Don't look at me that way, Virgil, she's my niece and they ought to get everything they can out of it.

"Alan, I'll be honest with you. The next five years are going to be tough. You know there are new Reapers in Glarus. I've already got orders to make up lists of who is going to make the cut and who isn't. Your farm is doing good now, but what if you have a bad year? What if the cows catch something? You'd be damn glad you had that bond if something like that happens. And even if you're not on the list, maybe a vampire is passing through and happens to get hungry by your place. You know it happens as well as I do. The lists don't mean shit when they're prowling, but bonds do."

After a moment to let the threats, spoken and unspoken, sink in, the major continued. "It ain't like she'd be gone permanent. I have that from the bishop himself. Touchet is giving talks in Platteville, Richland Center, and Reedsburg, then going back through Madison. Three weeks, she'd be gone. He said he wanted some companionship on the trip. And the bond starts as soon as she shows up at the Church Center in Monroe, so she'll be safe in Madison, even. What can I say, Alan. You've got a real honey of a daughter. She caught his eye."

"Quite a time for this to happen," Carlson said. "I wonder how Saint Croix would like her disappearing with that old lech. So much for them settling down."

"Don't worry about him. Worry about your family, Alan. Saint Croix might understand, after all. I'll have a word with the bishop. Since Saint Croix is practically family, maybe we can offer him the bond, too. Even make getting married to her a condition. That might close the deal. If he's a smart kid, he'll know five years is just what he needs when he's trying to get a farm up and running."

"He's a smart kid, all right," Valentine breathed. "Smart enough to blow your ass off through the floor."

"Let's talk to Molly tomorrow," Mrs. Carlson suggested, obviously to her husband. "And maybe David, too."

Valentine counted twenty heartbeats.

"Okay, Gwen. Listen, Mike, I'm sorry I got riled. You, too, Virgil. I was just a little surprised is all. When you're a father, your little girl is always six years old. She's a grown woman; I forget sometimes. But why her? There were prettier girls at the meeting."

"Not according to Touchet. Virgil, go wait outside. Alan, if you don't mind, I'd like a private word with Gwen."

"Okay, Major. I'll sleep on it. Call you tomorrow. Good night."

"Night, Alan."

Valentine listened to the footsteps move about as Virgil was escorted to the door and Mr. Carlson retired to the kitchen. Valentine thought he heard him exchange a few words with Frat.

"Now listen, Gwen," Valentine heard Flanagan say to his sister, keeping his voice low enough for it not to travel out of the room. *Not quiet enough for my ears, though,* Valentine thought.

"You know I'm not the law. The law is whatever the Triumvirate says it is. This Touchet is a big wheel in Illinois, one of the biggest outside of Chicago. The New Church wants him happy, and I'm going to see that he's happy. I'm making it look like Alan has a choice in this, but he doesn't. Neither does Molly. You follow me?"

"I follow you," Mrs. Carlson said in a low tone. Valentine picked up the anger in her brittle voice. He wondered if her brother did.

"Touchet's going to have her one way or another. I know what you have to say cuts a lot of ice with Alan. So you might as well profit from it and get that bond."

"Is there a bond in it for you, too, Michael?" she asked.

"Can't fool you, can I, Sis? Maybe there is. This is pretty important. I think the Kurians want Touchet to consider moving here permanently. That is, if we can pry him away from the Illinois Eleven. They want him running the Wisconsin farms like he does in Illinois."

"*We,* Michael? Are you a we with the Kurians?"

"Always have been. I know which side of the bread my butter is on. I always figured I got Mom's brains. I think all you got was Dad's stubbornness."

Mrs. Carlson sighed. "Okay, Michael, you're right. I'll see what I can do."

"There, that wasn't so hard now, was it?"

"Harder than you'll ever know."

"Wow, man, you're losing it," Frat exclaimed, eyeing the mountain of cordwood.

Valentine was turning logs into firewood with his usual vigor. He stood outside one of the many little buildings budding from the barn's walls, filling the woodshed with fuel. During his stay with the Carlsons, he had chopped a little every day to keep himself exercised. Valentine did not use an ax. He preferred a saw to reduce the trunks into manageable two-foot lengths, which he could then split with a wedge. He followed his routine with robotic precision. He grabbed a length of trunk and placed it on his chopping block: an old stump that had no doubt served in this capacity for years. Then he picked up the wedge in his left hand and the twenty-pound sledgehammer in his right, gripping the latter right up under the rounded steel head. A vigorous tap seated the triangular metal spike. Then he'd step back, shift his grip on the sledge by letting gravity pull the handle though his callused fingers, and whirl it in a sweeping circle behind him, up and then down to the wedge. He would then stack the halves and quarters in a nice, tight pile.

The day's woodcutting began after a halfhearted appreciation of one of Mrs. Carlson's epic breakfasts. Everyone ate with a preoccupied detachment, as if the family dog had gone rabid and no one wanted to talk about who would have to shoot it. Molly looked drawn, her mother pale and tight-mouthed, and Mr. Carlson sported a dark crescent under each eye. Frat gobbled his breakfast like a starving wolf and fled to the backyard and his chores, taking the dog with him. Even young Mary seemed to pick up on the tension; she shifted her gaze from her sister to her parents and back again.

Valentine decided Frat had the right idea, cleared his plate, and went outside. He had played the role of a forester the past few days and brought down several likely looking trees from the wooded hills to turn into split-rail fences and fireplace fodder.

He lost himself in the chopping, thinking about how to improvise a pack for his Morgan and some spare saddles. He could tie together a sawbuck rig, and there was enough worn-out leather and canvas in the old tack trunk to strap it to his horse. By having the Morgan carry feed for itself and Gonzalez's horse, and with Valentine loaded, as well, they should be able to get within striking distance of the Ozarks before the oats and corn ran out. He planned to cross the Mississippi farther north and move quickly across Iowa, returning to the Free Territory somewhere southwest of St. Louis.

But despite the hard work and plans to get his crippled Wolf home, thoughts of Molly continually shifted his train of thought to emotional sidings.

Frat's comment brought him out of his sledge-swinging meditation.

"What was that?" Valentine asked.

"You've been chopping wood almost every day since you got here; you're a regular Paul Bunyan. We've got enough to get us through two winters. It's going to rot before we can use it."

"Well, maybe your dad can sell some of it."

Valentine realized his back and arms ached. He looked at the sun; the warm September afternoon had already begun. Even better, his mind was relaxed, tranquil.

"Hey, David, why are they watching the house?"

Valentine put down the sledge, leaning the handle against his leg. *So much for tranquillity.* "Who is watching the house?"

"The patrols. There's a car down the road toward LaGrange. One guy in it, so his partner is probably in the hills somewhere with binoculars or a spotting scope." Frat shaded his eyes and looked up into the hills and shrugged.

"How do you know there are two?"

"They always go in pairs. Uncle Mike talks about it. They switch around the partners a lot so no one gets used to working with anyone. Keeps them honest, I guess."

"You're pretty sharp, Frat."

"Naw, it ain't that. It's just when it's the same thing day after day, you notice the patterns. Like you—anytime you're worried about anything, you cut wood."

"I do it for the exercise."

Frat shook his head, a triumphant grin on his face. "You sure needed a lot of exercise before meeting Uncle Mike. And when you and my mom talked about the damage to Gonzo's arm, you cut a lot then. Before you went riding with Molly, too. And that same day, after you got back and cleaned up your horse, you chopped until dinner."

Valentine sat down on the stump, staring at the youth. "Hell," was all he could think to say. He looked over at Frat. "Do you know about the deal with your sister?"

"Yeah, Mom and Dad were up most of the night talking about it. They talked about packing up and asking you to lead them out of Wisconsin. My mom said that wouldn't work because Mike was having us watched. Turned out she was right. They woke Molly up early and talked about it upstairs first thing this morning."

"Did they decide anything?"

"I don't know. Molly started crying."

Valentine concentrated on keeping his face blank.

"Frat, do me a favor. You have a few rabbit snares around, don't you?"

"Uh-huh. There's a warren up in one of the pastures, and there's rabbits in the hills, too."

Valentine scanned the hills. "Go up and check your traps. See if you can see where that other patroller is. Can do?"

"Sure. Can do."

"Come and look for me in the stable if you spot him. But first of all go in the house for a few minutes. Like you were just sitting around, and your parents came up with something to get you out of their hair. Now get going."

Frat scampered off toward the house.

Valentine forced himself to put away his tools for the benefit of the hidden observer. He wandered to the stable, in no particular hurry. The ancient stalls, missing their doors, enclosed the horses with short lengths of rope. The rich smell of horse sweat and manure filled the warm afternoon air.

Five horses, he considered. *Three belong to the Carlsons, then his and Gonzalez's. Mrs. Carlson on one, the girls on the second, Gonzalez sharing the third with Mr. Carlson, taking turns riding it. He and Frat could walk; the boy looked lean and capable. They're farm and riding horses, not packhorses. Best keep the load under 150 pounds for travel up and down hills. Blankets and tenting, rope and equipment. Farrier supplies for the horses, or losing a shoe means losing a horse. Maybe a week's food for man and beast. Would a week get us out of reach? God, the lifesign. Extra Reapers in Glarus to think about, they'd cover the thirty miles to LaGrange between dusk and midnight, running. Shit, we'd be drawing to an inside straight. And Gonzalez can't shoot.*

"Hi, David," a scratchy voice said.

Molly.

"Phew, you're sweaty. Frat said you were cutting wood."

"Oh, yeah. Well, I thought I'd leave your dad with a good supply. Or he could sell it, help pay for all the food we ate. Don't know how to pay him back for saving our lives. Are you okay?"

She ran her hands through uncombed hair, pulling the sun-kissed blond strands behind her. "So you know, then."

No point in lying, he thought. "Yes. I sort of eavesdropped last night through the basement air vent. None of my business, I know, Molly. Your uncle painted a pretty ugly picture. What did your parents say?"

"They just told me to do some thinking, and we'd talk about it more today. But I've already made up my mind."

"Not the Masada solution, I hope."

A hint of her old smile crossed her face. "No." She took a deep breath. "I'm going to do it, of course." It came out as a single word: *I'mgoingtodoit.* As if by saying it faster, it would be over with all the more quickly.

Valentine had a feeling all morning that would be her decision. What alternative did she have? Perhaps he could offer one.

"Did you tell your parents?"

"Not yet. I . . . wanted to tell you first. I know that sounds dumb. I mean, it's not like you're my husband, but—"

"Molly," he interrupted, "I've been thinking about getting your family out of here. And not just since yesterday, either. It's a slim chance, I'll admit. Here's what we do—"

"David, don't start. It's okay."

"No, listen to what I've—"

"No, I want you to listen to me. Your slim chance, it involves us trying to slip out, becoming runners, right?"

"Not just us, everyone. Your parents, the horses, even the dog."

"Listen, David, you're crazy. None of us are in shape to ride or walk for days and days. And they're watching us. If my uncle's letting us see two men, that probably means there's six more all around somewhere. He's no doubt let the Breitlings know that if we try something stupid, they can get the five-year bonds just for calling the patrols.

"They're only giving me an illusion of choice in the matter. My mom didn't say it, but I think that one side of the coin has the promise of the bond, but the other has a threat. If the bishop says *frog,* my uncle jumps. He's not going to let something like family get in the way of orders."

Valentine opened his mouth, but she stepped toward him and gently cupped her hand over it. "David, I'm glad you were thinking about getting us out. Before this stuff with Touchet, it would have worked, I'm sure. No one would have expected us to up and disappear. We could have done it with you guiding us. You know, almost nobody has maps anymore. None of the roads have signs. I couldn't find my way to Madison if I wanted to, or anywhere else outside a twenty-mile circle." She pulled her hand away and hugged him. He put his arms around her, strangely unhappy at the embrace. "You're being good and brave," she said. "But let's face facts. I'm not a damsel in distress, and there are too many dragons anyway. This guy is a big shot. He's going to get what he wants. I see a few cow farms I've never seen before, and some backwater towns. I get a trip to Madison. Maybe he just likes having a girl on his arm to impress people, who knows. So I sleep with him. One thing's for sure, I don't want a baby. My mom said there's a way—"

"Molly, don't say it. I don't want to think about you doing that," Valentine said, twisting his mouth in disgust.

"What, pregnancy? Well, you're a man. I guess you don't have to think about it if you don't want to. You seem a little old not to know the facts of life, but women have to consider the possibility."

"No, I've just heard things. About women dying that way, you know."

She looked down the aisle of horses and patted Lucy on the nose. Valentine looked at her, in an old pair of her father's pants cut off at the knee, breasts swelling under a T-shirt. In her disheveled state, she looked younger than her eighteen years, too young to be cold-bloodedly discussing abortion.

"Well, with luck, the old fart's incapable," she said, closing the discussion. She walked down the line of horses. "Great, the hay nets are empty. Mary only wants to ride and groom horses; she leaves the mucking out to Frat and me. Poor things! Sorry, guys, we can't turn you out in the new field until the fence is done! These two new horses ate up what grass you guys left in your pasture. Do me a favor, David. Can you get two bales from the loft? I'm going to water these two."

Valentine crossed to the barn and climbed into the hayloft. He liked the sweet smell of hay and alfalfa up there, masking the cow odor from beneath. A couple of sparrows hopped and played in the air, and spiderwebs caught the sunlight like little silver flowers.

He heard the ladder rungs creaking. Molly joined him in the loft, a determinedly cheerful smile showing off her good teeth. She had washed her face at the horse-pump, her T-shirt had a wet, face-shaped patch over the belly where she'd used it to dry herself.

"Thought I'd give you a hand with the bales. They're really loose. Sometimes they're hard to handle. But if you bale hay tight, it gets all mildewy and rots. We can't afford to waste anything."

Valentine sniffed a bale. "Hey, you're right. I didn't know that. All the hay I've ever seen has been packed too tight. Doesn't smell as good as this."

"That's the clover. We grow that on the other side of the road."

She cut a bundle and spilled it onto the floor of the loft.

"Very funny," Valentine said. "How are we going to carry it now? Or do you want to make a scarecrow?"

"Sure, David," she said, her eyes big and bright. "We can use your clothes. Why don't you take them off and give them to me."

"What's that?" he said.

She knelt in the hay. "Too shy? Okay, I'll start."

With a quick, graceful movement she pulled her T-shirt up and over her head. Her shapely young breasts bobbed enticingly as she leaned back into the hay. Valentine stood and gaped, feeling his groin swell, otherwise utterly dumbfounded.

"David, do I have to spell it out for you? Let's make love. I need you to do this for me."

"Molly . . . I mean, we've never even kissed, this is kind of—"

"Sudden?" she finished. "Well, yes, I suppose you're right. Actually, I've only kissed a couple of guys. And one, he was in the patrols, I didn't even want him to kiss me. But he did, and he put his hand on my chest. I yelled, pushed him away, and ran for it. That's the sum total of my sexual experience.

"David, I'm a virgin. I'm going to be with this guy, and the thing that bothers me the most about it . . . well, other than that I'm being forced to do it in the first place . . . the thing that bothers me the most is that he'd be my first time. Not a memory I want to have for the rest of my life. I know you, I like you a lot, and I think you like me. You're nice. You're better-looking than some, and brighter than most. You're an officer. A gentleman, too, otherwise you'd already be on top of me."

"It's not like the thought hasn't crossed my mind, Molly."

"Just go slow, okay, David?" she said, scooting her hips up off the floor of the loft and slipping the oversize shorts down to her feet. She kicked them off with the flick of a leg.

Valentine sank to his knees beside her, placing his mouth on hers. He was also inexperienced, his innate shyness and quiet manner made even youthful kisses and pettings few and far between. Molly Carlson, perhaps the most beautiful girl he had ever known, was in his arms and his for the taking. Animal instinct came to his rescue. His young, demanding lust took him where his self-confidence feared to tread. He felt her probing hand reach the hardness in his pants. She fumbled with his belt. He wanted to take off his shirt, but her soft, yielding mouth felt so exquisite against his, it was impossible to break contact. She undid his belt and the worn-out stitching of the fly gave way to her hearty pull; skittering buttons flew in all directions. He managed to tear his mouth away from hers, laying a series of gentle kisses across her face and down her neck. She giggled and squirmed, thrusting her breasts against his chest. He pulled his shirt up and off his head and thrashed out of his pants.

She came up to his mouth, pressing him with a hard kiss that went all the way down to his soul, and he lost balance, falling onto his back with her on top of him. Coppery-blond hair tickled his face and neck like tiny dancing fingers as she kissed him. Her hand trailed down across his stomach and found him, first touching, then exploring, and finally gripping his hardness. His own arms traced the muscles on her back and caressed the soft skin of her buttocks. She responded, rubbing herself against his thigh, one of her hands playing with his black hair as the other stroked him below.

"God, Molly, that's good," he groaned, a deep and sensual rasp in his voice. He returned the favor, his gentle hand tracing the outlines of her sex, from the curly triangular mat of pubic hair to the soft folds of flesh between her legs. Their kisses became a rapid staccato, and he felt a rush of moisture come to her.

"Please, David. Slowly, okay?" she breathed in his ear. She turned over on her back, and he followed her movement as if in time to a waltz. She gazed up at him, pupils dilated in the dimness of the loft. He suddenly wanted this moment to be forever, Molly in his arms and the smell of womanhood and clover and a hint of lavender-sweet nepenthe in his nostrils. He pressed himself against her, kissing her softly and slowly as she guided him inside, and they were one. He took her in a series of slow strokes, each one slightly deeper than the last. A wince of pain washed across her face and then turned, as an ebb tide gives way to the flow, into a flush of passion. Her hands alternately clawed and caressed his rippling back with each deep, slow penetration. They lost themselves, together and yet apart, until at last he climaxed, emptying himself into her as spasm after spasm racked his body, mouth gaping open as if in a scream, but producing only an intense, unintelligible moan.

Afterwards she lay in his arms, drowsing away the afternoon. He teetered on the pleasant point between exhilaration and exhaustion.

"Are you okay?" he asked.

"Wonderful," she said, drawling out the word. She reached between her legs and brought up her fingers. A smear of blood coated her forefinger and thumb.

"Funny. I figured it would be gone after all the horse riding," she mused.

He kissed away the blood from her hand. The girl named Molly who walked into the barn that afternoon would have been disgusted at the gesture, but the woman in her lover's arms thought it touching.

"Ha, fooled you. My time of the month," she said.

He glanced up at her, eyebrows lifted.

"Joke," she said, twitching her nose at him and rolling her eyes.

"Well, since this chore is done, I really have to look into making a pack for my horse," Valentine said, not letting her get away with it. She restrained him, tightening her grip around his neck.

"Chore indeed! When I took off my shirt, you about passed out."

"Yeah, the blood drained out of my head, all right," Valentine agreed.

"I know where it all went. I'm going to be walking funny for a while, I think."

They kissed, laughing into each other's mouths.

"Seriously now, David. This whole thing actually helps you, too. If you and Gonzo pack up and go right after I do, it will fit perfectly. I'm sure they're expecting you to get pissed and leave. You can keep the story about looking for a place to farm west of here. Your work cards are legit. Even if they call Monroe to check it out, your story will stand up."

He rolled onto his back in the hay with a sigh. He did not want the afternoon to end.

"When are you going to Monroe?"

"Tomorrow afternoon. Touchet is leaving for Richland Center the day after tomorrow. Tuesday morning, I guess. That's what Uncle Mike told my dad on the phone today. Is this guy that important that they kidnap young ex-virgins for him?"

Valentine shrugged. "You'd know better than I. But if he gets production out of the farms, I suppose he's pretty important. Their army has to eat, too. Speaking of eating, I wonder if Frat found any rabbits. Your mother makes a great game pie. Oh, God! Your parents . . . I'm going to have a hard time acting normal in front of them."

"You and me both. But—what do we have to feel guilty about? You're my fiancé, right?"

He chuckled, nuzzling her with his chin. The shyness had magically vanished. Or perhaps it had been exorcised by a far stronger and more ancient magic.

"Molly Valentine," she mused. "Ugh!"

"Hey!" he objected.

"No, I just hate the *Molly* part. I love *Valentine*. Melissa Valentine? That's better. Nobody ever called me Melissa. Molly is way easier to shout."

"Put your pants on, Melissa. Or we'll be here all night," he said, looking out at the setting sun.

"That wouldn't be so bad. I wonder if the patrolman watching the place got an eyeful."

Dinner passed self-consciously, but Valentine found he could talk to her parents without feeling too uncomfortable. Her parents seemed to have other things on their minds. All Valentine could do was look at Molly's red, raw lips. *How could they not notice that?*

Gonzalez noticed something else in the basement as they got ready for bed.

"Hey, Val, what happened today?" he asked.

"Split a lot of wood."

Gonzalez snorted. "You stuck your wedge into something."

Valentine turned around. "What's that supposed to mean?"

"Well, your fly's been unbuttoned all night, and your back looks like two alley cats went about fifteen rounds on it. Unless you've been rolling in barbed wire, I'd say someone was moaning in your ear."

"Just go to sleep, funnyman. I was just doing some chores for the family, really. Molly had something she needed fixed, so I took care of it for her."

Gonzalez shook his head and turned over, carefully positioning his injured arm. "You officers get all the good jobs," he observed.

*   *   *

Valentine awoke in the middle of the night to a light tread on the stair. In the dim light shining down from the kitchen, he saw Molly cautiously entering the basement.

"David?" she whispered

"Over here," Valentine breathed back.

"No, over here," Gonzalez answered.

"Shut up, you," Valentine said, throwing his pillow at the scout.

"I wanted to talk to you. Sorry, Gonzo," she said.

Gonzalez swung his feet to the floor with a groan and pulled on his pants with his good arm. "I just remembered how long it's been since I've watched a sunrise. Don't make too much noise 'talking,' you two."

"Thanks, Victor. I mean it," Valentine said.

"You owe me one. See you at breakfast."

He moved soundlessly up the stairs.

Molly scuttled into Valentine's arms. He kissed her, grateful for her surprise.

"Did you want to talk?" he asked.

"Sort of," she said. "But not anymore. Let's go into the secret room. It's dark, and we can make a little bit of noise. But just a little."

Valentine opened the panel in the wall, and they nipped into the deep shadows, holding hands.

"Hey, you used one of those soaps," Valentine whispered, smelling her clean skin.

"Yes, this one's—"

"Roses," Valentine said, caressing her hair. "Beautiful."

She shut the door, and they were in blackness so total there was nothing but touch, and the faint smell of roses.

They kissed and kissing, lay down together. They melded in the darkness, learning new ways to please each other, delight each other, and, finally, love each other.

They said good-byes in a steady, spirit-sapping drizzle. As Flanagan and his ubiquitous shadow waited out of the rain in the patrol car, family, friends, and lovers shared a few parting hugs. Valentine, Molly, and her parents all wore the same air of false cheerfulness that appears at a funeral, after a septuagenarian drops dead in perfect health. "Never knew what hit him," one relative will say to another. "Yes, I'd love to go that way. No pain, no suffering, no illness. Lucky man," the other will agree, jointly looking for the tiny patch of sunshine among the dreary clouds.

The same forced tone was present in Mr. Carlson's voice as he said good-bye to his daughter. Molly wore her oldest cow-mucking work clothes, clean but nevertheless permanently stained. "Country girl he wants, country girl he gets," she had said to her mother after turning down the suggestion that she wear her prettiest dress, a blue-checkered barn-dancer that matched her eyes, to cheer herself up. "No, give that to Mary. Something to remember me by," she said, leaving the room before her mother could ask what she meant.

"Take care of that arm, Victor," Molly said, shaking his left hand. "My turn to see the big city, Frat. At least Madison isn't Chicago, thank God. Mary, there's more to horses than riding and brushing them. I'm putting you in charge of the stables while I'm gone, and you'd better keep it clean."

Her words to Valentine, in hindsight, also hinted at her dark mood under the steel-gray clouds. "David, you're going tonight, right? When it gets dark?"

"That's the plan. I'm still working on that pack for my horse. We'll be miles away by morning."

She smiled up at him, satisfied. They wandered to the side of the house, where they could kiss without watchful eyes on them. "I'll think of you fighting Reapers, David. You know, now that I've thought of it, maybe your Masada solution is the better one. Take a few of them with you."

"Molly, don't get so grim. You'll look back on this in a couple of years and laugh. Or maybe throw up. But it's not forever. It's really kind of pathetic of him if you think about it. Sending your butt-kissing uncle out into the woods to bring him a dinner date at gunpoint."

"That's the first thing I'll tell him," Molly said, beaming at the thought.

"Come back and work the farm. And just because my plan won't work right now doesn't mean it won't three years from now. Some night a team of Wolves will show up at your back door. We'll get your whole family out."

"If my dad will go. He's pretty committed to smuggling people out of here."

"Well, I owe your family a very big favor. You're going to collect on it. I'll come for you someday in the fall, if I can."

She looked into his eyes. "I think three years from now, you'll have more important things to worry about. Be careful with promises. You know that saying, 'Tomorrow is promised to no one,' right? That's like the law of the Kurian lands."

"You've got five years promised to you and your family."

"We'll see, David. That bond might be as worthless as the ring he tossed into the audience. Just go tonight, okay? But can you tell me one thing, David? Was I your first time . . . you know . . . lovemaking?"

Valentine owed her the truth. "Yes. I hope you liked it. I've never been very . . . lucky with women."

"Good. You'll remember me, then."

"I'll remember you as the Wisconsin beauty who was really good at pointing out the obvious," he said, giving her nose a gentle tweak.

They embraced, kissed, and touched each other's faces as if trying to record memories with their fingertips.

"Believe it or not, I'll come for you. It's a promise, Molly." He read hurt disbelief in her eyes. "No, not a promise: a vow." Now only the hurt remained.

"Don't," she said, unable to look at him. "A lot can happen in three years."

"A lot can happen in three days. Like falling in love, Melissa."

"David, stop. You're just making this hard, making it painful. This is an end. I don't want you to talk like it's a beginning."

He kissed her, trying to win a concession through sheer sensual power.

"No," she said, lowering her eyes from his. "I can't. Not when I have to . . . go like this."

She turned and fled.

At dinner that night, Valentine and Gonzalez decided to leave with the first light of dawn. A morning departure, with a quick good-bye to the Breitlings, would seem less suspicious than a midnight escape.

After a final farewell talk with the Carlsons, Gonzalez and Valentine lay in the basement, their guns and packs stored for the last night in the secret room. Gonzalez hid his anxiety about his injured arm well, but Valentine knew the worry dragged at his scout. Gonzalez worked best when the only thing worrying him was what might be around the next bend or over the next hill, so he talked frankly about how they would accommodate his injury on the trip home. The rest of the household had long since retired, and they burned only a foul-smelling tallow dip for light.

"You'll ride," Valentine said after rolling his maps back up into their tube. "I wish we could hang around longer, but it might be months before your arm is totally healed."

"You think it will get better?"

"Of course, Gonzo. Nerve tissue just takes forever to heal."

Gonzalez moved two painful fingers. "I don't know about that. Might never grow back."

"Well, you can move your hand a little. I think that's a good sign. In fact . . . Hey, an engine."

Both Wolves used their hard ears. It sounded like a truck engine. Perhaps one of the semi drivers was passing through with another foundling. But it stopped in the road, idling with thick coughs of exhaust.

Valentine and Gonzlalez exchanged looks. Without another word, they got up and moved to the secret door. They carried the tallow lamp behind the false wall with them and shut the panel behind. They ignored their packs, grabbing knives and guns. A crash sounded from above through the air vent, the house-shaking sound of a door being kicked in.

A whisper came from the other side of the secret door.

"Guys, are you in there?" Frat whispered.

Shouts from upstairs, a man's voice issuing orders to search the house.

"Yes," Valentine answered softly.

"Two men in a big van and two more in a patrol car. They're all armed and coming in. Gotta go," Frat said. Valentine finished tying his parang sheath on his leg and picked up his rifle.

"Hey, kid," an unknown voice barked. "Get outta that bed and get up here."

"I'm coming," Frat answered, voice cracking from strain. "Don't point that shotgun at me, okay?"

Gonzalez blew out the tallow dip in case the smell was wafting up to the living room.

They heard Mr. Carlson's voice, angry and scared, as he descended the stairs from the second story into the living room. "What in the heck is all this, Toland?"

"Orders. You're wanted for questioning."

"Orders? We'll see what Major Flanagan has to say about that!"

"He gave the orders, pard," the harsh voice answered. "Think your days of being under his wing are over. Your little girl stuck a steak knife into Mr. Brass Ring's neck—"

"Oh, my God!" Mrs. Carlson gasped.

"—a couple of hours ago," Toland continued. "Your brother is fucked, and he knows it, and he thinks the only way out of the jam is to arrest everyone here."

"Can I at least tell my hired help to take care of things while I'm gone?"

"The Breitlings? We're supposed to arrest them, too. Where's those two from up north, the guy who was seeing your daughter? The major wants him brought personal to his office."

"They left after dinner," Frat volunteered. "David was pissed about the whole thing with Molly."

"Shuddup, Sambo. If I want your opinion, I'll slap it out of you. Carlson, is he right?"

"Yes, you searched the house, didn't you?" Carlson said, voice still tremulous.

"Which way did they go, and when?"

"After dinner. They didn't even eat with us. I think they went north, but I dunno. I've had other things on my mind today than watching them leave. You should leave us alone and go after them; they probably put her up to it."

A rattling came from above. "I got them leg irons, Sarge. Should we link 'em up now?"

"Yeah. Pillow, go out to the car and radio that we got the Carlsons in custody. Also put out a general call to pick up two men on horseback. One's got a bum hand. You other two get busy with those shackles."

Valentine touched Gonzalez on the shoulder in the darkness, and they felt for the door. They cut across the shadowed basement, listening to the rattle of chains as the patrollers fixed the family into the leg irons. Valentine led the way up the basement steps, keeping to the edges to lessen the sound of boards creaking. They padded through the kitchen barefoot, Valentine with his repeater to his shoulder and Gonzalez with his held against his hip. Valentine paused for just a second to listen at the corner between the kitchen and the front living room, attempting to place the occupants by sound. All he could hear was a frightened crying from young Mary Carlson and the sounds of shackles being clicked closed and chains passed through steel eyes. He gestured to Gonzalez, who moved to the kitchen door of the house.

With a quick sidestep Valentine rounded the corner, gun tight to his shoulder, a shotgun-wielding man already in his sights. "Nobody move," he said, in a low tone. "You with the shotgun, put it on the floor, holding it by the barrel. You two with the chains, facedown on the floor!"

As he spoke, Gonzalez opened the back door, holding the rifle in his armpit, and disappeared into the darkness.

The patrollers, conditioned by years of practice in using their guns to bully unarmed farmers and townspeople, complied with alacrity. The Carlsons, dressed in their bedclothes, kicked the weapons away from the uniformed Quislings.

"Okay, you with the stripes, facedown, too. Good. Spread eagle, gentlemen. I've got eight shots in this repeater; the man who moves gets the first one. Frat, get the guns away from them, before they get any ideas."

Frat began collecting pistols and shotguns. "This'll cut it, Carlson," Sergeant Toland said, speaking into the floor. "Before, you were just wanted for questioning. This means you're all dead within a day or two. Not an easy death, either, if the Reapers—"

A pistol thrust into the sergeant's mouth cut off the imprecations. "Shut up, Sarge. When I want any of your lip, I'll blow it off," Frat said, cocking the revolver.

"Mr. and Mrs. Carlson, start putting the shackles on them, hands and feet, please," Valentine said.

The screen door swung open, and the fourth patroller entered, his fingers laced behind his head and the muzzle of Gonzalez's gun pressing him behind the ear.

"Pillow here just reported the situation as being under control," Gonzalez said. "Is it, sir?"

"Seems to be. Where are the Breitlings?"

"They hadn't gotten around to them, yet," Mr. Carlson said. "They're probably still asleep."

"Mrs. Carlson, after you've finished, do you think you could go get them?" Valentine asked.

"Could I get some more clothes on first?"

"Of course." The patrollers were now securely shackled and handcuffed. *They're scared,* Valentine thought, looking at the sweat stains on the blue uniforms. He was also pretty sure that the one named Pillow had pissed himself. *Scared people confuse easily.*

"Boy, that major is fucking things up, Carlson," Valentine said, winking at his benefactor. "Hey, Sarge. Do you know what you've stumbled into?"

"You're a corpse, boy. You're a corpse that happens to be walking and talking for a few more hours."

"Don't think so, Sarge. Look at this," he said, thrusting his rifle butt under Toland's nose. "You've just busted in on a Twisted Cross double-secret blind operation."

"What the fuck is the Twisted Cross? 'Double secret' bullshit!" Sergeant Toland said, unimpressed.

"You wouldn't know, would you? We wanted Touchet dead, but we couldn't get at him in Illinois, because he's bought off so many of the people around him. But why am I telling you this? He was trying to spy out the operation at Blue Mounds."

"Bullshit," the sergeant responded. "Bangin' the Carlson girl ain't going to accomplish that, nor giving speeches, neither."

"Sarge, you don't have to believe me. But let me give you two facts. One is that you're still alive, and the other is that all this is way over your head. Something's gone wrong with our operation, or you wouldn't have gotten those orders to bring these folks in. I suggest that in the future you have Madison confirm everything before doing what Major Flanagan says. Gonzalez?"

"Yes, sir," his scout replied.

"We're switching to plan Red Charlie."

"Er . . . you're in charge, sir," Gonzalez said. Valentine hoped the patrollers would interpret Gonzalez's confusion for reluctance.

"Let's go outside and discuss it. Mr. Carlson, Frat, keep an eye on these four."

In the cool night air, Valentine patted Gonzalez on the back. "Good job with Pillow, Gonzo. You still haven't lost your touch, injury or no."

"Sir, what's our next move? Are we going to leave now?"

Valentine nodded and walked down the road toward the vehicles. A dirt-covered patrol car and a delivery-van-type truck stood in the blackness. The clouds had still not dispersed.

"Gonzo, I'm going to have to give you a lot of responsibility. Maybe it will take your mind off the pain in your arm. I want to get the Carlsons and the Breitlings out of Wisconsin. All the way to the Ozark Free Territory."

"We can do it."

"Maybe we could. But, Gonzo, it's not going to be a *we*. It's going to be a *you*. I'm going after Molly."

Gonzo's eyes bulged with surprise. "My friend," he said finally. "She's probably dead already."

"If she is, she's going to have some company. That asshole of an uncle, for one."

"What is more important, getting you and me and these people back safely, telling about what we saw behind all those skulls, or killing one Quisling? I hate to tell you your duty, but—"

"Fuck my duty," Valentine said. Just the words themselves could subject him to a court-martial and firing squad, but he might as well be hanged for a sheep as a lamb. "I've had too many people I care about die. Not this one, not this girl."

"I've already forgotten what you just said, sir. But you will still have to explain this if you get back. What am I supposed to do with these civilians? The prisoners? I'd have a tough time making it back to the Ozarks, just me and my horse, let alone all these people."

"Here's the plan . . . ," Valentine said. Gonzalez listened as his lieutenant gave his final orders.

An hour later, everything was ready. The patrollers were locked in the feed shed, still shackled. The feed shed had the best lock and was the only all–cinder block construction on the farm. The delivery van waited with its ramp brought up and rear liftgate closed; horses were saddled and tied to the rear bumper. Inside the spacious interior, empty except for numerous eyebolts for fixing prisoners in position, were the Breitlings, Mrs. Carlson, and Mary Carlson, clutching a few blankets and some travel clothing, along with the family dog. Mr. Carlson was at the wheel, and Gonzalez rode shotgun. Both were dressed in blue patroller uniforms taken from the Quisling captives.

Valentine and Frat stood outside the passenger door. Valentine wore the best of the uniforms and carried the identity papers of the patroller who most resembled him, the pants-wetting Pillow.

"We meet south of the bridge outside Benton, okay, Frat?" Gonzalez asked, rolling Valentine's map back up and returning it to the tube. Frat nodded.

"Mr. Carlson, if I can't get your daughter, I'm going to leave one hell of a trail of dead Quislings," Valentine said. "They'll come after me with everything they've got. Should make it a little easier for you."

"No one's asking you to do this, son," Mr. Carlson said from the driver's seat. "Molly's probably already dead. Maybe she used the knife on herself after killing Touchet." Carlson's lips trembled as he spoke.

"I don't think she'd give up that easy, Alan. If she's alive, I'm going to get her back. I'm coming back with your daughter, or not at all." He turned to Gonzalez and shook his friend's good hand. "Gonzo, I know you can do this," Valentine said quietly. "You've got the brains and the skills. Just keep them moving. Eat the horses one by one if it helps. When you get back, tell them everything you remember, even if it doesn't seem important. They've also got to get a Cat or two up here to find out what's going on at Blue Mounds. One other thing: Get Frat into the Hunters, or at least have him posted as an Aspirant. He'll make a better Wolf than either of us, at least someday. Take every buckchit I've got and draw it to get the Carlsons started. I've got some friends in a little place called Weening."

Valentine racked his mind, searching for another suggestion to increase Gonzalez's chances. There was always one more order to give, one more contingency to consider.

"I will do it, all of it, sir. *Vaya con Dios, jefe.* And I'll be praying for you, sir. Every day."

"Back to praying, Gonzalez? I thought your mother was in charge of that."

"She's in charge of my soul. I'll take care of yours."

"You're going to have plenty to take care of in the next couple of weeks without my soul thrown in. But thank you anyway; I'm honored."

Carlson started up the truck, and Valentine hopped to the ground. Gonzalez gave a little salute from his perch. "Good luck, Lieutenant."

"Send my respects to the Zulus, Gonzo!"

The truck rolled off into the darkened west. Hours to go before daylight.

"Okay, Frat. You and me now. I wish I had learned how to drive better."

"It's okay, Lieutenant," Frat said, moving around to the driver's side. "I know the way, so it's just as well."

"You can call me David, bud. Drive slow and careful. Keep the headlights off."

"I know, I know. You told me. Where to?"

Valentine checked the contents of his pack and a spare feedbag, which held extra restraints and a few packets from the Carlsons' kitchen. "Your uncle's house. You can tell me everything you remember about it on the way."

Frat covered the twenty miles in just over an hour, switching to tractor trails and cattle paths as he drew close to Monroe. The roads were empty, and the night seemed to be waiting for the curtain to go up on the last act of the play. The radio squawked occasionally, reporting from the patrols looking for two men on horseback. Valentine mentally prepared himself for a tragic ending to the drama. As Frat drove, leaning far forward as if the extra foot and a half of viewing distance made a difference, Valentine applied a hacksaw to the double-barreled shotgun, taking off the barrels from the edge of the wooden grip onward. He then filled the pockets on its leather sling-bandolier with buckshot shells. A second pump-action shotgun lay on the wooden backseat of the car.

"Okay, we're in the fields behind his house. It's right beyond that line of trees there," Frat informed him. "We've stayed over here a few times, back when he had a wife."

"Whatever happened to her?" Valentine asked.

"Don't know. Nobody does. One day she was just gone, and we learned not to ask."

"So he's not much for answering questions, then?" Valentine stepped out of the car and took the pump-action shotgun, pocketing shells into his stolen uniform. "I'll try to change that. Keep the scattergun handy, Frat. Don't be afraid to use it, and pull out if something comes after you. Keep alert."

"I will, sir. You be careful."

Valentine walked silently up to the line of trees, listening and smelling for the guard dogs. Their scent seemed to be everywhere across the lawn. Perhaps they were around front.

The extravagant house had bright security lights mounted high up just under the roof, angled out to bathe the lawn in white light. Their brilliance threw the surrounding terrain into harsh, black-and-white relief, blazing white wherever the lights touched and utter black in the shadows. Valentine whistled softly.

One of the great black rottweilers appeared from around the garage corner. Valentine reached into his feed bag and placed a few strips of meat on the flat of his parang. He whistled again. The dog growled and took a few steps closer. Valentine stayed very still, offering the meat from the brush at the edge of the woods.

"Good dog, good dog," Valentine said soothingly. The dog licked its chops and padded forward. Valentine lowered the blade to the grass, and the dog began eating. Flanagan obviously used the dogs only for show; a real guard dog would be trained not to take food from anyone but its keeper. Having made friends, Valentine stood for a moment patting the hopeful-looking dog.

Valentine watched the sleeping house for a few moments then jogged across the lawn to the back door. The rottweiler trotted along happily. The second hound, curled up on the mat at the door fast asleep, startled at their approach. Seeing the other dog, it came forward to greet the late-night visitor. Valentine issued more tidbits to the dogs and began feeling along the top of the windowsill to the left of the door for the key Frat said was hidden there. He found it, placed on a small nail hammered into the top of the windowsill.

The key fit the dead bolt on the back door, but Valentine was able to open the door only an inch or two. A heavy chain across the inside of the door barred further progress. He reached into his bag of tricks for the rusty crowbar from the patrol car's trunk, fixed it to the chain near its mounting on the doorjamb, and pulled. The chain parted with a loud *ting*.

Valentine entered the kitchen behind the business end of the shotgun. The tabletop was a mess of dirty dishes and paperwork. The main light over the table was still on, bathing the littered octagonal surface in a puddle of yellow. A heavy electric typewriter sat before a chair, a cold mug of coffee next to it, nestled like a small brown pond in a forest of empty beer bottles. A raspy snoring echoed from the living room.

He looked at the typed report on the table, flipping to the second page. Apparently it was a statement by the one patroller standing sentry outside Touchet's VIP suite door at the New Universal Church building. A paragraph caught Valentine's eye.

When the cook entered with Mr. Touchet's nightcap of coffee, I heard him scream. I drew my gun and entered the bedroom. Mr. Touchet was facedown on the bed, nude except for a pair of socks. The young woman was trying to force up the window of the bedroom, not knowing that it was nailed shut. As I entered, she smashed it with an ashtray but I was able to restrain her.

After she was handcuffed and held down by the cook, I examined Mr. Touchet for a pulse. He was dead. He had a steak knife handle sticking out of the back of his head right were the neck meets the skull. His back was coated with some kind of oil and he lay on a towel. There was very little blood on the towel. Mr. Touchet's brass ring had been removed from his finger and was placed around the handle of the knife. The young woman was screaming obscenities at us, so I hit her. She had not been injured by Mr. Touchet; the bruise on her face was from me.

Valentine walked to the living room and looked in. Virgil Ames lay stretched out on a leather sofa, sunglasses finally off, pistol belt looped around his arm. The air around him smelled of beer breath and stale flatulence. Beyond, in the glass turret-room, he could make out Maj. Michael Flanagan. The major slept in his chair, phone in his lap, widespread feet propped up on his desk.

The prowling Wolf shifted the shotgun to his left hand and took up the parang. *No making friends with this dog,* he thought, putting the wedge-shaped point just above Virgil's Adam's apple. At the swift inward thrust, the late Virgil Ames opened his eyes. Valentine wiped his knife on the rich leather sofa and moved toward the office.

Major Flanagan woke when the blued steel of the shotgun barrel poked him between the eyes. As Flanagan sputtered into surprised wakefulness, Valentine changed the angle of the shotgun barrel, pointing it between Flanagan's outstretched legs.

"You wanted to see me, Major?" he asked.

"What the—? . . . Virgil!" Flanagan shouted.

"Dead, sir," Valentine reported. "Better speak up, or you'll be joining him in five seconds. Tell me, is Molly Carlson still alive?"

"Virgil!" Flanagan cried.

Valentine stuck the shotgun toward Flanagan's screaming mouth. "Major, your screaming is not doing you any good, and it's giving me a headache, so cut it out. Or I might cut your tongue out and have you write down your answers."

"Fuck you, Saint Croix. We don't just have Molly, we've got all the Carlsons, as of eleven this evening. If you back out of here and never let me see your face again, they might live. You might even live."

The powerful, spearlike thrust of the shotgun shattered two incisors and left a worm-tail of lip dangling as it hung from a thin strip of bleeding skin. The major's hands flew to his wounded mouth, and Valentine clipped him on the side of the head with the shotgun butt. The major fell over, knocked senseless. Valentine busied himself with handcuffs and rope.

The house was dark when Major Flanagan came to. Valentine splashed cold coffee into his face. Groans rose from the Quisling just before he vomited all over himself. The paroxysm showed how securely he was tied into his office chair.

Handcuffs fixed his wrists against the arms of the chair, and heavy lengths of rope cocooned his chest and shoulders into the back. His legs were tucked under the chair and secured by ankle shackles with a short length of chain winding behind the central column that attached the chair itself to the little circle of wheels below.

No hint of morning could be seen through the windows of the office. Valentine stood next to the desk, a breathing shadow.

A metallic *ping* sounded, and Valentine picked up the silver cigar lighter, waving the lit end hypnotically in front of Flanagan's face. Its dim red glow reflected off piggish, angry eyes. "Okay, Uncle Mike, do you want to talk to me, or do I have to use this thing?"

"Talk about what?"

"Where Molly is."

"She's in the Order building in Monroe."

Valentine grabbed his pinkie and thrust the cigar lighter over it. An audible *hiss* was instantly drowned out by the major's scream. Valentine pulled away the lighter and stuck it back into its electric socket, pushing it down to turn it back on.

"Wrong answer. I read some of the papers in the kitchen. According to your report, you put her in a car for Chicago."

Ping.

"Why Chicago, Major?"

"We called the Illinois Eleven as soon as it happened. That's what they told us to do, send her to Chicago."

"Where in Chicago?" Valentine asked, extracting the lighter.

"How should I know? The Illinois Eleven don't like being questioned any more than the Madison Kurians," Flanagan said, watching the lighter wave back and forth in the darkness. "No! God, Saint Croix, I don't know."

This last was addressed to the approach of the lighter to his left hand. Valentine forced Flanagan's fist open and inserted his index finger into the cigar lighter. The smell of burnt flesh wafted up into his nostrils as he ground the glowing socket home. Flanagan screamed again, and Valentine withdrew the lighter. He pressed it back into the socket, reheating it.

"The pain will stop as soon as you tell me where she is in Chicago. You want me to stick your dick in this next?"

The tip of Flanagan's forefinger was a blackened lump of flesh and blisters. Even the fingernail was burned back.

Ping.

"I think they're putting her in the Zoo," Flanagan gabbled, seeing Valentine's hand move to pick up the lighter. "I've been there, it's on the north side of Chicago, near the lake. Lots of boats tied up permanent."

"Why there? I thought they just put everyone in the Loop when they wanted to do away with them."

"They knew Touchet. They asked me if she was a real looker. I told them about her. I mean, if she weren't my niece, one of the patrollers would have raped her a long time ago. Saint Croix, you haven't been around much. I've risked my job—my life even—to help my sister and her family. Molly was never going to be hurt." Sweat coated Flanagan's face, wetting his bushy eyebrows and running down his neck in rivulets.

"So what's this Zoo?"

"It's in a place called Lincoln Park. I've got a little map of Chicago in my desk, bottom drawer. Even has phone numbers for cab companies. The Zoo is . . . a big brothel, that kind of thing. There are a lot of bars there; they do sports, too. Kind of a wild place, anything goes, like Old Vegas."

Valentine popped up the lighter and left it resting lightly in its socket. "Good enough, Flanagan. There's one more thing I want before I go. I need a travel warrant made out for one Private Pillow. Giving him a week's leave or whatever you call it to go to Chicago. And some money to spend."

Flanagan's massive eyebrows rose in surprise. "Madison paper's no good there. Our guys bring things to barter. Jewelry, beer, food, stuff like that. But what you're thinking is nuts. I'd like to see Molly alive as much as her parents, but it ain't going to happen. There're hundreds of soldiers from Illinois, Indiana—Michigan, even. I've heard of officers coming all the way from Iowa and Minnesota to go to the Zoo. Even if you can find her, you'll never get her out. The Black Hole's a one-way—"

"Black Hole?" Valentine asked.

"I dunno where she would go for sure. But the Black Hole is kind of a prison. Women don't last long there. They're used . . . treated badly. Some of the men like that kind of thing. Never went there myself, but you hear stories."

"Just tell me where to find the papers to fill out."

Flanagan gave detailed instructions, and soon Valentine had his travel warrant. The major applied his seal and signed it; Valentine had freed the man's uninjured right hand to do so. The major wiped his face with his good hand. "You're tough, Saint Croix. I had no idea."

So he thinks fawning is his ticket to safety. Interesting. Has it gotten him out of jams with the Kurians? Valentine thought. He put his new papers and the folded map in one of the front pockets of his shirt. He then walked over to the front of the desk. The shotgun leaned up against one of the carved wooden lions.

"Take my car. It's in the garage, and the keys are in my breast pocket here. I'll tell them you went north. I'll keep the Carlsons under lock and key for a few days, then release them. We'll shout questions at 'em for a few hours; don't worry, they'll be fine. Of course, Molly can't ever come back here, but I'm sure you can get her somewhere safe up in the woods if your plan works. Watch yourself in Chicago, though. Must be a hundred Reapers there, easy. But if . . ."

The major stopped in openmouthed amazement as Valentine brought up the shotgun, pointing it at his head. "No, Saint Croix. Be fair! I gave you everything . . ."

Valentine put the butt tightly to his shoulder and placed his finger on the trigger. "You once said that if it were up to you, you'd hand me over to the Reapers for not having a work card. Well, now that it's up to me, I'm going to follow a little rule we have in the Wolves. I call it Special Order Twelve, section Double Ought. Any high-rank Quislings bearing arms against their fellow men shall suffer death by firing squad."

"You said you wouldn't kill me!" Flanagan shrieked, holding out his hand, palm outward.

"I said the pain would stop," Valentine corrected, pulling the trigger. The dark room exploded in noise and a flash of blue-white light like an old-fashioned flashbulb. At the last instant, Flanagan flung his arm across his face, but the blast of buckshot tore through his arm, head, and the back of the chair. Bone, blood, brain, and wood from the chair splattered the brick wall behind the chair.

Valentine went through the house, filling a pillowcase with anything of value he could find: Virgil Ames's sunglasses and beaded pistol belt, Flanagan's cheroots and electric lighter, a solid silver cigarette box, gold jewelry belonging to the missing Mrs. Flanagan. The liquor cabinet contained two bottles of bonded whiskey. They joined the other contents of the pillowcase.

He went into the furnished basement and flicked on one of the electric lights. A pool table filled one end and a small workshop the other. Three rifles hung from an ornate gun-rack, set between two eight-point deer heads. Valentine's eyes lit on an old Remington Model 700. He shouldered it. Then he crossed to the workshop and found a tin of kerosene. He opened it and splashed it along the pool table, carpet, and wood paneling. He struck a match and tossed it into the puddled liquid on the pool table. Flames began to race across the green baize surface. Sure that the fire was well on its way, Valentine climbed back up the stairs.

Frat pulled the car out of the field and onto the little path leading back to the road. "Now what, Lieutenant?" he asked. Oddly enough, Frat had asked no questions about what had transpired in his uncle's house.

"Where can I catch the next train to Chicago? Not a station, though. I mean to jump on."

Frat considered the problem. "The line connecting Dubuque goes right through Monroe. A train goes along that every day. Takes you right into Chicago, or the meatpacking plant, that is. You'd be in the city by tonight. You'll know you're close when you go through this big stretch of burned-out houses. Reapers burned out a huge belt around the city. Great Suburban Fire, it was called. Happened before I was born. Then they did something to the soil so nothing but some weeds grow. Mile after mile of old street and rubble. Of course, I was pretty young when I saw it. But you'll never find Molly in the Loop. You could look for days. How you gonna get her out again?"

"They didn't put her in the Loop. She's in someplace called the Zoo."

Frat smacked his head. "Zot me! I shoulda thought of that! They would put someone who looks like her there. My momma used to tell my older sister, 'What you trying to do, get a job at the Zoo?' whenever she didn't like what Phila was wearing."

"What else can you tell me about Chicago?"

Frat turned the car onto a road heading south. "It's big, really big. But what you got going for you is that there's people from all over, so strangers don't get noticed. If you cause any trouble, they grab you and throw you in the Loop. They use the old United States money there, too, but it has to be authorized. The bills they've authorized have a stamp on them, kind of like the stamp on our work cards. I'm pretty sure some of your people who fight the Kurians are there, but I don't know how you would ever find them. And I'd hide that big curved knife of yours. Too many of the soldiers know about those."

They reached a bend in the road. Frat pulled the patrol car to the side.

"Frat, you've been a great help. You know what to do now, right?"

"Drive fast with all the lights on, like I'm hurrying somewhere," Frat recited. "Put the car in a ravine and then walk to that bridge. Go cross-country and keep out of sight. I think I can manage."

"I'm sure you can."

"All you have to do now is go south, and you'll hit the railroad tracks. They curve where they run along the Sugar River, and I bet they'll slow down. Lots of guys bum rides. As long as you got identity papers, you're okay getting into Chicago. Just take my advice and don't cause any trouble until you're sure you can get away with it. Getting out again isn't so easy. They check the trains heading out for runners."

Valentine offered his hand, and Frat shook it. "Listen to Gonzo on the way back, pup. You can learn a lot from him."

"Yeah, he's cool. He thinks a lot of you, by the way. Says the Wolves in Zulu Company call you the Ghost."

"The what?"

"The Ghost. On account of you walk so smooth and quiet, like you're floating. And there's another reason: Mr. Gonzalez says you can tell when there are vampires around. He says it's spooky, but kinda comforting."

"The Ghost, huh? Well, have Gonzo tell them to keep their rifles clean and oiled, or I'll come back and haunt them. Good-bye, Frat."

"Good-bye, Lieutenant Valentine. Don't worry, I'll get everyone out, if Mr. Gonzalez just points the direction. You ain't the only one good at smellin' out Skulls."

While Valentine waited for the train in the morning shade beneath a willow, he ate from a bag of crackers and a brick of cheese he had taken from Flanagan's kitchen. He had already improvised a shoulder strap for his pillowcase of loot and admired the manufacturing on the stolen Remington rifle; he figured it would bring enough money for a bribe or two, or serve as one itself. He studied his map of Chicago, memorizing as many of the street names as he could. *It must be quite a city, he thought. Over a hundred Reapers. Great place to visit, but I wouldn't want to die there.*

Twelve

Chicago, October of the forty-third year of the Kurian Order: The Second City is still a town on the take. A resident twentieth-century Pulitzer Prize-winning journalist once suggested that the motto for the city should be "Where's Mine?" Nowhere is the art of bribery, corruption, and widespread beak-wetting more common than in the Kurian-controlled, Quisling-run City of Big Shoulders. No one is even sure exactly how many Kurian Lords run the city, as the Kurians divide it not by geography but by business and property ownership. A Kurian Lord might control a steelworks in Gary, an automobile-parts plant on the West Side, several apartment buildings on the Gold Coast, and a few antiquated airplanes that fly out of O'Hare. His Reaper avatars will travel among holdings, going into the Loop for regular feedings.

To prevent the Reapers from taking too much of an area's vital labor force, the Loop system was developed after twenty years of fractious and chaotic rule. The Kurians had little use for the high-rise business centers of the downtown, and after emptying the assorted museums and stores of anything they fancied, they created the walled enclave as a dumping ground for undesirables. Here the Reapers could feed without worrying about taking a vital technician or mechanic and starting a series of inter-Kurian vendettas that might escalate into a full-scale feud.

The workers of Chicago enjoy a security that few other communities under the Kurians know. But their existence depends on paying their way in old federal greenbacks. The destitute receive a quick trip into the Loop. But the elite Quislings who run the city for the Kurians amass sizable fortunes in a variety of barely legitimate ways.

One might wonder what the point of wealth is with the Kurians in

control, but the Kurians have become infected with the viruslike cor-
ruption that seems to thrive in Chicago and are often bought off by
their ostensible slaves. The top Quislings use their money to bribe the
Kurians not with cash, but with vital auras, the one thing the vampiric
Kurians prize above all else. The Quislings buy captives from a soul-
less body of men and women called the Headhunters, who in turn buy
them from wandering bounty hunters who lurk on the fringes of the
Kurian territory, grabbing everyone they can. These latter-day fur
trappers pick up strays in a circle moving clockwise down from north-
ern Michigan, across southern Indiana and Illinois, and then up the
eastern shores of the Mississippi to the northern woods of Wisconsin.

When a wealthy Quisling has turned over enough vital aura to the
Kurians, a brass ring is awarded. Only in Chicago is this practice of
"buying" brass rings allowed. With the security of cash and a brass
ring, these robber-baron Quislings then retire to Ringland Parks, a
twenty-mile stretch of stately homes along the shore of Lake Michigan
just to the north of Chicago, the only large area of suburbs to survive
the flames that desolated greater Chicagoland. But as brass rings can-
not be passed down to sons and daughters, their progeny are left with
the tiresome task of doing it all over again.

Chicago has become what Vegas was to the pre-Kurian world:
an anything-goes city where anything, including human life, can be
bought or sold if the price is right.

The Chicago skyline looked to Valentine like the bones of a titanic
animal carcass. His position atop the freight train gave him an unobstructed view as the train bore southeast, straight as an arrow in flight,
toward the city. He would have felt naked and defenseless riding the
rocking platform, clattering across the uneven points on the rail line,
but for the companions scattered across the last few boxcars. Now and
then other hitchers made the run-and-vault onto the line of cars.

He first spotted the skyline in the blackened ring of former subur-
bia that encircled the city like a burned-out belt. It reminded him of a
picture of the town center of Hiroshima after the atomic bomb: nothing
but rubble and cracked pavement. He wondered what the Kurians had
done to the ground to poison the plant life; just dry-looking brown
weeds and the occasional withered sapling grew from the bare patches
of soil. He wondered why the Kurians wanted to create this vista of
desolation. He asked an Illinoisan, a thirtyish man who had hopped on
as the train left the hills north of Rockford.

"The Chicago Blight?" the man said, looking at the expanse as if
seeing it for the first time. "You got me. My brother is in the Iguard,

and he says it's a no-man's-land between the Chicago Kurians and the Illinois Eleven. They depend on each other, but they had a big fight back when I was just five or six. Anyway, the Blight makes them refrain from wandering out of their territory to feed. Then I got a sister-in-law in Chicago, and she says it's to make getting out of Chicago harder. Guess burning everything was easier than building a wall that would have to run for fifty or sixty miles. But I've still heard of a few people managing to run across it in daylight. If they get lucky and dodge the Security Service and make it out by nightfall, I've heard of people escaping Chicago just using their legs. A lot of times they run right back, though; it's more dangerous downstate. I've been trying to get a good-paying job in Chicago for years, but I don't have the toke for a good position."

"You don't have the *toke?* What's that?" Valentine asked.

"You must be on your first trip to Chicago, blue boy. A toke is like a tip, but it's more of a bribe. Money's the best, but it's got to be their authorized stuff. You try to palm off a bill you picked up in Peoria, and you're asking to get your face smashed in. Cigarettes are good tokes, too. And if you are doing anything major, like getting a cab ride or checking in to a hotel, you toke twice, once when you arrange it and again when you're done. If the first one is too small, they might blow you off and look for someone else. If the second is too small, they'll just swear at you, but you'd better not expect any more favors. I've seen fistfights over too small a toke at the end of a cab ride, so be careful. But getting back to my point: For me to get a decent factory job, I'd have to toke the doorman, the union boss, and the manager. Maybe a couple of managers. And those would be big tokes, in the thousands. Hard to scrape up that kind of money on the farm."

Valentine reached into his bag and extracted one of the major's cheroots. "Thanks for the tip," he said, handing it to his fellow traveler.

"Hey, you catch on fast. Listen, if you want, you can come with me when we get off. I know a good route out of the railroad yard. That's a fine rifle, and some Chicago Security Service officer is gonna quote regulations and take it off you if you go through channels. Unless you can cough up about a hundred bucks worth of toke, that is."

"You're a pal. My name's Pillow," Valentine said, using the name on his identity papers.

"Norbu Oshima. Most of the guys call me Norby. Pleased to meet you, Pillow."

"My friends call me Dave. It's my middle name."

They made small talk as the city grew steadily larger. At last the train pulled into a bustling rail yard spread out over several square miles and dominated by a thick concrete tower. The train eventually switched to a siding near a series of livestock pens. Produce trucks and horse-drawn carts waited nearby, ready to accept the contents of the boxcars as the shipping clerks sorted them.

"C'mon," Oshima said as they jumped off. "Through the cattle crushes. There's a storm drain to the Halsted Bridge."

Other figures were hopping off the train and scattering, pursued by a few police in navy blue uniforms. A corpulent CSS cop jumped out after them from between two cars, but Valentine and his guide vaulted over a series of fences as they ran across the pens, and their pursuer gave up after mounting the first two bars, settling for yelling a few obscenities after them.

"Fuckin' yokels," the distant voice protested. "Where's my toke, you bastards!"

They rolled under a chain-link fence and slid into the concrete drainpipe, dragging their bags after them. "Welcome to Chicago," Oshima said, panting and slapping dirt from his clothes.

"Looks like he lets his uniform do his fighting for him," Valentine observed.

"Yes, those CSS guys got it made. Everybody tokes them. He's had one too many free burgers and beers at the Steak and Bun. Speaking of which, I'm starved. After I drop my stuff off at my sister's, you wanna eat?"

"Thanks, but I have to find someone. You know where I can find a bunch of bars in a row called the Clubs Flush? On Rush Street, I think."

Norby whistled appreciatively. "You must have some good barter in that sack. Those are some nice places. Never been in 'em myself. They take up a whole block. Rush is easy to find; it runs at an angle to the rest of the streets. Watch yourself around the vacant lots. I'll get you to Division Street and point you in the right direction."

"Thanks," Valentine said, and meant it. He handed Oshima two more cheroots.

"Don't worry, David. You'll do fine. As long as those cigars hold out, anyway."

Valentine walked down the street, consulting his tourist map. Even in the afternoon, there were more people on the street than Valentine was used to seeing in the most populated parts of the Free Territory. Despite the people, he felt strangely alone. The city smelled noxious; a mixture of tar and garbage assaulted his nostrils. Sewage odors wafted up from the storm drains, and trash overflowed from Dumpsters in the alleys. Public sanitation was not a priority with the Kur.

"Hey, blue boy, want a ride?" a man in a straw hat called from the front of a carriage. A horse stood patiently in harness. "Take you to the Zoo. I got a friend at one of the entrances, let you in half-price. Your buddies in Wisconsin won't believe their ears when you get back."

"Maybe later," Valentine said.

Cats seemed to be everywhere, especially in the rubble of the empty blocks. Hungry-looking stray dogs prowled the alleys, sniffing the gutters.

Valentine spotted the Clubs Flush. Had it been night, he would have seen it from farther off; electric lights on the building illuminated a ten-foot mural of a hand holding four kings and a joker. In sight of his goal, Valentine realized how tired he was. His last night in bed had been interrupted by Molly's visit, and he had been active ever since. He unbuttoned his shirt and smelled his chest. Molly's rosebud-soap scent still clung to his skin. The memories gave him new strength, even as he considered the hopeless task ahead of him. How could he have imagined a city this size?

He reached the bars, but there seemed to be no way to get inside. Nor could he see through the dark-tinted glass windows to get a hint of what waited within. He passed a woman wearing a dirty smock, standing out of the wind and smoking a cigarette.

"Entrance is around the side," she informed him, pointing her thumb over her shoulder. She took a long pull on a cigarette. "I work there, three-to-eleven shift. Good luck getting past Wideload. You looking for a job?"

"No, just a little fun. Thanks."

"Hey," she said conspiratorially, removing a brown-paper-wrapped package from under her smock. "Check it out. Sixteen-ounce porterhouse, right out of the Diamonds' cooler. Twelve bucks, what do you say?"

"No, I'm fine for food."

"Eight bucks. Can't do better. You can sell it for at least twenty on Michigan Avenue."

Valentine turned the corner and found the entrance. It was a decorated alley, with a brick arch above, wide enough to allow a wagon inside. Red and black painted wooden double doors with the Clubs' hours stenciled on showed that it must still be before six, as they were closed and locked. A smaller door was fitted into right side of the gate, and Valentine knocked.

A face that would not encourage casual conversation scowled out from a crack in the door. "What?" it said in a deep, monotone bass.

"You Wideload? I want to see the Duke, if he's in."

"Not for you, hick. Beat it."

"I'm forgetting my manners," Valentine said, reaching inside his pack. Looking at the fleshy face, he opted to hand over the brick of cheese he had snacked on earlier.

"That's more like it," the heavy-framed man said, opening the door and engulfing the three-pound brick in a paw that resembled a gorilla-hand ashtray. Valentine watched Wideload as he sampled the Wisconsin dairy gold. Both of the Wolf's legs would have fitted in the man's shirtsleeve, and he and Gonzalez could have slept out of the rain in his trousers. "Mmmm, not bad, blue boy. Go up the spiral staircase. There're two doors at the top. One's marked 'office.' Go in the other one."

Valentine nodded and entered the courtyard. Plants sprouting through a mulch of cigarette butts decorated the brick-paved enclosure. Beautiful brass and glass doors, one facing in each direction, indicated the locations of the four bars. Each was named for a suit of cards.

Curious, Valentine looked in each door. The one marked SPADES seemed to be devoted to gambling; the kidney-shaped green baize tables could mean little else, and brightly lit slot machines filled the walls. The Diamonds bar looked like a dining room. Valentine had heard about, but never before seen, white tablecloths, polished silver, and flowered centerpieces. All were in opulent abundance inside the restaurant. The Clubs room was the only one open for business. Comfortable leather chairs lay scattered around next to small tables, and the bar appeared as devoted to cigars and pipe tobacco as to alcohol. A few men, some even wearing suits and ties, lounged around, reading newspapers or playing cards. Most were smoking. The Hearts bar looked like a glitzy brothel. It was the largest, taking up two stories, and had an open space in the center that featured the traditional stripper's pole mounted on a circular stage. Valentine counted three bars within the mirror-decorated main room.

"Hey, Tori," Valentine heard Wideload say from his door.

"Hey," a bored female voice answered, and a woman who seemed mostly made of blond hair and legs strode into the courtyard, carrying an angular purse over her shoulder big enough to sit in and paddle down a river. She glanced at Valentine with an appraising eye and disappeared down a narrow hallway branching off from the central area.

Valentine shrugged to the cheese-eating doorman and climbed the metal spiral staircase. He went to the unmarked door and knocked.

"It's open," a familiar female voice sang out.

He entered, and recognized the Duke's escort sitting behind a desk larger than the one in Flanagan's office but somehow more delicate and feminine in its rich glossy sheen. *Debby? No, Dixie.* Valentine's mind cast about for her name. *Denise, of the revealing décolletage dress,* he remembered. Today she was wearing a simple gray sleeveless outfit.

"Hi, Denise. Can I see the Duke?"

She looked up at him, puzzled. "Does he know you?"

"Sort of. We met at the Bunker in Madison. He said to drop by if I was ever in Chicago. David Tiny, remember?"

"That's it. I thought I saw you before. You're the guy with the nice hair. The Duke says some wild stuff after a few drinks, but you might be able to see him for a minute before we, er, he goes to dinner. Hey, you wouldn't have an extra toot of that happy-dust, would you?"

"I'll see what I can do later," Valentine said.

"Great, thanks. If you want to sit, there're a couple of chairs. He's meeting with the guy who brings in the drinks and eats. They've been at it all afternoon, so they should be done soon." She favored him with a smile.

Valentine offered Denise a cigarette. Her smile widened, and she tucked it away in her desk. He sat, trying to stay alert. Faint, muffled voices came from the inner office behind a door painted with a king of clubs. Trust someone with the Duke's taste in clothes and women to carry an idea too far.

Needing something to occupy his mind to prevent himself from dozing off, Valentine hardened his ears and listened to the voices inside the office.

"I tell you, it's hell, Duke. The whole Kurian system would work better if they just formed a New Order bank or something and had a currency that was good everywhere. This business of shuttling around boxcars full of people is just ludicrous. 'All I've got is a two-hundred-pound male, can I get a hundred-pound woman and a fifty-pound kid as change?' "

Valentine heard the Duke laugh.

"Okay, I'm exaggerating again. It's a little better organized than that. It's one thing for the Kurians here to send a few boxcars full of people up to Milwaukee and then bring the cars back here loaded with beer. But let's say I want to buy beef in Texas. If it's hot, some of the 'currency' is going to drop dead on the trip. Plus you got the local Reapers in Tennessee and points south looking to take some people off you in exchange for riding their rails."

"Well," the Duke countered, "you got to look at it from their point of view. Money doesn't mean much to them. Some of them like art and stuff, but auras are the only recognized currency. They're like a bunch of damn junkies."

"Yeah, you're right. But it still makes me nuts. Plus the people know what's coming at the other end of the ride, which makes them tough to control. And finding good men to do the work of keeping them in line ain't easy. Most of the ambitious ones are in the military. Leaves me with the idiots and thugs who just want to push people around."

"I hear that," the Duke agreed. "Listen, if the side meat is a little late, we're okay. I'll just do a special on pork chops or something. But you gotta get home to those pretty wives of yours, and my stomach is growling. Call me tomorrow and let me know if you've made any progress."

They said their good-byes, and the man, richly dressed in a matched set of pin-striped pants and a vest, walked out and waved at Denise. She picked up the telephone and pressed a button.

"Hi, big guy. Can you see someone really fast? It's that sailor with the black hair, David Teeny. . . . No, we met him in Wisconsin last month. . . . Yeah, at the buy . . . I dunno, he said he might have some later. . . . Okay."

"You can go in, Dave," she said, getting up and opening the door. The empty eyes of the pale painted king stared into his.

The Duke, who seemed to draw his fashion inspiration from Elvis Presley, wore a white silk jumpsuit with the four suits of cards printed as racing stripes going down his arms and the seams of his pants, which were tucked into white leather boots. His office was all business, save for a rug made out of a polar bear. Its snarling mouth pointed at the door.

The Duke was putting away papers and clearing his desk. Valentine noticed a gleaming revolver in easy reach used as a paperweight.

"Well, well, well. David Tiny, right? Didn't expect to see you so soon. I heard a boat from the Fleet was in, but it wasn't yours. What are you doing in Wisconsin blues? You jump ship?"

"Bull's-eye," Valentine said with a smile. "There was some bad blood with the captain. I'm searching for fairer horizons."

Valentine reached into his bag and pulled out one of the bottles of bonded whiskey. "Here you go, Mr. Duke. A little token of my esteem. Thanks for the great party that night at the Bunker."

"Hey, thanks, Tiny, you're two flavors of all right," the Duke said, reading the label. "So you're seeking a new opportunity. Ambitious fellow. Good for you. Hey, you wouldn't have another load of that high blue, would you?"

"Sorry, sir. But if I did, you'd get it." *All of it,* Valentine thought. *Wonder how you'd look after swallowing a pound of cocaine?*

The Duke seemed to lose interest. "Too bad. So, you gave up life on the waves and are toting a gun in Wisconsin. Any other plans?"

"Just a brass ring."

"Well, I wish you luck. Here's a card; you can get an evening's drinks at any of my clubs. And here's a backstage pass for the Hearts room. You're good-looking. One of the girls might take a shine to you. You'll find they're a lot more fun than those would-be dykes on that ship. Have Denise endorse it on your way out, would you?" the Duke said, putting his hand significantly on the phone.

"Sir, I'm new in town. I've got some barter I want to turn into cash. Where won't I get ripped off?"

The Duke's interest returned. "Sure, buddy, I can give you an opinion on that. What you got?"

Valentine placed the contents of his sack, save for his parang and Virgil Ames's pistol belt, on the Duke's desk, finishing by laying the Remington carefully on top. The Duke picked up the gun and worked the action. "Not bad, Dave. How'd you come up with this stuff after only a month in uniform?"

"Same way as I got the pass to come down here for three days. I did my captain a big favor."

"A favor? What kind of favor?"

"I promised not to say."

The Duke smiled. "I get it," he said, flicking the side of his nose with a finger. "I bet you took out the captain's rival. Or did the colonel get shot by insurgents and the captain take his place?"

"You're warm, but I can't tell you, sir. Sorry."

The Duke examined the rest of the loot. He plugged in the silver cigar lighter and worked it. "Hey, that's aces. Look nice down in the Club Room. Tell you what, since you're an old friend and all, I'll buy it all off you. Make it three grand, plus free drinks in the Hearts room while you're on your pass. This your first trip to Chicago? You can have a lot of fun on three grand."

"Yes, it is, Mr. Duke. But I think I can do better on Michigan Avenue."

"Hold on, son. Okay, five grand. I wish I could do better, but jewelry just isn't worth what it used to be."

"Mr. Duke, some patrollers told me about the Zoo. What's that?"

The Duke laughed. "The Zoo, huh? I guess your balls are working again after that kick you took. Well, the Zoo is the place for you, then. It's pricey, but it's a blast. Every night is anything-goes night. Ever seen a Grog fuck a woman? They got one there with a dick like your forearm. Hey, Tiny, tell you what. Just to seal the deal, how about I give you a three-day pass to the Zoo. Save you a grand right there."

Valentine reached into his pocket and pulled out the mirrored sunglasses. "You do that and give me a place to crash while I'm in town, and I'll throw these in."

"Let me see those," the Duke said. Valentine passed the shades over, and the Duke looked at the wire-thin frame. "These are twentieth century, maybe." He gently flexed a bow. "Hell, real titanium. Okay, Dave, you got your place to sleep. Have Denise set you up in one of the rooms above the Club Room. There's even a shower down the hall. You can get yourself all squeaky clean for your night at the Zoo."

"And my five grand?"

"Coming, coming. Gotta hit the old bank."

The Duke walked across his office to the rear and swung a velvet painting of a grinning jester's face away from the wall. A gray, formidable-looking safe sat in the wall behind. Whistling, the Duke spun the combination and opened the door, which was layered with multiple panels of steel. He extracted a pad of bills with a thick rubber band around it and walked over, handing it to Valentine.

"Five thou, my friend. Pleasure doing business with you."

Valentine pulled up the first bill and flipped through the others. "Hey, most of these aren't authorized!" he objected.

The Duke slapped him on the shoulder. "Good eye, Dave, good eye. I knew you were sharp! That was just a test to see what kind of an edge your mental blade has. Here, give me that back, I'll get you the real stuff."

The Duke wandered over to a decorative roulette table stacked with bottles of fine liquor. He spun the wheel to a point Valentine could not determine and pulled up the spinner. He reached into the space beneath the wheel and took out a sheaf of bills. He hurriedly counted.

"Okay, all this is authorized, Dave. Scout's honor. But spend it all—that stamp's good only for a couple more weeks. Then you gotta stand in line for a new issue. Counterfeiters make it tough on us hard-working smugglers."

Valentine checked again, seeing the red circle with cryptic squiggles stamped over the face of Ben Franklin on each bill. He picked up the now almost-empty sack. "Thanks, Duke. I want my first trip to Chicago to be a memorable one."

"Don't mention it. If you decide to move here, I might be able to connect you to a job. For, say, fifteen percent out of your first year's paychecks. I could even need a favor myself someday. You might be able to help me with that, and I'd be able to give you a hell of a lot more in return than your captain, or whatever he is. And Chicago beats the hell out of living up in Cheeseland."

"It's my kind of town," Valentine agreed.

*   *   *

Valentine arranged for his room with Denise. The room was small and clean and had a mattress to die for. Valentine inspected the late Virgil Ames's pistol again. It was an old army Colt automatic, firing the powerful .45 ACP cartridge. It wouldn't necessarily stop a Reaper, but it would give it something to think about. The gun belt also held four spare magazines, all of which were full. With the ammunition in the gun, that gave him thirty-five rounds. More than enough, as he did not want to use the weapon except as a last resort.

Valentine stretched out on the bed and forced himself to sleep for two hours. He showered and put the gun belt and his knife back in his pillowcase sack.

He ate downstairs in the Club room. The food was simple, satisfying, and overpriced: He paid twenty-five dollars for an overloaded sandwich and a pot of tea. He looked at an employee working on a case that held smoking paraphernalia and had a thought.

"Excuse me, sir," he said to the server behind the counter. "Do you have any waterproof matches?"

"Huh?" the waiter asked, flummoxed.

"He means the big matches in the tins," the man arranging cigars in the display case said. Valentine noticed a tattoo with a dagger stuck through a skull on his arm. "They work good even in the rain."

"Yeah, that's what I'm looking for," Valentine agreed. "I'm outside a lot, and it's a bitch to light a cigar in wet weather."

"Here's what you want," the cigar man said, putting a circular tin in front of Valentine. Valentine unscrewed the lid and extracted a three-inch match. The entire thing was lightly coated with a waxy substance. Valentine struck one on the strip at the side of the tin, and it flared into a white light. He could feel the heat on his face. "That's magnesium," the man explained. "It'll get a cigar going in any wind, unless your tobacco is soaked, of course."

"Hey, thanks. Can't find these in Wisconsin. How much for a tin?"

"They ain't cheap. Fifty bucks for a tin of ten matches."

"If I buy five tins, will you give them to me for two hundred?"

"Sure, seeing as you're a friend of the man upstairs."

"Done," Valentine agreed, and toked the man the other fifty.

"You must not get to Chicago often."

"No, there's lots of things here that you can't get in Wisconsin. Like the Zoo."

The tattooed man looked wistful. "Yes, but I can't afford to go there often. Once in a while I buy a cheap pass off the Duke."

"Ever been to the Black Hole?"

"Oh sure, I've checked it out a couple of times. I've got a strong stomach for that kind of thing. Some of it even turned me on."

"Do they ever let regular guys get at the girls, or is it just shows?"

"Oh, if you've got a couple thou in cash, they got these rooms in the basement. Soundproofed, you know. And you can do anything you want. Anything. After all, the women and men in the Black Hole, well, they're the people that the Kur decided deserved something worse than the Loop."

"You don't know anyone who works there, do you?"

"Nahh, sorry. Wish I did. But you seem to know how to toke. Just get the money in the right hands, and you'll be fine."

Valentine paid for his matches and took his leave of the eatery. He approached Wideload, still on duty, blocking the door like a parked dump truck.

"Leaving?" Wideload said, stepping aside to open the door after a glance outside. "Fun starts soon."

Valentine squeezed past the human obstacle and entered the street.

He turned and looked up the sidewalk in the direction of Lake Michigan. A black van, its windows reinforced with wire, stood on the curb in front of him. The initials *CSS* and a small logo were stenciled in white on its side. *The Chicago Security Service?*

Two grubby youths leaning on a corner stubbed out their half-smoked cigarettes.

A silent siren went off in Valentine's head. Tobacco in Chicago wouldn't be wasted by street punks. He heard footsteps behind him.

For a moment his body betrayed him: His legs turned to bags of water. When the handle on the back door of the CSS van turned, he knew the trap was being sprung.

Two massive arms enveloped him. Wideload locked his hands in a deadly variation of the Heimlich maneuver, but instead of pushing up into his diaphragm he pulled Valentine to him in a rib-squeezing embrace. Valentine's breath left him.

A second pair of men approached from across the street. One, tall and thin wearing a red tank top and pair of chain-mail gloves, removed a pair of familiar sunglasses as he ran toward Wideload and his victim.

"You're—," Wideload started to say, when Valentine brought his booted heel down hard on his captor's instep. He thrust back his head, and felt a solid *thunk*. The bear hug ceased.

The four men closing on him were trying to trap him between the Clubs Flush wall and the CSS van. Its rusty back door swung open. He lashed out with his foot, kicking the door closed again. It shut on something, fingers or a foot; muffled howls echoed from inside the van.

He ran across the street, accidentally spilling a pair of riders on bicycles as they turned on their rubberless wheels to avoid him. The four pursuers tried to triangulate in on him, but he called on his speed and his legs answered. He cornered around a parked horse wagon so fast his feet skidded on the pavement. But he maintained his balance . . . just.

With open sidewalk ahead of him he broke into a loping run. A few loungers on doorsteps stared as he passed. He chanced a glance over his shoulder; the four were sprinting to catch him.

Thirty seconds passed, and the four became three. In another minute, the three were two. By the time Valentine turned a corner, running up a series of short cluttered blocks, the two had become one: the tall man with the chain-mail gloves. His red tank top was dark with sweat.

Valentine turned down an alley and found breath in his body to do one more sprint. He zigzagged around fetid mountains of refuse, scattering rats with his passage. His pursuer just managed to start down the alley as Valentine turned the corner at the other end. To the east down this street he saw an end to the buildings. *I must be near the lakeshore . . . and the Zoo.*

He pressed himself up against the corner and listened to his pursuer's heavy breathing and heavier footsteps as he trotted up the alley. The man slowed, sucking wind as he approached the alley's exit.

When he knew the man was about to come around the corner, Valentine lunged. He brought his knee up into the winded man's groin. Chain-Mail Gloves managed to avoid the blow, but Valentine's thick thigh still caught him in the stomach. The blow was just as debilitating: The Chicago air left ChainMail Gloves's lungs in a gasp, and he bent over in breathless agony. In no mood for a fair fight, Valentine grabbed his assailant by his hair and brought his knee up again. Cartilage gave way with a sickening crunch. The man went down, now out of what wasn't much of a fight to begin with.

The Wolf shuddered, still keyed up. He pulled the gloves from the unconscious man and added them to his sack of weapons, then trembled again. But for a different reason.

A Reaper. Coming, and already so near.

Valentine tried to clear his mind, make it as empty and transparent as a paneless window. He stepped back into the shadows of the alley, moving away from the Reaper. At the other end, he dug himself into a pile of trash, burrowing on his knees and elbows into the filth. He felt cockroaches crunch and crawl as he joined them at the bottom of the sodden refuse pile.

The alley grew colder.

up, you, up, Valentine heard a Reaper say, seemingly in his ear.

The Wolf almost leaped to his feet, ready to fight and die, when he realized the voice was at the end of the alley with the Duke's thug.

Center, center, I've got to center or . . . , David thought frantically.

you, foodling—where is the terrorist?

"Murfer . . . motherfucker jumped me," the man groaned, in the sharp honking tones of a man with a broken nose. "I dunno . . . speak clear, willya? Who? Ohmygod!"

awake now?

"Yessir . . . umm, I think he went . . . toward the lake? That's where he was running. Sorta."

you were supposed to follow him, not take him.

"The Duke said—"

the duke isn't here, or he would be taken . . . instead of you!

A motor at Valentine's end of the alley drowned out the Reaper's low hissing voice. He looked out from beneath his garbage and saw a gleaming red car stop. One of the punks who had dropped out of the footrace sat on the hood, directing it. Rats scattered again as the man jumped off and the passenger door opened.

Valentine heard screaming, the terrible gurgling sound of a man being fed on, from the other end of the alley. The cold spot on Valentine's mind marking the Reaper swelled and pulsed as it conducted the aura to its Master Vampire. All around the neighborhood Valentine heard doors slamming and windows closing.

From beneath a mass of flattened cardboard Valentine watched the Duke, in all his gauche splendor, blanch as he looked down the alley. The Duke gulped, and slunk into the alley toward the scene. His henchman trailed him for two steps, then thought better of it and returned to the car. The Duke rubbed the brass ring on his finger. Valentine wondered if he sought comfort in its touch, or perhaps imagined what having his finger pulled off would feel like. The Wolf read mortal fear in the Duke's eyes before he passed. He let his ears take over, afraid to shift his position. The Reaper had senses other than that which allowed it to read auras.

the good duke, the Reaper whispered, slowly and thickly. *eight years with a brass ring courtesy of his aura-drunk lord. dealer of powder-white chemical joy. harborer of terrorists.*

"How was I to know, sir?"

*you are too ready to do business first and ask questions not at all.
you have tap-danced close to the edge of the law too many times: others in the order are beginning to take notice. like this fiasco. my instructions were not clear?*

"I just thought—"

you're kept alive to do, not think, the Reaper hissed.

"Well, why should that damn renegade get my money anyway, sir?
He's up to no good; throw him in the clink and be done with him."

*that "damn renegade" is something special. one of my clan sensed
him coming into the train yard. we want to know, who he is going to
meet, what they know, and what they plan. his kind do not just wander
into town to look around. he's one of that breed our foe-kin use for
their dirty work. clean up this mess and return to your club. we will
take over the search.*

"He said he was going to the Zoo."

a cover story. or perhaps . . .

"What shall I do with my man?"

*throw the corpse to the snappers. i go now, to find what you have
lost. i felt his aura hot and clear for a moment as he fought with your
man, i can find him again.*

The chilling spot in Valentine's mind moved away. He waited
while the Duke had another henchman carry the corpse to his trunk.
By the time they left the alley, it had grown dark.

Valentine emerged from underneath the garbage and left the alley.
He concentrated on keeping lifesign down, casting about for somewhere to get some clean clothes. He found a used-leather-goods store
and purchased four cheap belts and a long leather trench coat that was
missing some buttons. He put the black coat on after paying for it. In
an alley, he put on the gun belt and the parang and filled his pockets
with the tins of matches. He tucked a belt up his left sleeve and rolled
the others up and put them in his pants pockets. His remaining cash
lay folded in his breast pocket, next to his identity papers and a small
white card.

Well, I'm as ready for the Zoo as I'll ever be, Valentine thought.
Pray God the Zoo isn't ready for me.

Thirteen

The Zoo: Lincoln Park, a green oasis between the shores of Lake Michigan and the shattered city, is considered the premier entertainment tract of Chicago, and indeed the Midwest. From what had been the oldest zoo in the United States at the south to the Elks' temple in the north, Lincoln Park as run by the Kurians is a mixture of Sodom and Mardi Gras. Along with its adjacent gambling ship tied up at the old Chicago Yacht Club in Belmont Harbor, it offers diversions to suit the most jaded palate. From late March to November, "Carnalval" is in session. This nonstop party provides much-needed relief for the favored Quislings who are allowed to attend. During Chicago's dreary winters, the action is limited to the indoors but remains just as wild. With good behavior, a Midwestern Quisling can expect a trip into Chicago to visit the Zoo every few years. They are released in groups, and anywhere from two to a hundred go to Chicago together, with the direst warnings about what will happen to the rest should any desert. Parties from places as far away as Canada, Ohio, and even Colorado and Kansas visit for up to a month. But as the money runs out to the point that even shoes are sold to pay for unholy delights, the trips are ended early by mutual consent. Everyone knows the destination for those left penniless in a city where there is no such thing as a free meal or room.

Within the confines of the Zoo, there is no curfew as there is everywhere else in the city. There is ample if poor-quality food and drink to be had at any hour from street vendors, tented cantinas, and permanent restaurants. Mounted officers, equipped like the statue of Phil Sheridan with sword and pistol, patrol the area from their headquarters in the old Chicago Historical Society building. They do very little to break up disturbances, and only a fistfight that threatens to grow into a riot will cause them to do anything but pause and sit their horses to watch. Everyone from magicians to three-card monte operators to street musicians tries to make a living on the streets, but nothing can be sold on the grounds of the park save food, drink, tobacco, drugs, and flesh.

It is this last that is the real attraction of the Zoo. Under every lamppost, at every corner, and inside every barroom, women, a few men, and the occasional child can be found for a price. At the top of the carnal hierarchy are the showgirls, performing everything from stripteases in the clubs on Clark to variegated sexual displays behind the bars of the Zoo that would make those performed in pre-Kurian Bangkok seem tame. Next come the geishas. These women, found in some of the better bars, act as short-term girlfriends to the Quislings on vacation who want more than just sex, providing a sympathetic ear as well as other favors. The full-time companionship of a geisha for a week or two is out of the price range of all but the wealthiest Quislings, but bar girls in the saloons will do the same as long as the soldier keeps buying them watery drinks. Finally there are the colorful street-walkers in a variety of flavors, offering their services anywhere from alley and bush to the little flotilla of old boats anchored in the park's Lake Michigan–fed waterways.

The careers of the Zoo women are short, and most come to a sad end in the Loop. A few make enough money to retire to Ringland or open an establishment of their own. A few more leave the Zoo permanently in the company of a Quisling. But for most, it is a degrading road that leads to servicing the most perverted and violent customers before the final trip downtown.

As for the Quislings, like carnivorous flowers attracting insects with bright color and perfume, only to trap and devour them within, the wanton joys of the Zoo leave many too broke to get home and, unless they are smart or lucky, they become prime candidates for the Loop.

The night breeze no longer blew just cool, but downright cold. Scattered clouds crossed the full moon like inky stains. Below, the color had drained from Chicago's streets, leaving a world of low-contrast black and white. As Valentine drew farther away from Rush Street, the streetlights became irregular, and those that still functioned gave light to a few square yards around the pole. Scattered figures clutched their coats or thrust hands deep into their pockets, shoulders hunched against the wind as they brushed past Valentine without a word or a glance. Beater cars and small trucks chugged along the streets, most without benefit of headlights, as clattering bicycles dodged out of their way. Valentine could hear the clopping sound of hoofbeats on pavement down a nearby alley. He cast about with his nose; the city seemed overwhelmed by an oily petroleum smell and dusty coal smoke. The gutters reeked of urine.

Valentine glanced up again at the moon. Its chalky whiteness comforted him somehow. *Full moon, good night for a Wolf.* But a sudden wave of fear passed through him, leaving his back running with cold sweat and his hair bristling. He paused under a light, ostensibly to check his map, when motion ahead caught his eye.

Pedestrians parted like a school of fish swerving to avoid a cruising shark. A Reaper garbed in a shirt, trousers, boots, and a cape—rather than the usual robes—moved toward the dead heart of the city. It ran with great multiyard leaps, like a deer bounding through the woods. Valentine's hand fell instinctively toward his gun, but he managed to change the gesture into a simple thrust of his fist into his coat pocket. The Reaper passed without a glance in his direction, its sickly yellow eyes blazing like tiny lightbulbs. Valentine turned and watched it go. It reached the back of a slow-moving car, a ramshackle vehicle with wood planks where the panels and roof used to be. The Hood leaped over it in a single bound, cape flapping like bat wings in the night, and disappeared out of sight as the startled driver stood on his squealing brakes.

Somewhere to the east, Valentine could hear Lake Michigan lapping at its breakwaters. He sensed lights and music somewhere to the north, a mass of noise that could only mean the Zoo. To either side of him, ruined blocks of rubble sprouted shanties like wooden toadstools. Some buildings still stood and showed signs of irregular maintenance— everything from glass to iron bars to wooden shutters covered the windows, and the smells of cooking wafted out into the street. He could make out trees in the lights ahead, and now several figures had joined him in moving toward the Zoo. Most of them had brightly colored cards dangling from thin beaded chains around their necks.

He noticed a line at a kiosk on the edge of the park and joined the cluster of waiting men, almost all of whom wore assorted uniforms. An elephantine redheaded woman sold the white cards on chains to the lined-up men under the supervision of a cigar-smoking baldie with the watchful, sullen air of a pit boss. Valentine looked at the prices, which started at five hundred dollars a day. He extracted the pass he'd obtained from the Duke and passed it to the meaty hand of the redhead.

"Three-day pass, huh, boy?" the woman said, reaching under her counter for a card on a chain. "You one of the Duke's couriers?"

The supervisor's eyes narrowed as he evaluated Valentine.

"Sort of," Valentine said. "What do I get with the pass?"

She did not really smile so much as smirk, but her eyes favored his with a friendly twinkle. "About anything your heart desires." She peeled a covering off the paper and began to recite the rules in almost a singsong manner. "This card will stay green for seventy-two hours; that's guaranteed. When it turns red, you gotta leave the premises. But while it's green you can see any show, go in any bar, and get free coffee or iced tea on the *Lady Luck of the Lake* if you're playing. That's the gambling boat," she added, breaking out of the recitation. "Real plush carpets and more lights than you've seen at once in your whole life, I'll bet."

A gruff voice broke in from over Valentine's shoulder. "Hey, there's people waiting."

"Shut your trap, you," she barked, "or I'll start readin' to him outta the '22 yellow pages." She turned her attention back to Valentine, drawing close enough for him to smell the beer fumes on her breath. "You take my advice; just spend your three days here. The food's cheaper than most anywhere in Chicago, and when you want to sleep just pay one of the girls for an all-nighter. You'll get a woman and a bed for what you'd pay for a bed alone in one of them ripoff hotels by the Michigan Avenue Market. And a guy with your looks will maybe get another tumble in the morning, free of charge."

Valentine slipped her a bill. She slid the toke into her udder-size bosom with a deftness that belied her size. "You got a map?" he asked.

"Listen to him," the voice from behind grunted. "Kid thinks he's in Dizzyland."

"Naw, it ain't that big a place. You'll find your way around. Why, you lookin' for something in particular?"

"The Black Hole. I heard it's really weird."

She did not look surprised. "It's always you nice-looking, quiet ones," she mused. "You can't miss it. North side of the Zoo, a big lit-up pit with walls all around. Last night the Grogs worked over this little beauty from Michigan. By the time they were done, she didn't have enough blood in her to fill up a Reaper's tongue. I hear the main attraction tonight's gonna be some real cute young thing from your Wisconsin. Enjoy."

"Nattie, you got other customers," the cigar-chomper said.

"Okay, okay. Just talkin' to the Duke's friend. The Duke would want us to make sure he got happy here. Geez, where'd he go?"

Valentine heard her expostulation as he strode off across Clark Street and into the Zoo, but the noise of music and shouting soon drowned her out. Bars lined the road on Clark, marching up north toward darkened high-rises. He glanced at a few of the names: Paradise Found, Jack Off With Jill On, the Gold Coast Grotto . . . Heavily made-up women enticed customers inside, strutting and promising greater delights within. He ignored the twinkling tableaux and moved into the cluster of old Zoo buildings. Women in assorted stages of undress challenged him with everything from a throaty "Hi, there," to a bellowed "Best head in the Zoo, twenty bucks!—Over here, handsome." A sickly stench struck him, and he stepped around a pool of vomit half covering the sidewalk. A shoeless drunken shape in bright orange overalls leaned against a boulder with the words EVERYTHING GOES scrawled in white paint across its chipped surface.

There seemed to be nothing preventing people from coming and going as they wished, but security troops mounted and on foot wandered the grounds, mostly looking at the colored cards dangling from the revelers' necks. One of them motioned to an apelike Grog, pointing at the shoeless drunk. Valentine watched as the Grog hoisted the man into a wheelbarrow cart and trotted off, pushing the drunkard south on wobbly wheels.

A long lagoon filled with little boats bordered the Zoo. Couples got on and off in a steady stream. Far to the north, Valentine spotted a glittering wedding-cake shape of light, obviously the *Lady Luck of the Lake*. He circled back into the Zoo's cluster of buildings from the north. A couple of small Grogs were picking up trash from the sidewalks and grass. Valentine walked up to them and pressed some very special toke into their hands before moving off toward another crowd.

A domed cage the size of a tepee stood in the center of a little depression. A ring of twenty or thirty laughing soldiers stood around it, hurling small stones and pieces of fruit through the bars. An extraordinarily tall man, dressed in a simple khaki uniform, stood before the crowd with a long pole with a metal club on one side and what looked like a noose on the other.

"Hey, let's have him change shape again," one of the men called, throwing a small rock into the well-lit center of the cage. He passed some bills to the khaki-uniformed man.

Valentine craned his neck to look within the bare cage. A single tree, barkless and dead as a piece of driftwood, decorated the twelve-foot circle within. A serpent lay coiled around the tree, hiding its head in the crotch between two branches.

"I can get him to switch, no fail," the keeper said, and poked the metal end of the pole into the cage. He rapped the snake twice on the head.

A shiver seemed to course up the body of the snake, a shiver that turned into a blur. Before Valentine's astonished eyes, the snake transformed into an orangutan, which hung from the tree by one long arm and then dropped to the ground. It thrust a rotten apple in its mouth and worked its jaws hungrily.

"How the hell did you do that?" a voice called from the crowd.

"I didn't do it, he did," the keeper explained. "What you have here is a relative of the Kurians. It's the only one that's been captured and put on display. They can change their shape at will, and they can practically go invisible. They're the masters of some of the terrorists and rebels that hide out in the hills. The rebs worship them as gods. Only way to please them is to bring scalps, and the rebs aren't particular about whose hair they take. They tell me this one had fifteen, twenty little blond scalps. God knows what the rebs did to them before lifting their hair."

"Motherfucker," one of the soldiers said, throwing a stone in at the seated figure. The rock made an impact in the sand next to the orang, kicking dirt up onto it.

The orang's eyes gazed sadly over the crowd. A few more stones flew in, some hitting the illusory ape on its broad back. Its eyes met Valentine's, and he jumped as if shocked by the spark that passed between their eyes.

Lee . . . Lee Valentine, a voice said inside his head. *Please let this not be the madness again. Oh, Lee, is it you, can you be here? It's Rho, the Ancient. Of the firstwalkers. By the Bonds and by the Gates, have you come to end my torments? Please say Paul Samuels is with you somewhere, and Ghang Ankor. The years . . . the years have sung their songs and moved the earth itself since we last met. Please say I will be finally free of their smacks and stares.*

All this passed through Valentine's mind in a flash. He responded. *No, I am not the Valentine you knew. I am his son, David. My father has been dead for over ten years.*

Son? Son? I can sense you are a Hunter. I do not know what brings you here, but I feel it is not I. You are anxious to be gone and fearful and worried and hateful and hopeful and . . . in love. Oh, I would cast myself into oblivion if I could, but they watch, always watch, with their dull eyes. You cannot know what I've been through. Years of abuse and bad weather and no food and torment. The orangutan stared at Valentine. *Please just kill me if you cannot get me out. If my life runs its course, I could be here for hundreds of years until these bars turn to rust and new ones replace it.*

Something sought his mind. Valentine pulled back and into himself.

I'm sorry, so sorry, Valentine thought, breaking out of the ring and filling his mind with *sorry* over and over again. The agony of the trapped Lifeweaver had been palpably transmitted through its thoughts. Valentine could not let despair overtake his mind with Molly waiting in some cage and a Reaper hunting for his lifesign.

He hurried past the converted animal displays. Inside one, a nude woman cavorted upon an artificial tree, alternately hiding and exposing herself to the whistling admirers. A few men threw money into the cage, and she picked up a thick green cucumber and sucked on it. More bills littered the floor of the cage, and she began to move one end of the spit-moistened vegetable down across her breasts and belly.

He reached an open pit. Black paint covered the stone barriers surrounding it and forming the deep walls of a large hollow. A uniformed Zoo patroller sat on the wall, idly smoking a sharp-smelling cigarette. Valentine approached the pit and looked in. A central mound, built up to the point that it was almost level with the ground outside the pit, sported two stone lions facing each other. From the mouth of each dangled a long leather strap, and the ground between the opposing lions had badly stained rugs spread out, covering the dirt. A Grog was scrubbing at the broad back of one of the lions, trying to remove bloodstains. To the far south in the pit, a gallowslike structure had a pair of ladders leaning against it and numerous hooks embedded in the posts and lintel. To the far right on the north end, a simple pole lay buried in the ground, with four sets of shackles dangling from the top. Valentine took in this three-ring circus of de Sade and moved over toward the smoking patroller.

"Is there going to be a show tonight?" Valentine asked, handing him one of the few remaining cheroots.

"You bet your ass. In a couple hours. You lining up for a good view?"

"Maybe. What do they do?"

"Make the ladies here scream themselves to death," the patroller said, putting the cheroot in his mouth and lighting it with the end of the hand-rolled cigarette. The scrubbing Grog paused in his work and watched the glowing red tip of the cheroot as the patroller inhaled.

A group of soldiers, civilians, and hookers walked by. Half-empty bottles dangled from their hands. While passing the pit, one of the prostitutes whispered something into her escort's ear. "Yeah, I seen a Black Hole show before," her john answered. "I've even seen Reapers in the audience."

"I heard that private parties can be arranged," Valentine ventured, after the party passed on.

The officer blew out the rich smoke with an air of approval. "If you've got the cash, just about anything is possible."

Valentine slipped the officer a hundred dollars. He glanced at the bill for a second before it disappeared into his shirt pocket. "I'll get you in to see the Head Keeper, sport. Wait here. He agrees to talk to you, you gimme another toke the same size."

"Fair enough," Valentine agreed. The patroller moved off toward a long brick building with a busy rooftop eatery.

Valentine looked at the Grog, who was similar in size to the one at the Miskatonic University. He lit a match from the tin and waved it back and forth. The Grog applauded with a childlike, patty-cake motion and waddled down toward the edge of the pit by Valentine. It looked up at Valentine expectantly.

"You want to see more?" Valentine asked. The Grog cocked its head from side to side like a woodpecker looking for termites. Valentine looked around, but the few Zoo patrons close by were paying no attention to the empty Black Hole.

The Wolf took out one of his tins of matches and rattled it for the Grog. The Grog held out both of its hands, just like the inhabitant of the Institute's catacombs. Valentine tossed the tin down to it. The Grog gave a little hoot of pleasure and thrust the matches into a pocket in its tattered trousers. Valentine made a slow circle of the Black Hole and found another Grog changing lightbulbs on a lamppost. He tried to hand a few more matches to the low-caste worker, but it shook its head and put its hands behind its back. Perhaps it had been punished in the past for something to do with matches.

Valentine's patroller, still smoking the long cheroot, returned. "You're golden," he said. "It's getting toward the end of the year, and they're not so busy anymore. You want to visit before or after the show? Sometimes it gets a little crowded after. Plus, there's a few less girls to choose from, you know?"

Valentine forced a smile. "Thanks. I'll see him now, if that's okay with you." Valentine handed over another hundred dollars in toke.

"Wise choice. After the show, Burt's usually drunk and ornery anyway. He tries, but he's just not smart enough to come up with new ways of killing people every week. Plus, he's pissed 'cause they're making him do a show tonight. He'd rather wait until the weekend, advertise it a little bit and work up a decent crowd. They toss in money and tell him what to do. But I guess the management wants this girl done fast and dirty . . . ho now, button up a sec," the patroller said, looking up at a Reaper moving down the path. It felt similar to the one who had pursued him to the alley. David assumed it was still searching for him. Or perhaps it was one of his siblings, animated by the same Master Vampire.

Valentine breathed slowly and deeply, letting his eyes go out of focus. Death passed in silence.

The officer led Valentine though a wooden fence screened by trees and overgrown shrubbery. The patroller rapped on the door and called, "Open up, Todd, it's me. I've brought a customer for Burt."

The brown-painted door swung open, and Valentine followed the patroller past a shotgun-toting guard and into a long brick building with a green peaked roof. It was half barn, half fort. The patroller brought Valentine to a metal door and opened it with a key from a small ring on his belt. He entered, holding the door open for Valentine.

They walked down a hallway and entered a linoleum-floored room. An unshaven man sat in a chair, legs extended and arms dangling tiredly. A few more chairs stood against the walls, and an empty desk at the corner shone under a hooded light. The cop gestured toward one of the open chairs.

"Take a seat. Looks like there's not much action tonight. I'll go get Burt."

Valentine sat down opposite the rag-doll figure. The bedraggled man wore a jumpsuit, new and shiny, made out of what looked to Valentine like nylon. He had long, unkempt black hair and a mustache. A prisoner-like pallor made his skin seem anemic against his dark beard. A pair of comfortable-looking black sports shoes with new soles covered his feet. Obviously a favored Quisling, if a tired and dirty-looking one. The jumpsuit had a high collar, almost a turtleneck, and Valentine had to look twice at the insigne in silver stitching just under the man's chin: a reversed swastika. *The Twisted Cross?* Valentine thought.

The man, noticing Valentine's stare, yawned and looked across the room at him.

"Howdy, pal," the man in black said. "Burt's kinda slow tonight. He's probably in one of the bars on Clark drinking. I've been waiting almost an hour." He had a drawling accent which Valentine identified as more western than southern.

Valentine looked at the pattern on the linoleum floor. It resembled a cross section of sedimentary rock strata. "I'm in no hurry. Got a three-day pass, and it's my first night."

"You in the Service?"

"Yes. In the patrols. Madison Triumvirate. How about you?"

"I get around. I'm on the General's Staff."

Valentine hazarded finesse. "You're Twisted Cross, right? You guys work pretty tight with the Reapers. Where are you operating now?"

"Some people up here call us that. Can't discuss it, though. You know, security."

"Oh, I hear you. Looks like they work you pretty hard."

The man smiled. "Depends on your definition of work. But it is exhausting, in its own way."

Valentine nodded. "You look kind of sick or something."

"This is nothing. You should have seen me when I first got out of the tank. I'd been connected for six days. Couldn't even stand up until they got some orange juice in me."

Valentine nodded. "Sounds like tough duty. I'm sure it's more interesting than driving around in an old car, though, making sure nobody's hiding milk cows in the hills."

"Funny, I've never been to Wisconsin, but damn if you don't look familiar," the man mused.

"You been up in the north woods?"

"No."

Valentine fought the urge to lower his face, but he looked the man square in the eye. "Then I don't know where else you might've seen me. I've never been south of Indianapolis."

The man shrugged. "I dunno. I never forget a face, and—"

A heavy tread echoed from the hallway, and the cop returned, escorting a shuffling man with the bulky build of a power lifter. He had a battered face that looked like he drove railroad spikes with it. "Burt, this guy wants to do some business with you," the patroller said.

"Sure, sure. Be with you in a minute, kid. Hey, Jimmy King, you look tuckered. You need the usual?"

"A nice juicy one, Burt."

There was a look of raw lust in the man's eyes like nothing Valentine had ever seen. It sickened him, but he was glad of it; the mystery of Valentine's face was plainly the last thing on Jimmy King's mind at the moment.

Burt grinned. "Then follow. Pickings are a little slim this time of year, but I know you ain't particular. Some of your friends have been through, and I have a lot of empty cells."

As Burt and Jimmy King left the room, Valentine toked the cop yet again. "Thanks again," he said.

"Have fun, kid. Pleasure doing business with you."

As soon as the cop had passed out the metal door to the yard, Valentine hardened his ears. Burt and the Twisted Cross man seemed to be going down some stairs.

"Got the old thirst, huh?" Burt asked.

"You know it," King said, his rubber-soled feet squeaking a little against the stone stairs.

"Your bro recovered from that shotgun blast yet?"

"Yeah, sure. He won't win any dance contests, but he gets around well enough. For a while there, I was limping even when I wasn't in the tank."

"How long were you hooked up this time?"

"Almost a week. Fucker fed three times. Made me want it so bad I almost bit the guy pulling me out. But the general was happy with what we did; gave the whole team two weeks off. We wiped out a whole nest of rebs in the Smokies."

Valentine heard keys rattling and the sound of a door being opened somewhere below.

"General shouldn't make you pull such long shifts. I heard some of your guys went nuts after . . ."

The clang of the door shutting echoed loudly enough for Valentine to hear with soft ears. The voices were gone.

He waited fifteen minutes before the basement door opened again, and Burt's ponderous step ascended the stairs, key ring jangling. Burt returned to the linoleum-floored room, and Valentine rose to meet him.

"My name's Pillow, sir. First visit to the Zoo."

"Burt Walker. Chief of One-Way Exhibits."

"One-Way?"

"Now and then we get troublemakers the management wants to make an example of. Don't matter how they die, as long as it's ugly. Whatcha lookin' for, Pillow? Something the girls out there can't handle?"

"You might say that. It's something I don't like talking about."

"Hey, kid, I heard it all, believe me," Burt said, in a rich, world-weary tone. "But I respect people's privacy. You just gotta let me know one thing. . . . Will she still be alive when you're done? 'Cause if you kill her, I gotta charge you big-time."

"She'll live, Mr. Walker. That's a promise."

"Okay, then, but remember what I said and don't get carried away. I gotta see the cash, though."

Valentine flashed his breast-pocket wad. "I want to see the girls first. I'm willing to pay, but I don't want anyone whose already used up. Someone kind of innocent and fresh," Valentine said.

"Hey, Pillow, you want innocent and fresh, you have to come to the special show tonight. When I saw her, I almost decided to come out of retirement. But I'll let Clubber and Valkyrie and my two best Grogs do her."

Walker took Valentine to the basement stairs.

"This'll be private, right?"

"Kid, there's curtains on the cells. Don't worry about noise; no one's going to disturb you."

They came up against the metal basement door. Walker thumbed through a ring of keys and opened it. They passed though to a spacious lower level.

It reminded Valentine of a stable, except for the dirty white tile everywhere. A series of cells with barred doors lined the walls. Valentine smelled blood, urine, and feces without even using his hard sense of smell. Another man in a khaki uniform sat at a desk, talking animatedly over a phone.

"Hey, Burt! There are problems up top. There's a fire in the Grog pens, and the stables. Can you believe it?"

"Oh, fine," Walker said, disgusted. "Stupid Grogs. 'Cause they're cheap and eat anything, we gotta employ 'em. They're more trouble than they're worth. Find Clubber and go help out at the stables. I don't give a shit if the Grog pens burn right to the ground. They can spend the winter under Lakeshore Drive for all I care."

The man nodded and disappeared up the stairs to the first floor.

"Okay, kid. Check out the cells, and then we'll talk price."

One of the doors slid open, and Jimmy King staggered out. He was nude, hollow chested, with spindly arms and legs. His face was covered in blood, and it ran down his chest into a mat of sticky black hair. He wiped blood from his eyes with slow, tired movements.

"Hey, King," Walker called. "Go use the hose, will ya? You're dripping all over the place."

The Twisted Cross man went to a washbasin with a floor drain beneath and began to hose himself off. Valentine walked up and down the cells, looking at the battered, pathetic figures behind the bars. Most of the stable-stall-size rooms were empty, and one held the remains of King's purchase, lifeless legs spread wide and throat torn messily open. Valentine reached a smaller hallway, empty of cells with another gate at the end of it, and wandered down it. The sliding barred door blocked his way, and he could see a long, poorly lit tunnel on the other side of the bars.

Something from down the tunnel tickled at his nostrils. He hardened his sense of smell and sniffed at the air. His heart skipped a beat as he recognized the odor of rose-petal soap. He returned to the tiles of the wide central hallway.

King had dressed again and was leaving, almost scuttling out the door to the upstairs. Walker shook his head and hefted his bulk up from behind the desk.

"Okay, boy. I'm a busy man. Which one? King's left me with a mess for the Grogs to clean up."

"Sir, how about you let me have the one for tonight's show? I won't even bruise her."

"Naw, sorry, kid. I'm already in Dutch about her. One of the guys got a little rough when she first got here, and I caught hell. They want her with a lot of energy for the show, you know? The guys always like it better if they aren't half-dead to begin with."

Valentine looked in one of the pens at a curled up, sleeping black woman. "This one looks unspoiled. But I think she might be dead. I can't see her breathing."

"Eh? What's that?"

"I don't see anything moving. And her head's at sort of a funny angle."

Walker came over to the cage, reaching for an old-fashioned key. He looked inside.

"What the hell are you talking 'bout, junior? I can see—*graak!*"

Walker's last choked cry came as Valentine whipped the thin leather belt, wrapped tightly in each fist around the man's neck. The chief's massive frame heaved, and latissimus muscles the size of halved watermelons bulged against his shirt. Valentine leaped onto Walker's back, wrapping his legs around his thick waist, and pulled on the leather garrote until his muscles flamed in agony. Walker crashed over backwards onto Valentine, trying to crush him with his weight, but the Chief of One-Way Exhibits weakened. Valentine rolled him onto his stomach with a heave, digging his knee into his opponent's kidneys. Walker flapped like a landed fish as the muted crackling of his throat's collapsing cartilage sounded through his gaping mouth. Valentine continued pulling until he could no longer hear a heartbeat. Then he stood, the odor of Walker's feces and urine rank in his nostrils.

He turned the chief over, avoiding looking into the bulging eyes. Removing the key ring and a club from Walker's belt, he pulled the body feetfirst into an open stall, closed the curtains, and slid the door shut, locking it. His hands shook as much from nerves as from muscular exhaustion as he went to the smaller corridor. The rose smell calmed him as he tried the barred gate. It did not yield until after he tried several different keys.

Perhaps the corridor had been brightly lit once, but now only a dank gloom filled his eyes. He used his nose to guide him, following the homing beacon of the rose smell to a cell door. The sound of quiet breathing behind the door reassured him.

"Molly, it's me, David . . . I'm here to get you out," he whispered, trying the keys. She did not respond, and he grew frantic. The lock finally yielded. He pushed the squealing door open. The cell was bare and dark, the cracked cement floor sliding down to a drainage hole.

Molly Carlson lay curled up in a corner, arms around her drawn-up legs, head resting sideways on her bare knees. She wore the tattered remnants of her white shirt from yesterday—*yesterday,* he thought, *or a year ago?*—and blood smeared the side of her face where it had dried from a bloody clot of pulled-out hair. Valentine's heart ached at the purple bruises on her face and in her eye sockets. He knelt next to her.

"Molly, Molly! *Molly,*" he almost shouted, gripping her hand. He patted the side of her pallid cheek and futilely searched for a response. He felt a strong, steady pulse under her wrist. *Was she drugged?*

He reached around her shoulders and under her knees. "I'll carry you out, then, Melissa," he said, lifting her into his arms.

Like a jinni summoned by the use of its name, her eyelids fluttered open. "David?" she croaked. "No . . . yes . . . how?"

He bore her out of the cell and down the tunnel, away from the basement. "Explanations will have to wait. We're both in a fix. But we're getting out of here," he said, quietly but with all the confidence he could muster.

Tearing himself away from the smell of roses on her skin, he caught the scent of fresh air and followed it like a bloodhound on a trail. Soon they reached a small corridor, jutting off from the main one at an empty doorframe. Following the now stronger odor of the outdoors, Valentine reached a short set of stairs.

"Can you walk?" he asked.

"I think so, David. I thought I was dead. I made my mind die."

Valentine looked into her battered features. He wanted to kiss her, but something in her haunted eyes held him back.

"Did they hurt you? Were you—?"

"Don't ask, David. Maybe I'll tell you someday. Now . . . now it's out of my mind, and it's staying out for a while. Where are we?"

"Chicago. The Zoo."

"That's where they said they were taking me. They said some big shots from downstate were going to come here and watch me . . . die."

"You're going to disappoint them, Molly."

"But you can't get out of Chicago. Not with me, anyway."

"Watch us."

"David, just shoot me. Shoot me and go, because after . . . I want you to get out, no matter what."

He looked down at her, shaking his head. "Oh, no . . . 'promises to keep, and miles to go before I sleep.' We'll be out of their reach by midnight, one way or the other."

"But how?"

"A Reaper is going to help us."

The arena of the Black Hole glowed under bright arc lights. Valentine heard distant fire bells and smelled smoke; the Grogs had made good use of their matches. He covered Molly with his leather coat and took her wrist, then brought her out into the bright lights of the pit. Giving her a boost up the side of one of the walls, he followed, taking her offered hand.

The cool night air chilled his skin, and Molly gripped the coat around her as her teeth chattered. Confusion hung in the air along with the smoke from the fires. Through the scattered trees, Valentine could see two fires burning, and noisy crowds clustered around, perhaps helping, perhaps simply enjoying the excitement. Valentine got his bearings and hurried along the deserted sidewalks, ignoring the knots of people rushing to and fro. He sensed Reapers searching near the fire.

In the little dome-shaped cage, the Lifeweaver now wore the shape of a large sloth. The audience that had been present earlier was gone now save for two drunks passing a greasy bottle back and forth. Ignoring them, the tall keeper snapped shut a final shackle to the sloth's curved paw and rapped it across the nose with a short black club similar to the one Valentine had taken from the body of the strangled chief. "Looks like you're done for the night," he said. "Everybody's watching the Grog Quarter go up in flames."

Valentine brought Molly around to the low cage door. "Hello, in there," he called, flashing a handful of bills. "When you're done, I need a favor."

A look of tired distaste came over the keeper. "Hey half-breed, beat it. Go get your Big Medicine elsewhere. Just 'cause it looks like an animal doesn't mean it actually is. It's just a trick. If you're looking to fuck an ostrich or something, you're outta luck."

The keeper fastened the last cuff to the dried-out tree limb and approached the door. Valentine passed him the bills with his left hand, casually holding the right behind his leg. The keeper grabbed the money, counting it with his eyes. "Okay, okay, you got my attention. Now what—," he began, bending almost double to squeeze his frame out of the low door to the cage.

The keeper never ended his sentence; the hard wooden shaft of the club crashed into the back of his skull with a *kraak*. The keeper dropped, unconscious or dead.

Valentine added the keys to his growing collection and hurried to the tree. The ones for Rho the Lifeweaver hung from a second, smaller ring. *If we make it, we live. If we don't, nobody's going to be an exhibit,* he silently promised himself, and Molly. And Rho. As he unfastened the leg irons on the sloth, he patted it gently on the head.

A Hunter? The other mind inside his head asked. A fleeting mental touch. *Valentine, it's you.*

The shape blurred again as it fell to the ground, released from its bonds. Valentine knelt and grasped it by the shoulders. He found himself looking into the rugged face of his own father.

"Dad?" Valentine found himself saying without even thinking about it.

The shape blurred again and became a hawk-nosed, deep-eyed old man with a tuft of white hair at the temples. "Sorry, Valentine the Younger. I was thinking of your father. My control isn't what it was," it said in a croaking voice.

Molly grabbed at the bars behind him. "David, we don't have much time. Those two drunks just took off!"

Valentine helped the Lifeweaver to his feet. "Sir, we have to move. Can you walk?"

"I would love to walk. Run even, Valentine. But I fear I won't be able to go far."

"I'll see what I can do. Now let's see what you can do," Valentine said, explaining his plan. "But we have to hurry."

Somewhere, somehow, the Reapers knew. He felt them coming.

Following a Reaper through the crowds made negotiating the press of humans a simple task. People parted for the Reaper like the Red Sea before the Israelites. Valentine and Molly only had to stay a respectful distance behind the flowing cape.

"Open your stride a little more," Valentine said in a low tone. The Reaper complied, almost goose-stepping into the street. "That one, the cab," Valentine added.

A dirty yellow lump of dented metal sagged to one side on a broken suspension. The Reaper stepped to the driver's side, reaching up to tap at the window, and paused, finding no window to tap on.

i need your ride, the Reaper breathed down at the driver. The grizzled driver looked up and lost perhaps two pounds while staring at the death's-head face gazing down at him.

Valentine and Molly climbed in, and the young woman sagged against Valentine the instant they were seated on the badly sprung bench. The Reaper joined them, squeezing into the backseat. The driver did not offer to have the Reaper sit up front.

"Where to, sir?" the driver asked, the effort to sound normal sticking in his throat.

the great pier, the Reaper said as Valentine pointed to his small map, which was illuminated by the streetlights shining into the car.

"Be there in five minutes, sir." The driver started his car. Valentine wondered if the man's hair had always been that gray. The taxi began to roll, engine sputtering as diesel fumes leaked into the car.

The Lifeweaver switched to his telepathy. It gripped Valentine's hand to make a more secure connection. *Valentine, you have saved me. In ways you cannot imagine.*

Don't fool yourself, he thought back. *We're not out of it yet.*

The audacity of this . . . It is worthy of your father. Once a Cat passed through the Zoo, but she was so sickened by the goings-on she barely touched my mind before hurrying away.

How well did you know my father?

I trained him, Valentine the Younger. I invoked him as a Wolf and saw in him the potential to be a great Bear. He and others forged Southern Command out of a few camps in the mountains. The worst days. But the Kurians grew to know and hate your father. He killed five of them. Not Grogs, not Reapers. Kurian Lords. They had a fortress in Saint Louis, suspended from the arch like a spider's egg sac. He stole a small plane and parachuted onto it. When he finished, no Kurian within ever drank another aura.

I never knew this, Valentine thought back after a moment.

He was the best of men, beyond our design.

Design?

He once had a family in the Free Territory, but they were swallowed in a battle that raged years before your birth. He sought solace in the remoteness of the north, and I never met him again. I hope he found some measure of happiness before he died.

He did, Valentine responded.

They made their way through the pier, checkpoints and all, with the same simplicity granted by Rho's Reaper aspect. Guards looked busy elsewhere, and port officials sprang into action, driving their work gangs into greater and greater efforts. Valentine urged them on, sensing a Reaper approaching from behind.

What had been Chicago's Navy Pier was now only an ill-lit and deserted utilitarian warehouse for merchandise moving into and out of Chicago by water. The great concrete pier sprouted wooden docks like leaves from a branch. Valentine found a responsible official by searching out the most well-maintained uniform.

"You there," he said, stepping from behind the Reaper. "Is there a ship here, the White-something-or-other?"

"*Whitecloud,* sir?" the officer said briskly. "She left this evening. Just under two hours ago. Probably halfway to Milwaukee by now."

Valentine's disappointment may have helped with the act. He thought for a moment. "Is it possible to still catch her?"

"Yessir. We have a fast motorized patrol boat. She could catch up in an hour."

bring it, the Reaper said, searching the dark horizon of the lake.

"Uh, follow me, sir," the man stammered. "There's only a skeleton crew. If you want more men for boarding, the *Whitecloud* is pretty big, crew of a dozen or so—"

"I think we'll be enough. The woman there just needs to go on board and identify someone. There's a terrorist on board," Valentine explained.

The port official walked them down a long, narrow wooden dock extending into the lake, held up by thick wooden pilings. The warped wood creaked under their feet.

Ahead they could see a long, low shape. The aged speedboat gleamed in the distant reflected light of Chicago. Valentine prayed that they would still get away with no one questioning a Reaper's orders.

The Reaper.

The real Reaper was somewhere close.

Valentine tried to hurry the other three along by trotting out ahead toward the boat, his hackles rising like a wary dog's. Rho seemed to blur, but his Reaper aspect re-formed.

They've found me. They are homing. I give off lifesign like a firework, Valentine the Younger, the Lifeweaver thought to him.

The Reaper grew closer. Valentine knew it was just behind them now.

The port official scuttled up the gangway. He began speaking to a pair of figures on board. Valentine pressed the pistol into Molly's hand. "Keep this in your coat pocket," he whispered. "Don't let them take you alive."

The Reaper approached. Its cold shadow was at the jetty, moving down the boards.

Valentine drew his parang, turned, and went to meet it.

*   *   *

When Valentine was fourteen, he had read Livy. Tonight his was the role of Horatius at the Sublician Bridge. What had seemed heroic now felt suicidal, with two meters of genetically engineered death moving toward him at cheetah speed.

At first he was afraid that the Reaper, coming out of the dark like a bounding tiger, would simply leap over him to tear and toss his charges lifeless into the lake. But Valentine stood, legs planted with the balanced blade of the parang resting in his hand against the back of his thigh.

The Reaper stopped.

It regarded him, drawn skull-face expressionless and yellow eyes sunken in bony sockets.

ahh, the foodling stands, curious after the long chase. it is your nature to run, human, it breathed. *did you think you could steal and escape with our bauble? you would not get out of sight of this pier.* It crouched, froglike.

Valentine tried to keep the fear out of his voice even if he couldn't banish its shadow from his mind. His bowels suddenly seemed made of water, and his tongue was thick and dry.

"Your time is up," Valentine said, speaking quietly to keep his voice from cracking. "In a few seconds, your Master is going to have one less drone."

Go, Rho. Take Molly and haul out of here, he mentally implored.

The Reaper did not laugh, did not smile. It pulled back its lips to reveal obsidian pointed teeth.

oh, no, foodling. it is high night, and your world is mine. soon you will be as cold and empty as the moon, your woman, too. all you have done is spit into a hurricane.

Behind him Valentine heard the motorboat sputter into life. The thing looked for a moment at the vessel. *ahh, a boat, i thought so. your luck has run out.* It reached into its robes and pulled out a short, thick gun. Valentine took a step back in confusion; he had never heard of a Reaper using a gun, but it fired into the air, in the direction of the speedboat. A parachute flare opened, bathing the pier in red light.

"Do you know me, creature?" Valentine asked.

i know your kind, boy. weak and easily emptied. i feast on your fathers at will, as i shall consume you, the Reaper hissed, rising and opening its arms for the deadly embrace.

Valentine brought his blade up. "Not my father. My name is David Valentine. Son of Lee Valentine. Have you met my kind, creature?"

The thing's face lost animation. Perhaps the Kurian Lord at the other end knew dismay.

Valentine attacked. He lunged, hitting it with a backhand swipe that narrowly missed its neck. His blade struck the skull, cutting and glancing off its face with a resounding *thwack*.

It lashed out with a foot, almost caving in Valentine's chest. He fell backwards onto the dock, gasping for air, his parang teetering at the edge of the wooden jetty.

With a soft *plop* it dropped into Lake Michigan.

And David Valentine knew he would die. The vampire-avatar advanced four steps, then bent to take him up in its long arms. But Valentine would meet it on his feet. He rolled away in a blur and got up with the balance of a judo champion recovering from a throw. Exhilarated, he felt a rush of power, a presence that lifted the fear away.

With him stood a phalanx of spirits who had also faced the Kurians. His father and mother, holding hands. Steve Oran and Gilman DelVecchio formed an unflinching wall to his right and left, and behind him Gabriella Cho went on tiptoe to reach his ear.

Go on, Davy. He's not as tough as he seems, she seemed to whisper in his mind.

A terrible strength filled Valentine as the rush infused his belly with fire. The thing paused to wipe sticky black blood from its eye, and Valentine was upon it. The force of his leap knocked it over. Valentine clawed at its back, pinning an arm that tried to tear him off. He wrapped his arms around it. The Reaper flopped and rolled like a netted fish.

It rose, bearing Valentine like a backpack. It began to totter down toward the boat, which seemed to Valentine bathed in a red mist. It tried to shrug him off, but Valentine's arms had turned to steel cables.

Molly Carlson stepped out of the darkness, sighting down the pistol's barrel with tear-streaked eyes. The Reaper moved toward her, no longer struggling with Valentine but reaching for the woman. Valentine shifted his grip and tore open the Reaper's robes at its chest, baring the rippled surface of its rib cage.

"Shoot! Molly, shoot!" he yelled.

She fired, putting bullet after bullet into the vampire's chest. Valentine felt the impact against his own body as the heavy slugs tore into the Reaper's flesh. Black blood fountained out of its mouth.

He slid off the thing's back to avoid the bullets, falling to the ground. It turned its armored back to Molly and staggered toward Valentine, leaning over him as if it sought to at last crush and smother him under the fall of its body. Its deadly jaws opened wide, revealing the pointed tongue behind its fangs.

Valentine brought his knees to his chest and grabbed at the Reaper's sleeves. He brought the creature's weight to the soles of his feet, using its momentum against it. Now almost standing on his head, Valentine kicked out with both legs.

The hissing nightmare flew, thrown upside down into Lake Michigan, arms clawing at empty air. It splashed into the water.

Valentine rolled onto his stomach, looking at the circle of waves emerging from where the robe-weighted Reaper sank from sight. Turbulence broke the water; perhaps the thing was still struggling as it descended into final darkness. . . .

Now it was Molly's turn to help him up. The pair returned to the motorboat, where the fake Reaper still glowered at the two-man crew.

"What the hell was that back there? Who called the Snappers to the pier, of all places? They'll kill us all!" the port officer yelled as they climbed on board.

nothing for you to know about, if you wish to see the dawn, Rho said in imitation of a Reaper's breathy hiss. *return to your duties, and let us catch the* whitecloud.

The port officer ran.

Molly sat next to Valentine, leaning against his shoulder. He watched the two men nervously casting off the boat under Rho's glowing eyes. Just in case, he reloaded the gun. While moving out of the slip, the boat hit something and rocked to a halt.

"What the—?" the man at the wheel said.

The engine sputtered and died.

"You have more guns?" Valentine asked. They ignored the question and stood looking out at the water around them in confusion, He fired a bullet into the windscreen. It spider-webbed, and the men turned to him.

"Get your damn guns!"

The pilot grabbed a shotgun, and the other followed his example and took a revolver from the map case. The boat rocked, and Valentine lurched toward the side. Molly threw herself down, pulling him into the bottom of the boat. Rho clutched at the throttle levers.

Humanlike hands and a dripping face appeared over the side. The Reaper. Valentine fired the pistol and missed, but the face disappeared nevertheless.

"Grenades on this boat?"

"We have a few," he said. He reached into a locker.

"Drop them over the side."

"Can't we get away?" Molly asked.

"The propeller's wedged," the pilot shouted.

"Here!" the man at the locker said, finding a canvas bag with soup-can-style grenades.

Valentine handed his gun to Molly and grabbed a sharpened boat-hook. He listened and tried to guess where the Reaper would appear next while the mate yanked the pin of a grenade and turned to throw it overboard.

An arm lashed up out of the water, catching the man in the temple. The unpinned grenade fell into the bottom of the boat, bounced and rolled toward Valentine.

Molly scrambled for it on her hands and knees. She scooped it with a shoveling motion, as if it were a hot rock. The grenade spun into the water. It exploded, sending a column of water into the air.

The Reaper climbed onto the front of the boat. It had shed its robes and boots. Bullet wounds showed as black patches on its chest like three extra nipples.

"What the hell?" shouted the man at the controls.

Valentine raised the boathook and leaped onto the bow of the speedboat, but the Reaper knocked him aside. It went straight for Rho, jumping into the back of the boat. The Reaper struck the Lifeweaver with a raking blow across his chest.

Rho's masquerade blurred for a moment as he fell, giving Valentine a glimpse of an amorphous blue-green shape. Molly reached for Valentine's gun.

His vision blurred from pain, the Wolf grasped the boathook in both hands. He moved toward the Reaper as it bent to take up the Lifeweaver, a hungry light shining in its eyes.

now, i take—

Valentine buried the curved prong into the thing's back. It reared up, and reached for the boathook in its back by using its elbow joints in the opposite direction from how they worked on a human being.

shoot him, stupid foodling, the Reaper hissed at the pilot, pulling at the hook.

"Don't," Molly shrieked. She pointed the Colt at the pilot.

The Reaper lunged at Valentine. The blow sent him flying. He landed on the prow of the boat. Something hard poked him in the back: he had fetched up against the anchor.

The thing launched itself in the air, landing astride him. It bent, yellow eyes blazing.

Blue-white light flashed, and a shotgun blast tore through the side of the Reaper's face. Skin and stringy black hair exploded in shreds from the skull. A second shot caught it in the back, toppling it over Valentine and into the water.

"Always wanted a crack at one of those sumbitches," the pilot said, breaking open the shotgun to reload it.

Valentine could only lie and watch as a pair of ghostly white hands gripped the tube-steel of the low front rail of the boat.

"No, goddammit," Valentine said. "You're through." He put the pain away and unclasped the anchor, making sure the line was not attached.

Mechanically, the Reaper pulled itself onto the boat. Its face had lost all animation, its limbs moving in uncoordinated jerks.

Valentine lifted the Danforth anchor by the shank, and turned it so the twin flukes pointed down. He brought it down on the Reaper's spine, burying the steel into its torso. Still holding on to the anchor, the Wolf strained every muscle and picked up the Reaper. He heaved and threw the weighted abomination into Lake Michigan.

Beyond the splash, he saw gray humps in the water moving toward the boat.

"Shit, the Snappers are coming," the pilot said.

Rho rose to his feet, the Reaper disguise gone. His human form looked like a wind-bent old tree, white hair streaming in the lake breeze. A misty patch at his chest throbbed with a faint blue light.

"I'm so tired," he said. "But perhaps I can help."

The Lifeweaver closed his eyes and gripped the boat. It began to move.

The boat picked up speed. Valentine saw more humps closing in from the sides. But they avoided the boat, gathering around the turbulence where the Reaper had disappeared in its final plunge.

"I've got the other grenade," the pilot said.

"We won't need it," Molly said, looking out over the stern. "Whatever they are, I hope they have strong stomachs."

Once clear of the harbor, Valentine and the pilot went over the side and unwound the Reaper's robe from the propeller.

"You two just helped three terrorists escape Chicago," Valentine told the Quisling as Molly helped them back into the boat. His friend was still unconscious, under a blanket in the forward cabin. "You can come with us and be set down somewhere, or join the fleet if they'll have you. It's the least I owe you for your help. That is if you don't want to paddle back and have a talk with the Reapers."

"I think we'd better come with you, sir. The name's J. P., by the way. My mate's name is Cal Swanson."

"Thought you might, J. P."

With the powerful motor again in action, they spotted the two-masted ship's lights before dawn. The speedboat tied up against the *Whitecloud* in an easy swell. The sailors, a mixed group of ten men, women, and children, came on deck to look at the visitors.

Rho stood still as a carving for a moment, looking at the new faces, then sank to his knees.

Valentine rushed to his side. He turned the Lifeweaver's face to him, but Rho did not react.

"I'm exhausted, Valentine the Younger. You are among your kind now?"

"Close enough," Valentine said. "We're safe, if that's what you mean."

The masklike expression did not change. Valentine looked into eyes filled with thousands of years of memories. "I will go in peace, then." Something that might have been a smile appeared on his lips. "I escaped them after all."

"Maybe you just need rest and food, sir. I'll help you up."

The Lifeweaver's mind touched his.

Too tired to talk. You've helped me more than you know. They would have dined long on me, but now I'll fly away free in death. Bring me to the cabin, the others should not . . .

"Molly, you and J. P. clear out the cabin, would you?" Valentine said.

He picked up the featherweight Lifeweaver. The former Quisling dragged his comrade Cal out into the night air.

"Help us, please," Molly implored to the faces above. Two sailors from the *Whitecloud* swung down.

Valentine took Rho into the dim compartment. A pair of tiny bunks angled together into the sharp prow of the vessel. He laid the Lifeweaver down.

Thank you, Lee . . . David. You have a strong aura. It might be best if . . . the others didn't see me, after . . . The mind's touch faltered.

"It's not over, sir. Just rest."

It . . . , Rho began, but never finished. He flickered one final time, before shifting back to his natural form. The thing he knew as Rho collapsed into a rubbery mass the size of a teenage boy. Rho sagged—there was no skeleton to support his body—into something that looked like a blue octopus with a bit of bat in the evolutionary tree. Leathery fins ran the sides of his tentacles, the longer limbs at the back of his body joined by the veiny membranes almost to the sucker-tipped ends like a ribbed cape, the shorter ones at the front unattached and with smaller, more delicate suckers. His aqua-colored skin, more blue around cephalopod skull, changed to sea-foam green along his limbs, with a latticework of delicate black lines covering the skin that he found eerily beautiful, though if they were decorative or functional Valentine could not say. Spicules and flaps formed a band under the brain-in-a-bag of its head, but whether they were noses, ears, breathing tubes, or even sexual organs was anyone's guess. The bulging eyes, lids opening wider and wider as it relaxed into death, drew Valentine's gaze back every time he looked elsewhere. They were like yellowish crystal balls flecked with red, with a black band running across the middle.

God, it was ugly for an angel. Or a devil, for that matter.

Valentine hugged the moist, limp form to himself. He owed his and Molly's life to the dead Lifeweaver. When the warmth had left the body, he covered it with a blanket.

He should stuff Rho's body in a bucket or a big jug, preserve it with alcohol, and get it back to the Miskatonic. The researchers there might be able to find a weakness, some flaw that would allow them to kill the Kurians without blasting into their lairs and blowing them to bits. Duty, and loyalty to his species, demanded it.

He exited the cabin and went to the engine.

"Take any gear and fixtures you want out of her," he said to the crewmen of the *Whitecloud.* "But don't go in the cabin."

He found a hose and siphoned some gasoline up into a water bottle. He took the fuel down into the forward compartment and splashed it on the carpet and wood paneling. He repeated the process until the gas was gone and the speedboat reeked of fumes. He followed his shipmates into the sailing vessel as the sailors pulled the powerful outboard up out of its mount with a block and tackle.

Valentine reached into his pockets and found one more tin of matches. He struck them all at once, and tossed the flaming handful into the cabin. Flames raced through the boat, and the *Whitecloud* sailors cast it off.

He watched and waited until the lake consumed the flaming wreck. The smoke dissipated into the fresh breeze.

Sailors are used to the unexpected. A woman with a long, thin-boned face introduced herself as Collier, the captain of the *Whitecloud,* and offered them blankets and hot coffee.

She invited them below to the cramped galley. Valentine showed the captain his card, the chit given him by Captain Doss of the *White Lightning.* She agreed to take them north, where they could transfer to another ship, which could take them anywhere in the Great Lakes they wished to go. "I'd do it anyway, even without Dossie's card. Something tells me you went through a lot to get here."

He, Molly, and J. P. discussed their options on the coming voyage. They decided to winter in the familiar (at least to Valentine) reaches of the Boundary Waters. He would see Father Max again. Only when spring came would he have to make new decisions.

A very weary David Valentine took Molly into the clean, cold air of the Lake Michigan morning. They looked west as the shoreline slowly became distinct and the sun penetrated the clouds. He thought of all the doomed souls beyond the distant, mist-shrouded shore. He had saved Molly, but how many others had died to feed the Reapers in the last three days?

He remembered a story that Father Max used to tell, and a quote he had to memorize from the green blackboard, of a tireless nun named Mother Teresa. She and her Sisters of Mercy had worked with the multitudes of impoverished, disease-stricken people in India. A journalist had asked her how she managed to keep her spirits up, when despite her unceasing labors there would always be more suffering than she could possibly cure.

Mother Teresa had thought for a moment, and then said: "You start with one."

David Valentine turned to watch the dawn, Molly's hand in his.
One.

CHOICE OF
THE CAT

To Paul, for opening the door

"Cat 'e no yoke. You no see 'im, you no 'ear 'im. Den yomp! 'E come."

—Richard Adams, *Watership Down*

One

The Great Plains Gulag, March of the forty-fifth year of the Kurian Order: Only the bones of a civilization remain, monuments to mankind's apogee. Nature and time gnaw away the rest. Derricks still stand in this corner of oil country, giant iron insects surveying the countryside. Beneath them, the pumps rust, scattered in the long yellowish grass like metal herbivores, snouts thrust into the earth. The former wheat fields, fallow for generations and returned to native forest or prairie, feed longhorns, deer, and canny wild pigs. It is a land of receding horizons, a stopped watch, timeless.

The soil under cultivation bears the turned over, trampled look of spring plowing. The tools and methods used on the stretches of farmland would make a twentieth-century resident either stare in wonder or spit in disgust. Horse-drawn plows, some with just a single blade, sit at the edges of the fields, where they were abandoned at quitting time, plots fertilized only by what comes out of the back end of an animal.

The agricultural settlements at the center of the remaining fields, always near a road or rail line, look more like chain-gang camps than family farms. Surrounded by barbed wire and watchtowers, the clapboard barracks that house the workers and their families cry out for a coat of paint and a new roof to replace the flapping plastic tarps covering assorted holes. Trash heaps and pit toilets decorate the compounds among pitiful vegetable gardens. The children playing amid the tight-packed buildings flirt with nudity, so worn away are their clothes.

Near the gate of these camps a more substantial building usually stands at a respectful distance from the barracks, avoiding contact like a visitor to a leper colony. Often a sturdy pre-22 brick construct; the windows hold glass behind bars or shutters, and curtains behind the glass.

A few miles north of Oologah Lake along old State Route 60, one of these collective farms, known to its residents as the Rigyard, is nestled between gently rolling hills. Two rows of tall wire fencing encircle the camp. Barracks laid out foursquare sit in the shadow of two watchtowers, dwarfed in turn by two cavernous garages like enormous Quonset huts. The garages are patchworks of earthen wall, structural iron, and corrugated aluminum. On the other side of them, in a commanding position near the gate, an L-shaped cinder-block building dating to the 1950s folds itself protectively around a set of gasoline pumps. A water tower—a recent addition, judging from the new shine to the steel—leans slightly askew above, adding a jaunty top hat to the guardhouse. Behind the cinder-block building, a fine two-story house stands in splendid isolation at the farthest point upwind from the barracks, circled first by a porch and then a set of razor-wire fencing with padlocked gate.

Each watchtower contains a single sentinel dressed in green-brown-mottle camouflage fatigues and black leather hunting cap. The sentry to the south is the more alert; he occasionally crosses his little crow's nest to glance up and down the highway bordering the camp's southern fence. The one to the north chews a series of toothpicks in appropriately beaverish front teeth. He watches a trio of smock-clad women wash clothing in the community sink set between the barracks.

Were the other guard equipped with an excellent pair of binoculars (unlikely, but possible), perfect eyesight (still less likely, as guarding farmers and mechanics is reserved for older members of the Territorials), and intelligent initiative in carrying out his duty (the phrase "cold day in hell" springs to mind) he would have paid attention to the gully winding up the hill that shelters the Rigyard from the prevailing winds. The wooded cut in the hill offers ample concealment and a commanding view, whether for simple observation or an organized attack.

A figure possessing all those qualities lies on that hill, surrounded by the white and yellow and red wildflowers of an Oklahoma spring. He is a muscular, long-limbed young man with coppery skin and wary brown eyes. Dressed not so differently from his ancestors on the Sioux side of his family, he wears a uniform of buckskin, save for a thicker cowhide equipment belt and boots. Lustrous black hair is drawn back from his face into a ponytail, giving him the illusion of closely cropped hair from every direction but behind, where it dangles to his shoulders. He wears an intent expression as he examines the camp. A young cheetah watching a watering hole might exhibit such wariness, unsure whether the vegetation contains game or a lion ready to pounce. His eyes wander from point to point in the camp with the aid of a pair of black binoculars, lingering here and there while his forearm acts as a monopod. Like the bucktoothed guard in the southern tower, his mouth is also working, thoughtfully nibbling on the tender end of a blade of seed-topped grass.

His gaze returns to the wire-enclosed yard of the two-story house. In the grassy back lawn of the house, two T-shaped metal posts face each other, missing the clothesline that once joined them. Instead of wash drying in the afternoon sun, three men and a woman are painfully attached to the improvised gibbet. Their wrists are clasped behind them and tied to the metal crossbeam above, tight enough to dislocate a shoulder if they slump in their bonds.

He knows that death awaits the four—not from pained exhaustion or exposure—but from something quicker, more horrible, and as sure as the setting sun.

The senior lieutenant of Foxtrot Company set down his binoculars and focused his eyes a few feet in front of him on a flowering coral bean, its delicate red spindles inclining toward the sun. The diversion failed; though they were a good kilometer away, he could still see the agonized figures in the yard. His shoulders throbbed with sympathetic pain. After four years' service to the Cause, his sensitivity to suffering had grown more acute, rather than less.

Lt. David Valentine looked back down into the gully. His platoon, numbering thirty-five in all, rested with backs up against leafing trees, using their packs to keep their backsides off the rain-soaked earth. They had covered a lot of ground since skirting the northern edge of Lake Oologah that morning, moving at a steady, mile-eating run. Rifles rested ready in their laps. They wore leather uniforms frilled in variegated styles to taste. Some still wore their winter beards, and no two hats matched. The only accoutrement his three squads shared were their short, broad-bladed machetes, known as parangs—though some wore them on their belts, some across their chests, and some sheathed them in their moccasin-leather puttees.

They didn't look like mixture of legend and alien science, part of a elite caste known as the Hunters.

Valentine signaled with two fingers to the men waiting in the gully, and Sergeant Stafford climbed up the wash to join him in the damp bracken. His platoon sergeant, known as Gator off-duty because of his leathery skin and wide, toothy grin, worked slowly to Valentine's overlook. Wordlessly, the lieutenant passed Stafford his binoculars. Stafford examined the compound as Valentine chewed another inch off the grass stalk clamped in his teeth.

"Looks like that last sprint was for nothing," Valentine said. "The tractor trailer pulled in here. We wouldn't have intercepted anyway—this must be a pretty good stretch of road."

"How do you figure that, sir?" Stafford said, searching the compound in vain for any sign of the tanker truck they'd spotted crawling through the rain that morning. The platoon dashed cross-country in order to ambush the tempting target. Thanks to the state of the roads in this part of the Kurian Zone, the rig couldn't move much faster than the Wolves could run.

"Look at the ruts by the gate, turning off the road. They've got to have been made by an eighteen-wheeler," Valentine said.

"Could have been from yesterday—even the day before, Lieutenant."

Valentine raised an eyebrow. "No puddles. Rain would have filled in something that deep. Those were made since the shower ended—what?—a half hour ago?"

"Err . . . okay, yeah . . . so the truck's in one of those big garages getting worked on. We get in touch with the captain, the rest of the company is here in a day or two, and we burn the compound. I figure fifteen or twenty guarding this place at most. Ten's more likely."

"I'd like nothing better, Staff. Time's a problem, though."

"Val, I know food's short, but what else is new? There's enough game and forage in these woods—"

"Sorry, Gator," Valentine said, taking the binoculars back. "I misspoke. I should have said time's running short for *them*."

Stafford's eyebrows arched in surprise. "What, those four tied up down there? Okay, it's ugly, but since when have we gotten dead over the punishments handed out by these little Territorial commandants?"

"I don't think it's just punishment," Valentine said, his eyes now on the two-story house.

"Hell, sir, you know these collaborator creeps. . . . They'll flog a woman for not getting the skid marks out of their skivvies. These four probably were last out of the barracks for roll call or something. God knows."

Valentine waited for a moment, wondering whether to give voice to a feeling. "I think they're breakfast. There's a Reaper in that house, maybe more than one."

Sgt. Tom Stafford blanched. "H-how d-do you figure that, sir?"

Valentine read the sergeant's fear with a species of relief. He wanted a subordinate in mortal fear of the Reapers. Any man who did not tremble at the thought of facing a couple of Hoods was either a fool or inexperienced, and there were far too many inexperienced Wolves in Foxtrot Company. Whether or not the whole lot, officers included, were fools was a question Valentine sometimes debated with himself on long winter nights.

"Look at the first story of the house, Sergeant," Valentine said, passing the binoculars back. "It's a nice day. Someone is letting in the spring air. But that second story now . . . shuttered. I think I even see a blanket stuffed in between the slats. And that little stovepipe coming out of the wall—that's got to be for a bedroom, not the kitchen. See the vapor? Someone has a fire going."

"Dark and warm. Hoods like it like that," Stafford agreed.

"My guess is that after the sun's down, the visitor will rise and go about its business. It won't feed till almost morning. It wouldn't risk taking them before it could sleep safe again—you know how dopey they get after feeding."

"Okay, sir, then that's the time to hit 'em. Tomorrow morning." Stafford couldn't keep the excitement out of his voice. "Maybe the captain could even get here by then. That refinery he's scouting can't be more than thirty miles away. They feed, dawn comes, and they button up in that house. We burn them out, even if it rains again, and have enough guns to knock 'em down, and keep 'em down till we can get in with the blades."

"That would be my plan exactly, Sergeant," Valentine agreed. "Except for one thing."

"What, you think that house won't burn if it rains again? Those phosphorous candles, I've seen them burn through tin, sir. They'll get the job done."

"You missed my point, Staff," he said, spitting out the thoroughly chewed blade of grass. "I'm not going to let the Hoods get their tongues into those poor bastards."

Valentine knew the word *incredulous* was probably not in his platoon sergeant's vocabulary, but Stafford's expression neatly illustrated the meaning of the word. "Errr . . . sir, I feel for them, too, but hell, it's too much of a risk."

"Having thirty Wolves within a mile of the Reapers is a risk, too. Even if we all concentrate on lowering lifesign, they still might pick up on us. Then we'd be faced with Reapers coming at us in the dark."

Stafford's left eye gave a twitch. The Reapers hunted not by sight or scent, but by sensing an energy created by living beings. Energy the Reapers' Masters desired.

"The sun isn't waiting," Valentine continued. "We're going to hit them now, while most of the guards are off in the fields. Keep an eye on things from up here—whistle if anything happens."

The lieutenant returned to his platoon, scooting backwards on his belly until he reached the cut in the hillside. He gathered his three squads around him.

"Heads up, Second Platoon. The captain detached us with orders to raise a little hell if we get the chance, and we just got it. There's a pretty big civvie compound on the other side of this hill. Looks like farmworkers and maybe some mechanics—there's a couple of big garages behind the wire. Two guard towers with a man in each. I figure most of the able-bodied are out in the fields to the north, and the garrison is keeping an eye on them. Chances are, there are only a few left in the compound, counting the two in the towers. Looks like there could be Hoods in there, too."

Valentine gave them a moment to digest this. Newer Wolves composed the majority of Foxtrot Company, rebuilt after being bled white in action east of Hazlett, Missouri, in the summer of '65. Each of his three squads had only one or two reliable veterans; most of the experienced men were with the captain or leading smaller patrols on this scouting foray into the Gulag lands north of Tulsa. While all had gone through the arduous training of Southern Command, the gulf between training and experience had been crossed by only a handful of his men. But the newbies were eager to prove themselves as true Wolves, and all had reason to hate the Reapers and the Quislings assisting them.

Valentine's eyes searched the expectant eyes for a pair of almost cherubic young faces. "Jenkins and Oliver, take a map and head south. Sergeant Stafford will show you where the captain's headquarters is supposed to be. If he's not there, go back to summer camp south of the Pensacola Dam and report. If you do find him, tell him we're about to hit some Reapers. I expect the Territorials'll react, and there'll be columns from all over converging on this spot. Maybe he can bushwhack one. We're going to run east and wait at camp. Got it?"

Marion Oliver held up her hand. "Sir, can't we be in on the attack, *then* go find the captain?"

Valentine shook his head. "Oliver, I could sure use you, but just in case this goes to hell, the captain would want to know what we found, where we were when we found it, and what we were going to do about it.

"Now when it was raining earlier, I saw a few of you with those new rain ponchos you lifted outta that storehouse we broke into a couple days ago. I need to borrow three of them, and two volunteers. . . ."

An hour later, Valentine walked down the empty road toward the camp, watching clouds build up again to the southwest. He hoped for more rain overnight. It would slow pursuit.

He wore a green rain slicker—an oily-smelling poncho borrowed from one of his men. Two of his best snap-shooters trailed just behind, brisk and bold in the open daylight, also wearing the rain gear stolen from the Quisling Territorials. Valentine had his sleeves tucked together to hide his hands—and what was in his hands.

As the trio approached the camp, the guard in the south tower near the road waved lazily and called something down to the cinder-block guardhouse below. Valentine smelled concentrated humanity ahead, along with the odors of gasoline and oil.

Like all Wolves, he possessed sharpened senses of hearing and smell and a mule's endurance, gifts from the Lifeweavers, humanity's allies in the battle against their fallen brothers from the planet Kur. Valentine made use of that hearing as he approached the camp, concentrating on the two guards walking up to the gate.

"Guy in front looks Injun, if you ask me," one uniformed figure commented to his associate. Valentine, still a hundred yards away, heard every word as if from ten feet. "Mebbe he's Osage or something."

"Didn't ask you, Gomez," the older of the two replied, scratching the stubble on his chin in thought. "Better go tell the looie, strangers comin' to the gate on foot."

"Franks is having a beer with that truck driver. They've been through six by now, prolly."

"You'd better tell him, or he'll have you stripped. He's jumpy what with the Visitors."

Valentine worked the safety on the pistol in his left hand. The gun in his right hand was a revolver; he covered the hammer with his thumb so it would not catch when he pulled it from the baggy coat sleeves. The seconds stretched as the Wolves approached the gate. The Territorial named Gomez returned with a tall thin man, who threw away a cigarette as he exited the gatehouse.

"Shit, four at the gate . . . ," Alpin, the young Wolf behind him muttered.

"Stick to the plan. I just want you two to get the guy in the tower," Valentine said, quickening his step. "Hi, there," he called. "I'm supposed to see a Lieutenant Franks. He's here, right? I got a message for him."

The bored guard at the southern tower leaned over to hear the exchange below, rifle held ready but pointed skyward. Valentine took a final glance around the compound. Back toward the barracks, a few women and children squatted on the steps or peered out of tiny windows at the visitors.

The tall lieutenant stepped forward and eyed Valentine through the wire, hand on his stiff canvas holster. "I don't know you, kid. Where's the message, and who sent you?"

"It's verbal, Lieutenant," Valentine answered. "Let me think. . . . It goes like this: You're a shit-eating, traitorous, murderous disgrace to the human race. That's about it."

The guards inside the gate froze.

"Uuh?" Franks grunted. Franks's hand seized his sidearm, the Velcro on the clasp making a tiny tearing sound, but Valentine had the two pistols out before the Quisling's hand even got around the grip. Valentine squeezed off two shots from the automatic and one from the revolver into the lieutenant's chest, the officer's limbs jerking with the false nerve signals generated by the impacting bullets as he fell.

Behind him, the two Wolves raised their carbines. One had some trouble with his poncho, delaying him for a second, but Alpin put a bullet through the guard's chin while the sentry was still shouldering his rifle. The other Wolf got his gun clear in time to put another shot into the lurching figure even as the magazine-fed battle rifle fell out of the tower.

In the time it took the guard's rifle to smack into the wet dirt twenty feet below, Valentine emptied his two pistols into the other Quislings at the gate. The three Wolves dived for the roadside ditch, splashing into puddled rainwater. Valentine abandoned the empty revolver and slipped a fresh magazine into the automatic, sliding the action to chamber the first round. A shot fired from the northern tower whizzed overhead.

Alpin slithered along the ditch as Valentine popped his gun arm and one eye over the crest of the depression, gun following his gaze as he checked the door and windows of the old guardhouse. An unlatched metal screen door with the word WELCOME worked into the decor squeaked in the gusty breeze. Valentine rolled back into the ditch.

"Should I make a try at the gate, sir?" Baker asked, muddy water dripping from his face.

Valentine shook his head. "Stay put, and wait for the sarge."

Farther down the ditch, Alpin popped up to swap shots with the northern tower.

"Alpin, stay down!" Valentine yelled.

The Wolf brought his gun up again, and a bullet burrowed into the ground right in front of his face. Dirt flew, and with a pained cry, Alpin dropped his gun and covered his right eye. Valentine crawled toward the youth, swearing through clenched teeth, when he heard a wet smack followed by the report of the shot. Alpin toppled backwards into the ditch. Valentine risked a dash to his trooper, whose one good eye fluttered open and shut next to the bloody ruin of the other.

The challenging wail of a hand-cranked siren sounded through the camp as he pulled Alpin along the ditch, seeking to put the gatehouse between them and the rifleman. Stafford had the platoon attacking the northern fence. Valentine heard a shot and the sound of breaking glass, where his other gunman was shooting at God-knows-what in the guardhouse.

Valentine found the wound in Alpin's arm and pressed hard to stop the bleeding. Thankfully, the sticky flow welled up underneath his palm in a steady stream rather than short arterial bursts. He called the other Wolf over.

"Baker! Alpin's hit!"

"Someone came to a window there. . . . I missed," Baker gabbled.

"Keep your head down. C'mere and help me put a dressing on," Valentine barked.

Baker scuttled over, but seemed at a loss as soon as he looked at Alpin. First-aid training always took place in a quiet meadow, not stretched out in a wet ditch with no elbow room.

Valentine blew out an exasperated breath. "Never mind. Just put pressure right here," Valentine said, placing Baker's hand on the underside of Alpin's arm, just below the armpit. "Press hard. Don't worry—he's in shock. He doesn't feel anything."

Valentine popped his head up again—still no sign of the other Wolves, although no more shots came from the direction of the northern tower. The guard had either run or been shot. Baker seemed to catch on, and he took control of keeping tension on the tourniquet.

"Mister, mister!" someone yelled from the guardhouse. "We surrender. . . . I surrender, I mean. I'm coming out, no gun. I got a woman with me."

"I'm just a housekeeper. I ain't one of the Territorials!" a woman's voice added.

He cautiously looked out of the ditch. "Come on out, then!" Valentine called. "Hands up in the air!"

The WELCOME door opened, and a young man in camouflage fatigues emerged, followed by a woman in a simple smock. Valentine aimed the pistol at the Territorial. "You in the uniform—facedown on the ground—now!"

The Territorial complied. No more shots came from the other side of the compound, but Valentine could see Oklahomans running from the barracks toward the north fence. The Wolves must have reached the compound.

"Open the gate, please." The woman rushed to comply. The unlocked gate swung easily on its hinges, and Valentine entered the camp. He walked up to the Territorial, still on the ground, face turned sideways and fearfully eyeing Valentine.

"Terri, you better tell me who's in the house, unless you want to piss off the man with the gun aimed at your head."

"Mister, it's four Skulls, and some administrator guy out of Tulsa. And I ain't really a Territorial, I just wear the uniform because I'm in the transports. I drive trucks. I just drive trucks, I swear."

"Did you drive a tanker in here today?"

"Yes, sir . . . that was me. They got a pump for the road vehicles and tractor. I'm s'posed to spend the night here at the Rigyard, then—"

"I found the lieutenant," a voice called. A Wolf pointed his gun around the corner of the guardhouse, covering the door.

"Sarge, Lieutenant Valentine's here. He's okay," another added.

"Keep an eye on these two," Valentine ordered. "Sanchez, help Baker carry Alpin in." Baker's head and shoulders popped up like a curious prairie dog. Wolves rushed to help him with their wounded comrade.

Chaos in the compound. Oklahoman civvies, mostly women and children, milled everywhere, shouting and crying with excitement. Wolves had taken up positions around the two-story house, pointing their rifles at it from cover, but no one was eager to get any closer than absolutely necessary. A pair of Wolves had grabbed a horse, interposing it between themselves and the house while they cut down the four figures hanging from the old T-shaped metal clothesline. Sergeant Stafford directed this last among a cluster of riflemen with barrels trained on the back door of the house.

Valentine waved over a corporal. "Get some men in that south tower. I want to know if anything shows on the road." He glanced at the horizon—with the thick clouds, it would be dark in less than an hour. He had to work fast. If he even had the hour: should the Reapers feel sufficiently threatened, they would simply bolt. He doubted he could stop four from getting away. And once night returned, bringing the Reapers back to full use of their senses, the triumphant Wolves might become tempting sheep. The Rigyard could turn into a death trap.

Valentine watched the rescue of the four bound victims, and then he trotted back to his truck-driving prisoner. A pair of Wolves stood above him, forcing him to squat, face to the wall, with fingers laced behind his head. Valentine waved them off and lowered himself to his haunches, facing the man.

"Here's the deal, friend. Usually when we catch a man wearing the enemy uniform, we take care of it with a bullet, or a rope—time permitting. Do you know what the Ozark Free Territory is?"

"Yes, sir. It's you folks in the hills there in Southern Missouri and Arkansas."

"I can arrange to take you there," Valentine said.

The young man's eyes widened. "What, to hang?"

"No, as a free man. I just need you to drive your truck one more time."

"Let me guess: a suicide mission?"

Valentine grinned. "Maybe. But I'll be riding shotgun."

The engine started with a growling, mechanical *grrrrrr grrrrrr grrrrrrrrrrrrr.* The brakes lifted with a hydraulic shriek; the tractor and its trailer pulled out of the barnlike garage.

As the vehicle accelerated, a Wolf gave the drop hose beneath the tanker a final twist of the cap. Valentine watched gasoline spray as his man jumped out of the way of the truck. The tanker moved across the compound, leaving a rainbow-catching trail.

Jouncing in the cabin of the tractor, with a pump-action shotgun ready to keep the Reapers off, Valentine glanced at the driver. The trucker wore a smile that was more than half snarl. "What's your name, anyway?" Valentine asked, raising his voice over the unmuffled engine.

"Pete Ostlander. Always dreamed of plowing this rig into something. Yours?"

"David Valentine."

Ostlander angled for the spacious front porch of the house. "Brace yourself, Valentine!" he shouted, changing gears. The truck shuddered and picked up speed, churning the wet turf of the lawn. Valentine put his feet against the dashboard and pushed himself tightly into the seat back.

The ancient hauler barreled onto the porch, taking out decking, supports, and roof. The aged wood collapsed like cardboard under the force of the truck's impact. The side of the house caved in, and Valentine could see the homey furnishings through the driver's-side window.

As the truck ground to a halt, Valentine opened his door and launched himself out of the cab, holding the shotgun with his finger across the trigger guard. He tumbled, turned it into a bone-jarring shoulder roll, and came to his feet running for the cinder-block gatehouse. Valentine glanced over his shoulder and saw Ostlander struggling with his seat-belt hook, which had caught on his boot. The driver freed himself and slid to the passenger side.

"Light it! Light it!" Valentine shouted.

Back at the garage, a Wolf touched flame to the gasoline trail. Fire raced across the pooled gasoline. By the guardhouse, three more Wolves waited with grenades ready in case the fuel failed to ignite the tanker. They yelled and pointed behind Valentine, who read the alarm in their expressions. One fired his gun. Valentine turned around, body twisting and following his gun barrel like a sidewinder coiling to strike.

Ostlander jumped from the tanker. Death knelt on the top of the truck, long monklike hood covering its head. The black-caped figure lashed down and grabbed Ostlander by the neck. The driver gave a spasmodic jerk—Valentine's ears caught to snick of vertebrae separating—then sagged with his head flopping forward. Shots from the covering Wolves tore into black robes. The Reaper ignored them; the heavy cloth dampened their kinetic energy, and the Reaper's tough frame did the rest.

The Reaper probably heard the approaching flames, rather than seeing them. It dropped the dying Ostlander and sprang up and over the roof of the house in a gravity-defying jump. When Valentine saw his Wolves fling themselves to the earth, he followed suit. He dropped to the ground with hands at the sides of his head, covering his ears with his thumbs and closing his nose with his pinkies. The tanker exploded with a *whump*. Valentine felt a hot blast of air lick across his back before the concussion knocked him senseless.

He awoke, with vague memories of a delightful dream. The drifting, blissful feeling bled away as his eyes focused on Corporal Holloway, the junior NCO.

"Good news, Holloway," Valentine murmured, still half-awake. "I like the way you handle yourself and the men—I'm recommending you to the captain for promotion to lance. Want the job?"

Holloway started to smile; then his brows furrowed. "Tell the sarge the lieutenant's awake, Gregg. He's kinda groggy."

Grogs? Danger! Valentine returned to Oklahoma with a rush, a long slide back into reality. He smelled burning tires and charred flesh and realized he lay in the cold confines of the gatehouse. He looked around at the rough, bare furniture and sat up, feeling nauseated.

"Okay, Holloway . . . better now. Water, please," croaked a voice that he had to convince himself was his.

Holloway handed him a tin cup, and Valentine gulped it down. "How long was I out?"

"About fifteen minutes, sir. Closer to twenty now."

"The Reapers?"

"Better let the sarge explain, sir. But I don't think there's anything to worry about right now."

Stafford bounced in, a relieved smile on his face. "It's getting dark, sir. No sign of the work details or their guards. They probably saw the smoke and put two and two together. I've got everyone set to pull out. There are a couple high-clearance pickups we can use. I put Alpin in one. Big Jeff volunteered to drive it. We could get you out in the other. Holloway's good behind a wheel."

Valentine stood up, the dizziness fading. "No ambulance required, Staff. Anyone else hurt?"

"Not a one, sir."

"The Hoods?"

"Only one made it out of the house, the one that jumped over the roof. He was on fire, took off like a scalded cat. We chased him down, but the light was fading. Looked like he fell over—his robe was still burning. We put about twenty rounds into it and threw a couple of grenades. Turned out it was just his robe. He must have dropped it and scuttled off flat-assed. My guess is he probably can't see—he plowed right into the wire and had to claw through it. We shouldn't have to worry about him."

Valentine thought for a moment. "What about the dependents?"

"That's your decision, sir. We're feeding those poor bastards that were tied up outside the house. They're in pretty poor shape. Some of the women were asking me, but I played dumb. Gave them the keys to the storeroom, though. They're emptying it now."

"Okay, I'll talk to them. We're going to head for the Pensacola Dam. Put the prisoners in one of the pickups, and find a driver. I'm putting you in charge of the vehicles. Make sure you got food, water, and fuel, spare tires if you can find 'em. Drive slowly with your lights off; you'll make it. Cross country where you can, especially after the old expressway."

"Beats walking, sir."

"Get rolling before the Territorials can organize themselves."

Stafford nodded and started calling men to him. Valentine turned to a level-eyed NCO with a single stripe on his tunic. "Corporal Yamashiro, you're in charge of getting the men ready for a march. Pass out the weapons to the Oklahomans. Wreck any machinery except the two pickups. Were there any more Territorial prisoners?"

Yamashiro coughed meaningfully. "We found two more in uniform hiding in the garage, sir. They say they're just mechanics."

"I'll let the women decide what to do with them. We'll give them guns—they're welcome to shoot them."

"Yes, sir."

Valentine offered his hand. "Good luck, Staff. See you at the dam."

Stafford shook it, his face grave.

Night crept over the compound, the ramshackle barracks now illuminated by a bonfire of the flaming wreckage of the house. Valentine watched preparations on the two pickup trucks for a moment. Both trucks seemed well maintained, with heavy-duty tires and plenty of ground clearance. He nodded to Big Jeff, who was already behind the wheel of one and gunning the engine, listening to its harsh roar like a concerned doctor with a wheezy patient.

Valentine walked over to the barracks, where Wolves were handing out weapons. A grizzled oldster selected a rifle and pocketed two boxes of ammunition. He examined the sights, opened the receiver, and peered down the barrel. The man knew weapons. Valentine caught his eye and beckoned him over.

"Sorry we can't do more for you folks just now, sir. We have to move fast," Valentine explained.

The man worked the action on the rifle. "Don't give it another thought, feller. Best thing to happen around here in years, you taking a poke at the bastards."

"What are you and the others going to do?"

"Well, that ain't been decided yet. Most will sit tight—the women want their men around. Even if something bad happens, they want it to happen to them together. I expect them Territorials'll move back in. A couple of the younger ones have already run for it, heading for your parts east, I expect."

"And that rifle in your hands?"

"I'm sixty-six. I just do odd jobs around the camp. I could feel my time coming. In fact, I bet I was on the menu for them Skulls you burnt out, if 'n they were to hang around much longer. I've got a little spot picked out in the old junk pile back of the garage. Real nice view from there of the whole place. There's a certain sergeant in the Territorials stationed here. I'm hoping for a chance to get him in the sights of this here repeater. And one or two others after him, mebbe. I gotta thank you, Lieutenant. It'll be a good death. I'll go now with the biggest damn smile."

Valentine opened his mouth to argue, but read something in the hard set of the wrinkles around the man's eyes that closed off debate.

"Right." Valentine groped for words. It seemed inappropriate to wish him luck. "Shoot straight."

"Don't worry on my account, sonny." With a nod, the man slung his rifle, picked up a shotgun, and moved off into the shadows of the open garage, whistling. Valentine heard the tune long after the figure disappeared.

A woman tugged at his sleeve. "Sir, sir!" she implored.

Valentine turned.

She thrust a diapered baby into his arms, cocooned in a plaid blanket. "His name's Ryan. Ryan Werth. He's only eleven months. Just mash any old thing up real good, and he'll eat it," she said, tears streaming down her cheeks.

Valentine tried to give the baby back to her. "Sorry, ma'am . . . but . . ."

The woman refused to take back the child. She put her palms over her eyes and fled into the crowd.

"Mrs. Werth! Mrs. Werth, I'm sorry, but we can't do this," Valentine called, going after her. He looked down at the baby, which was now squalling lustily. He could understand the mother's motives. The Kurians might do anything in the camp as a reprisal if they thought the inhabitants had cooperated.

He looked around for someone, anyone in the camp to hand the baby to, but they'd disappeared. He couldn't just set it down. Feeling more than a little ridiculous, Valentine returned to the pickups, trying to comfort the child. Perhaps Stafford had room for a bawling baby.

"Lieutenant Valentine, sir?" A young Wolf named Poulos stepped forward, saluting smartly. Poulos was a thick-muscled, good-looking young man who tended to keep to himself. He was one of the few survivors of the old Foxtrot Company, and wasn't going out of his way to bond with the new recruits, or else he'd have been promoted by now. Valentine understood his reasons.

"Yes, Poulos. What is it? I've got my hands rather full at the moment."

Poulos smothered the beginnings of a smile. "Sir, I have to ask your permission to take a dependent with us. Corporal Holloway told me to ask you, sir." Poulos stepped aside to reveal a beautiful girl in her late teens, wrapped up in a long coat with a bag over her shoulder. "Sir, this is Linda Meyer. She wants to come with us. Her ma was one of the ones tied up behind the house. I'll feed her off my rations. She'll keep up, she's healthy, and she can run, sir."

Valentine shook his head. "A girl already, Poulos? How many hours have we been here? I'd have thought with the Hoods afoot and the perimeter being secured, you'd have other things to do."

"She was showing me where the Terris hid the supplies, and we started—"

"Never mind the story. You know that's against regulations. Dangerous for her to be seen talking to us." *Bad for discipline for soldiers to go sniffing around for companionship in the KZ*, Valentine added to himself silently. Then there was the chance that she could be a plant. Two years ago, his first command in the KZ was almost destroyed by a boy leaving notes to the Reapers.

Poulos and the girl exchanged desperate looks. "But sir, company rules do allow wives along with the commander's permission." Miss Meyer let out a small, shocked gasp.

"Not on a patrol, Poulos. I'll listen to tent-pole lawyering in camp, but not in the KZ." Valentine wondered if he had really regained consciousness. The flame-lit compound was growing more and more surreal by the moment. Even the fussing baby seemed quieter in the orange-tinged drama of the scene.

"There's a preacher here, sir. He can marry us right now. We're heading back. It's not like we're going into action, we're coming back from it. Doesn't that make a difference?"

"I can keep up, Mr. Valentine," the woman said. They took each other's hands.

"I don't want to hear another word about it," Valentine said, avoiding the hopeful eyes of the young couple. Standing orders from Regiment, enforced by the captain to the letter, discouraged the practice colloquially known as "rounding up strays." The prisoners from the yard were one thing: the Kurians might have reasons for wanting them dead, for all he knew one or more were captured Southern Command soldiers. Aid and assistance were always offered to refugees who made it to the Free Territory on their own, but unless an operation went into a region supplied and equipped to bring out people, taking on stragglers led to innumerable problems. Valentine twisted in the opposing mental winds of his humanity and his duty. He suddenly thought of the girl's mother. While she probably wasn't an Ozark POW, she certainly needed medical attention and care. A loophole, perhaps big enough to squeeze a teenage girl through, opened before him. He could also get rid of the squalling baby.

"Okay, Poulos. You got yourself a wife—and child."

He passed the babe into the girl's arms, and little Ryan quieted. "Poulos, you take them and ride with Stafford and this woman's mother. Miss, take care of this baby. His name is Ryan . . . errr."

"Ryan Werth. Born April last, Mr. Valentine. Thank you, sir. I'll take good care of him."

"I'm sure you will. Hurry, or the trucks will leave without you."

The young couple hugged in as close an embrace as possible with the baby in her arms. They turned to run to the pickups even now crawling toward the gate in a chattering of diesel valves.

"Poulos!" Valentine called after them.

The Wolf about-faced smartly as the truck stopped for the Meyer girl to climb in. "Sir?"

"Congratulations."

Two

On the banks of the Lake o' the Cherokees: Foxtrot Company waits in a forward camp. Tepees, tents, wagons, livestock, and a smokehouse cluster around a stream running down from the hills into what remains of the lake behind the breached dam. A few eagles fish beneath the ruined arches, lingering along the flight paths most have already followed north up the Mississippi Valley.

In this border country, the Wolves of Southern Command imitate the eagles, moving quickly here and there to survey the countryside and striking at prey small enough to take. Their duty is to scout the Kurian Zone, pick up information, and warn the Free Territory of any impending threat to the human settlements in the hills and dales of the Ozark Freehold. Similar military camps lie scattered in the foothills of the Ozarks and Ouachitas throughout Missouri, the eastern edge of Oklahoma, Texas, and Arkansas. Beyond this uninhabited ring broods the Night of the Kurian Order.

The Kurians on the other side of no-man's-land wait for a chance, perhaps some combination of weakness and error, to engulf the Free Territory and put an end to one of the last bastions of human civilization.

"Congratulations, Valentine," Captain Beck said, emerging from his tent to receive the report of his tired lieutenant. "I hear you got four Reapers. You're a credit to the Regiment." Beck held out his right hand, back straight as a telephone pole, smiling at Valentine through clenched teeth.

The young lieutenant shook the proffered hand. "Three, sir. The fourth was a little burned, but got away."

"Stafford said he was blinded. That's one less Reaper to worry about, in my opinion."

Valentine never stopped worrying about a Reaper until its corpse quit twitching.

"Could be, sir," Valentine said, massaging his aching neck. He was so tired, he had a hard time organizing his thoughts, but he had to snap to for this particular superior, fatigue or no. Captain Beck had a reputation as a man-driver and courageous fighter. After being promoted as the senior surviving officer after the Battle of Hazlett in the summer of '65, he'd pushed his company through training and once up to strength requested a forward posting.

"I got Stafford's report on the action at the Rigyard," he said, inviting Valentine into his tepee with an outstretched arm. Valentine entered; the shelter smelled of leather and cigars. Socks and underwear drying on a line added a hint of mustiness. "How was the trip back?"

Valentine collected his thoughts. "It rained after Stafford drove off. Slowed us up. The next day I sent out details to start some fires to the north, make them think we were moving across the flatlands for the Missouri border. We spotted a couple of patrol toward evening, one on horse and one in a truck. We lay low and cold-camped. The next—"

Beck held up a hand. "What's that, Lieutenant? A single truck? Sounds like a good opportunity for prisoners."

"It had a radio antenna. Even from ambush, they might have got off a message. We had been lucky with casualties. I didn't want to press it."

Beck frowned. "I'd like my officers more worried about what they are going to do to the enemy than what might get done to them. Your return would be easier if the Territorials were too scared of losing patrols to send them out."

"We'll have a hard time scaring them worse than the Reapers, sir."

The captain clucked his tongue against his teeth, and the tepee seemed to grow warmer. "I'm not questioning your judgment, just telling you how I might have handled it, had I been there."

"Thank you, sir. The next day, we really put on some mileage. By nightfall we passed the old interstate. When did you get back, sir?"

"Two days ago, morning. We scouted that refinery outside Tulsa. It's fortified, but I think the whole Company could hurt it, if we could bait a chunk of the garrison out somehow."

Valentine nodded. Months ago, he had learned the best way to change his captain's mind was to make any objections he had seem like Beck's own. "Certainly, sir. While we're trying to draw the garrison out, what orders would you give if a flying column comes up? Or Reapers?

I'm sure we could take it, leading some Bears and a regiment of regulars as a reserve. That or have the help of a really good Cat, sir."

"Getting Southern Command to launch something like that isn't so easy to do," Beck said with a knowing chuckle. "That's enough for now. Take tonight off, get some food and sleep, then give me your full report tomorrow."

"Has anyone talked to the four Okies Stafford brought out, sir?"

"Stafford got their vitals. None of them were military. Feel free to interview them yourself. Add it on to your report if you get anything. Nice work out there, Valentine. Dismissed."

Valentine saluted. "Sir," he said quietly, and backed out of Beck's tepee.

A night off. Exhausted from the fight at the Rigyard and eight days in the Kurian Zone, he longed to fall into his cot, into oblivion. A hot bath first was tempting, but the platoon needed to be checked over, and he wanted to have a word with the liberated prisoners before they were taken east into the Ozarks.

He found Stafford with the platoon, engaged in an impromptu celebration for Poulos and his new bride. Someone had produced a jug, and Freeman, the company's oldest ranker, was pouring generous portions into the cluster of wooden cups held under the spout. The mugs were pieces of off-duty artistry: Free Territory hardwoods had been carved into wolf heads and fox ears. Some had handles chiseled to resemble curved tails. Even the rawest recruit in Foxtrot Company had his individual mug.

"Stafford, a word please." Valentine had to raise his voice over the ribald jests being directed at Poulos and his new bride.

The ruddy-skinned platoon sergeant left the guffaws and joined Valentine. They watched the festivities from the edge of the campfire light. Though himself a teetotaler, Stafford allowed his men to indulge after hard duty. The 120 miles covered on foot in the last seven days qualified.

"Poulos and the Meyer girl tied the knot, Gator?" Valentine asked.

"This morning, Val. They did it up right and proper. She's got her mom's wedding ring on now."

"It'll be a story for their grandkids. Hope nobody takes the hooch too close to the fire; I think Freeman adds a little turpentine to give it that woody, aged flavor."

Gator snorted, and Valentine returned to business. "I looked over your report on the drive back. Anything happen that you didn't want to put on paper?"

"No, sir. Except that I was cutting the engines about every fifteen minutes to listen. God, it was like I was driving around, setting off firecrackers. It's a wonder I didn't get every Territorial for fifty miles around me. But all we saw were a couple of deer we flushed. Came leaping at us in the headlights with glowing eyes and twelve-foot jumps. It took about two minutes for my heart to start beating again." His left eye twitched at the memory.

"I need to talk to that girl's mom and the others you brought out. Where can I find them?"

"The captain had to deal with that when we pulled in. Since they were your responsibility, he put them up in your tepee. Maybe he's sending a message about picking up strays. Lieutenant Caltagirone is still out on patrol with a chunk of third platoon, so Beck figured he might as well give that space to them. The little old guy, though—the one with the really long hair—you won't get much out of him. I think he's cracked. Hasn't said anything that makes much sense the whole ride."

"I don't even remember what they look like. Can I borrow you for a quick introduction?"

"Follow me, Val." Dodging dancers, they moved toward the ring of Company tepees at the center of the camp.

Valentine followed Stafford through the flap of the tepee he shared with Lieutenant Caltagirone. The refugees were relaxing. Their faces had been washed, and plates that looked as though they'd been licked clean were stacked by a washbasin.

"Here's the lieutenant; just a few more questions for you," Stafford said.

Valentine looked longingly at his cot. What was left of last night's charcoal was cold gray ash at the center. Caltagirone's cot and a tiny folding table paired up with a rickety stool completed the furnishings. A folding wood lattice stood behind the beds; spare equipment and clothing belonging to the Foxtrot's lieutenants hung from hooks.

As the prisoners sat up, Valentine walked over to his paperwork pouch bearing his stenciled name—months ago, someone had sewn a patch of a floating white cowl with two black eyes beneath the letters, a reference to his nickname, "the Ghost"—and extracted a clipboard. A new letter was clipped to the top of the assorted forms. He recognized Molly's hand by the deliberately printed black inscription, like a schoolchild's. Temptation to let the questions wait in order to peruse its contents almost overwhelmed him, but he stuck it back in the pouch.

Knowledge that a letter awaited him lifted the fatigue. He swung his leg over the little camp stool, sat, and awaited introductions. Stafford gave the names of the three men—Mrs. Meyer still being at the wedding celebration—and then returned to the platoon.

Their stories were the usual sad tale of refugees from the Kurian Zone. When they relayed the usual Kurian propaganda stories about life in the Ozarks—that a Rule Eleven existed condemning anyone who ever cooperated with the Kurians to either execution or being worked to death, and further, Free Territory soldiers were allowed to rape any woman they wished—Valentine only shook his head and returned to the routine questions. He had taken hundreds of statements in his time from refugees, and the picture was always the same bleak snapshot: a hard, bland life of labor until the inevitable end in the draining embrace of a Reaper.

Only one statement stood out, and that was from the man Stafford had described as "cracked." He was a smallish man with a permanent squint that gave him a wizened look. His name was Whitey Cooper, no doubt a reference to his snow-white hair. He wore blue-striped ticking, a shirt in the last stages of decay. Not a button remained, and the collar and cuffs were gone, so his bony forearms and hands had a false appearance of unnatural length. It was trying work getting anything out of him. Valentine finally managed to learn that he worked in the main rail yards of Oklahoma City.

"And for better than thirty years, junior," Cooper pointed out, stabbing one of those fingers at Valentine as if threatening him with a dagger. "Nope, not a bird to change its tune, not me. So many came and went there. Ducks—the lot of them, quack-quack-quacking out their lives before flying south. I wasn't set to fly, though, not by a long shot."

"No?" Valentine said, having given up the fight to make sense out of the man after an inquiring glance or two exchanged with the others. He wondered what Molly had written, and if her mother's health had improved.

"Naw, I was quiet as a broke television. If you're up to your neck in shit, don't make waves. Kept me kicking these years. Till them Nazis showed up on their way north and spoilt it with that big train. They messed me up, but they'll get theirs. Now, I know my history, boy. I've read mor'n books than you got fingers. I know the Nazis got beat once, and we'll beat 'em again."

Valentine stirred from musings. "Nazis?"

"That's the problem today, nobody's got no schooling. Yeah, Nazis, Mr. Lootenan. They were the bad guys way back when the world had the old-time black-and-white life."

"How do you know they were Nazis?" he asked, picking up his pencil.

"First I thought they were just train men like me. Most of 'em weren't much to look at. Thin and sickly kinda, so I assumed they was just railroad men on short commons. What I call the old "gun to yer head" Railway Local Union Nine Em Em. See this good-sized train come through, not the biggest I've ever seen, not by a long shot, but armored engines and caboose and all. I see these guys drinking coffee when it's stopped between, relaxing between the cars on break like. So I figure I grab a cup while it's hot and say howdy, 'cause I had a spare cigarette to trade. I climb up, and they get all exhilarated. Haul me to the caboose, where this big shot fancied-up general starts giving me the once-over. I got thirty years' worth of work stamps in my ID book, but does that cut anything with him? Prick. No, sir. Says I'm spying, as if a bunch of closed boxcars are anything worth spying on. Everyone's all saluting and calling him Generalissimo Honcho or something. Then they take me when the train leaves and start all zapping me with this electric stick. Oh man, I cried, no no not a spy."

"This general, he was in charge of the Nazis? Did you see a name, perhaps on his uniform?"

Cooper winced, as if the memory slapped him. "Oldish, sir. Not oldish and healthy, oldish and dried out, skin like a wasp nest in winter. Thick, wiry gray hair, cut real luscious 'n' full. Little shorter'n me, and I'm only five seven. Pink-eyed, too, like he was hungover. Had a voice like an old wagon running on a gravel road. I've never heard a young man talk like that. Old and squeaky and tired."

"Could you tell from the way they talked where they were from? Did they mention any cities?" Valentine asked again, keeping his voice casual.

"No, if he said it, I forgot."

"What about his men—you said they were thin and sickly?"

"Jest the ones hanging round the wagons. The ones that grabbed me, big burly fellows they were. Plenty of guns, high-quality iron from back then, or as good. Had somun'em oversize gorilla-men with him, too—tall, tall they were, those snaggletooth varmints. It was them that held me when they started in on me."

"I still don't see how they were Nazis," Valentine said.

The man rocked as he sat hunched over, eyes screwed shut. "No, I got a good record here. Check my book. Me a spy?" Cooper trailed off.

Valentine switched tactics. "I think you're wrong, Mr. Cooper. You probably just mistook them for Nazis when they were hurting you."

"I'm learned, I tell you. I can read, just don't get the opportunity. How could I tell? The flag, like they had by the millions in them pictures. On the uniforms, and on the flags in the caboose behind the

General Honcho's desk. Wore it proud, the bastards. You'll show 'em, though, like you did at the house."

Valentine wrote something on his clipboard. "Like this?"

"That's it, Mr. Lootenan. That's it. I bet you beat on them tons of times before, right?"

Valentine just nodded, to himself rather than to the poor man's words, looking down at the clipboard. He had seen that design before, here and there, and wherever he had encountered it, there had been trouble.

Written in pencil on the slightly yellow paper was the backwards swastika he'd heard called "the Twisted Cross."

"You're sure you don't know where they come from?"

"Naw. Why you need to know that?"

"You said we had to beat them."

"Course you will, Mr. Lootenan. Of course. But you don't have to go looking for them. They're coming for you."

It took Valentine a moment to come up with, "How can you be sure of that?"

"All summer, new lines is goin' in. Labor and materials already arranged. I was supposed to second a section chief. A new north-south running Dallas–Tulsa–Kansas City, and after that then three branch lines."

"Branch lines? Where?"

"Pointing like a pitchfork right at these hills."

Valentine camped in an accommodating wagon that night among three other Wolves who had given up their tepee to Poulos and his new bride. As the final earthy taunts and wedding-night stories died down, Valentine reread Molly's letter by the cold light of the rising moon.

January 18, 2067

Dear David,

I hope this letter finds you well and doesn't take too long—you'd think they could find your unit in less than a month, wouldn't you? Everyone here in Weening is good the winter passed with hardly any sickness but the food is all starting to taste the same though I shouldn't complain as I am certain it is worse for you. I read your last letter out loud during Sunday Services and received many greetings and well wishes to pass on to you that are too numerous to list. Mr. Bourne has something he's going to send you as soon as he can find one of the Wolves passing through the area since he doesn't trust the post with it—the package is a box or trunk of some kind so be on the lookout for it. He was working on it all winter and made me promise not to tell—and he can be sure I'm not telling as he is helping me with this letter! As you know I am somewhat behind in my education, the 3 Rs not being taught in that part of Wisconsin where we met. Have you heard anything from Frat? I think he's still an Aspirant down by Louisiana, but you all move around so much my information is always out of date. I am told the mail is even slower to him and just collects until he can return to his camp.

Graf has been recommended for Lieutenant—I think he's going to ask me to marry him if he gets the promotion. It may mean leaving the village but Mom is doing much better. Mary is old enough now where she can take over a lot of the chores and the Hudson brothers help out with the hardest. My mom and dad pretty much handle everything to do with veterinary work for the town livestock, if someone's having trouble with a calving they run and get them. With Mom better Dad's going to take a larger place in the Village, there's talk of him becoming a Director. To think when he first got here the town gave him a cow and two piglets and some chickens, and now we've got eight good milkers. Of course, in a way our start here is because of you. I should just say it, we owe everything to you: getting out of the badness in Wisconsin and everything that happened in Chicago.

Your letters are very cheery and polite in the way you ask about Graf. But you always are very casual and polite when you are upset. David, you're one of the finest men I've ever known. I still love you in a way, but a different way than I feel about Graf. I think you have a Purpose. I know we talked that our futures were woven together at one time, but something in me associates all the badness back there with you and every time I see you I remember. I should not say it was all wrong, before Chicago our time was wonderful, and precious, but I've sealed up everything that happened with Chicago, it's kind of like a memory of an old nightmare, not very clear. You were so patient with me all that winter, God did I even talk at all while we were in Minnesota? I think you need to be free of me to become whatever it is you are going to become (as you are all bound up with the Lifeweavers and Mr. Bourne says it

*is a hard way and the choice to follow them doesn't make for
a normal life) I need to be free of you to start here with a
clean slate. We tried last spring and it was just bad, I was
cold—God it was the last thing you deserve!—and you were
distracted.*

*The way things are now is for the best, I'm sure of it.
You've written that you think it's great that I have a man like
Graf and those words meant a lot to me and I hope they
weren't painful to write. I suppose we both have mixed feelings
for each other. One thing is certain though, you will always
have a home among the Carlsons in Weening no matter what
happens to you. You've been my friend, my love, my protector,
my healer, my guide, and now I hold you as a dear brother
in a Very Special Place in my heart. I look toward your next
letter, and pray that your duties will allow you to visit soon.*

> *Yours truly and
> always,
> Molly*

Molly was a bright young woman, and painfully right about them.
Valentine returned the letter to his dispatch bag. He played a mental
slide show of the Molly he had known: from when he first met her in
Wisconsin when her family hid him at great personal risk from the
Kurians, to his trip to Chicago to rescue her from violent public death
after she had killed a Quisling official. They'd escaped by ship to the
Minnesota shore, near where Valentine had been born and grew up, and
stayed a season at his adoptive father's house.

Valentine and the old priest sat up night after night, discussing
what he'd learned of the Kurians. It was the Padre who'd first taught
him about ancient civil war that divided the Lifeweavers and led to the
Kurian Lords, who—through their vampiric Reapers—killed sentient
beings to harvest the energies that sustained their endless lives. They'd
been thrown off Earth long ago, the interstellar gateways sealed and
destroyed, but they'd come again in 2022, and won.

Valentine made no attempt to renew the intimacy that had briefly
existed between himself and Molly, concentrating instead on feeding
everyone. Each night he read to Molly by the light of a single candle
out of the Padre's collection of old books. Books that had become his
family, in a way, after his orphaning. They'd taken him out of his mis-
ery, and he'd hoped they could do the same for Molly.

That spring, Valentine was determined to rejoin Molly with her family, although he had no idea if the Carlsons had even successfully escaped to the Ozarks with his fellow Wolf, Gonzalez.

Molly strengthened and blossomed on the journey in the spring sunshine of the north. Valentine had a good nose for trouble, and skirted wide around areas controlled by the Quisling servants of the Kurians. They reached the outskirts of Southern Command on the first day of May, and the young pair caught up to Molly's family at one of the small fortress posts in the hills watching the old roads and trails up from St. Louis. That reunion on the soil of the Ozark Free Territory was perhaps the proudest moment in his life. As if some silent bargain had been fulfilled, he and Molly renewed their intimacy that night, making love with giddy, laughing abandon.

But it was not the same. The desperation and danger of their situation in Wisconsin was absent, and Valentine felt the pull of duty. He had been posted missing and presumed dead, and upon hearing of his safe return to the Ozarks, Gonzalez and a few other Wolves of Zulu Company showed up to welcome him back. He settled the family with old friends in the little borderland settlement of Weening in northern Arkansas near the Saint Francis River and returned to his duties.

It was a frustrating return. Southern Command read, and promptly forgot, his report on the mysterious Kurian operations in the hills of southern Wisconsin he and Gonzalez had stumbled upon, and shrugged their shoulders at Valentine's suggestion of a new organization under a reversed-swastika symbol Valentine had heard called the Twisted Cross.

Zulu Company had replaced him, and Valentine was assigned to Captain Beck and Foxtrot Company, mostly freshly invoked Wolves who had never seen a live Reaper and knew Grogs—the variegated, semi-intelligent beasts bred to aid the Kur in their subjugation of humanity—only by their oversize footprints.

Constant training drained him, and he found it impossible to visit Molly in far-off Weening; they exchanged letters less and less frequently. Molly was young and beautiful, and soon found herself under the attentions of a sergeant in the regulars, the well-turned-out Guards who formed the main body of Southern Command's armed forces. Twinges of jealousy vied with genuine hope for her happiness on the unstable emotional teeter-totter that described his feelings for her.

Valentine shifted his weight on the hard boards of the wagon, causing the springs to squeak in complaint. That trail of thought led to a dead end. He returned to present problems, reviewing Cooper's ravings. He still knew little of the Twisted Cross. Only that its members were human, at least some of them, and that they were objects of dread in the Kurian Zone and on its borders. He had briefly met one in the bizarre garden of unholy entertainments of the Zoo in Chicago while searching for Molly. A man who talked like a soldier and acted like a Reaper, even to the extent that he thirsted for blood. And whoever they were, they were now somewhere just outside the no-man's-land separating the Free Territory from the KZ.

Despite that unsettling thought, he finally slept. Above his hard bed, the stars whirled away in the bright clear night.

"Grogs, Mr. Valentine. Hundreds of 'em. Five miles off and coming hard," a pubescent voice intruded on Valentine's deep predawn slumber.

Valentine woke like a startled animal, instantly alert, and the boy ceased shaking his shoulder. It was Tom Nishino, one of the teenage Aspirants who traveled with the Wolves and performed assorted camp duties in the hope of someday joining their ranks. The youth almost danced with excitement beside the wagon. Captain Beck had taken Nishino, the brightest of Foxtrot's teens, under his wing and used him as a messenger.

"Whose are they?"

Nishino looked puzzled at the question. He'd never served down south, where Governor Steiner had his unique and independent enclave of humans and Grogs. So far, Steiner had never let his militias off his lands, which formed a buffer in the south between Kurian Louisiana and the Free Territory. Valentine had always hoped to hear of closer cooperation—he'd played a small part in that alliance his first year as a Wolf.

"Don't know, sir. They're coming out of Oklahoma."

"Are we supposed to sound assembly?" Valentine asked, letting his ears play across the campsite for sounds of the tents being struck and men gathering.

"The captain asks that you have your platoon turn out with full weapons and equipment, and you're to report to his tent, sir," Nishino reported.

"Thank you, son. Please walk, *walk* mind you, back to the captain and tell him I'll be there in five minutes. Sprinting in the dark is a good way to turn an ankle, or have a sentry put a bullet into you. Take it easy, boy."

"Sir," the boy said, showing his best salute, and turned neatly to begin a stiff-spined walk back to the captain's tent. Valentine tried to remember if he'd acted like that when he'd first joined the Cause at seventeen.

The Wolves sharing the wagon with Valentine still lay in their bedrolls. The pose was deceptive—Valentine had seen them lay hands on their rifles at the first hint of action in the air.

Valentine pulled on his boots. "Benning, find Sergeant Stafford, please. Tell him to get the platoon together, ammunition and two days' rations. Gabriel, please go and get the draft animals together on a line. We may be moving fast without the wagons. Thank you."

He hopped out of the wagon as the men exchanged knowing looks. They'd already seen through his facade. Whenever their young lieutenant spoke in that crisp, politely affected manner, action was in the air.

Valentine walked to the command tepee, unconsciously registering the clatter and curses in the night air as the camp came to life. Grogs were significant. The battle-bred warriors of the Kurians were rare in Oklahoma; Kur relied on Quisling troops in the plains. Might be they'd been brought down from Northern Missouri, and that could mean an attempt to thrust into the vitals of the Free Territory. Valentine ticked off the possibilities in his brain: a raid, an attempt on the Fort Smith region, or perhaps a thrust northeast to link up with others pushing south into Missouri, catching the forces and populace in that corner of the Free Territory in a meat grinder. Or most likely of all, it was a rushed-up retribution for the recent raid by Foxtrot Company. If that was the case, the Wolves could do what they did best: skirmish and ambush. They'd lead the Grogs on a chase until they could be decoyed into the Ozarks and cut off.

Captain Beck stood outside his tepee in the pink dawn, his hands behind him in the at-ease position.

Valentine came up beside him. "What's the situation, sir?"

"Pickets spotted the Grogs crossing the lake about midnight, five kilometers north of here. Tango Company might have picked them up; that's getting up in their area. They turned south right away, moving along the banks of the river. I sent the camp squad out to keep an eye on them—they're freshest. They'll bushwhack any scouts if they can. That'll slow the Grogs some."

"Strength?"

"Probably won't have any idea of numbers until daylight, but they're on those legworms—it's how they crossed the river so quick and easy. Pickets said they spotted harpies above the treetops. No sign of them here, so I'm hoping it's just their imagination."

"Coming here or just trying to raid into the Ozarks?"

"They're after us, no doubt about that. Maybe some Kurian is down to his last Reaper thanks to you, Valentine. We're going to make them sorry they caught up to us."

"How's that, sir?" Valentine asked, adding a silent prayer. It wasn't what he thought.

"I've already tele'd to Decatur for reinforcements and put the sick and wounded in the trucks you captured. Oh, and the children. There's a cavalry regiment of Guards in the area, and more behind them. The Grogs have got to be planning to burn this camp and maybe catch us pulling back toward the Free Territory. They've moved fast, so it can't be a well-planned assault. If we pull up onto Little Timber Hill, we can hold out there for days. It would take more artillery than the Grogs have in Missouri to blast us out of those rocks." Beck reached for the waxed linen packet in which he kept his cigars. With his usual courtesy, he offered one. Valentine shook his head, gathering the right words.

"Sir, there's nothing here worth fighting for. There aren't any of our farms within twenty miles at least. Let the Grogs burn some wagons and barrels of pork. If they follow us toward Fort Smith, the farther they go, the fewer will get back alive."

Beck's dark brows dueled like bighorn sheep. "Dammit, Valentine, you know how I feel about that kind of crap. Until we start making those Jaspers more afraid of us than we are of them, they're going to keep pushing into us whenever they feel like it. Besides, you're forgetting Lt. Caltagirone. He's still out with his short platoon. I don't want him coming back to a camp crawling with Grogs."

"I know that sir, and I agree. But we're Wolves, not Guards. Even a couple of our men are worth more to us, worth more to Southern Command, than every Grog in that column is to the KZ."

"Are you suggesting I'd throw away men's lives? Because if you are—"

"No, sir, certainly not, sir."

"The toughest decisions are always where to fight. I appreciate you speaking your mind, Valentine. That takes a kind of courage, too. Just because we disagree, it won't be held against you."

He waited, as if expecting a thank-you, then continued. "Someday you'll get a company of your own. When you get it, command it. No councils of war. This is a screen of Grogs who are about to get their noses lopped off. And even if it isn't, we can hold them until the regulars arrive. You know how long I held outside Hazlett, Val? Five days. By the second day we were low on ammunition, and by the third even the Grog guns were empty."

Valentine had heard the story of those five days several times.

Versions from the senior surviving Wolves of Foxtrot Company did not match the commander's account exactly, but this was not the time to bring that up.

"Your orders, sir?"

"Your platoon is going to haul as many supplies as possible up Little Timber Hill. We've already got trees down all around the hill, we've been working on the fortifications since we got here. Fill a couple wagons, triple-team them if you have to, and get them up that hill to Rocky Crown. Water's not a problem this time of year, but I want food and ammo. And every hand grenade we have. Drive the livestock up, and make a pen."

Valentine took the orders like bitter medicine. Now he had to decide how to carry them out, quickly. Grogs on leg-worms ate miles, skirmishing pickets or no, and with daylight they would move even faster.

"Yes, sir."

"Good. Clear the camp as soon as you can."

"And the spouses?"

"Some left with their kids. The others have to get up the hill, too. Any further questions, Valentine?"

"No, sir," Valentine said, already wondering if he could even get the wagons up that slope, triple-teamed or no.

The whole camp was stirring now as the Wolves gathered their weapons and equipment. Valentine returned to his platoon to find Stafford sitting on top of a wagon, issuing orders and equipment to the assembling men.

"We'll be ready to pull out in fifteen minutes, sir," Gator reported. "If we aren't moving the wagons, some of the women can ride on the draft animals. We'll make good time, probably hit the outskirts of the Territory by sundown."

"Good work, Staff, but we're not leaving. We have to hitch up some wagons and fill them from the stores. We've got to get the ammo and food up to the redoubt."

Stafford's face fell, lacking only an audible thud. "The captain wants to fight it out?"

Valentine hid his own misgivings with his best airy smile. "Gator, it's probably just a screen of Grogs to flush us. The Guards are already on their way if it's not. And besides, Caltagirone is still out with his men. We can't abandon them to the Grogs. Get the men moving; they've got fifteen minutes to get something in their stomachs—then we have to hitch up a couple of wagons, fill them with food and bullets, and haul up that trail. Minutes count, okay, Sergeant?"

"Yes, Lieutenant."

Gator turned and began bellowing orders. Poulos's new bride, her mother, and a few of the other camp casuals were already passing out ersatz coffee and the morning's biscuits. The men squatted around their NCOs, cramming food into their mouths while they discussed how best to get the supplies up that hill. The smell of bacon frying brought saliva to Valentine's mouth, and he moved over to the cooking fire. A seven-year-old girl, the daughter of Corporal Hart of First Platoon, scuttled past him in a flutter of tangled dark hair chasing a chicken.

Valentine swore under his breath. She should have left with the trucks. Hart and his wife must have decided to keep the family together despite the risks. The girl got the chicken and hurried off to the coops. Valentine tried to put her out of his mind. It was too easy to imagine a Grog loping after her.

By the time he had eaten two heels of bread dripping with bacon fat and a pair of still-sputtering strips of meat, the platoon had the outlines of a plan. Stafford and the other NCOs decided to run two wagons, one from the camp to the base of the steep hill that served as the Company redoubt, and a second double-teamed one to run light loads up the hill. Valentine watched the first group of men move off with axes and two small horses toward the hill. They would improve the trail and check for deadfalls, then improvise a corral at the rocky top of the hill. The camp dependents would follow, bringing a few necessities and driving the goats, geese, and cows that made up the Company's livestock.

In the early hours of the morning, Valentine left everything but the ordnance to Stafford. He personally supervised digging up the Company's reserve grenades and ammunition. Some of the explosives used black powder, and he wanted to make sure that in the rush, the volatile mixture was not mishandled.

"Mr. Valentine," said O'Neil, uncovering the last case of grenades from the shallow trench that had covered them, "gimme half an hour, and I'll set a little booby trap here. We leave behind a case, and the first Grog tries to shift it gets blowed into pieces that wouldn't fill a spoon."

"If we had time, we'd leave surprises everywhere, O'Neil. But they're going to be here any minute."

It promised to be a cloudy morning. As Valentine walked behind the load of ammunition, eyeing the balance of the load in the wagon bed as it ascended the first gentle slope toward the redoubt, a running Wolf broke cover from the tree line to the north. Valentine watched

him disappear into the thick trees of Little Timber Hill, making for the
new command post.

"Let's keep it moving, men. The Grogs are on their way. We want
to have this load to shoot at them, not the other way round."

O'Neil quickened the pace of the four horses, and the last of Valentine's platoon soon disappeared into the trees at the base of the hill.
Stafford waited there, with more horses ready to be hitched to the rest.

"Everything and everyone's up at the top, sir. The corral took no
doing at all—there's a little hollow in the rocks that we just closed off
at one end. The captain's going to use the other wagon to block the trail
once we make it to the crest."

"Good work, Staff. Let's get a man at each wheel with a rock,
ready to brace it up if the horses need a breather. Get a few hides between the crates, just in case the load shifts. I don't think even a bad
bounce would set it off, but better safe than dead. Where's the platoon
supposed to be once we get up?"

"We're to form a reserve. He wants the dependents armed, too. The
rest of the platoon will cover the south and the saddle to the east where
it joins the rest of the hills. First platoon is going to be on the main line,
covering the trail. The captain figures if they'll come, they'll come up
the trail, where the slope's gentle."

The newly double-teamed wagon ascended the hill, with men ready
to prop the wheels with rocks when the horses could no longer take the
strain. Even this, the "gentle" part of the hill, had an exhausting slope
to the grade, running way up Little Timber Hill like a long ramp.

A little more than halfway up the hill, they came upon the fortifications. Whatever Valentine's other disagreements with the captain, he
had to admire the planning and execution of the redoubt. Trees were
felled at the crest of the steepest part of the slope, pointing outward
with their branches shorn and sharpened into abatis. Earth-and-wood
fortifications, complete with head-logs in many places, frowned down
on the steep slope. If the Grogs wanted Little Timber, they would pay a
steep price, as steep as the hill the wagon now climbed, exacted by the
marksmen of Foxtrot Company. Valentine put himself in the enemy's
canoelike sandals at the base of the hill. How would he go about the
assault to minimize the cost?

He knew his men would fight like cornered rats, but Valentine disliked being in a corner in the first place. The Wolves lived and fought
through their mile-devouring mobility, striking where and when the
Kurians were weak and disappearing once the enemy concentrated. He
dreaded the coming hammer-and-tongs battle, but what could he do in
the face of orders?

"C'mon, men, push!" he shouted, throwing his weight against the wagon when the horses began to shift sideways in exhaustion. His Wolves hurled themselves against the wheels, sides—anywhere on the wagon where they could get a grip. The wagon and men groaned on up.

At the line of fortifications, Valentine braced up the wheels and passed out cases of ammunition and hand-bombs. The slope from here was easier to the crown of the hill. A little above them a small boulder-strewn spur off the crown marked Beck's designated command post. He saw the captain moving down the slope toward the trail.

"Keep it moving, Sergeant. I'm going to talk to the captain for a moment."

He found Beck, legs stiff as though rooted among the rocks.

"Nice work, Lieutenant. That was a big load at last."

"The ammunition took a while to dig up, sir. What's the word on the Grogs?"

Beck looked grim. "It's in the hundreds, at least. The scouts marked a dozen legworms. There're men with them, too, but they were too far away to see if it was Quisling regulars or just the supply train."

"Grogs don't move with much in the way of supplies. I think they eat rocks if it comes to it."

"Valentine, you and I both know what they eat. Let's just try to stay off the menu for a few days. I want your platoon covering that ravine to the south and the saddle where the rocky crown meets the other hills. Keep your best squad as a reserve, back up wherever they decide to hit us first. I've put a squad in reserve, too, and we're going to shift them as needed. Twenty or so extra guns will make the difference wherever they come."

Valentine did some quick mental math. Beck's deployment put a man every ten feet or so in the tree-trunk fortifications on the crest of the little hill. Maybe a little more to the west and on the saddle, a few less at the steep ravine on the south side. Lt. Caltagirone and his twenty men would be a godsend, if they would just return. The two flying squads would be very busy.

He jogged up to the crown of the hill, a windswept expanse of rocks on the heavily timbered rise protruding from the trees like a cal-lused spot on an ox's back. Stunted specimens of scrub pine grew among the rocks, in what looked like just a few handfuls of dirt. A goat bleated from a little depression in the hill's crown. The stock drank from a muddy pool of rainwater caught in a basinlike depression. The camp casuals stood by, armed. Everything seemed to be in place here. He found a moment to smile and nod at the Meyer girl—or rather Mrs. Poulos now, the baby still in her arms, and tried not to think about their fate if the Grogs overran the hilltop. He turned to the men taking their positions at the breastworks.

Sergeant Stafford had already arrayed the men, stretching them painfully thin at the ravine to the south, and clustered them in two groups on the saddle that connected Little Timber Hill to a larger ridge to the east. Beyond that line of hills to the southeast stood the comforting mass of the Ozarks, blue in the distance.

Valentine made only one improvement in the Sergeant's defenses. He had the men drape a few hides, hats, and bits of clothing over appropriately shaped saplings. The Grogs were remarkable long-range snipers, and a few extra targets to absorb potshots during an assault might save the life of a real soldier.

The Wolves took to making scarecrows with a will, even going so far as to naming them Fat Tom, the Hunchback, Mr. Greenshoots, and other colorful monikers. As a few aged felt hats were being fixed atop the faux Wolves, shots echoed up from the west side of the hill.

"Looks like they found us," Valentine announced, seeing his men stiffen at the sound. "Keep your heads down, gents. Let them shoot, and mark them. Then shoot when they reload their pieces. Or when they psyche themselves up for a charge."

Valentine fought the urge to go to the other side of the hill for a glimpse of the opposition. His place was with his men.

"Gator, I'm putting you in charge of the reserve squad at the top. That'll be the final line if this one goes. Get the ammunition in there with the stock, and fill every bucket and canteen with water. Understand?"

"Ahead of you, sir, at least as far as the ammunition goes. I'll get first squad to work up there. Whistle if there's trouble?"

Valentine extracted a little silver whistle on a lanyard from beneath his buckskin jacket. Stafford winced at the sight; the whistle had belonged to Valentine's predecessor. It would have been buried with him, too, if Stafford hadn't rescued it from before sending the body on to the field morgue. "We might be in for a long fight. Work the men in shifts."

A leaping figure raced up the hill from Beck's spur. It was the Aspirant, Nishino.

Valentine checked his carbine and pistol while he waited for the racing teen.

"Lieutenant Valentine, sir," Nishino said, again out of breath. "The captain wants you in charge of the flying squads. He says to assemble them behind the command post. They found us, and it looks like they're coming up the hill!"

"Thank you, Nishino. Tell the captain I'll be there at once," he said, granting the boy the formality of a salute.

He turned to Stafford. "I guess that leaves you in charge here, Gator. Put Corporal Holloway in with the dependents and the livestock at the last line."

"Yes, sir."

"The Grogs should be a while probing the hill. If they come in your zone, it'll be across the saddle. Put two men with good ears on the other side of it, and tell them to make sure the Grogs don't get between them and the crown."

"Good luck, Val." Gator shook his hand, hung on for an extra moment.

"You, too, Gator."

"See you soon."

"Soon."

Valentine trotted up the hill, feeling liberated. He'd done all he could. The Wolves would do the fighting now. All he could do is offer to stop a bullet like the rest of them. The day might see him as a hero, a coward, a fool, or a corpse. Like a drunk anticipating a hangover, he knew that the fear would come later, leaving him shaking in a cold sweat and nauseated.

He stole over to the command post, crabbing carefully between the rocks. Grog snipers could already have a view of the spur, and he wanted to avoid a rendezvous with one of the fifty-caliber bullets fired from single-shot rifles they favored.

Beck was scanning the bottom of the slope with his binoculars, listening to the popping of sporadic rifle fire, turning his head at the shots like an owl following mouse scratches.

He glanced once at Valentine and returned to the binoculars.

"Lieutenant, scouts are back. The legworms will be up this slope in a few minutes. They're lining the damn things up now in the camp. We've counted only ten. They'll have to do some winding to get around these trees, so they can't come up at a rush. Take the flying squads, and reinforce at that wagon. If I want you to pull out for some reason, you'll hear three short blasts from my whistle."

"Three blasts—yes, sir," Valentine repeated.

Beck put down the binoculars. "Give 'em hell, Val. Captaincies grow from days like these."

"Yes, sir."

Valentine hurried up to Yamashiro and his squad, wondering what sort of stress Beck was under, to make him think his lieutenant would fight harder if he thought there was a set of captain's bars in it. He had served with Beck for nine months, and his superior still had no idea what kind of man his senior lieutenant was. It was a disturbing thought on a day that already had many other unsettling mental threads unraveling.

He gained the tree where Yamashiro waited with the most veteran of the squads of Second Platoon. The expectant, confident expressions on the men's faces were a tonic to Valentine.

"Here's the story, gentlemen. We're going to have about ten legworms in our laps in a few minutes. But this isn't the open prairie; those big bastards are going to have a tough time in the woods. Corporal, do you have two reliable catapult teams?"

"Sure, sir. Baker can hit the strike zone from center field, and Grub is pretty near as good."

"Very well. I want one team just below the CP."

"Just below the command post—yes, sir."

"There's a pair of boulders kind of leaning together above the line of fortifications on the south side of the road—the other team should be posted there. Take a sack of bombs, men, and make them count. Remember, the brain on a legworm is buried in the middle."

The Wolves began putting together the catapults. They were improvised weapons for hurling the baseball-size grenades of Southern Command. Essentially larger versions of the classic childhood slingshot, they consisted of a broad U of one-inch lead piping, with thick surgical tubing attached at the top. The grenade rested in a little hardened leather cup at the center of the tubing. Two men held the U while a third pulled and aimed the catapult, launching the grenade twice as far as it could be thrown, often with uncanny accuracy in the hands of a skilled puller.

Valentine took Corporal Yamashiro and the other four men down to the breastworks. He looked around the makeshift "gate" in the trail, made up of a wagon with rocks and timber piled around it.

"Sergeant Petrie, you in charge here?" Valentine looked up at a man kneeling with two others behind a long log stretched across the length of the wagon.

"Yes, Lieutenant Valentine."

"Nice job spacing the men. Pass the word, Wolves—we've got legworms coming. It does no good to shoot the damn things; they won't even feel it. Knock the Grogs off the top. And don't be afraid to use the grenades. We've got a whole summer's worth." The last was not quite true, but Valentine wanted to encourage their use. Explosions had been known to make legworms reverse themselves and creep away as quickly as they came forward.

A few of the men had bundled bunches of grenades around a hefty branch, making a throwable stick bomb. Valentine moved up and down the line, checking the men's positions and equipment. Most gripped their rifles and stared down the hill with hard, alert faces.

Valentine let his hearing play all along the bottom of the hill. Muted light from the cloud-filled sky gave the woods an eerie, shadowless uniformity. A woodpecker beat a tattoo on a distant tree, as if drumming a warning of what was to come.

"C'mon, apes, if you're gonna bring it . . . let's get it over with," a Wolf said as he peered down the leaf sights of his rifle to the base of the hill.

The answer came: a distant horn sounded a hair-raising call of three blasts, each slightly louder and higher than the preceding: *awwwk Awwwwwk AWWWWUUK!* It made Valentine think of trumpeter swans he had heard in his Minnesota youth. A few of the newer soldiers looked at each other, seeking reassurance from their comrades after hearing the otherworldly sound.

"Good of them to let us know they're on the way," Valentine said. "Let's return the favor." Then more loudly, "Stand to your posts, men, and let them know that Wolves are waiting!"

The men cheered and began howling, imitating the cries of the canine predators. The cries were picked up and amplified by other Wolves up and down the thinly held line until the hills echoed with them. Valentine spotted skinny young Nishino a little way above in the rocks of the command post, red-faced from yelling his lungs out.

A steady rustle, like a wind through dry fall leaves, came from the base of the hill. The cheers ceased. Valentine brought up his carbine, comforted by its reliable weight and smell of gun oil.

The pale-yellow legworms advanced, slinking up the hillside like gigantic centipedes. Each individual limb rippled one at a time along the thirty-foot length of their bodies, faster than the eye could follow. The motion fascinated Valentine; it reminded him of quickly falling dominoes. He tore his gaze away from the hypnotic sight of the legs. A probing maw ringed with catfish whiskers waved to and fro, finding the way for the rest of the creature between the tree trunks. Gray troll-like figures, proportioned like huge apes, sat astride the long, tubular legworms. They held metal shields in cordwood-thick arms, with long-barreled rifles resting in eyebolts projecting from the side. Each legworm in the assault carried six of these Grogs, already firing up into the Wolves' breastworks. Their shooting was worse than usual, owing to the unsteady motion of their sidewinding mounts.

A few shots rang out from the Wolves as bullets zipped overhead. Explosions tore through the trees when grenades fired from the catapults detonated on the hillside. One Wolf whirled a stick bomb on a short lanyard, sending the grenades bouncing down the hill and into the approaching line.

Between the legworms, Grogs on foot jumped from tree to tree, covering each other with steady rifle fire. A few shots told among the Wolves. But the infantry Grogs could not keep up with their mounted comrades.

A stick bomb rolled under a legworm's middle. The grenades detonated, sending black digits flying. The creature collapsed at the middle, dead, but both ends still writhed on reflex-driven legs.

Another grenade exploded close enough to one's nerve center to send it into convulsions, throwing or crushing its Grog riders and trees alike as it whipped and rolled like a scorpion stinging itself to death. A legworm on the northern end seemed confused, moving sideways, forward and back amongst the trees as if looking for an escape, giving the Wolves a chance to pick off its riders. Freed of their control, the legworm moved back down the hill away from the chaos. Two more followed it despite the frantic efforts to control it on the part of its simian riders.

"Pour it into them, men, pour it on," Petrie yelled above the din, blood spilling down his face from a gash across his temple. The bullet that nearly killed him had taken his hat. White bone glistened red under a ragged flap of skin.

Valentine squeezed off shot after shot at the lead Grog on the nearest legworm, but the bullets seemed either to miss or bounce off the piece of armored shield it held in its hand. Vexed, he knelt to reload. Grog snipers put bullets where his head had been a moment before. He noticed the Wolf to his right had the whole right side of his head torn away, as if sawn off with a precision tool.

Carbine ready, Valentine rolled and came back up behind the breastworks at the dead man's notch. He squeezed off three shots into the same leading Grog from the shield's off side. This time his shots found their mark; the Grog toppled off its mount. Its fellows tried to grab the reins, but the legworm already began to arc off to the right. At the rate of a Grog a second, the Wolves dropped the other five riders like ducks in a shooting gallery.

Cordite filled Valentine's nostrils. Another legworm thrashed in tree-cracking pain, badly wounded by a grenade. But two more were atop the breastworks, forcing their way through the abatis, ignoring the sharpened branches, which first impaled, then broke off in their soft, puffy skin.

Valentine saw the flash of a fuse and heard a faint, wet *pop*. A legworm's mouth exploded, leaving a greenish-yellow wound open across the whole front of its body. The thing reeled and sped back downslope, shaking its riders like a bucking bronco. One of the catapults had managed to put a grenade right down its throat, using the basketball-hoop-size maw as a target. But the remaining legworm was up and over the head-logs in a flash, and the Grogs dropped off it and onto the men below, closely followed by a second yellow giant. As it climbed onto the logs, heavy and pulsing above Valentine's head, he ignored his own advice and fired shot after shot into its belly at the approximate middle. The bullets left green-goo-dripping holes, but the thirty-caliber shells fired muzzle-to-skin found nerve ganglia. The legworm collapsed; as it fell, he threw himself out of the way, but it still trapped him below the knees. A few legs hammered against his thighs as they twitched out their final spasm.

The Grogs fought hand to hand with the Wolves, tossing the smaller humans right and left, firing oversize pistols and swinging double-bladed battle-axes that gleamed red with blood. Volleys of fire from above cut them down: the grenade teams had dropped their catapults and turned their rifles on the Grogs fighting at the barricades.

He got one leg out from beneath the fleshy mass.

A Grog from the legworm Valentine shot hopped up onto the abatis. Valentine brought up his gun, but the carbine's hammer came down with an impotent click. A misfire, or he was empty. The Grog raised its battle-ax, and Valentine read death in its purple eyes just before two holes opened in its chest, throwing it backwards. Valentine had no time to look for his unseen marksman-savior; he pushed free of the dead legworm and brought his gun up and over the breastworks, only to see the Grogs retreating through the trees. Valentine looked one second too long; a bullet whizzed past close enough to feel the pressure of its passage against his ear.

He dropped to his knees, seeking safety in the thick comfort of the breastworks. To either side of him, Wolves were still shooting down the slope. A bloody-knuckled man helped another stop the flow from a head wound as Valentine counted the cost of the attack. Four dead. Many wounded.

Valentine looked down at a Grog pistol by his knee. The weapon looked like two revolvers joined at the bottom of the grip, with a thick trigger guard running between the two. A single lever cocked and fired both barrels.

"They're going," someone shouted. The survivors of the legworm assault sagged against the protecting logs, many with tears of relief running down their faces.

"They'll be back," Petrie said as another Wolf wrapped a bandage around his head. "They'll keep coming until they're all dead . . . or we are."

They came six more times that cool spring day. Each time, like a rising tide, the Grog wave crested farther. And when they receded, they left snipers among the rocks and trees, sappers who could be silenced only by grenades and concentrated rifle fire. The Grogs wrapped their lines around Little Timber Hill like a python coiling around its prey, waiting for it to weaken and smother under its irresistible pressure.

Noon came and went, and afternoon brought a two-hour lull in the fighting. Valentine let the men leave the breastworks in small groups to steal away to the rocky crown for food and water—even a brief washup if they could get it. Although the last might be rendered moot: the rain clouds were piling up on the horizon again.

A sniper wounded Captain Beck when the Grogs came, thick and screaming, up the long slope at about three in the afternoon. Tom Nishino, not knowing what else to do, blew his captain's whistle. Valentine heard the trilling above the shrieks of the Grogs and looked up to see the boy waving to him. Valentine gestured back, outflung arm trying to motion Tom to keep down, when a slug took the youth, spinning him in one quick, 360-degree revolution to drop dead among the rocks.

Valentine left Petrie in charge and scrambled up to the command post. Two Wolves and one of the camp women knelt around Beck. The captain's left shoulder was shattered, leaving his arm dangling.

"How are the men holding?" Beck asked through paingritted teeth. The woman bound the wound with quick strokes, ignoring Beck's gasps. Valentine paused a moment, admiring the sure motions of her hands.

"They're holding good, sir. But I've got nine dead around the trail, and a lot of wounded."

"I don't know how long I'll be conscious here, Valentine. So I want you to take command. Hold this position; the Guards are on their way. Bring the wounded up to the rocky crown. They'll be safe there. Sooner or later they're going to figure out that the easiest way to get at us is from across the saddle, so you'd better reform your flying squads."

Valentine wished Beck would stop talking. If he was going to relinquish command, he should quit giving orders.

"Yes, sir," he said. "Let's get you up into the basin."

The two Wolves helped Beck to his feet, supporting him with his good arm. The captain's face contorted in pain as he made his first halting steps toward the rocky crown, the trio keeping hidden from the snipers at the bottom of the hill.

Valentine picked up Beck's dropped binoculars. The odor of the captain's cigars clung to their casing and strap. What had been Beck's was now his. Responsibility for Foxtrot Company's future put his stomach into a knot of Gordian proportions. He watched the ragged young woman who had bandaged the captain as she picked up Beck's bolt-action carbine, examining it. She had brassy red hair cut very short, freckles, and pretty, if angular, features. She looked like she had been on short rations for a week: her eyes had a wide, alert, and hungry look. Valentine suddenly realized he didn't know her.

"I'm sorry, who are you?" Valentine said. "I thought I knew everyone in camp."

"I've been in your camp for only a couple hours, Wolf. Are you missing about two dozen men?"

Valentine frowned. "My name is David Valentine, Second Wolf Regiment of Southern Command. I'm in charge of what's left of this company. I'd be obliged if you'd give me your name."

"I'd prefer not to be put in any official reports. My code name is Smoke, if you have to say something."

An occasional shot from below punctuated the conversation.

"Code name? You're a Cat?"

"Yes, Mr. Lieutenant. Since the age of sixteen. Normally I work the plains of here, but I'm on the trail of something."

"What was that you said about missing men? Some Wolves under a lieutenant named Caltagirone are missing."

She looked grim. "Don't expect them back. They got caught on the banks of the Verdigris. Slaughtered."

Valentine froze his features into immobility to hide his shock. *Another friend gone.* "Grogs?"

"No—Reapers, at least sorta." She licked her lips, like an animal that comes across an unpleasant smell.

The news sank in. Caltagirone was as canny as Father Wolf made them. Not like him to get taken unaware. "What do you mean, sort of?"

"It's a little hard to explain. It's a band of about twelve Reapers. I've never come across a group that big just roaming before. They're also using guns, which is odd from what I've heard about them."

"I've never heard anything like that before." It didn't make sense to him. Reapers served as conduits for vital aura between the victim and their master Kurian. Unless they were close enough to touch, the psychic energies were lost. Even in battle, Reapers killed so their masters gained the aura they craved.

"Saying I don't know my own eyes, Wolf?"

"No. Not at all. Thank you for the news about . . . about the Wolves on the Verdigris."

The redhead sat, removed a high-laced boot and two sets of dirty socks, then rubbed the instep of her right foot. Her bony feet had the calluses of someone who'd done a lot of walking.

"Now's not the time to discuss what the Kur are up to. Whatever or whoever these Reapers are, they still rest during the daylight hours. But I'm pretty sure they're headed here. If they wake at dusk, they'll be on you by midnight, maybe before. I about killed a horse getting here. I think the Grogs are just flypaper to stick you in place. The Reapers will be the ones to swat you."

She smelled of horse lather and swamp water.

"They might get their chance. The Grogs are all around us."

"Lieutenant, if I find a hole in their line, do you think you could raise a little hell somewhere else? It looks like you have enough horseflesh to drag your wounded out."

Valentine did not need any convincing to abandon the hill, as long at they could put some distance in between themselves and their gathering enemy.

"Night still comes early this time of year. Let me get my sergeants up here, and we'll talk."

The first mortar shell hit the rocky crown as they moved up the spur, and the pair threw themselves to the ground together. "This day just keeps getting better and better," Valentine said, spitting dirt.

Valentine had to raise his voice to be heard over the animals and gunfire sputtering below. The Grogs lobbed sporadic mortar shells into the hill, but they didn't make much more of a bang than the Wolves' hand grenades. The Grog column either did not pack much ammunition or lacked the ability to fire their piece very often. Maybe technology, maybe training.

The sun settled. Darkness crept up the hill, engulfing the wooded slope like a rising flood.

"One more time, Wolves. Stafford, you are with me on the diversion." Valentine had his best NCOs—save Hart at the breastworks—all around him, and he rotated like the second hand on a watch, issuing orders. "We're going to give the Grogs something to think about on the west side while everyone else pulls out east. Yamashiro, you cover the litters for the wounded. Make sure the drags stay attached to the draft horses and the wounded are ready to go."

Yamashiro nodded.

"I don't want to hear anything about some of them being too bad to move. We're not shooting anybody, and we're not going to leave anyone behind. Petrie, if you're still feeling up to it, I need you to handle the rear guard. I want the shell in the line ready to collapse as soon as the diversion gets going."

"Hell of a headache, sir. Not your instructions, the Grog's little tap, I mean."

Valentine looked into the sergeant's eyes; the pupils were normal, though he had a black eye worthy of a medical book forming on the left side of his face near the wound. He turned to the next man.

"Holloway, you take five good Wolves and go with our Cat here. She's going to pick the trail. Your job will be to make sure everyone gets on it. Avoid gunplay if you can."

The Cat in question shoveled hot beans and rice into her mouth as she listened. The pockets in her ratty overcoat bulged with bread, and she had more food wrapped up in her blanket roll.

"Sure the Grogs won't smell you coming now?" Valentine ventured.

A few snickers broke out among the Wolves, but the young woman just eyed Valentine coldly. "Not a chance. You just make some noise this side of the hill, and keep everyone moving hard for at least an hour. Can you handle that, Lieutenant?"

Valentine suppressed the urge to shrug his shoulders. In an hour he could be dead. "We'll see what we can do." He reviewed the faces of his NCOs, reassured by their self-reliant expressions. "Questions, gentlemen? No? Then let's saddle up, please. I want to be very far from here by morning."

As he slid down to the breastworks with Stafford and the other four crack riflemen, Valentine considered the fact that he was ignoring Captain Beck's final orders. But Beck was in a drag-litter now, unconscious from shock or pain. Even if the Cat's guess that these mysterious Reapers were on the way was wrong, Valentine doubted he could hold Little Timber for the problematical arrival of the Guard Cavalry. If the Grogs were reinforced at all, they could sweep over the top of the hill by making one more effort that matched the first legworm assault.

His team approached the wagon. The darkening sky was turning the woods to shadow.

Sergeant Hart had modified the wagon for a one-way trip down the slope. Each wheel now had its own hand brake with a new leather shoe at the end of the lever. Some Wolf who had read *Ben-Hur* had fixed knives, blades outward, on the hubs of each of the four wheels. The sides and front had small tree trunks added, interwoven and lashed together around sandbags for added protection. A case of grenades and a box of phosphorus candles were secured to the reinforced sides.

The volunteers climbed in, rifles, pistols, and sawed-off shotguns at the ready. "Be pretty funny if a mortar shell dropped in here after all this work," Stafford commented, helping Valentine up into the wagon bed.

"I've heard of toboggan rides to Hell, but I never expected to sit in one," another Wolf said, putting two rounds of buckshot into a scatter-gun. He snapped the breech closed with a grin.

Valentine picked up a captured Grog rifle. Another like it lay in the bed of the wagon, loaded and ready. It was heavy and unwieldy; he decided he could aim and shoot it properly if he could rest it on the side of the wagon. The bolt and trigger were oversize and strange to work—the bolt was drawn all the way up and across the gun to the other side to eject the expended shell, like a large switch. Even the lever looked odd, until Valentine remembered the strange head jerk of the Grogs after they shot—they opened the chamber and popped the shell with their chins. He placed one of the Grog fifty-caliber shells in the weapon. The bullets were as long as his hand and thicker than his index finger.

As the shadows deepened, Wolves slunk away from their positions, leaving Petrie's picked few to hold the breastworks.

Valentine assigned a man to each brake, taking the right front one himself. The shadows turned slowly purple in the growing night as the minutes ticked by.

Darkness.

"Okay, let's have a little covering fire, men. Give us a shove back there! Heave!" Valentine yelled over his shoulder at the waiting Wolves.

The wagon began to roll down the long, straight slope. The ruts in the trail would serve to guide the wheels in the absence of horses, as long as they didn't pick up too much speed.

"Keep on those brakes, there," Valentine called to the other three men at the levers. He wanted to be moving fast enough to be a difficult target, but not so fast that the wagon got outside of the brakes' ability to halt it. Bullets from both sides whistled and zipped around them. "Stop before we get out of the trees."

Stafford and the other free Wolf threw grenades to either side, for all the world like parade dignitaries tossing taffy to children lining the road. A Grog jumped out onto the trail in front of them, rifle raised to its shoulder. Valentine had an instant flash of his life ending in the bed of the wagon, thirsty boards absorbing his blood, but the report of the gun was not accompanied by the impact of a slug. The Grog threw down his rifle and drew a knife the size of a machete. It ran up to the wagon's side, throwing its arm across the side logs in an attempt to climb in. Its fierce snarl turned into wide-eyed surprise as the knives on the hub rotated their way across its belly. The eviscerated Grog dropped off the side as quickly as it had leapt on and fell writhing on the trail behind them.

Snap! The Wolf at the rear brake looked down in stupid amazement at the broken handle—or more precisely, the piece of wood that had attached the handle to the body of the wagon.

"Keep the pressure on—we're almost to the bottom," Valentine said. The grade lessened. They would be out of the trees in a few seconds. "Okay, hard brake, everyone. Stop this thing!"

Damn, damn, double damn! The wagon was slowing, but not stopping. It rumbled out of the trees to the tune of squealing wood: the leather pads had peeled off the brakes.

Gun flashes peppered the night around them. A Wolf fell, gripping a shattered arm and thrashing in the bottom of the wagon. The others fired back. Grogs ran forward, throwing themselves prone to shoot at the wagon.

"Stafford, the candles," Valentine yelled. He picked up a pair of flares and handed some to Gator, who coolly threw a grenade into the night.

Valentine and Stafford ignited the fireworks on a glowing piece of slow match. They burst into eye-cutting, blue-white light. Squinting against the glare, Valentine flung his as far into the night as he could. Grog shooters appeared in the pool of light where it landed, giving the riflemen in the truck a mark. Stafford threw two more off to the left.

"More! If we can't shoot 'em, let's blind 'em!" Valentine shouted. A form appeared out of the dark into the blue light of one of the candles, cloaked and hooded.

Reaper!

Valentine pulled up a Grog gun, balancing its overlong barrel on the log in front of him. The Reaper went into a defensive crouch as the Wolves fired at it, inhuman joints bent like a spider's and ready to spring.

The Grog gun roared like a cannon, flipping the Reaper neatly onto its back, feet twitching. Grog iron packed a kick at both ends: Valentine's shoulder felt as though he'd been shot, as well. But it was worth the pain; the bullet went through the Reaper's protective cloak. He reached for the second gun, but by the time he brought it up, the Reaper had already fled.

Splinters flew as Grog bullets pounded into the sandbagged logs the Wolves used for cover. The distance between the wagon and the trees at the base of Little Timber was a dark, deadly chasm. They had to try for it before the Grogs clustered too thickly around the wagon.

"Now! Break for the woods!"

The firing men seemed not to hear him. "Move it!" Stafford barked, shocking the men out of their firing with his field-filling bellow and slaps on the back of the neck. The sergeant pulled the wounded Wolf to the rear as the men jumped out of the wagon.

At the sight of the Wolves abandoning their mobile fort, the surrounding Grogs came running, hooting to each other. Valentine dropped one of the chargers with the other Grog gun and rolled off the wagon.

Stafford suddenly sagged, gripping his stomach. "Go, go!" he gasped at the Wolves, folding and falling.

Valentine caught Gator as he fell, reflexes in top gear.

"Go . . . go," Stafford repeated, though whether he was still calling out his final order or encouraging his officer to leave him, Valentine couldn't say.

Valentine hoisted him on his shoulders in a fireman's carry. "Uh-uh. Not getting out of Foxtrot that easy," he puffed as he lumbered toward the woods. The howls and shots of the Grogs in pursuit spurred him on.

Another Wolf fell, sprawling dead on the field, a mere ten yards shy of the trees. The flash of a shotgun illuminated a Grog leaping at them from the woods, gray skin ghostly in the glare of the flares. It toppled, almost cut in two by the blast. Some acoustical trick made the shot seem as though from a great distance.

Valentine started up the slope, Stafford's hot, sticky blood running down his back. Nothing mattered but getting the sergeant to the top of that hill. Valentine forgot the Grogs, the other Wolves still hurrying beside him, covering him as best they could. The flaming agony in his legs, the thick, coppery-tasting burn in his chest—they were the here and now, all else faded into the noise and confusion of the running fight. He felt Stafford go limp. . . . *Please God let it be unconsciousness.*

"Get . . . to . . . the . . . wagon," Valentine gasped. The Wolves would be up the hill already, if they would only quit covering him and Stafford.

One worked the lever of his rifle. "After you, sir," he said, kneeling to shoot back down the hill. Valentine heard an inhuman scream of pain.

He found the strength and breath to keep moving.

"Lieutenant, get down!" Sergeant Petrie called from somewhere above.

Valentine sank to his knees, dropping one arm from Stafford to hold himself up.

A volley crashed out from the breastworks. A second ragged one followed as the Wolves worked the actions on their rifles.

"Now, sir!" Petrie called out. A tiny red dot, the fuse on a grenade, flew overhead.

The seconds of respite worked wonders on his legs. He struggled to his feet, still burdened by Stafford, and reached the breastworks at a run. Wolves squeezed off shots from a twenty-yard stretch of the breastworks.

"The rear guard should be off this hill already, Petrie," Valentine admonished his savior. "But I'm damn glad to see you."

"The feeling is mutual, sir. Shall I light the fuses?" the sergeant asked.

"Be my guest."

The second wagon, like the first, was lined up in the ruts leading down the hill. Only this one was filled with tinder, ammunition, black powder, and grenades, and manned by four smiley-face scarecrows pulled from the hill. Petrie nodded to a pair of Wolves who kicked out the rocks bracing up the wheels, and as the wagon began to roll, Petrie lit a spaghetti tangle of black fuse cord dangling off the end. Six individual threads hissed as they burned down toward the explosives.

The cart picked up speed.

"Let's not stay for the fireworks. Gavin, Richards, help Sergeant Stafford. Put him in that stretcher. I've got another man hit in the arm. Where's Holbrooke?"

"He didn't make it," one of the volunteers said. "He fell on the trail."

Valentine pushed Holbrooke, a newly invoked Wolf with the makings of a good officer, out of his mind. "Let's catch up to the others."

The Wolves fell back as explosions rumbled from the base of the hill. The small-arms ammunition and grenades cooked off, as well, adding their own notes to the destructive symphony.

The escape route Smoke scouted wound through the deep ravine on the south side of Little Timber Hill. Valentine and his weary men moved as quickly as they could along the crown of the hill to the Wolf posted at the point in the breastworks where the line of retreat began.

"Lieutenant Valentine," said the soldier, tears of relief in his eyes, "I'm to get you caught up with the rear of the column. That Cat sure knows her stuff, sir. We found two dead Grogs at the break in the ravine. Two others farther up, too. Did it without firing a shot."

With four men on Stafford's stretcher, they caught up to the rear guard in a matter of minutes. The Cat lingered at the back of the column, waiting for them.

"And they say we have nine lives," she said, eyes sparkling in the darkness. She twitched and turned at tiny sounds, pure nervous energy beneath her freckled skin. Her face was coated with black greasepaint, and she had turned her overcoat inside out to reveal a black shell on the reverse side. "Good to see you made it, Lieutenant. That was some stunt."

"Thank you, thank you for finding us a bolt-hole, that is. From everyone in Foxtrot Company." Valentine favored her with a little bow. "If there's anything the Wolves can do—"

"Sure. I'll take a carbine like the one I saw you with and a scattergun. A revolver would come in handy, too."

"Of course. Tomorrow morning you can have your pick."

"No, sir—now, if you don't mind. I'm going back to the hill."

Valentine stopped in his tracks, causing the Wolf behind to plow into him. Other men swore as the file sorted itself out. "What's that?" he asked, stepping aside and gesturing to the Wolf to keep moving.

"Look, Lieutenant, someone should keep the campfires going there. Fire an occasional shot at the Grogs. Tie up the stock so the lifesign fools them—at a distance, anyway.

"We already used some wounded Grogs for that," Hart cut in.

She flashed a smile before turning back to Valentine. "Besides, I think those Reapers we spoke of are going to hit your camp sometime tonight. I want another look at them."

Valentine was startled into an unguarded comment: "You're crazy."

"Mmmm. I'm not trying to take heads. Just a look and a listen. I'm pretty slippery; they won't get their tongues into me. If I stay back there, it improves your chances of getting away about a hundred percent. When I do leave, I'll leave noisy. I'll try to lure the Grogs down toward Fort Smith."

"It's your aura. Take whatever you want with my gratitude."

She grabbed weapons from the astonished Wolves. She moved lightly, making no more sound on the forest floor than a breath of wind. "Thanks. Maybe we'll meet again, Lieutenant," she said, throwing her new carbine over one shoulder and cradling a shotgun.

"Hope so. Let me know what you find out. You can get in touch with me through the Miskatonic. I drop in there whenever I can."

"Those ghouls? They always want me to bring in Reaper blood bladders. Fresh ones. Like I walk around with a jar of formaldehyde."

"I've got friends there." He offered his hand, and the woman took it.

"You don't look like an egghead, Valentine. Until a better day."

"Better days," he agreed.

She disappeared into the darkness as quietly as she came, and Valentine was left with a grease-stained hand.

*   *   *

They buried Stafford at dawn the next day.

Foxtrot Company laid him to rest on a forested ridge overlooking a little ruined roadside town from the Old World.

The sound of the occasional shot from Little Timber Hill faded once they put the first ridge between themselves and the Grogs. With a couple of miles between him and the hill, Valentine relaxed into his after-action jitters, sticking his hands in his side pockets to keep them still. The news that Stafford had died barely registered through the worry and fatigue; he had been half expecting it. When he was told that Poulos, the handsome new bridegroom from his platoon, had succumbed to shrapnel wounds from the Grog mortars, he felt more of a shock. Poulos had been bleeding a little, but insisted on walking one of the litter horses instead of riding.

They paused to rest, eat, and bury the dead. Rain turned the dirt into wet lead for the diggers and as the little clusters of miserable people stood over the freshly covered mounds, saying the final good-byes of the graveside.

Good men and mediocre men, veterans and youths—all in all, Foxtrot Company had lost twenty-two Wolves, without counting Lieutenant Caltagirone and his short platoon. Adding in the wounded brought the casualty rate up and over 70 percent. A disaster. And he'd been in command.

Three

Fort Smith on the Arkansas River, March: HELL ON THE BORDER *reads the sign hung just beneath the foot-tall stencils of the post's official marker. The slogan goes back to Fort Smith's days as a station at the edge of the Indian Territory, when prisoners brought in from the Nations waited in a dank series of cells for their turn before the Honorable Judge Parker, U. S. Grant's "hanging judge."*

Now the buildings around the Reynolds Bell Tower—the bell still serves as the post's alarm system; it last rang in the fall of '66 during an air raid by harpies—still see their share of prisoners. Runaways from the Gulag, deserters, captured Quislings, and troublemakers from the western half of the Free Territory are brought here to be interrogated, and either sent downriver into the Free Territory or brought up before a military court.

Fort Smith is the responsibility of the Guards, the uniformed defenders of the Free Territory. It marks the end of the commercial line on the Arkansas River and four eastern roads. There is a civilian presence supporting the soldiery and schools and a hospital to accommodate them. It is a hard-duty station. Only the posts south of St. Louis on the Free Territory's border see more alerts and action. Hardly a month goes by without the departure of a regiment or two of Guard infantry with their supports to cover some portion of the border against a real or threatened attack out of the Kurian Zone. Lesser patrols depart and return at reports of everything from Reapers to horse thieves, downed telephone wires and hayloft arsonists.

The graveyard south of Belle Point is filled with the Guards who came back in the morgue wagons.

Duty at Fort Smith is not without its diversions. Traveling per-

formers entertain at the Best Center—singing groups and acting companies inevitably called the "Worst Enters" by the sarcastic soldiers. The women at Miss Laura's, the most opulent of Fort Smith's brothels, provide assorted horizontal refreshments, but unlike the free Best Center, it takes a week's pay to enjoy a few hours of diversion. The local beer, Smith-Knoble, is well thought of throughout the Territory, and entrepreneurs who don't mind the occasional sound of artillery fire operate restaurants and pubs.

Hunters in from the KZ stick to a few boarding houses and pubs that welcome their kind. Neither civilians nor Guards, they are nominally subordinated to the Officer Commanding Fort Smith while within the broad boundaries of the post. But something about the Hunters, even in civilian dress, makes the civilians wary and Guard hackles rise. Perhaps it is the intense stares or the too-quick-for-the-eye flinches at unexpected movement or the tribal clannishness that sets them apart. But when word comes that a Reaper is on the border, Hell on the Border is glad to have them there.

The orders in Valentine's dispatch pouch that read "Survivors leave ending 9MAY2067" amounted to an epitaph to Foxtrot Company.

It meant the Second Wolf Regiment considered the company destroyed as a fighting force; even those still unwounded after Little Timber would be distributed to other units. If they decided to rebuild the company, he'd get a second set of orders soon enough. As the senior unwounded officer, he might even be selected for command. If so, he'd try to get a few of the veteran NCOs, perhaps arguing that "third time's the charm" for ill-fated Foxtrot, now decimated twice in three years.

After getting the flimsy, Valentine decided to spend his leave in Fort Smith. It would be easy for orders and mail to find him there; he could visit the library; perhaps he'd even be able to spend a few days fishing in the river or one of the lakes around the post if he could obtain a skiff, rod, and reel. He needed quiet and solitude to help the memories of Little Timber settle.

He'd thought about spending his leave in Weening. Molly had invited him to visit in her letter, but she was no doubt enmeshed in a celebration of her engagement or wedding plans—he'd seen in the spring issue of the *Service Bulletin* that her swain had been promoted. Molly didn't need Valentine hanging around like the proverbial skeleton at the feast. Her beau might even consider it an insult.

The part of him that wanted to get away was strong enough that he considered fleeing to Hal Steiner's enclave in the Arkansas bayou country. Frat had written that Steiner's unusual community of man and

Grog had thrived since he'd first visited it years ago. But Steiner's independent land wasn't part of Southern Command's communication system. He'd have to journey to the nearest post to check for orders.

So he settled on Fort Smith. Besides, he had another report to make. This time he'd do it in person.

The afternoon he arrived he first went to the communications office on the old university grounds. There he reported his presence in person to the duty officer, and by phone to Second Wolf Regiment Headquarters. With that done, he drew a portion of his accumulated pay and was a free Wolf.

He asked about the town at the civilian liaison officer's station, but the sergeant behind the open, circular desk spoke with such enthusiasm about the food and beds at a particular boarding house that Valentine decided he was getting a kickback. He just picked up a mimeographed map and walked toward town.

Blue-steel storm clouds rolled in the distance, so he decided to look around town while the weather held. There were Guards in their charcoal-gray uniforms everywhere. Those on duty moved about under camouflage ponchos, rifles slung and helmets bumping from their hooks on their belts. As he got farther away from the fort, he met more off-duty soldiers, undershirts white in the spring overcast, thumbs hooked in their suspenders, hats pushed back to reveal close-cropped hair. The men and women of the Guards clustered about the pubs and markets in groups, laughing and talking with animated energy. Valentine with his dirty buckskins, mud-crusted ponytail, and meager possessions rolled in his hammock felt like a country hare wandering amongst hyperactive city squirrels.

Constant war had not been kind to Fort Smith. Every other lot was a reclaimed "rubble garden" with neat shelves of ruined masonry supporting wildflowers and surrounded by bushes. A few old homes were still standing in a section of town the map called the Grove. One of them, Donna's Den, was listed on the map as a boarding house. He'd heard the name from one of the Foxtrot Wolves. After getting his bearings off the Immaculate Conception Church, he found it.

Donna's Den was a white two-story house with an antique iron railing running around the roof. There was a chicken run and a garden in back. The front had a flower garden, with a pair of wooden sofas and a lounge chair sitting among the blossoms. The outdoor furniture supported domestic animals. Cats snoozed, and a dog twitched an ear as he passed. He smelled pies baking.

His knock on the screen door summoned a shirtless boy who thundered down the stairs. The boy had modified a laden tool belt with shoulder straps so it would go around his tiny waist. "Lieutenant Valentine, Second Regiment, Foxtrot Company," the boy said, looking at Valentine's collar tabs and sewn-in nameplate. "But the tunic is cut Zulu Company style, Lieutenant, sir. What's the story?" The boy sounded bored.

"David is fine, to a veteran like you." That got a brief smile out of him. "Do I speak to you about a room?"

"Mom!" the boy bellowed over his shoulder before vanishing back upstairs. "One of Dad's kind."

Donna Walbrook had flour in her hair and on her overalls. Valentine's nose picked up the scent of strawberries. She wiped her hands on a towel as she came to the door, showing more enthusiasm for Valentine's presence than the boy had.

"Brian has no manners," she apologized. She had a nice, though practiced, smile and a good deal of ragged beauty. "He's got his teeth into building armoires. Can I offer you a room?"

"Until the second week of May, if it's not inconvenient."

"No such thing for a boy in buckskin. Come into the parlor—just leave your bundle at the foot of the stairs."

It turned out the parlor had a small shrine to Hank Walbrook under a framed commendation letter. Valentine looked over a photograph; it showed a Wolf with an old United States Army beret set at a jaunty angle on his head. Walbrook's belt and parang lay in a case, a few rifles—Valentine noted that they smelled of gun oil and appeared well cared for—hung over the fireplace. She poured Valentine water out of a pitcher and presented him with a glass.

"Your husband?" he asked, feeling he already knew all the answers.

"Yes. A sergeant, First Regiment. Captain Hollis was his commanding officer, but I understand he's retired."

Valentine had never heard of him.

"My husband was killed in February of '55."

"I'm sorry."

She saw him glance upstairs as he did the math. "Brian isn't from Hank, but he thinks he is. I'll explain it to him when he's old enough to work it out. We have two other Wolves staying at the moment, convalescent leave," she added, putting the smile back on. "I'm sure you'll be eager to meet them."

"I would, Mrs. Walbrook."

"First rule of this house is to call me Donna."

She went through the other rules. They were brief and clear, militarily precise, and covered visitors, mealtimes, the gun locker, and the necessity for stoking the boiler if there was to be enough hot water.

After negotiation involving Valentine reducing some of her cordwood to kindling, they settled on twelve dollars Southern Command script a day for his room and two meals. If he did his own bedding and laundry. Lunch he could scrounge, buy, or have for free if he cared to walk all the way to the Guard canteen.

"Any questions? I've been here fifteen years. There's nothing about the town I don't know."

Valentine wondered how to phrase his request. She wasn't officially part of Southern Command, but—

"Out with it, young man. I've heard it all." She covered her ample décolletage with a hand. "You got a case of something you don't want down in your Q file? I won't scream and faint." Her eyes sparkled with interest.

"There's supposed to be a Command Intelligence Division office about somewhere. I've seen bulletins issued from them, and the Western Border ones are marked 'Fort Smith.' But I didn't see it on the guide at the Fort, or the town map." He held out his map. "You wouldn't know where it is?"

She looked disappointed. "It's hardly a secret. They just don't have enough people to staff an information desk for every Tom, Dick, and Jane off the riverboat who saw a strange footprint."

"I need to file a report, in person." He'd tried through channels once, and nothing came of it. "It's more than a footprint."

"They're in the old museum building. Three stories, red brick, curved windows at the top. There's still a nice little one-man museum on the first floor. Schoolkids and recruits spend some time there for lectures. CID has the rest. You go in through the museum."

"Thank you."

"And there's a wonderful laundry just catty-corner. Tucks, it's called, and they will make those buckskins look like they've just been sewn. They can get the bloodstains out. Along with the . . . ahem . . . natural masculine odors."

The museum filled out about one quarter of the first floor of the building Donna had described. Valentine had bummed a pair of jeans and a clean shirt off one of the convalescing Wolves—Gupti had a head wound and Salvador a knee brace; Salvador's advice was to borrow from Gupti because there was every chance of him not remembering he'd ever lent out his clothes. Valentine borrowed clothes from Salvador and reported to the fort to let them know where he was staying; then went into town.

The museum was on his map.

He spent a few minutes chatting with the curator, a one-legged veteran with a solid build and a pistol in a quick-release holster—a former Bear. A single key dangled from a breakaway chain around his neck; Valentine suspected it was for a case of captured assault rifles.

He took a polite look at the exhibits, tracing everything from the last newsmagazines, stained and dog-eared, covering the earthquakes, tidal waves, and volcanoes of 2022 before Big R hit. The next cabinet covered the Ravies plague—photographs of wild mobs caught in action, cities aflame, stacked corpses riddled with bite marks and bullet holes. Then the hopeful headlines from the few remaining newspapers about the Kurians, visitors from another world who had come to restore order to a shattered civilization. Alongside these were pamphlets, amateurish and smeared and filled with horrific sketches about how the Kurians were the cause of it all. There were drawings of the robed Crisis Governors with captions asserting that the "Reapers" were nothing but death-collectors, vampirelike creatures who fed on humans for their masters.

Then came a few fuzzy shots on bad stock of the Lost War. Drawings of the Grogs, a polyglot of beings brought by the Kurians from other worlds. Blasted tanks. Crashed planes. Mushroom clouds. Ruins. Flags being hauled down as bases went up in smoke to save them from capture.

A room, shielded from the rest of the museum by a black curtain, was devoted to the Kurian Order as practiced across the planet save for a few remote Freeholds. Valentine decided not to look in there. He'd seen enough of the KZ with his own eyes.

Valentine stated his business. The custodian picked up a phone and dialed, and he told Valentine one of the "upstairs men" would be with him in a minute.

Bone Lombard was about Valentine's age and had thick glasses. He introduced himself as a CID "filter."

"What's that?" Valentine asked.

"I'll show you."

He took Valentine back to the loading dock. Like a big garage, the dock had a series of metal doors on rails, a wide-open interior devoid of anything but structural supports. Painted lines crisscrossed the floor. The lines organized a sea of wire crates and metal trays filled with documents, binders, folders, and books.

"We get a lot of captured paperwork," Lombard said. "*We* meaning a big we—Southern Command. Anything that isn't obviously useful, like the details of a column, where and when it'll be, ends up being carted here. We get everything from Quisling cookbooks to personal letters, complete with perfume and snips of hair. I don't want to bore you with all the procedures, but the filters read through it." He waved at another young man and a woman. The other filters sat on wheeled chairs with a built-in desk, pencils handy under a droplight hanging from a hook attached to the back of the chair, going through loose paper. "It can sometimes give us a picture of what's really going on outside our borders. Where there are shortages, weak spots."

"You divine trends from paperwork?"

"Once, based on requisitions that the logistics commandos found in a hospital, we saw that huge amounts of bandages and surgical supplies were going to Shawnee Oklahoma. Turned out that the Fassler Revolt was in full swing."

Valentine remembered hearing something about it while he was studying for his lieutenant's bars at Pine Bluff. "It ended badly."

"Fassler and all his men got hanged, yes."

"I heard crucified," Valentine said.

"Maybe. Couldn't get them enough guns in time. The Oklahomans really locked down the counties in revolt. But again, if it weren't for some paperwork, we might not even know the name Fassler."

"I've got a name for you. What do you know about the Twisted Cross?"

Lombard shrugged. "I don't know. Let's index it."

One of Lombard's associates kicked out sideways and sent his chair-desk rolling down an alley between the boxes. A white cat jumped out of the way.

The "index" turned out to be an old library card catalog in a separate room, thickly insulated behind a safelike door. There were several of the huge wooden cabinets filled with index-card-size drawers. Valentine opened a drawer; under typed headings there were handwritten notations in a mix of letters and numbers.

Gannet, Pony A. (Capt. "Chanute Leadership Corps")
MIL-KAN ACT206928 11NOV61
Append CAP -6 INT -15(m, v) EX 61-415

"Don't even try," Lombard said. He took the card. "Seems this Pony—strange first name—Gannet was a captain from a Quisling body called the 'Chanute Leadership Corps.' Action Report 206-928 describes the fight. You see the date. Looks like he was taken, and there was something interesting about the capture—it appears as a separate appendix. His interrogation is also appended, and copies went to Division V, which deals with atrocities, and M, which deals with people missing in action. They must have caught him more-or-less red-handed at something. He was executed in '61 sometime between eleventh November and the end of the year. That's pretty fast nowadays. If you go to a card for the 'Chanute Leadership Corps,' you'll see—"

"I'm impressed. But the Twisted Cross?"

"Quisling unit, I bet," Lombard said.

"Yes."

Lombard went to a file drawer. "They have any other names?"

"I don't know. I wrote out my report. You want to read it?"

"Sure, in a sec. Okay . . . Twisted Cross. They're designated a Quisling unit. Looks like they get around by train. That's odd. They're cross-referenced to Eastern Division."

"Why's it odd?"

"They provide railroad security, maybe?"

"Why is it odd?" Valentine asked again.

"Usually Quisling units stay in one area, under a lord or a group of lords. You wouldn't find the late Captain Gannet's Chanute Leadership Corps operating in, say, Illinois. Unless that particular Kurian family was invading Illinois, I suppose."

Valentine gave him the copy of his supplemental report that he'd attached to his description of the battle at Little Timber. Lombard looked through the three pages at the rate of ten seconds a page.

"Aren't you going to read it?"

"I did. Shall I quote the key passage? *Ha-hem* . . . 'The destruction of Lieutenant Caltagirone's platoon and Smoke's report of heavily armed Reapers employed in groups as a cohesive fighting force demand investigation. Any information on the General—' "

"Sorry. I wrote a report on these guys once before. I might as well have tossed it in a swamp."

"Fear not. I'm sure it lives forever in an index just like this one, so it can be located in a climate-controlled warehouse. Wish we filters got the same treatment—you should smell this place in August. Let's go talk to Doug; he's our Quisling expert for everything west of the Mississippi."

As he followed Lombard to the stairway, Valentine congratulated himself for passing through the filter.

Lombard took him to an office this time. Doug Metzel had a nameplate on his door, which opened only partway thanks to the volume of binders in his office. They lined shelves, filled corners, and cut off the light from the room's big, arch-topped window. A cat napped in the sun atop one labeled BRIDGE SECURITY. But the man himself wasn't in.

"Two weeks' leave. His mother—cancer, I guess," his assistant reported. She was a slight woman, perhaps in her late thirties, and wore a Guards uniform. Her nameplate read SGT. LAKE.

"Shows you how often I make it to the third floor," Lombard said. "What is it, Bone?"

"I've got a Wolf just in from . . . ah . . ."

"Lake of the Cherokees," Valentine supplied.

"Memory's great short-term." Lombard shrugged. "Five minutes later, it's mush. Comes from doing sort after sort after sort."

Lombard made further introductions. Metzel's Southern Command associate shook hands with Valentine. "I'm honored," she said gravely. Valentine hadn't heard that expression very often from either a civilian or a Southern Command Guard. He wasn't quite sure how to respond.

"It's a pleasure," he said.

"I'm Doug's liaison, and I'm filling in while he's gone. What do you have, Lieutenant? Sit down and give me the highlights."

Valentine sat across from her and began with his first encounter with the Twisted Cross swastika logo when he'd seen it on a canoe belonging to some Reapers hunting a Cat named Eveready in the Yazoo Delta. The Illinois Quislings who feared an organization with that insignia called the Twisted Cross. The Twisted Cross man he'd met in Chicago who spoke of a comrade who "fed" and suffered a bad leg wound. The man's own feeding, somehow inspired by the others. Then more recently, Smoke's description of Reapers with guns.

She listened attentively and brought down a binder. Inside it were pages of snipped insignia from uniforms. She consulted the legend in the front and then opened it before Valentine. "Like this?"

The card within had a black piece of fabric attached. On the fabric was a white piece of metalwork, a reversed swastika.

"That's their insignia. I saw one just like it in the Zoo in Wisconsin. The owner . . . he fed like a Reaper." Valentine's voice cracked, embarrassing him.

The liaison and Lombard grimaced. "Maybe just a sicko? Monkey see, monkey do?"

"I only saw him for a few minutes. He was definitely Twisted Cross."

She made a note on a pad of paper. "We don't know much about them. We think it's railroad security. They've been spotted in a couple different places." She looked in another folder. "Looks like the current theory is they run what we call 'Q-trains.' Trains filled up with soldiers that look just like normal cargo trains. You Wolves or whatever hit the train, thinking you're going to score some tires and penicillin, and out jumps a regiment of men. But there are no action reports having to do with the Twisted Cross attacking Southern Command, so we can only theorize about methods or numbers."

"It's got to be more than that," Valentine said. "There were border trash in Illinois that were scared——-"

She turned the book around and looked at it again. "I don't doubt it. Lots of Quislings use Nazi insignia. Trying to be tough or scary." She waved at the binders. "I can name half a dozen groups that use that crap. There's a gigantic biker gang in California's Silicone Alley that has SS death's-heads and the twin lightning bolts plastered everywhere. Up in Idaho, there are brownshirts with those goofy cavalry pants and boots. The Quislings open a history book, find something that looks intimidating, and copy it. Hell, even our own guys—Colonel Sark's Flying Circus in the Cascades uses the Iron Cross as a decoration for valor. I'm sure there are others in the East; the West is my field."

"Will you read my report?" Valentine asked.

"It's informative," Lombard added.

"Of course."

Valentine passed it to her. "While I'm here."

She smiled at him. "You always been a Wolf, Valentine? Seems like you don't trust our department."

"Always been a Wolf, unless you count my year in the Labor."

"The millstones of Southern Command grind slow but exceedingly fine," she said. She rotated a pencil in her mouth as she read, looked up, and extracted it. "Sorry. Old habit."

Lake finished it, put a star in the upper righthand corner. "That means 'interesting,'" she explained. "I'm kicking it higher in the food chain."

"What would two stars mean?"

"Immediate threat," Lombard said.

"I don't see anything like that here. Southern Command has other fires nearer its foot to piss on. But thank you for bringing it to our attention. I'll see if I can find that Cat's report; I'll send them on together. Thanks for bringing him up, Bone."

Valentine had done all he could. Perhaps he'd given his story enough inertia to keep the Twisted Cross moving through Lake's millstones. He thanked her for her time, and Lombard escorted him to the door. A calico cat rubbed itself against his boot as Lombard fumbled with his key.

"What's with the cats, Bone?"

"Mice. They love to eat paper. We've got a lot of it here."

"Do you think what I came in with is important?"

Lombard took off his glasses and cleaned them with his shirttail. He didn't bother tucking it back in. "Yeah. Anything that can surround and kill a platoon of Wolves is dangerous. But your Cat's story—it's hearsay, kinda. Operating out in the KZ for months on your own, it's enough to queer anyone's judgment. I've read a few Cat reports. . . . Some sound like the products of a disordered mind."

"Will you make sure the paper trail stays in view?"

"I'm just a filter, like I said. I'll do what I can."

They shook on it at the museum door.

The weather turned sunny, almost hot. Valentine sweated on his walk back to the boarding house.

"You missed a courier, Valentine," Donna Walbrook said when he returned to the Den.

She handed him a sealed envelope. "Bad news when it comes special delivery."

He read the sender's imprint. It was from the colonel's office, Second Wolf Regiment. Maybe they'd cut his survivor's leave short so he could take command of a reborn Foxtrot Company. Foxtrot deserved to live after the fight they'd put up at Little Timber. He broke the seal.

Mrs. Walbrook watched him, saw his face, patted him as he read. "Sorry, son. Someone you know die?"

"I've got orders to report to Montgomery next week." The rest of the words were hard to say; he had to force them out of a thick throat. "Under escort. There's a court of inquiry being formed to investigate my actions. I'm subject to court-martial."

Four

Southern Missouri, April: Even the rebuilt islands of humanity sur-rounded by the bloody sea of the Kurian Order no longer resemble the quiet past. The settlements and towns are in the tradition of medieval villages, with stout buildings huddled together like a threatened ele-phant herd, presenting horns and hide to the world as the mothers and young shelter within. People take care to be indoors by nightfall, and trust only the faces known to them. A few radios and even fewer print-ing presses distribute the news. A telephone call is a rarity. Trusted elders and community assist the smallholders with everything from education to sanitation.

On the north "wall" of the little town of Montgomery, folded into the foothills of the picturesque Ozarks of southern Missouri, Jackson Elementary School stands stolidly as one of the hamlet's oldest build-ings. Architecturally uninspiring but thickly bricked, it protects the north side of one of the newer towns of the Ozark Free Territory. A series of classrooms, with windows bricked up except for a few rifle loopholes with sandbags ready on nearby shelves, look out on a play-ground cleared of swings and trees. The roof of the school is covered with a slanted shield of fireproofed railroad ties, which, along with a thirty-foot watchtower are the only additions to the school in the last half-century of its existence.

Inside the building, in the old half-underground library on the lowest level of the school, three long scarred wooden tables have been rearranged into a U. At the center of the table, a sober-faced woman in a heavy uniform coat sits with three small piles of paper in front of her, sorting through the handwritten and typed pages with the aid of a younger officer. To her left, another gray-haired officer waits in self-important isolation, his fingers laced primly in front of him, tired-looking eyes gazing across the empty space in the hollow of the U at another figure.

The object of his gaze is David Valentine, wearing the closest thing to a uniform the Wolf officer posesses: creased blue trousers, boots, and a pressed white shirt. He has bound his shining black hair close to his scalp out of respect for the occasion. Valentine has none of Foxtrot's complement in Montgomery, but were any of them to look at him, they would know he was angry. His chin is down, jaw set, and he wears the fixed expression of a wounded bull about to try a final charge at the matador. A brother Guard officer leans toward him, speaking calmly and softly into his ear.

Col. Elizabeth Chalmers, who rumor said had written the book on Southern Command's military jurisprudence, cleared her throat. After the days' proceedings, Valentine learned that the sound was her version of a judge bringing the court to order with his gavel.

"This investigation is drawing to a close. Captain Wilton," she said, addressing the older man who sat facing Valentine, "you've had the unhappy duty of attempting to substantiate the charges brought by Captain Beck against Lieutenant Valentine. Namely that on the date in question Lieutenant Valentine willfully and without cause disobeyed orders and withdrew from Little Timber Hill, turning Foxtrot Company's hard-won victory into a defeat."

Two weeks ago, when Valentine first heard that Beck, from his hospital bed, had ordered charges brought against him, he had been shocked. During the course of investigation to determine if a court-martial should be convened, Valentine came to the slow realization that Beck was using the investigation of his subordinate as a smoke screen to obscure the debacle at Little Timber Hill. Foxtrot Company, so laboriously built up and trained over the last year, was again well below half-strength and rendered useless to Southern Command for the rest of the year at least. Judicial proceedings against a disobedient subordinate would befuddle the issue.

Who knows, Valentine thought, a touch of gallows humor appearing, *Beck might even get another promotion out of it.*

Captain McKendrick of the Advocate General's office, the tiny legal team that handled most of the military and civilian justice in the Free Territory, had been assigned to Valentine as his official "friend and spokesman." His counsel consisted of, "Keep your mouth shut," and "Colonel Chalmers prefers to be addressed as *sir*, not *ma'am*."

He did not inspire much confidence in Valentine. Especially after he heard that if brought to court-martial and convicted, he could be shot by firing squad.

The colonel's voice broke him out of his dark musings. "Captain Wilton, your summation, please."

The prosecuting officer stood up, a slightly bent figure with the slow voice of grandfatherly wisdom. "Yes, sir. I think we should concentrate on two essential facts. The first being that on March sixteenth, the day in question, Foxtrot Company was victorious on Little Timber Hill. In no small part due to the courage of Lieutenant Valentine here, the Grogs were thrown back each time they tried to take the hill. Their attacks grew less and less frequent as the day progressed, until finally they were reduced to sniping and the occasional mortar shell. Lieutenant Valentine's own report, read out at this hearing, states that plainly. They were beat, and they knew it."

"Colonel, please," Valentine's adviser interrupted. "There's no evidence to support that last statement."

"Don't let rhetoric carry you away, gentlemen," Colonel Chalmers said. "Let's stick to facts, please. The statement about the Grogs being beaten will be removed from the record."

"My apologies, Colonel. But that would have been my judgment, having served in the field most of my career. Within minutes of Captain Beck being wounded, Lieutenant Valentine assembled what subordinates he could and began planning a withdrawal. Despite the fact that Captain Beck, before relinquishing command temporarily owing to wounds, ordered that hill be held."

"Colonel, sir . . . ," McKendrick said, holding up his hand.

"You'll have your chance to speak, Captain McKendrick," Chalmers shot back. "Please continue, Captain."

"Lieutenant Valentine's reasoning for disobeying his Captain's orders is given in his report. This Cat out of Oklahoma somewhere believed that some kind of 'paramilitary Reaper unit,'" Wilton read, referring to a copy of Valentine's report, "would be there by midnight, having already destroyed Lieutenant Caltagirone's short platoon of Foxtrot Company. Unfortunately, this Cat disappeared as quickly and mysteriously as she came."

Captain Wilton let that hang in the air for a moment.

"We know she is no figment of the imagination, but wild stories about Reapers behaving contrary to everything we know about them might seem more frightening on the battlefield with Grogs prowling the woods than here. Lieutenant Valentine acted on this intelligence, for whatever reason"—Valentine gritted his teeth and dug his fingers into his thighs to keep from speaking—"and left a strong defensive position with a long column on night march through territory of unknown enemy strength and disposition. I think we should count ourselves fortunate that any of them returned at all.

"Of course, I must leave it to the colonel to decide whether the withdrawal from Little Timber Hill constitutes a court-martial offense."

Colonel Chalmers turned to Valentine's side of the table. "Captain, are you ready to give your final statement, or shall we break so you can reread the record before your response?"

McKendrick stood. "Colonel, I believe there is no basis for a court-martial; in fact this hearing should never have been called. Charging Lieutenant Valentine with disobeying orders makes no sense, for as soon as he assumed command when Captain Beck was wounded, no one of superior rank was present. The only orders he could disobey were his own.

"Lieutenant Valentine holds a commission in the Wolves, an honor that says we trust him to make decisions about the lives of those under him. As a commander, he made a decision to abandon the position under the same authority that Captain Beck had to order its defense. Wolves in the field usually operate outside the formal command structure; he had no one to refer to, so he used his own judgment. He made the right decision, in my opinion, but even that is a moot point for the purposes of this investigation. Even a handful of Wolves are worth more to us than the entire Grog force assaulting the hill is to the Kurians. A Grog force that was being reinforced as the day progressed as evidenced by the artillery fire that started that afternoon.

"As to the issue that Captain Beck's final orders should have been obeyed, I agree that it is traditional to follow the orders of a wounded commander being carried from the field. But we are talking about a court-martial here, and a sentence that could include this officer facing a firing squad. So we must be very careful about how we apply the law, as opposed to applying tradition.

"As soon as Lieutenant Valentine assumed command, any action he took that did not violate the Stated Rules and Regulations or Emergency Articles was by definition legal. We have had Guard colonels withdraw their forces despite orders to the contrary from immediate command authority, and at each instance, we have deferred to the judgment of the officer in the field. This proceeding should go no further. The fact that it has gone this far speaks more eloquently of the nature of the officer who brought these charges than I—"

"Colonel Chalmers! This—," Wilton protested, but Chalmers cut him off.

"Captain, Lieutenant Valentine is being discussed here, not Captain Beck. I believe this is the second time I've had to warn you about this. I want those remarks removed from the record," she said to the young officer typing on the recorder. "Another statement like that, and I'll put my own censure of you on record, Captain McKendrick. Please continue."

Valentine would infinitely rather have been back at the breastworks on Little Timber Hill than be subject to this cross-court sniping. He shifted in his seat, a bitter taste at the back of his tongue.

"Thank you, Colonel," his defender continued. "I just want to ask the colonel to keep the good of the service in mind. If we hamstring our officers by court-martialing them for decisions made under fire, we are going to get a very timid group of Wolves. Lieutenant Valentine was at Little Timber Hill; we were not. What's more, he was in command. For us to punish him for exercising that command would be the height of folly."

McKendrick sat in his wooden chair and pulled it forward with an authoritative scrape.

Colonel Chalmers looked at the piles of paper before her. "Lieutenant Valentine, do you have anything to say before I make my decision?"

McKendrick elbowed him and gave the tiniest shake of his head.

Valentine stood up to address the colonel. "No, thank you, sir."

"Then would you please step into the waiting room while I discuss this with the captains."

"Sir," Valentine said, and left the room.

A very welcome face met him in the tiny room. Baker, the Wolf who had aided him in the attack on the Rigyard, was stretched out full on the sofa, reading a yellowed book.

"Hi-yo, Lieutenant. What's the story?"

The sight of a familiar face was like a cool breeze in hell. "Baker!" Valentine said, trying not to drop his mask of assumed stoicism too far. "What are you doing here? Foxtrot is supposed to be at mustering camp getting replacements."

"I'm outta Foxtrot Company, sir. I applied for a post in the Logistics Commandos."

"You, a scrounger?"

"Yeah. 'The backbone of the army is the noncommissioned man' and all that, but we need beef and shoes that aren't made out of old radial tires."

"Good luck, wherever you end up. The Wolves'll miss you."

Baker shrugged, his big shoulders making the gesture evocative of a turtle withdrawing to its shell. "I liked serving under you, but by God if it weren't for you and that Cat, we'd all be dead. And what happens to you over it? A court-martial."

"Not a court-martial. An 'inquiry.' There's a difference." The words came easy. Valentine had told himself the exact same thing hundreds of times a day for the past week:

An inquiry can't shoot me.

Baker began rummaging in his rucksack. "Now, where is that—? Here Mr. Valentine, I brought you some liquid morale." He said, extracting a sizable corked jug. "This ain't no busthead, either. It's genuine Kentucky whiskey. Berber or some such. Every man in the platoon chipped in and bought it off a cart trader. Bill Miranda from second squad grew up in Kentucky. He tasted it and vouched for the authenticity. Tasted a couple times, as a matter of fact, but we'd bought a big jug, and no one thought you'd miss a sip or two. Taste?"

"I'd love to. But I've got to go back into the courtroom, or whatever they call it. Not the best time to show up drunk."

They chatted over the small doings of the platoon and the company, from the smooth-faced kids who were supposed to be turned into Wolves to the lack of adequate blankets to replace those lost.

"This last batch," Baker was complaining, "turned to mush when they got wet. How the hell do you make a blanket outta sawdust, that's what I want to know. They'd unravel, if only there was material in 'em to unravel in the first place. Does all the wool go to the Guards' fancy dress uniforms?"

The young officer who transcribed the inquiry poked his head into the room. "They're ready for you, Lieutenant."

"Good luck, sir," Baker said, suddenly serious.

As he walked back to the table-filled room, the stenographer walking next to him at a wedding-march pace, Valentine fought the urge to ask what the verdict was. He would find out soon enough, and the last thing he needed was this kid looking down his nose at a weak sister of a Wolf.

He stood in the center of the U of tables, the faces of the three officers conducting the inquiry impassive.

"Lieutenant Valentine," Colonel Chalmers began, "by all accounts, you are a fine young officer. I have tried, behind the scenes so to speak, to see if we can just drop this with some kind of simple reprimand. The basic facts of this case are in your own report, which you have sworn to and stood by, that Captain Beck ordered you to defend Little Timber as the new commander of Foxtrot Company. In that you heard and acknowledged that order, I have decided it would take a court-martial to decide whether you disobeyed said order."

Valentine's heart fell at her words. Innocent or guilty, the very fact of being court-martialed would ruin his career. No commander would want a junior under him whose ability to obey orders was the subject of a military trial.

"However, I do have certain powers. I am going to give you a choice. Face the court-martial, and take your chances. If it means anything to you, your friend at this inquiry, Captain McKendrick, has offered to defend you before the court. And, interestingly enough, Captain Wilton also very passionately offered his services in your defense. You can come away from this assured that the officer investigating on behalf of the complaint against you is sympathetic to your situation.

"I am also giving you the option to resign your commission rather than face court-martial. You can serve as a Wolf, or go into one of the other branches of service discreetly, or return home to Minnesota if you wish. I advise you to consider this option. In my experience courts-martial are tricky affairs—no one on either side ever comes out smelling like a rose, so to speak. What say you, Lieutenant?"

Valentine felt the room reel around him for a moment, and then he straightened. "May I think about it for a day, sir?"

"Of course. I am holding a hearing in the matter of a theft of civilian property tomorrow, and I believe there are two more cases before I move on in the circuit, so you can answer me at your leisure. Good luck to you, Lieutenant Valentine."

She rose, as did Wilton and McKendrick. She left the room by a back door, walking a little oddly with her artificial left leg, and carried away the formality of the proceeding with her.

"Damn shame, Valentine," Wilton said as soon as the door closed behind her. "The colonel of the Second Regiment should have shut Beck up, but good. Does he have friends in Mountain Home?"

"I don't know, sir."

McKendrick approached him, and Valentine offered his hand. "Seriously, do you have enemies in high places, Valentine? I can't see why this is being pushed through. She should have rolled that complaint up and tossed it in the fireplace. Bullshit like that usually walks with the colonel."

"Captain, you want a drink? There's enough bourbon for you, as well, Captain Wilton," Valentine offered.

"No thanks, son," the old man said. "Gives me a sour belly."

"Good," said McKendrick. "More for us, then."

*   *   *

The informal party, which Valentine dubbed "the Wake in Honor of David Valentine's Lieutenancy, May It Rest in Peace" broke up about 2 a.m. Baker had left around midnight in the company of a very companionable "widow lady" who joined them in the shanty bar just outside Montgomery's walls. But not before he turned over his pocket watch and most of his cash to Valentine. McKendrick proved to be a loud, roaring drunk who recited obscene jokes at each round but exhausted himself at the stroke of one. "The stronger the wind, the quicker it blows itself out," Valentine quoted to the other drinkers, not sure if he was quoting himself or someone else. Valentine shared the rest of his jug with the barflies and ne'er-do-wells of Montgomery, assuring himself of their undying friendship while the liquor lasted.

Nobody seemed to own this oversize shack; the pack trader who had been selling drinks went to bed at midnight. Valentine decided that returning to his room at the old school was too much effort. The dirty linoleum floor seemed much more cool and soothing than any bed. Clean sheets were not worth the walk, anyway. He was a Wolf, by damn, at least for now, and used to sleeping rough.

"This how you always take bad news, Lieutenant?" a sarcastic and vaguely familiar female voice sounded from the whirling world above.

"I'm the king of bad news, lady. Ask my parents. Ask Gabby Cho. I'm King Midas and the Angel of Death all rolled into one. Whatever I touch . . . dies."

"Ahh, the jovial kind of drunk. My favorite. C'mon, Ghost, let's get you up." She lifted him to his feet. Her compact body had a good deal of wiry strength, Valentine noticed through the drunken haze. She also smelled good, a faint, soapy aroma.

"Errhuh?" Valentine said, not sure that he wanted to be pulled to his feet by the Cat he knew as Smoke—even if his nostrils were attracted to her. "They used to call me that in the Wolves. Which I'm not anymore, and neither are you."

"You're coming with me, Lieutenant Valentine. Can't have you doing yourself any harm, not on my watch, anyway."

Valentine cleared some of the bourbon fog with an effort and a few lungfuls of the cold spring air of the Ozark Plateau. It really was Smoke, the Cat from Little Timber. "Okay, okay, I'm fine. Hey, how did you get here? I could have used a deposition from you today, you know. My asshole captain intends to salvage his next promotion by putting me in front of a firing squad."

She escorted him to a caved-in house on a hill overlooking Montgomery. Tree branches through a window held up the one remaining wall.

"It's got a good basement," she said, leading him to a still-standing door within the ruins. She shoved open the door and helped him down the steps. The embers of a dying fire glowed within an old backyard grill in the center of the room, the wisps of smoke drawn up through the remnants of furnace vents.

"All the comforts of home. There's even a washtub. Until I got here three days ago, I hadn't had a hot soak for a month. I had to kill some rats to claim the room. I'm worried that they're reorganizing for a counterattack, though." She reawakened the fire and stared into its orange-yellow dance for a long moment.

Valentine sagged onto a pile of musty discarded clothes piled in a corner. "Three days ago?"

"Yes, I've been listening in to the trial."

"Funny, I didn't notice you in the room. Were you disguised as the colonel?"

"Valentine, you're talking to a Cat. The militia cretin in the watchtower wouldn't see a hundred gargoyles flying in a V-formation on a sunny day, never mind me sneaking into the building before dawn. I found a spot in the basement where the echoes were favorable and listened. We Cats have about as good hearing as you Wolves, you know. You didn't say much in your defense."

"I didn't want to spoil anyone's fun. They were having a fine time dissecting me."

"The words you use. You're a regular dictionary, Valentine. I can read pretty good, and I've been doing a lot of it lately. I've been checking some of your reports they have copied at the Miskatonic. I'm starting to think we were fated to meet."

She avoided his eyes, laying out blankets and matting.

"How's that?"

"I'll explain when I'm rested and you're sober. Too tired now."

"Give me a taste."

"No. Shape you're in, you wouldn't remember anyway." She crawled into her bedroll. "*Brrr*—I've been waiting for you to come out of that dive for hours. What are you going to tell them tomorrow? I notice you didn't ask anyone's advice."

Valentine rubbed his 2 a.m. shadow thoughtfully, making the bristles rasp. "They got me pegged as a retreater. I was thinking of fighting it out. Beck would have to take the stand, and there are a few questions I'd like to ask him."

She kicked her shoes out from under the blankets. "Do yourself a favor, Valentine. Just resign. Go quietly. There's more important things at stake than your ego."

"Just a second, lady. Where do you get off talking to me like that? I've got four years in the Wolves. I don't see what my choice has to do with anything you're interested in."

"Valentine, go to sleep. We'll talk tomorrow. Now be quiet before I start asking myself those exact questions."

"Speaking of questions, you've never even told me your name."

"Duvalier. Alessa Duvalier."

"Appreciate the assist, Duvalier. Never thanked you properly." He reached out and gave her shoulder a gentle squeeze.

"Don't press your luck."

Gold-plated bitch.

"I meant for back in Oklahoma. You saved—"

"Cats need their sleep. Good night, Valentine."

With a diamond setting.

Frustrated, Valentine wrapped himself in a blanket and let the booze win. He turned his back to the fire, feeling as though he were in the bottom of a canoe in white water. The pair vented their mutual hostility in deep, regular breaths. As Valentine drifted away to calmer waters, he noticed that they were also breathing in unison.

Valentine hadn't smelled real coffee more than twice in the last year. So the aroma of Duvalier brewing it in an aluminum percolator over the rebuilt fire startled him into wakefulness.

She saw his head rise. "I figured you could use some coffee. I'm glad you're not the puking kind of drunk."

Valentine's tongue felt and tasted like the defensive end of a skunk. "The morning is still young. That can't be coffee."

"You'd be surprised at what I get out of the KZ. Here, have a cup." She poured a generous amount into a scratched plastic bowl. Valentine wondered if he was supposed to lap it up, but eventually got some down without burning his lips.

The sharp, stimulating taste made the morning appear rosier.

"Ever read detective novels?" he asked.

She shook her head. "Where I usually circulate, I'm lucky to have old dishwasher warranties to read."

"They're stories about really smart people who solve murders. They always spot a tiny little clue everyone else missed, and explain themselves to the rest of us poor idiots at the end. Once you start reading them, they're kind of addictive."

"And?"

"My point is I feel like one of the idiots, waiting for the puzzle to be put together under my nose."

She smeared something in a skillet and reached for her jacket. "Your file said you were well read. Wish I could help. My puzzle is missing a few pieces, too. Maybe together we can fill in the blanks."

He met her gaze, but she didn't elaborate.

Depressed, half-sick, headachy, Valentine wished he could just spend half the day in bed, as he had during the long Minnesota winters when there wasn't much else to do but read away the short days and long nights.

She cracked a pair of eggs in a pan, and they immediately began sputtering in the hot grease. Her elfin features were the picture of concentration as she poked at the eggs with a handleless spatula. "Don't get used to this. I don't know if it's because I feel sorry for you, or because I know what it's like to have a hangover. The bread might have a little mold on it, but the eggs were freshly swiped this morning from one of the good citizens of Montgomery. The only trade good I have right now is the coffee, and I don't want to part with it. Besides, I'm keeping my presence here quiet. I've got only one plate, so I'm just going to eat out of the pan if you don't mind."

She passed him the cooked over-easy egg and a hunk of green-dusted bread. Valentine mopped up the egg with the bread and ate the sticky combination. "This is great, thanks."

"You like it that way, too, huh?" she said with a smile, eating her own egg-yolk-smeared bread. "Okay, how do you want the story, from now working backwards, or from the beginning?"

"I don't think I can think backwards, so you'd better do it from the beginning."

"Easy enough. I came across some interesting stuff reading your reports. Four years ago you had a run-in right after you were invoked as a Wolf. You stumbled onto some Reapers hunting a Cat in the Yazoo Delta."

"Yes. That's the first time I saw that Twisted Cross insignia."

"At first we just brushed it off as another faction of the Kur. Sometimes they use little symbols to note their houses, or clans, or whatever you want to call the groups of Kurians." She consulted a thin notebook in a leather case, like a waiter's order pad he'd once seen in Chicago. "The summer you ended up hiding in Wisconsin, one of the Freeholds we communicate with went silent. It was a small one, really just a valley or two in the Smoky Mountains. Scouts from the New England Freehold found buried Quislings. And some mass graves. But back to the Quislings, they had Twisted Cross insignia on their uniforms. A swastika is another name for it, I'm told. So the Cats kept their eyes open, and now and then these Quislings were seen in other parts of the country. So the insignia did not mean just one geographical group of Kurians.

"The people at Miskatonic have an idea that the Kurians have taken some of their Quislings and created Reaperhuman half-breeds, kind of a specialized striking force." She looked at him expectantly.

"Is it under someone called the General?"

She looked puzzled. "Where did you hear that?"

"From an old railroad man we brought out of Oklahoma. A little addled. Not much of what he said made sense, so I abbreviated it in my report. He stumbled across some Quislings under this Twisted Cross banner in a yard. They took him before this General, who then decided to kill him as a precaution."

Duvalier digested this information along with her moldy bread and egg. "This General is someone we've heard of now and then. I think he's a very highly placed Quisling. So they have a special train?"

"Yes, he said it was a sizable one."

"That doesn't fit with the rest. As far as Miskatonic knows, they go in small groups, without heavy weapons or a big escort. Do they just want to look like another supply train?"

"Guessing is interesting, but facts are better." Valentine returned to a subject much on his mind lately. "What happened at Little Timber Hill after you went back?"

"I was getting to that, because I think it's important. I built up the campfires and shot down at the Grogs from various points in the line. They didn't come at night. Some Harpies flew overhead, but they didn't risk dropping down for a close look, so they never saw that the breastworks in the trees weren't manned.

"Well before dawn, could have been three a.m., eight Reapers came up the hill. I just hid and watched. They were loaded for bear, assault rifles and everything. Mean-looking Kalashnikovs with banana clips.

"But here's the kicker. They make the top of the hill, and they get . . . confused. I've never seen a Reaper that looked like it didn't know what to do. So they group together and talk. Who ever heard of Hoods talking to each other? Usually when you see a group of them, they're all puppeted by the same Kurian, so they don't have to talk. Same hissy voices. If these were some kind of Reaper-human cross, they sure left the human parts in their other pants. They looked and sounded like Reapers to me. Just didn't act that way."

Valentine put down his plate. "How did you get away?"

"They picked up your trail, sent out the Grogs. I just slipped away back to the south in the dark. I wanted to have another talk with the

Miskatonic people about this, so I caught a barge from Fort Smith to Pine Bluff. That's where I heard about all this. I was told to come up here and talk to you."

"Told? Told by whom?"

"Don't worry about that right now. An old friend of mine, who knows some old friends of yours. I was hoping you'd do some work with me in the KZ for a while."

Valentine narrowed his eyes, wondering what she was getting at. "I thought you Cats worked alone."

"We do. Unless we're training another Cat."

Dear Sir,

It has been my privilege to serve in the Wolves for four years. I wish to spare myself, my company, and my regiment the pain and disruption of a court-martial that would be the inevitable result of my fighting the charges brought against me. Please accept my resignation from duty in the Second Regiment of Wolves, Southern Command, immediately.

I have the honor to remain, etc.,
David Stuart Valentine

Duvalier looked up from the handwritten, slightly smeared note. "Brief and to the point, Valentine. I expected more flowery 'the clock has struck the hour of fate' type stuff out of you. I like you better already."

"After I turn this in, where are we headed—north or west?"

She shook her head as she shouldered her pack. "Back into the Free Territory, actually. You have to meet with someone. We also need to outfit you with a little better blade than that sawed-off machete before our little welcoming ceremony with the Lifeweavers."

Valentine remembered his. The cave, Amu the Lifeweaver and his retinue of hairy, sleeping wolves. Amu had called it an "operation," though he'd never opened Valentine with anything but a tasteless drink and his mind.

"Another invocation? Like when I became a Wolf? I felt like I was wearing a different body the first few days. Nothing worked right. I couldn't pick up a mug without knocking it across the table."

"Same here. Maybe it'll be different for you. I've only been a Cat. But don't let it worry you."

Valentine buttoned up his buckskin tunic, thoughtfully running his finger up the familiar fringe. The Wolves of Southern Command decorated their jackets with leather strips of varying length on the arms or chest or some combination of both, a token to friends and enemies alike of their clan. Supposedly they helped shed rainwater, but Valentine had been soaked to the marrow enough times to smile at that bit of frontier myth.

They took the short hike into town in silence and parted at the main gate. His first duty was to hunt up Baker and return the ex-Wolf's money and pocket watch. Then Valentine made for the old school to see Colonel Chalmers. Duvalier went into the Montgomery market with Valentine's remaining money to acquire some provisions for the trip.

Valentine found Colonel Chalmers in the court's temporary offices, going over the organization of her schedule with her ubiquitous shadow, the young clerk. Valentine smelled sawdust in the air and heard distant sounds of construction. More rooms in the school were being renovated.

"Ahh, Lieutenant," she said. "I take it you slept on your decision. I haven't seen your counselor yet this morning; they tell me he's a little indisposed. Kenneth, would you excuse us, please?"

The clerk exited, shutting the door behind him.

Valentine tried to stand as straight as possible. The letter in his hand trembled a little, and he fought to still it. "I've thought over your offer, sir, and I gratefully accept. Would you forward this with the report of the inquiry to Headquarters, Second Regiment?" He handed her his spidery-scripted letter.

She glanced down at it, and back up into his eyes. "I'll handle it for you, Valentine. The colonel will be relieved. Everyone ends up looking bad in a court-martial. Although I'll bet my next quarter's pay that he's sorry to lose you as an officer."

"Thank you, sir. In any case, I'm lucky not to be in the ground next to Sergeant Stafford."

Valentine got the feeling he was being judged for the second time in twenty-four hours.

"He died for something, David. Most people just end up dead."

"I'll let you get back to your work, sir."

She held up a hand. "Valentine, I did what I could for you. Off the record, I sympathize with your situation. I can't say very much about the inner workings of Southern Command, but we make more mistakes than we admit. This may not turn out to be a mistake after all.

"You know, I met your father once. At a ball. I was a lieutenant in the Guards, perhaps your age. The dance was in this fine old convention center right across from the hospital. Electric chandeliers, if you can believe it. Good food on gold-rimmed plates, an orchestra. But I didn't feel like dancing. I had just lost my leg from the knee down at Arkansas River; a sniper got me when I was spotting for artillery. Your father had been in the hospital, too. A piece of shrapnel had taken a chunk out of his arm. I just sat in a corner by myself, feeling like it was all over. I didn't do my physical therapy. I didn't want to get used to walking with a prosthetic. Just wanted to sit. I suppose I would have been in tears if I were the crying type.

"Your father came over and made me dance with him. I would have said no to a man around my age, but your dad was maybe fifteen years older—it made him seem like an uncle or something. We had to have been the worst-looking couple on the floor: I was sort of hopping on my good leg, and his arm was in a sling. We lurched our way through a waltz, and I could tell everyone pitied us—or rather me, I suppose. So he goes to the band and makes them play a polka. Now a polka you can sort of hop to, and before I knew it, we were flying around the floor. I had a tight hold on his shoulders and he just sort of bounced around, taking me with him. The band started playing faster, and he kept spinning us in a wider and wider circle. People got out of our way rather than get run over. When the song stopped, we were in this big circle of people, and they applauded.

"I got a look at myself in a mirror. I had this huge smile on my face. I was laughing and crying and gasping for air all at the same time, and very, very happy. Your father looked down at me and said, 'Sometimes all it takes is a change of tune.'"

She stared at the wall, plastered with poorly printed handbills, but Valentine could tell the wall wasn't there, just a big room filled with a band, food, and dancers in some broken-down corner of Southern Command. Colonel Chalmers returned to the present after a moment's silence.

"I read you were orphaned. How old were you?"

"Eleven."

"I didn't really know him, apart from that dance and talking to him a bit afterwards. He was kind of remote, in the nicest possible way, and I think the wound hit him hard. He left the Free Territory shortly afterwards, moved up to Minnesota and married your mother, right?"

Valentine could deal with his own memories of his family. Other people's left him feeling wistful, wishing he could talk to his parents again.

"I never even knew he was a soldier until I was older. The man who raised me afterwards didn't exactly keep it secret, but I think he wanted me to make up my own mind about things."

"You're probably wondering where I was going with that story. I ended up in the Advocate General and never found anything else I could do half as well. I just wanted to tell you that perhaps you just need a change of tune, so to speak. .

"Good luck to you, Valentine."

"Thank you, sir." He saluted and left, closing the door behind him.

"They don't waste any time," she said quietly after he shut the door. But not quietly enough. Valentine still had his Wolf's ears, if not his commission; she might as well have shouted it.

They don't waste any time. He passed the loitering clerk with a nod, already analyzing her words. Did somebody want him out of the Wolves for a reason? Duvalier seemed to be a veteran Cat for one so young, but could she have the pull to get him dismissed from the Wolves just to help her run down the Twisted Cross? He doubted it.

He walked out of the school. The hardworking residents of the town were in the fields surrounding the village. A flock of sheep passed through the main gate under the stewardship of a boy and two dogs. Valentine looked at their heavy coats—they were due for their spring shearing.

Duvalier rounded a corner, pack already over her shoulder and Valentine's hammock roll in her left hand. She waved a knotty walking stick with a leather wrist strap in her right hand.

"That was fast, Valentine."

"It takes a long time to build a career. You can wreck it in a couple minutes."

She handed him his pack. "Crackers and cheese to get us where we're going. I lost my taste for dried beef a long time ago, so I got us each a three-pound wurst. Some new cabbage, turnips, and a few beets. I make a pretty good pot of borscht. No rice and not much flour to be had, at least not for strangers."

"Where are we going?"

They passed out of the gate, waving to a half-awake deputy at the gate. "First stop is not far at all, just over the border in Arkansas. Why couldn't you have been one of those officers with half a dozen horses, Valentine?"

"Try covering thirty or forty miles, mostly at a run, with full equipment sometime. I'll never mind just having to walk somewhere again."

Duvalier looked up into the wooded hills of the Ozarks. "I can never get over it when I'm in the Free Territory. No checkpoints, no ID cards, no workbooks. You were in the KZ once, right?"

"Yes, in Wisconsin and Chicago."

"Never been to either; my ground is between here and the Rockies. I was in the desert in the Southwest once, too. Lost all illusions about how tough I was when I ran with the Desert Rangers there for a winter. Sometimes out there you get . . ." She let out an exasperated breath.

"You feel impotent against it all. You'll die, your friends will die. . . . ," Valentine said.

"Yeah. But then you get back here, where the kids don't have that quiet, haunted look. Then you pick up and do it again, because . . . you know."

"I know."

As the day progressed, they moved deeper into the old growth of the Mark Twain Forest. At the crossroads, there were new maps, burned into planks and painted and anchored, sometimes covered with glass, showing which road led where. People clung to the old names, as if as long as the names existed, the past existed, and a future that might be like the past.

Valentine's nose picked up life everywhere in the rich, rain-soaked spring soil. The trees and undergrowth flourished in green tangles all around the walkers. An empty tanker truck returning to one of the Free Territory's minuscule "backyard" refineries in eastern Oklahoma gave them a ride up old Route 37, the driver and his shotgun letting them ride atop the tanker, giving them a bumpy entrance into Arkansas. By evening, they were south of Beaver Lake in Spring Valley, when the truck turned southwest for refilling.

A pig farmer by the name of Sutton hailed them off the road and offered them lodging that night. He was an older man, in need of a couple of strong young backs for a few hours, and glad for the company. The men who helped him run his place stayed with their families in the evenings, and visitors to the rather pungent farm were limited to days with a stiff easterly breeze. Valentine was happy to cut firewood in exchange for the hot meal and lodging.

Reducing tree trunks to cordwood and kindling was Valentine's way of sitting cross-legged and chanting. He often lost himself in the steady, muscle-draining effort. He had chopped wood as a kid in Minnesota, bartering his labor to the neighbors for a few eggs, a sack of corn flour, or a ham. Even as an officer, he cut wood on mornings when he could get away from his other duties, causing his sergeants to shake their heads and find other forms of uninteresting labor for the men who fell into their bad books. The satisfying, rhythmic *chop* of ax blade or wedge into wood cleared his mental buffers, a psychological reset that left his torso rubbery with fatigue.

He finished up with the wood by moonlight and returned to the house in time to say good night to the obliging Sutton. "You and the missus got the whole upstairs to yourselves. I don't like trips up and down them stairs any more than I have to; I got a nice bed now in the office. I showed her where the linens and such are—sorry if they're a little mothbally."

Valentine padded up the creaking staircase in the faintly piggy-smelling house. A steaming bucket of water, soap, a basin, and a towel waited for him.

"Whoever last used this had a lot more hair than me," Duvalier commented, looking at one of the long hairs caught in the brush she held. She had a towel on and was playing with the three-plated mirror in the small bedroom vanity.

"He's a widower. He told me when we stacked wood. Her name was Ellen. They had two kids, Paul and Wynonna, and she died giving birth to Wynonna. The kids are both dead in the Cause's service."

Duvalier set the extracted hair carefully on the marble tabletop.

Valentine stepped into the old bathroom across the hall. The fixtures were operational, though they gave only cold water, and the electrical lighting in the house was a pleasant surprise. Sutton must be fairly well-to-do, or the area between Fayetteville and Beaver Dam better maintained than most parts of the Free Territory.

He washed up with the pail of hot water and returned to the bedroom. "So you're 'the missus,' huh?"

She peeped out at him from under a thick quilt. "My conversation with him wasn't quite as serious as yours. He assumed, and I didn't correct him. I'm not looking for sex, but you are a warm body. It's a cold night."

"Your hot water bottle is turning in. Ready for light's out?"

"Mmmmph," she agreed, turning facedown in a feather pillow.

Her rich, female smell both lulled and excited him as he lifted the covers to climb into bed next to her. His nostrils explored her even if his hands remained tucked under his pillow. He toyed with the scents in the room, locating them with his eyes shut: the wet hair of the woman next to him, the out-of-mothballs sheets, the dusty quilt, the warm, soapy water remaining in the bucket and sink, wood smoke, and the faint, omnipresent smell of pigs. He counted scents like some people count sheep, and was asleep when his companion Cat pressed her back against his.

The next morning, after sharing two steaming cups of coffee from Duvalier's shrinking supply of beans, they packed up again. Sutton drank the coffee with lip-smacking pleasure and presented them with a slab of cured bacon wrapped in brown paper.

After exchanges of gratitude and good-byes, the pair turned east. The ground grew more rugged, and the roads began to break down into trails. Worn-down mountains loomed ahead. They walked in companionable silence, pausing at little streams for water and brief respites.

"I've never been to this part of the Territory," Valentine said. "Where are we headed?"

"Cobb Smithy. One of the best weapons men and all-around blacksmiths in the Free Territory."

"I think I've heard of him. I recall some of Major Gowen's Bears talking about him."

"Actually, it's a bunch of them. There's old Cobb, his son, his daughter, a couple of journeymen, and apprentices. It's quite an operation. They probably made that chopper of yours."

"My parang? How can you tell?"

"What, you never looked at the blade closely?"

"To oil it, sharpen it . . . Wait, the *CFS* on the blade, in little letters right by the hilt?"

"Cobb Family Smithy, Valentine."

He drew his old, notched parang with its hardwood handle. He held the blade so the light fell on it, and looked again at the faint letters scrolled in tiny, precise calligraphy up against the hilt. "Funny, I never thought to ask what it meant."

They reached the smithy and outbuildings early in the afternoon. Faint hammering sounds from two different workshops sounded in the little hummock of land between Arkansas ridges. A stream ran down from the high hills to a half-pond, half-swamp on the other side of the road.

A pair of sizable but indefinable dogs trotted up to greet them, warily hopeful. Valentine took a step forward to greet the canines, and the pair began barking to raise the dead. A boy on the short side of ten ran down the drive to meet them.

"Who are you, and what's your business?" he squeaked. Then to the dogs, with more authority, "Still, you two! We know company's come."

"Smoke, Cat of Southern Command. Her Aspirant, Ghost. He needs a weapon or two."

"You're welcome here, then," the boy said, swelling with self-importance. "Follow me."

The house was a single-story conglomeration, a long rambling rancho growing like a rattlesnake's tail: an extra part every year. Whatever their skill at steelwork, the Cobb family knew little about architecture esthetics.

A middle-aged woman came out onto the nearly endless porch and squinted down at the visitors. She broke into a grin and clapped floured hands together. "Why it's Smoke, our little Kansas State Flower. How's that straightsword working out for you?"

"Needs a professional edge put back on. The hilt could use some rewrapping, too—the cording is a little frayed."

Valentine looked at the Cat, puzzled. "Did you bring it? It must be awfully small."

Duvalier exchanged glances with the woman and shrugged. "He's new, Bethany." She twisted her walking stick at the knob on the head and exposed a black handle. In a flash, she had the sword out from concealment within the stick. Valentine guessed the blade to be about twenty-two inches, single edged, with an angular point. The metal was dark, burnished so as not to reflect light.

Bethany examined the hilt with an expert eye. "I'll get a man on this. Can't have our precious Smoke losing her grip in a fight. What does your Aspirant need?"

"Apart from about two years' training in the next two months— which is my problem, not yours—he's going to need a set of claws. I'd like to see about getting him a decent blade, too. He's a Wolf, but by the look of it, he's been digging holes with that cotton chopper of his. He needs something to bite a Reaper."

"You want the old man to work with him, or my brother?"

"The Ghost here has had a hard enough week. Nathan will do."

"I'll be happy to oblige," Bethany said, moving to the screen door and holding it open. "C'mon in, and I'll make some tea."

"I've got better than that. Coffee," Duvalier said, handing over the rest of the bag.

Bethany Cobb smelled the beans. "I declare! You are just too good, rosebud."

They went into the kitchen, a vast cavern with two stoves and a large brick oven. After ringing a bell on the end of a carved wooden handle, Bethany reached high on a shelf for a coffeepot and grinder, and began to work on the beans while the water heated. "My brother will be with you shortly."

Nathan Cobb was a lumbering man with bulging arms and a substantial potbelly. He clapped Duvalier on the back, a blow she absorbed with some grace, and came close to crushing Valentine's hand in a vigorous shake. "Always, always happy to see a new Cat out there. Raise some Hell for me, would you, ummm, Ghost?" he said before getting down to business.

"I take it you need a set of claws?" he asked Duvalier.

"Yes, please, and time is a little bit of an issue."

"He seems to have average-size hands. You want talons like yours, or blades?"

"Talons, and make the fingers stiff—concealment won't be an issue on this job. I want him to be able to climb with them as well as fight."

"That'll save some time. Let's measure you up, son." Cobb extracted a stained tape measure from his work apron, and wrapped it around Valentine's palm. He then measured each finger from the little well in the center of his hand to its extremity, making notes in neat block numbers in a little pocket pad. "How about a weapon or two, Smoke? Are you going to train him?"

"I'll have to."

"Then you'll want a sword for him, I suppose. We may have something already made up."

An old man appeared at the kitchen at a door from one of the adjoining rooms in the endless house. "Is that coffee I smell?"

Bethany began pouring. "Sure is, Dad. We have visitors, and they brought it. Smoke Duvalier and her apprentice, Ghost."

The elderly man paused in his appreciation of the java. "Ghost? What's your real name, son? Don't worry, my memory's going so fast, I wouldn't be able to tell anyone if I wanted to."

Valentine looked at Duvalier.

"He's named Valentine," she said.

"Then your father was—"

Valentine rose. "His name was Lee Valentine, Mr. Cobb."

The senior Cobb's eyes narrowed suspiciously. "You sure don't look like him, except a little round the eyes. You sure you're mother wasn't just making a brag?"

Valentine ignored the insult. "My mother was Sioux, sir. North side of the Great Lakes."

"You're a fair size, but not as tall as your father. Nat, he needs a weapon?"

"Something for a Cat, not a Bear," the son answered.

"C'mon, boy, follow me," he said, blowing on the scalding mug of coffee and shuffling off down the hall. He opened a door to a stairwell and slowly started down into the basement.

Valentine looked around at the others, who simply smiled. He followed the senior Cobb.

The basement had a collection of everything from swords to antique farm implements. Daggers hung next to sickles on one wall, and opposite, pitchforks shared a rack with long pikes. A cavalry saber occupied a place of honor over a fireplace. Valentine stepped up to it and looked at the rather ordinary hilt and scabbard.

"That belonged to Nathan Bedford Forrest, son, but I don't expect you know who that is."

"Confederate cavalry commander in the Civil War. He wasn't a West Pointer, but he sure outwitted a bunch of them."

"Glad to be wrong once in a while. Bound to happen every year or two. See anything you like?"

Valentine picked up a heavy blade with a basket hilt sharing a rack with a similarly sized claymore. He swung it experimentally.

"Valentine, what are you thinking?" Duvalier chided him from the bottom stair. He hadn't heard her on the stairs. "You don't want to be lugging that halfway across the country. Mr. Cobb, let's look at something he can draw fast and swing quick."

"Hummph," Cobb grunted, not exactly disagreeing, but not wanting look like he was taking her advice, either. "I have a beautiful blade and scabbard. Last carried by a Guard with a different taste in sword. They usually like sabers and épées. Let's see what you think of this."

He opened a footlocker and began sorting through long, slightly curved shapes wrapped in blankets and twine. "Which sumbitch is it? Here we go," he said, extracting a shape. He handed it to Valentine.

Intrigued, the would-be Cat unwrapped it. As soon as he saw the hilt, he recognized it as a samurai sword of some kind. His brain searched for the term.

"Called a katana, Valentine. That's a helluva piece of fighting steel. Looks old, but it's actually from this century. We'll have to fit you with a new hilt, but that won't take too long. Only twenty-four inches of blade."

Valentine drew it experimentally. The blade carried a few cryptic ideograms etched in the metal.

"Can you cap the scabbard like mine?" Duvalier asked.

"Easy enough, missy. You should use it two-handed, boy, lets you put your whole back into it. But you can use it one-handed, from horseback, say, or if you want to parry with those damn fighting claws.

"I like it," Valentine said. "What's the cost?" he asked, wondering where he would come up with the money.

"That's Southern Command's problem, not yours, Valentine. You and little missy here will just have to sign a chit for what you take."

Duvalier wrinkled her freckled nose. Valentine could tell that the *missy* was getting under her skin.

The claws, he learned the next day, were a pair of metal hands held to his palms by thick leather straps. They arced out like a second skeletal system from there, ending in sharp talons that capped his fingers.

"You can climb a tree with 'em, and they do gruesome in a fight if you use 'em right," Duvalier explained. She put on her slightly smaller pair and looked around for a tree. "It takes a little practice," she said, stepping to the bole of a mature oak. She jumped up the side of it, reaching around either side until her palms were opposite, and began climbing. She was among the branches in no time.

Valentine imitated her and learned to his chagrin that if he failed to grip the trunk with his legs, a single set of the claws weren't enough to hold him up. He arrested the slide before falling off, then managed to hump his way up the trunk neither as quickly nor as gracefully as Duvalier. But he succeeded.

He also learned about putting a new hilt on his sword. A craftsman named Eggert showed him how to encase the naked tang in a wooden handle shaped more or less to fit Valentine's hands. Then he wrapped it in wet pigskin, applying a series of small bumps to the blade side in fastening the leather. "They used to use skin from stingrays and sharks, but those aren't too common hereabouts," Eggert explained. Finally a fine cording was wound round and round the hilt. Duvalier insisted on tying the last knot herself.

"For luck," she said, planting a tiny kiss on the newly reconstructed hilt. They worked on the scabbard together, fitting an old rifle sling to the mahogany wooden tube. Valentine decided he felt most comfortable carrying it over his shoulder.

"We can add a spring to the bottom—it'll help you draw faster," she observed, after watching him pull the sword a few times.

They moved on as soon as Valentine's sword was finished. They shouldered their packs one more time, newly laden with food supplied by the generous and Southern Command–compensated Cobbs.

"Now for home," Duvalier said, turning on the road east once more.

Five

The Ozark Mountains, May: The Free Territory had its genesis here, among the river-cut limestone, caves, sinks, and thick forests of America's oldest mountains. Like the armadillos and scorpions found in these timbered, rocky hills, the residents here are scattered, alert, tough, and dangerous. They know the stands of oak and hickory, trout-filled lakes and streams, and each other. But one area they avoid out of respect for its inhabitants, more wary and hermitlike than the most remote woodsmen. That is the ground around the headwaters of the Buffalo River, home to a cluster of Lifeweavers.

The locals call them wizards. Some fear them as a branch of the Kurians and their otherworldly evils. When the residents come upon a Lifeweaver, perhaps among the beeches running along the river as he fills a cask with water, they gather their children and avert their eyes. The Lifeweavers draw trouble like corpses draw flies. The Reapers, when they break through the border cordon to stalk and slay amongst the Freeholders, gravitate to this area in the hopes of killing Kur's most ancient and bitter foe: their estranged brethren.

Perched halfway up Mount Judea, a stoutly built A-frame lodge stands in a thick grove of mountain pine. The foundation of the building was cut from the old seabed a few miles away, thick slabs of varicolored stone that support the massive, red-timbered roof. Two monolithic lodgepoles of granite, etched with obscure designs that suggest Mayan hieroglyphs, gradually narrow toward the peaked roof. The building dwarfs any other house in the area; you would have to travel to the old resorts of the Mountain Home region to find a larger construct.

The Cats of Southern Command call it Ryu's Hall or just the Hall. They also call it home.

*   *   *

Valentine liked the look of the building from when he first set eyes on it, in the afternoon of the day after leaving Cobb Smithy.

"I was expecting another cave," Valentine said as they walked up the hill-cutting switchback leading to the Hall. "This part of the Ozarks is full of them."

"The Wolves like to lurk in their holes. We Cats like shared solitude and comfort," Duvalier said, leading the way with her swordstick used as a staff.

"Shared solitude? Sounds like 'fresh out of the can' to me. Or 'military intelligence.' "

"Watch it, Valentine. What 'military intelligence' Southern Command has feeds you now."

He didn't need his Wolf's nose to scent pine trees and wood smoke. They were cheery and welcoming odors after their days on the road.

The pair walked across a pebbled path to a metal-reinforced door. A cylinder of wrought iron with a thin steel bar hanging down the epicenter hung next to the door, and Duvalier rang it until the hills echoed.

A face appeared at a high, horizontal window. Female, amber skinned, with sharply slanting eyebrows. "Duvalier! You made good time with your new boy. Let me get the door."

Valentine heard a heavy bolt being drawn back and noticed there was no knob or handle of any kind on the outside of the door. It moved, and he got a good view of the six-inch-thick timbers that constituted the main door.

"David Valentine, meet Dix Welles," Duvalier said by way of introductions. "Dix was the toughest Cat between here and the Appalachians once upon a time."

He noticed that the darkly attractive woman held herself very stiffly and used a cane. "That was a long time ago, before my back got busted up," Welles explained. She was wearing ordinary blue overalls and had a bag of tools hanging from her hip.

"Pleased to meet you, ma'am—," Valentine began.

"Dix does just fine, David. For the last—I guess it's nine years now—I've been the Old Man's assistant, or majordomo, or whatever it is I do here. Have you ever met Ryu, Valentine?"

"No."

"He's met his brother Rho, though," Duvalier said. Intrigued, Valentine looked at the two women. It never occurred to him that the Lifeweavers had families.

"We can talk later," Welles interjected. "Come in, come in. I'll find you some space. We're almost empty right now. The Cats that wintered here left for the summer. About all that's here are some Aspirants like you, Valentine. What are we going to call you, anyway?"

"Ghost," Duvalier answered. "Some of his old friends gave him that name in the Wolves."

The conversation barely registered to Valentine. His eyes had adjusted, and he stood and gazed at the cavernous interior of the lodge.

Ryu's Hall was one big room built around a central fireplace. The fire pit was a good thirty square feet, with a wide metal chimney that disappeared up into the dark rafters. Valentine's eyes followed the metal tube up to the peak of the ceiling, which he estimated to be at least sixty feet high. A series of beams crisscrossed above his head halfway to the roof, holding up two chandeliers. They glowed with formed drops of liquid illumination, bathing the entire lodge in a golden light and deep shadow.

Welles saw the direction of Valentine's gaze. "Those little fancies are something the Lifeweavers brought across the worlds. Leave them out in the sun for an afternoon, and they'll glow like that for weeks. But don't ask me more—I only work here."

The main room of the Hall was subdivided around the edges of the room into a series of six-foot-by-six-foot platforms projecting out of the walls like shelves, all at various heights and connected by little staircases, climbing poles, and even rope ladders. A handful of figures lounged on the platforms, eating, reading, or simply sitting and looking at the new arrivals. Tapestries and sheets and rugs hung from the rafters or from the platform above provided some measure of privacy. Plates and mugs and casks were stacked at the centers of two long tables at opposite sides of the fireplace.

"You like it small and cozy or open and airy, Valentine?" Welles asked as they walked into the hall. She moved with a back-and-forth motion of her upper body that reminded Valentine of a metronome.

"Open and airy, I suppose. That's what I'm more used to."

"I'll take my usual spot," Duvalier said. "Just put him up above."

"Easy enough. These tables are the common eating area." Welles led them into the depths of the lodge. "You are free to make your own food, of course, but we usually have a morning meal and a night meal made up by the Aspirants. That's you now, Ghost-man. We have genuine toilets in the back, along with two showers and a tub, but you have to attend to the boiler. When there are a few more bodies here, we take turns with that duty so there's always enough hot water for all. There's a sauna that works whenever we got the boil up. This place is built practically on top of a mountain spring, so there's the best drinking water you've ever had whenever you want it. We don't even have to work a pump handle. Sweet, no?"

Valentine felt the warmth of a few dying charcoal bricks as they passed the massive fire pit.

"The fireplace is more for heat than cooking, but we've had a pig roast here on occasion. The main kitchen is in back. You wouldn't be any good at making bread, would you Valentine?"

"In an emergency."

"Great, you're our new baker. These kids go bluescreen whenever they try to bake anything but flatbread. Ryu has the rooms above the kitchen, and he doesn't take to visitors, so stay away from the back staircase. Questions so far?"

"Just as long as you don't have him in the kitchen at all hours," Duvalier grumbled. "We've got a lot of work to do if he's going to be ready to come out with me in a couple months. When can we see Ryu?"

"You know that's not up to me. Okay, here we are. Your usual spot, Smoke, and the Ghost will be in the attic."

Duvalier had a small space beneath Valentine's platform and its stairs. Valentine noticed she already had curtains up, blinds made from some kind of wicker. She dropped her pack under the stairs and sat on a footlocker to unlace her boots. He looked up at his own platform directly above, bare and featureless.

"I can find you a futon if you want, Valentine," Welles offered.

He didn't relish spending too many nights in his ever-ready hammock. "Thank you, I'd appreciate that."

"I'll let Ryu know you've arrived," she said, and rocked her way back to the doors at the rear of the Hall.

As he placed his possessions on the platform, connected by a stairway to the main floor and by a little walkway to still another platform, it occurred to him that his whole life amounted to two little heaps of gear: his carbine and the new sword, a pack containing a few tools and utensils, pans, and spare clothes, and one moldy-smelling nylon hammock. He had a locker back at Regiment with some heavy clothing, books, and odds and ends that he would have to write to somebody about.

"Hey, Duvalier," he called.

"Yes?" she answered from below, like a fellow camper in the bottom bunk.

"Where am I?"

"Southern Command calls it Buffalo River Lodge, Newton County. We call it Ryu's Hall. You confused about something?"

"What are we going to be doing here?"

"Didn't you listen? You're going to bake bread. That and learn how to kill Kurians."

Ryu himself woke Valentine the next morning. The nearly window-less hall slumbered in darkness, lit only by the red glow in the fire pit.

The Lifeweaver chose to appear as an ordinary man, with a hooked nose and a regal bearing that made Valentine instantly think of Pharaoh from illustrations in the Padre's storybook Bible. He wore a simple black loincloth and sandals.

"I am glad of this opportunity to meet you, David," he said as Valentine sat up, a little startled. "Would you share the sunrise with me?"

"Yes, just give me a moment," he said, rubbing the sleep from his eyes. The futon didn't look like much, but it was bone-deep comfortable. He slept heavy in the hours before dawn, but duty seemed to require him to awaken then more often than not.

Ryu turned and slowly walked down the stairs. Not sure whether that was a yes or a no, Valentine hurriedly pulled on his pants and followed. The Lifeweaver led him, with slow, graceful steps, almost floating back through the kitchens and spring-cave. They stooped into a rocky passage cut into the side of the mountain. They walked, and at times climbed, in silence through the shoulder-wide tunnel. They arrived at a wooden ladder, and Valentine smelled outside air.

"This is my private entrance. The ladder ends at a little fissure in the mountain."

Sure enough, the predawn quasi-light came faintly down the tunnel. The Lifeweaver began to climb the ladder, and Valentine followed. They emerged in the trees on the north side of the rounded-off mountain with birdsong all around them.

"It will be a fine morning. My spot for dawn-keeping is up the hill."

Valentine followed him up the slope, eventually coming out at a pile of boulders. Ryu sat down on the cold stone without even wincing, and Valentine joined him on the broad slab of rock. To the east, the green-carpeted mountains of the Ozarks bent away to the southeast. The high, scattered stratus clouds were turning from pink to orange as the unseen sun began to touch them.

Ryu said, "It will be a morning of rare color."

"What should I call you, sir?" Valentine asked. Amu, the Lifeweaver who'd been in charge of the Wolves, had acted like an old man who enjoyed teasing his grandchildren with riddles, and spoke as though he knew Valentine his whole life. Rho, the Lifeweaver who'd trained his father, he'd known only a few hours before he died. Ryu seemed cold and detached compared with the other two.

Valentine shivered in the chill morning air. The rock they sat on leached his body heat, but that was not the reason for the shudder. Ryu looked solid enough—he brushed aside small branches and flattened grass with his feet—but the Lifeweaver had no *presence*. Valentine thought it like having a conversation with an unusually lifelike portrait.

"Just Ryu. In our Old World, we had long and complex names describing our family, profession, planet of origin, and planet of residence. My brother and I were young then, born when the old Interworld Tree was still intact, and the rift with the researchers of Kur just beginning. We are old now, but not what we consider ancient. I mention my brother because my first duty to you is to thank you for getting him free. The torments and humiliation he suffered at the hands of the fiends . . . I had no idea until you brought him out of there. His death was free of grief. He went in peace, among friends."

Valentine couldn't find the proper words, so he resorted to a quiet yes.

They sat side by side, staring off into the warm palette of the coming sun.

"You have questions for us. You have an inquisitive mind."

"Sometimes I sense the Reapers. They say there are others like me, but I've never met one. Is that something Amu did? When I was invoked as a Wolf, one of the men said that I'd been 'turned all the way up.' "

"Some bodies are more ready for the change than others; the genes are there to do more. Your family had an aptitude, I understand. But as to this *sense*—I cannot say."

" 'I cannot say' isn't the same as 'I do not know.' "

"In the earlier war, before you wrote your histories, we tried a great many modifications to humans. Some we shouldn't have. Vestiges of those live on. It could be that."

Ryu let that sink in a moment before he continued. "Another possibility is that you could be a genetic wild card, a leap in natural selection brought on by the new stresses on your species. If I knew for certain, I would tell you."

Valentine felt like a bug under a light. The Lifeweavers were strange sort of leaders. They didn't inspire the Hunters to die for them, for all that they helped in their own secretive way. They just happened to be on the same side of a war—a very old one, in the case of the Lifeweavers. "You use us," Valentine said, and then thought that the fact had sounded like an accusation.

"Yes, we do. Do you know why? When we fell under the first

onslaught of the Kur, we were in panic. We had no aptitude for fighting. We needed a weapon, something flexible and powerful, a species we could both use to attack with and hide amongst. A sword and a shield all in one. Your race fit the bill, as you say. In a span of nine planets, you were the material that best answered our need: cunning, savage, aggressive, and organized. You are a unique race. The deadliest hunter in the world is a tiger, but put five of them together and they still hunt no better than a single tiger. A beehive is a miracle of organization, but three beehives cannot cooperate. Army ants make warfare, plan campaigns, and make slaves of their captives, but do all this on group instinct and could never work together with an ant from a different queen. In microcosm, that is what we found on the worlds we explored: individual greatness or collective ability, but never both. You humans, you are tigers alone and army ants together, able to switch from one to the other with ease. You're the greatest warrior species we have ever encountered."

"Considering all that, the Kurians beat us pretty handily."

"They had surprise on their side. Had we known they were coming, we might have been able to warn you in time. Unlike Kur, we had no friends in your various governments; we did not wish to reveal ourselves to you. Perhaps it was a mistake, but we felt your society needed a chance to develop on its own. We had no idea Kur could organize such an effort, had bred such a variety of what you call Grogs, or that so many of your so-called leaders were willing to sell their species for some iteration of thirty pieces of silver. Ah, here is the dawn. Let us enjoy it."

The sun tinted the clouds above and trees below, renewing the world in its warmth. Its welcome touch restored him; Valentine felt ready for whatever challenge Ryu might put in his path.

They sat together in silence. When the shining orb separated from the horizon, Ryu turned and sat facing Valentine.

Valentine tried to pierce the psychic disguise, to see the real shape of the Lifeweaver beneath—a grotesque mixture of octopus and bat—through sheer force of will, but Ryu did not change.

"David, you've proved yourself as a Wolf. It may not seem that way to you right now, but we think well of you. Amu's Wolves succeed through hearing and smell, speed and endurance. My Cats are different. They depend on stealth and surprise, and a certain amount of pure daring that we cannot give but only encourage. To become a Cat, your body will undergo some difficult changes, and there is a risk. Perhaps you remember a Wolf or two who could not adapt."

"Yes," Valentine said, remembering a cabin mate who had thrown himself off a cliff in the confusion brought about by the Wolf invocation. After Val's own invocation, the tiniest noise and movement made him jump, before he learned to soften his new senses. It was too much for some.

"It is a hard, lonely life, often without even the comradeship of your fellow soldiers. You lived once in the Kurian Zone. Are you willing to go back? Perhaps to disappear, nameless and unavenged? Every year there are Cats who do not return."

"Ryu, I've heard enough stories about the Cats to know all this. The only time I ever knew I'd made a difference was when I got Molly and her family out. If there's any way I can help the people in the lost lands . . . I'll take the risk."

"Good words. But are they enough? Is there another reason? A personal one? Forget about your father, your fellow men and women, the Carlson family, or the graceful Alessa. Forget all that's happened with your old captain. You don't have to prove anything to us. Are you going to do this because you want to?"

Valentine sat back a little, perplexed. "Ryu, if that's the case, you should count me out. My desires are at the bottom of my list of why I'd like to do this. Of course, I agree with her about what we need to hunt."

"Forget about the Twisted Cross for now. I want to know what's in you."

So do I. "It's because of my parents, and for my people, that I want to do this. You talk about what an amazing species we are, like we're some kind of work in progress. We're a species that's either headed for extinction or permanent branding as livestock. Whatever potential you saw in us is going to waste as long as the Kurians are here.

"Sir, given my druthers, I'd like a house with a lot of books in the woods on a lake where I could fish in peace. I volunteered for this life, and I've sought responsibility because somebody has to, or there's not going to be a future for any of us. So if you're looking for a samurai mentality, dedicated to its own perfection in deadly self-annihilation, it's not me."

"Nothing more? David, do you like to kill?"

Valentine's heart stopped for a moment, then restarted with a thud that bounced off his ribs. How far into his mind could Ryu see?

"The old Cat took your tongue?"

"I can't—," Valentine said.

"David, how did you feel when you knifed that sentry on the bridge, when you killed that policeman in Wisconsin, the one who disparaged you as an 'Injun.' What did you feel when you strangled that man in the Zoo?"

"How—?"

"Hows take too long. What was in your soul?"

"Guilt, but—"

Ryu waited.

"I felt guilty."

"Guilty because you chose one path over another, leading to their deaths? Or guilty because you reveled in it?"

Valentine shrank away. Ryu suddenly frightened him; he wasn't sure he wanted this conversation to continue. But he had to answer, and no answer would do but the truth.

"I don't know. I don't know myself well enough."

Ryu nodded. "Then leave it at that. I like to know what is in my Cats' hearts. Once you've learned what's in you, I hope you'll share it with me someday. Very well, you'll have this opportunity to aid your people in their crisis. And perhaps one day learn why David Valentine feels guilty."

"Then I'm in?"

"You are in."

The ceremony could hardly have been simpler. Valentine was brought to a warm little room in the back of the Hall, escorted by Duvalier. He wore only a towel wrapped around his waist. "It's a waste to wear clothes for the Change," she said as butterflies began to beat their wings on the inside of his stomach.

It resembled a wedding in a way. Ryu entered, wearing a heavy robe with more cryptic designs woven into the lapels and cuffs of the garments. He had Valentine stand next to Duvalier.

"Alessa, are you ready to take on the responsibility of training this one?"

She nodded. "I am."

Ryu turned to Valentine. "David, are you ready to take on the responsibility of joining our ranks?"

Valentine nodded. "I am."

"May the bond between you meet with success."

The Lifeweaver emptied a small vial into a plain ceramic bowl of water and swirled it in his palm like brandy in a snifter.

"Drink this, and become a Cat," Ryu intoned.

Valentine drank it, as tasteless as water.

Ryu handed Duvalier a small knife. "Now share your blood."

With a quick slash, she opened a small cut across her right palm, then took Valentine's left hand and did the same. They then clasped hands tightly. Valentine felt the sticky warmth pressed between their palms.

Ryu looked at Duvalier. "Explain to your bloodshare what is coming."

"David, the next few days are going to be a little difficult. Within a few hours, you're going to feel jumpy. I had trouble breathing, and it made me very panicky. Most people get very dizzy; people who've been on boats say it's like seasickness. Your heart will beat very fast. There's no real physical pain, but a whole new part of your body that you didn't know was there is going to be waking up. We'll keep you in this room for a couple days, safe and warm. Relax and ride it out. Try not to tear your hair out or gouge yourself."

Valentine stiffened. He'd been awkward and twitchy after his first invocation, but hadn't felt the desire for self-mutilation.

She continued: "If you have to bite something, we've got a leather-wrapped plastic tube in there for you; gnawing at the wood's no good, you'll just wreck your teeth. After the second day, I just did jumping jacks till I collapsed; then it was done. Maybe that will work for you, too."

Ryu shook his head. "David, she's making it sound worse than it is. If it helps to have a goal, keep this in mind. The first test of a Cat is how silently one goes through the Change. And you're lucky; the Wolves who've come into our caste adapt quickly. There will be someone outside the door at all times. We'll be keeping an eye on you."

The Lifeweaver clasped Valentine's blood-smeared hand between his palms in a gesture that was half-handshake and half-bow. Duvalier gave Valentine a tight hug, then showed him the old white scar across her left palm.

"You'll be fine. See you in three days."

They shut and locked the door to the little room. It reminded him of a sauna, right down to the little glass window in the rough cedar door. A single slatted bench was the extent of the furnishings, and a drain hole in the center of the wood-paneled room evidently served as the sanitary facility. There was a water spigot fixed into the wall, and Valentine gave it an experimental turn. Cold springwater cascaded onto the floor.

They left him the hunk of leather and plastic, like a dog's chew toy. He did not feel uncomfortable, at least not yet. He spread the towel on the unyielding boards of the bench and stretched out. The light shining into the little room illuminated one edge of the bench, and Valentine recognized human teeth marks.

The human psyche has a wonderful capacity to remember pleasant things: the taste of a superlative meal, the feel of a lover's lips, a refrain of inspiring music. It hurries to dispose of the unpleasant. Valentine was always grateful for that ability later: the three days in that little room were among the worst in his life.

The first tremors hit within an hour, and by the afternoon, his muscles screamed for action. He wanted to run until he dropped. Sweat poured off his body, his ears pounded, the tiny amount of light coming in through the window hurt his eyes. He felt disoriented. The room seemed to be a tiny cork bobbing on a sea of five-story waves. He did not vomit—he would have loved to do so, but it was one long stretch of nausea absent the relief of vomiting. His stomach alternately cramped and spasmed, leaving him twitching and listening to his own overloud heartbeat. To keep his heart from exploding out of his chest, he curled into a fetal position and locked his arms around his body, at war with his own desire to climb the walls, pound down the door, then run and run until the maddening electricity coursing through his body left him.

He bit the leather loop to keep from screaming.

The second day was better. His wooden cell seemed oddly shaded, the red browns of the room became muted and faint, the shadows more sharply defined. The room no longer swooped and plunged around him; it rocked like a cradle moved to and fro by a cooing mother.

But he wanted *out*.

He did push-ups until he collapsed in exhaustion, drank a little water, and passed out into electric nightmares.

The third day was a hangover to end all hangovers. His empty stomach hurt, his head ached, his hands would not stop trembling. When Duvalier's face appeared in the little window, he threw himself at the glass, clawing at the door and leaving a smear of saliva where he'd tried to bite.

Then he slept.

When she came again, he was too drained to react.

She entered cautiously, a tray holding a shallow bowl with some kind of soup in her hand. "How do you feel, cousin?"

Valentine eased himself onto the bench, feeling lightheaded. "Weak as . . . as a kitten?"

It turned out that the soup meant the general consensus was that his ordeal was over. While he ate, Duvalier went to get him some clothes, leaving the door open to air out the stuffy room. Forty-eight hours ago, he would have run howling into the hills, but now he was content to just sip at the soup and wait for her to return with something presentable. The blood-and-filth-smeared towel deserved a decent burial; all four corners were gnawed to shreds.

He finished the meal and got dressed, still trembling a little. When he followed Duvalier into the brighter light of the little honeycomb of rooms that composed the toilet and washing facilities at the rear of the Hall, he put a hand on her shoulder. She, and everything around her, didn't look quite right. There was little color in her skin, and the wooden walls were ashen, like bleached-out driftwood.

"Just a second," he said. "Why do you look different? The light is all odd."

"I know what you mean. It's not the light—it's your eyes. A Cat with some medical training explained it to me once. It has to do with the cells in your eyes. I guess there are two kinds; he called them rods and cones. The rods are good at picking up low light levels. You've got a whole lot more rods now. Your color vision will return once your eyes get used to it; right now your brain is just not processing it right. That was his theory. You'll adapt. In any kind of light short of pitch black, you're going to have no trouble seeing from here on out."

"Did the doctor explain the drunken feeling?"

"That was even more confusing, and it's got to do with your ears. We have these little bags of liquid in our ears that help us keep our balance. Some animals, cats in particular, have a whole different set of nerve fibers attached to them. You know how a cat always lands on its feet, or at least nearly always? It's from these nerves. Their balance corrects as involuntarily as your leg moving when your knee gets tapped. Right now you're oversensitized again."

She walked into the kitchen and picked up a sack of flour.

"Stand on one leg. Raise the other one like a dog marking a tree. Higher. Okay, keep it there," she ordered.

Valentine obliged, noticing that as he raised his leg he barely moved. Normally he would wobble a bit.

"Now catch," she said, tossing the ten-pound sack of flour with a shoving motion.

He caught it a few inches from his chest, causing little puffs of flour to shoot in the air. What's more, his leg was still raised.

"Interesting," he said, returning his leg to the floor. He shifted the bag of flour in his hands, and quick as a flash hurled it back at her.

Her reflexes were no less than his. She snatched the bag out of the air, but while she was strong enough to halt the ten pounds of flour aimed like a missile at her head, the bag wasn't quite up to the task. Its weakened fibers opened, and a white bomb detonated full in her face.

"Mother—!" she screamed, emerging from the cloud in kabuki makeup and fury.

Valentine let out the first squawk of a laugh and then read her expression. Their eyes locked for a second, like a gazelle and cheetah staring at each other on the veldt. He ran for his life.

"Dead meat, Valentine!" she shrieked, after him in a flash. Valentine went to the stairs up to his little flat, and jumped. To his astonishment, he made it up to the top of the flight in a single bound. With only one foot down, he changed direction and leapt onto the next platform over, a jump he normally would have needed a sprint to cover.

He slipped on the landing and sprawled. Duvalier was on his back in a moment—she must have equaled or exceeded the speed and power of his bounds. He tried to wriggle out, but as he turned over, she pinned him with legs that felt like a steel trap. She nailed his arms down in a full pin. He found the situation arousing: Duvalier in the classical position astride him, the flour liberally coating her from the waist up adding its own strange zest to the moment. But her eyes were lit only in triumph.

"Okay, gotcha," she said. "Let's have it."

"Sorry," he panted. "Didn't mean to make you the monkey's uncle."

"What's that?

"A monkey's uncle!"

"Can't hear you, Valentine, speak up."

"Uncle!"

"That's better," she said, rolling off him.

He took a deep breath, still goosey with the half-drunken, half-hungover sensation.

"Ghost, how do they do it?"

"Do what?"

"Change us like that."

He shrugged. "I've wondered about that myself. Some of the Wolves used to say they were just awakening something already inside us. I was talking to a cabin mate named Pankow one time, and I remember he took a gas lamp that was barely on, just a flicker, and turned it all the way up. It hissed and roared and lit up the whole room. He said that's what the wizards do, they just 'turn up the heat.'"

Valentine wondered if he could share his fears with her, as well. He looked at the healing wound on his hand. "But the bigger the flame, the sooner the gas runs out. You swap heat and light for longevity. It worries me. I haven't met many elderly Hunters."

She shook her head, flour cascading off her face. "Gimme a break, Val. You know how long the average Cat lasts in the KZ? Two or three years. Ask Welles—she'll confirm it. Me, I'm already well past my 'lifespan.' I'd like to switch subjects.

"Now that you've been tuned up, it's time to start training. We'll be cutting a lot of corners. I'll try to fill in the holes on the road."

"Okay, Sarge, what's next on the agenda?"

She began to dust herself off. "Sarge? David, as a courtesy, Cats are treated as captains by the other ranks in Southern Command. So you got promoted after all. But rank doesn't mean much to us. As far as the *agenda* goes, you're going to get some food and sleep in you. Then we're going to run your ass ragged. When I drop, Welles will take over. So you take it easy while you can."

Over the next weeks, Valentine decide that Duvalier held an epic grudge against him for the flour bomb and wanted to see him lose life or limb if at all possible. When she was unavailable to personally torment him, Dix Welles made sure he sweated.

He had to carry the sword everywhere, to ridiculous extremes like the shower and the toilet. If Duvalier caught him exiting the head with a dog-eared copy of *Reader's Digest* instead of his sword, he got to spend the rest of the day running up and down the mountain. He learned a few basic stances, cuts, and thrusts from Duvalier the first day, then practiced them endlessly, first with a wooden replica until he got the motion right, and then with the naked blade. One day Welles took him outside and had him climb up the sharply slanted lodge roof, and draw, swing, and move with the sword back and forth across the narrow peak, carefully straddling the top as he fought wind and momentum.

He took bundles of twigs, wrapped them in old rags, soaked them, and then attached them to poles. The target was then placed on a gimbal-mounted teeter-totter. He tried to hit it while Duvalier, at the other end of the ten-foot plank, made it dodge his blows. She succeeded in knocking him over with it more than once. When she wasn't bashing him with straw men, she was doing it herself, in fencing duels with wooden swords. She struck like lightning, and more than once laid him out with stars in his eyes.

Even when he was off his feet, he had to read. Poisons, explosives, powders both natural and chemical that blinded or sickened. Acids and bases. A grizzled old Cat, toothless and bent, lectured him on how to sabotage everything from tank engines to hydraulic brakes to a backyard water pump.

He learned to climb and fight with his claws. Duvalier taught him to always keep them in the pockets of an old overcoat, so that all he had to do was slip his hands in to become armed. He clawed, climbed, and parried with them until they felt like old friends, but that wasn't good enough. Duvalier had him practice with them until they felt like a natural extension of his body. A couple of the other Cats-intraining shook their heads and privately made fun of Duvalier's fixation with them.

"Waste of time," one of them said at dinner. "You end up using them one fight out of a hundred, I've been told."

Welles overheard and stiffly turned on the other Aspirant. "That one time in a hundred he'll be alive. And you won't."

Ryu appeared now and then and took Valentine in order to work his mind. First Valentine had to reduce his aura at rest, and as the days progressed, he had to do the same while running or climbing, or even practicing with his sword. He'd learned the basics of hiding lifesign from an old Cat named Eveready the summer after he'd been invoked as a Wolf. Now he was learning from the Lifeweaver who had taught Eveready.

Valentine could satisfy Ryu at rest, but in action, the Lifeweaver upbraided him again and again. One afternoon, as he crossed a rock-strewn creek under the Lifeweaver's eye, Ryu lifted his arms, the signal to stop. "You're still in your own mind, David."

The obvious joke about "the perfect Cat is always out of his mind" had to be bitten back—again.

"You're not a Kurian. You don't need it to survive. How can you sense it?"

"Aura is a lot of things, David. Thought, emotion, sensitivities, fear. I am able to perceive these to an extent. So can you, by the way. There's more to intuition than guesswork. Sometimes I can read you as easily as you read printed words."

"Sorry. I saw a fish dart away."

"Forget about your empty stomach for a while."

Valentine stood in the shin-deep water and tried to reduce himself again, become a part of the stream and the rocks rather than a traveler over them.

"The energy they feed from, what we call lifesign, is as individual as a fingerprint," Ryu continued, "and you're putting out far too much into the world. You're the wind on the rocks, the water flowing on its natural course, a swarm of gnats over the dead log there."

Valentine imagined himself part of the stream. The fish he'd alarmed resumed its vigil, waiting for a meal to drop onto the surface of the slow-flowing pool. *Just water and rock, trout . . .*

"Quit thinking, David. Just float across."

Valentine followed the water, ignoring the fish and the gnats until he stood beside Ryu.

"Better. Look back at the stones. Try to trace your path."

He squatted and looked for marks of his field boots on the stones. He'd come up and out of the stream without overturning a stone or leaving a telltale track of mud.

He didn't say anything, just felt the breeze.

"Now be that wind and let's talk again at the top of that hill," Ryu said, pointing to a limestone-scarred slope.

He worked inside the lodge, as well, leaping from rafter to rafter with his arms tied behind his back.

"Everything is balance, Valentine," Duvalier shouted up at him from the floor, a long hard fall below him, as he teetered for a split-second after a jump. "It keeps you from being hit in a fight, lets you hold your rifle steady, and makes you silent when you walk."

A Cat named Cymbeline—a tattooed woman with a milky eye and hairless even to her eyebrows—taught him unarmed combat. Her philosophy for unarmed combat was to arm yourself as quickly as possible with anything handy, even a piece of chain or a good solid stick. From her, Valentine learned to use everything from his instep to his skull—Cymbeline called it a readily available, ten-pound brick—to disable an opponent.

His spare locker from the Second Regiment depot found him after five weeks at the Lodge, along with another padlocked case of back-straining weight. A note and a small key came in an envelope forwarded with his other mail. He looked at the unfamiliar handwriting and opened the letter. Written in heavy block printing was

Dear David,

    This better make it intact, or I'll have something to say to the Territorial Post. I've become good friends with Molly and her family. They told me what happened and what you did for them in Wisconsin. We're glad to have people like the Carlsons in Weening.

    I don't have any family worth speaking about. I never served with your father but I know he'd want me to help you along if I could. I'm enclosing a very dear friend of mine, one of my favorite guns from my days in Jorgensen's Bears. It's over a hundred years old now, and been rebuilt a time or two, but it's a damned murderous weapon and I want it in your hands. It's an old Soviet PPD-40. Reliable in any weather and dirt. I've enclosed a thousand rounds I loaded myself, plus tools and casts to make reloads. I've also sent a little

*manual on it I wrote myself. I suppose it was captured by the
Germans when they invaded Russia. The German Army loved
this gun and grabbed every one they could. It got captured
again by our troops and brought back here. I got it from a
collector in Missouri who was handing out his guns left and
right in the Bad Old Days of '22. Later taught me to take
care of it.*

   *Hope it takes care of you as well as it did me. Watch the
full auto—you'll empty that big drum in less than eight
seconds if you hold the trigger down. You can get shells for it
at Red's in Ft. Smith, or the Armory in Pine Bluff, or go see
Sharky at Gunworks in Mountain Home. Just tell them you
need* 7.62 × 25 *or* .30 *Mauser. Better yet, learn to do your own
reloads. More reliable that way.* READ THE DAMN
INSTRUCTIONS, *kid.*

   *Always liked you when you spent that season in Weening.
I respected the way you went after them Harpies and took
that Hood that got the Helm boy and your Labor Regiment
pals. Stop by anytime, there's always a bed and a beer
waiting for you at my place.*

> *Your friend,*
> *Bob Bourne*

Valentine remembered the man named Tank from four years ago
and the firelit night when Gabriella Cho, the closest thing Val had had
to a childhood sweetheart, died.

He put the memories away.

So the gun was the mystery mentioned in Molly's last letter. He
took the key from the letter and opened the case. The gun was smaller
than a carbine, but solidly built, with a thick wooden stock. The barrel
was encased in a larger, vented handle. Amongst the little reloading
tools and instructions were three heavy ammunition boxes. He picked
up the gun, ruggedly manufactured from heavy steel. Cyrillic characters were printed above the trigger.

"Thanks, Tank."

Tank had enclosed three drums and a banana magazine. The fully
loaded drums held seventy-one rounds. Valentine hastily referred to the
manual, a mixture of weapons jargon and how-to hints, like instructions for replacing a worn spring in the drum and using a piece of
leather to cushioning a part in the gun's simple action. He stripped the
weapon experimentally, an operation that involved simply opening the

hinged receiver to expose the bolt and spring, and found that it broke down as easily as it went back together. Valentine, who had some experience with various guns used by both the Free Territory and their enemies, was all in favor of simplicity, but he had his doubts about using exotic ammunition. The stock was clearly new; perhaps that was what Molly was referring to when she said Tank was working on something for him that winter. Gleaming with rich stain and polish, the stock had been fashioned out of a beautifully grained piece of ash.

Duvalier joined him on his little platform. "Heard a Logistics wagon was by with some stuff for you. Did your locker arrive?"

Valentine replaced the gun in the case.

"Yes. Even better, an old Bear came through."

The next night they ate dinner alone. Dix had led the rest of the Cats to the nearest Southern Command trading post for supplies. Valentine was grateful for the quiet—he'd spent the day running pursuits on Duvalier. If he was unlucky enough not to catch her after an hour, they'd turn around and she'd chase him. He hoped he'd get time for a long shower and then a sweat in the steam room.

Ryu emerged from his refuge, a beautiful woman accompanying him. In fact, she was so striking, Valentine assumed she had to be another Lifeweaver. Such beauty had to be illusion, the stock-in-trade of all Lifeweaver interactions with humanity.

The Cats greeted the stranger with short bows.

"My courageous ones, please greet my sister from the East, Ura," Ryu said, standing aside so she could come forward. Radiant in a simple teal gown with a roped belt of gold, she walked without bending blades of grass beneath delicate feet. Valentine thought she looked like a princess out of a storybook.

"A little rough around the edges, like everything here, but you seem capable," she said, smiling. She shook each of their hands with a cool, firm grip.

"Ura, Alessa Duvalier and David Valentine are also concerned with the Twisted Cross. Could it be that the evil has been reawakened, like so many others?"

"I fear so. Certainly they have unfurled the old standard. Perhaps they march again."

"What's this, Ryu?" Duvalier said. "When you tasked me with this, you didn't tell me you knew anything."

"I thought it might be coincidence. Many things appear to be different now. Certainly they never used Reapers before."

"Maybe you should start from the beginning." Valentine mined his memory, trying to bring back every detail, every word of the brief encounter he had with a member of the Twisted Cross in Chicago. All he could remember was the unknown man's kill in the grotty Zoo basement, the sight of the gaunt figure's blood-smeared face, the ripped-out throat of that poor condemned girl.

"Come and sit then," Ryu said, leading them to one of the long tables. "Ura, would you care for food or drink? No? David, to start from the beginning would take years. As you should well know, you've learned more of these matters in your youth than many of your elders, even ones who should know better.

"The Twisted Cross go back to the first onslaught, when the Kurians came across the Interworld Tree as the great schism turned to war. On Earth and six other planets, they attacked us without warning. Their first human allies were a group known as the Aryans, originally from the middle of Asia.

"Because of their favored status with the Kur, the Aryans considered themselves superior to other men. The baubles the Kurians gave them made them able to convince others of this, and soon the Aryans led armies that would do the bidding of Kur."

Ura held up her hand. "It is worth remembering that the Kurians failed in their first invasion, and the Aryans' power was broken."

"So what does the Twisted Cross mean?" Valentine asked.

"I do not know," Ryu said. "Some have interpreted that glyph to mean 'life.' As an extreme example, there is no physiological reason that a human couldn't live off vital aura and gain what amounts to immortality. It requires not much more of a Change than the one that you recently experienced, David. Your body already generates and uses vital aura; it is the loss of this in the declining years that causes you to age. It is just a matter of being able to acquire and utilize another's aura."

Valentine took a moment to consider this. Perhaps that was the carrot dangled before humans who betrayed their own species. If offered eternal life, what would his answer be? How different was it, truly, from eating a steak or a slice of ham?

"Alessa, David, do what you can to learn about this new threat. In the mountains of the Eastern seaboard, my sister tells me, we suffered a mysterious loss two summers ago. One day there was a thriving freehold in a guarded valley. Ten thousand of your people. And the next, a wasteland. Last summer we lost all contact with some allies on the Gulf Coast at the Florida peninsula. We fear the Ozarks may be next. I've sent out other teams with the same orders I'm giving you: Find out all you can about this General and those who follow his banner."

"Of course we'll learn what we can," Duvalier responded. "I've got an idea of where to start. But the trail's already cold. We may be back soon."

"You're not ready yet, but then neither am I," Duvalier told Valentine a few days later. "Doesn't matter, though. We're leaving."

The lodge echoed emptily. Aside from Valentine, the lone remaining Cat was Duvalier, and even the other Aspirants had left to join their tutors for the summer. Of course the ubiquitous Welles still lingered, but she was a permanent resident. They busied themselves with last-minute preparations: putting together an assortment of photographs—Welles had a pair of cameras and a darkroom—that could be used on identification papers, collecting blank forms they might need in the Gulag, going over the latest news summaries so they understood conditions in their operational area.

Valentine had grown into his new senses and skills. He handled his sword with the same confidence he once felt in his rifle and parang. He practiced with the gun Bourne sent him—it wasn't any use at all over two hundred yards, but in the rough and tumble of close-quarters action, it would be a deadly asset.

His night vision rivaled that of daytime except at the most extreme distances, and he could play follow-my-leader with Duvalier over a single-strand rope footbridge without thinking twice. As he did it, he concentrated on "quieting his mind," obliterating his higher consciousness as Ryu instructed. He needed no training in moving quietly; his skill at that had earned him the nickname "Ghost" long ago from his Wolf teammates.

Even Duvalier found his ability to move silently a little eerie. He overheard her discussing it with Welles one evening when they assumed he was asleep. Duvalier explained that she was resting against a tree one afternoon and knew he was next to her only when he touched her shoulder.

"Hmmph, maybe it's the Indian blood. He got the hair, anyway."

"His mother was Sioux. Listen, there's more. I read this in his Q-file: he can sense Reapers. It happened on a couple of occasions, and there are witnesses. But only if they're active. He picks up on them when they're moving around, but if they're asleep . . . nothing. He can almost locate them with it. It's like their reading of our lifesign, only reversed."

Welles paused, perhaps thinking it through in her mind. "Weird shit. Maybe he's sensitive to the connection they have with their Masters, do you think?"

"Could be. I've heard of people being able to ping off them; never met one, though. I'll feel a lot more comfortable sleeping at night knowing he's right there."

"I bet he could make you a lot more comfortable at night," Welles said with a very uncharacteristic giggle.

"Get off, Dix. My interest in him is purely professional."

"Mmmmm-hmmmm. Good thing I just fell off a turnip truck, otherwise I might not believe you. I will miss the fresh bread and biscuits, though. He worked that cute ass of his off in the kitchen. Never mind the firewood to last until next spring."

The Hall echoed with the sounds of their packing. Valentine looked up at the glow bulbs, tempted to take one. It would be a useful souvenir.

"Feel free to store your gear here," Duvalier said. "We all do. This is the closest thing to a home you're going to have for a while."

Welles appeared, a bundle tucked under her arm.

"Made this for you, young Ghost. In return for a lot of tasty bread and some great fireside stories. Who ever thought I'd like hearing about Roman emperors and moldy old English plays? Here you go," she said, handing it over. "I can't move around so good anymore, but I still sew like the wind."

"I don't know if I'd call *Richard the Third* a moldy English play, but you're welcome," he said, taking the folded green cloth. He untied the twine around it and unfolded a long riding overcoat.

"Sorry some of the buttons don't match, but you know how it is. I used wooden pegs at the stress points—they hold up a little better."

Valentine held it up and then tried it on. It was a faded, slate-colored green, reversible to black like Duvalier's natty relic. It hung to just above his ankles, and was split up the back for saddle use, including loops for his legs to go through. There were pockets galore, and a built-in muffler that could strap around his throat and closing heavy collar. A hood hung neatly down the back, cut so skillfully it looked like decoration. "So you weren't taking my measurements for 'statistical reasons' a month ago, huh?"

"Guilty. Keep out of sight, would you, Valentine? It'll keep out the wind, but not bullets. The damn Bears grab all the Reaper cloaks, you know."

"You going to cry or thank her, Val?" Duvalier asked.

"Thanks, Dix. I really appreciate this."

"You'll appreciate it even more the first rainstorm you walk through. Wear it in good health, Ghost."

*   *   *

They opened the heavy front door and stepped out into the morning light. A pair of roan horses browsed amongst the grass and weeds of the front lawn. As Ryu followed the Cats out the door, the horses raised their heads and nickered.

"A farewell gift," Ryu explained. "This pair is out of a very wily herd of wild horses that runs the mountains. I called and they came."

"They won't do us much good, then," Valentine said. He had spent some time training wild horses to pull timber in Minnesota. "It'll take days to break them properly."

Ryu patted Valentine on the shoulder. "That will not be necessary, David. I imprinted the two of you on them, if that is the proper expression. They should take to you quite readily. Try it."

The horses, as if listening to Ryu's words, walked up to the pair.

"I'll go grab some oats out of the kitchen," Dix said. "That'll last you until you reach a border fort for supplies."

Valentine looked at the mare a trifle dubiously, but she looked calmly back at Valentine from her white-freckled face as if she had known him her whole life. She gave the collar of his new overcoat an experimental nibble. He grabbed a handful of mane and slipped onto the horse's bare back. He pressed against the horse's side with his calf, and it sidestepped to face Ryu and his ethereal companion.

"We have some saddles and blankets in the outside shed, do we not?" Ryu asked.

Duvalier looked over at the little outbuilding next to the smokehouse. "Yes, I think we can rig something up. Thank you, sir—this means a lot to us."

Ryu turned his piercing eyes to Valentine. "Seventy-one days ago, you accused us of using you. At times I think my people take you humans for granted. We share the same war, but you do most of the dying. Some hold that if we do too much for you, you will become dependent on us and cease growing. I sympathize with that belief, but arguments over not interfering with a civilization become moot when the Kurians have already reordered your world to suit their purposes. So if I can help my children with a simple trick, I do it.

"Speaking of simple tricks, I have one for you, David. A small gift," he said, holding out his hand. In it a tiny, triangular glow bulb glimmered faintly in the daylight. " 'May it be a light to guide you in dark places, when all others lights go out,' " he said. Or did he? The quotation seemed to drop into Valentine's brain, a windfall from the abundant orchard of his reading, without benefit of the Lifeweaver's lips moving.

"You know how to charge it, I believe," he said, again speaking with his voice.

"Leave it in the light," Valentine said, taking the little pyramid-shaped object.

"In the Old Days, we had ones that generated heat, as well, which would be far more useful. But that Art, like so many others, is lost to us in the here and now."

Ryu and Ura exchanged a long look, making Valentine wonder if in that time they shared the mental equivalent of an evening's discussion.

"Alessa, follow your spirit when your mind falters. David, if you keep an open mind, you will find friends unlooked for," Ryu said. He drifted up off the ground, touching their foreheads, first Duvalier's and then his, with his fingertips and spreading his arms before them as if in benediction.

"Go, the two of you," Ura added, imitating the gesture. "Turn away this old evil, and in doing so, change evil fate into good fortune for our Cause."

While you are at it, find King Solomon's mines and a splinter of the True Cross, the contrarian part of Valentine's mind added. He looked over at Duvalier, standing next to her newly appointed horse with a rapt expression on her face. She looked hypnotized. Did she know more than he, or was she just more gullible? Evidence of the Lifeweavers' special abilities stood quietly between his legs at that moment, or were the magically appearing horses some kind of elaborate put-on?

He could not argue with his enhanced senses, from vision to balance. He could spend most of the day running, but not be exhausted. There was no question that they had awakened something inside him, but did they create it, or just ring the alarm clock?

Duvalier and Valentine bowed in thanks and left their horses to see if they could find bridle and saddle in the jumble of odds and ends housed in the outbuilding.

Valentine looked at the Hall one more time. He remembered something his mother used to tell him: *There are two kinds of people in the world—those who look back and those who look forward.* She also said that most people in their youth look forward, and a sign of advancing age was looking back. *Always look forward, David,* she'd told him.

Being atop fresh horses and under the summer sun felt fine. The Kurian Zone was far away; if it were not for the July humidity, the day would have been ideal. After an easy stretch to warm them to travel again, the well-shaded old highways of the Ozarks guided them back up to the Missouri borderlands in a second hard day's ride. Duvalier showed her usual flair for finding discreet shelter in a pre-Overthrow ruin.

Valentine always bedded down in the old homes and businesses with a certain amount of trepidation. He would sometimes find an old weather-stained family picture and stare at the carefully combed and braided hair on the children and wonder what the fate of this or that family member was. The Ravies plague that swept the world in 2022 took the majority; war and upheaval claimed the rest. He had seen enough death at close hand to wonder how any of the old-timers had come through it with sanity intact. The population in the first years of the Kurian rule was thought to be somewhere around 10 to 15 percent of its pre-2022 height, with the urban areas suffering the worst losses. Valentine once passed through the nuclear blast site in Little Rock on a trip up the Arkansas River, where nature had returned but not man. Trees now grew amongst the naked girders and piles of rubble, but people shunned the site as if it lay under a curse.

"What's on the agenda for tomorrow?" Valentine asked after they had seen to the horses.

"We're a team now, Valentine," she said, lugging her saddle indoors. "We both share the decisions. You're sensible enough."

"That sounded an awful lot like a compliment."

"You cut me off before I could say 'most of the time.' I was thinking we should stop tomorrow at Fort Springfield. That's the last stop before we hit no-man's-land. That old man from the Oklahoma City rail yard, he said the 'Nazis' traveled by train, right?"

"Yes. He also mentioned that new lines were going in west of here."

She set down the saddle and dug out a tin of some kind of tallow from her pack. She worked the tallow into a rag and then used the rag to clean the summer dust off the saddle. Valentine began to put some dinner together using the fresh food they brought with them from Ryu's Hall. The best of the summer vegetables had come in, and he began to peel and pare into a pot of chicken stock.

"There's three sides to a job, Valentine," she said, drawing a triangle in the dirt. She put three letters at the corners. "Fast, safe, and right. You get to pick any two when you're out in the KZ. You can do something fast and right, but you sacrifice safe. Or safe and right, but you won't get it done fast."

"Then there's fast and safe."

"That's how most Cats operate. In and out quick. Me, I like to live around my objective for a while. Then when it comes time to act, I know what I'm doing. Your lead from the old nutcase is the only trail we have, at least in this part of the country. I'd just as soon not go stumbling around in the Smoky Mountains, where I don't know anybody."

"Then you know people in the plains?"

"How does that old song go? *'I got friends in low places . . .'* Sure, Valentine, not everyone in the Gulag is a Quisling."

Valentine covered the little pot hanging over the fire burning in an old stainless-steel sink they had propped up on two cinder blocks.

Duvalier unfolded a map of the Old United States. "We know the General moves by train, right? They didn't raid into the Free Territory, which I kind of suspected they might do. Could be he doesn't have the muscle for that job yet. They were heading north out of Oklahoma City. The Kur don't have a reliable east-west rail line south of Iowa and Nebraska—your old buddies the Wolves raise too much hell between Kansas City and St. Louis—they don't even try to keep that line repaired anymore. In Kansas or Nebraska, they could have turned west, to hit Denver or one of the Freeholds in the Rockies. I can't believe they turned back east. Why come west in the first place?"

Valentine looked at the map. "North out of Oklahoma, they might have turned west at Wichita, Junction City, or maybe even Lincoln. Lincoln seems like a long shot, but if I were trying to recruit, Iowa might be the place to do it. It sounded like a long time ago, there was a pretty big army under that Twisted Cross banner. Maybe they're trying to do the same thing again. A lot of loyal Quislings have land in Iowa granted to them in exchange for services rendered. We used to draw a two-hundred-mile circle around Des Moines and call it Brass Ringland. I imagine these Quislings are raising families. Could be they want some sons and daughters to join up."

Duvalier looked at the map for a moment and thought. "Funny, I'm just not picturing these guys as leaders of a huge army. They seem secretive, more like a tight elite unit. In a way, if they had a huge army, it would be better for us. We could track—hell, even infiltrate. I feel like they're more the Kur's answer to our Bears: small teams of very serious badasses who crack nuts the Kur don't want to risk their own Reapers on."

"Reaper mercenaries? Okay, you've seen Reapers, I've seen men. Maybe it's their version of a tag team. The men guard the Reapers when they sleep away the day, and the Reapers do the killing at night."

"That system's in place already, Valentine."

"Perhaps they're just perfecting it."

"I still heard Reapers talking on the hill where we met. That means they weren't being operated by the same Master."

A Kurian Lord animated his Reapers through a psychic bond, the same bond that fed him the vital aura of humans killed by the Reaper.

Nothing made sense to Valentine. "How about if a group of Kurian Lords decided to spread the risk in destroying common enemies. They each contribute one Reaper, a flying strike force to . . . No . . . damn, that makes no sense. A Kurian's hold gets weaker the farther the Reaper is from him."

Duvalier nodded. "That would mean the Kurians had to travel around the country. To much risk. Nothing, but nothing, gets them out of their little fortresses once they are established. They're the biggest cowards in creation."

"Yes, you're right. Doesn't make sense." His stomach rumbled at the smell of cooking food. "But I can understand my insides. Let's eat."

They turned to their bread and soup and concentrated on the hot food. For dessert they shared a bag of summer plums, seeing who could spit the pit most accurately. Valentine won on distance, but Duvalier expelled hers with bull's-eye control. They laughed at the wine-colored stains left on their faces and turned in, giggling like kids.

"How'd you get to be a Cat? Were you always a troublemaker, or is it just the training?"

"Both, in a way. I grew up under the Kur in Emporia, Kansas. It's a town about halfway between what's left of Topeka and Wichita. My daddy had been shipped off to some work camp God-knows-where. My mom made clothes, mostly for the labor. We call that part of the country the Great Plains Gulag. Gulag: I thought it was some kind of hot dish until someone told me it means concentration camps. My mom was a little too young and pretty, though. Some of the Society used to visit her. Society is what we called the Quislings. She got extra food and stuff out of it, but I hated Society calls."

"You don't have to elaborate."

"I have the high ground on you, Valentine. I've read your Q-file. But you don't know much about me, other than that I saved your ass, then recruited you.

"I started causing trouble, sneaking around, spying on the Society guys. They lorded it over the rest of the Labor, driving around in their cars. God, I hated them. I started lighting fires. A real dynomaniac."

"Pyromaniac," Valentine corrected and instantly regretted it. The habits of growing up in the Padre's schoolroom, where he helped teach the grade-schoolers, died hard.

Duvalier didn't seem to mind. "Pyro-maniac. It started with the uniform of one of the Society. I swiped it while he was with Mother and torched it in a culvert. I used to watch them burn off fields when I was little, and after a fire everything was clean and new for the spring, and the bean sprouts coming up were always so bright green against the black. The uniform just started me. Ever afterwards I liked to see things go up in flames, especially if they belonged to Society. One time I burned up a police van that had a bunch of equipment in it. They hauled twelve people off to the Reaper, one every twelve hours, waiting for a confession. I knew old Mrs. Finey saw me do it, too, but she didn't turn me in. I've always wondered why not. I felt so bad about it, I told my mom. . . . I mean, people were being taken off to be killed because of something I did. My mom about died on the spot. She sat down and put her head between her knees and started crying. She had been sick a lot that year—I think now she had syphilis. She grabbed my baby brother and went to the phone—the phones worked in that part of Kansas. I figured she was going to call one of the Society guys and turn me in. I ran out of the house with just the clothes on my back.

"I lived for nearly a year on my own. I got picked up by the law once, pretty early on. An old guy and a young guy in a car." Her voice got low and monotone. "The young one convinced the older one to pull off the road so he could haul me into the woods and rape me. The old one just opened a bottle of beer and said, 'You have ten minutes.'

"He took me into the woods, I can't imagine why—I was dirty and thin, didn't look much different from a boy at that time. My boobs had shrunk from not eating to practically nothing. I had handcuffs on. He bent me over and got my pants off, then threw me down on my back. He was getting set on entering me, fumbling around with his prick, I think. I got my teeth around his Adam's apple and bit for all I was worth. Then blood was everywhere, and he was making this weird wheezy sound. He tried to get up and was drawing his gun when he tripped over his own pants. I stood up and started just kicking into him, right in the face, with my heel. He was stunned and about half bled to death, and I jumped in the air and landed with both feet right on the side of his head. His jaw broke, but he might have been dead already, I couldn't tell.

"I knew what a handcuff key looked like, but it took me forever to find it and then get it into the cuffs. I was doing everything by touch behind my back, and I was shaking so bad, I kept dropping the key. It seemed like it took hours and I kept thinking his partner was going to show up and kill me.

"I got the cuffs off finally and picked up the gun. It was a revolver with this really nice white handle and scrollwork on the barrel plating. He had probably stolen it somewhere. It had bullets in it. I sat there for five minutes, hiding in the bushes with the hammer of the gun pulled back, waiting for the partner to show up. Finally I hear him honking his horn on the car.

"I got up and left my pants off, and wiped the blood off my face mostly. I pretended I still had my handcuffs on and came running out of the woods up onto the road with my hands behind my back holding the pistol. I was screaming and crying, which wasn't too hard to do given what had just happened. The old guy was looking at my crotch when I ran up to the car, and he said something like 'Where the hell's—' or 'What the hell's—' and I never heard the deputy's name because I shot him right in the face from three feet away. I shot him twice more just in case through the window of the car, even though his brains were all over the place.

"I got a nice leather jacket, some food, blankets, a compass, camping stuff—all kinds of things I needed from the car and the dead Society men. Guns—pistols, a shotgun and a rifle, too, but I threw the rifle away after the first day because it was so heavy to carry all the shooters and my other stuff, too. I burnt the car with them in it, which was a dumb idea because it attracted a lot of attention and I only just got away by crawling through a swamp. I knew from when I was little that there was a place in the mountains to the southeast where they didn't have to live like us, and I decided to go. I made it just as winter was setting in. A nice family named the Duvaliers took me in. They didn't know what to make of me: I talked almost nonstop. You'd think I would have been quiet, but no. The poor bastard who had to take my statement had a lot of writing to do. I had a good eye, noticed a lot of things: where there was militia, what kind of vehicles they had.

"So the next spring they had this raid planned into Leavenworth. There are all these prisons there that the Reapers use. They needed scouts and guides, and my name came up. I was young, but they put me out ahead of the column. I got pretty chummy with the other scouts; one was a Cat named Rourke. He liked what I did, and before I knew it, I was his disciple. I've been back to the Free Territory only four times in the eight years since then. Five now, if I count this time with you."

Valentine woke early with a plan. While Duvalier slept, he turned it over in his mind.

"We ride the rails," he said as they split what was left of the fresh bread for breakfast.

"Hmmm?" Duvalier said. Valentine had learned that she was something of a bedbug; it took her a while to wake up.

"Have you ever bummed a ride on a train? Not a military train, just one hauling corn or potatoes?"

"Not too often. Being on a train means pulling into train yards. They're well guarded."

"I did it in Wisconsin. It wasn't without risk, but it's doable. In fact, it seems to be a pretty common way for the people in the KZ to get from A to B. I think it's kind of winked at. But you have to be somebody."

"You mean a Quisling?"

Valentine nodded. "In this Gulag, what do the Quisling militia wear?"

She thought for a moment. "Generally they're called the Society in most of Kansas. They wear kind of a khaki police uniform with epaulet. From Nebraska on north, they're a little more anything-goes. They're generally called Marshals for basic law enforcement, but since it is a borderland, there's a military unit called the Troop. Individually, they're 'Troopers.' The Marshals wear this black uniform, usually with a tie and everything. The Troopers wear any old thing, but they almost always have old police bulletproof vests with insignia patches on them and their name stenciled across the back."

His mind gaining momentum; he put down his tin. "Okay, we go up into Nebraska and get our hands on a uniform and some papers."

"I've got a few forgeries for us. I worked on them while Welles was giving you a hard time. Or I can make them as we go. It's a talent you should learn, Valentine."

"We just pose as a couple of travelers. Better if one of us could be a Somebody, or at least military. Everyone in the KZ lives in fear of offending a big shot and winding up in the hands of a Reaper."

"Pretty nervy. I like keeping away from towns and stuff. Too easy for something to go wrong."

He turned the thought over in his mind, looking for holes. "We could pull it off, I've met a few Quislings. Having you along would add a little realism."

"How's that?" she asked.

"Anyone who is anyone in the KZ travels with a woman. You're attractive, just the kind of pretty young thing a Quisling officer might have hanging on his arm."

"Dream on, Valentine!"

"Just a suggestion. Even if you're in uniform, too, we're just a pair, traveling to see relatives in Kansas, or an old friend in Omaha."

"Omaha ain't ours no more, Valentine. It's a ruin on the Missouri River. Hip deep in Grogs. Harpies, Tunnel-Snakes, Bigmouths—"

"Sorry, I forgot. Anyway, we can crisscross the Gulag and try to pick up the scent. Maybe your sister ran off with a Twisted Cross guy and I'm helping you look for her. Are there a lot of checkpoints—say at the Kansas–Nebraska border or something?"

"No, the Gulag runs from northern Oklahoma to the Dakotas, from the Rockies to the Missouri River. Just little princedoms, you might say, with Satan's own on the thrones. Something for bribe and barter would be handy. I've found tobacco pretty useful."

"We can pick up all the tobacco we need in Fort Springfield. They might have some whiskey that's hard to acquire in the KZ, too. Thank God we're still in Southern Command. Cash crop."

She smiled at him. "Okay, Valentine, you sold me. A-riding-the-rails we shall go. But I've got a few visits to make, so let me do the navigating once we get into the KZ."

They requisitioned feed for the horses at the Fort Springfield depot, the last post on borders of the Ozark Free Territory. Duvalier and Valentine turned in their Southern Command ID to the officer commanding; he'd hold it until they returned or a year passed, when the next-of-kin protocols would be put into effect.

Valentine found a healthy pack mule and did not even have to throw their weight as Cats to acquire the beast. The stable master handed over the pack and leads with a chuckle. "He's a damn thing. Fifty bucks says you'll be eating mule steak two days from now."

They also signed a chit for enough script to load up on cheap cigars, cigarette makings, and rolling paper, and a few bottles of labeled liquor. Some feed for the mule and provisions for themselves went onto the mule's pack.

At Duvalier's insistence, they went out of town and traveled a half day east back into the Ozarks.

"We aren't the only spies in Missouri. Kur has eyes in every border fort we have, without a doubt," Duvalier explained.

Valentine made sure they weren't being followed, dropping off the horse behind high points in the rolling ground and letting Duvalier lead his horse while he scouted. The pair turned north after a column of patrolling Guards jumbled their tracks.

"Nice work. You're shaping up, Valentine."

"How about you just shorten it to *Val*?" he asked. "It's what most of my friends use."

"Funny you should say that. Duvalier gets shortened to *Val* a lot, too. Can't say that I want to be the Val twins, though. You can use Alice or Ali if you want."

"Okay, Ali. I'll answer to David, then."

"We'll see. Every time I say *David*, I hear Ryu in my head using that fatherly tone of his. I like *Val.* But if you want to wake me up in a hurry, use *Duvalier.* That's what old Rourke used to bark in my ear when he wanted me on my feet."

They decided that for now they would stick to Missouri, keeping to the west side of the state in the hilly region east of Kansas City. Then they would cross the Missouri River somewhere north of St. Joseph, angle into Nebraska, and start hitching rides on westbound trains around Lincoln.

They switched over to night travel while still within the nebulous borderlands of Southern Command. If they were to encounter enemies, daytime was more dangerous than night, for the Grogs that lived along the Missouri Valley preferred to fight in daylight. After a long afternoon's rest, they turned up an old road at nightfall. The mule had its own ideas about nighttime travel, and took a good deal of convincing to get it in motion. It then showed a tendency to stop at every opportunity, leaving them with the task of getting it in motion all over again.

"No wonder that stable master parted with him so fast," Valentine said.

"Maybe we can tempt him with something," Duvalier suggested, pushing on the back end while Valentine hauled away at the front. "Do we have any plums left?"

"That would work, until we ran out of plums. Then he'd never move without one."

The quest seemed to be off to a mule-stalled start when Valentine finally solved the issue with what Duvalier laughingly called the "wugga-bugga dance." The mule bit Valentine, nearly clipping off his ear, as he tried to pull it by the throatlatch. With blood running down the side of his face, he ran into the woods, returning with the better part of a poplar sapling. He yelled gibberish at the mule, thrashing pack, ground, air, and mule with the noisy branches. The leaf-shaking spectacle sent the mule trotting down the road of its own accord. Any time thereafter that the mule balked, Valentine just brandished his leafy shillelagh, imprecating against it in the glottal nonsense that worked on the recalcitrant beast. The mule put itself into high gear to get away from nasty voice and noisy leaf.

"We'd better start taking turns scouting soon," Duvalier said later, after a break for a cold meal.

"Why's that?"

She pulled down a young sugar maple bough. "Stripped clean," she said. Something had torn off the leaves and bark, leaving the thin limb as naked as a rat's tail.

"Grogs?"

"Yeah. They don't digest much of it, if you've ever looked at the droppings close."

Valentine swept the woods with ears and nose and picked up only a distant owl. "Duty in the Wolves denied me the pleasure. I've never patrolled Missouri, just passed through it a few times. More east of here, though."

"Don't know if it aids their digestion, or they just put something in their stomach to fool themselves out of being hungry. Anyway, if you see stripped branches, you can tell they pass through. The evidence hangs there a lot longer than footprints. Or droppings."

"First point goes to—"

She tweaked his nose, held up to better catch the soft nighttime breeze. "Me. God knows I can't keep that mule moving."

Mule problems aside, Valentine found he enjoyed nighttime travel. With his cat's-eye vision, the color-muted landscape looked clearer than he remembered the brightest of moonlit nights. His ears worked to their best advantage, as well; the sounds of nighttime insects carried farther, though they made a good deal less noise than their daylight counterparts. The Cats bedded down after dawn with a hot meal and dozed away the heat of the day. Even the mule grew accustomed to the routine.

They cut a few trails of Wolf patrols, but these grew more and more rare as they approached the old Kansas City–St. Louis corridor. If there was a danger point on the first leg of their journey, this was it. They took turns leading the mule, with one of the pair on point a hundred yards ahead, looking and listening, and the other guiding the mule. As Valentine peered down onto the area around the old interstate that the Grogs frequented, the mule decided to bellow into the night. He swore he'd dine on a mule steak for breakfast. Either nothing heard the animal, or whatever did hear it did not want to bother to investigate the source. In any case, they crossed the corridor without seeing anything but tire tracks and footprints.

Valentine was on point when he scented them. Three Grogs, sleeping upright back to back like Buddhist statues, rested on a thickly forested knoll.

He drew his sword and waved Duvalier forward.

"Pistols or blades?" he whispered.

"Neither."

"They're snoring."

"Of course we could kill them. But ten would come looking for them. You're good; we would probably kill those, too. But then a hundred would close in from either side."

"In the Wolves—"

"Don't ever want to hear that again. You're a Cat now, and it's all about the mission. Killing a Grog patrol has nothing to do with that."

By dawn they were miles off the corridor and pushing northwest. The land began to flatten out with the beginning of the Great Plains. They supplemented their dwindling supplies with, and fed the animals on, the wild corn and beans common to the area. They set small game snares on likely ground, two or three every morning, and it was a rare day when they could not come away with at least one animal for the stew pot. Even if it was only a wild rat.

Valentine and Duvalier began to know each other's minds. They approached abandoned buildings communicating through hand gestures and learned to rely on each other more and more as the days passed. When Duvalier spent a day in the cramped agony of dysentery— she would devour meats the new Cat wouldn't even touch—Valentine gathered a shirt full of elm bark and poured boiling water over the strips, then picked out the floating parts once it had cooled. He made her drink the infusion three times over the course of a day, and the symptoms subsided.

They released the mule and horses at the Missouri River. Valentine gave the mule its freedom with a kind of sadness; he would miss their combative companion. Like parents with a rebellious child, dealing with the bloody-minded beast together cemented the relationship between the two Cats. They left the beasts grazing in a grassy field thick with white clover-heads, shouldered their newly heavy packs, and crossed into the Gulag.

Six

Southeastern Nebraska, July: The Great Plains Gulag produces the wheat and corn of the Kurian Order. Collective farming settlements, managed under discipline that would make Stalin envious, dot the flat expanses of the Plains. Good farmland is divided into roughly fifty-mile-diameter regions from the main railheads with their towering grain elevators. At the center of the circle, like the spider in the middle of its web, is the well-guarded fortress of the local Kurian Lord. His eyes and ears and appetites are in his Reapers. The Reapers pass the Master's orders to the Marshals and Managers below them, making sure they attend to duty with the devotion expected of ones absolved from any chance of providing auric fodder for the Kurian Overlord.

The trade in this part of the country is a tragic exchange. Boxcars full of grain and corn leave the Gulag to feed the urban population else-where and return with a few dozen assorted captives, criminals, and disposables as payment. The Marshals then unload the unfortunates from the boxcars and route the prisoners to their doom with the knowl-edge that each unknown fed to the hungry Kurian Lord means one less friend or neighbor selected and sacrificed in the dead of night. Rumor has it that in Dallas, Chicago, Atlanta, and Seattle there are trading pits, run with the same frantic energy of the Old World, and devoted to buying and selling wheat, corn, soy, barley, and legumes with human lives. The trades are administered and run by the accountants and deal-ers for their Kurian Lords, seeking the best deal in living bodies per ton in what might be called a futures market for those who have no future.

Lincoln, formerly the capital of Nebraska, is a good example of the Kurian Order in the Gulag. The Dark Lord lives, appropriately enough, in the fourteen-story stone tower that looms over the reduced city skyline.

Its solid construction, commanding view, and numerous carvings and statues appeal to the megalomaniac temperament within. Though one valuable statue from the pre-Kur days is missing: the Daniel Chester French study of a pensive, standing Lincoln. Some say that the Kur destroyed it as they did the larger, more famous seated one at the memorial in Washington, D.C., but others maintain it was spirited out of the city and now resides in one of the Western Freeholds, a hidden icon of liberty.

The people within his realm call the Kurian Lord "Number One," and nothing gets the local Quislings' attention like someone walking in a room and announcing, "Orders from Number One." Just across from the dreaded tower is the old City-County Building, now just referred to as the Hold. The local Marshals are quartered here, and the ample prison space is the last stop for those on the way to the Reapers. The city is now home to artisans and technicians in the employ of the Kurian Order, as well as being a main depot of the Troop. Their armored cars and trucks are maintained in a huge garage, once the Pershing Auditorium. The Regional Director, a Quisling in charge of the thick belts of farmland within the Kurian's realm, lives (at the pleasure of Number One) in the Colonial-Georgian governor's mansion. The house has a sad history: assassination and suicide, as well as the occasional Reaper-led housecleaning, have plagued the series of Regional Directors and their families. The suicides especially drive the Kurian to distraction—he sees it as a tragic waste of aura.

The Lincoln Lord has six Reapers. One or two are usually at the Capitol Tower serving as bodyguards and mouthpieces. Another is circulating in the city, checking up on the doings in Lincoln, and another will almost always be on tour in the farmland with a dreaded retinue of Marshals, spreading fear wherever he goes. Finally two more hunt in the unclaimed buffer zone between the Kurian principalities, looking for threats to the realm and feeding their lord with drifters, runaways, and the occasional sleeping-on-duty Trooper.

"Why'd it do that?" Valentine asked, peering through the empty window of the parked patrol car.

It was a ridiculous-looking vehicle, an old police cruiser on a jacked-up suspension, sitting on fat on-and-off-road performance tires and missing its trunk hood. Camouflage greens and browns replaced the old state-trooper markings.

"Haven't you ever seen a Reaper hole?" Duvalier said, looking at the grisly scene within. Bronze-colored flies clustered around a ragged wound. "They poke their tongues in right above the collarbone. Pretty good chance at hitting the heart or a big blood vessel."

"This just happened." Valentine's hair was standing on end from something other than cold river water hitting his nethers. The Reaper must have been just over the hill when they crossed.

"Lucky for us he was here." Duvalier grabbed a key ring off the body's belt. "Crap—no codes."

"But what I meant was, why would a Reaper take out one of his own militia?"

Duvalier touched the corpse. "Not quite cold. Either it was a Reaper from down Kansas way poaching—which is pretty unlikely, they might grab some farm boy but not a soldier—or the Hood caught him sleeping on the job."

"Kurian justice is efficient, I'll give them that."

"Solves one problem. You were talking about scrounging a uniform. Here's your chance."

Valentine ignored her buttocks as best as he could as she rooted in the car through the window.

"The vest you mean? We'll have to clean it. We'd also better take the whole body."

"Why, you want to give him a Christian burial?" She summoned a tongue full of spittle and let it drop on the Trooper's forehead.

"No, they're going to be a little suspicious if they find a body missing a vest and identity papers."

"Your idea. You carry him, then. Better get him over the shoulder. Rigor will be setting in," she said, putting on her claws.

"Why the metal? Think the Reaper is coming back for seconds?"

"Nope. Omaha is Grog country. We're near enough to make it look like they made off with the body."

"Would they touch a man in uniform?"

"They're kind of freebooters. I've heard that they don't take orders from the Quislings to the east or the Kurians to the west. As long as they don't interfere with the rails or roads, they do as they please. Maybe a few Harpies smelled the blood and came down for the body."

She scratched the paintwork on the roof and hood with the claws, a sound painful to Valentine's sensitive ears. She looked inside. "I'd put marks in the upholstery, but I don't think anyone would notice. Three generations of corn-fed Troopers have done their worst."

Valentine searched the car, but was disappointed at the results. A little bit of food, some tools, a pump-action shotgun, and a box of shells were the extent of the booty. He also carried a fist-sized key ring, which had a number of varicolored disks threaded on it like beads on a string. Duvalier explained that the disks served as money, useful enough in Lincoln itself but no good in another Kurian's territory. He pocketed it nevertheless. Grogs would definitely take the shotgun, for trade if nothing else, so he took it and the shells. "Not even a radio. Kind of primitive up here, huh?" he said, shouldering the body.

Duvalier erased their footprints as they moved off the road and to the west.

They weighted the body with rocks and sank it in some swampy water along the shallow river they'd been following when they came upon the car. In the distance they saw a few lights, the first they had seen since Missouri.

"We're on the outskirts of Number One's land around Lincoln. If we keep heading north, we should hit the rail line between Lincoln and Omaha. Then it's just a matter of catching the first westbound."

Dawn brought a blush to the sky, and they found some tall growth at the banks of the river to sleep away the day's heat. Duvalier believed in hiding in plain sight, so to speak, when this close to enemy territory, rather than looking for concealment under old bridges and in barns. She examined the vest and papers of the dead Trooper.

PRICE W was stenciled across the back of the body armor, and the identification card had "Price, Wesley" typed in the blank for name.

"Hmmmm. Okay, Val, how does 'West Rice' sound?"

"Like a Texas side dish. Can you do it?"

She took out a small scalpel and a bottle of ink. "O ye of little faith. Think I'll get some rest first, so I can concentrate. Wake me with some lunch at midday, Rice."

"Sure thing, Beans."

She was good to her word and spent the afternoon removing the *P* from the back of the vest, then dabbing black ink in to cover the worst parts. Valentine tried it on; the Trooper had gone to some trouble to make it more wearable by adding leather panels to the inside with a layer of cotton mesh sewn over them. It was still hot and heavy even with the side panels open all the way. Duvalier did a masterly job with the ID, right down to placing a new photo over the old complete with imprinted seal. This last she managed with the tip of a small screwdriver. After the ink dried, she folded it and had Valentine place it under his armpit for an hour. "Nothing like a good sweat stain to add some realism," she said.

"You'd think they could make these up for us before we left," Valentine said, unfolding the damp ID papers and looking at the details again to refresh his memory.

"Sensible if we were just going one place, but there are many, many different Kurian Camps just in the Gulag. A lot use different kinds of ID.

We'd have to carry a whole satchel just with forged papers. We're safe enough around Lincoln, as long as we don't run into one of Price's close personal friends. If we go in the town, it should just be Marshals."

"The sword won't be suspicious?"

"You got it off a dead Grog. It was valuable, so you took it. I once saw an Oklahoma Territorial walking around with a battle-ax, God knows why. The thing must have been heavier than hell."

"You're the boss."

"I'm more worried about the gun. That big round magazine, it makes it look pretty memorable. Anything no one's ever seen before is suspicious. It makes sense to stand out a little, but not too much."

"I've got a regular clip for it. Or better yet, I could leave it unloaded."

"That would work," she said. "It's such an ugly thing, except for the stock. Looks like you put it together yourself."

They angled around the village that night, moving through fields of tall corn. Most of the houses showing lights were clustered in little groups, but an isolated farm here and there appeared to be occupied. "Not many big harvesters and combines left," she commented as they passed a tall John Deere that looked well maintained. "Most everything is done with horses again. The Kurians like having a lot of labor under them."

"Where do you figure on jumping on the train?" he asked.

"I thought you were the expert on train travel. Maybe we should stick to the Platte River—it's between Omaha and Lincoln. Follow it north until we hit a bridge, and jump a train there. They always slow down crossing a bridge—you never know when one of those resourceful long-range Wolf patrols are going to take out something like that."

When they settled down for the evening, Valentine had the first watch. He stood above the camp, wishing they could run across some Wolves. It would be good to see the beards, the hats, the sweaty buckskins again. Hear the rude jokes. Life was simpler in the Regiment: you followed orders, camped, moved, slept with the assurance of your comrades all around. He felt naked moving in the Kurian Zone without the companionship of his pack.

On the other hand, being a Cat brought independence and its concomitant responsibility. Best of all, freedom to use his judgment.

All things considered, he'd take it. Even at a price of loneliness. Of course, he'd been paying that bill since he was eleven years old.

Duvalier opened sleepy eyes. "Val, relax. I can hear you grinding your teeth all the way over here."

"Sorry."

He watched seed-laden grass bend in the soft summer breeze and tried to quit thinking, to be that breeze. The tension left his neck and shoulders.

"That's better." She rolled over onto her side.

By dawn they struck the Platte where it threw a wide loop south around Omaha before joining the Missouri. They camped in a thick patch of timber, about halfway up the slope to the crest of the river valley. Their spirits rose for a moment at the distant clatter of a train, but they realized it was eastbound when they found a vantage point allowing them to see the line of cars.

As Valentine ground some stolen ears of corn into flour in the predawn clamor of rising birds—it was Duvalier's turn to set the traps or try for a game bird with the wrist rocket they carried for small game—he suddenly felt his luck was in. They would catch a train that day, or at worst the day after. He felt confident enough to walk into the Tower in Lincoln and see what Number One was up to, for that matter. Or maybe he just looked forward to the excitement of train travel after weary weeks of walking.

Duvalier returned, bearing a pheasant. "I think it was asleep. It never knew what hit it. I probably could have just reached up and grabbed it," she said, sitting down on a rock and opening her small clasp knife. She cut the bird's throat, nearly severing its head, and bled it into her canteen cup.

"Pretty feathers, these things have," she said, beginning to pluck it. She picked up the cup. "Blood, Val? Nice and warm. Chock-full of vitamins."

Valentine chewed dandelion leaves and young fern buds, among other things, for his vitamins. "Thanks, no. I only like it with lemon and sugar."

"Great for the eyes, my friend. But it's your choice. I can use the iron anyway." She drank it down, smacking her lips in appreciation, and continued plucking the bird. Valentine enjoyed the taste of fresh blood only in cold weather for some reason, perhaps because it reminded him of winter hunting trips with his father.

The pheasant turned out to be an old and stringy specimen, so they made soup, plucking the painfully hot joints out of the broth with their fingers and gnawing the bones clean.

"Is this breakfast or dinner, Ali?" Valentine asked, watching the sun come up.

"That's a philosophical question; I'm too tired to care, Valentine. Put the fire out and let's get some sleep."

Valentine relaxed, and she stretched on the rattan mat she rolled out to keep herself off the cold ground. He listened for trains and watched her nod off. Her angular face softened in sleep; and he decided she was altogether desirable. *You've been without a woman for a good year now,* the responsible part of him said. *Keep your hands to yourself. She's a comrade, not a lover.*

It was a three-day wait for a westbound train. Valentine hoped his lucky feeling regarding the train timing was an aberration, and the rest his premonition of good fortune would come through.

They spent the time reconnoitering the bridge region, making a few cryptic notes in Valentine's journal. You never knew what knowledge might come in handy to Southern Command. A small sentry shack stood at each end of the bridge. Only the western side post was manned during the daytime, but both had a pair of soldiers at night. The sentries were supplied by a little guardhouse at a settlement called Gretna, which marked the start of the unoccupied area leading to the Omaha ruins. Trooper vehicles patrolled north from there on the east bank of the Platte and rolled out due west, probably as far as the Missouri River south of Omaha.

They heard the train before it appeared atop the lip of the shallow river valley.

The western side bridge post was a good spot to hop on. It would give them the added authenticity; a pair of deserters or runaways would hardly shelter somewhere run by the local Authority.

With the train still well in the distance, they approached the guard post. A single middle-aged sentry, with a functioning radio and a bicycle for his commute, stepped out of the slant-roofed little blockhouse with his shotgun in his hands. He had the hairy, crusty look of someone who spent a great deal of time in the elements.

"Howdy," Valentine said, breathing heavily as he climbed up the hill. He paused, put his hands over his knees, and faked exhaustion. "We didn't think we'd make it. I sure want to hop this train."

"Then you have a lot more running to do," the guard said, gun pointed at Valentine as he watched the pair suspiciously. "Train doesn't stop here."

"Oh, great, the difficult type," Valentine said to Duvalier, loudly enough for the sentry to hear. He looked back up at the guard. "Listen, I'm in a jam here. I just want to ride it, not blow it up. My name's Westin Rice, and this is my bride-to-be, Ali. We're getting married in two more weeks out by Grand Island, where I'm stationed, and we were here visiting my folks out by Fremont. They never met her, you see? I've been away from my unit—it should've been just the weekend, but old friends and relatives showed up, you know how it is."

"Can't say that I do," the man said, but at least he didn't move for the radio. Valentine noticed a brown stain at the side of his mouth.

"My sarge is covering for me, of course. If we can catch this freight, everything's Toyota."

"Not on my watch, kid. Don't know how you do things out there, where about all you got to guard against is prairie dogs, but here where we're staring down the wildthings in Omaha, rules mean something."

Valentine was about to reach into his pocket for some cigars when Duvalier unexpectedly burst into tears. "Th-th-there goes your promotion, or w-w-worse," she sobbed. Valentine looked almost as startled as the sentry. She sank to her knees, pouring tears into palms clasped against her face. "Your mom b-b-being so n-n-nice an' all, and giving me her mother's wedding ring. Wh-wh-what're we gonna do?" she blubbered, staring up at him with tear-strained eyes.

Valentine picked her up. "Don't worry, hon, I'll figure something out. Don't I always?"

"Look, er—you two," the man said, rubbing the back of his neck. "Hop the damn freight. But if anything happens, I was taking a break in the bushes, you follow me? You never even got a good look at me, I was too far away."

Valentine pulled out a cigar. "Thank you, sir. My pa gave me these. He has a connection over in Cedar Rapids with those rich big shots across the river. They're for the groomsmen, but I want you to have one."

"Save it for the groomsmen, then. No, I won't take it, and that's final. Just take my advice, and don't do stuff like this. The way I got to be this age, pulling easy duty, is by not bending the rules. Get me, you two?"

The train started down the opposite bank of the Platte and rolled onto the bridge.

"We get you—thank you, sir!" Duvalier said, kissing him on the cheek as they hurried past him. "Sometimes the rougher they are on the outside, the more tender on the inside," she added sotto voce as they took positions alongside the tracks. "It's the ones who just seem not to give a damn one way or the other who make me worried."

Valentine took a good look at the train. It burned oil, judging from the blue fumes emerging from the engine. Behind the engine came the main guard car: a mountain of sandbags and a tripod-mounted machine gun. Behind the guards was a pair of passenger cars followed by the freight and tanker cars. A caboose, looking like it was modified from an old observatory car, brought up the rear. Most of its windows were missing.

Valentine and Duvalier ran for the little balcony welded onto the rear of the armored caboose. A bored-looking guard started to wave, then stared at them as they dashed to catch the train. They both leapt up onto the platform and grabbed railing.

"Help her over, dammit!" Valentine said to the paralyzed soldier, who complied.

Valentine swung his legs over the rail. "Good arrangement here," he said casually as a sergeant appeared with an infuriated look on his face. "If there's one thing I hate, it's riding on top of a boxcar. Can't even roll a cigarette, you know?" he said, carefully taking out a paper and a pouch of makings.

"Look, Trooper, I dunno what you two think you're . . . Hey now, is that the real thing?" the sergeant asked, looking at the aromatic brown shreds going into the cigarette.

"Real Tennessee Valley Tobacco, or so they tell me."

"You wouldn't be able to spare a puff? Haven't had a real cig in a week, just chew that's half sawdust. Bastard Chicago clip-joints."

"The Zoo, eh?" Valentine said with a knowing wink. "Only thing I ever came home with from there I needed gunpowder to cure, you know? I'll do better than a puff or two—you can have the whole thing, how's that. Can never have too many friends in the New Federal Railways, you know?"

"This train is Consolidated Overland. Federal has the gray uniforms with the black epaulet. We've got patches."

Valentine looked over at Duvalier, who appeared to be making herself agreeable to the sentry who helped her over the rail.

"Stopping in Lincoln, right?"

"Of course, and then on west. End of the line is McCook."

"Passing near Grand Island?"

"Err, Grand Island . . . I don't know the Plains that well, beyond our route. Let's see the map." They went inside the caboose. Only one more soldier was on duty there, looking forward from the observation platform. The sergeant checked at a map pinned to the wall. "Okay, yes. We stop in Hastings, that's just south of Grand Island. What's in Grand Island?"

"Our wedding. I'm bringing her back from meeting my folks. My unit and her family are up there."

"You two are carrying a lot of iron for just visiting relatives," the sergeant observed.

"I have to have my piece, Sergeant. Regulations. But even if that weren't the case, you can't be too careful near Omaha, sir," Valentine said. "Ali got us a pheasant the other day, too. She shoots well for a civilian."

"You could get in a lot of trouble back east letting a civilian carry a gun, even if it is yours, West. But hell, this calls for a drink, celebrate you two taking the bonds," the sergeant said, but the guard chatting with Duvalier looked disappointed.

Valentine grinned. "Yes, it does, and I'm buying. If you'll bend regs for a shot."

"If we took duty that seriously, you wouldn't be here, Trooper."

Valentine took out a bottle of whiskey, and three glasses appeared as if conjured out of wind and dust. He poured everyone two fingers' worth and faked a swallow from the bottle himself.

"Be sure to save enough for the wedding toast, baby," Duvalier said. "Your dad went through some trouble to get that."

"Have pity, miss," one of the guards said. "Awfully hard for a man to walk around with quality likker like this without having a sip now and then."

The rest of the journey passed in a much more convivial atmosphere. They discussed various kinds of duties, comparing being in the Troopers in Nebraska with guarding trains. In the process, Valentine and Duvalier learned a good deal about railroad routine. A second round of drinks, with formal toasts for the would-be newlyweds, cemented the temporary friendship. Unfortunately for Valentine's sense of satisfaction with the day's events, they learned what two of the boxcars held.

"Food for *them*. You know what I mean," the sergeant confided. "Twenty in each car this run, but we've crammed in as many as sixty. Half getting off in Lincoln. Glad it ain't our job to clean the cars out afterwards. We're just making sure they don't break out. They're chained up in there like dogs in kennels, but you never can tell."

"How long is the stop in Lincoln?" Valentine asked, desperate to change the subject.

"Four hours. We'll get some sleep. But don't worry, West. Some nosy-new comes checking in here, you two can hide in the john. We'll get you back to your sergeant and your wedding on time."

"Four hours?" Duvalier said, unusually enthusiastic. "I can do me some shopping in Lincoln. You know they have a real shoe store in town, Sergeant?"

"Knock me over with a feather, miss," the sergeant said. He winked with the eye on the side of his face turned toward Valentine. "I was really hoping to pass the time with a deck of cards and your fiancé here, though."

"Oh, he doesn't have to come with. Shopping bores him to death. Honey, can I please have some of the money Uncle Max gave you?"

"Money?"

Duvalier glared at him. "You aren't playing tricks on me now, are you, Westin? Uncle Max, I saw him give it to you through the window of his patrol car. The one you said looked dumb, all jacked up."

Valentine reached into his pack. "I guess I can't fool you. Here, but don't spend all of it, okay? It's supposed to be saved for starting us off." He passed her the ring of money.

The three Overland guards exchanged half sneers. One made a tiny motion with his wrist that might imply a whip being cracked.

The train pulled into Lincoln Yard for unloading, and Valentine dived into the card game to avoid looking at the doomed souls being unloaded. As long as he didn't see the faces, he would be fine. He started a game of gin with the soldier who had to stay on duty in the caboose, while the sergeant and the other guard left to lend a hand at the off-loading.

Duvalier gave him a peck on the cheek and disappeared into town, leaving her pack in Valentine's care and twirling the ring of coins as she went.

"Hooo . . . welcome to married life," said the sergeant, returning to the caboose as Duvalier left.

"You married, Sarge?" Valentine asked, trying his best to let the other sentry win a cigarette off him at gin.

"Is he married? You might just say that!" Valentine's partner said. "What are you up to now, Sarge, four?"

"Seattle, St. Paul, Chicago, and Atlanta," the sergeant said, leering at Valentine. "Each one waiting for the next run that will allow me to return to hearth and home. Travel has its advantages, Trooper."

"You don't say," Valentine said, picking up and laying down a card. "How do I get into this outfit?"

"I could put in a good word. You could write Capt. Caleb Mulroon, care of Overland Consolidated in Chicago. That is, if you think you could get out of your present post with no hard feelings."

"Gin!" said the sentry, laying down his cards and picking up the cigarette ante.

"I think I can make the Troopers happy to be rid of me," Valentine said, passing his cards across to be shuffled.

Four pairs of eyes widened when Duvalier returned later. Her appearance wrecked a perfectly good game of poker.

The transformation was nothing short of incredible. She had changed from slightly grubby scarecrow to head-, neck-, and shoulder-turner in the space of the afternoon. Her short red hair was now in carefully arranged, slightly curly disarray. She wore a midriff-revealing, sleeveless jeans jacket unbuttoned to a hint of lacy red bra and more than a hint of cleavage. Short shorts hugged assorted curves where they didn't reveal long, athletic legs ending in white canvas rubber-soled shoes. Her lips matched the fire in her hair, and her eyelashes seemed longer and thicker. Valentine was not used to makeup, especially not on Duvalier.

"Better, sweetie? Hardly spent any money at all."

"You are a lucky son of a bitch, West," one of the Overland guards said.

Valentine got up and took her hands in his. "Much better. That's the Ali I dream about at night." He gave her a hug and experimentally patted her on her backside as he planted a kiss on her ear.

"Now, now, Westin, can't have these men thinking you're a *pig*," she said, locking her eyes on his. "Don't let's get carried away now—we still have a lot of traveling to do before we're home safe."

The miles rattled off pleasantly until Duvalier killed the Overland guards.

She had been napping in one of the little bunks set atop the caboose's wooden storage cabinets. It had tiny rails to keep her from rolling out.

As evening fell, the card game had died off, and Valentine put some clothing in to soak in a soapy basin, getting in a badly needed laundry between stops. One Overland guard kept watch from what the sergeant called the "catbird seat," a cupola high at the train-side end of the caboose, and the sergeant retired to the bunk opposite Duvalier.

The other guard, suspenders dangling and in a sweat-yellowed tank top, kept up a pretext of conversation with the man on top as he eyed the sleeping Cat from an angle that allowed the best view down her décolletage. Valentine heard her stir as he wrung out a pair of socks, and she looked up in alarm at the presence looming over her.

"Ever think about trading up?" the guard asked, touching her hair before sending his fingers walking down her shoulder and across the exposed top half of her freckled breast.

Duvalier locked on the guard's eyes and wrist at the same time. Valentine felt a horrid trill of danger from some inner alarm as she pulled the exploratory hand down under the sheet and between her thighs. "I thought so . . . ," the guard said, giving Valentine a wink across the rocking caboose interior.

She clamped his hand there.

The knife came up fast—so fast, the guard never saw it. He let out a surprised cough, gaping at the handle sprouting from his armpit. Duvalier rolled out of the bunk, walking stick ready.

Valentine smelled blood. His pack and weapons were in a locker at the other side of the room. He grabbed the washbowl. He needed something—anything—in his hand.

Duvalier thrust with her stick just as her would-be lover opened his mouth. She caught him solidly below the breastbone; the yell for help died into a gasp of a contracting diaphragm. He grabbed at the weapon, and Duvalier left him holding the empty scabbard as she drew twenty inches of naked blade.

She became a blur. To Valentine, it was like trying to watch a hummingbird.

"Hol-huh?" the waking sergeant asked just before she stabbed him up and under the chin. The guard in the catbird seat brought down his rifle. Not knowing what else to do, Valentine threw his bucketful of water and laundry in his direction.

The splash of water brought the man with the blade in his armpit out of his shock. He dropped Duvalier's scabbard and pulled the bloody-handled blade out of his armpit. Duvalier danced out of the way of the arterial spray and spun to slash up at the legs of the seated guard. At one time or another, Valentine had heard the expression "cut off at the knees." Now he saw it in practice.

Blood pouring from under his arm, the guard made one half-swipe at Duvalier with her knife before he sank to the floor, face calm and beatific as though relaxing into sleep.

Tchick-BANG went the guard's rifle and splinters flew and Duvalier stabbed up and up through the seat and the blood came down as though from a broken pipe and the rifle fell on the man bleeding to death on the floor. *BANG*—Valentine ducked as the rifle fired again as it landed and Duvalier pulled the mutilated guard out of his seat and threw him to the floor and jumped on his back and pounded his face again and again into the bloody floorboards until broken teeth lay like dropped candy and clear fluid ran out and the screams ended.

Valentine pulled her off the guard.

"Damn them all," she said, leaving a bloody smear as she wiped her nose with a trembling hand.

"What was that?" Valentine asked.

"A helluva killing." She moved some of the spilled laundry out of the way of the blood. The thirsty wood could absorb only so much. She smiled and planted a bloody kiss on his lips. "Good work with the water."

"Are you insane?"

"Maybe. We have to beat the heat. Let's jump off."

"Just a minute." Valentine couldn't leave it at that. If they set the caboose on fire and fled, there'd be a pursuit as soon as the engineers radioed for help. They had to make the deaths look plausible, sow a few doubts for when the train pulled in at the next stop to drop off people and take on corn and cattle.

As Duvalier gathered their gear, plus wet laundry, and rooted for supplies, Valentine put the sergeant and the half-dressed guard among spilled cards and whiskey on the floor, bloody utility knives in their hands. The guard who had been on duty they set out on the open rear galley for the moment, until they were ready to jump off. As the train slowed at the top of a gentle slope, they threw dead man, their packs, and themselves off. After the train disappeared into the night, Valentine concentrated on making it look like the wounded guard had somehow got caught under the train and succumbed to blood loss at the side of the tracks.

Duvalier removed traces of their presence from around the body. He watched her, greenish gray to his night-widened eyes.

Only after they were well off the rail line and moving south in Nebraska incognita did he vent. They cut across ancient fields, now returned to the prairie plants and insects.

"I thought we were 'all about the mission'?"

She let out an exasperated breath. "I don't like being pawed."

"You could have said something."

"You ever been attacked? You know . . . for sex?"

"You led him on."

"I woke up, and there's a soldier with a hand on my boob. Maybe they had a gun on you. I didn't think, I reacted. Panic."

"So you just lost it?"

"Something like that."

"And when a posse comes?"

"Posse? Val, we killed some Overland rail guards. It's Overland's problem. You think the local Kurian is going to round up a bunch of men to search deserted silos? Hell no—he's got better things to do. At most, Overland will bitch to whoever's running the show here, and something will get negotiated. Meanwhile that sergeant's wives are going to be in for a surprise when they try to claim pension."

"This negotiation—it'll probably involve some aura changing hands, you think? It's the only thing Kur values."

She reached up and slapped a fly out of the air. "Not necessarily. Could be just corn."

"Hope it was worth it."

They took another twenty paces in silence.

He thought he heard a sniffle. "You want to talk abou—?"

"No!"

They caught a road at dawn, and Valentine stopped and unrolled a map. As they tried to guess their whereabouts, she was as calm as though they'd spent the last few hours berry-picking. Valentine couldn't help thinking that she'd killed the three Overland men for touching an old wound. A woman like Duvalier might attract male attention anywhere they went. A reaction like that in the wrong place—

His mind went back to when he had first met her. The shapeless old coat, the dirt, the half-starved flesh. Was she at war with her own looks, as well as Kur? He wondered if he was chasing the Twisted Cross under the guidance of a woman who was, to use Bone Lombard's phrase, of "disordered mind."

He couldn't think that. He'd lose hope. She'd just reacted. She wasn't disordered. Disordered wouldn't find the General and then get them home again safe.

Duvalier found them a little town the next day, and they walked in with a tale of stolen horses. They didn't get so much as a suspicious glance when they said they had business south. There was a truck loading for a southbound trip to Manhattan, Kansas; the driver was making notes as townspeople listed their needs. The Cats needed a quick ride, so they entered Kansas in the back of a diesel truck baby-sitting a load of eggs.

The driver was glad to have them. If there was anything besides eggs in the back—for instance, black market clothing or jewelry, the driver hinted—it might be a good idea to have a uniformed Trooper visible riding shotgun.

Duvalier had a contact near the truck's destination.

"Who?" Valentine asked as Duvalier did everything but lick her lips in anticipation.

"A friend."

She described her contact as they rattled south in the back of the carbon-spewing truck, which due to some idiosyncrasy in its suspension shimmied side to side like a duck shaking its tail feathers.

"Roland Victor is an odd sort of black marketeer. Lots of contacts in the Militia; Roland's so well connected, he might as well be part of their logistics support."

Valentine didn't hear her refer to other men by their first names.

"He deals in items appealing to Kansas Society's women, but ninety percent of his clientele is men. He's also something of a loan shark. I think every Militia officer above the rank of lieutenant owes him money or a favor. He gets clothes, jewelry, wines, chocolates, teas, and almost any kind of luxury you can think of, little favorites that powerful men like to give to their whores after giving the wife a new apron for her birthday. He's not the sort of man you invite to your daughter's wedding, but when you and your brother officers are planning a binge, he's the one to see for a case of Canadian whiskey. You wouldn't think wealth meant anything anymore, but it does to Roland."

"Know him well, do you?"

"He has very good manners, and he has a lot of—what's the word, style?—no, call it class. He plays he's a baron and looks the part. You're going to have to see him to believe it."

"I suppose he knows better than to paw at you."

Her eyes pleaded with him as much as her voice. "Drop it, Val. Please? I'm sorry about back there in the train, okay. Cross my heart."

"We got away. I'm ready to forget it."

"Start trusting me again. You've been all stiff and watchful lately."

"I don't mean to be. Sorry."

"Buddies, you know? Like before?" She held out her hand, turning her palm up so he could see the scar she'd made at his Cat invocation.

He shook it, their common wounds touching. But it was still hard to meet her eyes. He'd found a soft spot in a woman he'd come to respect as he respected only a handful of other teachers in his life: the Padre, Eveready, Captain LeHavre. He relied on her, and up until the incident on the train, would have gladly followed her into any danger.

He sneered at himself: Who was he to judge? Had he always made the perfect decisions?

The Kurians would have relished the moment. Sworn allies suspicious of each other despite the danger all around. They would have gladly sacrificed the Overland guards to set a pair of Cats against each other. He had to quit letting his sensibilities do the enemy's work for them.

By the time they reached Manhattan, Valentine knew as much about Roland Victor's operation as Duvalier did. She explained that his couriers always showed a *V* somehow when in public. For example, the driver of the truck they had swayed southward on had a pocketknife open in a V shape resting on his dashboard. Victor had his own network, which extended to Canada, the Mississippi, and down into Mexico—a web of friends of friends of friends who specialized in the underground trade the Kurians didn't bother to suppress, as long as it was furs instead of firearms.

The driver had his own legitimate market to visit at a Militia camp, so they had to travel on foot the last few miles. They walked through the empty husk of learning that once was Kansas State University. They saw crates being taken out of a from a three-story hall, with new bars on the tall windows, but most were burned-out shells.

"Just warehouses now," Duvalier explained as Valentine instinctively counted trucks and guards.

She turned them up a road, the asphalt as black and smooth as molasses.

Valentine marveled at Victor's well-tended grounds on the shores of Lake Milford. The smuggler made no attempt to hide the fruits of his luxury-goods labor. Clipped lawns, statues, neatly trimmed trees, decorative gardens, flower beds, and shrubs arranged to form secluded grottoes were a new experience to Valentine. He found himself estimating how many potatoes could be grown on the front lawn before him.

The sturdy pinkish-gray brick house seemed built to flaunt its ostentatiously oversize door. Val wondered if guests dismounted outside or rode their horses into the entryway.

"We'll go around the back. He uses the front door for Society. He has a smaller door to his office for business."

Roland Victor greeted them after a discreet tap from Duvalier on the plain wooden door. He already had company in the form of a sawed-off-looking man in a leather cap. Or perhaps Victor's companion just looked small in comparison with the big, bluff smuggler. Victor had the hearty, meaty features of a beer-and-beef diet, concealed to advantage by a well-fitted suit. Valentine had seen only a half-dozen suits in his entire life, and never one with a starched shirt underneath.

Victor's square face, framed by thick black sideburns and an equally bristly mane, broke out in a welcoming smile. "Ahh, out-of-town guests. From Nebraska, judging from the uniform, Trooper. Please, come in and don't worry about the boots. Can this be my dear Dee? It's been too long." He turned to his current guest. "I'm sorry, Mr. H, but we'll have to cut our pleasant afternoon short. Can I look forward to the pleasure of your company when you get back from your commission?"

"Gladly, Mr. Victor," the man said, aping Victor's pleasantries if not his educated accent. "I'll be sure to stop by directly."

Victor escorted his courier to the door. Mr. H was slightly hunchbacked, and seeing the two of them move toward the door together made Valentine think of an entertainer with a trained monkey he had glimpsed during his time in Chicago.

The smuggler returned to his new guests. Duvalier introduced Valentine as simply *David,* and Victor shook his hand and gripped him by the upper arm as he did so. From another man his size, the gesture might be intimidating, if not overpowering, but from Victor it conveyed only bonhomie. "Coffee? Something to drink?" he asked, moving to a mirrored liquor cabinet.

Valentine and Duvalier accepted Victor's coffee with appropriate *oohs* and *ahhs* at its aroma, and sat. At the first taste, Valentine's eyes widened in pleasure; the coffee had a rich, smoked chocolate taste and a stimulating kick. He watched Victor pour something from a crystal decanter into his own coffee and looked around the room. Victor had a fondness for statues, mostly blackened bronze interpretations of cowboys, riding like fury with horse, lariat, and gun. Valentine looked at the label. He'd never known the old Remington gun company made art, as well.

"Now what can I do for you children?" Victor asked, taking a sip of his Irish coffee, hardly enough to wet his lips.

"Information," Duvalier said. "We're hunting something. Or someone."

Victor leaned forward in his leather chair, which silently bore the shift in his respectable weight. He braced his massive head on a bipod created by his forearms, chin resting on the back of his right hand. "Yes? I shouldn't wonder the hunt isn't going well, if you don't know whether you're hunting a *who* or a *what*."

Duvalier took a breath. "That's because it's a little bit of both. The *what* is some kind of new military organization the Kurians set up. Their banner is sort of like the old swastika one from the twentieth century. Only backwards. The who is a man. We don't know his name; he goes by the rank of General. 'The General,' his people seem to call him."

"How do they get around, truck or train?"

"We know they use trains," she answered, "disguised to look like ordinary freight cars. The last solid information we have is that they were in Oklahoma in March. Headed north, we believe. No information on trucks."

"Hmmm, I've not heard anything about a 'General' from the Kansas Society. You never learned where they were going?"

"No," Valentine chipped in, wishing to contribute to the conversation.

"How large? Do they have enough men and equipment to make a try to conquer, say, Denver?"

Duvalier shrugged. "We just don't know. It can't be too large an army. Anything bigger than a couple of regiments, and some of the other Cats would have picked it up and brought it to Southern Command's attention."

Victor's jaw worked as he stared at the ceiling in thought. "I know there's a new line being driven west into Colorado. First new construction in that direction I've heard about in ages; our venerable Masters don't go in for civic improvement. You do know that they're also putting in new lines on your western border, right?"

"We've had some word. Southern Command isn't taking it seriously," Valentine said. "They think it's just another rail corridor to make defending the border easier."

Victor brushed out his sideburns with the backs of his hands. "I wouldn't be seen around where they are building. They'll either shoot on sight or impress you. Best case is you'll be cutting embankments and driving spikes for a daily issue of corn bread for what's left of your future. But you could ask my man out there. I've got an agent that does an occasional run into the Denver Zone. He sometimes comes back with word of what's going on in the mountains."

Duvalier brightened. "How do we get there?"

"I'll put in a word with the East-West Line Chief, and that'll get you as far as the high plains. I'd recommend horses once you're out there. I'll give you a letter of introduction to Cortez. He'll get you supplies and mounts if you want to head west from there. He might even agree to guide you."

A gentle knock at the back door announced the arrival of another visitor.

"It never rains; it just pours," Victor quoted. "Last week I sat and twiddled my thumbs, but today you're my fourth caller. You will stay the night, of course."

Victor told his visitor that he would be just a few minutes, and introduced the Cats to a combed, pressed, and manicured servant named Iban. He charged Iban with preparing meals and bedrooms for the pair, and returned to the door to greet his latest arrival, a dust-covered man with a hat so wide it was just short of a sombrero.

The well-tended rooms, rugs, and furnishings made Valentine long for a bath more than for a meal. Iban somehow telepathically picked up on his desire and suggested, "If you want to wash up before you eat, there is fresh soap and towels in the first-floor bathroom."

"Dibs," Duvalier said quickly. "Victor's bathrooms are incredible. Hot running water at the twist of a knob, and a razor so sharp, you can shave with its shadow."

"Prove it. What are you going to shave, anyway? I'd like to watch."

"Oh fu—Dream on, Valentine."

Valentine plunged into the prewarmed tub after a quick washup in the sink, fearing he'd leave a ring like a moon crater if he dipped immediately into the steaming water. The servant had poured some sort of scented oil in the tub; it smelled vaguely of cedar. Valentine lathered and shaved with a small hand mirror placed in a tub caddy, lingering over the rasping strokes and enjoying himself immensely.

Iban discreetly knocked and entered, taking Valentine's dirt-encrusted clothing and replacing it with a heavy cotton garment, a thin robe the servant called a *kimono*. Valentine lingered in the tub, then finally rose and put on the wheat-colored wrap. His hiking boots had disappeared, as well, and as the efficient Iban had not replaced them with anything, even socks, he left the bathroom barefoot to find Duvalier wolfing a fruit salad in an airy corner room. French windows let in the warm afternoon air.

"Quite a place," Valentine commented, feeling the rich texture of the draperies as he parted them to take in the lawn and sky.

"Quite a person," Duvalier countered.

"I didn't know they still made fabric like this."

"Probably just well preserved," she said. "Every time I'm here, it makes me think of stories I heard of the Old World. It's like a museum or something."

"Some of the higher-ups in the Kurians' favor live like this, I'm told," Valentine said. "You sure he's not one of them? How does he get away with it?"

She paused to finish a forkful. "He doesn't fight the system. He provides things the Society wants, and that the Kurians can't be troubled to deal with. The nearest Kurian is seventy miles away. The Quisling who runs Manhattan has a brass ring, but all he knows is a lot of shiftless types come around this house. I've heard of Reapers visiting the area, and I know the Milita searched his house and buildings. No guns, no problem. The Kurians don't seem to realize that wealth and influence can be a weapon, maybe a better weapon than a battery of howitzers. He uses that wealth now and then to help us. Or Denver, I suppose."

"What does he ask in return?"

"That's the funny part. Nothing."

They rested for two glorious nights on clean sheets, groaning from stuffing themselves at Victor's table. Rack of lamb, roast beef, and delicate baked rolls that fell into buttery quarters left them torpid, barely able to make conversation. Their host asked no questions beyond pleasant inquiries about after-dinner drinks.

After a hearty breakfast of pork chops and fried potatoes, Victor saw them off with the dawn. Wearing cleaned clothes and bearing Victor's letters of introduction, they shouldered their refilled packs bulging with canned food and hearty biscuits, and thanked their host.

"I hope it puts you back on track," Victor said. "The length of Kansas is a long way to go on a wild-goose chase."

Valentine said, "We'll be riding most of the way. You've made it a quick trip."

"I'm a little worried about those guns. Nebraska Trooper's uniform or not, somebody might decide you shouldn't be carrying weapons. They'll be taken for 'safekeeping,' and you'll never see them again. The Line Chief will give you passports, but his stamp won't help much in that case."

Iban produced a small, two-wheeled basket cart.

"On the road you can pull it," Victor said, "and if you can't use the wheels, you can carry it between you. Negotiables. The usual assortment: tobacco, alcohol, watches, pens, and good paper. I've put in some real gold coins and some fake pearls that are very good. Optics are popular with the soldiers: you have two binoculars, a spotting scope, and two spyglasses. Once you get rid of those, it'll be a lot lighter. Always better to bribe your way out than fight your way out."

"Amen," Duvalier agreed.

"If you have to, use my name as an IOU with anyone in my network, but please use discretion. If you're caught burning down a police station, Dee, my name won't help you and will only hurt me."

"Thank you. We're worth your trust, sir," Valentine said.

"Then go out and prove it. I hope you'll have another Kurian notch in your scabbard the next time I see you, Dee."

"Seems to me you're doing pretty well for yourself under them," Valentine said. He just as quickly regretted it.

"Val!" Duvalier said.

"It's okay, Dee." Victor looked at his nails, bitten to the quick. "Am I well? You try living your life smiling and dancing at parties and picnics and weddings of people you despise, boy. Cheering at Militia games where the teams are made up of murderers who keep their one sorry life in exchange for hundreds of their fellows. I've got a chronic ulcer, and my doctor says my liver is going to throw in the towel."

He seemed to sag, ruddy skin now almost purulent. "It's not as easy a life as you think. I only hope my liver gives me enough warning so I can go to the Governor's New Year's Ball wearing an explosive belt."

Valentine felt his face go hot. "I'm sorry. I should be grateful. Not my place to criticize unless I'm in your shoes."

"Live and learn. Emphasis on *live*."

Seven

The High Plains of Eastern Colorado, August: A better name for this upland might be the Dry Plains, as running water is scarce much of the year. The pumps and sprinklers that fed circular patches of crops, which had dotted the flats like some giant variety of lily pad, are now nothing but rusting empty skeletons and dry as marrowless bone. A little more rainfall, and the high plains would be a lush paradise: the sun shines three hundred days a year, and the winters are comparatively mild.

Perhaps it is the sun that keeps the Kur away, or just the lack of sustainable population for their feeding. The inhabitants of Denver and the Eastern Slope might also have something to do with it. Their outpost garrisons scattered in this empty land imitate the forts of the Old West, with wooden walls high enough to prevent a Reaper's leaping over them.

The few souls living in this expanse hide their paths and habits from both the vigorous Denver Freehold in the West and the Kurians to the East. The Denverites have been known to "relocate to safety" anyone found on their borders, confiscating property too large to move at the point of a gun. As for the Kurians, it is the old story. Any group larger than a family is too hard to feed, and too big a risk of becoming a lifesign lure for a roaming Reaper.

So only the occasional house is inhabited, though the isolation can be as hard to live under as the Kurian avatars.

Valentine did not know whether to call it a sod house or a cave. The House of Cortez had none of the scope and glitter its conquering namesake inspired. The front of the structure protruded from the side of a

grassy hill, as if it had been fired from a gigantic cannon and embedded there. An overhang sheltered the wide porch, with rough wooden
trunks holding up the dirt-and-grass-covered roof. Flowers in hanging
baskets and planters added a splash of color to the weather-beaten
wood and straw-colored grasses covering the hillside and the crown of
the house.

They drew near the house to a crescendo of barking. Valentine
guessed three dogs, and he and Duvalier approached empty-handed.

"At least we know we have the right house. We haven't seen another one for five miles," Duvalier said.

"I've got a gun," a female but not very feminine voice called from
the shadows of the house. "You're welcome to water from the pump,
but there's no food or roof here for strangers."

"We're here to speak to Tommy Cortez," Valentine called over the
barking.

"No one here by that name. You're lost, sounds like."

"We have some messages from Mr. Victor. We got the directions
from him."

The unseen figure contemplated the news for a moment, and even
the dogs went silent. "My husband's not home. Your business is with
him. If you want to wait, just tell me where you'll be, and I'll tell him
when he returns."

"Ma'am," Duvalier said, "we've come clear across Kansas, and
we're heading farther west. We've lugged this case all the way from the
railhead, hoping for some help when we got here. Food and horses, in
other words."

"Horses? You see a barn here?"

Valentine put a restraining hand on Duvalier's shoulder.

"Mrs. Cortez, we're here to help if we can. Is your husband missing?"

Valentine felt the hard casing of the unseen woman's manner break
inside the shadowy interior. "Three weeks and two days," a much
smaller voice said from the shadows. The door opened, and a short rai-
sin of a woman in a denim smock stepped out onto the porch, gripping
a rabbit gun. Years of dusty Colorado summers were written on her
face in vertical lines. "Never been gone this long. I'm about out of my
head with worry. It wasn't even much of a trip, just up to Fort Rowling."

They ate a meal of corn bread and drippings and drank prairie tea
under the low ceiling of the Cortez home. Like a rabbit warren built for
humans, the house behind the half-buried facade was a series of rooms
and passages, mostly filled with cobwebbed relics as a sort of indoor

junkyard. A generator chattered away; judging from the piping, it burned local natural gas to light and ventilate the house. The musty smell was offset, to Valentine's mind, by the welcoming, earth-insulated coolness of the interior after the hot August sun.

"My husband brought me out of Garden City, Kansas, almost thirty years ago, now," Mrs. Cortez explained while moving about the tiny kitchen. She had grown garrulous after letting them in. "He always was a traveler. Tall and handsome, he was. Still is, even with the mileage. Just his size made most of the varmints in Kansas avoid him. He made money getting messages into Denver, New Mexico, wherever. The New Order had just got itself worked out by then, everything all organized to suit them. After years of fighting and starvation, lots of folks were happy to stay put where they were told and do what was ordered. But I saw there was no future in it, and when Tommy asked me to go, I went. He had found this place in the middle of a whole lotta nowhere and had been slowly fixing it up. We were happier than we had a right to be, considering what was going on beyond the horizon." She removed a pistol from her apron and sat down to her own meal.

"It's always been just the two of you?" Duvalier asked.

"Yes, we couldn't have children. Something wrong with one of us, I expect, but no way of knowing these days. Not that we failed on account of trying," she said, a shy smile creeping across her face. "There was Karl, an orphan boy Tommy picked up on one of his trips. He stayed with us about three years, but moved on to Denver when he was seventeen. Nobody around here—he was lonely, poor boy. Or I should say nobody around here worth knowing. These lands get all sorts of trash passing through, and I'm not as brave as I once was. I get scared if I'm left alone. That's why we've got the dogs."

The curs in question snored in a companionable heap on an old sofa. They sported the curled tails and short-haired, irregular coloring of mongrels, and as soon as their mistress had dropped her suspicions, they turned into a tail-wagging, tongue-lolling trio of family pets.

Valentine cleared the table and worked the pump in the sink. As he washed the dishes, he noticed a half-folded note on the counter. Making sure that his body blocked him from the table, he dried a finger and turned it open.

> *To Who Finds This Note:*
>   *The house and all in it are yours. Tom's been gone these days and I must find him. I can't stay alone in this house no more or I'll be a suicide God forgive me the nights are too much and I don't sleep with him away. I will find him or . . .*

Valentine folded it closed again. "I'm sorry he's overdue. Bad for us—we were hoping he could serve as a guide to this part of Colorado. But of course that's not important compared to you."

Mrs. Cortez brightened. "I used to know the land between here and Denver real well. In the years since, I've changed but the hills haven't. With you two along, I'd feel safer following the trail to Fort Rowling. And yes, we do have horses. The stable's just hid; it's in an old foundation you'd think was just a collapsed house unless you got within spitting distance. There'll be news of him there. Whether he's there or not, you can pick up a guide. Good place to hear news, too, if that's what you're after."

"Sounds like the best plan for all of us," Valentine said.

Valentine enjoyed riding the dry, lonely country. The horses, tough mustangs with muscles of steel and adamantine determination to accomplish whatever the rider asked, whether bearing packs or saddles, were in better condition than most horses he had known. The three dogs added an air of a picnic to the trip, for they explored the countryside with such canine joie de vive that the accompanying humans could not help sharing in their high spirits. They were out of the KZ, no checkpoints to dodge, watchful eyes of the residents no longer on them. Finding water was the only problem, but between their guide's memory and Valentine's nose, they went from waterhole to waterhole without too much searching.

The nights passed a little more nervously. There might be slim pickings for any Reapers wandering away from Kansas, but human lifesign in such an empty land would show up all the brighter on a Hood's psychic radar. Mrs. Cortez must have thought the Cats a quiet couple. Valentine and Duvalier sat at the tiny, shielded campfires, in a lifesign-lowering trance that had many of the benefits of sleep. Her small talk continued despite her unresponsive companions until she drifted off to sleep.

Then came glorious dawns. The horizon always seemed a little higher than the observer. To Valentine, it felt as if he were in a vast shallow arena, with only high, wispy stratus clouds watching their performance.

They were a matter of "a few more hours' " ride from Fort Rowling when the dogs alerted. All three narrow snouts pointed northwest at the same moment, ears cocked to attention. Valentine's ears picked up the sound of vehicles.

"Motors. Maybe two," Valentine said, and Duvalier nodded agreement.

"It's most likely Denver soldiery, but we might want to get under cover anyway," Mrs. Cortez said, sliding off her saddle. "Guess my ears aren't what they used to be."

They took cover in the lee of a horseshoe-shaped hill among a spread of scraggly oneseed junipers. Mrs. Cortez held the horses, which took the opportunity to nose among the branches for the dark blue berries, and ordered the dogs down next to her. Valentine and Duvalier chose a spot on the crest to observe.

Two wide-framed cars, minuscule in the distance, bumped along the remains of a former road, moving south. As long as they stuck to the road, they were little threat.

"Just brownish off-road cars," Valentine called back down.

"You sure they aren't green? Denver folks have their rigs painted green, sometimes they got a white star on 'em, too."

"Maybe they're just dirty," Duvalier suggested, but even she did not sound convinced.

They traveled more carefully after that. They found the road the jeeps had used, but the tire tracks told no clear tales, except that the jeeps weren't the only vehicles that had used the road recently. A mile past the road, Valentine picked up the smell of humanity on the light afternoon breeze as they walked their horses.

"People up ahead," he said to Duvalier. "Don't look startled—it's probably a stillwatch. Let's worry about it behind some cover."

They wound around a bend in a hill, cutting off the scent, and stopped. After that it was a matter of outwatching the watchers. Sooner or later curiosity would force them to reveal themselves. Duvalier volunteered to go after them while Valentine and Mrs. Cortez made a pretense of tending to the horses.

Valentine was wondering how to phrase it when Duvalier let out an exasperated breath. "Don't look like that, Val. I'll be gentle."

Within an hour she descended from the grassy hills carrying an unfamiliar rifle behind a matched pair of uniformed soldiers. A second gun bobbed on her back.

"Look, she found one," Valentine said.

Mrs. Cortez narrowed her eyes. "Good-size boy. That's a Denver regular, not one of the Rangers they use here on the Frontier. Something must be going on. I hope she was polite; the Denver troops get riled easily."

Duvalier walked her prisoner into camp, chatting with him as they approached the horses. The soldier spoke first.

"Look, friend, you're in Colorado now. Ambushing and hitting a soldier brings a heap of trouble your way, especially now. Better tell your girl to give me my rifle back. In about five minutes, you'll have twenty guns pointed at you from these hills."

Valentine shrugged. "'My girl' is actually in charge here, more or less. I wouldn't get too heavy-handed with the threats, Private. Your sergeant might ask us some questions, and if he finds out this 'girl' about half your size surprised you and got your gun without even having one of her own, well, I wouldn't care to be you."

The soldier, who had PARKSTON stenciled on his breast, glanced around at the crests of the low surrounding hills, as if the unnamed sergeant were in danger of overhearing that someone had taken his gun.

"But we don't want that to happen," Valentine continued. "As far as we're concerned, you hailed us from good cover, having sense enough to ask questions first and shoot later, and from our conversation you decided to bring us in to see your officer. If we give you your gun back, can we trust you not to do anything foolish?"

"Yes, sir," Parkston agreed. His comrade nodded, dispelling the suspicious air hanging between them.

Duvalier returned his rifle, a restored version of the old M-16 battle rifles of the U.S. Armed Forces. "What are you doing so far from home? I've never seen a Denver regular this far out on the frontier before," she observed.

"I probably shouldn't say," Parkston said. "Maybe the sarge can tell you more—he's leading this patrol."

The patrol in question chose this moment to reveal themselves. A line of men came over the top of the hill from the same direction Duvalier had appeared with the boy. Valentine heard others moving at the crest of this hill, staying hidden from sight but not being quiet enough to fool either him or the dogs, who at this moment were startled out of making themselves agreeable to Parker by the new arrivals.

The sergeant and a small team approached, rifles ready but pointed down.

"Howdy, folks," said the thirty-something man with the stripes. He exuded calm confidence, which was just as well since none of his team looked over twenty, and nervous boys with guns in a potentially hostile situation needed a lot of reassurance. "What are you doing this far into the DPZ?"

Mrs. Cortez ended up doing the introductions, her nasal western twang being similar to the sergeant's own. "My name is Cortez, and I'm looking for my husband, a pack trader last on his way to Fort Rowling. These two are with me—you might say they're helping a nervous old woman."

One of his men opened his mouth to say something, but the sergeant cut in. "Seen anything unusual west of here?"

"Two vehicles a couple hours back, moving south," Valentine spoke up.

"They were too far away to tell who they belonged to, you or someone else," Duvalier spoke up. "Sergeant, I'm no stranger to the Protective Zone. I've been to the South Platte Trading Post before on a cattle drive. None of us are friends of the New Order."

The sergeant lit a cigarette, and Valentine recognized the noxious smell of clove tobacco. "The jeeps were ours. But whether you're friends of Kur or no, it won't hurt you to know that Fort Rowling's gone. Burned right to the foundation. Done from the inside too, not artillery or any kind of heavy weapon as far as we know."

"What?" Mrs. Cortez and Duvalier said, nearly simultaneously.

Valentine rooted in his pocket and came up with a pack of cigarettes. He passed out two or three each to the sergeant and his men. The youths hooted, and the sergeant lit his and threw away the homemade smoke.

"Only bodies left to tell the tale," the sergeant continued. Valentine saw that the sergeant still held his gun in a way that wasn't threatening, but the barrel had to rise just thirty degrees to put a bullet through his chest. "Never saw anything like it before. They must have been surprised; there's a secret bunker in the gulch well back of the fort where the dependents are supposed to go if trouble's coming. Not a soul in there, or any sign of a fight, for that matter, at least at the refugee bunker. Fort Rowling put up a struggle, judging from the shell casings. They were at the walls for a bit. The gate was blown to bits. Some officers say a rocket, but I think demolition charge. The blast was just too big for anything else that you wouldn't need railcars to haul. Whoever planted the charge must not have minded machine-gun bullets."

"What was the garrison?" Valentine asked.

"Full complement is around eight hundred, but about half that is almost always on patrol or doing escort duty. Arming the camp casuals would mean six hundred men available for the defense. Fort Rowling wasn't just some little hole in the wall either. It was our strongest Frontier post. Mortar pits, two howitzers, I don't know how many support weapons. There's even a rail line that goes out to within ten miles of the fort, a project that don't look like it's going to be completed now."

"Tell them about the dependents," one of the sergeant's men said.

"Mrs. Cortez doesn't want to hear that."

"No, go ahead—I need to know. Please, Sergeant," she implored.

The sergeant tossed away his butt. "I've seen plenty of death, but not like this. Heads stuck on the ends of sticks, babies flung against walls and left on the ground like some sparrow that hit a window, houses burned with the people handcuffed inside them . . . I'm gonna be thinking about what I saw there till the day I die now, and I thought I was a hardcase." He paused to take a gulp of air and to swallow. "Mrs. Cortez, I'm sure your husband died on the walls if he was in there—if he could have carried a gun, they would have armed him."

Mrs. Cortez let out a deep breath, blinking back tears. "Maybe he ran for Denver. Oh, I do hope so."

"We'll get you there and you can find out, ma'am," the sergeant said. Valentine met his eyes and gave the NCO a tiny bow of his head in gratitude.

"Don't make sense," Parkston said. "I mean, whenever the Reapers hit somewhere, they take prisoners. It's the whole point. If people go dying on them in the fight, they're no use for . . . for food."

"I'll tell you what really doesn't make sense," the sergeant said, recovering from his memories somewhat. "The tracker's report. He said that his best guess was three two-and-a-half-ton trucks carrying about fifty men. Fifty men. Fifty Reapers couldn't have taken that fort, I don't think, not that I've ever heard of that many Reapers all together anywhere but a big city. What fifty men could wipe out six hundred in a defensive position?"

"I think you'd better take us to whoever is in command now at Fort Rowling," Duvalier said.

Valentine saw what was left of the fort up close. It had been in a good defensive location, with water for man and livestock and stands of timber nearby. The wooden parts of the walls were burned, the block-houses and bunkers demolished. The first order of business of the troops on the scene had been to decently tend to the bodies; long rows of fresh graves stood a little distance from the fort, looking out over a gully through which a sluggish stream still flowed in this, the hottest month of the year.

After surveying the burnt ruin, Duvalier asked for a chance to speak privately with Colonel Wilson and his adjutant, Major Zwiecki, of the Denver Free Colorado Corps. They left Mrs. Cortez hunting through the personal effects of the dead, looking for evidence of her husband. The colonel obligingly gave them his time. He was as desperate for an answer as any of the Denver soldiers or what was left of the Fort Rowling garrison, now returning from the patrols and convoys that had preserved their lives.

Rather than reoccupying the fort, he had pitched his men's tents on some high ground a half-mile from the fort, so the men didn't have to spend the night among the bloodstains and burned timber. Night had fallen, and the tent was lit by electric light provided by a mobile generator.

"Gasoline we got," the major said when Valentine asked about the logistics that allowed mobile electricity. "There's a lot of shale oil in Colorado. We make it in blasting furnaces; you get the shale hot enough, and it bleeds oil. I've got a brother-in-law there. He says the refinery is really something. Up in the mountains. They call it Hell's Penthouse. The name comes from the huge slag heaps everywhere, and the furnaces that run over nine hundred degrees."

Duvalier cut in. "We're here to find out what happened—let's stick to the subject at hand."

"If you've got an answer, or even a good guess, I'd like to hear it," Colonel Wilson said as the major turned to pour coffee.

"Colonel, have you ever heard of Reapers using guns?" Duvalier asked.

"No, but I'm ready to listen to anything. Because other than an attack by a few thousand flying Harpies who carried off their dead and never landed so's to make tracks, you have to get to really weird theories to explain this."

The major added, "The more I see of the Kurians, the more my definition of 'really weird' gets pushed further and further out."

"We work for Southern Command," Valentine broke in after a look and a nod between him and Duvalier. "We're looking into some new unit the Kurians have, a group called the Twisted Cross under somebody known as 'the General.'"

The major and the colonel exchanged looks. "That's substanial," Wilson said, "and I'll tell you why. We've kept this from the troops, but there was one survivor of the Fort, a very old woman who lived there with her daughter and her daughter's family."

"Pretty tough old bird," the major added.

"She didn't see anything of the fight—they were in a basement. She heard a lot of gunfire. Some men busted into the basement, dressed in body armor with heavy black helmets. They dragged the others off, but they pulled her up into the compound and made her watch what was going on. She said when they were done, one of the men in body armor 'hissed' at her *'Tell them the General did this.'* Also something about coming back. That's why we kept it from the troops."

"Hissed?" Valentine asked. "Those were her words?"

"Yes, 'hissed,'" the colonel said. "I've never been close enough to hear a Reaper, but I guess they have kind of a breathy voice."

"That big tongue doesn't leave much room for vocal cords," Valentine said. "They hiss, all right. I'd like to speak to her."

"Then you'll have to chase her to Denver," the colonel said. "She's been sent there for debriefing. I didn't want the men worried about what happens if this General comes back. I'm doing enough of that for the whole regiment.

"I don't know what could stop them. If they can do this to Fort Rowling, I don't know that any of our posts outside Denver could."

They said good-bye to Mrs. Cortez inside the Denver Corps camp. She had found a bloodstained hat belonging to her husband; a bullet had come in through the side of the wide-brimmed ranch fedora.

"At least I know it was quick," she said fatalistically.

Duvalier hugged her and whispered something in her ear that Valentine did not even try to hear. Sometimes using his "hard ears" just depressed him, giving him glimpses into others' private lives he wished he had not heard.

"You two take the horses, and mine besides. I'm going west to Denver with the dogs. Make myself useful in a hospital or stable. Been out there so long, it'll be nice to be among people, even if you're living under a set of rules long enough to choke a horse." The tears were in her voice, but not in her eyes.

They held a final meeting with the colonel and his adjutant. The colonel had requested a briefing about the Twisted Cross for all his officers, but Duvalier demurred, wishing to keep a low profile in camp. They told all they knew of the General, speaking on the record as Cats "A" and "Z" of Southern Command as Major Zwiecki took notes. As far as everyone else in the Denver Free Colorado Corps was concerned, they wanted to be known as just a pair of concerned relatives looking for one of their dead at Fort Rowling. That they also were remembered as some drifters who inexplicably had their horses shoed, were given a pack saddle, canteens, food, fuel, and a pass allowing them on Denver Protective Zone Territory at DFCC expense, Valentine never learned.

They followed the Republican River east out of Colorado, traveling slowly and carefully. Avoiding contact with farm, camp, or town, they worked their way back up into Nebraska. Valentine changed back into his Private Rice attire when Duvalier judged it safe enough, and they worked out yet another cover story to explain their presence. But this corner of Nebraska, so close to the Colorado border, was empty enough to allow them to move without being noticed. And so they came to the river Platte and its adjoining roads and tracks. After looking for their faces on wanted posters at station offices and finding none, they traded the horses for travel warrants from a corrupt rail-yard chief. Soon they rode again on the railroad, this time working for their passage—riding in and cleaning out eastbound cattle cars.

They were inside an empty cattle car on a siding outside their original pseudo-destination of Grand Island, sharing a bag of corn bread, when a train approached from the west. It moved with a mile-eating speed as the powerful engines pulled it. When the train roared by, Valentine counted an extra guard-car, thirty nondescript freights, and another heavily armored guard-car before the steel-colored caboose passed by. Whipped by speed and wind, two flags fluttered next to each other on the caboose: black with a spiderish design centered on the standard.

It was the white swastika of the Twisted Cross.

Eight

The Sand Dunes, September: Stretching north from the Platte River is the rolling, empty expanse of Nebraska's dunes. Sitting above one of the great aquifers of the world, the coarse, dark brown soil is not suited for crops, but supports some of the world's best ranching country. It is the Sahara transformed into a grassy garden. The Dunes, a beautiful green ocean in the spring before being burnt into straw by the summer's heat, cover an area larger than the state of Connecticut. They start to the west, and like the ocean, the great rollers are found the farthest out, thousand-foot-high, wind-rounded ridges a mile across and ten miles long, almost all running east-west according to the prevailing winds. East from the great ridges are smaller hills of varying squiggled shapes but still mostly long and thin. These gradually fade off into tiny steep hillocks, as the great rollers of the Atlantic turn into the chop of the English Channel. So like little waves are these hills that the residents use a nautical term for them: choppers.

While much of the soil is too dry to easily grow crops, the area is anything but a desert. It is ideal ranching country and supports more than horses and cattle. The little valleys between the hills are thickly wooded: lakes and ponds, marshes and soggy meadow can be found among the teeming cottonwoods and box elms. Trout streams and lakes filled with pike are dotted with beaver homes and dams, and a newcomer is sometimes startled to see a pelican fishing after descending from one of the high, dry ridges as seagulls ride the breeze overhead. Game is plentiful, mule deer bound through the long grass like giant jackrabbits, and antelope herds graze while the younger males at the edges keep watch for coyotes. Bird hunters come home with everything from waterfowl to wild turkey, pheasant to sharp-tailed grouse. But the residents of the Dunes ride with rifles for reasons other than shoot-ing game.

They hunt the minions of Kur.

Valentine and Duvalier caught up to the Twisted Cross train at the fork where the North Platte and South Platte converged their sandy banks. The town of North Platte no longer existed on the spit between the rivers, having been burned in the chaos almost fifty years ago. A hand-lettered sign announced that they were pulling into Harvard Station.

Their train did not stop, even though they had been assured by the engineer—this being a cattle car, unguarded except for a few rifles in the hands of the railroad men—that it would pause at Harvard Station before moving on to Ogallala and Scottsbluff. As they passed through the station, they saw squads of Troopers milling all over the yard, crates being unloaded and organized, and sentries posted on either side of their track for the express purpose of making sure no one got off. A small, single-engine plane came in for a landing on the old airstrip southeast of town, adding to the panoply of war. He and Duvalier openly stared; in fact, had they not watched the plane, it would have been even more suspicious, flying machines being a rarity even in the Kurian Zone. Valentine looked at it through his binoculars: it was tiny bush hopper, white with red markings. He half expected to see a swas-tika on the tail, like in pictures in World War II books, but could iden-tify no markings.

"I've been here before," Duvalier told him, "but I've only seen it from the other side."

Another Twisted Cross train was on a siding by a dock with some chutes and pens for livestock. They could see figures lounging in the sunlight, wearing what looked like black jumpsuits, but unlike the men at the other train, they seemed to be in no hurry to unload the contents of closed boxcars. Around the caboose, a team of the most formidable-looking Grogs Valentine had ever seen stood guard, taller than the slab-skinned gray ones he had fought at Little Timber and partially covered with fawn-colored fur.

A concrete blockhouse, surrounded by razor wire and gated, looked out over the ruins of the town and the river below. Men in a sandbagged platform smoked as they stood watch with machine guns. The black-and-white banner fluttered from the blockhouse's flagpole.

"They're setting up shop," Valentine said as their train pulled away westward. "Supplies, men, weapons, a plane. But what's the target? We haven't heard any news of a uprising in the local Gulag."

Duvalier gazed off northward into the rolling, grassy hills. She looked terribly, terribly sad. "If there were, it would be news they'd keep quiet. This isn't even a Kurian center—this is an outpost of the one down in McCook, right on the border."

"Border? Border with what?"

"The Dunes. They must be after the Dunes." She sighed, as she had done one day in Kansas, when they saw a police truck lumbering down the road with human fodder for the Reapers chained in back.

Valentine followed her gaze, not exactly doubting her, but waiting to hear more. "Who or what are the Dunes?" he finally asked. Duvalier liked to make him ask questions for some reason, perhaps as revenge for his occasional corrections to her English.

"It's more of a where, Val. The Dunes are that," she said, pointing. "It runs from here up to the Dakotas. Kurians never really controlled any of it, and every time they've tried, they got their ears pinned back. It's a huge area, maybe half the size of the Ozark Free Territory. I don't even think the Reapers dare hunt there."

"Why is that?"

"The Trekkers. Wanderers. The only way to describe it is big moving ranches that go with their cattle and horses. Everything in their life is packed onto their wagons, they move from winter to summer pasturage and back again, but not always the same spot. Their whole world is their cattle; the herds feed them and buy what they can't make."

"Buy from whom?"

"There are a few outfits that trade with the Quislings, no doubt about it. Oh, they call Quislings 'Jacks' out here. I've asked six different people and got six different stories. Some say its short for 'jackals,' but I'm not even sure what those are."

"They're a sort of scavenger dog—in Africa, I think," Valentine explained.

She ignored the zoology. "Others say it's because they used to be led by a man named Jack. Some more say it's because they run like jackrabbits if someone starts shooting at them. I forget the others. Doesn't matter. They're Jacks to folks out here."

"You know the people in the Dunes?"

"I do. Good people, damn good people. I got friendly with one of the larger clans, a group of families under the Eagle brand. They identify themselves with the marks they put on their cattle, you see. The brand looks kind of like an old set of air force wings, or an American Indian thunderbird. I guess it got its start from some Strategy Air Controller people who helped them fight off the Kurians in the worst years."

Valentine wondered if she meant "Strategic Air Command."

"They don't care for strangers too much, but I got to know them when they were running stock to Denver. I ended up riding scout for two cattle drives. Good days. Learned a lot about the land between here and the Rockies. The area between the two Platte branches is real anything-goes country. A couple Kur ranching settlements, bands of Jacks riding for the Kur, Crow Indians trying to live on the Pawnee, and a few little villages just trying to keep out of everything."

"So you've been to Denver?"

"No, the Denver Outriders would meet us outside the city. I always wanted to go, though. See a city. Of course, they tell me it's pretty empty, just like everywhere else. A fair amount of damage, but it's still free soil, and that always feels good."

Valentine watched Harvard Station disappear into the distance behind them.

"So you think they're going to clear out these Trekkers?"

She nodded. "It kind of fits the pattern. That other Lifeweaver, Ura, she mentioned that a couple of small Freeholds got torched by these guys. Maybe they're training before taking on bigger game, like us or Denver."

"If Denver depends on these people for food," Valentine theorized, "could be this is a step in a campaign against them. That might go a long way to explaining the attack on Fort Rowling. It was a probe."

"This will be a chance to see how they operate," Duvalier said. "We can see how they organize, scout, prepare for a battle. Find out about these Reapers with guns. Do they have artillery? It looks like the Twisted Cross has an air force, even if it's just one plane. Southern Command will need to know what's coming."

Valentine felt another, more important battle coming on. His duty and his humanity, his conscience and his code silently warred within. It wasn't much of a fight this time. Too many lives at stake.

The wind at the top of a rise pulled at his hair. He pulled it back into place, and as he did so came to a decision. As if a yoke had been lifted from his shoulders, he straightened.

"Ali, that's exactly what we should do. But first we've got to warn those people."

They jumped from the train as it slowed to climb a hill east of Ogallala. Rather than leaping immediately into the bushes, they waved at the railroad men watching from the caboose. The railroaders waved back, smiling.

"That's always fun," Valentine said, pulling a teasel weed's prickly head out of his hair and picking up his pack. "You okay?"

"Did it knock some sense into you?" she said as she changed back into her stained traveling clothes. At least she was speaking to him again. They had argued briefly, until she quit talking to him after he asked her if she could just watch her friends from the Denver cattle drives die.

"Not yet. Ali, I didn't say that you had to come. I didn't even suggest it. One pair of eyes can see as much as two. You can keep an eye on the Twisted Cross, and I'll try and get the word out to the people in the Dunes."

"You did suggest it. You said, 'We've got to warn those people.' *We* is plural, Mr. Professor."

"Okay, I hoped you'd want to come with me. After all, you're already known to them."

"Irresponsible. What we're doing—recon—is *really* important. As far as Southern Command is concerned, the Twisted Cross is just another gang of Quislings. I wanted to take you on because after reading your reports, it seemed like you were just as worried about them as I was. But you want us to go up into the Dunes, where all that's going to happen is we'll be on the receiving end of their attack, instead of evaluating it and learning about their numbers and methods."

Tears trickled down her face. "I liked those people, Val. They're good people, as good as I've met anywhere. There are families in those wagons, Valentine. They're going to be dead in a little while, and there's not a thing we can do about it—and it's killing me. Now you just want to throw our lives away, too.

"Our duty is to Southern Command. What about warning them? Didn't you take an oath when you became an officer, or a Wolf or whatever they put you through when you joined up?"

"Maybe if I can warn them they can hide the kids. We, or I— whatever—I just have to let them know about what's coming." He tightened his pack. "I'm going in there. Unless you want to try to stop me."

The stare-down was brief.

It ended when Duvalier looked at the dirt beneath her hiking boots, poked the loose soil with her walking stick. Then she gripped it firmly by the middle, and for a second Valentine thought she was planning to knock him out with it. But the tears disappeared.

She even looked a little relieved.

"Okay, David. We warn them. But that's all."

*　　*　　*

The Cats decided to risk crossing the North Platte River during daylight, starting as early as possible in their race against time and death.

It wasn't hard; at this time of year, the brown-streaked river was at its lowest point. They crossed into the Sands at the wreckage of the Kingsley Dam, passing a sign that read UNSECURED TERRITORY TRES-PASSERS SUBJECT TO SUMMARY JUSTICE. Although the road had been destroyed, a drift of sorts existed, allowing them to make the treacherous crossing without wetting anything below their knees. A few anglers, perhaps out of Ogallala, plied their rods from the banks. If hidden border sentries also watched the pair, Valentine's Trooper vest perhaps confused the guards enough to keep them from shooting.

Rather than disappear into the Dunes right away, which would look more suspicious to a stillwatch, Valentine decided instead to walk up the banks of the Platte among the birches and poplars of the floodplain.

After a rest, they found enough wooded cover to cut up into the Dunes, running parallel to the old State Route 61 north into Dune Country.

Valentine pushed the pace. He carried Duvalier's pack across his chest, so Duvalier, who hadn't spent years running from point to point in the Wolves, was light enough to keep up with his trot.

They jogged carefully along the hills, making sure they did not skyline themselves. At sunset they stopped to rest and watch the daylight go out in a blaze of glory. Valentine had been in some wide-open spaces before, but something about this rolling sea of straw and grainy soil felt endless.

"It's funny," Duvalier said. "What we're trying to do is just . . . nuts. Hopeless. I feel liberated, though. Like I'm about to go shoot some rapids in a barrel and it's too late to worry."

Valentine looked at her as he massaged his aching legs. The fading sun tinted her skin the color of beaten copper. "No, it's not that. You're doing the right thing. When I was a kid, the man who raised me after my family died, he was a teacher. He used to have the older students read about the Holocaust. The Holocaust was when—"

"I know what the Holocaust was," she said, but without her usual vexation. "Kind of a dress rehearsal for all this."

"He made us study it for a couple reasons. One was to learn that there were people who went through times as bad as these and survived, although it wasn't that bad in the Boundary Waters of Minnesota. I think the other reason we read about it was to learn that evil, even if it seems all-powerful for a while, always collapses eventually. He used to say evil was like a rabid animal: it was very dangerous and should be destroyed as soon as possible, but even if it couldn't be attacked from the outside, the sickness within would put an end to it.

"But back to this one book I read about the Holocaust. It started with this diary kept by a little Jewish girl in hiding. She was killed, but her diary survived, and the rest of it went on about people who helped the Jews and others hide from or escape the Nazis. People would ask them afterwards how they found the courage to do it, when the Nazis killed people who helped the Jews. They said it took no courage at all; it was the easier choice to make. By doing the right thing, they kept their humanity. I think being able to keep their self-respect gave them strength. There's a power in doing right."

Valentine opened an old tobacco pouch and took out his little pyramid-shaped stone so it could absorb the remaining sunlight and charge.

Duvalier looked at the tiny crystal pyramid. "Do you ever think the Lifeweavers are angels?"

"What? Err . . . no, I heard you. What do you mean, I should say."

"When I first got to the Free Territory, and that Cat Rourke began to sort of be a father to me, he took me to see Ryu. It was a sunny day, and he was wearing that white loincloth he goes around in, only he had another white thing he was sort of wrapped up in, too. I remember I was looking at him, and something about the sun must have warmed him—he turned to it and spread out his arms. Suddenly I saw this man with a halo, and these big white wings billowing out from his back. Of course, it was the white shawl or whatever he was wearing and the sun in his hair."

"Be a funny kind of angel, making killers. The Lifeweaver who turned me into a Wolf, he said the only kind of people who were going to be able to beat the Kur were ones filled with hate and fury, not so much soldiers as berserks. At least that's how I remember it. The whole thing is a little hazy."

"I never heard anything like that out of Ryu. He always seems"— she sought for a word—"lonely. Lonely and sad."

Val shrugged. "You want to get a little rest before we push on?"

"I think maybe you should get some. You always carry most of the load, plus that god-awful gun and ammo."

Back in the Regiment we should have been called mules rather than Wolves. They selected us for a sterile life of endurance. He stretched out on the grass with his coat as a pillow. "I can handle it."

"You still carry too much," she said, and suddenly leaned over and kissed him on the forehead.

He opened an eye. "It's a good thing you didn't do that while you were still wearing that bra-and-shorts combination. Otherwise I would have performed a very convincing newlywed act on you."

"Dream on, Valentine," she said, sending a peanut shell his way. They had picked up a bagful somewhere during a trade.

"I wish I could have seen you buying that red bra. That would have been a memory to treasure. No one at the hall would have believed me. I suppose you burned the evidence."

"No, I didn't buy that in Lincoln. Actually I found it, still hanging on a little plastic hanger in a ruined store in Amarillo a year ago. Still wrapped up in tissue paper and plastic. It fit so well, I decided to keep it for days when I just can't deal with my boobs."

He laughed. "You carried a red bra around with you for a year?"

"It's a hidden little piece of me, okay? You're a man, you don't know how important a good bra is."

"Your little pieces weren't so hidden under that jean jacket. What does it feel like to have a tan inside your belly button, anyway?"

"Cretin."

"Bitch."

"Quit being an ass. Get some rest—we're up again in an hour."

A day later, they cut a broad trail moving east. Cattle, wagon ruts, and horse hooves all churned a wide swath through the grassy dunes.

"You don't have to be Red Cloud to follow this," Valentine said, pushing the dirt in one of the deep wagon ruts aside to see how far down it had dried.

"Red what?"

"Red Cloud. He was a Lakota Sioux chief. My mother used to say that when I tracked mud across the kitchen."

She tipped her head, a faint smile on her face. "Do you have a picture of her?"

"Only in my mind."

"I bet you have her hair."

Valentine shrugged, and they began to follow the trail. A distant, buzzing *errrrrrrrm* made them take cover as the little plane they spotted at the Twisted Cross depot came up from the south.

"Now wouldn't that be a timesaver," Duvalier said, looking up at the scout plane. That little thing can do in an hour what it takes us days to cover."

Once it had moved off to the north, Valentine and Duvalier continued on their course, trailing the marks of the mass of men and cattle into the Dunes. They walked hard for an hour, and then rested for fifteen minutes, then got up again to jog for a while. After six hours, even Valentine began to get dry-mouthed and rubber-limbed. Duvalier groaned whenever they rose from a rest break, but otherwise endured the hard miles in silence.

It was afternoon when they spotted a pair of riders, the rearmost part of a rear guard, cutting across the path ahead. The pair rode smart, avoiding the skylines, and frequently paused their horses just to look and listen.

"Those are Trekkers," Duvalier pronounced, passing the binoculars back to Valentine. They began to jog in the open, trying to catch up with the outriders.

The riders spotted them soon after they started running, and moved with their horses to intercept. Valentine had his gun slung where he could get at it, but he had no weapon in his hand, and Duvalier just had her walking stick.

The men sat their horses, rifles on their hips, and awaited events.

"That's close enough, Trooper," one of them called from beneath a wide-brimmed Western hat. "What are you, a deserter?"

"Parley, riders," Duvalier called. "He's no Trooper. We took that off a dead 'un for disguise. What brand do you ride behind?"

"Barred Seven. Glad you're not a stranger here, little lady. What brand do you ride behind?"

"The last time I visited here, I rode with the Eagle's Wings. We have to speak to your Wagonmaster."

"Always happy to talk to a brother brand, 'specially when the visitor's such a pretty one. Does your boy here talk, or did somebody fork his tongue?"

"I can talk, friend. I just like to see which way the wind blows."

"Out here, it's usually west-east," the other man said, his lips hidden by a long drape of a mustache. The wide-brimmed man guffawed.

"You still got a good two miles to go before you hit the wagons, I'm afraid," he said. "But we'll get you to the edge of the herd." They turned their horses neatly and began to follow the trail.

"Bar Seven," Duvalier said quietly. "Not one of the larger groups, but tough as nails. They keep to the border country. Rumor has it that they trade with the Jacks, but let ye who are without sin cast the first stone. A lot of the Trekkers do, one way or another."

"What about your Eagle's Wings?" Valentine asked.

"No, they have a serious feud with Kur. Lots of memories from grandfathers in the military. And too many losses while running cattle to Denver. But in a way, this is good—Bar Seven might not want to offend the Eagles by being difficult, since the Eagles are the biggest of the Trekker groups. Once in a while there are disputes over winter pasture, and Bar Seven can't afford to make enemies."

They caught up to the herd, mostly Herefords that looked like they had been toughened up by the addition of a long-horn bull or two. Beyond the herd they could see a little spread of twenty or so wagons. A cowboy with a yellow bandanna tied at his hatband had a few words with the scouts and then rode up to the Cats.

"You want to see the Wagonmaster, huh? You got anything that's worth Mr. Lawson's time?"

"I think Mr. Lawson would like to be able to make that decision, friend," Valentine said.

"Ain't your friend, half-breed. Would like to be your friend though, miss."

Duvalier reached up to shake his hand. "Mister, we've come a long way. Could we please see the Wagonmaster?"

"I'll ride in and ask. Best I can do."

"How about you bring us with you. Saves a little time."

The man pursed his sun-dried lips. Either he had trouble thinking on his own or he had a very strict set of orders to follow.

"The Wagonmaster is a busy man. Where do you come out of?"

"The KZ, to the south," Duvalier said. "But I've ridden with the Eagle's Wings."

That seemed to make the decision easier for the rider. "Be back soon," he said, putting his horse into a trot toward the wagons.

Night blanketed the grassy hills. The Bar Seven cooks rang the supper bell as Valentine and Duvalier finally caught up to the loose ring of wagons. After a boring wait among the cows, the yellow-marked foreman rode back out with news that Wagonmaster Lawson would see them.

Lawson was a broad-shouldered individual with a heavy scar over his forehead, giving him a scraggly eyebrow that looked permanently raised in surprise. He used the back gate of a large wagon as a combination desk and supper table, and was tearing into a blackened piece of beef when they were introduced to him.

"Boy, you might want to take off that vest in here. One of my men might take a shot at you, just out of habit."

Valentine removed the vest, feeling strangely naked without its weight.

"I hear you two rode with the Eagles?"

"Just me," Duvalier said. "Actually, I'd like to get back to them in a hurry. We think the Kur are planning a major raid into you out of North Platte. A real clean sweep."

"Uh-huh," Lawson said. "What makes you say that?"

"A sizable force offloaded from a train in North Platte. Everything from Reapers to Grogs, armed for bear. Even the Reapers will be carrying guns."

"Haw, that's a good one. Skulls with guns! Since when?"

"We both saw it. They're fighting with new tactics. They're scouting the area, and they're going to strike soon. Haven't you seen that little scout plane?"

Lawson looked suddenly uncomfortable. "Ee-yup. As a matter of fact, it circled here a couple times. You think they might be aiming to hit us? Bar Seven, I mean?"

"That we don't know," Valentine said. "We're just trying to warn you."

Lawson scratched his growth of beard. Judging from the whiskers, he shaved only once a week, and according to Valentine's sensitive nose, bathed even less often.

"We really need to get to the Eagle's Wings," Duvalier said, almost pleading. "It's a lot to ask, but if you could loan us a couple of horses . . . We don't have much to barter with. A few cigars, a little tea."

The Wagonmaster stared at them through narrowed eyes and sucked in his cheeks. "Nice-looking lady like you always has something to barter."

Valentine watched cords pop out on Duvalier's neck. She glared at the Wagonmaster.

He lost the staring contest and shrugged. "But charity's always been my middle name. Okay, looks like I might be out two horses. How's this: if what you say is true, as far as I'm concerned the information is worth two good horses. If you're wrong, I'll be relieved but expecting either their return or payment. Tell Mr. Hendricks that a couple calfs out of one of those big reds he breeds would be adequate. Sound like a deal?"

Valentine looked at Duvalier. "Deal," they said in unison.

"I'll even throw in saddle blankets. Sorry I can't do any better, good tack is hard to come by. We ain't short of leather by a long shot, but good saddle makers are rare."

"Do you have any idea where we can find the Eagles?" Valentine asked.

"You aren't leaving now? It's getting dark in an hour or so."

"Afraid so, sir," Valentine said.

"Hope you know what you're doing. Hard riding in the dark is a good way to lose a horse. The Eagles are about forty miles northwest of here. It's calving time, so they're in a good anchorage, with water and wood under one of the big ridges."

"And where's that?" Valentine asked.

"Go dead northwest until you come to a big ridge, runs the whole skyline, a good ten or fifteen miles long it is. If you hit a little stream, turn left; if not, turn right. They're at the head of that little stream. You should see the cattle a long way off—Eagle's got thousands."

"Thank you, sir," Duvalier said.

"Good luck to you, Mr. Lawson," Valentine added.

Lawson began barking out orders, and his men hurried to comply.

"Nice diplomacy, Smoke," Valentine said as they left the wagon with one of Lawson's riders. "Never would have guessed you had it in you."

She squeezed his hand. "You'd be surprised at what I've done with my mouth, if it gets me where I need to go."

They rode out at nightfall, heading northwest. Valentine's stomach sometimes got ahead of his brain, and his insides were doing flip-flops from fatigue. And he had a new worry. When they dismounted from the improvised, blanket-and-rope saddles to walk the horses for a while, Valentine's concerns finally made it to his voice box. "I don't get it, Ali. How does he know so exactly where the Eagle's Wing camp is? They camp in different spots every year, don't they? You said Bar Seven and the Eagles aren't even friendly."

She stopped for a second, then shook her head.

"Valentine, their horsemen range pretty far. Hunting, rounding up strays. Sometimes looking for other Trekkers' strays, if I know the Bar Seven. He gave us the horses, didn't he? If he were in cahoots with the Twisted Cross, which is what you're suggesting, why not just hand us over to them, dead or alive? They had a good twenty guns hanging around those wagons, and their men know how to use them. We wouldn't have had a chance. Stop being paranoid. The Bar Seven are on the shady side of the line, sure, but I've never heard of one group of Trekkers betraying another. Every other Trekker brand would come down on them from every direction but up, and they'd try that if their horses could jump high enough. It'd mean the death of—"

"Enough. You win. You get hold of a man's ear so he has to chew it off to end the arguments."

The hard miles crossing the Dunes left Valentine's brain swimming. He finally convinced himself that the disquieting feeling he had from the Bar Seven came from lack of sleep.

They cold-camped for a couple of hours, deciding rest was more important than hot food. Duvalier kept his spirits up by promising him a sizzling steak on their finding the Eagle camp. While the horses cropped grass, they shared a soda-cracker-and-cheese meal that brought them back to their first journey together.

At noon the next day, they caught sight of their destination. Lawson was not kidding about the ridge. The grassy monster loomed like a tidal wave over little lines and clusters of trees at its base, following the eastward-flowing stream he described. Herds of cattle were scattered on the floor of the valley and the steep slopes of the dune.

Valentine traced the base of the hillside with his binoculars. At last he spotted it, an irregular triangle of wagons parked on a hummock at the base of the hill. The base of the triangle spread out as a concave arc, and the peak trailing up the hillside. On top of the ridge, like the mast of a ship, an observation post stood on a single trunk of timber. He whistled in appreciation.

"You don't know the half of it, Val," Duvalier said. "They've got other herds we can't even see. Counting all the families, there're over sixteen hundred people in this traveling circus. There's about a five cows to every person."

"What about that steak," Valentine said, training his binoculars across the red and red-white herds.

"Coming right up, sir," she said, touching her heels to the horse's sides lightly. Their horses broke into a trot, catching the smell of their kind coming from the three-sided enclosure.

On closer inspection, the wagon laager was even more impressive. Hundreds of wagons made a wall centered on the little spring in the hummock.

"They have three kinds of wagons," Duvalier explained as they cut through the herds. A bull or two stared at them, but most of the cows took no notice. Valentine noticed a lot of calves—a few still knock-kneed newborns—dutifully trailing behind their mothers. "Most of them live in little house-wagons, which they told me are based on Gypsy wagons, whatever Gypsies are. No, I don't want any history lessons, Val. Those are drawn by horses. Then there are the supply-wagons; those are the ones with the big rear wheels and the small front ones. They take oxen because of the heavy load, sometimes as many as sixteen. Most of what you see on the walls are those or the long battle-wagons. The battle-wagons are drawn by draft horse teams, and when they stop anywhere for longer than a day or so, they fortify. The battle-wagons have sheets of metal that they put on the outer face, joined kind of like double-paned windows, with rifle loopholes. They fill the space between the aluminum sheets with sand. The kids even help with this. They have little shovels and buckets they carry. In the space of an afternoon, they can build a pretty substantial wall by hooking the wagons together, and within a couple of days, they have trenches dug and the walls filled in."

As they grew closer, Valentine saw the battle-wagon scheme in practice. The triangular fort even had little mini-forts at the corners, clusters of four wagons projecting out like towers at a castle's corner, covering the main gate.

"Keeping the fires going, that's the teenagers' job," she continued. "Whenever I tell this story to people with kids, they laugh. The Trekkers don't cut down trees for firewood unless it's an emergency—they use deadfalls and trim branches, sure, but when the wagons first used to roam, they'd cut down too many trees and screw up the whole area for everybody. So they conserve wood. They use the cowshit. They mix it with grasses and twigs and leaves and press it into dried bricks. It makes a good fire, practically smokeless. Gathering the droppings and turning them into fuel is how you spend your youth from twelve years old to sixteen, or whenever they allow that you're ready to get your own horse and gun.

"Wherever they stop in a camp, they plant, potatoes, tomatoes, and peas mostly. They mark the crops with stakes before they move on if they can't harvest themselves. It's called 'leaving something for the future.'

"The Eagles have some allied brands, groups of families that have split off to form their own brands. It happens every generation or so. These wagon trains can only get so big before they become impossible to feed and water without permanent digs."

Valentine noticed that no outriders came up to ask them their business; the men watching over the cows just looked at them from under the brims of their felt hats. Presumably some sentry in the observation tower signaled strangers coming in long ago.

The wide gap in the wagon wall that served as the gate was also the outflow of the spring that watered the camp. It splashed down a rocky watercourse to meander into the trees to the east. They dismounted and led their horses up the final slope to the camp. Valentine expected it to reek of burning dung after Duvalier's travelogue, but he smelled only people, cooking food, and cattle. He eyed the layout of the camp, the trench and fortifications, with admiration.

A lanky man with a thin beard and a dusty top hat waved and came out to greet them. He recognized Duvalier with a smile.

"Glory be!" he said, stamping his foot and tossing his head like a horse. "If it isn't Little Red outta Kansas. It's been nigh on three years, sister."

"Hi, Deacon. I see you're still in the baptizing business. I've brought in another stranger from the south. This is David Stuart, out of Minnesota originally. We've traveled hard and ask your hospitality."

"The Eagle's Wings grant it to both you and the brother. With pleasure, Little Red, with pleasure."

"We're also going to need to speak to you, the Wagon-master, and anyone else concerned with the Common Defense."

"This has anything to do with that plane that's been passing overhead?"

"Yes, Deacon."

"I knew that machine was a bad omen, soon as I saw it. We'll talk later, woman. Why you're thin as a rake! Let's get you into camp and get some food into you. Boy, come here!" he hollered at a scrawny kid gaping at the new arrivals. He spoke a few urgent words to the youth and sent him running into the camp.

They passed through the wagon barricade. An inner ring of wagons, a mix of the house-wagons and larger supply-wagons, formed a second wall within the first. A corral held a reserve of horses with saddles draped on the trek-tow fence. Valentine guessed the camp could mount a hundred men in a matter of minutes. Another wide loop of wagon wall sheltered a mass of oxen downwind, and more could be seen just outside the walls, grazing. "Animal husbandry must be second nature to you," Valentine remarked.

"We live and die by the stock," the deacon agreed.

They made their way past women washing clothing in the stream, lines of laundry drying on ropes stretched between the house-wagons cracked in the fresh breeze. At the center of the second circle of wagons, another pole-mounted crow's nest held a sentry, and above him a flag with the symbol that looked like a thunderbird—or perhaps a set of United States Air Force wings.

A train of dogs and curious children followed the deacon and the Cats as they walked their horses into the center of camp. The children were dressed in the final tatters of hand-me-downs, but they looked healthy and energetic.

"The widow knows you're coming in," Deacon said. "Since a fever took Mr. Hendricks, rest his soul, last April she's been running things. They had a son and a daughter, if you remember, Red, and Josh and Jocelyn have both grown into fine people. Good woman. Those were some big shoes to fill, but no one's missed the old Wagonmaster except in their hearts."

Mrs. Hendricks did not look like a Wagonmaster to Valentine; she looked like your favorite aunt who always bakes a thick cherry pie with a perfect lattice crust. She wore a simple dress with an apron containing everything from pen and notepad to scissors. Her sun-streaked hair was tied back into a bun, and she had meaty, work-reddened arms, well-padded hips, and cherubic cheeks. The only thing hard about her was her eyes.

Seeing the deacon and the visitors, she waved over some young women with platters from the cooking pits. A long table with a blue-and-white checkerboard tablecloth was filled with still-sputtering food, joining tall pitchers of water and prairie-herb tea.

"You poor tired things. We're in the middle of calving festival, so I want you to try this rib roast and tell me what you think. Doris, what's keeping those peas?" She turned back to her guests. "Now, clean up in the bucket over there, don't spare the soap, and tell me what brings you in. Red Alice, I remember you from a few years back, but this young man is new, isn't he? Have you taken a husband?"

"Some days it seems like it," Duvalier said, freckled skin going a trifle redder. "Other days it's like I've had a son. Questions all the time."

After washing his hands, Valentine swung a leg over the bench when the woman motioned them to sit. He reached for his knife and fork, mouth overflowing with saliva, when Duvalier grabbed his hands and thrust them in his lap. The deacon had just bowed his head at the end of the table.

"Heavenly Father, for what we are about to receive may we be made truly grateful." He raised his head. "Lord, that looks good. Let's eat."

Valentine could not have agreed with him more.

With supper cleared away, the dinner table became a council of war. The hot meal had left Valentine sated and sleepy. Through some internal resource, Duvalier was as bright as ever. Valentine struggled to imitate her.

"Red Alice" summed up the threat in a few concise sentences, giving her experiences with the Twisted Cross in Oklahoma, and their supposition that the Dunes were on the list to be cleared out.

The Hendricks woman listened impassively, shaking her head in sadness when Duvalier described the dead Caltagirone and his Wolves and the massacre in Colorado. Her son, Josh, and her daughter, Jocelyn, joined them at the table, mostly listening. Waldron, the Camp Engineer, who looked as though he had a bit of longhorn in him, asked sensible questions. The leader of the outriders, an almost baby-faced young man named Danvers, who proudly claimed he was eight years old on the ground and eighteen years old in the saddle, wanted to know details about the Twisted Cross weaponry.

Around the tables, many other members of the Eagle's Wings Brand stood, squatted, and sat, all listening. The Wagonmaster was not one to hide her doings and decisions behind closed doors. The others kept a respectful silence, allowing the words to carry, and the few who asked questions held up their hands and waited to be called on like disciplined schoolchildren.

"I wish we had a better idea about what you're facing," Valentine said in answer to a question from Danvers.

"We only ever worried about artillery," Waldron said. "So far, every time those Troopers have brought it into the Dunes, they've lost it. We even have a couple of their pieces in camp, but the mortars are the only ones that still have something to shoot out of them. Air power or armor would whip us, but if any of that's still being made, it's not finding its way to Nebraska."

Valentine nodded. Duvalier had briefed him on how the cavalry harassed invading columns, assembling and striking at them like sparrows pecking at a hawk, and dispersing again to leave the Troopers capturing nothing but hoof-prints and air.

"Fact is, those creatures can't cooperate for shit, or they'd of took us long ago," Josh Hendricks said. The boy's clothes didn't fit; his adolescent body was lunging out in all directions.

"Language, Josh," his mother warned. "I should say English, too. I didn't teach you to talk like that."

"Sorry. But one time that bast—that bad' un in Scotts-bluff came at us with everything he had, trying to take the whole land up to the Niobrara. He was doing pretty well until his cousin in Cheyenne hit him from behind. I hear he lost half his territory. Been all he can do to hold on to the rest ever since. I can't see a bunch of them ganging up on us. Not like 'em."

As darkness fell, a bonfire and music started, almost at the same time, from the south end of camp by the gate-stream.

"It's still calving festival," Mrs. Hendricks said. "I hope you young folk will join in the fun after your hard ride."

"Just some sleep would do nicely, ma'am," Valentine said.

"We won't keep you, then. We're going to talk over what you told us and decide what to do. Don't let the music fool you. We're taking this very seriously. We'll have extra riders out tonight and people on the walls. Please feel free to stay here as long as you want—we'll handle the Paul Revere job from here on out. Jocelyn, show our guests to the visitors' cabin."

A saddle-muscled young woman stood up. Jocelyn Hendricks wore a man's moleskin hand-me-downs brightened by a red neckerchief wrapped around her thick brown hair. She stepped around behind the Cats.

"Thank you for the dinner, Mrs. Hendricks," Valentine said, swallowing the last of his milk.

"Yes, it was wonderful. Thanks for the bed, too. It's going to be very welcome," Duvalier added.

They zigzagged through the maze of wagons, tentage, washing lines, and campfires.

Jocelyn paused at the little ladder and door of one of the house-wagons, set apart from the rest. "People are going to be asking me what our chances are. What should I tell them? They'll be worried about their children."

Valentine looked at Duvalier, who shrugged.

"I can't tell you what to say, Miss Hendricks," Valentine said. "If there's somewhere safe they can put their kids, I'd recommend that they do that right away. Reapers move fast at night when they want to. They could be here tonight."

"We'll be here with you, at least tonight," Duvalier added. "I believe that if anyone in the Dunes can beat them, it's your brand."

Jocelyn showed them the cozy little cabin, with its bunk beds, tiny cabinets, and built-in basin. "There's water in the pitcher," she explained. "Clean bedding on the mattresses, real horsehair stuffed, and a thunderbucket in the corner in case you don't feel like a trip to the pits. I'll check on your horses and tack before I turn in; they're in the north corral.

"There will be dancing until midnight or so. You sure you aren't up to it? A lot of the folks would be interested in meeting people from elsewhere."

"We just spent two days traveling hard," Valentine said. "I'm sure you understand."

Duvalier added, "Another time."

"Maybe tomorrow night, then," Jocelyn said, smiling as she closed the door.

Duvalier placed her sword where she could reach it easily. "If there is a tomorrow night, Val."

No call to arms, no attack from the darkness disturbed their dreamless slumber. It seemed only a matter of minutes before Valentine heard a gentle tap on the door and opened his eyes to light pouring through the window.

The door opened, and Mrs. Hendricks entered, bearing a tray. "Good morning!" she half sang, half whispered. "Anyone up? I've brought you a little something to get your eyes open."

Valentine realized he had collapsed in his clothes, and guiltily looked at the mess he'd made of the sheets. Duvalier had stripped down to her shirt, and she swung her legs from the bottom bunk with a groan.

"I thought I might kill two birds with one stone. So I brought some sausages and wheat bread and a cup of tea for each of you. Nothing happened over the night. The meeting went until late, and we decided to scatter some of the herds and families. We sent out riders to warn the other brands and asked them to send what men and guns they could this way. We're going to have to unite to stand any chance at all, from what you've told us."

"How soon will they be arriving?" Valentine asked.

"Days. The Dunes are big, and in the summer the smaller brands get to the most remote places they can. If the Troopers raid into us, it's usually between May and September."

Valentine removed the fly-cloth from his breakfast and began eating. Duvalier nursed her tea, content to listen and look out the window.

"How can we help?"

"You've done enough, by my reckoning. But if you want to, go around, speak to the men, maybe tell them a little more about those Reapers. We don't have much experience against them, and what we do know has us all frightened."

Duvalier nodded. "We'll do what we can." After the Wagonmaster left, she looked at Valentine. "I'm frightened, too."

"Never thought I'd hear that from you."

She went to the basin and wrung out a washcloth, wiped it across her face. "Hear me admit it, you mean."

Valentine shrugged.

"We've warned them, Val. Let's head out."

"I'm staying. You've got more experience at this. You'll be better without me."

"Staying? Staying like in desertion?"

"Staying like in helping them fight. We've been over this before."

She lowered her voice in case anyone was outside the wagon, listening. "I figured once you saw them, you'd either figure there were enough guns for the fight so that you being here wouldn't make a difference, one way or the other. Or you'd see it was a lost cause."

Valentine stood for a moment. He feared the coming fight but wanted it, as well. *Do I have a death wish?*

"I'll quit trying. You're a lost cause, Valentine. No wonder your captain had you court-martialed."

She must have seen the hurt in his eyes, because her tone softened: "Sorry. You—well, you deserved that, but I shouldn't have said it. I'm going to scrounge up some supplies. Think about it before I ride out."

Valentine spent the day with Waldron, the Camp Engineer, trying to forget about Duvalier by inspecting the defenses.

The Eagles had a trench around the camp, hurriedly being made as wide and deep as the sandy soil would allow. Shovelfuls of thrown dirt rained dust and pebbles that made skittering noises as they bounced off the metal panels of the walls. Some of the corrugated sheets that served as armor on the outside of the battle-wagons still had sections of vaguely familiar logos from the Old World.

"We took a lot of these facings from old rigs. Big engines called semis used to haul these trailer affairs. The metal is light and strong."

Valentine ran his hand along the dirty old surface, printed in huge letters, ADWAY. Farther down, the red Coca-Cola label protected one of flanking corners. Strange that one of the most persistent holdovers of the Old World was its product marketing; like the advertisements for gladiatorial contests that he'd read could still be seen on a wall or two in Rome.

"Been a long time since we've had to shoot from the walls of the camp. Last time it was because we got surprised," Waldron said as they walked the perimeter. "A few years back, the Troopers reinforced a bunch of their trucks and loaded them with men. Came barreling at us across the plain; I think the idea was to ram through the walls. Sure, tin and sand stop bullets, but not a truck moving at forty miles an hour or more. They either didn't know much about physics or they forgot about the trench; they hit it and killed most everyone in the trucks. We hardly had to fire a shot."

He lifted up his shoe, and Valentine smiled at the serrated pattern of a truck radial. "Got a darn long-lasting pair of shoes out of it, and a good laugh."

"You said you had some artillery?"

"Ha! A pair of mortars and less than thirty shells. Eighty-one millimeter. Let me show you what we have come up with, though."

They cut through a hidden angle in the battle-wagons, and climbed up into the bed. A shiny cylinder that Valentine recognized as an old artillery shell casing, probably a 155-millimeter, sat in a metal trough secured by a heavy steel cover. A fuse, curled like a pig's tail, dangled behind. The whole affair stood on a tripod welded to an old metal wheel.

"This is kind of based on a swivel gun. You can point it using the mount, but your aim doesn't have to be very precise with this cracker. It's an artillery shell casing sitting in the half-cut pipe there. We loaded it up with powder and put a bag of taconite pellets on top of the wad. No range to it whatsoever. But it'll sweep twenty yards in front of the gun like you were using a broom, and more beyond if you get lucky. We've got a version that goes on the ground too, in a wooden holder. Strictly one-shot, takes us a good while to clean and reload it if the casing doesn't crack." Valentine thought it looked like as much of a threat to the men behind the weapon as the enemy in front, but he kept silent.

"We also have some grenades we took off the Troopers, but not enough, and coal-oil bombs—which are really just sawdust and the oil mixed in an old vodka bottle. And that's our artillery."

After lunch he met with Duvalier. She had spent the morning after her scrounge riding with Danvers, going from point to point looking for signs of the Twisted Cross.

Eagle Brand families took a portion of the cattle and dispersed to hiding places among the dunes. "They're great trackers and the best horse-riding guerrilla fighters since the Apache—plenty of rifles but not enough support and artillery," she said.

Valentine was happy to find her equitable—or just resigned to him staying. "Same thing in camp. The Reapers will tear this place apart from a couple hundred yards, and there won't be much they can do about it. All the guts in the world aren't much of a help against Kalashnikovs in the hands of something that isn't disturbed by catching a bullet."

The little red-and-white plane appeared just then high in the sky, hardly audible even to Valentine's ears. He felt a chill as it threw a wide circle around the camp before moving off eastward. It was like the ravens of the Middle Ages, who would gather along with the armies in anticipation of the coming carnage.

"Rider coming in," the sentry mounted in the crow's nest at the central cluster of wagons called. Valentine saw Josh Hendricks go toward the gate with the deacon. Valentine and Duvalier looked at each other, shrugged, and joined the cluster of people, wondering what new calamity the rider portended.

It was a boy on a lathered horse. Valentine guessed him to be somewhere between fourteen and sixteen. He was dressed like a Comanche, in a leather loincloth and vest, and had a blanket-saddle on his black horse. His mount dribbled, foamed, and glistened with sweat.

"Boy's out of the Q or Twin Triangles Brands, is my guess," an older man by Valentine predicted. "Don't look like good news either."

The kid rolled off his horse, half-fall and half-dismount. Josh Hendricks poured him some water out of a canteen.

"Triangles' camp's been burned," the boy said flatly, once he had caught his breath. "Last night. We were camped between the Middle Loup and the Middle Branch. I was outrider to the north, and I heard shooting. All a-sudden the wagons was going up in flames. Then up came the Grierson family. Mr. Grierson was shot and looked real pale; his sons were carrying him. Mrs. Grierson told me to ride and warn you. She said they weren't no Troopers, they came with guns and explosives, and the bullets didn't seem to touch 'em. I asked about my pa and ma, and she didn't know, she said she was sorry," he said, his voice cracking before he realized he'd voiced his thoughts.

"Damn," the older man next to Valentine said. "That isn't far at all. Just east of here maybe four hours' ride—and not a hard ride, neither."

"Big difference here, though," Valentine said. "We know they're coming."

The elder man spat. "We know the sun's going to set in about five hours, son, but there ain't a thing we can do about it."

The deacon handed the boy the reins to his horse. "See to your horse, son."

Then he turned on the gloomy man next to Valentine. "Have a little faith, Brother Tom," the deacon said. "The Lord's seen fit to bless us with warning and some help. He'll be with us tonight."

Tom's words troubled Valentine as the sun lowered toward the horizon, as slow and deadly and inevitable as Poe's pendulum. He learned more about the Twin Triangles: though not numerous, they were as good a group of riders and shooters as existed in the Dunes.

The Eagles had more fighters, but would that just mean more bodies to be buried? With the teens and older men armed, the Eagles could horse a force of five hundred men. But nearly a hundred of these were with some of the women and children and livestock who had scattered into hiding after the decision by the Common Defense Committee last night. Dozens more were riding across the Dunes now, as messengers to the other brands. The foundation of the brand, their wealth and their sustenance, was the cattle, and the animals had to be moved and protected. This deducted another hundred and fifty riders. That left a force of a little over two hundred women and men able to stand in the wagons, backed up by teens old enough to shoot for the camp.

One of the scouts sent back word during supper that a convoy of vehicles had been spotted west on the old Highway 2. The Trooper-marked column wasn't making good time—weather and actions of the Trekkers had reduced the road to little more than a bad path—but they were clearly heading for the Eagle camp. The Twisted Cross were intent on smashing the largest brand in the Dunes, probably sometime after nightfall.

A few voices suggested that they pull up stakes and move at dusk, leaving nothing but empty space for them to attack, but Hendricks vetoed the idea with the weight of the Common Defense behind her. Valentine explained that with the Reaper's ability to read lifesign, the mass of moving wagons would shine like a lighthouse across a calm sea, and they would be able to cover whatever miles the wagons put between them and the camp that same night. They were better off fighting it out from behind trench and wall.

As the sun set, a mist began to steal across the valley beneath the great rolling hill.

"That's strange for this time of year, especially in the evening," Mrs. Hendricks said, watching the veil thicken around the camp.

"It's the Kurians. They can shape the clouds when they have a mind," Duvalier said. She'd lingered through the day, saying she wanted to rest her legs and her horse. "Val, I'll ride now. You still staying?"

Her tone was nonchalant, but he read concern in her eyes. "Yes."

There wasn't a fight this time.

The pair went to their packs in the guest wagon. Duvalier stripped down to a utility vest, perhaps some old angler's jacket or photographer's rig at some time, now dyed. She now loaded it with everything from her claws to screw-topped pipes filled with chemicals designed to burn or blow up. She began to apply black greasepaint across her face and arms as Valentine sharpened her sword. The straight, angle-pointed blade had a dull coating everywhere save the very edge, where it glinted with cold reflections.

"I'm going to be outside the camp before the sun goes down," she said. "I plan to stick to them like a tick. You live through this, you can catch up to me south of Omaha, where I got that pheasant. Remember? Just head east till you hit the Missouri."

"I'm not leaving these people until things are decided one way or the other," Valentine said.

"Neither am I. This column means there's a headquarters for it. I'm going to find those Troopers and see what I can see. Could you help me with this greasepaint?"

Valentine coated her shoulders and the back of her arms with the ebony grease, leaving the occasional strip of sun-darkened flesh exposed to break up the human pattern. She looked like a black-and-tan tiger. Her torso finished, Duvalier slipped into baggy black pants with enormous cargo pockets on the thighs and her trusty old hiking boots. She tucked her red hair under a dark, insignia-less kepi. It was the standard-issue hat of Southern Command dyed black.

"Technically I'm in uniform, not that it makes a difference if they catch me. If I learn anything useful, I'll try to leave you a message somewhere outside the Twisted Cross camp. Look for a pile of four of anything sticking up, rocks, sticks, whatever. I'll leave a note under it."

"Be careful."

"You, too. Don't get your head blown off, Ghost."

"Don't get caught lighting any fires, Smoke."

She took a step toward him, and evidently thought better of it—instead she opened the door. She touched the side of her hand to her eyebrow and then dragged her index finger down her grease-painted nose, and left.

Fog and night closed in on the camp; the lantern lights glowed like amber gems, each surrounded by a tiny halo. Valentine stepped out of the guest house-wagon. He wore his old Wolf buckskins instead of his traveling coat, now like Duvalier's night gear darkened to a chocolate color. The heavy vest weighted his shoulders. His parang and revolver still hung from the sweat-darkened leather-and-canvas equipment belt he could not bring himself to let go. But now it had additional gear added: the old curved sword hung across his back, and the two spare drums for the submachine gun were clipped above each buttock where once canteens had ridden. His fighting claws, worn more for luck than because he expected to use them, hung around his neck from a break-away leather shoelace like Eveready's old necklace of Reaper teeth.

Even with the seventy-one-round drum in it, the submachine gun had a nice balance. He sat down on the tiny steps to the wagon, broke down the gun, cleaned and oiled it, and put it back together again. He flicked the little switch in front of the trigger from full automatic to semi-auto, and back again, listening to the inner workings of the gun. He put the drum back on and chambered the first round.

He looked at the stock, and looked again, before he recognized what he saw. Someone had marred Tank Bourne's carefully stained and lacquered finish and carved a little heart in the stock, no bigger than the nail on his pinkie. A valentine? It must have been Ali, in one of her sentimental fits. He wondered if she kissed it after she had etched the icon. Of course he knew many soldiers with strange little rituals they practice to bring fortune. One of his Wolves used to chew a terrible gum made of pine sap before action, as though as long as his jaws worked, he knew he was still alive.

Valentine tried to relax, but his body refused to cooperate. He rose, deciding to walk the perimeter as darkness fell.

The inner ring of wagons had been drawn into a tighter circle, trek tows lashed under the wagon in front of it, with the little house-wagons parked in the gaps. The remaining women and children were huddled in a quiet mass around the main campfire. Jocelyn Hendricks read by firelight from some children's books, reciting the well-known tales of Pooh and Piglet. Piglet was voicing his worry over meeting something called a Heffalump when she looked up and met Valentine's eyes.

"Rin, read the rest of this, would you?" she asked a boy, handing him the book before getting an answer. She stepped lightly between the children in her pointed-toe boots and joined Valentine.

"These are the kids whose parents won't let them go. They figure if anything's going to happen, they want it to happen to everyone. Is it as bad as that?"

Somewhere on the walls a sentry started up a tune with a Native American flute. He or she was skilled; it sounded like two instruments accompanying each other. The woven notes soothed.

"Are the kids okay?"

She shrugged. "The little ones just know something is wrong. The older ones are so busy pretending to be brave, they don't ask questions, but I can tell they're listening. Not to my story or the music—they're trying to listen for the sounds outside the camp."

"And you're pretending to be brave reading, and I'm pretending to be brave walking around with a gun."

"It's not pretending. At least not with you."

Valentine looked down at the young woman, scarecrow-lean in her hand-me-downs. Duvalier was the bravest person he'd ever met, and she voiced her fears. Why couldn't he admit to them, as well?

"I'm scared all the time. Scared of dying, scared of doing something stupid that causes others to die. Scared that no matter what I do—" Valentine stopped, not wanting sink into nervous garrulity. Especially not in front of this young woman he had just met.

"No matter what you do? What's that mean?"

"Not making a difference."

A quick, embarrassed flush came over her, and she rose to the points of her boots and brushed her lips against his cheek. "I feel safer with you here. With our wagons. So that's a difference, isn't it?" Then she fled the kiss's rebuff, or return, to the circle of children.

*   *   *

Outside the central ring, he met Waldron, setting up the last of his one-shot cannons to cover the outlet for the spring. More battle-wagons, ready to roll, had been placed to block the gate. "The lookout up on top of the ridge says the fog isn't thick at all, doesn't even come up to the hilltop. Says he thought he saw movement on Stake Ridge. Where's your lady?"

"Out there," Valentine said, gesturing with the ugly muzzle on the gun.

Waldron whistled in appreciation. "No kidding? You wouldn't get me out there on a night like tonight, not with them Reapers on the prowl. They can see through fog, right?"

"Fog, night, rain—it's all the same to them. They can read off of something else."

"Body heat, like old infrared equipment?"

Valentine shook his head. "No, but it's generated by our bodies. Some kind of energy. It's what they, or rather their Masters, feed off of. Your cattle create it, too. . . ."

"Rider coming in," someone called from the wall. The observation tower was useless in the fog.

Mrs. Hendricks hopped down from the wall, where she had been talking to some of the men on guard, showing fair athleticism for a woman her age. The deacon stepped forward, putting on his tall formal hat, but she moved in front of him.

Valentine half expected one of Tolkien's nazgul-shapes to appear out of the misty darkness drifting thick around the camp, but it was only a tired-looking rider.

"Don't shoot, now," the man said, riding forward with his reins in one hand and his other in the air. "I'm Deak Thomas, with the Bar Seven, speaking for Wagonmaster Lawson. Where's Wagonmaster Hendricks?"

"Dead, son. I'm his wife, I'm filling in. Say your piece."

"He heard you were gathering outriders, and he's come himself with ninety-five, horsed and equipped. We came as fast as we could, so we need provisions."

"Glory be!" the deacon muttered, raising his eyes to the fog-shrouded heavens.

"Tell him he's welcome. Tell him he'll get his payment for helping those messengers along, and a lot more besides. Tell him I'm grateful for his help, and I'm glad to see that the bad blood between him and my man is forgotten. Now's the time to put aside our differences if we're going to get through this."

Thomas nodded out his understanding. "He's a half hour away at most. We've had to ride carefully, before this fog set in we spotted some Troopers. They must have forgotten what happened the last time."

"With your Wagonmaster's help, we'll teach 'em another one, Mr. Thomas," Josh Hendricks said, coming up in support of his mother. Thomas walked his horse back into the fog, and they heard it break into a trot.

"That's news we can use. Close to hundred!" Josh said. "He must have emptied his camp."

Valentine felt his stomach tighten in turmoil.

All wrong. Something's all wrong about this.

"Funny . . . ," said Mrs. Hendricks out loud.

"Ma'am," Valentine said, wondering how to say this. "I don't like the sound of this. When we spoke yesterday, Mr. Lawson just didn't seem right to me. He looked nervous when I asked him about that scout plane. He was sure of your camp's location—like it'd been on his mind."

Josh Hendricks interrupted.

"Nothing unusual in that," Josh said. "Are you trying to start something, stranger? Didn't the man help you on your way? He could have just killed you or turned you over to *them* when you were in his camp."

"Quiet, now, Josh," his mother said. "Let the man speak. I've got a worry or two, and I want to see if his are the same."

Valentine lowered his voice, not wanting to have rumors spread in case he was wrong. "First, it sounds like there's some history between your brands. I don't know what it is, but bad blood can make people do crazy things. Especially if the hurt is recent. Second, is he the type of Wagonmaster to strip his wagons, leave his herd almost unguarded with enemies in the area, to come to the aid of someone else? Unless he was sure they wouldn't be touched, that is."

"That's true enough," the deacon said.

"Third, he knew a lot about your camp, where it was, the calving, but none of his men must have talked to yours or he'd know you were the new Wagonmaster. Finally, his brand was also on the line of march from the Platte, but the Triangles got wiped out and his wasn't. You'd think his whole brand would've spent the last day running for their lives."

Josh Hendricks shook his head. "Pa used to say I could think better than most, Mom. I'm thinking this is plain stupid."

"Hush now, Josh."

The boy ignored her with fifteen-year-old certainty. "No Trekker has ever rolled over for them, and I don't think even Lawson would be that low. His men would string him up. They can't all be bad apples. I'd bet my life on it."

Mrs. Hendricks looked out into the fog. "I've got to think about more lives than just my own. But we'll see. You may have to bet just that, with the help of our new friend here."

Twenty minutes later, Lawson and his outriders came into the camp through a gap in the gate battle-wagons. Two tables laden with food and drink stood near the gate on one side, opposite the little shallow with the stream running out of camp. A fire burned cheerfully in the center. The deacon stood in the light enjoying a bottle of beer and one of Valentine's cigars.

Valentine watched events from beneath a house-wagon in the second line in the center of camp. Rocks, cases, kegs, and dirt were piled up under the wagons, hiding him and two dozen men good at rapid rifle fire. A few feet in front of him Josh Hendricks stood, Valentine's revolver tucked in the back of his belt.

"Look at those guns," a man sighting down his lever action muttered to Valentine. "There ain't a man there who isn't ready to shoot. Think they suspect us?"

"No, I think they're supposed to do this in a hurry," Valentine breathed. His heart sounded loud in his chest. A fight was coming; he felt it in every raised hair.

At the sight of all the ready guns and the antsy-looking men, Josh Hendricks seemed to shrink back into his clothes as he stepped forward. Lawson stood up in his stirrups and looked around the walls, where a few of the Eagles were on guard. He scratched his heavy growth of beard with the front sight on his pistol.

"W-w-we sure are glad to see you, Wagonmaster Lawson," Josh stammered. The deacon edged closer to the boy. "We're short men on the north wall. After you eat, you think you could get your outriders to screen us from the ridge side?"

"Those your orders, boy?" Lawson said, squinting at Hendricks.

"No, my mother's. She's Wagonmaster of this camp."

"Not anymore," Lawson said, pointing his pistol like a striking rattlesnake. He shot Hendricks in the chest twice, and the youth toppled backwards, falling almost in front of Valentine.

Valentine's riflemen brought their guns up as the Bar Sevens wheeled their horses toward the walls. The men and women to either side of him fired in a long, ragged volley, followed by a second as the Eagles worked the bolts and levers on their guns. The food and drink tables upended, men appearing from underneath like shotgun-armed jack-in-the-boxes, blazing away at the surrounding horses. From the walls, men fired down into the mass of emptying saddles and screaming horses. Three Bar Seven outriders managed to get outside the gate before the battle-wagons were pushed together behind them, but explosion-flashes from the swivel guns swept them into a bloody, dying heap in the trench.

The deacon crawled through the flying lead and dancing hooves, pulling Josh. He dragged him beneath the wagons and stayed put.

It was over in less than a minute. With the gate shut, a few of the Bar Seven men flung their rifles down and dived off their horses. Some tried to crawl out out under the wagons, only to be rounded up by the men from behind the tables who advanced into the slaughter-yard to pistol the crippled horses and pick up the wounded men.

Valentine raised his gun over his head and waved it. He and the snipers emerged from beneath the wagon to join the deacon and Josh. "How is he?"

"Gasping for air, scared, and a Godly man for the rest of his days, I'll bet," the deacon said, pulling apart Josh's shirt to reveal Valentine's bulletproof vest on the coughing youth. The deacon extracted out the flattened remnants of a slug and tossed it from hand to hand like a hot chestnut. Josh Hendricks got to his feet and removed the vest, handing it to Valentine.

"I guess I owe you an apology, sir," he said, rubbing his breastbone.

Valentine looked at the deacon. "No harm letting them think the sneak attack worked—"

The deacon's eyebrows came together; then a grin split his face. "Good Lord, yes." He turned to the walls. "Fire off a shot now and then . . . like they're mopping up." A few shots cracked off into the night.

"Ghost! Ghost!" Valentine heard a female voice call from out of the mist.

Duvalier.

He ran to the front gate. His fellow Cat stood, barely visible in the mist in the light thrown by a reflector lantern.

"Can't stop for more than a moment—can you hear me?"

"I'm here," Valentine said.

She spoke quietly, but Valentine's ears picked up her words. "A Trooper and another of these Bar Seven turncoats were waiting about a couple hundred yards out."

"What did she say? Why's she so quiet?" one of the men on the wall asked.

"Anything we have to be worried about?" Valentine asked.

"No, I took care of them. One's just behind me, and the other's in the stream, if you want to get their weapons. I listened in at their camp; they're waiting for a signal. Watch your north wall, too."

"For what?"

"No idea."

"Get out of here."

"It's a good night for hunting, Ghost. You were right about the Bar Seven after all. I'm impressed. Good luck." She disappeared into the fog-weighted night.

Waldron was replacing the expended charge in the trough of the swivel gun with a new shell.

"Signal, huh?"

"Yes. I think I need to ask a few questions."

The deacon was finishing his cigar as a woman in a white calving smock tied a tourniquet around the leg of Wagonmaster Lawson. Lawson looked around at his shattered outriders, tears of pain or anguish streaming down his cheeks.

"Shot up bad," the deacon muttered.

"They made all kinds of promises," he confessed to the deacon as Valentine approached. "I thought I'd become the biggest cattle king in the history of Nebraska, able to run the Dunes as long as I didn't cause them trouble. But as soon as they got into camp, they started showing who was boss. That damn General guy, ordering us around, treating my men like dirt. But what could I do? All the women and kids are in their hands now."

Valentine approached the pair. The medic looked up at him and gave a tiny negative shake of her head. The ground beneath Lawson was black with blood.

"Damn, that tobacco smells good, Deac," Lawson said weakly. "I haven't had a real smoke in months."

"Give him one, Deacon," Valentine said.

"Thanks," Lawson said, through a grimace of pain. He took a deep puff on the cigar and closed his eyes. For a moment Valentine thought he would die; then they opened again. "Hey, you're the one with the horses, trying to warn people. They asked me some questions about you two. I gave them a wagonload of bullshit."

Valentine whispered something into the deacon's ear. He nodded.

"Lawson, here, hold my Bible. The Good Book's about the only comfort I got for you. You don't have much more time in this here world, so maybe you want to think about the next. You can help us, tell us what you were supposed to do once you took the camp."

Lawson's breathing became labored. "Sure. In my pocket. Flare pistol. Fire when we . . . got the camp."

Valentine found the wide-mouthed pistol, listening to the occasional shot or two still ringing out.

"My men . . . have pity . . . wounded . . . ain't . . ." He faded away.

The deacon checked his pulse. "Not dead yet, but soon," he decided. "God have mercy on you, Wagonmaster," he said, taking his Bible back from the relaxing fingers and mumbling a prayer.

Lawson gave a faint gurgle, and Valentine waited for the deacon to finish. When the deacon's hat was back on, Valentine picked up Lawson's pistol and handed it to Josh. "Souvenir for you, Josh." Valentine turned back to the preacher.

"Deacon, get me Waldron."

Mrs. Hendricks looked out over the slaughtered men and horses, shaking her head and patting down her hair, as the bodies began to be dragged away and lined up. Valentine didn't need his Wolf's nose to tell she smelled like gunsmoke.

"Wagonmaster," Valentine said. "This may work to our advantage. They were supposed to send up a flare when they seized the camp. If we send it up, the General's men might come in. I expect they'll be careful about it, but they'll still get close enough to have a look. I think if we can hit them then with some of Waldron's one-shot wonders, we can shorten the odds."

Waldron joined Valentine and the deacon. The four hashed out a plan, and then gave it to the leaders to pass among the Eagles. They would fire the flare, and the gates would be opened. When the Twisted Cross, or the Troopers, or whatever walked or rode in, they would fire every one of Waldron's cannons on command. Valentine described the main targets: "Tall humans, probably in body armor or at least heavy robes. They'll also have some serious hardware, battle rifles with curved magazines. Don't waste your cannon on the Troopers if they come in— just try to get the Reapers."

Mrs. Hendricks fired the flare herself, which arced up into the mist and bathed the camp in its red light, glowing as it descended from the heavens like the Star Wormwood.

"Remember, cheer as they approach the gate," Valentine said to the men, some standing and some hiding in the battle-wagons flanking the gate. Every cannon Waldron could load was clustered around the gate, and the wooden mine versions were hidden behind dead horses and in front of the wagon wall. They would explode in a hail of splinters and scrap metal. Valentine crouched in the cold waters of the spring, waiting.

He heard an engine approach, filling the night with the rattling, wheezy sound of a big diesel.

"What the hell?" one of the men on the wall said, peering into the mist.

"Cheer, yell your heads off!" Valentine called up at them.

"Would you look at that Goliath," the deacon said, crouching behind a dead horse. His cigar tip glowed above the cannon fuse.

"Let it in, let it in," Valentine called over the increasing noise of the engine. "The troops are coming in behind it." He half closed his eyes.

Quiet.

Centered.

Valentine pictured his consciousness as a large blue ball filling the horizon, and breathing deeply, he shrank it and shrank it, all the while inhaling and exhaling from a point at the bottom of his rib cage. He felt his heart slow, felt the whole world slow. The people around started to look like mannequins, dummies like he'd seen turning round and round in shop windows in Chicago. With his mind faint and open, he felt the presence of Reapers. A lot of them, terribly near. And coming closer, cold will-o'-wisps of death drifting toward him out of the fog.

Valentine's first view of the Twisted Cross, coming straight at him out of the midnight fog, froze him in place. A tracked vehicle, like a bulldozer with armored plate on its arms and front instead of a blade, towed a tanker-trailer that someone had torch-cut and welded into a mobile fortress. Crew-served machine guns pointed out of each side of the trailer and the windows and doors of the tractor were covered with slitted armored plating.

Behind them, in two columns, came the Reapers of the Twisted Cross. More like insects than men, they wore carapaces of heavy body armor, topped by visor-covered helmets that hung down at the sides and back like old samurai versions. The battle-Reapers held assault weapons at the ready and bulb-headed tubes in a harness on their backs.

The Eagle men cheered, some of them almost hysterically, others tentatively. A few inched away, ready to run for cover at the first shot.

Valentine crawled and flattened himself into the depression cut by the stream of water as the battle-rig rolled overhead, its bulk straddling the little spring with ease.

C'mon, Waldron. Now!

A whistle trilled in the night, to immediate effect. The swivel guns began to go off in such quick succession that it sounded like one continuous roar; an avalanche of sound and air pressure washed over Valentine. From beneath the still-moving trailer, he saw armored figures knocked down, some never to rise again. Others seemed not to even feel the blasts, and they turned to fill the night with muzzle flashes like yellow flowers blossoming.

Valentine, deafened by swivel-gun blasts and the gunfire, crawled out from beneath the trailer.

A Reaper ran toward the back of the truck, trying to take cover from the cross fire streaming down from the battle-wagons.

He rose to his feet with his gun at his shoulder. It pulled up and stared, perhaps surprised by his sudden appearance. It brought up its gun but caught a chattering blast from Valentine's PPD through its visor and into its face.

He heard the machine guns in the armored trailer firing, stitching the side of the battle-wagons to either side. Men toppled and dived for cover.

Valentine turned. He took two steps toward the rear of the sawed-off tanker and leapt, vaulting into the air as if lifted by an invisible pole over the ten-foot moving wall. The Cat landed on a walkway that ran along the spine of the converted tanker. The top hatch was round like a manhole, locked tight. He found a fan mounting on one of the sloping sides, the exterior closed by wire designed to keep grenades out.

Quisling mechanics take no pride in their work. Quick and cheap does it every time.

He squatted next to it, ignoring bullets whistling all around. Balancing on the balls of his feet, he coiled his body, grabbed, strained, and tore the thin grating free. Then he kicked the plastic blades out of the way.

He tucked the gun and dropped inside.

Only one had time to even look in astonishment at the intruder who had appeared in the their midst as if conjured out of the fog before Valentine swept the forward half of the gun bay with a burst from the submachine gun. The PPD roared in the confined space of the platform, sending men sprawling.

Valentine sensed movement behind—ducked as a pistol shot ricocheted off the armored wall where his head had been. He put a burst up into the soldier, lifting the man clear from the deck. He squeezed a second blast into the other rear gunner as the Twisted Cross man struggled to put a new magazine in his rifle.

Eight dead or dying men lay inside the back of the truck. Valentine moved forward to the crew-served weapons, shooting one crawling soldier in the side of the head as he did so. The semi was turning, bringing its deadly sides to bear on the main gate, the drivers in the cab still unaware of the destruction wreaked in the rear.

He pulled the machine gun facing the wall of wagons out of its mount and looked in the box magazine at its side, half-empty of shells. He decided it was enough and climbed up to the firing position at the front of the old tanker, using a step that gave him a clear view out over the top of the tracked dozer. The driver and his companion traded shots with the Eagles on the wall from within their reinforced cockpit. Nothing but canvas and wire mesh stood between him and the two men in the cab. He shoved the gun tight into his shoulder and pressed the trigger, snarling down at the unsuspecting Troopers. The muzzle flash blinded him. When he lifted his finger and could see again, both men lay dead in the bullet-riddled cab.

He went to the other machine-gun slit in the tanker wall. It was a well-designed weapons bay: a slit cut in the armored side of the trailer, with the gun mounted on a tripod behind a second bulletproof shield. Through the slit, he could see a triangle of Reapers. They had made it past the gate, firing all around as bullets hit their body armor. They seemed invulnerable. A grenade exploded amidst the three, causing one to drop to its knees. It righted itself and continued firing.

Valentine sighted the weapon and loosed a long burst, the tripod easing his aim. The weapon hardly shook as the bullets poured out of it, cartridge casings sounding in the gun's deafening chatter like faint bells as they tumbled to fall through the holes in the wire grid deck, where they wouldn't be tripped on before they could be collected from the belly of the tanker.

The first Reaper went down, broken in half by the machine gun. Another's head vanished when it turned to look at the first, and the grenade-wounded third tried to crawl away after he knocked it over with a blast. Valentine must have put a hundred rounds into it—in short bursts that alternated with mindless obscenities—before it finally lay still.

Get a hold of yourself. Use your brain as well as this gun.

Fighting the madness still heating his blood, Valentine dropped two more Twisted Cross off the wall. Another team vaulted into one of the battle-wagons. One removed the head of the defender in the wagon with a single hand-thrust up and under the Eagle's chin; its companion fired a weapon that looked like a plunger with a football glued to the end of it. The warhead took off in a whoosh of rocket-sparks and exploded under a battle-wagon, tossing men and debris into the air.

Valentine emptied the weapon into that pair, knocking one—its midsection torn to a pulp of black goo—into the bullet-riddled wall and blowing the other off the parapet. It fled, swinging over the wagons and into the trench minus an arm and a leg.

Working as though possessed, he lifted a new ammunition belt from the locker at the base of the weapon and opened the feeder at the top. As he placed the first round in the gun, a Twisted Cross rushed out of the darkness. In two seconds, it covered the distance to the truck.

When Valentine saw it leap, he drew his sword, and by the time it ripped through the top hatch, he had the blade held ready.

It came through headfirst.

His first slash removed the thing's arm at the elbow; it just dodged his backswing designed to take off its head. Had it immediately dropped in clawing fury on Valentine, it might have ended the fight there, but whoever was animating the Reaper decided to use its gun.

It dropped and spun to land on its feet; as it fell, it brought up the Kalashnikov, giving Valentine the instant he needed to roll forward under the burst of bullets. He opened its stomach just beneath its vest, where the groin-guard joined the armor above, then used the return thrust and skewered it under the armpit.

It turned, plucking the sword out of Valentine's hand like a wounded bull taking off with a banderilla. It staggered a step away as Valentine reached for his parang, drawing the machete-like knife and striking the back of its neck with one fluid motion. The body took one more step with its spinal cord severed before crashing to the deck, smearing a tarry black substance on the wire flooring as it rolled and flopped.

The men at the walls and figures outside the gate were still exchanging shots. Valentine heard a great deal of fire on the hillside at the north end of camp, not the chatter of the Kalashnikovs but the *pop-pop-pop* of aimed rifle fire. An occasional heavier *whump* sounded as one of the swivel guns discharged, joined by sharper explosions Valentine knew now to be rocket-propelled grenades.

Feeling thick-limbed and dull-eared, he retrieved his PPD and replaced the drum. Shaking himself back to coherence, back sore from adrenaline-burn, he readied the mounted machine gun and trained it on the gap at the gate, but even the muzzle flashes of the Twisted Cross guns had ceased. The gunfire around the camp faded into a moaning chorus of the wounded calling for help or screaming out their pain.

There was nothing left to kill.

Valentine sagged against the butt of the gun, aware of nothing but the smells of cordite and hot metal; he waited for someone else to make the decisions.

As the Twisted Cross Reapers withdrew, the barrage started, a fall of mortar shells blasting man, animal, and wagon into pieces. Valentine had never experienced anything like it. Though they fell all around the wagons, each explosion seemed aimed at him.

Thirty minutes later, it stopped. Then the cleanup began.

"If this is victory, I'd hate to see a defeat." The outrider leader, Danvers, looked across the smoldering ruin of the campsite as dawn burned away the fog. Valentine had joined him in the survey, asking that he might also employ the outriders in looking for a "pile of four" message from Duvalier.

The Eagle's Wings Brand dead lay in a long row, blanket-covered bodies with feet, at least in the cases where the deceased had both legs, protruding from beneath the earth-toned shrouds. Among them was the Camp Engineer Waldron, killed by a Reaper while reloading a swivel gun.

As they waited for the dawn and organized what was left of the defense, Danvers told Valentine about his outriders' fortunes on the hill above the north wall. During the Twisted Cross retreat, they discovered insectoid Grogs they called "Sandbugs" scattered on the hill above the camp.

"Sandbugs we can handle. They're out of the Dakotas—they live mostly in the unoccupied prairie and Badlands area," Danvers explained. "They look kind of like big sow bugs—they grab you in their front choppers and stick a needle with some kind of venom into you. If you're lucky, it kills you; if you're not, you get paralyzed. Either way, they throw you in a hole with a bunch of their eggs."

"Weaknesses?" Valentine asked mechanically, watching a widely spaced line of men on horses checking the grounds around the camp.

"They're the dumbest damn things, they don't organize at all, just scuttle in to the attack whenever they spot motion. Of course, if they had made it to the walls, there would have been trouble, they can dig like hell and they would have just hit the trench and gone right into the sand, come up in camp. That wouldn't have been pretty. What's left of my men are trying to hunt them down. They'll be hiding from the sun now that it's coming up. All we need are Sandbug nests on top of everything else."

Valentine's business was with the Twisted Cross, not new Grog physiognomy. He hadn't seen Duvalier, or discovered any message from her.

He found the deacon overseeing the care of the wounded and preparations for interment of the dead.

"I can't find Mrs. Hendricks, Deacon, so I thought I'd say good-bye to you, and ask you to tell her I'm on my way."

"Hold on now, son. You need a break as much as everyone else. Mrs. Hendricks is riding with the outriders. Let them see what those people have found out. No point in you wandering off half-cocked. Besides, we still haven't found sign of your friend. Don't you at least want to see her given a decent burial?"

"I think she's alive, Deacon."

"Now look, here comes the Wagonmaster now. Talk it over with her."

Mrs. Hendricks rode in, bearing her exhaustion and loss with the same mild manner she used to order her camp. A man ran up to help her off her horse.

"Thanks, Brent," she said. Valentine and a few others approached her, anxious for news.

"Yes, they're gone—their camp is empty," she announced. "And no, we haven't found any of the missing people yet, except for Peter and Judith Reilly. They're down amongst the trees, shot. That should take care of most of your questions."

The crowd mostly turned away, but Mrs. Hendricks chose to speak to Valentine first. "No sign of Alice, young man. But no body, either."

"Wagonmaster, I don't think you have to worry about the Twisted Cross for the immediate future. They'll need time to regroup after this. I'd like to move on. Maybe I can follow them back to their hole. Seems like they're retreating."

"We've survived before; we will again. You'll always be welcome among our teams, David. I saw you with that mobile bunker," she said, looking at the battered tanker. It had been emptied of weapons; the automatic guns were now in the capable hands of the Eagles. "I didn't grow up in this area—I was born into the Freehold out in the Wind River in western Wyoming. I was a dispatch runner at one time, before I met my husband while he was scouting for the Eagle Brand cattle drive. I know the Hunter's Arts when I see them. Back in those days, I used to use my ears and nose just as much as my eyes. I'm sure you know what I mean."

She turned to her son. "Josh, we'll need a good saddle horse and rig for our friend here. He has to be riding on. Put a couple of bags of feed for the horse and something to keep him going on the saddle, would you?"

"Yes, ma'am," Josh said briskly, despite the pain and fatigue in his eyes. The boy had changed from opinionated adolescent to dutiful outrider in a single night.

Danvers added, "It might take a while. The horses that had bolted during the mortar barrage are still being rounded up."

She smiled at her son's back. "I think they pulled out south." Her rosy features turned fierce. "We really gave them something to choke on. Oh, there was a pair of burned trucks, and one heavy tow-rig that looked like it plain blew up. Could be your Alice got in their camp when they were busy with us. Hope she didn't go up with their powder."

"She said she'd leave word if she could," Valentine said. "Did you see any markers, any piles of stones or wood?"

"No, but then the camp was a mess. She sure can cause a lot of trouble when she sets her mind."

"You could say that," Valentine agreed. "And now I need to find her."

"You've been up all night, son. Crossing the Dunes with Lord-knows-what still out there bleeding and angry isn't a job for someone who's half-asleep. You need two hot meals and some sleep in between before I let you walk out my gate."

He opened his mouth, but shut it again when Mrs. Hendricks planted hands on her hips. She jerked her chin down in a nod, putting the same authority in the gesture as a Chalmers tapping her gavel.

Valentine returned to the house-wagon, grateful to give in to the wisdom of her words. Jocelyn Hendricks sat on the wooden steps, a cup of something steaming in her hands that smelled faintly of whiskey.

"I put breakfast in there for you," she said. There were circles under her eyes. "There's so many dead. It felt . . . strange to make coffee and food with bodies laying in rows. I feel like everything should stop for a while, but the cows still needed to be milked."

She got up and opened the door for Valentine. He dragged himself inside and sat at the tiny table. Rolls and a slice of pie stood on the table next to a pitcher full of milk.

"I couldn't touch meat, let alone cook it. Sorry," the young woman said, opening a window.

"I'm not that hungry," Valentine said. He poured himself some of the still-warm buttermilk and drank. The rich taste triggered something in him, and he raised the glass, gulping it down. What did not go into his stomach went down his chin. He put the glass down with a shaking hand.

She stared at him, biting her lower lip. Valentine, in a fog matching last night's, couldn't bring himself to make conversation.

"Was this a bad battle?" she finally asked.

"No. You won."

She shifted her weight closer and brought up a rag to wipe off his chin.

"There's . . . blood or something all over your clothes. From when you were in that truck, so I hear. Though it's already turning into a tall tale: they've got you jumping like a deer, practically flying. . . . Let me wash them for you; they can dry while you sleep."

He stood, still chewing, his mind taking in her movements, the taste of the food, and the little cabin, but not processing the information. He began to undress. She blushed and stepped outside, and he handed her the bundle through the window.

"Thanks, Miss Hendricks," he said.

"Jocelyn."

When he woke, Jocelyn was sitting on the cabin's tiny stool, oiling his boots. He either felt safe in the Eagle camp, or she had sneaked in during his deepest cycle of sleep: he did not remember her reentering the house-wagon.

"You're leaving?" she asking, getting up to show him his newly washed traveling clothes.

"Soon." He sat up, still wrapped in the blanket, and tried to blink the gum out of his eyes.

"To find your wife?"

"Wife? She's more of a guide. I suppose I rely on her better than some men do their own wives."

"I know it's none of my business, but do you and she—?" She trailed off, darting an embarrassed look at him from her lowered head.

"No—we joke about it. Maybe under different circumstances I'd think differently."

"I had a boyfriend. He went on a drive to Denver, never came back. That was over a year ago now. I guess he wanted to see the city. I was hoping for a letter, a message, but he never explained himself."

"I'm sorry."

"He used to make me feel . . . all warm and safe. Last night, when you talked to me, I felt warm and safe again. I wanted to kiss you."

Valentine felt lust and compassion war within him. She was an alluring young woman, but he was leaving almost within minutes. "Jocelyn, I'll bet every young man in this brand would walk through fire to kiss you. We're strangers."

"The guys here are good men. I've known them all my life. All the older ones act more interested in the fact that I'm the Wagonmaster's daughter. The young ones are just . . . kids in men's boots, if you know what I mean. You're . . . serious."

Valentine thought it a strange word. Perhaps it was apt.

She placed the boots on the floor and sat at the edge of the bunk. "Since that meal after you rode in, I've been thinking about you. You probably think I'm just some silly hick girl. I'm not looking for a man permanent. If anything, you going away makes it better for me—I can just lose myself in it without worrying about the future. Know what I mean?" She took off her bandanna and shook out her thick chestnut hair. She planted her palm between his pectorals; his heart thumped hard against his ribs, as if it were trying to touch her.

Valentine rose from the bed toward her, and they fell into each other's arms, need making the embrace smooth and unembarrassed. Even better for Valentine, it was unselfconscious. Instincts sublimated during months without touching a woman surged inside him, spilling out like rising floodwaters over an earthen dike—in an instant the barriers dissolved. He took her rich, sage-sweetened hair in his hands as he kissed her.

"David, who *are* you? I . . . feel like I'm in heat," she gasped as he explored her neck with his mouth, the rest of her with his hand. He helped her wriggle out of her clothes. His blanket had already fallen away, leaving him nude and aroused and pressed hard against her.

He laid her down to the sheets, and she parted for him. Her hands gripped, pulled at his back as he entered. She melted around him, greedily taking what he gave her, but what she gave him was even sweeter. Forgetfulness. For those minutes there was no battle, no hunt, no responsibilities or fears, only a trembling woman in his arms. Their lovemaking was just kisses and softness and warmth and wetness and lust and motion, thrusting motion in which there wasn't a last night or tomorrow just a climax like a lightning flash in the dark of the angry void that was his life, a paroxysm that left him even more hungry for her and the oblivion of her body.

He trotted out of the Eagle's Wings camp on a bay quarter-horse gelding. It was like riding on a mobile tower: the horse measured over seventeen hands and had a rear end like a rowboat. The Eagles lined up to see him out of the gate. Valentine felt honored by the gesture, though he flushed at the little half-wave Jocelyn gave. He saw her hands clasping and unclasping as he rode out, and felt guilty.

Valentine's only souvenir of the fight was a metal helmet, a piece of Kevlar with coal-scuttle flanges protecting the neck. With his battered vest, it would add to his disguise should he have to resort to posing as a Trooper again. Whoever had worn it invested in a cork-and-webbing liner and khaki cotton sun sheath, which did an admirable job of keeping him cool.

He searched the Twisted Cross camp. It stood in the lee of the little ridge south of the larger, horizon-filling one that sheltered the Eagles' camp.

A pair of outriders scavenged the wreckage, throwing everything from useless-looking scrap metal to expended shell casings into a wagon. Valentine rode up to them.

"The man with the tommy gun," one of them said, waving back. "Hey, mister, we got word you were looking for piles of four of anything. I think we found what you're looking for—that or these boys sure have a funny way of taking care of their dead. Look at Sam beside the trail yonder." He pointed down the rutted cross-country trail.

Valentine joined the waving outrider and found a little collection of four Reaper heads, arranged in a neat pile like cannonballs in an old fort. Bluebottle flies were already thick on the dead flesh; in places, masses of maggots had already exposed black bone.

He closed his nose and mouth and knocked over the pile with his toe. Beneath the gruesome marker was a folded piece paper. He picked it up and recognized Duvalier's hand.

Ghost,

I'm moving south to the Platte. I listened to the camp, and there's another contingent over in Broken Bow. Just go south to the highway and follow it east, or read your map. If they've pulled out of there, let's meet south of Omaha where we talked about. I listened in on their General, and their Headquarters is there. They call it the "Cave," whatever that is.

Don't be impressed with the pile. This is wounded I finished off while they were trying to get back to their camp.

—Smoke

Valentine folded the note and put it in his map case. He returned to his horse, which already had its nose down in the dry grass, cropping some green weeds beneath the longer growth.

"Broken Bow it is."

He camped that night near an old highway intersection, in a former Nebraska national forest.

The indefatigable horse covered nearly sixty miles that day. Valentine was astonished at the distance. In his first year as a laborer in the Free Territory, the horsemen in the Ozarks had passed on their preference for mustangs, saddlebreds, palominos, and tough ponies, claiming quarter horses lacked stamina. The bay's energetic, mile-eating walk proved the Ozark horsemen wrong.

Valentine had seen some wisps of smoke to the northeast in the afternoon, but decided that whatever happened was probably over with before dawn. He had no desire to investigate another gruesome battle-field and risk being seen by a straggler. He saw fresh tire tracks on and beside the old highway, but even the little plane that had appeared every day previously was grounded. His only companionship was the occa-sional wary coyote and a few far-away hawks.

The campsite felt lonely. He missed Duvalier's jabs and sarcasm, and the smell of the woman's sweat over the campfire. He made a cold camp, and not knowing what might be out there, decided that his old Wolf habit of switching campsites around midnight was called for. He waited for the moon to go behind a cloud, and then he picked up his blanket, pack, and saddlebags.

As he placed the western-style saddle on the bay, preparing to walk to a new campsite, the horse grew restive. Valentine tried to stroke the horse's forehead, making soothing sounds, but the animal wouldn't be quieted. It danced backwards. Alarmed, Valentine turned to see what the bay was backing away from. A hummock of grassy ground bulged beside him, and he caught a wet moldy smell, like decayed wood swol-len after a rain.

Valentine agreed with the horse. He vaulted into the saddle. The animal turned, but the saddle did not turn with it: Valentine had just placed it on the bay's back in preparation to walk the animal and never fixed the girth. He tried to grip the horse's barrel chest with his calves, but saddle and rider slid sideways off the fear-crazed animal.

He rolled to his feet and drew his sword. He felt the ground shift under his feet and sprang away. Something attacked the saddle and bags in a spray of dirt. He ran a few steps to the old highway, wanting broken pavement beneath his feet instead of soil that might conceal an enemy.

Something crashed through the woods and brush on the far side of the embankment. He saw a boulder shape bouncing downhill. It altered its course slightly—and intelligently. It headed for him, even as he sidestepped to get out of its way.

He dived, and the thing bounced over him. His peripheral vision picked up movement from another direction, and he put up his sword. A carpet of living muscle threw itself on his legs. Something poured liquid fire into his calf. He shifted the grip on his sword and plunged it into the thing, working the blade like an awl right and left in search of something vital. Valentine gasped for breath, and his sword and the pinned Sandbug suddenly looked distant to him, like the optical illu-sion a glassless telescope creates.

He had no inner sense of peace as consciousness died, his life did not flash before him . . . just a confused *What the hell?* And then darkness.

His little sister's puppy liked to nibble feet. It would lie down and cross its paws over his shin in the yard, and chew at his toes with sharp young teeth. David would lie in the yard and shriek out in ticklish agony while his sister sat on his chest and her mutt worked at this foot. Then his sister started in on the knee on his other leg. He felt her tearing at the soft flesh at the back of his leg. "Ouch, Pat—cut it out!" Then someone put a pillow over his face, and he had to struggle to breathe.

Valentine felt dirt in his mouth, but he couldn't spit it out. His tongue felt dry and withered, like a desiccated toad. He was in darkness, every muscle frozen. He tried to shake his head, move his arm, but his body wouldn't answer. Something was thumping at his chest. It was easier to fade back into sleep. *You sleep, you die,* a little voice told him, and he fought to stay awake, to break out of the enclosure binding him, but it was too hard, and he faded again.

Pat was at his face, strong beyond her years and trying to force a tube into his mouth. Using his last iota of willpower, he kept his jaws clenched.

"David! David!" his mother called from the back door.

"Mom?" he called back. "Pat's being—"

A hard probe entered his mouth, and some kind of fiery liquid hit the back of his throat. He couldn't breathe through his nose; he swallowed.

"David!" Jocelyn implored. "David, I'm here, it's okay. We killed the Sandbug grubs, you're going to be all right."

Valentine felt neither one way nor the other about the matter. He was too tired.

"Give him another jolt of whiskey. Best thing for the damn Sandbug venom," a gruff voice said, but his foggy brain took its time with the words.

More liquid forced in, his mouth held closed, and his nostrils shut. He had no choice but to swallow.

He woke feeling like a broken victim of a cattle stampede. But he could see now through blurred eyes. Jocelyn, the deacon, and Danvers sat around a campfire, staring into the flames and sipping something out of tin cups.

"Water," he croaked.

Jocelyn grabbed a canteen and knelt beside him. Danvers got behind him and lifted him so he could drink properly. The cool water infused him with enough strength for him to look up at Jocelyn.

"What?"

"Your horse wandered back yesterday. We knew something must have happened," she said, her hair tickling at his face as she stroked his brow.

"The Sandbugs are loose everywhere," Danvers explained. "We're losing cattle right and left. But the Wagonmaster, when she saw your horse come in, had us drop everything and track you down, just in case. We've pulled guys out of Sandbug holes before, and if they ever come out of the coma—well, they're like stroke victims a lot of the time. You being a tenderfoot and all, I figured about all we would be able to do is kill the grubs and bury what's left."

"It hurts. . . . Anything help the pain?" he said.

"I've got a soda poultice on it now," Jocelyn said.

Danvers patted Valentine's scratched and dirt-covered hand. "You'd clawed your way to the surface. We saw your head and arm sticking out of the burrow. You must not have got much of a dose."

"Don't let him scare you," the deacon said from the campfire. "You'll be fine. They only nibbled on you a bit, and all your fingers and toes still twitch. You were buried at least a day. Have another swallow of whiskey. That old saw about it being good for snakebite is bullfeathers, but some alcohol in the bloodstream sure helps with whatever it is they sting you with."

Danvers uncorked the bottle, poured another mouthful into Valentine, and gave him a chaser for good measure when he swallowed the first.

"That good, eh?" Danvers said. He took a swig.

"Chuck, you stop that, don't forget we're far from home," the deacon admonished.

"Sorry. First drop since calving festival, Preacher. Lot's happened since."

"It's your last till we're among the wagons again. When dawn comes, I'll ride back and let them know to call off the trackers."

Dawn came, and Danvers roused the deacon from his watch. The old Bible-thumper went to his horse and eased himself in the saddle.

"Time was, life got easier when you got old," he grumbled, and walked his horse over to Valentine. "Young man, you're welcome at our wagons anytime you like."

The deacon pulled his hat down firmly on his head.

"Thank you," Valentine said. He still felt drained, but his mind was back in the alcohol-numbed world of the living. His left leg throbbed at the ankle, but it was the healthy pain of a body healing. "Now I know what Sandbugs smell like, sir. I'll be fine."

"Jocelyn, he doesn't saddle his horse for two more days. Lots of water and rest will flush the stuff out," the deacon ordered. "Danvers, I'll send out some of your men to take your place so you can get back to work."

"Thanks, but no, Deacon. I'll keep an eye on Jocelyn."

"As you like. Good-bye again, Mr. Stuart. God be with you."

The poultice cooled the wound. Valentine bowed his head and shut his eyes. "He was when I met the Eagles."

Valentine napped in the shade whenever he wasn't drinking. His Eagle companions fed him on bread soaked in broth. Jocelyn put vinegar-soaked compresses on his wound, and the cool antiseptic bite of the vinegar brought some relief. Valentine watched the two work: Danvers's eyes never left the girl when he was in camp. But there was restlessness to the man; he continually went out to fetch water or survey the road, or set snares for small game, and hallooed from a quarter-mile off when he returned.

"He likes to be on the move, doesn't he," Valentine said, as Danvers rode off to exercise Valentine's bay on another sweep of the ground to the south.

"He was born and raised in the saddle, more or less. His mom climbed off her horse and had him two minutes later. His pa says she climbed back on five minutes after that, but no one takes him seriously. He's leaving us alone out of politeness."

"I like your company, but there's no need."

"He . . . I made kind of a scene at camp when your horse came back. I told my mother I was going to find you and go with you."

Valentine read the anxiety in her eyes.

"I think your people need you," he said after a moment. "More than I."

"They'll be fine."

"I'm not going to tell you you couldn't keep up, or that I wouldn't want you next to me, Jocelyn. So I'll rephrase. You need your people."

She looked at him, eyes wet. Perhaps she had expected a different argument.

"They're your family. You're at exactly the age where that doesn't mean much to you, but as the years go by, you might regret your choice."

"I might not, too."

"I wish I had the chance to regret my family. I had parents, a brother and a sister, a home. It all was taken away when I was eleven. If you've got any respect for me, set aside whatever it is between us, and listen to this: Stand by your mom and Josh. We're two people who needed each other for a little while. Your family will always need you."

"You're just saying this to keep me from . . . tagging along. Tell me you don't want me to go with you, and I won't."

"I don't want you to go with me for the reasons I just explained."

Her face hardened. "That's not what I meant. You, David, the man."

"Man? Am I?"

"Well, you're not a mule, except you're stubborn as one."

"You need a man with possibilities. I'm—"

"Used up?"

"What makes you say that?"

She sat still for a moment. "It's what my father used to say. About the older generation, the one's who'd seen too much death and change. He said they were still walking and talking, but something in them died—'used up' in the wars. Their families, if they had any, had a hard time."

"I was going to say you need someone to grow old with. I've had . . . bad luck with friends."

"It can't be better to be alone."

He shook his head. "Of course not. But it's easier."

Jocelyn was chipper as a robin in spring sunshine for the rest of his recovery. Valentine couldn't tell whether it was a mask or not. The three of them talked long across the firelight as the stars circled overhead, until the embers dimmed and they were only shadows and voices in the darkness.

The next day Jocelyn and Danvers rode southeast with him for a few hours, before saying their good-byes. Danvers shook his hand, and Jocelyn hugged him when they rested their horses at the farewell. Jocelyn broke off the embrace and resaddled her horse; perhaps she was not as eager to leave her brand as she seemed.

"Thank you," Danvers said, taking his reins. His gaze darted to Jocelyn and back again. "For everything."

"Remember . . . us," Jocelyn said.

"I will. Your people helped more than you know. The General's been given a bloody nose. Maybe he'll run home to his hole for a while. Then I can catch up to him."

With the good-byes said and an annoying mist in his eyes, Valentine turned his horse's head to the road, and tried not to listen with his hard ears to the slow hoofbeats of friends leaving.

This land was thick with stands of cedar, with small, irregular hills sheltering wetter country and woods. Wildflowers and bees ruled this part of the Dunes. He saw no sign of cattle or the trails of the Trekkers. He was into the borderlands.

He tried to remember what Kurian controlled this area, and thought it to be the one in Kearney. He doubted he would see any Kearney Marshals out this far yet, but there was a chance of a Reaper at night or Trooper patrols in the day. He walked his horse and rode with more caution, keeping to low ground farther from the road.

He approached Broken Bow by throwing a wide loop around to the south. He had known some Quislings to be suspicious as hell of someone riding in from the no-man's-land, but let that same man just circle and come from the other direction, and they were nothing but smiles and "have a cup of java."

Night was falling by the time he approached the little cluster of pre-Overthrow gas stations and markets, houses and roadside stops.

He came across an old railroad track and dismounted to inspect it. There was no question that it was both little used and had recently had a train pass over it. The rails and ties were in poor shape—even for Quisling-maintained lines—yet the overgrowth had been damaged by a passing train.

He paralleled the tracks and the road, coming into town as the shadows disappeared and evening claimed the town. Only one building, a whitewashed cinder-block corner shop of some substance, had any light burning from windows covered by makeshift shutters. Only the wind moved through the streets.

If there had been a train in town, it had passed on.

Valentine saw the glow of a cigarette in the shadows of an alley, and a Trooper appeared, gun held ready in sentry duty. He pointed the barrel down the road at Valentine.

"Hold it right there. Who are you?"

Valentine halted his horse. "It looks like I'm too late. Did the General's men pull out? I was supposed to deliver a message."

"I don't know you."

"I wouldn't expect you to. I'm from Columbus, not Kearney. I'm going to turn right around, friend. He's obviously gone, and I just had a hard day's ride for nothing."

"Why didn't they just radio it in?"

"Not that it's any of your business, but the General likes to see certain things on paper, or so I'm told. Could be they didn't want everyone with a scanner picking up the transmission."

"Well, go on inside if you want. You could at least have a bite before turning around. Leave the horse and gun out here, though. Better leave that oversize shiv, too. Where did you get a thing like that?"

"A Grog in Omaha, two summers ago. It better still be here when I come back outside. I have a revolver, too—can I put that on the bench over here?"

The gun didn't waver from Valentine, but he could see the soldier relax a little. "Sure. You're well armed."

"You'd be well armed, too, if you were this far out, riding alone."

The sentry went to the door. Its glass was badly scratched but intact. "Dispatch rider coming in. I got his horse and guns."

Valentine strode into the little corner building. Four soldiers, two of whom were sleeping on cots, filled the post with sweat and smoke. Sandbags filled the windows, and a line of rifles hung on the wall. There were new sheets of paper lying here and there on the freshly swept floor; perhaps the building had recently been a headquarters.

"Evening," one of the men said gruffly. He looked like a sergeant, even if he wasn't dressed like one.

"Good evening," Valentine answered. "I'm a day late and a dollar short, story of my life. I was supposed to deliver a packet to the General or his most immediate subordinate. Looks like he pulled out."

"Yep, you're about eight hours late of a done deal. Don't know about a General, but that Twisted Cross bunch were here. I understand they burned out three whole brands in just two nights. There was some orders came through, and they left."

"Hell. To where?"

"How should we know? Those guys are damn closemouthed. They gave me the shakes, I can tell you that."

"I know the feeling," Valentine said, honestly enough.

"They said they'd be back. Not that I'd recommend you waiting. Some snafu out west with the goat-ropers. Bank on this, though, when they do come back, it's going to be with enough guns to plant every last cowboy out there. Not that it's any blood outta my veins."

"Mind if I help myself to some coffee? I have to be moving on back, then."

"No, go ahead. It's old, but it's hot."

Valentine poured himself some of the acorn-and-hazelnut swill. He missed Duvalier's stolen coffee.

"Hey, son, if you want to take a real break, in the back room we have a nice little piece of runaway. If she's over seventeen, I'll eat my hat. They found her family by the river two days ago, and I sort of inherited her from a buddy of mine who drives a squad. Spooks got her parents. You're free to take a turn."

Valentine took a step over to the doorway and peered in. The other soldier stepped over to his NCO and whispered, "Don't like the look of him, Bud." Not that a whisper mattered to Valentine's ears.

Valentine tossed down the rest of the coffee. "No, but thanks for the offer. I'd just get all sleepy, and I have some riding to do." He walked up to the sergeant, putting his hands in his pockets. "Let's see, I've got a tin of Indian tobacco in here somewheres, and if you'd be willing to swap a—"

He lashed out in an upward swipe, fighting claws on his fingertips reducing the sergeant's eyes to red jelly. With his left hand, Valentine raked the other Trooper across the face, opening four furrows to the bone from his ear to his nose. As the sergeant staggered backwards, palms to his bloody face, Valentine kicked over the cot holding one sleeping Trooper.

The other rose in time to have Valentine almost sever his head from his shoulders.

Valentine slipped off the claws and grabbed a rifle from the wall, aiming it at the soldier rising from the overturned bunk. The hammer came with an impotent click. Misfire or unloaded—he reversed his grip and laid the man out with a swing the Jack was too slow to duck. He struck the other Trooper solidly over the head, breaking the stock at the grip. The Trooper fell to the floor, dead or senseless.

Valentine finished the grisly work, killing the wounded with his parang. He took a pump-action shotgun from the rack, made sure it was loaded, and crossed to the sandbagged window. There was no sign of the sentry; he had either run or was crouched somewhere, covering the door.

Keeping below the windows, Valentine set the shotgun carefully next to the door, picked up one of the dead Troopers, and launched him through the window. Glass shattered, and he heard a shot. Valentine burst through the door, shotgun at the hip, and saw the sentry standing over the body, pointing his gun at the prone figure. Valentine's first shot caught him in the shoulder, and the second load of buckshot tore off part of the man's head.

The quarter horse was dancing in fear, pulling at the bench he had tied it to. Valentine calmed the animal, retrieved his gun and sword, and went inside.

The girl, the object of all this death, was in the bare little back room. She huddled in a corner, wearing only her fear and a ratty blanket. Two large brown eyes stared out at him from under a tangle of almost-black hair. She screamed when she saw Valentine take a step into the room, but he lowered his gun and spread his hands, palms out.

"My name is David. I'm not going to hurt you." He took another step toward her.

"No!" she shrieked, closing her eyes and turning her chin to the wall.

He stopped. "Sorry, this isn't much of a rescue. You're going to have to do all the work. Do you like horses? Do you know how to ride?"

"Ride?" It was only a whisper, but it had hope in it.

"Yes, ride. Ride away from here, on a horse that can run all night."

"Away from here?" she said, a little more loudly.

"Now you're getting the idea. Do you want something to eat, some water?"

"No . . . I'd like to be away from here. Like now."

"Get dressed. Take some blankets."

Valentine returned to the room and looked out on the intersection, if two unused roads sprouting sunflowers from the cracks could still be called an intersection.

The girl had seen enough. He threw bedding and jackets over the dead eyes of the Troopers and returned to the back room.

"Are they dead?" she asked.

"Are who dead?"

"The Authorities. They came in the night and took them. Took them for-forever."

"Who, your parents?"

She nodded, tears reawakening in her eyes.

"Yes, little sister, the Authorities are dead."

She walked out of the room, the blanket draped over her skinny frame like a poncho, in a torn pair of pants and some thick military-issue socks. "Wow," she said with a sniffle, looking at the corpses.

Valentine took her out to the horse. "I want you to ride on this road, straight as an arrow. I don't think you'll see any trucks, but if you do, hide. Find some people who have lots of cows and wagons—you got that?"

"Cows and wagons, sure."

"You know how to take care of horses, right? I've never seen a teenage girl who couldn't do it better than any man alive. Now that I think of it, I never did name this guy. I guess you'll have to do it."

She patted the big horse on the neck, making friends. "Yes, sir. He sure is a big one. I think I'll call him Two Tall. He has two stockings, you see?"

"When you reach the cows and wagons, find someone called a Wagonmaster. Tell the Wagonmaster that you need to get to the Eagles, and they'll help you. Are you okay with that?"

"Wagonmaster. Eagles. Sure."

"There's a woman with the Eagles who just lost a lot of people to the Authorities. She'll look after you. Now what road are you going to follow?" He asked, taking his pack down from the horse but leaving the food and water.

"This one," she said.

"Any questions, little sister?"

She climbed onto the saddle with the agility of a monkey, a skinny young girl in the saddle of a very big horse. She pulled back on the bit and turned Two Tall. The excited horse sidestepped; she knew how to neck-rein.

The girl's eyes followed the road into the night, confidence rather than fear on her face, and then turned down to Valentine. Her eyebrows furrowed. "Who are you?"

Valentine wondered himself sometimes. He adjusted her stirrups as she looked at the dead Trooper lying in the street.

"I'm the one who comes in the night for the Authorities."

The rail terminus turned out to be a treasure trove of equipment abandoned by the hastily departed Twisted Cross. Valentine found the Troopers' pickup truck, a heavy-framed conglomeration of dirty windows under wire grids, wooden cargo dividers in the bed of rusting bodywork over a double axle. But the mechanical heartbeat within the diesel cylinders was still strong. He examined the engine, added motor oil, and loaded the bed with food and fuel, all the while keeping his ears open for approaching patrols.

The Jacks had either stolen from or been equipped by the Twisted Cross. There were stenciled crates everywhere. He read the labels using the light from Ryu's stone. It fit easily in his palm, allowing him to shine it this way and that. He found a case of grenades and another of thermite bombs. The aluminum–ferric oxide mix, when ignited, burned hot enough to weld metal, and was a favorite incendiary device of the more destructive-minded Quislings. He loaded up with maps, guns, and ammunition from the dead "garrison" and got behind the wheel— looking through a newly cleaned windscreen and the armored wire grid over it.

As he drove—not very well at first, he was inexperienced with such contraptions—he tried to get to know the ancient truck as he would a horse.

Valentine would never know it, but his slow drive through Northeast Nebraska became the stuff of local legend. He wanted to avoid any chance of encountering either patrols or hunting Reapers, so he stayed well clear of the Number One's territory north of Lincoln. He crawled along on the backest of back roads through an area claimed by Kurian, Grog, and Man. He stopped at the occasional lonely homestead, trading guns and boxes of ammunition for a meal and a night's rest.

The residents at each stop asked no questions of him, but were eager to tell him about their problems. He cleared out a nest of Harpies that were plaguing a little bottomland settlement from the old college at Wayne by burning their roost, and ambushed some armed ex-Trooper thugs who prowled in a two-vehicle convoy as they camped at night. He killed one of the deserters as he went to relieve himself in a gully and returned in his hat and shot the others before they could rise.

He finally gave away the truck from Broken Bow to a co-op of families in the picturesque country north of Blair. On his legs again, he proceeded afoot into the ruins of Omaha.

Omaha was a burnt-out husk. The outskirts of the city were falling apart, the inner regions a charred and collapsed wreck, and everything south of the city between Council Bluffs and Papillion flattened by the nuclear air and ground bursts designed to knock out the old Strategic Air Command base at Bellevue. He planned to move around the edge of the ruins, perhaps along the old I-680 line, when Fate decided to lay down one of the face cards that She sometimes used to change his life.

Nine

Omaha, September: The Old World transportation hub set in the wide, wooded valley of the Missouri is a sad shadow if its former self. The skeleton of the Woodman building looks out over smashed walls and collapsed roofs, where people and commerce once thrived. Like its sister St. Louis, farther down the wide Missouri, Omaha proper is now the breeding ground for assorted Grogs and human scoundrels. The city and its surrounding lands were deeded to the Grog tribes in exchange for their help during the Overthrow, and the Grogs have shaped it to their taste. Control over the vital communications lines passed to the Quislings in Council Bluffs, who oversee the railroad bridges and the river traffic. On the western shores, the nineteenth-century brick buildings of the Old Market are now home to an assortment of human smugglers, traders, and plug-uglies plying perhaps the second-oldest profession—that of getting goods into the hands of those with the ability to pay. But even that nest of vipers just south of what's left of Heartland Park now thinks about relocating to a new city; there have been stories of fighting throughout the city between the Grogs and tall, well-armed men. The city is being cleared of its Grogs.

Which would be fine with the smugglers. But the recent destruction of a barge full of contraband and the death of its entire crew have the Old Market gangs worried. The Quislings always winked at the trade that supplies them with a few luxuries from other parts of the country, the Grogs in the ruins depend on them for weapons, and since the Freeholders are too far away to go to such lengths just to burn a few barrels of rum and brandy, they are forced to wonder if they have also been selected for destruction.

Someone with a plan is making a power play for the city, and playing for keeps.

He was on the northwest side of the city, near one of those multi-level, indoor shopping centers of the Old World. Now the cement structure was black and green and hollow as a diseased tooth. It reeked of Harpies from a half mile off, so he avoided it.

Valentine wanted to make time, so he walked well out in the open, intimidating-looking gun over his shoulder, sweating freely under the heat of the September sun. He pushed through the green chaos of what had been either a golf course or a park and moved out onto a series of parking lots in the midst of being reclaimed by forest, with the overgrowth-dripped roof of the mall in the western distance.

He came upon an east-west road, no more or no less clear than any of the others he had crossed, littered with the rusting ruins of weather-beaten cars, many with small terrariums growing in the sheltered detritus within, like a series of rust-colored planters. But he picked up a battlefield odor—flesh rotting in the sun.

He followed the smell and saw stains, recent but faded to brown, splashed on a car, and his nose located the fresh, overripe smell of bodies in the afternoon heat. A little farther down, Harpies, the snaggle-toothed, ugly, bowlegged, and bat-armed Grogs that Valentine despised from his earliest days in the Free Territory, lay dead on the road and tossed atop cars.

Among their broken forms he found a huge fallen backpack—far too large to be carried by a Harpy, even on its feet, in the road. It was fashioned out of wood and skins, grafted on a core of what looked like a tube-steel frame of a kitchen chair, clearly homemade but showing a great deal of delicate craftsmanship in the numerous leather laces and braces. Obviously some Harpies had survived the encounter with the backpack-wearer, for it was empty.

Curious for some reason, Valentine tried to read the story of the battle from the placement of the bodies. The Harpies first attacked their victim in the middle of the road, judging from the two that lay dead to the east with bullet holes. His restless mind welcomed the challenge; he got on his hands and knees to find discarded shell casings. Their victim tried to make it to the trees Valentine had just emerged from, killing one on the way by tearing a leathery wing, breaking its neck, and throwing it into a car. He was strong, whoever he was. And tall—the Harpy had been thrown through the sedan's sunroof. Around the fallen pack, there was more dried blood, an increasingly heavy trail that became a torrent as it reached the broken windows of an old McDonald's. Valentine saw a final dead flier, but nothing else, in the stripped-out lobby of the restaurant.

McDonald's built its restaurants to last; this one's roof was still more or less sound after nearly fifty years of Nebraska's seasons. Stepping softly, Valentine followed the blood trail into the back of the building, through the debris and growth springing up wherever swirls of dirt accumulated. The trail ended in the dark, cavelike metal walk-in that had once been a refrigerator, or perhaps a freezer.

Valentine smelled more blood and heard slow, labored, breathing. He opened the door to the freezer a little farther, and looked inside.

A Grog lay curled up on the floor. An enormous one. It looked to be a type he had glimpsed among the Twisted Cross trains, taller and not quite so broadly built as the fierce gray apes he was familiar with. This one's exposed skin, rather than resembling the thick slabs of armor plating like that of a rhino that the Grogs on Little Timber bore, was rougher and deeply wrinkled, pebbled like an elephant's. It was also wearing fitted clothing. He had never seen Grogs in anything more than simple loincloths or vests. It was dusted with soft, fawn-colored fur, in patches on its chest and somewhat heavier on its back and shoulders. Blood matted the sparse fur. An ugly brown streak ran from the Grog to a drain in the center of the floor.

It was unconscious, obviously dying. Valentine almost shut the door, to leave it to expire in peace, when he heard the slightest whimpering sound from the Grog, lost in some pain-diffusing dream. Whatever else, it had killed six Harpies, four with its bare hands. It deserved some thanks as far as Valentine was concerned. He began to rummage around for something that could be used as bandages.

The store was empty, but while exploring the basement, he found a few rags and old towels. The uniform closets and employee lockers had been stripped long ago, but he found a large red flag, well trodden on and obviously once used as a carpet on the cold floor by some unknown resident, long gone. He found an old box with packets of mix labeled SANITIZER, read the label, opened one up and experimentally added it to some water poured from his canteen into one of the buckets scattered around the basement.

Absently he stuck the empty packet in a pocket. Going over the Spanish instructions and comparing them to the English half would give his mind something to do later on.

Working with speed now, he went back outside and found rainwater in a crumbled sewer. He filled two buckets with water, and then rinsed out the rags and the dirty flag as best he could in the standing water. After that he filled two buckets and poured some packets of

sanitizer into one, starting the material in on a cleansing soak. Returning with the water, he gathered deadfall branches under his arm and
came back to the restaurant. Using a match for expediency instead of
his usual small magnifying glass, he built a fire in one of the old fry-
vats with the branches and set a metal bucket of water on a rusty grill
over the fire to boil.

Valentine wondered how long the material should soak in the sanitizer. He made more trips for water, until he had every portable vessel
he could find full up, then began to turn the cloth into bandages. He
stripped and tied the cloth with almost hysterical speed, and forced
himself to calm down. After a few deep breaths, he brought the boiled
water and the strips of chlorine-scented cloth into the metal-walled
room and began to wash and dress the limp creature's wounds. It was
wearing a sleeveless, short robe that tied behind it in the small of its
back, now badly torn and bloodstained. Valentine removed it and
tossed it in the sanitizer bucket, where it joined the bloodstained rags
that he used to dress the wounds.

Its cuts and gouges and bites bled again, but slightly. Whatever else
might be said about Grogs, they died hard. With more time now, Valentine took the bloody rags to the fire and threw them in another bucket
of bubbling water to boil clean.

He had a little brown sugar and a jar of honey, a gift from one of
the farms in Northeastern Nebraska. The bee enthusiast had also given
him pieces of dried honeycomb along with the syrup. In Valentine's
next boil, he dissolved some sugar, honey, and honeycomb, and brought
it in to the Grog. Using a washcloth-size piece of material, he poured
the warm sugar-water into the cloth and then placed it in the creature's
mouth, cradling its bearlike head in his lap. It began to instinctively
suckle at the liquid.

Twenty-four hours later, having given it six more feedings and another change of bandages, Valentine prepared to leave the Grog. He
arranged the honeycomb, a large supply of water, and some dried beef
within reach, along with a bag of all the edible fungi he could scour
from the nearby woods.

He hurried to pack up, for the Grog showed signs of returning to
consciousness. Its breathing was slow and regular, and it no longer alternately groaned and whimpered. The Grog's remarkable body, perhaps more than Valentine's fit of tenderness, had pulled it through its
numerous injuries.

Valentine took a last look at his patient. He had made a bed for it
out of some of the scraps downstairs and padded it with moldy-smelling
paper, but at least it was a cushion of sorts. Oddly enough, he felt the

time spent treating the Grog was not wasted. He'd needed a day or two's rest anyway, and the empty restaurant was as good a place as any. He wished to be off well before nightfall, however, since the Harpies evidently hunted the region.

Valentine turned to leave and began to walk out of the kitchen area, when his sharp ears picked up a hoarse croak. "Wait . . . man."

Valentine had never heard English out of a Grog before. Intrigued, he returned to the freezer.

"Was . . . this . . . you?" it asked, pointing to the dressings around its head and chest. It had a voice like a rock slide, a low, clattering rumble.

Valentine nodded. "Yes."

"Food . . . drink . . . also?" It tried to sit up, failed, but managed to raise its ursine head. Its pointed ears extended, sticking up on either side of its head like a bat's when unfolded. The ear tips tilted toward Valentine. "Why?"

He shrugged, before it occurred to him that the Grog might not know the meaning of the gesture. "You fought outside very . . . bravely. Call it a tribute. Do you understand?"

It closed its eyes for one long second. "No."

"It means I think you're strong, a warrior. Give help then."

The Grog chuckled, a low sound like subterranean grinding. "No . . . man. Your . . . words . . . I . . . understood. You . . . purpose . . . I . . . not . . . understood."

"That makes two of us. I will leave you now. I think you'll be all right."

"Thank . . . you . . . but . . . gratitude . . . is . . . owed."

"No."

The creature rolled onto its stomach. It lifted its chest off the floor with two muscle-wrapped arms. First one leg, then the other was drawn up under pectorals the size of manhole covers. Somehow it got to its feet, leaning as raised itself with an arm like a child's slide. It stumbled toward the door, and Valentine moved forward to catch it, forgetting that the Grog's full weight would probably knock him flat at the very least. But the Grog extended one of its five-foot arms, bracing itself against the wall.

"No!" it said between gasps. "A . . . gratitude . . . is . . . owed. Please . . . wait . . . one . . . day."

Curiouser and curiouser, Valentine thought. "Very well. One day."

"As . . . Men . . . do . . . I . . . am . . . Ahnkha . . . Krolph . . . Mergrumneornemn," Valentine thought it said. He got the first part, partially understood the second, but the final word in what sounded like its name was a set of trailing consonants as unintelligible as his old pickup's transmission.

"My name is David Valentine, errr . . . Ahn-Kha." He pronounced it best he could, as if saying, "Ah-ha!"

"Valentine is your clan name?" the Grog asked, catching its breath.

"You could say that. But it is a small clan. As far as I know, I'm it."

"David is your close name?"

"We say first name."

"My David, I am grateful to you," Ahn-Kha announced, crossing its left arm across its chest, palm outward, and bowing with ears folded flat.

"Ahn-Kha, I am pleased to meet you," Valentine responded. His knowledge of Grog habits was limited to what part of the human anatomy they liked to eat first. He extended his hand. The Grog either recognized the gesture or had some knowledge of human customs; he solemnly engulfed Valentine's hand with his own leathery palm and shook. "We didn't just get married or anything, did we?"

The Grog's features split into a wide smile. It threw back its head and opened its satchel-mouth, like a baby bird looking for a feeding, and laughed. The sound reminded Valentine of a certain braying mule of recent acquaintance.

"I hope that was a no."

Valentine gave Ahn-Kha one more day than he asked for.

Ahn-Kha's strength returned exponentially. Valentine admired the powerful construction of the Grog. Although he stood like a man and had longer legs than his "Gray One" relatives, when Ahn-Kha wished to move quickly, he made use of three or four limbs. Valentine eventually learned he could outrun him on the flat, but if it came to moving up or down a slope, especially one cluttered with trees or rocks, the Grog could vault and pull himself up using his enormous arms with an agility Valentine could match only with Cat jumps.

Fully erect, Ahn-Kha stood seven feet tall. His arms formed an inverted U, with an arc of muscle at the shoulders that bulged and writhed like separate creatures riding his back. He had three fingers and a thumb, the index and middle finger a good deal longer than the digit on the end, which was nearly as opposable as the true thumb opposite. His feet mirrored his hands, but he kept the former covered with something like a thick mitten shod with leather that allowed him to better use his toes climbing.

The two males of their respective species agreed that each was the ugliest thing they had ever met in Creation. Ahn-Kha thought Valentine looked like a flat-faced birth defect, and found the contrast between hair and skin revolting in contrast to the Grog's own all-over tan-blond body hair. For his part, Valentine kept thinking of the Grog as some kind of weird miscegenation between a shorthaired bear and an ape. He had something of the calm wisdom of a bear in his expression, with deep-set black-flecked eyes of the richest brown. The fanged mouth below marred the effect, making him look like a predatory beast of ravenous hunger. Ahn-Kha's snout was wider than a bear's. He bore a set of long white catfish whiskers that hung out and down from the sides of his mouth, though they looked more decorative than functional.

Ahn-Kha ate constantly, giving Valentine endless opportunities to examine the Grog's mouth. He watched Ahn-Kha eat with the same fascination that he once had when he studied a rattlesnake as it ate a rat. Hinged far back, Ahn-Kha could drop open his mouth like a steam shovel, wide enough to take a grapefruit down his gullet as easily as Valentine could swallow an aspirin. His front teeth, including the over-large incisors that projected up and down, just visible behind his rubbery lips, projected forward like a horse's, but his back teeth resembled Valentine's own, proving him omnivorous. The Grog sucked rather than lapped water. For the size of his mouth, he had a small tongue, preferring to use his lips to move food around in his mouth. When Valentine, while discussing eating habits over dinner, extended his tongue out of his mouth to touch the bottom of his own nose, the Grog choked back vomit and turned his back on Valentine for the remainder of the meal.

Valentine learned to watch his companion's ears. The pointed shells telegraphed his mood. When interested in something, they projected slightly up and forward and narrowed into points at the top, giving him a devilish appearance. When asking for a favor, even something as simple as passing a knife during a meal, the Grog flattened his ears against the sides of his head. When he was tired, they drooped; when something pained him, they went almost horizontal. When he and Valentine were moving over unknown ground, as they did when the Grog first got up and about and started to exercise, they twisted this way and that like radar dishes, fanlike flaps of skin spread wide.

One mannerism that took a good deal of getting used to was Ahn-Kha's habit of closing his eyes to mean no. Until Valentine got used to it, he kept asking questions twice, a practice that annoyed both of them no end.

They relocated a mile south as soon as Ahn-Kha felt well enough to travel. Neither said a word about accompanying the other as they set out, but the Grog's presence felt natural to Valentine. They explored and finally settled in to a ranch-style house by the wooded shores of a lake. The others in the neighborhood were burnt ruins, but this one had solid brick walls and a slate roof. The fresh air and movement had seemed to do the Grog good at first, but he fatigued quickly. The lake turned out to be rich in walleye, and Valentine decided they could feed themselves without going out of hearing distance from the house for the remainder of Ahn-Kha's recovery.

"How did you know about the mushrooms, my David?" Ahn-Kha asked the day they found the ranch, sharing a bowl of fungi-based soup with Valentine. "You say you have never lived among us, traded among us, yet you know our tastes?"

Valentine could take or leave mushrooms. They provided easily gathered protein, and in some cases fats, but given his choice, he would prefer to set rabbit snares or trap snakes rather than eat the chewy, tasteless growths.

"I've tracked a lot of your kind and watched them from a distance. What did you call them again, the gray ones with the thick hides?"

Ahn-Kha made a noise that sounded like he was getting ready to spit.

"That's not a word, that's a bodily function," Valentine demurred. "The Hur-rack? Is that close enough?"

The Grog nodded—a born diplomat, he adapted to David's gestures more easily than the other way around, as Valentine's ears were as fixed as his teeth—and concentrated on his meal. Cooking for Ahn-Kha was like trying to feed a lodge of lumberjacks.

"We've had some dealings with them down south. I knew a captive one once, he lived with some researchers. Loved root beer."

"Root beer? I know beer. I know root."

"It's a sweet drink—you wouldn't believe how good it tastes after a hot day's running."

"The mushrooms?"

"I've seen the Hur-rack stop and break off mushrooms from fallen trees and eat them on the march, even fight over them. I figured you found them tasty."

"Yours are adequate, no more. You have never tasted a heartroot, my David, which surpasses even your bread."

"How did you learn to speak so well?"

"We have a tradition, my David. When one asks a question needing a story to answer, the asker must then be prepared to tell a story in turn. Fair?"

Valentine nodded. "Fair."

"I was born here, my David, one of the first of my clan to be brought into this world once our people had settled. I am forty-one years old, and call this land home. The 'Gray Ones' you fight come from my parent's world, too; they are jungle dwellers—they do not write or shape metal and stone. We are the Golden Ones of hill and valley, builders of dams and bridges and makers of roads. Kur lured many of our clans and the Gray Ones' tribes to this world with promises of land and space, ours for the taking from a filthy and weak race. They gave us guns and trinkets, training and promises; we did the dying and helped win their victory. My parents despised your parents, many of whom sold their species for power and small wealth. In their opinion, you got what you deserved.

"We Golden Ones are happier as builders and planters than destroyers, and we claimed our land from Kur as soon as we could. Our clan settled around a fine stone building, once a library in this place you call Oma-Ha. My father was an overseer of our human laborers, and I heard your tongue. In my youth, I learned the English-speech and the English-script. I read many, many of your books, played your music on the electric toys, and grew in knowledge of your kind. I began to disagree with my parents, in simple rebellion at their narrow view at first, and later through conviction. A clan seer said my destiny would be with men, and so I chose as a profession trading. I was often in the house of the Big Man in Omaha, drinking his tea. I met smugglers who drove gasoline-powered off-roads. After being cheated more than once, I learned a valuable lesson: Know the man before sitting down to bargain; examine the product before making the trade. I learned that some men I could trust with my life—others were lower than dogs.

"By my thirtieth year, I sat at our Principal Elder's side during any meetings with your race, to help translate and advise. Men sometimes give themselves away when they lie. By my thirty-fifth year, I was an Elder, ten years before custom usually grants such an honor, and I looked forward to one day surpassing the achievements of my father.

"Our people had fine gardens of heartroot in the old brother buildings. Heartroot thrives on moisture and waste and little else. It is our staple. We learned to care for your animals, finding chickens tasty and easy to keep. We had a good land and busied ourselves tearing down the old and planting or putting up the new in our deep, rich soil.

"Then came the Twisted Cross, the emblem of our doom. I was optimistic when they first came; they showed us every respect. Their human 'ambassador' called for warriors to serve the new lord called the General south of the city, promising in exchange the General's protection for our lands.

"The ambassador, who had spoke fair words at first, turned foul when he learned we would not immediately give him all he demanded.

" 'We always protected our own before this day,' said the Elder. 'I suspect what you really offer is protection from the General himself. Look for your tribute of clan-flesh elsewhere.' "

Valentine tried to picture the scene, on the steps of the Grog-restored library, the Golden Ones talking amongst themselves, facing a uniformed contingent under the black-and-white swastika flag. Ahn-Kha, as he warmed to his tale, switched to the cadence of his native tongue, speaking slowly, his tone rising and falling like a ship in a heavy swell.

"After many words, sometimes hard, sometimes soft, the Principal Elder decreed that any free spirits who wished could go along.

"The General's man promised rich rewards of land after 'actions to destroy certain bands of rebels and terrorists' were completed. We Golden Ones had heard such before in the times of our parents and grandparents, and after much death and suffering were granted ruined lands near poisoned ground. Nevertheless, a number still returned south with the ambassador.

"He came again in the fall, again asking for a quota of able bodies. With fewer words and more anger, the Principal Elder turned him away, and only one or two malcontents went with him this time, rather than the dozens he had swayed before.

"Then came the third and final visit in the spring, now over three years ago. One of the malcontents who went with the ambassador on the second trip returned with him. The news they bore caused such shock that were it not for the many guns in the hands of the ambassador's men, there may have been bloodshed. Kur had named this malcontent, Khay-Hefle (may he forever wander from hell to hell), to be our new ruler. Not Principal Elder, but *ruler*. Of course, this Khay-Hefle did not voice himself with brazen demand, knowing the gods would not allow his treasonous tongue to speak such words. All were shocked into silence at the ambassador's announcement, even the Principal Elder.

"A great anger came upon me, and I stepped forward and said: 'Go, all of you, or you will be killed where you stand.'

"The ambassador ignored me and spoke to the Principal Elder. The Elder quoted the agreement that deeded us this land, ruined and poi-soned as it was, to us to be used and governed as we saw fit.

" 'Ah,' said the ambassador. 'It does say that, but as a Golden One would still govern, the agreement is still valid and Kur is still keeping its promise.' And many more words of deception like it.

"The Principal Elder grew angry, and his hair bristled. 'This is the second time in my life I have heard plain words twisted to mean the opposite of what they say, and both times your Masters are involved. Go back to your kennels, dogs, and never come again. Khay-Hefle and all who follow him no longer belong to our clan unless they return in seven days.' At this there was sorrow from the families of those who left in the two times before.

" 'You may try to enforce your demands and place this usurper over us, but do not think this task will be an easy matter,' said the Elder. 'You will go back with none of our warriors and less of your own.'

"I supported his brave words, and all the Elders stood silent and grim until the ambassador and his dog Khay-Hefle left. Then there was much argument, some saying that it would be better to preserve what we had built than suffer in a war that we would lose. Others said we must leave: go north at once beyond the reach of this General or Kur.

"In the end, the Elders sent away One of Ten, to travel north and then west to a range of mountains we knew of in the place you called Canada, beyond the reach of the Kur who care not for such cold. I was selected to lead the flight because of my skill in speaking to humans, but refused. I still felt the heat of my words before the Clan Hall and wished for nothing more than to see Khay-Hefle come with his new masters and try to enforce their wicked will."

Ahn-Kha paused for a moment and stared into the glowing coals of the fire kindled in the stone fireplace of the house. After their morning meal, it was still far too hot during the day to keep the fire going, so they let it die.

"For the rest, I shall be brief. We turned our gardens into trenches, or homes into forts, our halls into castles. Everyone carried a weapon at all times, and we gathered the children in the basements. I thought we stood a good chance, or at least would make such a struggle that in our destruction they would be destroyed, too, and our children would grow free of them.

"They came, and we had never encountered such soldiers. Our bullets knocked them down, but did not kill them. Even arm against arm, their strength matched ours by some demonic power, and we killed only one for each ten of us who died. They were as the Hooded Ones but they fought with the weapons and skill of men. They came with explosives, guns gushing streams of fire, and cannon mounted on tracked vehicles. The fire-guns were the worst. My people fear fire the way some of yours fear snakes or spiders, or great heights. Our end was bitter. Some comrades, and my father, as well as myself were holding a building in the garden before the Hall. They came with boxes of explosives, and when I saw this, I called for all to follow me out the secret tunnel going back to the old library. When the explosion came, it buried all behind me in the blast and rubble. I went to the Hall. A bomb or shell had gone off in the basement with the children, killing all there. I took another tunnel to the post where the Principal Elder commanded, but found nothing but bloodstains on the floor.

"I determined to avenge the Clan on Khay-Hefle, and lurked outside the ruins of our lands, waiting for a chance to kill him. But he set about ordering the lives of the survivors, surrounded by humans and a bodyguard of the Gray Ones. Imagine that illiterate rabble chewing on gum-root and watching Golden Ones toil as they scratch themselves.

"Strangely, I was shunned by the few other survivors who lurked in the city. Perhaps they had their minds poisoned by Khay-Hefle, who told them that I brought this on our Clan with my proud words, and the death and destruction of our Clan came about because a few mad ones controlled the mind of our Principal Elder.

"My people live now as many of yours, my David, little more than slaves who live under the lies of a Golden One who speaks the words he is told to speak. I have had to move to the outskirts of the city and live alone. I still hope for my chance, but sometimes I think of going north and seeing if the One in Ten ever made it to the mountains of Canada."

Valentine reached into his map case. "I have some maps here, if you think they would help."

"I recovered with some from the old human library. But I will not go north before I pay off my gratitude to you."

Valentine shook his head. "Do we have to talk about this again? You owe me nothing. I had to see what could have killed those Harpies barehanded, and then I felt sympathy for you. It was a tribute, not a favor."

"We shall see, my David. You agreed to tell a story in return for mine. To know yours would make me happy. I have not really talked to anyone in a very long time. We are brothers under the skin, I feel, for you also carry many sorrows that trouble you."

"I could use a drink," Valentine said.

"You mean wine, or liquor?" Ahn-Kha asked. "My people made a wonderful wine from a fruit we call *ethrodzh,* but I have none with me. I had none even before the fliers attacked."

"I'd like to try it sometime," Valentine said, looking around the cracked and peeled walls of the ranch, the stained ceiling and musty furnishings.

"You told me about your people; I'm not sure what to say about mine. We used to classify ourselves by color and language, where we lived and what we did. Not anymore, though. To me there are only three groups left: the ones who help the Kurians, the ones who endure the Kurians, and the ones who resist. The ones who help them, I have no sympathy for, and I've found that there's very little I can do for the ones enduring. If I think about it too much, I despair. I'm in the group that fights the Kur.

"So was my father. I'm not certain about his reasons for quitting the Cause, but now that I've done it for a couple years, I can guess. I don't know if he met my mother before or after he stopped fighting. I think it was after. But he left. He tried to live quietly about three hundred miles north of here, like your One out of Ten who looked for a place where the winters were too long and harsh for the Kurians to live. My parents raised a family—I was the first, and I had a younger brother and sister. In northern Minnesota every summer the people retreat deep into the woods and return in the fall. During the summer, the Quislings—you know what a Quisling is, right? Anyway, we hid out in the summer from them, as well as from the Reapers. In the winter, we were cooped up in our houses. Getting firewood and ice fishing were probably the only times we went outside.

"I guess my father didn't go deep enough into the woods. A Quisling patrol came by—I was away gathering corn. They killed them all, more for fun than anything. Another man, an old priest who was a friend of my father's, brought me up and educated me.

"When I was seventeen going on eighteen, some soldiers came by, from the Ozark Free Territory."

"I have heard of this place," Ahn-Kha said. "You cause a great deal of problem to the Kur."

"Problems," Valentine corrected absently. "But you would probably want to say, 'You cause a great deal of trouble for the Kur.'"

"Not troubles?" Ahn-Kha asked.

"No," Valentine said, causing Ahn-Kha to shake his head in disgust.

Perhaps we are some kind of kindred spirits, Valentine thought. *Who else, with death all around, would worry about grammar?*

"Go on with your tale," Ahn-Kha prompted.

"I went south with some other young people from Minnesota. I was curious about these men who fought alongside my father. I wanted to do something, avenge them in a way, or replace him. It was my way of learning who I was, by following in his footsteps. Or that's what I told myself then.

"I also wanted blood. Show the force behind all this that you might be able to kill the father and mother but the sons and daughters will take their place. A schoolmate of mine, a girl named Gabriella, came south with the group. I had . . . feelings for her."

"I see, my David. When do you humans mate, at that age?"

"The question is, 'When don't humans mate?' I think."

Ahn-Kha put his hands on his stomach—Valentine knew enough of him by now to know that the gesture showed quiet amusement.

Valentine continued: "The first year, they just worked us half to death in construction and farm labor. I think they were winnowing out the shirkers. We were toughened, learned to work together, and all the sweat helped the Free Territory. But that year Gabriella died—it had to do with those damned Harpies and a Reaper. We did manage to get the ones responsible. They made me a soldier after that, and I've been one ever since. But it didn't bring Gabby back."

"A strange soldier, who fights alone," Ahn-Kha observed.

Valentine did not want to say too much. "It's a long story. I guess you could say I'm a scout that went out a little too far."

"Now you go home?"

Valentine nodded. "Now I go home."

"I think we were meant to know each other, my David. We both have lost our clan. We both wander alone. You are half my years, but your feet have stepped where I have only ventured in thought. I read your eyes when I spoke of the General's men, the Twisted Cross. Would you change your mind about going home if I were to tell you exactly where they could be found?"

As they talked, Valentine idly wondered if this all was not some kind of elaborate trap. He discarded the notion; the Grog probably could have killed him in his sleep last night. Unless Ahn-Kha fabricated his story out of the still night air, he had more reason to hate the Twisted Cross than Valentine.

Valentine wanted a chance to examine the Twisted Cross base, but Ahn-Kha insisted that they first come up with more supplies, as they could not afford to wander and hunt near the Twisted Cross headquarters. And Ahn-Kha wanted weapons to replace the ones he lost to the Harpies. They were still debating the issue on the eve of their departure, as they packed to move on that night.

"My David, I feel naked without a gun."

"I offered you my pistol."

"Ha! I should have said I feel naked without a real gun."

"Ahn-Kha, I'm already overdue to meet my comrade. Your idea to go into the part of the city where the Golden Ones live seems a little risky. Why not try at this human settlement on the river?"

"There are Quislings there. We would certainly be noticed. My face might be remembered there. Besides, we have nothing to trade for a gun save another gun. Although we could get two good rifles for your automatic weapon."

"It still doesn't get me to the Platte, and there we can—"

Valentine was never able to finish the sentence. His nose alerted him to a strange scent, coming at them from the lakeshore.

"Danger," he whispered.

The Grog had reflexes. Ahn-Kha went down on all fours by the window before Valentine chambered the first round in his PPD.

"From where?" the Grog asked.

"The lakeside, to the north. Let's check the front." Valentine crawled for the front window. He stayed out of the light and examined the new stand of woods and brush between the house and what was left of the suburban road. Yes, there were Grogs out there. One of Ahn-Kha's Gray Ones had his long rifle in the crotch of a tree, sighted on the front of the house.

He returned to the common room. Ahn-Kha threw wet sand from their toilet bucket into the fireplace, killing the light.

"It is the Wrist-Ring clan, perhaps," Ahn-Kha said. "One of their scouts may have seen us in the house or read our tracks. There are six approaching from the lake. They have ropes. Perhaps they mean to take me back and place a harness on my back. If so, they'll find this old horse can still kick."

"Did they see you?"

"No, I believe not, they would have charged—or taken cover."

Valentine checked to make sure he had put his map case away in his pack along with the rest of his possessions.

"The way I see it," he said, "we have three options. Fight it out from in here—"

The Grog shut and opened his eyes. "They will burn the house around us, my David."

"The second option is to try to talk or bargain our way out of here—"

This time Ahn-Kha remembered to shake his head side-to-side. "The Wrist-Ring would make the best deal they could, so we do not waste our bullets fighting them, and then kill us afterwards."

"Or we could just run like hell."

"Often the wisest choice," Ahn-Kha agreed. "But they will shoot us as we run."

"Follow me," Valentine said. He picked up his pack and led the Grog into the garage. Light glimmered down from a hole under the peak of the roof, where the broken edges of a porthole window stood festooned with bracken. The wooden door still stood in its rusted tracks.

"They'll probably rush the house," Valentine said. "They'll come noisy, with grenades if they have them."

"No, my David. Grenades are too valuable to waste on drifters. There is always the chance that we have powerful friends, too. Perhaps you are a wandering Twisted Cross official. They would come in and shoot anyone not in a uniform they recognize. Why do we speak in this place? It has no exit, and it will take time to climb out of that hole."

"We're not climbing out the roof. You're making a new door."

Ahn-Kha gripped the submachine gun, cradling it tight to his body in his massive arms. When Valentine heard an unintelligible cry, and the breaking sounds of the Grogs crashing through doors and windows, he counted silently to five, and then nodded at Ahn-Kha.

The Golden One lowered one of his saddle-size shoulders and charged the closed garage door. He struck it with the force of a demolition charge going off, splintering the ancient wood.

Ahn-Kha spotted the sniper at the crotch-tree, just where Valentine described a moment ago, but now Ahn-Kha had a much better angle than he would have had shooting from the house. He loosed a burst that peppered tree and Grog alike, sending it reeling backwards. Ahn-Kha twisted to his right and fired another burst into the Grog covering the living room from outside as its clan-mates went in. The wounded Grog dropped the rifle it had just begun to aim in their direction.

As planned, his living battering ram turned and tossed the PPD to Valentine, who lay down with the gun pointed at the front door. Ahn-Kha loped out into the front yard, to the tree where the late sniper positioned himself. The fawn-colored Grog picked up where his distant relative left off, sighting on the doorway.

Valentine backed down the driveway, now pointing the gun at the corner leading to the backyard on the garage side. He heard something coming around that side. Half a face appeared, peeking around the corner. "Your eye ain't much good if it doesn't bring your gun along," a gruff old Wolf had told him once, and Valentine taught the Grog the same lesson by aiming a burst at the half-face. He missed, splintering the corner of the garage, and the face withdrew.

He turned to run, and heard Ahn-Kha fire the booming fifty-caliber at something in the doorway.

"Cover me!" Ahn-Kha urged, and Valentine slid to the ground again, this time with the gun pointed at the midpoint of the house. Valentine marveled at how he worked with this remarkable creature—a being that was technically an enemy he might have killed on sight until a few days ago. Ahn-Kha stripped the sniper Grog of a bandolier glinting with shells and reloaded the cumbersome—to a human—weapon. Valentine saw motion in the front window and gave the trigger a twitch. The bullets went in the window; whether they struck anything was a matter of luck. Hips never leaving the ground, he wiggled next to his companion and lay down behind the fallen Grog.

The dead Grog had a homemade "potato masher" grenade jutting out of its bag. He held the grenade up to Ahn-Kha. "Can you throw this over the house?"

"I can throw it over the lake."

Valentine pulled the fuse and handed it handle-first to the long-armed warrior. Ahn-Kha drew back an arm, putting the other forward in the classic javelin-throw pose, and sent the grenade spinning over the deadfall-covered roof.

They ran, Valentine in the lead, cutting away from the house at an angle in order to force their attackers to get them with a crossing shot. They went over a fallen log in the middle of the road, Valentine hurdling it and Ahn-Kha vaulting over it sideways, using his long left arm as a brace.

The grenade Ahn-Kha threw never went off; perhaps the fuse went out, the bomb malfunctioned, or some desperate Grog behind the house extinguished it in time. The pair sprinted southward. Shots thwacked into trees around them as they ran.

Six Grogs followed, loping into the young forest of the ruined suburban tracts. It became five when Ahn-Kha halted behind a tree while Valentine kept running and brought down the lead pursuer. After that, the chase proceeded with less speed and more caution, and when Valentine killed another from a rooftop Ahn-Kha had stirrup-lifted him onto, the pursuit broke off.

"We got away from them," Ahn-Kha said, breathing heavily and resting on all fours.

"You bet, old horse." Valentine marked the setting sun. "But they won't get away from us."

Ahn-Kha got his pick of weapons that night.

They swung around in a crescent, and Valentine left the exhausted Grog with his pack and gun well clear of the house while he went back to the brick ranch, approaching from the opposite direction from which they had fled. He took with him two grenades scavenged off the dead Gray Ones.

He crawled around the perimeter of the house in his black over-coat, listening to the grunts and barks within. The Grogs had gathered around their wounded, resting in the back room by the fireplace. He armed and activated the grenade as quietly as he could.

Gray Ones have good noses and better ears; one of them heard or smelled the fuse. It barked a warning, and Valentine let the fuse burn down two anxious seconds' worth before tossing the grenade through the window. While it was still in the air, he stuck his fingers in his ears.

At the explosion, he drew his sword and came in through the back door. It was a matter of killing everything that moved in the smoke-filled room that was not a part of him. The stunned and stricken Grogs might as well have played blindman's buff with a buzz saw—only one had the sense to run. It left a blood trail across the floor as it hurried to leap out of the gap where the front picture window had once been.

It didn't make the window. Valentine was after it like an arrow, opening it with a slash across the back.

Ahn-Kha returned to the house and ignored the carnage. He examined the various rifles and eventually selected one with a black-stained handle. The Grogs liked the butts of their weapons to be gnarled and burled and this one was no exception. "I must shape this before it truly suits me, but it is a good gun." He also pored over the finger-size bullets, sliding the formidable-looking rounds he selected into his bandolier.

Valentine lined up the Grog bodies according to Ahn-Kha's instructions, placing them on their backs with the left palm over the heart, the right palm across the nose and mouth, weapons laid to either side. Another patrol from the Wrist-Ring Clan, upon finding the bodies, might pause for the proper ceremonies. They would seed the bodies with the correct decomposing fungi, and perhaps be too busy mourning their dead to pursue.

"You men anger the Gray Ones when you just burn their corpses. They think you kill them not only in this world, but deny them the passage to the Hero's Woods their bravery merits. Better to leave them to lie on the battlefield untouched."

"Ever heard the expression 'When in Rome'? They wouldn't have their rites ignored if they weren't here in the first place."

"That's the fault of another generation."

Valentine thought of the wilds of western Missouri. Wolf teams could reach Omaha, find paths that more powerful forces could follow. "By working together, some of that generation's legacy might be wiped away."

"The Golden Ones have tasted the fruits of their alliance with Kur.

We found them rotten. Then came the Twisted Cross. Many would be ready to join your fight."

"I wish we could find explosives more powerful than these grenades," Valentine said, rooting through the Gray Ones' equipment. "We could hit the Twisted Cross in their own backyard."

"I can help you in that," Ahn-Kha said. "There are men in the Old Market who can obtain anything you need."

To Valentine, anything pre-2022 was "old." But this part of the city, set against the river, was aged even by Old World standards as he understood them.

The closely packed, square brick buildings had new windows where they weren't simply closed by masonry. The west and south faces of many still showed burnt-black smudges, lingering evidence of the airbursts that had destroyed the city and the old air force base to the south.

They came to the district walking along the Missouri. The river rolled south past the city, redolent of silt and algae, with only a hint of the sewage that Valentine smelled from many of the old storm drains. In the distance, a rust-colored dredger worked between the pillars of the rail bridge, bringing up masses of mud. Just upriver from the dredger, a few barges rested against a wharf. There were overturned canoes and even a few small sailboats sharing the riverside with the trim barges, baby versions of the huge transports Valentine had seen from a distance on the Mississippi.

Ahn-Kha told him a little about the settlement. Though all of Omaha and its surroundings had been given to the Grogs, the Golden Ones and Gray Ones still needed to trade—especially for tools and weapons. They invited a few humans to set up house, giving them protection for activities that were outlawed elsewhere in the Kurian Zone, and a little patch of land next to the riverside fields and C-shaped lake. The black marketeers flourished, and as the Quisling society in Iowa and parts of Kansas grew, they became semilegitimate even in the eyes of the Kurians.

Old Omaha had no walls. Once past the reeking piles of trash and the masses of feral cats sleeping in the sunny blown-out doorways and windows north of the wharf, Ahn-Kha led him to clean cobblestone streets. Every windowsill and rooftop supported a garden. Goats and calves grazed in open lots. The animals were marked with splashes of dye.

"The traders here run 'houses.'" Ahn-Kha explained. "When I came here, there were three. I am told it has been that way for years. The three tolerate each other, but no more. They share the common land but mark their animals. The gardens on the land of the house are their own. They tell me there are groves across the river for apples and cherries and chestnuts, but I have not been there to see how they divide it."

Men, most of them armed with gun belts, lounged here and there on the corners. Some rose from benches and made a show of standing in the sidewalk so Ahn-Kha had to step into the street to pass.

"You just take that crap?" Valentine asked.

"It is easier to receive an insult than a bullet."

Valentine saw the wisdom in that, but it still irked him.

"Which house do you wish to try?"

"House Holt. For the most part, they were good friends with the Golden Ones. It is run by the Big Man."

"What's he like?" Valentine wondered what to expect. He hoped it wasn't an Omaha version of the Duke in Chicago, alternately bluff and frightening.

"He was always evenhanded to me, though not friendly. He looked always to the future; I admired him for thinking, and speaking, in terms of decades rather than days."

"Not many can afford to do that."

"Here is his insignia. It hangs outside his house, and his men carry it as his token."

Valentine looked at the sign. He'd seen broken versions of it here and there; it was circular, green and white and black, featuring a serene long-haired woman surrounded by stars. Above the projecting sign on the second story, fans set in the window turned behind inch-thick iron bars.

"Electricity here?" Valentine asked.

"Yes. The three houses share the maintenance of a coal generator. Long ago I tried to get them to put one in for the Golden Ones. I failed."

As they approached the door under the sign, a man next to the door rose from his seat on a wooden locker and put his hand on his pistol. He had long hair and a longer stare.

"What's your business?"

"A meeting with your Executive," Ahn-Kha said.

"You let your Grog do your talking for you, kid?" the door warden asked Valentine. "Usually with you Black Flag types, the man's the mouth and the Grog's the muscle."

"I'm the bodyguard," Valentine said.

"That so. Put your weapons in this box, and I'll let you in. Whether you see the Big Man or not will be up to him."

Ahn-Kha gave Valentine a nod. The warden opened the box. Ahn-

Kha leaned his captured rifle against the door-jamb; the gun was too long to fit inside. Valentine placed pistol, parang, sword, and claws within, and covered it with his bedroll and submachine gun.

The warden shook his head. "More iron doesn't make you more tough, kid. I've got to check your pockets and pat you down. Anything sticks me, we'll float you back to your General on crutches. Anything else?"

Valentine removed a short clasp knife and tossed it in with the rest. It wasn't much of a weapon anyway. "Clean now. Enjoy."

The warden searched both of them from head to foot. "Strangers call," he shouted into the door.

"Opening for strangers," came the response after a moment. An older man, white at the temples, wraparound sunglasses worn against the glare outside, lowered a shotgun when he saw Ahn-Kha.

"Ankle! It's been years."

Valentine was glad he looked genuinely pleased.

The man nodded to Valentine, then shook Ahn-Kha's hand. "Thought you bought it in the Big Burn."

"I've been in hiding, my Ian. Please to meet my new brother, David."

Ian shut the door and sent a thick bolt home.

"You no longer run your route?" Ahn-Kha asked.

"The routes are drying up. Even north. Those of us who still want to draw food work carrying guns now. The General's giving us the squeeze."

"Then perhaps we can do business. We wish to see the Big Man about the General."

"Lost cause. That rat's got muscle from here to KC. Keeps trying to get us to come on base, wear his damned cross. Doesn't sit right with me—lots of us—going down there just to salute and put new heels on Reaper boots. This is House talk only, but immyho, the Big Man says that's the only alternative to just pulling up and leaving for God knows where. He's down to trying to get us a good deal and keep us off base."

Within fifteen minutes, they were speaking to the Executive of House Holt.

The Big Man wasn't big, or even of average size. Valentine guessed him to be about four feet nine inches, and a bantamweight to boot. He had lush black hair falling back from the crown of his head to his thick beard. An open-necked shirt, silver-buckled belt, and cuffed pants over pointed-toe boots. He was bowlegged, pigeon-chested.

Valentine guessed his age to be mid-forties. When Valentine was training to be a Wolf, he heard a senior Wolf talk about a generation

the veteran called the "children of chaos." In the years of what the Free
Territory called the Overthrow, many babies were born underweight
and malnourished as a rule, and in the tumultuous years that followed,
they never had a chance to catch up. Valentine had known only a few
from those hard years, compact-framed like the man before him, but
generous spirits. Extreme hardship, it seemed to Valentine, had polar-
ized that generation to extremes of magnanimity or selfishness.

Valentine hoped for magnanimity.

Their host stood at a window on the third floor, surveying Old
Omaha from a floor-to-ceiling window, the layered panes somewhat
distorting the view. He stood resting against a chair; the chair and its
mate sat to either side of a wooden chess table with gold and silver
pieces arranged on the board and beside it. The office was opulently furnished around an immense wooden desk and bookcase, but it seemed
crammed—with everything from statues to rugs to paintings to vases
and urns—rather than arranged, especially when compared with Roland
Victor's in Kansas.

The corner nearest them, separated from the Big Man by a folding
screen, was occupied by a squint-eyed assistant. She wrote in a ledger
resting upon a drafting table. The Big Man's burled desk had nothing
on the top except a lamp and a leather blotter.

"Ahn-Kha." The Big Man had a flat voice, a trifle reedy. "What
brings you and your 'bodyguard' to my house?"

"My compliment on your promotion," Ahn-Kha said. "What became of the Big Man?"

"Ravies. Some rats they'd released, I suppose on the Ozarks to the
south, made it into one of our barges. Bad luck; he was checking incoming cargoes and stuck his hand into a bag of rice without wearing
gloves."

"You took the name along with the Executive title?"

"Sort of a joke. I don't mind."

The Big Man walked around to his desk and sat down. He moved
stiff-leggedly, with the aid of a pair of canes. The canes disappeared as
soon as he sat.

"Shall we leave right now?" Ahn-Kha asked.

"Without introducing your friend?" the Big Man asked.

"His name is David."

He swiveled his gaze to Valentine. "I should explain. Ahn-Kha and
I have had our differences in the past. I didn't care for our house trading weapons with his kind." He returned to Ahn-Kha. "I accused you
of eating human babies, as I recall. Ten years ago I . . . anger tended to

get the better of me. Anger that had nothing to do with the Golden Ones."

"For my part, I challenged him to combat," Ahn-Kha added. "Aggravating insult with greater insult."

"Was there a duel?" Valentine said when neither offered an end to the story.

"No," the Big Man said. "Calmer heads interceded. Unless you wish to take up the challenge?"

Ahn-Kha closed his eyes, opened them. "No."

Valentine felt some of the tension seep away. "We need your help. House Holt's help."

"What do you offer? We're traders. Smugglers, to some. Quislings to others. I saw you take off a Wolf parang."

"My company was destroyed this spring," Valentine said. The truth, even shaded, was preferable to a plausible lie. "Our request is unusual."

"January, please get our guests some sandwiches and lemonade." The woman behind the screen slipped out.

"Lemonade?" Valentine asked, going over to the chess set.

"Thanks to the Kurians, they grow fine in some of the more sheltered parts of the Missouri Valley."

Valentine stared down at the pieces. The gold king was in trouble—nothing but a castle and a pawn protected him from a knight, two pawns, a bishop, and the silver king.

"Do you play?" the Big Man asked, turning his chair.

"A little. My dad taught me. I used to play it with my adopted father—neither of us were very good."

"Do you see a way out for the black king? I'm trying for a draw."

"*Black* meaning the gold one?"

"Yes. Sorry. Convention requires black and white no matter what the color of the pieces are."

Valentine looked, thought. "No. I think mate in three moves."

The Big Man sighed. "Two. The king can attack."

"How about a game? While we have the sandwiches."

Their host looked eager again and rocked his way back to the table. "You're the guest. White or black."

"Silver."

Valentine moved a pawn.

Eight moves later, behind leaping knights, the black queen came forth. "Checkmate," the Big Man said in his inflectionless voice.

Valentine shook his hand. "What's the General to you, Executive? An enemy bishop, or your king?"

The Big Man rested his chin on his cane. "An opposing king. I give him tribute, barges of food. He'd rather I were one of his pieces. My position isn't that different from the way the pieces were before our game. Though I don't have a castle. Just three floors of odds and ends."

The sandwiches arrived, pulling Ahn-Kha from an examination of oil paintings in dusty frames.

"January, I won't need you for a bit. You can go home for the afternoon if you wish," the Big Man said.

Valentine saw a look pass between them. "It's all right—I'm perfectly safe. They're not Twisted Cross." He began to put the pieces back in their starting positions. "Care to switch chairs for the next?"

This time the Big Man's silver bishops eviscerated him like a pair of dueling swords. Checkmate in eleven moves.

"What did you come here for?"

"Guns for the Golden Ones. Explosives," Ahn-Kha said, as Valentine and the Big Man switched chairs again. "My people would use them against the Twisted Cross."

"I'm only crippled physically, Ahn-Kha."

Valentine moved his queen, taking a knight. "Southern Command would help, too. Perhaps in a few months, we could have Bear teams up here. You know what they are, don't you?"

"A kiss and a promise. I'll believe it when I see the teams. Besides, I don't have that much time. The General has given me an ultimatum. Join, leave, or . . . be burnt. Your move."

Valentine saw it coming this time—the Big Man had sacrificed a knight to draw out his queen. He lost a bishop, and then it was, "Checkmate."

"Let's play again. No switching chairs, I like silver."

"Very well."

This time they were silent. Valentine lost a knight, and when the bishops came forward again, his pawns occupied them until his queen had space. She took a castle, a pawn, and a bishop before falling. Then his castles came forward. The Big Man let out a small noise, wrinkled his brows, moved a knight back. Valentine sent a bishop forward, took a pawn, lost his bishop, and brought out his last knight.

Valentine checked.

The Big Man moved his king, a smile on his face.

"Checkmate," Valentine said.

The Big Man offered his hand. "My compliments. I saw it two moves ago, but went through the motions. You deserved the gratification."

Valentine arranged the pieces the way they'd been when he first approached the table. "Sir, in your quest for a stalemate . . . suppose you could have gotten that pawn to the white side and converted it."

"Unlikely."

"Suppose the unlikely happened."

"Reliance on the improbable is a bad strategy."

"Even so," Valentine said.

Ahn-Kha's ears pointed forward, listening.

"The whole balance would change. I could get the draw. Depending on the white bishop, I might be able to squeeze a victory."

"If you got enough arms to the Golden Ones, in the ghetto, on the base, that lonely pawn could become a terrible weapon."

"No. I won't put my house's future in jeopardy."

Ahn-Kha's ears drooped as he stood. "Thank you for the sandwiches. I am glad we have put the past behind."

The Big Man nodded. "Good luck with your own future."

"What there is of it," Valentine said. "Thank you for your time."

"Thank you for the game. I haven't been beaten in years."

Valentine and Ahn-Kha went to the door. As they opened it, the Big Man spoke again. "David, a bit of advice: Practice the tried and true. You'll win more often. The intuitive player can be brilliant. Once in a while even beat the best. But most of the time, you'll lose."

The Cat nodded. The Big Man returned to his board. Valentine left a crack in the door and looked back through it. The Big Man wrinkled his brow in thought, then pushed his golden pawn forward.

"So much for explosives," Valentine said when they were in the street again.

Ahn-Kha looked at the sky. "There's one other place we could try. It's only a few blocks away."

"A different trading house?"

"None of the others deal in anything but hunting rifles."

"Then what?"

"The General's building where Khay-Hefle now rules. It lies behind the walls that imprison my people."

From what might have been a corner office within the skeleton of a high-rise, Valentine looked across central Omaha at the ghetto of the Golden Ones.

Flat on his stomach, he leisurely surveyed the quarter of the city's ruins allocated to them. Behind the old library, now the residence of their usurping chief and his Twisted Cross shield, were the twin buildings Valentine knew to be home to the dank farms of heartroot of which Ahn-Kha rhapsodized and home to Omaha's captive Golden Ones. Ahn-Kha said the lower floors and stairways of the buildings were sound, though the walls and windows had been blasted out by the overpressure of nuclear explosions. Many Golden Ones lived on the structurally intact floors in a warren of partitions and rebuilt rooms, complete with a gravity plumbing system that Ahn-Kha claimed to be the wonder of Omaha.

The Twisted Cross added on some changes. Piles of rubble topped with cemented-in broken glass formed walls all around the Golden Ones' quarter. Their new Principal Elder insisted on this measure for the safety of his people. Ahn-Kha maintained that the wall did a better job of keeping Golden Ones in than their enemies out, a belief supported by the slapped-together wooden guard towers that stood both inside and outside the wall.

Valentine guessed the whole area to be well over a square mile, in what was once downtown Omaha. As Ahn-Kha described, there had been a thriving population of Grogs controlling the heart of the city, but even in their reduced space behind the walls, the ghetto appeared far from crowded.

"I don't see many of your people. A few working in the gardens, some more clearing that field of rubble to the northwest."

"Every day a train comes through the rail-gate in the south. My clan is great builders; your Twisted Cross need them in the old base south of the city. Those who wish to eat adequately get on the train. They serve soup and bread for those who work. They even keep some of my people in pens on his base."

"Hostage taking. The General likes the tried-and-true as much as the Big Man."

"Once the Golden One who traded profitably, or spun the best poem-chant, or threw the *sook* most accurately at sport was considered a Great One. Now it is the back that moves the most dirt."

"Have you been back inside since all this happened?"

"Yes, brief trips. It is dangerous. But I have met many times with those who sneak out for trade and to hunt. My people are good engineers; they open a new hole as soon as another is blocked. It is a dangerous business, especially at night. The Hooded Ones of the Twisted Cross see through walls, sometimes under the ground."

"*Seeing* isn't the right word. An energy that a sentient being creates, called an aura, is something they sense."

The Grog nodded. "I heard of this, but I thought it was a tale to frighten us. The General's men roam outside the walls at night. During the day, my people are under the eyes of the guards in the towers. Some are men, some are Gray Ones, some are Khay-Hefle's lickspittles."

Valentine, his eyes still to the binoculars, broke into a smile. "You are well read, Ahn-Kha. I don't think I've ever heard the word *lickspittle* spoken in my life."

"I grew to love your language, my David. It has little logic or music to it, but there are some fine phrases."

"Agreed. My engineer-sergeant, when I served in the labor regiment, he had some fine phrases. No logic or music in them, either, but he got his point across."

Ahn-Kha laughed. "Foremen are the same everywhere."

"You said you had a plan for getting us inside. What do you have in mind?"

"We cannot go over the wall. There are many obstacles, traps, and noisemakers. During the day we would be seen; at night, the Hooded Ones could sense us. That leaves only two other ways in. The first seems less risky on the face of it, but involves a good deal of luck. I know of two tunnels in, but my information is months old. As I said, they do find the tunnels. We may get below ground only to learn it is bricked up. Or it may appear clear, but have explosives placed all around to kill us and close the tunnel at the same time.

"The second way requires more daring. Both the rail gate and the city gate are guarded by humans, those in the lowest ranks of the Twisted Cross. To them, every Golden One looks alike. There is only rarely a Golden One on sentry duty; more often it is Gray Ones. I could march in as one of Khay-Hefle's lickspittles—as you like this word so much—with you under guard. We might get as far as the Clan Hall. There, however, Khay-Hefle's bodyguards do stand sentry duty, and they would recognize me."

"How big is his bodyguard?" Valentine asked.

"There are twelve or fifteen. Three always attend to him, standing outside his door day and night. Another stands at the Hall Doors, and those off-duty gather inside the Hall or near it. They are well armed, for they fear my people whom they have betrayed."

"The Great Hall has the weapons of the Twisted Cross?"

"Yes, the armory is there, under the supervision of this General's men. I understand they also have a small post on the other side of the river. They have done much work on the old base south of town. This General recruits artisans and technicians from many places. He covets more than just Omaha."

Valentine nodded. "That's what I'm afraid of. From what you said, he means to destroy the lands I come from. He could succeed, given what I've seen. Southern Command is only just hanging on as is."

You're just one man, he told himself. *Get back to the Ozarks with what you have.*

One man can't wreck the factory, but he can drop a wrench in the works, another, more confidant part of him answered. *Southern Command wouldn't get an expedition organized until next spring, if at all, and by then it could be too late.*

Valentine had done some brazen things in his life, but walking up to a guard post with a well-spoken blood enemy holding a gun to his spine was the crowning act of audacity in his career. He dragged his feet down the cleared road through the rubble of what was once a wide thoroughfare with his hands over his head.

At first he asked Ahn-Kha to move him along with the submachine gun. "No, my David," the Golden One disagreed, "it would be noticed. The lowliest gate warden holds himself superior to my people, and would take your weapon without thinking twice."

So they hid the PPD and Valentine's pack in the rubble of the building they used to observe the Golden One zone. Ahn-Kha carried Valentine's sword, parang, and pistol in what had been Valentine's pack. The would-be prisoner's only weapons were his fighting claws.

Evening shadows began to settle across the city while a Twisted Cross noncom watched them approach with an interested air. He carried himself with the impatience of one who expects to be promoted to better duty. Valentine's ears picked up their conversation. "One of our valiant allies caught himself a real prize," the corporal with the silvered swastikas on the sleeves of his gray overalls commented.

"Wish they'd bring in a woman for a change, Corp," the private in an urban camouflage version of the same overall commented.

"Wish for a promotion, then. The officers get the mistresses, the sergeants get the whores, and the rest get the shaft."

"Ain't it the truth, Corp."

As the pair drew up to the zigzag of barbed-wire fencing blocking the gate in the daytime, the corporal stepped into the sun. "That's far enough," he said, assault rifle cradled in his elbow. One of his eyes was set higher in his face than the other. As if to balance it, he kept the opposite corner of his mouth turned down. "What's this, soldier?"

"Da-Khest, Railroad Security, sir!" Ahn-Kha barked. "I caught this man just this side of the old interstate, on the south line. He was armed, sir!"

The corporal turned back to the sentry. "Railroad Security," he said, sotto voce. "Three meals a day to sleep under a bridge." He turned back to the Grog. "Good work, Detest. We like to see results for a change. Usually we get stories from your *people* about bandits dragging their dead away. Let's see that gun."

Ahn-Kha pulled out Valentine's revolver and handed it over. "It was empty, sir."

The corporal examined the weapon. He spun the cylinder. "I'm not surprised. Private Wilde, you have any use for a .357?"

"No, sir. I know Ackermann is looking for a spare nine-millimeter."

"Who wants a wheelgun anyway?" another sentry put in.

Wilde nodded. "Those Troopers are the only ones who carry that hardware. Dumb goat ropers."

"It's too scratched up," the corporal commented, spinning the cylinder and working the double action. "Be worth something if it were chrome, or at least stainless. This blued steel looks like hell after a few years."

Valentine spoke up. "There's been a mistake, sir. I'm just a courier, but I have friends on both sides of the river. Both sides, sir. It would be worth something to the Big Man in the Old Market if I got back to him."

The low eye squinted on the corporal. "Listen, mook: I'm not some hungry Trooper or a Marshal on the take. I'm chiseled out of stainless steel. Bullshit slides off me."

You're also so busy being superior, you're not asking the right questions, Valentine thought.

"This isn't worth the sweat I'm working up in this heat," the corporal decided. "De-test, this man's in pretty good shape. Running packs of contraband builds the muscles. He'll find them useful at the Cave. Throw him in the hold for now; he'll go out on tomorrow's train."

The corporal returned to the little shed and made a note on a clipboard. The sentry moved aside half the wire barricade, and Valentine led Ahn-Kha home.

"Think about it, sir," Valentine called over his shoulder. "Get in touch with the Big Man. Tell him Blackie's in the cuffs, he'll be grateful. And generous."

"He'll do what he always does," the corporal laughed. "He'll claim he's an honest businessman and say he's never heard of you."

Exactly what I'm counting on, Valentine thought.

Ahn-Kha marched Valentine into the Golden Ones' ghetto and turned up a little lane that led up the hill to the library.

"About one more hour until the work train returns," Ahn-Kha whispered. "It will be dark then, and the Hooded Ones will be out to watch it unload. They always watch whenever great numbers of my people are together. We hide until then, my David."

They passed a row of houses built out of old cinder blocks and scrap metal. But these were no makeshift hovels—the Golden Ones worked with rubble like some artists did with broken glass, creating mosaics and patterns out of broken paving bricks and twisted structural steel.

Older Grogs—their fur had turned to gray white—lounged in front on wooden chaises, chatting in their rumbling tongue.

"In this door, quick!" Ahn-Kha said, and Valentine complied. He pulled the curtain aside, and they entered the rude home.

A white-haired Grog looked up from his evening meal. He blinked his eyes twice, and suddenly his ears shot up.

They spoke for several minutes in their native tongue, and the older one finally limped outside. Valentine watched out of the corner of the window, observing ghetto life from inside.

"He is an old friend of my parents," Ahn-Kha explained. "He goes now to tell the others to pretend they saw nothing; then he shall pay a call on another friend at the Clan Hall. Ahh, here, my David, taste this."

Ahn-Kha broke a tubular growth in half. It had a hole running down the center, as if it had grown around a spit. Valentine tasted it and found it pleasant, a little like pumpkin with the texture of half-cooked pasta. "We used to dip it in honey, but there's no honey to be had these days." Ahn-Kha opened up a locker and began searching through folded clothes, and he found a simple blue version of the robe-kimonos the Golden Ones preferred to wear.

"Not bad," Valentine said, taking another bite. "Tastes kind of like spoon bread. I'd like to try it with molasses. What is it?"

"Did I not tell you? This is heartroot, the staple of my people. From nothing but dead growth, night soil, mud, and time we get this. It grows year-round as long as the water does not freeze, although much more slowly in winter." He changed his torn and dirty old robe for the blue one he selected. They passed the time talking about the former library and the probable location of the armory within.

They waited until darkness and left at the banshee wail of the train whistle pulling into the ghetto. Valentine carried his revolver and sword, the former now loaded and in a holster at his hip, the latter strapped across his back under the black trench coat, with the hilt projecting out the loose collar behind his head. Ahn-Kha still bore the fifty caliber, the gun carried midbarrel in his right hand. The Grog had Valentine's parang tucked inside the fresh robe.

They traversed the common ground in the center of the ghetto, part cultivated garden and part parkland. Some sheep lay in the shade by a lily pad–filled pond.

Ahn-Kha stood very erect. "This way, my David."

The Grog took him to a little clearing bordered by another Grog shantytown. Valentine saw, and smelled, a latrine in the center of the field. Ahn-Kha halted and, using his rifle as a staff, gazed out onto the meadow.

"This is where they buried my people," Ahn-Kha said, slowly and quietly. "When Khay-Hefle took over, they dumped the bodies in a pit here. My parents were among the dead, along with the Principal Elder, and many of my people who fought back. Along with those who just got caught in the battle."

Ahn-Kha took off his mitten slippers and dug his long toes into the earth.

"My wife and sons are buried here. I wished them to go with the One in Ten to Canada, but she refused to leave her family. Two thousand of my people rest beneath this soil. They say if you are very silent, you can hear weeping.

"At first, after the custom of you humans, my people planted flowers here, I am told. Then one day, after the walls had risen, this General who accepts only submission or death came on an inspection. He saw the many beautiful flowers and ordered them pulled up. In their place he dug pit-toilets, and ordered all to use them. The first, of course, was Khay-Hefle, who always seems to find new insults to put upon those who had been his people. At one time they would march the workers all the way from the train station to here at the end of the day. Golden One workers are not considered fit to use human toilets at the Cave this General is building. They must go to the river bushes or wait until they return here."

"I'm . . . sorry," Valentine said, choking on the second word. It was inadequate. "Never said you were married."

"I play tricks on myself. When I do not speak of it or think of it, the pain lessens for a time. She was very beautiful, both in the looking and in the knowing. You own my apologies, I am speaking in English but my private voice speaks in the Golden Tongue. Let me try again. She was very beautiful to look at and to know."

"I'm sure she was," Valentine said, and meant it, although he did not have the first clue as to how a Grog measured physical beauty.

"My David, I am glad we could come here. I have only seen this place from afar. But we must hurry—we have business on the hill."

They moved among the wooded parkland up the hill to the old

library. From below, it loomed like a temple built to the specifications of a fortress. Valentine sensed a Reaper somewhere within. A coyote or feral dog crossed their path ahead, head and tail both held close to the ground. A few Golden One couples could be seen here and there among the trees, the smaller females walking just behind the males, touching the backs of their partners.

"Let's wait a moment, please," he asked Ahn-Kha. The Grog knelt and followed Valentine's gaze to the building.

Valentine quieted his mind. He felt his body relax. The Reaper came into focus. It was below ground.

"Are you all right, my David?" Ahn-Kha asked.

"Yes, now I am. One of your Hooded Ones is in there."

"You smell it?"

Valentine didn't have time to explain. "Something like that."

"You said you had a plan for getting in," Valentine reminded him, looking at the stoutly barred and shuttered windows around the first floor of the building.

"My father's old friend knows one of my people on Khay-Hefle's staff. She hates the new Principal and gives news to my people when she can. She has arranged to unlock the shutters on one of the windows on the second floor after the guard checks it. It is very dangerous for her; it means she must remain in the building all night. The windows on the second floor are not barred, for the climb is thought impossible."

"Then how are we going to get up there?"

The Grog pointed at a flagpole in front of a long low building, just to the right of the Great Hall.

"We shall use that."

Valentine looked up at the flag of the Twisted Cross hanging limp in the night sky.

"Don't tell me that's the barrack for the Twisted Cross soldiers."

"Yes, it is."

"That's quite a risk." Valentine checked the view of the guard at the Great Hall. Khay-Helfle's soldier wore padded leather at his shoulders, shins, and forearms, and a helmet cut to accommodate the flexible pointed ears. He could not see the barrack.

"There is no sentry in front of the barrack."

"No, the Twisted Cross close up tight in the evening."

They avoided the Golden One sentry standing outside the main doors of the ex-library, now the Golden One Great Hall, and moved around the side of the building. Valentine took a long look and listen. Satisfied, he slapped Ahn-Kha on the arm, and they dashed across the cracked cement sidewalk. The Grog made so much noise running, Valentine found himself wishing in vain for the absent Duvalier. Was she on her way back to the Free Territory? Waiting at the rendezvous, cursing him every hour on the hour?

"How many of these Hooded Ones are there in the ghetto?" Valentine asked.

"No one knows. The number seems to vary. On some days I've been told as many as thirty will be here. They use our lands for a base to operate elsewhere in the city, perhaps training, perhaps subjugating another clan."

The Reaper hadn't moved. Valentine hoped that whatever was occupying it would keep its attention for another few minutes. "Here goes." They jogged up to the flagpole.

"Put up by humans, not by the Golden Ones," Ahn-Kha said. He placed both hands around the pole. "Now to pretend this is the neck of Khay-Hefle." His muscles bulged and tightened as he first pushed the flagpole then pulled it. Valentine kept watch for a moment and then decided it was pointless. They were so in the open—if they were seen, it would be all over anyway, so a few seconds' warning would make little difference. He got on the opposite side of the flagpole and began working with Ahn-Kha, though he couldn't bring half the strength of the Grog's arms. When Ahn-Kha pushed, he pulled, and then they switched. Soon the pole was rocking in its dirt. Ahn-Kha wrapped his thick arms around the pole, hugging it as tightly as a constrictor taking a wild deer. With a mighty pull, he uprooted its concrete base.

The Grog took the heavy end, and Valentine the flag tip, and they managed to get it to the side of the building.

"It's a good thing the Twisted Cross don't garrison your people properly," Valentine observed, legs burning in protest of the load. "A few patrols in this area, and we could kiss this project good-bye."

"My people live in abject fear of the Hooded Ones and a return of the flamethrowers, my David. They are worked half to death for their daily soup. They need little policing." Ahn-Kha wasn't even breathing hard, though burdened by the heavy end. If anything, he looked energized.

They reached the base of the window, though not a crack of light showed from the supposedly unlocked shutters. The team managed a two-person raising of the Iwo Jima flag and carefully set the pole against the side of the building. Valentine winced at the *thunk*.

"Wait here," Valentine muttered, and began to shinny up the flagpole, wishing it were made of wood so he could use his claws.

The shutter pulled open silently. He hopped down the ledge into a dark office, smelling Golden Ones. Its shelves were lined with paint and cleaning supplies, and Valentine could understand why a roaming guard might check its window only once as the sun went down. Hardly worth stealing. Duvalier might want the turpentine to make—

—burn the place down!

It was a tempting thought, but he turned back to the window. "Get rid of the pole," he called down, sounding like a laryngitis patient in an effort to be heard without speaking loudly.

Ahn-Kha complied while Valentine wound and knotted a pair of canvas drop cloths. He soaked the canvas in a washtub—wet fabric would hold better at the knots and strenthen it. He wrapped the improvised line around his back, got a good grip, and sent his dripping line out the window for Ahn-Kha. The Grog grabbed it and began to climb. Valentine had all he could do, legs braced and quivering against the wall under the window, to hold up his end of the job by not letting go as what seemed like half a ton of Grog swarmed up the line.

The Grog made it through the window, his awkward rifle left outside. They opened the bag with Valentine's weapons. Valentine offered the Grog his choice of pistol or parang.

"It'll be knife-work if we have to fight in here," Ahn-Kha said, drawing the parang and passing it, blade out, between his lips. The Golden One's eyes blazed.

Valentine heard a step in the hallway on the other side of the door.

He put his fingers to his lips and pointed out the door. Ahn-Kha's ears went up and forward, listening for the tread.

"A Golden One," Ahn-Kha whispered.

There was a knock. Ahn-Kha gave Valentine a reassuring nod and opened the door to reveal a more petite version of himself, without the pronounced canines but with longer and more expressive ears. They gargled to each other. Valentine doubted he would even be able to generate the necessary sounds should Ahn-Kha decide to teach him the Golden One's language some day.

She passed two keys on a little metal ring to Ahn-Kha and left as quietly as she had come.

"She was hiding, waiting for us in the next room. Vihy has no business staying here after hours; she would be killed if caught. She asked for us to be sure to lock the shutters behind, just in case."

He showed Valentine the ring. "The keys are to an iron gate at the basement stairs. For our cleaning people to get in the basement, a Twisted Cross officer on duty must open it. She stole it from his office as he slept on duty. Not all are 'men of stainless steel,' it seems."

The bravery of some of the people who lived under the Kurians never failed to humble Valentine. Kur ruled through fear, intimidating their subjects into submission. But for some, after a certain point, even the threats of torture and death no longer work. These helpless people chose death, even welcomed it when it came, as long as they were able to strike some kind of blow against their oppressors. Not for the first time, he wondered if he had that kind of courage.

But such thoughts did not help mask his aura. Valentine brought his focus back within himself, until his worries were a hard little crystal locked in his brain.

"Ahn-Kha, there's still a Rea—a Hooded One to deal with. I think it's somewhere in the basement. I'm afraid it will sense or hear you coming. Would you be good enough to wait here while I deal with it, please?"

"Yes, my David. Whatever you ask of me. I would prefer if it were something other than waiting."

"You could get a bunch of rags together here, and open a can of turpentine. We may have to start a fire as a diversion."

Ahn-Kha nodded and began to pile some dirty towels in a janitor's bucket. "May your blade find your enemy's heart."

Valentine handed over his revolver. He half drew his sword, tested the edge with his thumb. "A Reaper has two hearts, one on each side of his body. I go for the neck; they have only one of those."

Ahn-Kha extended his fist, his long thumb up. Valentine smiled in recognition; the proportions were all wrong, but the thumbs-up nevertheless heartened him. He threw the sword's harness over his shoulder, tightened the straps.

He crept out of the storage room. A hall led down to a shadowed open area. Valentine could see a decorative rail looking out on the central atrium his companion described. Low-wattage electric lights cast patterns across the Golden Ones' renovated stone and woodwork overlaid on the older human design.

Keeping on his belly, Valentine crawled down the hall toward the atrium. He paused now and then to listen, but while there were sounds of activity on the floor above, he could hear nothing near him. He crawled out to the atrium and slithered to the staircase. Look. Listen. Smell. And then down.

On the first floor, he waited two full minutes in an alcove, feeling the rhythms of the sleeping building. The only sounds came from the guardroom just inside the main door, where the off-duty Golden One guards were eating and talking. He smelled heartroot, a rich smell like carrots pulled fresh from the earth. Following Ahn-Kha's instructions, he made it to the staircase down without encountering anything other than vague noises from somewhere below. As he moved down the stairs, listening and using his nose, he identified the sound and smell of machinery. A generator whined somewhere in the bowels of the building, and he picked up a faint medicinal odor, like disinfectant.

The Reaper definitely moved near him now. Life or death depended on the Cat continuing to sense it, and the Reaper being unable to read Valentine's lifesign until he was too close for it to matter. A silent contest, like the Old World books of submarines hunting each other in cold darkness. He waited until the Reaper was somewhere far from the gate door at the base of the stairs before employing the keys.

Valentine noticed an alarm bell mounted on the wall just down the hall, next to a door with light and the sound of voices coming from it. A switch with a conduit pipe running up to the bell probably activated it. The door was wired, a detail perhaps none of the Grogs knew. He thought for a long minute, but could not come up with a decent plan. That Reaper would not stay in the opposite corner of the building forever.

It had to be done, and if it had to be done, it had best be done boldly. He unlocked both locks, his sword hidden against his leg.

"Yo!" he called. "I'm at the door. Wanna get the alarm for me?"

"Coming," a tired voice said after the echo faded. A human in a white lab coat appeared at the door and absently turned the switch. Valentine threw open the door and covered the ten feet of hallway in a single leap.

"Hey," the man in the lab coat said. Too late. He reached up to hit the red alarm push button, but Valentine's sword intercepted his arm, removing it from the elbow down. Mouth gaping, the man looked at the interesting phenomenon of his amputation as Valentine's sword point came up under his chin. Valentine withdrew the blade as he rushed around the corner and into the well-lit room. A woman, also in a white lab coat, had time to scream before he cut her down. When it was over, the only movement in the room was the slow spread of blood across the tiled floor. The remains of a meal sat on a table under dazzling spotlights. Stainless-steel counters and white cabinets marked the room as a dispensary or examination room. There were medical supplies, bandages and iodine-colored bottles and instrument trays available. Valentine saw machinery in the room beyond, but had no time to investigate.

The scream was nearly as effective as the alarm. The Reaper was coming. Valentine hurried to the gate and locked it again, then stepped back into the dispensary, dragging the dead man behind. He readied his blade, holding in his favorite stance, like a batter at the plate, just inside the door. He heard the Reaper's step in the hallway and listened to it pause as it saw the slain man's blood and the severed arm Valentine forgot to retrieve. Then it did something Valentine would not have believed of a Reaper. It turned and ran.

Valentine pursued. Cloak flying, the Reaper turned a corner, and Valentine had to slow in case it was waiting just around the corner. It wasn't—it was in a room off the hall. He heard the Reaper's odd, faint voice speaking urgently.

case red! post twelve calling a case red! it breathed, pressing the transmit button on the microphone of the tabletop radio. While the voice was that of a Reaper, something was wrong about the cadence, the urgency in the voice.

It sensed Valentine. Turned—slit pupils wide as screaming mouths reflected Valentine's blade flashing for its neck. It ducked, slowly for a Reaper—meaning it took a full blink of an eye to crouch instead of half of one.

Which was half a blink too slow. The Reaper's body crouched without its head—now spinning in the air sprinkling black blood on the painted cement walls.

A man in the urban camouflage of the Twisted Cross stood next to an overturned chair, frozen in shock at the site of the Reaper's death. The communications center man reached for his pistol, and Valentine opened his stomach with a right-to-left slash, then stood on the man's wrist and pulled the gun and pocketed it. The man lay on the floor, gasping out his pain and trying to hold his intestines in.

Valentine tore the microphone off the radio, ignoring the Twisted Cross man, who coughed out his final breath. He unplugged the radio and cut the power cord.

The swinging cord end reminded him of something. That something was connected with the woman in the lab coat he had killed. An item that she was holding. An IV bag. An IV bag just like the ones hanging above the machinery in the room behind the dispensary. Why did a machine need an IV bag? It all came together in a rush.

Valentine flew back to the dispensary and into the room beyond.

Twelve oversize metal coffins were lined up on either side of the room, quietly humming with electric power. A thirteenth stood in the aisle between the two rows. They were wider and deeper than coffins, however. More than anything they reminded Valentine of defunct tanning beds he had once found while sheltering in an Old World strip mall. They had mysterious, unlabeled knobs next to telltale lights flickering on the side.

He closed the metal door behind him and barred it, using a pivoting arm that swung into a receiver on the frame.

From the lights and noise, Valentine determined that seven of the

oversize coffins were on and functioning; each also had an IV bag
hanging from a T-shaped rack above the machinery. Valentine went to
the humming, blinking center machine and circled it. His ears picked
up the sound of water being cycled through some kind of plumbing. A
cabinet-door-size hatch was fixed to the top at one end.

Not knowing what to expect, Valentine opened the hatch. Inside,
floating in the water like a piece of wood, was a very pale, thin man
with a bristling growth of beard. Wires were attached with little flesh-
colored cups all over his body, concentrated on his shaven skull. A
smell, both salty and rank, wafted out of the miniature pool.

The man's green eyes opened in surprise, and Valentine looked
into the confused gaze of the man who until a moment ago was animating a Reaper. How many years' service did he have in? How many
people had his avatar killed while under his control? Did he climb out
of the tank desiring to tear the throats out of victims, like the Twisted
Cross man he'd met in Chicago who'd been "in the tank" for weeks at a
time?

This was the reason the Reapers spoke to each other, as Duvalier
had observed. And killed with guns, wasting vital aura. The Twisted
Cross were a weapon, combining the minds of human soldiers with the
death-dealing bodies of Reapers.

Valentine grabbed the man's neck and shoved him underwater to
the bottom of the tank. The Twisted Cross Master struggled against
Valentine's grip, muscles that hadn't been used in days creaking, while
a sensor of some sort on his water-filled coffin beeped. The man clawed
against Valentine's face with long fingernails, and the Cat turned his
head away. Bubbles. The thrashing finally ceased, and the sensor added
an outraged, high-pitched whine to the beeping. Valentine looked back
down at the dead figure. His electrodes had come loose during the
struggle, and under each one was a tiny tattoo of a swastika.

Valentine turned off the annoying monitor-machine. In the fresh
silence, the crash that always came after a fight hit like a delayed-fuse
bomb, and it hit hard. Vomit made up of his heartroot dinner poured
into the salty water of the tank. But there was more to do. He rinsed his
mouth with a handful of the salty water from an unused tank and spat
it back.

Finish this.

Minutes later, six more dead bodies lay in their individual tanks of
now-bloody saline solution. Somewhere, seven Reapers were wandering in confusion, bereft of the controlling intelligence of their masters.
Valentine cleaned his sword with a spare lab coat and checked each of
the other capsules to make sure they did not contain further Twisted

Cross. He wanted to scream, to howl, to lose himself in a burst of activity, anything to push the last few minutes out of his mind.

Forget it. What you killed were not men. Not anymore, the old voice inside him said. Valentine wondered in a half-amused fashion if he were going mad. Had id and superego decided to launch a psychic putsch? He did not really care—perhaps another symptom of insanity.

The alarm, a mind-numbing Klaxon, screamed.

He cocked the pistol and carefully opened the door. The basement was still empty as the tomb it had become. Valentine checked the main hall and saw Ahn-Kha tearing at the cage door. He turned off the alarm. It refused to die, so he did the next-best thing and shot out the speaker. Elsewhere in the building, it still brayed.

"Easy on the metal," Valentine said. "Twist it enough, and it won't open. I don't want to be stuck in here."

"I am thankful that you are well, my David. Did you find the armory?"

"The armory?" Valentine said, with the tone of someone who had forgotten to pick up a pound of sugar at the store. He went to the door and opened it, legs rubbery, trying not to stagger.

"Are you wounded, my friend?" Ahn-Kha said, ears pointed at him the like the horns of a charging bull. The Grog sniffed the nail-marks on his face.

"No. C'mon, let's find it—it has to be one of these doors."

They discovered the armory behind a steel door that was not even locked. The arsenal was not as well stocked as they had hoped: automatic rifles and pistols, a few shotguns, some boxes of grenades and mines, and two flamethrowers. Valentine found a case of satchel charges, and there was ample small-arms ammunition in cabinets and cases on the wall. Valentine looked in vain for bullets for his PPD and ended up arming himself with one of the Twisted Cross assault rifles. He filled his pockets with magazines.

Ahn-Kha selected a shotgun and a machine gun with a bipod at the front. He draped ammunition belts for it around his neck like a priest's vestments.

The pair moved out of the armory and to the basement gate. Valentine placed part of his load at the base of the stairs and crept up them with Kalashnikov at the ready. Ahn-Kha followed—only the slight *klink-klank* of the ammunition belts giving the Golden One away as he followed.

He could hear voices of Grogs at the balcony and stairs to the upper floors in the Great Hall.

"You cover the upstairs. I'm going try for the door," Valentine said.

The chattering sound of Ahn-Kha's machine gun behind him spurred him on as he made it to the entry vestibule. The Golden Ones who had been on guard had fled.

He slid open a wooden panel. In front of the hall, a group of Golden Ones crouched on the hill just beyond the concrete sidewalk. They wore the simple smocks of common laborers. Two more sheltered behind a defunct and overgrown fountain, wearing stained overalls. They had improvised weapons: iron bars, sledgehammers, and lengths of chain.

Valentine lifted the heavy bar fitted to the double doors and unfastened the locks. He stepped out, tried to signal the Golden Ones to approach. They crouched and looked at him as if they expected him to open fire on them. A *zingpow* of a bullet chipping the doorpost got him out of the entrance.

After waiting for another long burst from his partner's machine gun to stop, Valentine called over his shoulder "Ahn-Kha, there are some of your people out front. I think they're ready for action, but don't know what to do. Let's switch. Talk to them."

Valentine ran to the base of the stairs and sighted his gun upward. "There's just one. You can't see him from the bottom of the stairs, but go halfway up and he shoots," Ahn-Kha warned.

The Grog went to the door and threw both the portals open wide. He began bellowing into the night, waving the gun above his head.

Golden Ones rushed in, brandishing picks and mallets. It appeared as though, without willing it, he and Ahn-Kha had started a revolt.

"My David, show my people the armory, I beg of you. I have business elsewhere," Ahn-Kha said, leaping up the stairs three at a time. The example inspired some of his fellows to follow despite their lack of weapons. A shot splintered the banister, and the giant sprayed bullets up to the third floor.

"Can you all understand me?" Valentine asked.

"Yes, sir," the growing mob said in various accents.

He led them down to the little room, wishing it had three times as many guns. He handed over the automatic he had taken off the dead radio operator. The Golden Ones just took the guns and grenades and left the explosives, Valentine was happy to see. Nothing saps the will to revolt like accidentally blowing up a dozen of your vanguard.

More and more Grogs gathered as the word spread. One of them, an oldster missing a hand, an eye, and with a pronounced limp, joined Valentine in handing out guns and the proper ammunition.

"My friend, was no-right at rail-gate," the elderly Golden One said in his halting, glottal English. "Own-eyes watched Hood-man drop dead. No-gun, no-hurt. Guard-mans watch their-eyes same-same, ranned away. Now my people done Hood-mans?"

"I hope so. I don't know," Valentine said.

The last guns left in the hands of their new owners. Valentine followed the flood of straw-tinted muscle to the door. He could hear shooting outside. The old Grog grabbed him by the arm as he went out the door.

"Careful-careful, sir!" he implored, and yelled something up the steps. "Or shoot you, maybe-maybe." The Grog led Valentine to the door.

In front of the old library, a bonfire had been constructed out of any wood the Grogs could lay their hands on, mostly in the form of railroad ties. Even now, pairs of what he recognized as females were carrying up more ties, adding to the blaze. Valentine heard shooting from the direction of the Twisted Cross Barrack, and saw further flames lighting the sky there. Guard towers on the other side of the wall were firing into the ghetto, but they were too far away for Valentine to tell whether they were achieving anything other than alerting every Grog in Omaha that something was seriously wrong in the Golden One quarter. Valentine, feeling that events were now well out of his control, just lugged his booty from the armory to outside the library and sat on the steps to watch. The old Grog barked orders this way and that to hurrying youngsters, but if they paid attention to his words, Valentine could not say. He could see the ears on the Grogs, twitching this way and that in excited confusion.

"My people were like that bonfire, my David," Ahn-Kha said, unexpectedly joining him. His machine gun was down to its last belt, and the Grog reeked like a sulfur pit as he kicked another of his kind, longer haired and fleshier, before him. "Sit, dog!" he told the prisoner. Then to Valentine: "The fuel was there. They just needed air and a spark. You provided both—"

"*We* provided both," Valentine corrected.

"*You* provided both," the Grog insisted, "when you destroyed the Hooded Ones. That was the air, allowing them to breathe. From what I am told, the Hooded Ones all dropped over unconscious at the same time. The spark came in this building."

"Interesting. When a Reaper's tie is severed with its Master, it acts on instinct. Dangerous, but not smart."

"Ah, but that is when the Master is still alive, is it not?"

"I don't know. Is this the esteemed Khay-Hefle?"

The wretch plucked at Valentine's pant cuff. "Sir, take me to—"

Ahn-Kha wrapped his long foot around the prisoner's neck. "Silence! Yes, my David. Though my dream of revenge is not to be. It is—well, it was—a law of the clan that none of my people may kill except in battle or duel of honor, and he was unarmed. With this pretender brought low, I believe the old laws will be restored. His fate will be for the new Elders to decide. Besides, he screamed for mercy. There is no triumph in killing such a One on his knees."

"That's so." Valentine doubted he would have been as charitable if his family had been buried under a latrine.

Other Grogs came and strung Khay-Hefle from the iron bars of his own palace, giving the General's surrogate a good view of events. He hung from his wrists, crying as Grogs came to shout what had to be abuse.

"He's right side up. Mussolini wasn't so lucky," Valentine said to Ahn-Kha. The mob surprised him with its restraint: it restricted itself to words, sometimes pointing and laughing. Humans probably would have set fire to him; he'd heard ugly stories from veteran Wolves about what happened when towns changed hands.

"This Mussolini, he once ruled your Free Territory?"

"Never mind."

Two more Grogs ran up to the bonfire, each with a huge kettledrum on its back. They were beautifully fashioned, carved so the different woods and metals looked as though they'd grown together. A third Grog with a pair of club-size drumsticks began to beat out a rapid-fire tattoo.

The pounding rhythm gave Valentine a welcome primal thrill, heating the cold sour ache in his belly. The drumming intensified until he felt the earth shake with the Golden Ones' stamps. Even the muzzle flashes from the distant watchtowers paused while the drums boomed. Then it slowed to a steady, ominous beat.

The sound galvanized the Grogs. Without a word, they knelt and rapped their weapons against the pavement, ears pointed up and out like the horns on a Viking's helmet. The drumbeat intensified, and its tempo increased as did the clatter of rifle butts hitting concrete. As a people, they tilted their heads back and began to bellow and howl to the stars.

Valentine took in the crescendo and he trembled for their enemies.

Ten

The Cave: Strategic Air Command's old headquarters at Offutt Air Force Base has seen better, and worse, days. Better when it was a buzzing hive of planes and blue uniforms, jet exhaust in the air, and the camaraderie of men who know that they're the best in the world at what they do. Worse in the summer of '22, when the nukes came, thundering blossoms of thermonuclear heat that reshaped the landscape. They turned sand to glass and flattened anything that wasn't built to bunker specifications in a hurricane of wind, pushing first out from the blast and then rushing back toward the mushroom clouds of the MIRV warheads.

Now some of the great hangars have been rebuilt, SAC's old underground catacombs reoccupied. A new general has come, with men in strange uniforms; the swastika flag flies, its spiderish black-and-white design stark and forbidding against the blue of Omaha's skies.

Thirty-six hours after the bonfires died, Valentine, Ahn-Kha, and a strong young Grog named Khiz-Mem watched the shadows lengthen across the old base south of Bellevue.

Ahn-Kha selected Khiz-Mem after the flame-lit night in the ghetto.

Valentine remembered the rest of the revolt as little but a confused series of impressions. The Twisted Cross barracks aflame. Screams of Man and Grog. The endless drumming. Gunfire clattering in the distance, dying off, then starting up again. Fresh ash lifted skyward, turning the wind bitter.

Valentine had stayed out of the struggle at the request of his friend, who feared that in the confusion, some Golden One would shoot him down as a one of their Twisted Cross overseers.

The killing did not stop until after dawn, when the last guards in the watchtowers outside the walls either fled or were brought down by snipers. The towers inside the walls unexpectedly revealed major structural faults as the revolt got going, and they came crashing down at a signal of one of the Golden One engineers. The Golden Ones shot as far and as well as their Gray One brethren, many of whom lay dead in the upper floors of the Great Hall and in the little barrack houses outside the two gates of the ghetto.

With a few hours' rest and some warm food inside him, Valentine decided to push on southward. He knew the Twisted Cross would not take the Golden One revolt lightly, and that they'd be back soon with everything the General had. Ahn-Kha shared Valentine's fear of the coming threat and refused to be parted from him.

"Ahn-Kha, your people need you more than I do."

"My David, here I am just one more set of hands. With you, I am half of the first alliance joining Golden Ones with the Freeholders, honored to stand at the side of a friend. In which role can I help my people more?"

Valentine wanted to go to the General's Cave and throw a little sand in the gears of the Twisted Cross war machine before it could return to Omaha and quash the Golden One rising. But now it would take more than blowing up a few hundred feet of bridge. In preparation, he and Ahn-Kha "liberated" flamethrowers and explosives from the Hall's armory.

Khiz-Mem made the pair a trio after Ahn-Kha drafted him to serve as packhorse and guide. Ahn-Kha assured Valentine that the young Grog knew every corner of the aboveground part of the old Strategic Air Command base. Khiz-Mem, in the full flush of his twenty-something strength, shouldered the weight of flamethrower, satchel charges, food, as well as his own pistol and rifle. Ahn-Kha carried the other flamethrower and a slightly lighter load. Valentine had an additional satchel full of grenades—white phosphorous incendiary grenades among the others.

Ahn-Kha examined one of the cylinders as they walked out of the ghetto. "With these, they burn the houses of those they would punish. I should like to give the Hooded Ones a sample of their own flame."

The Cave was a little more than a long day's walk south of the ghetto, but Valentine did not want to move straight down the rails connecting the base with the city center.

What was left of the Twisted Cross ghetto-police had taken that route; discarded equipment lay at the edge of the rail line like markers.

They were probably holding some intermediary point, waiting for their own chance at vengeance.

So the trio took off west before turning south, retrieving Valentine's submachine gun and pack from the little cache. Picking its way south with Valentine scouting well ahead, sweeping the smugglers' trails of Omaha with his ears and nose, the party took its time. He wished he had another few days to look for Duvalier, they weren't very far from the rendezvous point.

The day had a hint of autumn to it; even the afternoon heat had a cool quality to it that the summer days had lacked.

They spotted a scout plane midday. If the little ship was not the ill-omened red-and-white one from the Dunes, it was its twin sister. It flew up from the south and circled the city above the Golden One ghetto. As they watched it from a halt, Valentine explained to Ahn-Kha the story of its use in the Dunes.

"So that means they will attack soon," Ahn-Kha said.

"Yes, they'll hit your people before the Golden Ones can get organized."

"Our people, my David, our people. From this day forward, you will always be accounted a member of our clan, and welcome in the Hall."

"I hope there'll be a Hall—and people to do the welcoming," Valentine said, studying the little plane.

At another break, in the roofless ruins of a warehouse, Ahn-Kha showed Valentine how to use the flamethrower. It consisted of three tanks on a backpack frame, a small one with compressed air and two larger tanks containing gasoline with a thickening agent. The mixture was fired by what amounted to a heavily built garden hose attached to a wide-mouthed insecticide sprayer. It fired the jellied gasoline a good thirty yards with a frightening roar of flame.

"I saw some burnt-out ruins in Wisconsin once where the Kurians had been doing some kind of training under the supervision of the Reapers. I wonder if they were teaching their men how to use these things? None of us could figure out how so much damage could be done without explosives."

"You must be careful with your trigger finger, my David," Ahn-Kha said. "This pack is half-empty now. You must use very short bursts, and even then you have only a few. Why do we carry these all this way?"

"I want to do the same thing at the Cave that I did at the Hall. Just on a bigger scale. The Hooded Ones are terrible, but the ones working them are vulnerable. Maybe more vulnerable than the General knows."

After a final hard march, they came up on the damaged areas outside the base in the late afternoon. The scouts shared a heartroot meal in a patch of tall grass at the old interstate, looking down at the outer edge of the camp. The perimeter fence consisted of two lines of fence topped with concertina wire. The main part of the base was hidden behind a lip of low hills; concrete observation bunkers set among them like teeth. A rail track ran along this, the western edge of the base.

Khiz-Mem talked in his native tongue and pointed to the wire and the area beyond.

Ahn-Kha patted the youngster on the head and turned to Valentine. "Between the wires are mines. You cannot see them, but there are guard posts well concealed behind the wire. Not all are manned all the time. The General still does not have all the men he wants, but he has plans for this place. He trains new soldiers always. Omaha was thought to be a good post to give recruits experience."

"They got an experience, all right," Valentine said, trailing his binoculars over the open prairie surrounding the base. It would be a nightmare to get in—there were probably trip wires within the concertina, if not Reapers prowling like guard dogs. "I don't think marching up to the gate is going to work for me here."

"I told you—our people are resourceful. There is a small tunnel, which stretches very far. It opens out on the far side of the old concrete road behind us. A few have used it to escape. We cannot go through it in great numbers, for the air goes bad within. Khiz-Mem says it is very tiring. You have to crawl the whole way. It opens within the base in a livestock barn, at the pigpen sluice."

"Fantastic," Valentine said. He was not sure if Ahn-Kha's knowledge of English extended as far as sarcasm.

"No, my David, this is to your advantage. They use dogs on the base, some running free, at night to find intruders. Pig odor may confuse them."

After the meal and rest, they swung around to the west in a final arc to the exit hole for the escape tunnel.

"Strange how things turn out. We dug this to let our people get out, but we will use it to get in."

"Not we," Valentine said. "I. I don't think we should all go in, especially at night."

Ahn-Kha opened his mouth to argue when the noise of engines caused them all to drop to the ground. Valentine and Ahn-Kha climbed up to the cracked and uneven remains of the old expressway and looked out at the western border of the base.

A column of trucks bumped along a road running alongside the rail line bordering the Cave, turning out from the main gate that Valentine could now see farther to the south. A four-by-four scout car led the column, followed by a genuine armored car on fat tires. Then came truck after smoke-belching truck, twenty-two in all, mostly old two-and-a-half-ton army jobs, restored and painted and towing trailers. A few of these carried machine guns mounted in a ring on the roof above the passenger seat. Double-axle pickup trucks towing cannon followed the army trucks, interspersed with camouflage-painted U-Hauls. In the beds of the pickups, uniformed figures sat facing each other.

Valentine plucked a piece of grass and chewed it as the procession of motorized military might passed by.

"I see some of our people still wish to serve the General," Ahn-Kha observed, as more utility trucks rolled by, their slat-sided beds filled with armed Golden Ones and Gray Ones.

"My species hasn't cornered the market on betrayal," Valentine said. "There's good and bad everywhere."

"I would have more good," Ahn-Kha said, lifting a mule's worth of gear.

"Someday, old horse," Valentine said, watching dust settle as the column bumped off to the north at a steady ten miles an hour.

The sun was setting, the Twisted Cross Reapers would be in Omaha soon, and he had a tunnel to crawl through.

They went back to the outlet, an old cement drainage pipe by the interstate, broken open by some force of war or nature.

"I believe you should let me come, be another set of eyes, if nothing else," Ahn-Kha insisted.

"Suppose we are crawling through your tunnel as a Reaper passes overhead. He might find it strange that life-sign is passing a few feet under his boots, don't you think?"

Valentine turned over the PPD and his remaining ammunition. "Here's my gun. If I'm not back by tomorrow morning, go to the meeting place at the river I told you about. There should be a human woman there—if not, look for a pile of four of anything: rocks, firewood, whatever. There may be a note in there, and you can act on it as you see fit. Or go back to yo—our people in Omaha."

He unwrapped his old nylon hammock, placed the flamethrower, his sword, and the satchel charge within its webbing, and then wrapped it all up in a blanket. He climbed into the tunnel, pulling the sack behind him.

"See you at sunup," he said, and backed into the hole.

The escape tunnel was a wonder of improvised engineering. Valentine had expected to have to wiggle through it like a mole in a garden tunnel, but forgot about the Grog shoulder span. Wood held it up in some places, corrugated aluminum in others, and beneath the road and rail line Valentine crawled through a real concrete tunnel. The building of this thing must be a fascinating story in itself; he promised himself to hear the whole tale from Khiz-Mem should he come out of this.

It grew pitch-dark as he left the opening behind. Valentine hated the abyss of absolute dark. The dark of the grave, of death. Even his newly sensitive eyes were useless; only the Reapers could hunt here. He imagined steel-like fingers reaching out of the darkness behind him and closing around his neck. He reached into a pocket for a leather to-bacco pouch and brought out the diamond-shaped glow bulb that Ryu had given him as a parting gift. He had bound it in a little harness loop of leather, which he now hung around his neck. The comforting yellow glow was like a tiny little piece of the sun with him in the darkness, and he felt his fears shrink back to manageable size. He sniffed the damp air of the tunnel and smelled a faint piggy smell.

Dragging the burden behind him was an exhausting process; he had to stop every ten minutes to rest. He learned to do this under the too-infrequent air tubes the Grogs had poked through to the surface. Rats and field mice had taken up the tunnel as a convenient home; he smelled and heard them all around even if he couldn't see them.

With his back and shoulder muscles screaming, Valentine inched down the tunnel. It was kind of like rowing a boat, except for the ab-sence of boat, fresh air, and water. He would scoot his buttocks a foot down the tube, which seemed to stretch endlessly through miles of midnight, then drag his improvised blanket-sled along behind with a pull at the nonexistent oar.

The piggy smell was his holy grail, his stink-at-the-end-of-the-tunnel. As it intensified to the point where he no longer needed his Wolf's nose, he pulled with renewed energy. When he felt his probing hand come away smeared with filth, he knew he was at the end.

He left the pack where it was. Fighting disgust, he smeared his face and hands with the soiled mud. He would have to remember to carry a can of Duvalier's greasepaint from now on.

Telling yourself you're going to survive this, eh? It's a one-way crawl, and you know it.

The tunnel bowed into an upward slope. Above, he saw a length of ten-inch pipe with a funnel at the end—running vertically through the tunnel. He put away his comforting light cube and let his eyes adjust. Hints of light could be seen around the edge of the funnel. He listened with hard ears, but heard only faint animal noises from above.

Valentine moved the funnel. The wide part covered a hole chipped in a concrete basin, just below dirty grating apparently set on the floor above. The smelly sluice pipe and funnel came out of the ground easily enough. He climbed up through the hole in the bottom of the space just below the grate.

He paused to listen again and then lifted the grate. He peered into the cement-floored pigpen of the barn. In one warm corner, a heap of porkers lay grunting in a pile. Across a low partition he could see another pigpen and its cluster of sleeping livestock.

He climbed out of the grating hole. One of the pigs woke up and gave him the once-over, but flopped back on its side when it saw he bore no slop pail. Valentine reconnoitered the lowest level of the unlit barn. It sounded and smelled as if cows were above on the main floor. The pigs shared the basement with a tractor and a horse-trailer on blocks, now filled with chickens.

He dropped back into the tunnel and began to transfer his equipment. He sensed a Reaper roaming somewhere as an unsettling tickle at the edges of his mind.

He lifted his arsenal out of the tunnel. The pigs took one look at the flamethrower and decided it looked like some kind new trough-filling device and began to gather around and oink in excitement. Valentine escaped to the garage area, listening for sounds of investigation.

He hid the satchel charge and flamethrower behind the tractor and climbed up a series of ladders to the hayloft. The smell of alfalfa and hay brought back a rush of memories of Molly and their first tryst. Keeping to the shadows, he surveyed the land as best he could.

The barn stood behind the apartments of the officers' residences. In the distance he could see a concrete tower at the restored airfield. As far as he knew, the Twisted Cross air force consisted of a single two-seat scout plane, but perhaps the General had plans to increase his fleet in the future. A bunker-flanked hummock of ground marked the entrance to what Khiz-Mem called the Cave, the nuclear-blast-hardened headquarters of the Twisted Cross.

The biggest aboveground structure on the post was the massive Train Hangar. Valentine could see the front of the building from the three-story-high loft of the barn. Built on the concrete foundations of a hardened airplane hangar, a network of rail lines ran parallel across the wide area in front of it before turning toward the main gate. It reminded Valentine of pictures he had seen of the German submarine pens in the Second World War. According to Khiz-Mem, they were in the process of adding enormous steel doors running down tracks in the concrete columns that held up the reinforced roof. Valentine could see sparks thrown by welders even now, in the dead of night, as work proceeded on the multiacre structure. They lit lines of boxcars inside, and Valentine could make out a few laboring figures within the machine shops and workbenches inside.

Somewhere deep within the Cave, a natural-gas power plant supplied electricity for the entire base, including for the electrified perimeter fence he knew to be in the works. He moved to the north end of the barn and watched the guards at the main gate. He wondered if the tracks were wired with explosives—if so, it might be feasible to assault the camp by running a train through the gate. More barracks stood behind the low ring of hills that sheltered the base from prying eyes, and two more looked like they were under construction. Valentine did not know if the hills were natural, man-made, or the remnants of crater rims caused by nuclear explosions in '22.

A Reaper lurked somewhere, near the entrance to the main gate. He sensed another near the Cave and possibly two near the hangar, though those last were at the edge of his range.

Valentine forced himself to rest in the hayloft for fifteen minutes. He was exhausted from the hike and the cramped crawl through the tunnel, and he needed to think now that he'd seen the hangar. He had a lot still to do this night.

The rational part of him wanted to get back to Southern Command with what he had learned. Certainly the Twisted Cross needed to be taken very seriously. Left untouched, the General would eventually have enough Reaper–human pairs to consume the Free Territory. Teams of Twisted Cross could destroy the border posts and principal bases as easily as they'd destroyed the Denverites at Fort Rowling. He knew Southern Command had some kind of emergency plan to fall back into the more rugged mountains, but how long could you feed hundreds of thousands of civilians in the hills?

The Twisted Cross had weaknesses hidden behind their black-and-white flag of terror. This General, whoever he was, seemed still to be in the process of recruiting and building his army, testing it against easy targets as he trained more men. If Southern Command could be convinced, he would guide as many Bear teams as they could afford to send up here, and this General's all-conquering army might be stillborn in the act of creation.

Valentine's mind kept returning to the Golden Ones, betrayed twice by Kur, and now in full revolt. Perhaps there were other Grogs elsewhere, equally mistreated and exploited, who would follow in their footsteps if just shown the way. Given time and training, the Cats could—

But the Golden Ones didn't have time. The attack was already being prepared, and Valentine knew that the Twisted Cross Reapers would hit the ghetto in the darkness. They'd go in to kill, not occupy, and leave daylight mopping up of any remaining strongpoints to the support troops. The threat to Southern Command might be years away—the Golden Ones woud die tonight.

If Valentine could use the demolition charge judiciously, the General might lose a few more of his precious Reapers. Just the act of debating his course was an admission of surrender, in a way. If it was the fate of the Golden Ones against duty, duty would lose.

A few minutes after midnight, Valentine lurked outside the Train Hangar. He had found a blue jumpsuit hung up in the barn, and put it on along with a pair of muddy rubber galoshes. He piled the sword, flamethrower, and satchel charge in a wheelbarrow, threw the blanket over them, and headed for the gate to the officer's compound. He wheeled it slowly and tiredly toward the gate, and the sentry stepped out of the shadows and into the light, shotgun under his arm and collar turned up against the cool air.

"Sorry, that took way longer than I thought," he called to the sentry. "It turned out she had twin calves, and I just couldn't get the second out. I ended up having to pull it round by getting a piece of twine and drawing its head around," Valentine said, firing off the sum total of his calving knowledge in a single verbal broadside. But it got him ten feet farther toward the guard.

"Hold it, now—*now!*"

Valentine's arms were a blur, and his sword flashed. The guard fell over with a stunned look on his face, perhaps not believing that a human being could move that fast. Valentine put on the guard's jacket and hat and tossed the shotgun in the wheelbarrow.

He left his weaponry in a shallow depression in the middle of a field near the mountainous building, covered it with the blanket, and began scouting the Train Hangar. He found a four-wheeled pushcart, piled it with a few items of scrap metal, and began to push it around the pavement, looking busy. He counted twenty-eight boxcars in three rows in the Train Hangar, with guards and dogs protecting the cargo within. None of the workers approached the guards any nearer than they absolutely had to. Valentine looked in the open side door of one and discovered that the ordinary-looking boxcars contained more of the metal coffins, perhaps each with a Twisted Cross soldier floating inside and animating one of their Reapers.

Valentine let his hard ears roam, listened to the workers in the Train Hanger. The laborers were wondering what happened to the

Golden One labor that usually was here to help them. Earlier that day, guards had come through and collected the Golden Ones. They had been placed in a special compound. Some thought they were being searched for weapons; others believed they had been taken as hostages to ensure the reliability of the General's puppet on the throne back in Omaha. There were rumors of a fight in the city. Then orders had come through to strip the base of anyone who could be trusted to use a rifle properly.

"The General's really lost it," one commented after Valentine had wandered away and he checked over his shoulder. Valentine's Wolf ears still picked up every disgruntled word. "First he tries to bite off more than he can chew out west and loses a big chunk of his best teams, and now it sounds like there's a trouble in Omaha. Instead of letting it cool down, he always demands scorched earth. He can't win a war because he refuses to ever lose a battle. He always talks about how patient he is, but—"

"Watch it, you. I don't want to be put on a list because I was talkin' treason."

"It's not treason to say there should be more carrot and less stick. I signed on to this for the carrot, a big stretch of land to call my own and a brass ring like my old man has. It's been four years of step and fetch, and still no ring, no land."

"I'd be happy if they just got the hair-backs working again. I'm breaking my back here."

A concrete control tower stood within in the center of the hangar. It sat on a base that Valentine saw housed a spiral staircase, going down as well as up. The tower widened out to a bowl above, and four Twisted Cross soldiers stood atop it. Machine gun muzzles projected out over the edge of the bowl. Valentine pushed his cart past bunkers standing outside the hangar at the corners. The strongpoints didn't worry him. Their firing slits were designed to cover the approaches to the yard, not the interior. He looked across the cavernous interior, trying to figure out where the satchel charge might do the most good and how to deploy it.

He brought his cart outside again, ostensibly heading for the junk pile. When he returned, the weapons were still hidden in plain sight in the wheelbarrow. He put them on his scrap cart and pulled it toward the center of the Train Hangar.

As he approached the whitewashed guard tower, a sentry challenged him.

"Just a sec, buddy—where do you think you're going with that shit? Nothing's allowed to be stored by the cars, even temporarily."

Valentine kept pulling the cart, and pointed across the yard to a line of workbenches against the far wall. He bumped over the last set of tracks, deeply recessed into the floor of the Train Hangar next to the tower, and an eight-foot-long metal rod rolled off his cart, helped by the tiniest nudge of his leg.

The guard stepped around in front of him. "You want to get over there, dumbass, you go around. Just because the lieutenant ain't here doesn't mean I can't take your number."

Valentine picked up the steel rod and moved to put it back on the cart. Suddenly he uncoiled his body, swinging it up and catching the guard under his armpit. Ribs and shoulder bones cracked. The guard's rifle flew away, batted by the steel rod as its owner tumbled to the ground.

A whistle blew from somewhere near the boxcars. Valentine pulled the cart to the door at the base of the tower and shouldered the flame-thrower first, its nozzle clipped to the tanks. He put the satchel charge over the other arm and went up the spiral stairs with the shotgun in one hand and his sword in the other, the dangling nozzle of the flamethrower clanging on the metal.

A Twisted Cross guard was on the stairs above. Valentine could hear his rapid-fire breathing as if the man were panting in his ear. He put down the sword and heavy weapons.

He bent and jumped up five full steps, turning in the air as he went. He fired the shotgun in the man's face, sending flesh and bone flying.

Nearly at the top, he could see the ceiling above. Valentine pulled the pin on one of the concussion grenades, counted two quick heartbeats, and tossed it up into the balcony.

"Grenade," someone yelled, too late to do any good. Valentine was already running back down the stairs to his other weapons when the explosion hit.

Even with concrete and two loops of the metal staircase to protect him, Valentine still felt the blast of the grenade. Everything seemed to slow down, and he felt closed off from the world, as though swimming underwater. Off balance, he lifted his gear and climbed up the stairs, bracing himself like a drunk.

The men in the tower had either jumped or been blown out of the fifteen-foot-diameter circle. Two machine guns still rested in their mounts, and a pair of shoes lay incongruously on the floor.

A flutter in the air, like bird wings beating against a window—

—the Reaper almost had him when it jumped into the tower. But this was no Kurian-operated killing machine, owner and avatar seasoned by long years of psychic symbiosis. The man in the unknown tank pulling the wires of his puppet was an apprentice, not a Master, and the Reaper tumbled as it landed.

Valentine had time to take up his sword as it rose. Before it could point its gun, he slashed downward, catching it at the knee. He jumped out of the way of the rising gun barrel, and the bullets tore through the empty air where he had stood an instant before. Now the Reaper was seriously off balance, and another whirlwind stroke by the Cat caught it across the neck. The head wasn't severed, but the central spinal cord was; the Reaper dropped to the ground, helpless. Its black teeth bit impotently at its own extruded syringe-tongue.

Valentine ignored it, unhooking one of the strap-ends of the demolition charge. He flipped open the satchel charge and pulled both starter fuses from the top. The heavy bag began to hiss and smoke. Valentine spun like an Olympic hammer-thrower with the single strap held in his hands and sent the bricks of plastic explosive arcing off toward the lined-up boxcars.

They may have been easier to guard packed together like that, but they made an unmissable target for Valentine's explosives. He heard the *thunk* of the charge bouncing off a wooden boxcar's roof, and he dropped behind the yard-thick concrete wall of the guard tower. The part of his mind that always drifted around himself in a fight wondered for a moment why the General would use wood for his boxcars, and the answer came as he opened his bag of grenades. Metal would be too hot in the sun—it could cook the men in the tanks inside. But wood had disadvantages, as well.

He picked up one of the white-phosphorous grenades and covered his ears and nostrils against what was coming.

The thick walls of the hangar magnified the tower-shaking *boom* from the explosives. With debris still in the air, Valentine pulled the pin and released the safety handle on the grenade. He pitched the hissing grenade into the destruction in the center of the boxcars. Shots from the hangar's few guards whipped through the air around him, and he dropped back down before they could improve their aim. As he continued to throw as fast as he could pull pins, he saw the first grenades explode. The phosphorous bombs scattered burning white particles into the splintered wood all around it. Fires devoured paint and wood in half a dozen places.

He heard the sound of footsteps at the bottom of the spiral staircase and sent his last grenade bouncing down the metal stairs. It went off somewhere below, eliciting cries that brought a savage satisfaction.

He turned on the pilot light of the flamethrower and came up over the edge of the parapet with the nozzle pointed at the boxcars.

Valentine loosed a long stream of fiery rain on the sentries aiming their guns at him among the line of boxcars nearest the tower, painting the roofs with orange and yellow flame. The jellied gasoline roared as it consumed paint and wood, splattering and running down the sides and filling the Train Hangar with black smoke. Fire, the most ancient of terror weapons, was as effective on the Twisted Cross as on the Golden Ones. The boiling flames silenced the shots from the men around the cars.

The Twisted Cross guards ran for their lives, some dropping their weapons as they escaped flame and smoke.

Looking down from his concrete nest, Valentine exulted at the havoc wreaked below. No wonder Ali enjoyed lighting fires; the results *were* spectacular. The flamethrower ceased its napalm ejaculation, empty of everything but harmless compressed air. Valentine dropped it and moved to one of the machine guns. With precise movements, he opened the ammunition box mounted on the side of the gun and slapped home the belt in the receiver. Teeth gritted and a snarl on his face, he pulled back the bolt and fired a burst at a group of guards running toward the boxcars. The gun chattered, steady as a rock in its mount, with less recoil than he would feel tapping a pool ball with the cue. Crouching, he concentrated on keeping anyone from fighting the fires now vigorously burning among the boxcars. He could feel the roaring heat almost painfully on his skin from thirty feet away. Nothing mattered but keeping those boxcars alight and the fire growing.

Two thin, nude figures staggered out from the cars on shaky legs, arms waving in front of them. He cut them down with the .50 and fired a burst into the cabin of a train engine being backed into the hangar to tow out some of the cars. Peppered by bullets strong enough to pierce the thin metal walls of their locomotive, the engineers jumped out of the engine and ran. Another nude Twisted Cross operator crawled from the wreckage, burned on his hands and feet. Valentine fired until the pale form ceased twitching.

Valentine heard orders shouted beneath the tower. He looked over the side and saw automatic rifles pointed up at him. He pulled back his head—not fast enough. A bullet grazed hot across his skin and he registered a hard tap, as if a doctor had taken his reflex hammer to the ridge of bone just below his eye, and then a second later the pain hit.

My God, I'm shot.

Not quite believing yet, he put a hand to his face, tracing the heat and feeling open skin with his fingertip. The bullet had torn a furrow up his face from his chin to the corner of his eye.

The burn that lasted a few seconds was just practice for what came next as his nerves revved up.

It was like a white-hot poker being held to his face. He felt himself scream, but there was just a ringing in his ears, lightning in his eyes as he viewed the world through a glittering curtain of diamonds. Somewhere outside the fog of pain and disorientation, he heard steps on the stairs. Concentrating like a drunk trying to get his house key into a lock, he picked up the shotgun, went to the stairs, and fired blindly down the spiral staircase. Blood poured out of his face. Dripped onto the storm-cloud-colored concrete and the metal stairs going down. Fell across his chest, warm rain. An apple dropped from the sky and into his concrete tree house. No, not an apple, a grenade.

There was nothing to do but jump. He launched himself out of the tower, spinning and pivoting —*wow! just like a cat*—to land hard on the surface below and run toward the darkness outside the hangar. Running had never been so easy; he hardly felt his feet touch the ground.

Though there was no one around, someone managed to kick him in his left leg as he ran. No matter, the foot on that side wasn't working that well anyway. He could hop into the darkness. But the darkness could not wait—it came rushing at him, greeting him in its comforting embrace like a long-lost love.

"It'll be all right, Molly," he said, lost in a strange new tunnel he had somehow floated into, an ever-lengthening passage of closing mists. "If you can't walk, I'll carry you."

He found the strength to turn his head, the darkness having decided to put him gently on the ground. He could see campfires in the distance. The fires burned brightly, melding into a single fire like the sun coming up. The fire was what counted. The fire was all that mattered.

Too bad he was too tired to remember why.

David Valentine's body fought a hard war against waking up. Every time consciousness charged up the hill, his exhausted, pained, exsanguinated body held the line and at the last moment sent consciousness tumbling back into the darkness of oblivion. It tried to return when he was picked up and carried from where he fell, and tried again when he was placed on a table. A bright light in his face and surgical tape over his cheek brought other battles. Later, on a hospital bed, consciousness launched a series of sneak attacks. He had vague dreams of speaking to Captain Le Havre, then to his father.

Death never arrived to relieve his body from its war against the pain, so Valentine eventually awoke. He was disoriented; for some reason he wanted more than anything to know how long it had been since he'd been taken.

As he spun back to the awful real world, he reached up, but some kind of restraint frustrated his first instinct to touch his face. In fact, he couldn't even turn his body. The whole left side of his face throbbed in pain, and he felt a tired empty nausea. There was cold dampness between his legs, as well as a warm, sticky, solid presence in his undergarments. His left leg was missing its pantleg, though the rest of his clothes were still on. The pain was too much to deal with, so he sank back into a groggy sleep.

He did not sleep deeply enough. A woman eventually cut away the rest of his clothes and cleaned him up, a surprisingly agonizing process, though she handled him as gently as if he were a baby. When they changed the dressing on his face, under the care of a man not nearly so gentle, it hurt like the bullet cutting through his flesh a second time, and he passed out again, unfortunately for only a minute. He came round while they were applying more searing iodine and another dressing.

The hours ticked by, and he tried playing games with the pain, offering the pain thirty minutes of agony for just five minutes of relief, but pain would not agree to his terms.

He dropped into a fitful doze and came out of it a little further at a shake of his shoulder.

"Would you like some water?" a man in a lab coat asked.

"Yes, please," he croaked. There were more sensations now. The pain, always the pain, but he could also taste the air, and something about it told him he was underground.

The man brought the cup lower, and Valentine sucked cool water down through a surgical tubing straw.

"He can talk, that's good enough. Bring him."

Through the mists, he felt himself being lifted, carried down a hall to another room. They sat him up in a tube-steel chair with a hard wooden seat, the kind of chair that's been sitting in a neat row with five others just like it in some assistant principal's office since the school was built. They handcuffed his hands behind his back, which amused him. He was too weak to crawl, let alone fight. When they moved his leg to handcuff his ankle to one of the chair legs, the pain became so bad that warm urine flooded his pants. It felt like he was pissing nitric acid.

"Aw, Christ," one of the guards said, seeing the seat get wet and smelling the urine. "He pissed himself."

"So what."

Valentine's head lolled, and he looked at the pale green tiles on the floor. He tried to remember if he had ever seen such small tiles, so evenly laid out, when he again slipped into unconsciousness.

Later he had to wait. It felt like days, but perhaps it was only hours. His consciousness strengthened, and the haze began to fade. He realized that he desperately wanted to live, even if it was only for a few more hours. He wondered if they were just going to shoot him or if they had a more elaborate end in store.

They gave him more water. He was able to drink it, though it hurt his face to do so. The room was uninteresting, not even a desk or another chair decorated it. The little green tiles went from the floor about one third of the way up the wall. From there on up, it was unrelieved and undecorated concrete, marked only by a swirl or two of the mason's smoother. He smelled chalk somewhere and tried to remember if there was a chalkboard in the room from when he was brought in. The lone door to the room was also behind it, and he heard people passing in the hall at intervals.

When he heard a set of heavy steps in the hall, something inside him told him *This is it.* He tried to steel his mind, even if his body felt like worn-out rubber. But his mind was a slave to his body; intellect prostrated itself before the pain and fatigue just when he needed his wits most.

The door opened, and he was able to turn his head enough despite the pain in his cheek to see two tall Grogs enter. They were Golden Ones, dressed in black leather robes cut like a double-breasted trench coat of the Old World and shiny as a beetle's back. One stood to his right, the other to his left. Their fawn-colored hair was shorn down to stubble.

A dried-up husk of a man walked around in front of him. His skin had the waxy look of a cancer patient in the last stages of the disease; his lips chapped. Vigorous dark hair grew out from a widow's peak on his forehead and was brushed straight back across his head. His eyes could have been pale blue or pale green, depending on the opinion of the person looking into them. He wore a simple rust-colored uniform, and a Sam Browne belt very similar to Valentine's own. Red tabs with golden reverse-swastikas marked his collar. He wore no tunic, sidearm, or decorations.

"One of the best things about living so long," he said, in a vaguely European accent that Valentine was not experienced enough to place, "is that you get to see all the mistakes historians make, talking about something they don't really know.

"For example, the only history widely read since 2022 is that wretched pamphlet called *Fallen Gods* by that would-be Margaret Bourke-White named Kostos. She says the first of the new doors to Kur were opened in Haiti in the eighteenth century. She only missed by about a thousand years. How do I know? *I was there.* My eyes have looked on Charlemagne, young man. Kur had a door open in the Dark Ages, but they were not dark times for me—oh, no. During the Inquisition, we managed to get another open in Spain."

The General walked around behind Valentine and wheeled a cart into view. On it was his sword, his fighting claws, his little glow bulb, and a few other personal effects.

"So you joined long ago?" Valentine asked. "What did they offer for betraying a whole world?"

"What no price, no wisdom can buy. Time."

"So you feed."

"Yes. Long, long ago, I was given a gift, a revelation of biblical proportions, you might say. For my service, the scientists taught me how to achieve immortality."

"An immortality others pay the price for," Valentine said tightly.

"Don't cows, hogs, chickens pay the price for your life?"

"Not the same thing."

"That's where you and so many others are wrong. Cows and so on are eaten because they are tasty, certainly, but more important, because they aren't developed enough to keep themselves from being eaten. Mankind took a great leap forward when it learned to keep livestock, putting it ahead of all other creatures on the earth with a few bizarre exceptions like those honeypot ants that keep aphids. We were once no better than the cows, but we developed and the cows didn't. The cows pay the price, and we are better for it."

"Why are we talking about this?" Valentine asked.

"When you get to be my age, when you've seen people come and go over not just generations or centuries, but millennia, you become a good judge of men. In my days as a monk, before my awakening, I didn't think much of the human herd. No spark, no imagination, and misunderstanding even the simple concepts we tried to teach.

"As I've aged, I've found it harder and harder to suffer fools. Most people aren't much better than cattle. They've just inherited more complex stimulus-response routines. When you see men making the same mistakes, over and over and over again, you lose empathy and acknowledge only utility. That's what I tried to tell Kant when I lived in Prussia."

Valentine could hear someone outside the door asking for a message to be delivered to the General, and his aide accepting it.

"I think," the General said, "you are above the herd, a valuable piece of human capital. You, too, have been given gifts by the Lifeweavers. You have a talent I need badly. I'd like to have you on my side, rather than dead and in some Grog's stomach. If you found a tarnished bar of gold in the road, would you shine it up, or would you grind it up and toss it to the winds? I'm in a position to offer you what amounts to eternal life. A chance to grow your talent instead of wasting it."

"How can you have an opinion of me if you don't know me?" Valentine asked.

"When someone gets the better of me, I'd want to learn how they did it. I've done a little research, asked a few questions. A skilled man asked you some questions while you recovered. You were at the Eagle's Wings Brand out on those forsaken grassy dunes. Before that you were a promising officer, until you were sacrificed by an ambitious superior trying to keep his record clean. Yes, I have sources right in Southern Command. There are people you work for who want to live forever."

"You know me, then. Who are you?"

"Someone like you. A reader. A leader. More of a realist, but you are young, and idealism is the asylum of the young."

"I'm sorry you escaped the asylum."

The General ignored him. "I was, before my personal Enlightenment, a monk of the Dark Ages, one of those depressing, chanting celibates who claimed to be keeping culture alive after the fall of Western Rome, but were in fact dreaming up new ways to take advantage of the gullible. I was something of a historian, and I found hovering on the edges of certain ancient tracts pieces of a larger story. I convinced my superiors to let me go on a pilgrimage to the Holy Land and beyond. I ended up going far beyond anything my order expected of me. I found the ruins of the Kurian City of Brass in Central Asia and met a smooth-skinned Chinaman who claimed to be two thousand years old. Thus began my education into the Arts of Kur. Later they sought us out. But the Chinaman—old Zhao—he was my savior, in a way.

"When I got my first infusion of vital aura, I was old and sick. It— you have to experience it, I can't put it in words. Where there had been weakness there was new strength. I'd forgotten what the flush of youth was; it's the finest feeling in the world. The opportunities it opened . . . I could live my life all over again. I lived dozens of lives all over again. The Golden Horde knew me. I saw the Turks come and fade, I rode with Cossacks as the Grand Armée retreated from Moscow. I invested and let time work for me over generations.

"My wealth bought power and influence, which I put to the bidding of Kur. I owned prime ministers and generals, diplomats and writers.

Have you ever heard of major league baseball? Owners of teams used to buy, sell, and trade their players in an effort to get a team that would win the pennant. I was doing the same on a global scale, slowly and patiently. That is the great advantage of the Kurian scientists' immortality, Valentine. It gives you the luxury of patience."

Valentine looked at the dried-up old General. If anyone ever looked old and sick, except for his lush band of hair, it was the former monk.

"Where did you get the Twisted Cross?"

The General touched the reversed swastika on his collar tab. "This is an old symbol, a token of special status of those who are counted as a friend of Kur. You can find it on artifacts from prehistory almost the whole world over. I chose it to symbolize a reawakening of the old open alliance between Earth and Kur, men and their old gods. Men with the vision not just to accommodate the New Order, but to shape it for their own purposes, as well."

"So you're on a longer leash than most. It's still a leash." His croaking voice took some of the spite out of the words.

"Kur needs me, desperately, to do their fighting for them. They are too busy running their dominions, feuding and scheming amongst themselves. Now that they have won so much, they no longer want to risk their precious Reapers fighting with the pockets that are left. You've been troublesome in your obstinacy, unwilling to admit the war is over—like starving Japanese soldiers in an island bunker."

Valentine felt very tired, and began to wonder if he would remain conscious for the rest of the interview, or interrogation, or inquisition.

"General, I'm the one in handcuffs here. What's next for me?"

"You have a choice, a choice that you deserve, given your abilities and manifest intelligence, albeit talents wasted in the unrewarding service of the ungrateful. I am not just speaking of the pathetic Lifeweavers, either, I am referring to your so-called brethren who stay at home while you risk your life to protect their chicken-hearted existence.

"I will not insult you by asking you to join me. You need not say yes. All you have to do is ask for another week's life. And then another. And then another. I will show you visions, introduce you to possibilities that will fire your imagination, your belly, your loins. Someday you may be given touchstones and have knowledge at your disposal that Aristotle couldn't have dreamed of. The rewards are literally endless. What shall it be, son? The pistol—or another week's life?"

What'll it be, Cat? Die defending "the herd"? Or feed off it?

Valentine, hurt and tired, found an answer in his pain. Faces flashed through his memory. He saw Molly, the Carlsons, Sutton the generous pig farmer. Linda, who'd been Mrs. Poulos for a few hours, and the squalling baby from the Rigyard. Donna and her armoire-building son. The young Grogs gamboling with human children around the well of Steiner's little enclave. Ahn-Kha and the Golden Ones. Jocelyn Hendricks. Who would be sacrificed for whom?

His voice was strong this time. "Shoot me, Judas."

"A pointless end to the tale of the Valentines. You'll find your Golgotha lonely."

"How lonely is your bunker, General?"

The General struck the smirk from Valentine's face. Blood began to run out from under his bandage.

"You had defeated me in battle—well, defeated the men I trusted to fight my battles, which may mean the same thing. But that is a question for the philosophers. But what is a delay to me? Do you think you have really harmed me?" he asked, his eyes beginning to light up with angry fire. "Do you? Your pathetic little gesture was spittle in a hurricane. I can afford to think in terms of thousands of years. That is why this base is being built, not for one campaign in Nebraska, but for control of a continent. It takes years to select, grow, and train a fighting pair; I began this project before you were born and have seen it through setbacks worse than the fire you started.

"The science of Kur and my leadership has proved that this system works. Men can control Reapers, Reapers who fight like soldiers, without the weaknesses and desires of the Kurian from which they sprang. First principles, my son. I proved that I can do it with one, and if I can make one, I can make a thousand, and if I can make a thousand—"

The door opened again, and another shorn Golden One in the leather uniform of the bodyguard entered, almost dragging the protesting aide. The arrival said something to the other two in their own tongue. "I'm sorry, sir," the aide apologized. "There seems to be a disturbance outside in the Grog pen. We should go to the emergency shelter at once."

Valentine looked at the panting messenger, and his heart leapt.

The former monk let out a tired breath and nodded.

Valentine tried to stand, drawing the General's eye. "That may be true, sir, from a logical point of view. But I think someone is going to have to pick up where you left off. It appears you've fucked with the wrong species."

"Wha-*awk*," the General managed to get out, before Ahn-Kha wrapped his viselike fingers around his throat. The angry titan picked up the General, swung him at the shocked aide.

Valentine's chair fell over in the struggle, but he still could see the unique sight of a man being beaten to death with another man used as the murder weapon. With six blows, Ahn-Kha reduced both the General and his aide to bloody pulp. The General proved to be a poor choice of club; he began to fall apart after the third swing.

The bodyguard Grogs shrank away from the twitching corpses, as though the General might rise again in demonic fury. But it was just reflex of muscle and broken bone making wet sounds against the floor. The bodyguards exchanged a few tremulous words with Ahn-Kha and then embraced him.

The Golden One breathed hard after his exertion. "You do not look yourself, my David. Let me help you."

The bearlike face hovered over his. As the world slipped, Valentine tried to stay conscious.

Back. Feel the pain. Smell the blood. Hear the—gunfire. There's gunfire?

"What did you say to the bodyguards?" Valentine asked weakly. A few shots sounded from the hall.

" 'If you do nothing, all is forgiven.' It is a little more poetic in my tongue. I hope this does not hurt you further." The Grog's arc of muscle at his arms and shoulders tensed, and the handcuffs snapped in two.

The door opened, and Alessa Duvalier stood silhouetted in the frame, encased in Twisted Cross assault armor. The gear made her look a little absurd, like a turtle in too big a shell. She held a rifle to her shoulder, covering the hallway, and her naked, blood-smeared sword stuck blade-up in her waistband. A sweat-soaked headband kept flame-colored hair out of wild and hungry eyes.

"No time for kiss and tell, boys. Heat's on."

Valentine wondered if he were in some wild dream brought on by loss of blood. "Ali?" he said, "What are you doing here?"

She reversed the magazine in her gun, quickly substituting the full one for the empty one taped to it. "I'm milking a male ostrich! What does it look like, Val? I'm taking point for your pointy-eared friend."

Ahn-Kha scooped Valentine up in his arms and followed the female Cat out the door and down the hall. At an intersection ahead, Valentine saw another Golden One with a machine gun at his hip, spraying the corridor with fire. They turned at the corner opposite to where the Grog was firing, and Valentine got a brief glimpse of a corridor littered with bodies. Valentine felt himself being carried up some stairs, thinking that perhaps it wasn't so bad to be partnered with a mentally disordered woman—sometimes. Then he passed out.

"The hardest part was figuring out where you were," Duvalier explained the next day.

Valentine lay in his hammock in some thick woods on the Missouri River well south of the Twisted Cross base. Ahn-Kha was sleeping soundly, Valentine's PPD cradled in his arms. Valentine sipped some willow-leaf tea to ease the pain. According to Duvalier, he had the blackest black eye she had ever seen.

"I caused a little trouble with the column that hit the Eagle's Wings, but I mostly wanted to learn where their base was. It was just a matter of getting into camp and keeping my ears open. The stunts you pull are the type of thing only Bears are stupid enough to try—I'd just as soon stay out of the way of bullets, thank you very much. Not that I don't admire your balls."

She kissed the bandage over the left side of his cheek.

"Maybe I can introduce you to the twins and their big brother when I can walk again," he suggested.

"Dream on, Valentine. So I go to the rendezvous and wait, and naturally you don't show. So I leave a note and come hunting around the south end of Omaha. I pretty much mapped out the base, got an idea of the numbers the Twisted Cross had, and found out that oversize perimeter wasn't too well guarded. The General was planning for the future, I suppose. But his present couldn't do the job.

"So one day I'm checking out the west side of the wall, and I see this ugly ape trying to move through the brush, real sneaky-like but making more noise than a bulldozer in a bottle factory. I'm about to do him in from ambush, when I see this ugly, drum-fed gun in his hands. It's just too much of a coincidence for there to be two of those in Nebraska, so I stick my blade to his throat and start asking questions."

Ahn-Kha opened an eye and snorted. But he didn't disagree.

"It turns out you've disappeared into the camp, they heard an explosion from a mile off, but then you were MIA the next day. He sent his buddy off for reinforcements and had just about decided to try to bust down the main gate to go looking for you when I showed up.

"That night I went into the Cave and acted like a *Cat*—instead of a one-man army, please make a note of that Valentine—just looking and listening and hearing what was being talked about. It turned out that you were in the basement medical center below this Train Hangar. I saw the General return from Omaha, with what was left of his force after his Reapers mysteriously started dropping in the middle of the assault on the Grogs. He said something about wanting to meet the man they captured, and I knew you were still alive. I also found out you were going to be interrogated the next day.

"I got back to your big friend here, and he has a hundred armed-to-the-ears Grogs, wanting Twisted Cross blood. And you. And then more blood."

Ahn-Kha carried on the story. "The Big Man came to our aid after all. He hid a few pistols and grenades in the food going to the Golden Ones the General had hostage on the base. It was not much. But it got them out of their pen.

"I told them to start tearing the place down. After that, it was just a matter of sneaking in with your uncle over there and waiting for our chance to get you and the General both."

"What happened at the base?"

"They still had a lot of firepower. There were losses. It was really two rescue missions, a little one for you and a big one for the Grogs still on the base. I don't think we'll have to worry about the Twisted Cross for a while. They don't have many of those Reapers left. Maybe they can put the operation back together, but it'll take some time. Their underground is intact. We couldn't even get near that Cave of theirs. We'll need to get Bear teams up here to blow that."

Ahn-Kha yawned, showing off his tusklike teeth. "Ha! Not if the Golden Ones had anything to do with it. Whatever we built, we know how to destroy. Even now we use the great construction machines to build a cairn for our dead. On top of the Twisted Cross bunker, of course."

"Old horse," Valentine said, "I think the balance of gratitude has shifted back in your favor. Now I am in your debt."

The Grog's eyes were closed in his dozing, so Ahn-Kha settled for the human gesture of shaking his head. "I told you there could be no talk of debts between brothers, my David. I always wanted to see the wider world."

"We could learn from you, too. That heartroot could be grown on every farm in the Ozarks. Wherever people are, there's moisture and, uh, fertilizer. The idea might take some getting used to, though."

"I have pieces of spore-pod in my pack. No Golden One travels without it. This I can do."

"What about it, Ali, shall we go home?"

"You need to rest a little. Why do you always have to rush things?"

Valentine smiled. "Because life is short. Thank God."

She furrowed her eyebrows at him and went back to re-bandaging his leg.

He felt sleep coming on him again, and he looked over at Ahn-Kha. He wondered what would have happened if the Cat and the Grog had not shown up. His conscience pained him more than his face. Did they rescue him from a quick death—or endless life? He remembered the knot in his stomach, fearing his life had run its course. His words had been brave enough, but they were just words, stiffened by pain. When he felt the cold barrel of the pistol at the back of his head, what would have been his choice? *A question for the philosophers,* as the General said.

Eight weeks later, in the rich colors of autumn in the Ozarks, Valentine limped right into an ambush. Of course, since he saw the men watching and waiting, it could hardly be called an ambush, but the young Wolves were clearly proud of their work, hallooing to each other once they had the trio dead-bang. He, Ahn-Kha, and Duvalier put up their hands.

"Where the hell do you think you're going, Groglicker?" the leader of the close fire-team asked, squinting at them from under woolly eyebrows and a notched felt hat. Valentine would have handled the ambush differently were he in charge, letting the far fire-team make contact and keeping the close team hidden to provide a nasty surprise in case things got hostile.

"My code name is Smoke," Duvalier said, stepping forward. "This is my partner, Ghost. Verification November: five-oh-three. Take us to the nearest post—we're coming in with a priority report for Southern Command."

The sergeant in charge of the patrol pushed his coonskin cap back on his head. "That so? Well, Cats or no, we'll have to put you under guard. Unload your weapons and sling them, and we'll oblige right quick. What's that with you, a prisoner? Don't think I've ever seen a Grog like that before. Where'd you capture long-legs?"

"That's not a prisoner," Valentine corrected, leaning on his walking stick. "He's my brother."

"Hell's bells," one of the Wolves in the background said to his comrade out of the corner of his mouth, "what was his old man thinking? I've heard of a guy being desperate, but there are some things that just ain't right."

The Wolves, pointing their weapons away from the three, gathered around their charges, positioned to guard as well as to guide. The Hunters turned and headed home.

TALE OF THE THUNDERBOLT

To John and Laura Anne,
for getting me to the next level

From the east to the west blow the trumpet to arms!
Through the land let the sound of it flee;
Let the far and the near all unite, with a cheer,
In defense of our Liberty Tree.

—Thomas Paine, "The Liberty Tree"

They sailed away for a year and a day
To the land where the bong-tree grows.

—Edward Lear, *The Owl and the Pussy-Cat*

One

New Orleans, January, the forty-eighth year of the Kurian Order: Formerly glorious in its decay, under the New Order the city transformed from an aging beauty into a waterlogged corpse. Much of the Big Easy rots under a meter of Mississippi River water—save for the old city's heart, now protected by two layers of dikes. The rococo facades of the French Quarter, once browning into a fine patina, fall to pieces in quiet, unmourned. The stately homes of the two great antebellum periods, pre-1861 and pre-2022, have vanished under a carpet of lush kudzu or riverside saw grass. As if the flooding and years of neglect were not enough punishment, New Orleans suffered a major hurricane in 2028: a titanic storm that rose from the Gulf like a city-smashing monster in a Japanese movie. No FEMA, no insurance companies showed up afterwards to clean and repair the storm-battered city. What was destroyed stayed destroyed; the inhabitants found it easier to shift to still-standing buildings than to rebuild.

But the mouth of the Mississippi is too important, even to the reduced traffic of the Kurian Order, to be given up entirely to nature. The metropolis, both the section behind the dike and the Venice-like portions of the flooded districts, still support a mélange of denizens from all across the Gulf of Mexico and the Caribbean. Counting those living among the lakes, bayous, and in the Mississippi estuary, New Orleans boasts a population of over two million—a total that few other cities known to the Old World can match. The rich harvests of seafood, fish and game of the swamps, and mile after mile of rice plantations feed the masses concentrated at the sodden bend in the river.

The Kurian Order encourages fecund populations. A Kurian lord must breed his polis to supply him with enough vital aura, for only in feeding on the energy created by the death throes of a sentient being can he revitalize his immortal lich. The Masters of New Orleans have no regrets about its silenced music, its smothered culture, its reduced cuisine, or its broken history. Healthy, mating herds of humans, kept from escape and from the clutches of rapacious competing Kur, are the only form of wealth that matters.

For the human race, living to see another year is now the paramount pursuit in a city once known for its sensual diversions.

Though the Easy Street was only a waterfront dive, it was *his* waterfront dive, so Martin Clive took pride in every squeaky stool and chipped mug of his saloon. From grid shielded-electric lights to sawdust-covered floor, he loved every brick of it.

His customers, on the other hand, he could take or leave.

Not that he didn't need them. Clive's herd of cash-bearing cows, properly milked, provided for him. Clive surveyed the noisy, smelly Thursday-night crowd as the winter rains poured down outside. Safe behind the badge sewn to the money vest he seldom took off—even to sleep—and in the ownership of the biggest bar on the dockyard district of the dike-hugging waterfront, he passed his time and occupied his mind in sizing up the men as they talked, smoked, and drank. The few women in his bar were there on business, not for pleasure.

Clive perfected a three-step practice of evaluating customers over the years, now so ingrained that he did it unconsciously. Separating the "payers" from the "bums" came first. Knowing who had the cash for a night's drink and who didn't had been second nature to Clive since before he acquired the establishment. Distinguishing "gents" from "trouble" was yet another specialty. As he aged, and passed the responsibility of serving out drinks and rousting the "bums" and "trouble" to younger, stronger men, he took up a third valuation: that of predicting the remaining life span of his customers.

Clive looked at a bent longshoreman, hook over his shoulder and a pewter mug of cheap beer at his lips. The man had drunk, smoked, and wheezed out a few hours in the Easy Street six nights a week for the past ten years. Clive had watched him age under grueling physical labor, rotgut alcohol, and bad diet. If the longshoreman could stay in the good books of his crew chief, meaning handing over kickbacks out of his wages, he could probably spin out as many as ten more years if he stayed out of the hold. Sitting two seats down from him, a merchant sailor drank plain coffee, sixty if he was a day, dye rubbed into his hair to darken it in an effort to look younger. Soon no captain would hire him on, no matter how sober and upstanding a character he might be.

He was due for the last dance within a year or two. On the next stool, a boy kept an affectionate eye on the aged sailor, perhaps a relative, perhaps just a shipmate. The boy did not drink either, and with hard work and a clean nose could expect to live another fifty years as long as he kept indoors after nightfall.

Over at a warm corner table, a young officer drank with three of his men. The officer was a welcome combination of "payer" and "gent," to the point where Clive bothered to name him. The officer was "the Major" to Clive, and the Major always ordered a good bottle and never complained about the cheap whiskey substituted inside. That made him a fine payer. The Major and his men rarely caused trouble; therefore, they qualified for genthood. They wore the mottled green uniform of the Carbineers, one of the horsed troops of paramilitary Cossacks who kept civil order and patrolled the streets of New Orleans.

Maybe in other city establishments the Major threw his weight around, took food and drink without paying, and had his uniform silence objections. But not in the Easy Street. Clive had friends at the top of the city's food chain.

Clive learned in his youth that if you were in good with Kur, you could thumb your nose at the Port Authority, the Transport Office, even the police and militia. With Kurian patronage, he bid for ownership of the moribund Easy Street. A whiff of anything going on in the bar that Kur wouldn't like, and he picked up the phone. Clive wore his third ten-year badge on his chest, not due to expire for six more years, and he was certain of acquiring another. The badge put him off-limits to the Kurians' aura-hungry Hoods—well, mostly—and brought him peace of mind that muzzled any protest from his conscience.

The inner door of the entry vestibule opened, and Clive heard the wind and splatter of the rain pouring down outside in the moment before his doorman swung the outer portal shut. Clive liked the rain. It drove customers indoors and flushed the filth from the city's gutters.

A stranger stood silhouetted in the door.

The man didn't remove his raincoat. Clive took a closer look. A coat could conceal any number of unpleasant accoutrements. The Easy Street's owner relaxed when he caught a glimpse of uniform under the coat's heavy lapels. The flash of navy blue and brass buttons revealed the stranger as a Coastal Marine. From the fit of the coat and the good though mud-splattered boots Clive judged the man a payer. But something about his face made Clive reserve judgment on whether this man would be trouble or not.

The marine was tall and lean, but not remarkably so in either aspect. Clive put him in his mid-twenties: he had the narrow, crinkle-edged eyelids of a man with a lot of outdoor mileage, and the bronze skin of someone with a hefty dose of Indian blood. The stranger walked with a trace of stiffness in his left leg, not a false limb but perhaps an old injury. He was good-looking in a clean-shaven, sharp-jawed way, judging from the looks exchanged by a pair of whores keeping each other company at the end of the bar. Shining black hair hung in wet tangles, a ropy opal mane thrown back over his collar. A thin white scar traced his right cheek from the outer corner of his dark eye to his chin like the path of a milky tear.

With a moment to get a good look as the marine moved, Clive judged the man to be wearing a pistol at his hip, then the capped tang of some kind of knife appeared as the entrant turned. Clive knew how to spot weapons, long coat or no.

The new customer glanced around the room. His gaze flicked from the massive fireplace at the west end, big enough for a barbecue, to the game tables at the east.

The marine froze. Clive followed his gaze. Before he could determine whom he had recognized, the scarred stranger approached the bar nonchalantly. Clive guessed he had recognized the Major, for the table in the corner had gone quiet. Probably some old quarrel over a girl, or a smuggling deal gone bad. The Coastal Marines, with their mobility and lack of supervision, were notorious black-marketeers on the coast stretching from Galveston to the Florida Floods. Intrigued, Clive looked across the bar to the Major's table. The gents had their heads together. Clive's nose, after years of smelling the various aromas of a saloon—tobacco, liquor, sweat, urine, sawdust, and vomit (usually in that order)—was not as straight as it once had been, but he smelled trouble.

"Tea and rum, if you've got either," David Valentine said, dripping from head to foot on the sawdust-sprinkled floor. His coat trapped the wet of his shirt better than it kept the rain out.

"Got both, Coastie."

"The hotter, the better," he said, pulling his hand through his slick hair again to get it out of his eyes. The gesture gave him a chance to look at the corner table. A silent mental alarm had tripped a switch in his nervous system, warming him better than any fire. Details stood out: florid printing on the bar bottle labels, the meshed ranks of gray hair on the barman's arms, a blemish on a prostitute's neck, footsteps muffled by the sawdust scattered on the floor, the rancid smell out of a spittoon.

The officer leaned across the corner table to speak to his men. Valentine trembled as his mind raced.

"You cold, Marine?" a whore asked, brushing a wet lock of hair behind his ear. Gold lamé and blond hair covered what little skin she didn't have on display. "I got a way—"

She'd been attracted by the uniform. Ironic, because its thick, high-quality fabric and solid brass buttons repulsed him every time he put it on. Whenever he looked at himself in a mirror, he saw the Enemy looking back out of his own eyes.

"Some other time, perhaps." Valentine turned away from her.

His conscience hammered at him until his eyes shone wet with more than rain. *Fool! Lazy, irresponsible fool!* Over a year's worth of preparation, service to the Kurian Order under a false name, all turned to shit and flushed. Just because he'd been tired and felt like coming in out of the weather.

Valentine racked his brain for the name, picturing the hawkish face in the hammock that summer in the Yazoo Delta during his training in Free Territory. Lewand Alistar, a freshly invoked Wolf six years ago and posted missing, presumed dead. So the Reapers hadn't killed him after all. Perhaps he had been captured and turned; perhaps he had been planted in Southern Command as a spy who saw his chance to get away clean. Whatever put him in a Carbineer's uniform in New Orleans was immaterial. The fact remained that mutual recognition occurred.

Valentine remembered Alistar as a quick-witted, active comrade. A hot mug of spiked tea arrived, and Alistar chose that moment to rise and take up his coat. Valentine blew into the steaming crockery. Alistar's companions shifted their chairs around. They pretended to watch the barmaids and hookers, but all three heads were pointed at Valentine.

Valentine heard Alistar move behind him. He readied himself to turn and fight, should the footsteps approach. But the Quisling left the Easy Street in a hurry. Typical of Alistar—not heroic but smart. No wonder he wore a major's cluster in the Kurian Zone.

Valentine needed to get out of the bar, too, without being impeded by Alistar's comrades, who he guessed had been ordered to keep him from leaving. He reached into his pocket, wadded a ball of money in his hand. He raised his mug in a come-hither toast to the whore who had approached him.

"Interested in a little fun and a lot of money?" he asked, his rough voice low.

"Always," she said, smiling at him with a decent, if tobacco stained, set of teeth behind compound layers of lipstick. "My name's Agri. Like as in agreeable to anything."

Valentine thrust the money into her shirt, pretending to feel her up. "Glad to hear it. There's a hundred and then some, Agri. Which girl here rubs you the wrong way?"

"Huh?" she said.

"Quick, or a man. Who don't you like here?"

She dropped the attitude at the quiet urgency in his voice. "Umm, there's Star," the woman said, leaning out to look around Valentine's wide shoulder. "The head of hair with gold earrings. She's always breaking in and screwing my work up."

He followed her gaze. "Which one is she, in the pink?" he asked, spotting a prostitute with a mass of wavy hair framing her face like a lion's mane. "Okay, I'm going to go talk to her. I want you to start a fight, fast."

"And that's all I gotta do?"

"Make as big a scene as you can. Yes, that's all."

"Shit, Marine, I'd do that for free."

Valentine turned away from her and moved to the darker woman in a hot pink half-top. "I've heard you're quite a woman," Valentine said, raising an eyebrow suggestively. The whore cocked her head and smiled welcomingly.

"That's my up, you bitch!" his paid prostitute shrieked.

Noisy, even better, Valentine thought.

Star reacted with a speed that would have done credit to many of Valentine's former comrades in the Wolves. She planted herself, lowered her hips, and spread her arms.

The two women fell to the floor, fighting bobcats spitting and hissing at each other. A ring of hooting barflies formed around the combatants. Valentine backed through the crowd, snatched a hat off of an unattended table, and moved out the door before any of Alistar's soldiers had a chance to push through the crowd to guard the exit.

The conditions could hardly be worse for tracking a smart man in the crowded—and dangerous, thanks to prowling Reapers—city with a two-minute head start. Night, rain, and the rickshaw-cluttered streets all conspired to hide his quarry. Visibility nil—the big bosses never bothered much with public lighting. Most men would not have had a chance.

David Valentine was not most men. He was a Cat, one of the select specimens of humanity called Hunters trained by the Lifeweavers to fight against the abominations of their vampiric brethren, the

Kur. The Kur controlled most of the planet, and the regions that remained outside their grasp, like Valentine's adopted home in the Ozarks and Ouachitas, owed much of their freedom to the sacrifices of the Hunters.

The Hunters, outnumbered and weak compared with the Reapers and the other creations of the Kur, relied on enhanced senses, physical ability, and tight mental discipline. The last was of paramount importance. The Reapers, the Praetorian Guard of Kur, tracked human prey by reading lifesign, psychic auras sent out by sentient beings.

Valentine needed to wash the fear from his mind. At the moment he was alone among enemies, surrounded by thousands who could gain a ten-year badge protecting themselves from the Reapers by pointing him out as an enemy of the New Order. And somewhere in the rainy darkness, a man whom he knew to be no fool was hurrying to ring the alarm bell.

Alistar would not just run to the nearest phone. He had no idea if Valentine was working alone, or with others who might have picked up a surreptitious signal and followed him out of the bar. Valentine remembered him as a man who liked to be in command. It was possible that he would get a posse of his own Carbineers together, to better take the credit for his coup in capturing or killing one of Southern Command's "terrorists."

The barracks of the Carbineers would mean a long walk, too much time wasted. But Valentine knew from months of working the port that a contingent of them guarded their supply warehouse by the docks. Some of Alistar's men would be there.

It was only a guess, but as good a guess as he could make. Valentine ducked through an alleyway and broke into a sprint down a road parallel to the one Alistar probably took. Even if he had guessed wrong, the farther he got from the Easy Street, the better.

He loosened his coat to run. If anyone saw him, pounding down the center of the near-empty street, splashing through puddles, they might mistake him in the wet and darkness for a Reaper. His sprint did not end at the hundred-yard mark; he called on his reserves, and they answered, propelling him through the night with legs and lungs of flame. Astonishingly, at least to anyone who did not know what a Hunter was capable of, his speed increased.

The warehouse he sought was in an old, brick-paved part of town. Garbage lay in heaps on every corner, and better than half the buildings were fire-gutted shells. Empty, glassless windows gaped out at the street like skulls' eyes when they were not boarded up.

One closed-up window wore a freshly spray-painted skull with a heart around it. According to the graffiti of New Orleans's streets, some-one just lost a loved one to the Reapers within.

Any of the empty buildings around might contain a prowling Reaper. This was one of the districts of the city where it wasn't considered healthy to be out after dark, even for a man in uniform. He relaxed his mind, let his vision blur, tried to feel for the cold, hard spot on his mind the Reapers sometimes made.

Sometimes. He prayed his psychic antennae were working tonight.

He pulled up at a noisome alley, partially blocked at one end by a stripped car turned on its side. Its gutters served as the local populace's latrine, judging from the smell. Hand tapping at his pistol butt, Valentine cut down the alley and back to the main thoroughfare. Alistar was a former Wolf, and there was every possibility of him scenting Valentine before seeing him without some kind of masking odor.

A *thunk* and a metallic clatter sounded from one of the broken windows, hitting him like a shot. He spun, crouching against the half-expected leap as he drew his revolver. His keen ears picked up the sound of the skittering, scrambling claws of a fleeing rat within.

Valentine edged sideways down the alley, gaze flicking from pane-less window to window until his heart slowed again.

He paused in a deep well of darkness under a fire escape, rehol-stered his gun, and drew a stiletto from his boot, nerving himself for what he had to do. Killing in battle, with bullets cracking the air all around and explosions numbing his senses was one thing. Premeditated murder of a fleeing opponent required an entirely different side of his persona. It was a version of himself who had killed helpless men in their Control Tanks in Omaha; blown a bound policeman's head off with a shotgun in Wisconsin; and knifed lonely, frightened sentries on isolated bridges. Cold-blooded need provoked those killings, but his sense of exultation in the deeds bothered his conscience more than the acts themselves did.

Valentine heard footsteps over the steady patter of rain, coming from the direction he expected Alistar. Two people hove into view in the middle of the street, walking together under some kind of tarpaulin sheltering both from the weather. Not his quarry then, but—

One was definitely pulling the other along. The insistent guide was about the right size and sex. Clever. Trusting his hunch, Valentine collected himself for a leap. As he crouched, the analytical side of his brain appreciated the irony of Alistar using a woman as camouflage, paralleling his own subterfuge in the bar. The tarpaulin provided just the right touch of shape-concealing cover. He probably grabbed her out of a doorway, tucking himself under the improvised umbrella with her and ordering her to accompany him. Alistar had always been cool in a crisis.

As they passed, not seeing him in the rain and dark, Valentine leapt. His standing broad jump covered five meters, ending in a body blow that caught Alistar in the small of the back. The two tumbled down, the man ensnared in the wet canvas.

The girl screamed out her fright, and Valentine heard her stumble and right herself. He paid no attention, concentrating on getting his knife to the Quisling's throat. The man struggled in the folds of the tarry material like a netted fish.

He straddled Alistar, pinning his chest and arms with the full force of his body weight and muscle as he cut open the tarp. The stiletto dug into his former comrade's neck, eliciting a squeal. "Dave, no! Wait!"

Valentine paused, not moving the knife either farther in or back. He had not been called Dave since his days as a recruit.

"Not what you think," Alistar said as his face drained to white. "You think I wanted this? You remember how it was, we got separated. . . . The Reapers were after us. One got me, picked me up. They took me all the way back to Mississippi. After questioning, it was join 'em or die. Never really joined though, never really joined. That's why I ended up in this rear-area pisser, didn't want to fight against y'all. You have to believe me. I met a girl, got married. We've talked about running— every chance we get alone, we discuss it. Lois wants out."

"You could have contacted me in the bar, then. Quietly. What did you run for?"

"I—I got scared."

"Looked to me like you were running for help."

"I didn't tell the guys you were with Southern Command. I said we fought over a job. You threatened you'd kill me if you ever got the chance. I ducked out to go get my wife, I was going to have her go in there and talk to you. Make you see our way. Lois's honest—you can tell just by talking to her. I knew you could always read people, Dave. You'd be able to get us out."

Valentine listened with Lifeweaver-sensitized ears for anyone approaching to investigate. He let Alistar speak.

"We can be ready in an hour. Hide out wherever you tell us. I dunno why you're here, but maybe you need some advice about how to get away." Alistar paused. "Or not. Any way you want it. Just trust me—give me a chance to prove it."

Valentine put himself in Alistar's shoes. The summer of his eighteenth year, had their roles been reversed, could he honestly say he would not have followed Alistar's path, given a choice of death or grudging service? But how grudging? He wore a major's cluster, after all. Perhaps he wore other insignia.

He shifted the knife and used his right hand to pull open Alistar's raincoat. On his old comrade's breast was a row of little silver studs, projecting out of the green uniform over a shining five-year badge. Valentine knew that each stud represented five confirmed kills of enemies bearing arms, and the badge probably gained through turning over friends, neighbors, or comrades to the Reapers.

Alistar read his fate in Valentine's eyes and opened his mouth to scream for help. Valentine shot his hand up to Alistar's throat, crushing cartilage and blood vessels in a granite grip. A sound like a candy wrapper crinkling and an airy wheeze was all that came out of the Quisling's collapsing throat.

"Would've let you go another time," Valentine said, fighting his friend's final paroxysm. "But what I'm here to do is just too damn important."

Valentine got up off the corpse. Emptying his mind, quieting his thoughts with the aura-hiding discipline of the Lifeweavers had a succoring side effect: it kept him from thinking about what he had just done. He carried the corpse off to the stinking alley and went to work with quick, precise motions. Using his knife, he tore a ragged hole just below Alistar's Adam's apple, then picked up the twitching body and held it inverted. The warmth of the draining corpse nauseated him. He watched the blood mix with the rain on the cracked and filthy pavement, and stood shivering from wet cold and nerves.

Between the injury and the confused girl's story of a flying assailant out of the shadows, assuming she was brave enough to go to the Authorities, there was a chance that whoever found Alistar's body would conclude a prowling Reaper had taken him, draining him of blood with its syringelike tongue.

Valentine had seen enough Hood-drained bodies to mimic the injury and disposal of the corpse. He stuffed Alistar in a debris-filled window well. The Reapers usually concealed their kills so as not to disturb their human herds. But an investigation blaming the death on a Reaper feeding was too slender a thread on which to hang the success of his mission.

It would have to start tonight.

Two

The City Center of New Orleans: No matter what his or her status in the Kurian order, a human has to consider the risks before going abroad after dark, even at the busy city nexus of road and rail lines. At night, the vital aura of any sentient being shines bright and clear to the senses of a Reaper, drawing it and the Appetite that sees through the avatar's eyes. The Reaper, tall, thin, and cloaked, grabs its victim in a bruising grip and buries its long tongue in the food's neck. Sharp teeth keep its hold while the tongue searches out the wildly beating heart.

The "last dance," as the locals call it, leaves the victim emptied of blood. The rich fluid is absorbed into the Reaper's rudimentary digestive system, and life aura is transferred to the Kurian Lord animating the Reaper. The Kurian is a puppet-master working the million synaptic strings of the Reaper's nervous system. Rumor has it that the pain and fear of a victim enhances the Kurian's appreciation of aura. Reapers have been known to stalk and play with their food, even dragging it away to the Master's refuge for a cleaner "connection" for the draining transfer. What torments might be added, flavoring the aura like seasoning on a meal, do not make for pleasant speculation.

Valentine's night began with a call on the Station Rooms. Too comfortable to be called a prison, and too regimented to be called a hotel, the Station Rooms housed wives and families of the men at sea. In Imperial Roman tradition, the families of the men serving the Coastal Patrol remained under watchful house arrest until the sailors' return. The freedom from the Reapers provided by naval service required some kind of guarantee that the men would fulfill their duties, and with their usual efficiency, Kur settled on hostage-taking. While it was well-fed, curtained hostage-taking, the implicit threat remained no matter how bourgeois the surroundings.

With the grisly scene in the alley playing over and over in his head, Valentine wanted nothing more than a few hours' sleep, perhaps with a stiff drink to help him calm down. He could obliterate it all in the arms of a woman easily enough, but whores weren't to his taste even if he'd had the time. He had been up since well before dawn, making his way by boat and foot to the rendezvous at the outskirts of the city. Once again, the dozen Wolves had not shown, making them nine days overdue. He'd lingered as long as he dared among waterlogged ruins under the old water tower, its rust-scoured letters leaving only the vaguely menacing block capitals ORWOE still legible on its sides. Once back in the city, he'd bought an okra-and-rice dish from an open-air diner, not trusting meat that had flies buzzing around it in winter. It began to rain, and on his wet and weary journey back to the ship he'd decided to stop for a drink at a strategically placed waterfront bar his marines spoke well of: the Easy Street.

Now, chances were that the hunt was on and he was the game afoot. He would have to put into effect the plan he had been considering since the Wolves had turned forty-eight hours overdue. Phony repairs to the ship could only be stretched out so long, no matter how imaginative the chief engineer was in his delaying tactics. The captain had shown symptoms of apoplexy at being told the *Thunderbolt* would be laid up another few days, waiting for parts. Further postponements might mean a change of personnel in the form of a new chief engineer, which would be more fatal to the mission than the nonarrival of the Wolves.

Valentine's thoughts kept returning to details of his encounter with Alistar. The gleam of the wedding ring on the dead man's hand—how much of the story about his wife was real? Valentine wished he could meet the woman, and in an overwrought fantasy imagined the two of them having a conversation in private, where he could confess his regrets about her husband's death and the bitter choices, tonight and six years ago, that had necessitated it.

The rain slackened as Valentine approached the Station Rooms. The name came from the proximity of the building to the train station, an odd location for mostly naval dependents. As he neared the entrance, he walked loosely, mimicking the purposeful stagger of a man full of drink.

A sentry stood just inside the barred doors, rather than at his usual post on the first step. The rain had driven him into a minor dereliction of duty, but the Station Rooms contained nothing of value, and what security there was concentrated on keeping the Coastal Patrol families indoors at night.

Valentine rapped on the glass between the added-on bars, a relaxed smile on his face. "Hey Ed, open up, eh?"

The sentry, whose nameplate read HINKS, P, shrugged and spread his hands helplessly. "It isn't Ed, Mr. Rowan, sir, it's Perry."

Valentine raised his eyebrows. "Ed sick? He always has the duty Friday nights."

"He does, but this is Thursday, sir."

"Look, Perry, let me in, will you? I want to see my wife."

"Mr. Rowan, sir, you know the rules. Overnight visits have to be okayed beforehand."

"Coursh I know that," Valentine said, "but I don't want to shtay overnight. Jusht an hour or two. You know. Ship's ready for shea, parts came in, and we leave in the morning. Have a heart—it's a three-month out."

"Mr. Rowan sir, you're listed as active duty. You should be at your ship tonight, not ashore."

"Have a heart," Valentine repeated. "Jush don't log me. You don't catch the shit for letting someone in, and I don't catch the shit for vishiting."

"Be a little difficult for me to explain when you leave."

Valentine summoned a belch. "You've got the midnight to four, right? I'll be out by three. Not logged in, not logged out."

"Sorry, sir, what if you get delayed?"

"Look, call Mrs. Rowan. She'll promise you I'll be out by three. You know her—if she made the promise to you, she'd see to it I got out in time. It's a three-month out, for chrissakes."

"What about the desk?"

"I'll bullshit my way past. I've got an understanding with Turnip. Thesh captain's bars are good for more than just a spot at the front of a ration line, eh?"

"Sir, maybe that's the way they do things up in the Great Lakes, but not here."

Valentine held his breath, forcing his face to color and his tone to harden. "Do they stand their watches indoors here?"

Hinks blanched. "Aww, Mr. Rowan sir, have a—"

"Heart?" Valentine finished.

The guard looked inside the Station Rooms. "Okay, Mr. Rowan, three a.m. You're not here by three-oh-five, I'm phoning up. Okay? Mr. Turner isn't at the desk anyway. Reading in the john again. You wanna report someone, you should start with him."

"Forget about it, Ed, errr—Perry. You're a good egg. I'll bring you back a bottle of rum or something, how'sh that?"

"Just be out by the time my shift ends, or I'm perishable."

"Hey," Valentine slurred, "I promised, right? Just a quick visit, and we ain't spending it talking."

The guard opened the door. "Mrs. Rowan's some lady, sir. I hope I get some rank and get a chance to take my pick."

"That's the shpirit, Perry," Valentine said, coming in out of the rain and wiping his hair back. "One way to move up is to do favors for higher ranks. Maybe I can get you into the Coastal Marines. Quick advancement. Dishipline isn't too hard, if you do your job."

The sentry shook his head. "Like my outfit just fine, sir. Going ashore and attacking a blockhouse full of outlaws ain't my idea of a career."

David Valentine waited for the sentry to unlock the inner door, and moved across the stained carpet to the stairs. The night manager's desk was empty, as Hinks predicted. Most of the lights were off, and the remaining elevator that still worked was always shut down at night when the hotel closed up to conserve electricity. Valentine smelled soap and heard splashing water coming from the basement: someone was doing laundry in one of the slop tubs there.

He climbed to the top floor, remembering the intolerable heat of their arrival that summer, the last in a series of moves as he performed his duties as a Quisling Officer. His real home lay in the hill country of Arkansas, Missouri, and Eastern Oklahoma, on free soil, though since being recruited as a Cat, he'd hardly spent six consecutive months there. For the past year, he'd been dragging Duvalier all around the Gulf Coast, worming through the Kurian Order, obtaining a commission and a promotion under a dead man's name and background provided for him by Southern Command—it made him feel like a maggot in a corpse.

Though the Station Rooms predated climate control and therefore had fair-size windows, the bars prevented residents from escaping to the fire escape to nap out the heat. The bars and windows were the only part of the Station Rooms inspected and kept in prime condition. Elsewhere the paint was peeling, the walls were dimpled, and the plumbing fixtures were maintained in a condition that shifted back and forth between inoperative and barely functioning.

Valentine reached the chipped wooden door to "Mrs. Rowan's" apartment. He knocked softly, using a three-and-two rap to identify himself, three soft and two loud. The sole lightbulb in the hallway faded for a moment and then brightened; New Orleans's patchwork power system was having its usual nighttime irregularities.

The door opened, revealing an attractively angular face under short red hair sticking out in all directions.

"You're out late," Alessa Duvalier said, still half-asleep. She wore an oversize yellow T-shirt of tentlike proportions, which was coming apart at the shoulder seams. "What is it?"

He ducked inside and flicked off the light. To his Cat-eyes, the room remained lit and as detailed as ever. There was just the usual color-shift that came with low-light vision.

"I was recognized." He used old American Sign Language to convey this information as he said for the benefit of the microphones: "Baby, we're out tomorrow. Last chance for ninety nights." They'd found a bug when they'd first moved to the Station Rooms months ago, and asked for a different room—complaining, with justification, about bedbugs. Management moved them to the stifling top floor, and a Coastal Marine widow, Mrs. Kineen, took an empty room next to them the same day.

Duvalier woke up fast. "Somebody made you? How?" she signed.

He flopped down on the bed as soon as he got his coat off. He let out an occasional moan as he told her, spelling out some of the words with his fingers. They'd had training in sign language before setting out from the Ozark Free Territory, and though they practiced, Valentine's usually quick-acting brain faltered after the long day and the encounter with Alistar.

The woman who'd taught him to be a Cat sat in her chair, folded herself up so her chin rested on her left knee, and rocked the bed with her right leg so the headboard banged the wall they shared with Mrs. Kineen.

The room smelled of cloves and walnuts. Duvalier had picked up intestinal parasites in her travels, perhaps as long ago as their trek into the Great Plains Gulag when she first recruited him three years ago, and was dosing herself again in an effort to flush them.

"This week has been nothing but bad news," she signed, interrupting the tale when he began to describe his disposal of the corpse. "Laundry-room intelligence says there's been a lot of new faces in town. Troops moving in. Some say a push into the Tex-Mex borders; others say it's Southern Command's turn again. I know the train station's been busy. Lots of cars taking on supplies coming in from the Gulf Coast and moving west. This didn't turn into such a dull assignment after all. I've been able to watch the station and pick up a little." She peeked out the window. "Hope you can get going soon. Southern Command needs to know details."

"I don't think the Wolves are going to show," he decided. "I'm going to have to go with it and improvise. Figure out a way to oust Captain Saunders and get control of the *Thunderbolt*—"

She let out a yelp, faintly orgiastic, and winked at her partner.

"You'll improvise yourself right onto the Grog gibbet," she signed. Valentine never tired of admiring her quick, dexterous fingers. They were the first thing he'd noticed on her when she bandaged his former captain on Little Timber Hill. "Who will help you?"

"The crew."

"Quislings?" She added the question mark with her sharp eyebrows.

"They wouldn't be in the Coastal Patrol if they didn't like being away from the influence of Kur."

"All the more reason for Kurians to pick the men for loyalty. Remember what you had to do to get your commission down here, and then the promotion to captain."

"Don't remind me," Valentine signed. Elaborate fake papers showing his service record in the Great Lakes took him only so far. For the past year, Valentine had put his manifest talents to the service of Kur, assembling a good record in a rear area before being offered a promotion in exchange for "more active duty." He had seen men shot, hanged, or given over to the Reapers without batting an eye. And more.

He'd learned the reason for the elaborate groundwork only a few months ago, once he had received his commission on the *Thunderbolt*. Ahn-Kha appeared afterwards, bearing his detailed orders. In twenty-four hours, he memorized the instructions, based plans on the objective, and destroyed the letters, maps, and drawings. Since then, he concentrated on making friends in the crew and learning all he could about the Caribbean, and particularly Haiti.

"So are you ever going to tell me?" Duvalier asked. "Once you're at sea, it couldn't hurt for me to know." She stopped the headboard-thumping with her leg, waited a moment, then started again with renewed vigor.

"You know better. If you were really in on it, I'd have your opinion every step of the way. But I can't risk the Kurians finding out if it goes amiss."

Amiss. The word was a kind of shorthand between them. A euphemism for "capture, torture, and death."

She climbed on to the bed next to him, lay close so she could breathe in his ear. "We're good together, Valentine. Hope they haven't tasked you with a one-way trip. Some things shouldn't even be tried. Like turning that crew. We should blow and get out of here. The mission is down the drain, and Mountain Home needs to know about this buildup."

"Taking the ship's not the half of it," he whispered back, feeling his skin tingle at her scent. "Or I should say that's not your half of it."

She rubbed her hand through his damp hair. "David, I know I had the easy part this time. Maybe old Ryu thought I needed a rest. I got to look around, safe behind my ID, then disappear after you ship out. But now my stomach's hurting, and you have that never-say-die look like in the Dunes. You didn't come up here for a good-bye."

Valentine smiled in the darkness. "No. I have to ask you a favor. It would make my job easier if you could get some of the other wives and families out."

She quit toying with his cowlick.

The room waited in silent darkness. His sensitive ears could not even pick up the sound of her breathing. "How many families?" she finally whispered.

"As many as you can. Make contact with the pipeline, and have them help guide you all out."

She sat up, pulled her knees up to her chest, and thought before she started signing again. "Val, that involves getting about a hundred people out of New Orleans. On my own. I've no gear, no weapons but a skinning knife. Lots of kids, so I need transport for everyone and food to last us out of the KZ. It can't be done."

Valentine signed back: "Of course it can't be done. Since it can't be done, I don't think the Kur will be expecting it."

"No one expects me to step off a thirty-story building either. But if I do it and give everyone a big, effing surprise, that doesn't mean much when I hit."

"The only way I have a chance with the men is if they think there's hope for their families."

"Valentine, full abort. Set all this back up somewhere else. Mexico. There's got to be plenty of transport—"

"And blow a year's worth of work. It's the ideal ship. Who'd 'ave ever thought I'd get assigned to a gunboat? I figured we'd have to settle for a troop trawler full of men. If we get her, there's hardly a ship in the Carib that can say boo to us, plus she's seaworthy in case of bad weather. She's not some coast hugger."

"Good arguments in favor of a bad idea."

"Didn't you say you had made friends among the women? That a lot of them were discontented?"

"Who wouldn't be?" she signed back. "We get out of this building only twice a week when you're away, and even then it's to a fenced-in market. I'm sick of this place, too. If it weren't for the danger to some of the people I've met here, I'd torch it as soon as you're out of the harbor and vanish. They'd think I maybe . . . Whoa there . . ."

Valentine could almost feel her brain revving up. "You know, if you got everyone out and rigged some kind of explosion . . ." he suggested.

"Don't have the tools to collapse the building," she signed, "but this is an old structure. Set a fire somewhere hard to put out but not immediately dangerous, the authorities evacuate everyone, and I have someone from the pipeline who knows just where to be, and when. Maybe they would have a few people around to make sure we don't wander off, but they wouldn't expect an organized breakout. I can handle them."

"Be careful who you tell," Valentine advised. "I'd just let a couple of trustworthy people know. Wait until the absolute last minute to spread the word."

"Who taught who this game, Val? I was keeping myself alive in the KZ while you were still running with the Wolves, if you recall."

"Keep yourself alive. The Cause needs you. So can I count on you? Think about it while I sleep."

"I'll do it—if I can get the pipeline to open. You can tell your men that. Guarantees aren't my style. I like to bug out if things get hairy. I think you're headed for a noose, or maybe a long drag through the ocean back to the nearest port. Getting a mutiny started won't be easy. I've never heard of that being done before."

"All the more reason for it to work, they won't be expecting—"

She cut him off with a forceful thrust of her hand. "Oh God, don't start on *that* again!" she said, this time aloud. Then they smiled at each other. What would Mrs. Kineen make of that?

Valentine dreamt of the Ozarks. A fall breeze rustling a million leaves all around, cool streams running in the morning, the sounds of fish splashing as they jumped—

He felt Duvalier shaking him by the shoulder. The hour's rest was not nearly enough, but it would have to do. "Last chance, Valentine," she signed after handing him his coat. "Full abort, plenty of reason to justify it. I don't like the feel of this, not at all."

His doubts had also rested, and returned refreshed. *No! Ignore them!* "I'm not happy about it either. But if you knew more, you could see that I don't have a choice. This could turn the tide."

"You and your coulds." She hugged him, nuzzling her chin against his chest. Duvalier was seldom affectionate toward him, their bond exhibited more through ribbing than rubbing. Though he was attracted to her, she had a wall around her he couldn't break. Sometimes she lowered the drawbridge. Tonight was one of those moments.

"I grew up in Kansas," she whispered in his ear. "I don't know tides, except that they're caused by the moon. Oh, and a king tried to do something about them once but couldn't. In the end, the tide always wins. It's too strong."

He turned the risks over in his mind, then unholstered and tossed his heavy .44 service pistol on the bed along with the spare ammunition he carried. He'd hide the loss somehow. "No," Valentine signed, after buttoning his coat. "It's not too strong. The tide wins because it doesn't give up."

The look of relief on Perry's face made Valentine forget the gruesome events of the night. For a moment.

"See, Perry, I told you so," Valentine said, pointing to the clock. Its plain face indicated 2:40.

"You're a man of your word, sir. Thank you."

"No, Perry, thank you," Valentine said, smiling and waiting for the outer door to open. "I'll see you in three months."

"I hope so, Mr. Rowan. Word has it my unit's going to rotate out. They're saying West Texas, which is fine by me. I've had it with the humidity around here. I got mold allergies something terrible."

"Mobilizing for something big?" Valentine asked nonchalantly, looking out at the rain.

"Like I'd know. 'You'll find out when you get there,' is what we get told." The guard drained a cup of cold coffee.

"Enjoy the sun. I've got to get back to the ship before the captain gets up."

"Me savvy."

Valentine plodded into the rainy night, his hands thrust deep into his coat pockets. He had a good hour's walk ahead of him. The *Thunderbolt* sat moored well to the east in New Orleans's expansive but underused dikeside riverfront. High seas trade was not something the Kurians encouraged. They seemed so uncomfortable with oceans that Valentine wondered if Kur itself was not arid. Most of their sea traffic was made up of barges and tugs, hugging the coast as they moved from port to port in the shallow waters of the Gulf of Mexico.

Fear brought him out of his thoughts. A cold tingle ran down his spine. . . . There was a Reaper somewhere behind him in the fog.

Valentine stepped faster, shutting down everything in his mind except the animal reflexes required to keep moving, a fish swimming quietly and straight to avoid the prowling shark.

And he'd given his gun away to Duvalier. All he could fight with was the short service knife at his belt. Not enough steel to bite through a Reaper's neck—his sword was back at Ryu's hall with his other possessions.

The street was empty, almost unlighted. Doors and windows all around were buttoned up for the night.

He felt the cold spot growing as it came up behind. Its booted feet clipped along in the drizzle somewhere behind. He tore off his rain-coat. Perhaps it would hesitate to attack a uniform.

A massive figure appeared out of the mist ahead of him.

Ahn-Kha! Thank you, God.

Solid as the *Thunderbolt*'s icebreaking prow, ugly as commandment-breaking sin, and the closest thing he had in the world to a brother, the Grog waddled down the street.

He heard the footsteps following halt as the Reaper read the new-comer's lifesign.

Ahn-Kha carried a great boat hook across his shoulder and wore a brown Grog Labor Brigade sash across his chest. Like a bull gorilla, he used his arms as well as his legs in his slow, deliberate stride. Rain matted his fawn-colored fur and dripped from flexible, batlike ears. Ahn-Kha bore a face like some stony nightmare leering off a cathedral at travelers below, but his steady eyes, black-flecked with irises the color of a healthy acorn, could only be called "gentle."

Valentine clasped hands with Ahn-Kha. "Careful," he breathed, gesturing behind with his chin.

He heard the Reaper approach, and Ahn-Kha straightened to his full eight-feet-plus, planting the boat hook solidly before him like a pikeman.

Valentine met the yellow-eyed gaze, touched the side of his hand to his eyebrow, and lowered his head, the usual salute to a representative of the Kurian Order.

The Reaper responded by throwing its hood back over its scraggly-haired scalp and striding off into the night.

Valentine didn't relax until the cold spot on his consciousness faded. The Reaper probably could have killed the both of them, but perhaps the Kurian animating it was more risk-averse than most, and didn't wish to damage his living tool for the extraction of vital aura.

Ahn-Kha put the boat hook over his shoulder again.

In the three years since Valentine had met Ahn-Kha, he had learned to rely on him for thought as well as thews. Years ago, Ahn-Kha's people, the Golden Ones, had been brought with the other species, labeled alike by much of mankind with the epithet *Grog*, across worlds to help the Kurians with the conquest of humanity. But even the Golden Ones had been betrayed by Kur when they were no longer useful. Thanks to the pair's chance meeting, the Golden Ones were again thriving along the west bank of the Missouri River around Omaha.

"My David," Ahn-Kha rumbled, his bass voice sounding as if it echoed from a deep cave. "I began to worry when you did not arrive by the time we darkened the ship. I feared something might have happened to you, and I made for the Station Rooms. Is all well?" The Grog did a neat turn on one of his hamhock fists and walked beside Valentine.

"Yes and no, old horse. Someone recognized me tonight, in a bar. He's dead, but unless his men were born stupid and got worse, they'll be looking for me. We're going to have to set off with the dawn, before the Kurians can organize a manhunt."

"What about the men? Have they arrived?"

"No. We may have to go with the crew we have."

"And the captain and the executive officer? Perhaps you plan to have them both meet with accident?"

"I'm going to try to turn the crew."

Ahn-Kha snorted. "Maybe a few brave hearts will try. Not enough, my David, not enough."

"I'm going to promise them a new life with their families, if we can make it back to the Ozarks. Duvalier is going to get their wives and kids out."

"If she can manage that, the fates themselves fight on her side. But without the promised Wolves, I do not see how we win the ship."

"When we're at sea, I'll try Lieutenant Post first."

"The man's a drunk, my David, or he would be in command of the marines instead of you."

"Yes."

"How will you explain their absence to the captain? You told him the Coastal Marines were supplying a team of scouts, showed him fake orders."

"We'll use your Grogs. I'll tell him your laborers can perform the job. Besides, the men like having a few Grogs around to do the dirty work. Will they do what you say?"

"They're Gray Ones—brutes. They obey me; it is easier than thinking. On paper, they are a combat-ready team, but I've never seen them shoot. When they are done working the ship, they were supposed to be moved inland. But a request from the Coastal Marines would outweigh such a trifle. The Kurians have many to take their place."

"Better get them ready as soon as we reach the *Thunderbolt*. I'll have a word with the Chief, and we'll be under way by dawn. The radio is going to break down, as well. We can't be too careful."

The *Thunderbolt,* tied up to the dock, did not live up to her name. She looked like the swaybacked old icebreaker that she was, new coat of paint and polished fittings or no. Her 230-foot length had a high prow, a deep well deck, and her castle amidships. Just below the bridge in the bow was the five-inch gun, her main armament. On the other side of the castle, a twenty-millimeter Oerlikon looked like an avant-garde sculpture under its protective cover. Valentine's marines were responsible for it and the four 7.62-millimeter machine guns in action. They lay ready to be placed in the mounts on either side of the ship, more or less at the corners of the upper deck of the square main cabin.

As she was now configured, she carried four commissioned officers and seven warrant officers, supervising divisions of forty-five Coastal Patrol crewmen and thirty-four Coastal Marines. Usually she patrolled with a higher proportion of CP, fewer marines, and more space for all concerned, but she had been modified to carry troops this trip. The captain had made no secret of their mission. A nest of "pirates and terrorists" on the island of Jamaica had been bold enough to trouble the continental coast. The *Thunderbolt* and crew was to "capture, scuttle, or burn" the pirates' ships and destroy their base. The gunboat had little to fear in return: she could stand off and sink the pirates in their harbor or on the sea, for the sail-driven brigands had no gun to match the five-inch cannon, and nothing short of naval gunfire, mines, or torpedoes could penetrate the icebreaker's hull.

Whatever her hoped-for glories, the *Thunderbolt* looked dismal enough in the predawn gloom as she waited in her berth. A light burned at the entry port at the end of the gangway, and a glow from the bridge revealed the outline of the officer of the watch.

Valentine and Ahn-Kha walked up the gangplank.

A duty officer came to attention. "Mr. Rowan, sir," the CP said with just enough briskness to prove that he had not been sleeping. The man did not acknowledge Ahn-Kha.

Valentine looked forward and aft. Ahn-Kha's labor team lay in a snoring heap at the stern. Frowning, he turned on Ahn-Kha.

"If your gang is going to sleep like that on deck, you might as well get them some bedding," he said. "You have permission to get it out of ship's stores."

"Sir, thank you, sir," Ahn-Kha said, giving a quick bow.

The duty snorted. "Hope they wash it afterwards. We got enough bugs already."

For'ard, Valentine saw the red glow of a cigarette. The Chief sat on a stool, his legs up on the rail and an ankle comfortably cradled in a machine-gun mount, watching the rain fall. In a complement of more than eighty, Valentine's confidants consisted of the Grog next to him and the Chief by the rail. He moved forward. Obviously the Chief was waiting for him to return.

"Good evening, Captain Rowan," the Chief murmured as Valentine approached. The Cat paused and rested his elbows on the rail, looking out at the drizzle. Chief Engineer Landberg, like Valentine, had a strong dash of Native American blood in him, giving his title an ethnic twist which he bore with good humor. Though not a tall man, he had a wide wrestler's torso supported by pillarlike legs. Unlike his body, his face was soft and rounded, a textbook example of the kind of face described as "apple-cheeked." The Chief had been an informer for Southern Command since his youth, but until this run limited his service to simple intelligence-gathering.

The rain had washed the air clean of the usual fetid river odors. All Valentine could smell was the vaguely metallic tang of the ship, new paint, and the Chief's burning tobacco.

"What's the matter, Chief, can't sleep?" Valentine looked back over his shoulder. The sentry probably couldn't hear them over the weather, but no sense taking chances.

"No, the sound of rain on this biscuit tin keeps me awake sometimes, so I just come up and watch it fall."

"How's that fuel pump coming? I'd really like to get under way. The men are getting anxious."

Landburg looked up, swallowed. Valentine gave him a nod.

"They are, huh?"

The engineer pinched his lower lip between thumb and forefinger when overhauling a problem. He would pull out his lower lip then release it so it hit his upper lip and teeth with a tiny *plip*. "Well, I reckon good news shouldn't wait"—*plip*. "I got sick of waiting on the part, so I found something I could modify with just a little machining. I'll try it out right now, if you want"—*plip*—"and we can let the captain know if it works. These delays have been driving the old man nuts."

"Good work, Chief."

Valentine exhaled tiredly and left the Chief to finish his tobacco and thoughts. He was committed now. By this time tomorrow, he would be at sea, with only Ahn-Kha and the Chief set against the captain and crew, backed up by the Kurian system that controlled them. Were it not for the rock-steady support of Ahn-Kha, as imperturbable as a mountain, and the Chief's wily aid, his quest would have foundered long ago.

He climbed one of the metal staircases running up the castle side to the bridge and asked the watch officer to call him at dawn, and retired to his shared cabin. Originally only he and the captain were given their own cabins, but after he saw the crowded conditions on board, he invited Lieutenant Post to share his cabin. Post got quietly drunk each night, duty or no, and Valentine felt for him after hearing some of the gibes hurled with casual viciousness by the other wardroom members.

He looked down at Post, a sleeping ruin of what must once have been a physical archetype of a man. His six-three frame didn't fit on the bed, from his salt-and-pepper hair to rarely washed feet, breathing in the restless, shallow sleep of alcoholic oblivion. As usual, he hadn't bothered to undress before turning in, and would attend to his duties tomorrow in a wrinkled uniform, permanent stains marking the armpits and back. Post ignored even the captain's comments about his appearance, but in some fit of contrariness shaved each morning after Valentine had once privately mentioned over coffee that he would have a terrible time keeping his marines clean shaved if his lieutenant sprouted three days' worth of stubble.

Valentine sat on his untouched cot and began to remove his shoes. Above him, a railed shelf held his meager collection of books. Father Max's gilt-edged Bible—the old Northern Minnesota priest had raised him after his family's murder, and died of pneumonia while he was training Foxtrot Company. The Padre had willed the aged tome to him. It had arrived while he and Duvalier were seeking the Twisted Cross on the Great Plains. Next to the Bible were his battered old Livy histories, brought down when he first joined up with the Cause eight years ago. He owned copies of Clausewitz's *On War* and a Chinese Army translation of Sun Tzu, volumes he'd had to study at the military college in Pine Bluff, Arkansas, as he'd been studying for his commission. His American Civil War histories were next: Sam Watkins's *Company Aytch* and Frisch's *Lincoln: Leadership to Liberty.* Then came his little collection of fiction. *Watership Down,* its yellowed pages stitched together and ironically rebound in rabbit skin—given to him as a welcome-home gift by the craftsman, a Wolf named Gonzalez who'd survived their ill-fated courier mission to Lake Michigan in 2065. Next to it, and in much better shape, was a recent hardcover of the complete set of the *Sherlock Holmes* stories. Then there was his latest acquisition, a copy of *Gone with the Wind* bought at a New Orleans bookstore. He'd seen his fellow infiltrator Duvalier reading it last year while he was undergoing Coastal Marine training in Biloxi, Mississippi. Shocked to find her so deep into such a brick of a book, he'd made some comment about the four-color cover. "Ever read it?" she asked. When he admitted that he hadn't, she told him not to offer an opinion out of ignorance. Sensing a challenge when he heard one, he sat down with it his first free day, intending to mock it and her—but within twenty minutes was so captivated that he went out and treated himself to a bottle of cognac to enjoy with the epic.

The rest of the shelf held mostly unread Kurian propaganda and service bulletins.

There was a quiet knock at the door.

"Naturally," Valentine said to himself and two hundred pounds of alcoholic stupor a leg's length away. He rose and opened the door.

A twelve-year-old boy in a uniform two sizes too big for him stood in the corridor. The crew called him and his twin brother Peaone and Peatwo, being identical twins sent to sea in the care of their uncle, one of the petty officers. The captain, sick of not being able to tell them apart, flipped a coin and had all the hair shaved from Peaone's young head. Under a messy shock of sun-white hair, Peatwo looked up at Valentine with piercing blue eyes.

"Sir, the captain's passing the word for you, Mr. Rowan. He wants to see you in his cabin."

"Tell the captain I'm coming."

"Aye aye, sir," Peatwo said, turning and moving six feet up the passageway toward the captain's door. The captain was not the sort of man to just knock on the wall or come himself.

Valentine retied his boots, wishing he had had just five minutes out of them. He walked the short distance to the captain's cabin. He smoothed out his uniform unconsciously and knocked.

"Come," a sharp voice answered.

Captain Saunders fancied himself a species of tough old seahawk, but to Valentine, he seemed more like a rather aged rooster. The heavy wattles hanging under his chin were hardly hawklike, and the full head of gray hair that was the captain's pride and joy was brushed up into a bantam's pompadour. Perhaps something hawkish flickered in the stare of his hard hazel eyes, between which a beak of a nose matching that of the mightiest of eagles, if not a toucan, arched out in its Roman majesty.

"You passed the word for me, sir?" Valentine asked. The captain was in one of his work-all-night fits, and Valentine tried his best to look alert.

"Ahh, Captain Rowan. Are the marines ready to go to sea?"

"Of course, sir."

"Good. You'll be glad to know we'll be leaving in the morning—the fuel pump is repaired. I had to light a fire under the Chief, but if properly motivated, the man can work wonders."

Valentine blanked his expression. He looked around at the small day cabin. The captain sat behind a massive desk that must have been brought in sections, then reassembled. It dwarfed the other chairs in the room. A few pictures, all of Captain Saunders in various stages of his career or of ships he had officered, decorated the walls. "Glad to hear it, sir. The waiting has been hard."

"It's finally over. Keen to get to sea, I hope? Ready for the smell of burning sail?"

"At your order, sir. One thing though, sir. I still haven't had any luck finding a reliable team of rangers. Something must be going on inland. I've tried through channels and I've tried out of channels, but all I can find are kids or old men," he said, more than half-telling the truth for once. "The Grog labor team is a combat squad on paper. I'd like to just keep them, sir."

"What about quartering them? We're crowded enough—the men won't share with Grogs."

"We can rig some kind of shelter in the well deck, sir. Tents would do."

Captain Saunders thought for a moment. "Very well, they can eat the leftovers. Stretch the stores. I understand Grogs aren't too particular. Put that foreman of theirs in charge of squaring them away. I'd like to depart at dawn, and you'll be welcome on the bridge at six a.m. We'll take her out right after breakfast."

Close to two hours of sleep! Valentine sagged in relief. "Thank you, sir."

"One thing, though, Captain Rowan. I'd like you and the exec to do a final weapons inventory. You'll do your marines and the small arms locker, and he'll cover the heavy weapons. Wouldn't want to reach Jamaica and find your men's rifles had been left dockside by accident. 'For the want of a nail,' am I right?"

"Yes, sir." Valentine said, the prospect of sleep evaporating like a desert mirage. "Speaking of small arms, I had to give over my revolver for barter for some parts the Chief needed. I'll need a new pistol from the ship's arms."

"Rowan, you have to learn to throw your weight a little more. Greasing palms with your sidearms . . . Still, if it helped get us to sea, I'm grateful. Anyway, get that inventory done. That was item one, business. Item two is pleasure: I'd like your company at dinner tonight. A tradition of mine, to celebrate the beginning of what we all hope will be a successful cruise. Mr. Post is invited, too, of course. Number One uniforms, please. That will encourage your lieutenant to clean himself up."

"Yes, sir. Thank you, sir," Valentine said.

"That's all for now. See to your men, Rowan."

"Aye aye, sir." Valentine shut the cabin door softly behind him and began his day's work.

He hardly noticed the ship pulling away from the dock and moving downriver, so busy was he with final preparations. The executive officer, Lieutenant Worthington, started on the heavy weapons inventory then begged off as the engines were turned over to attend to duties on the bridge. Valentine, who had little to do with the actual handling of the ship, was glad to be rid of him and offered to finish Worthington's part of the barely begun job. The exec, though two years older than he, had not seen much action and assumed Valentine to be a man of vast experience, to be a captain of marines in his mid-twenties. He had the annoying habit of wanting particulars of the various real—and faked— incidents in Valentine's "Captain Rowan" dossier. Valentine did not wish to discuss the faked events out of fear of slipping up on some detail, and the memories of the real incidents seen from the sidelines in the service of Kur troubled him too much to want to talk about them for the entertainment of a callow fellow officer.

Inventory and inspection done, he just had time to change into his best uniform before dinner.

Naturally, the dinner began with a toast over the cloth-covered folding table that had been set up for the meal. Worthington raised his glass of wine, an import brought all the way from Western Mexico. The captain and exec sat opposite each other, stiff in their crisp black uniforms, the captain's solid-gold buttons engraved with illuminati eye-and-anchor. Valentine and Post in their brass-buttoned navy blue filled the other places on the square table.

"The *Thunderbolt,* Queen of the Gulf," Worthington intoned as they raised their glasses. Saunders sipped with a connoisseur's thoughtful appreciation; Post drained his glass in a single motion; Worthington barely tasted his. Valentine took a welcome mouthful, grateful just to be off his feet.

The wine hit him hard, and he fought to keep from falling asleep in his soup. A winter salad followed. The captain and the exec did most of the talking, discussing the pilot's navigation of the treacherous, shifting sandbars at the mouth of the Mississippi and the balance of the stores on the ship. Valentine was content to eat his main course, a fresh filet of Texas beef smothered in onions and mushrooms, in exhausted silence. Post, who had been encouraged by Valentine to mend his best uniform and press it to celebrate the freedom of being at sea and away from the humid air of New Orleans, finished the bottle and started on another of less illustrious vintage.

"Captain Rowan?" Captain Saunders's voice broke in through the mists of Valentine's fatigue.

"Sir?" Valentine asked, looking to his left at the captain.

"Lieutenant Worthington asked you a question. About the Grogs?"

"My apologies, Lieutenant," Valentine said, bringing himself back to the dinner with an effort. "I'm not myself tonight. What was the question?"

"Seasickness, Captain Rowan?" Worthington asked, a smile that was half sneer creeping across his face. "We're still on the river."

"Probably."

"I just wanted your opinion on Uncle's Grogs," the exec continued. "We were really hoping for some rangers for the inshore scouting work." The men on the ship called Ahn-Kha "Uncle," and Ahn-Kha was too well mannered among their enemies to correct them. In the Ozark Free Territory, he would have flattened someone who could not be bothered to learn to pronounce his name correctly.

"Uncle says that they are combat trained. I'll vouch for his word."

"It's your responsibility, of course," Captain Saunders said.

By now Valentine knew that the phrase was Saunders-speak meaning that if the Grogs failed in some way, the blame would be passed to Valentine.

"I'm sure we can keep them busy on the ship," the exec said. "I've never had any experience with Grogs in combat. I've heard they leave something to be desired."

"Properly armed and with a decent leader, I'll put them up against anyone," Valentine said. "I've seen them in action, once they sink their teeth into a fight, the only way to stop them is to kill them." He did not add to the speech that his experience mostly came from fighting against the Gray Ones, rather than with them.

"But as scouts, Rowan, as scouts?" the exec asked.

"Like dogs who can shoot guns. Fine marksmen. Good eyes and ears. Not a whole lot smarter than a dog, though. Decision making isn't their forte; they'll come back and hoot at you to let you know they've found something. Uncle can make more sense out of their tongue than I can."

"Very well, Captain Rowan," Saunders said. "That settles my mind, knowing you are confident in the matter. I'm sure they'll be an asset."

The rest of the evening passed in the captain telling stories to his captive audience. Valentine leaned back in his chair, keeping his eyes open while his brain turned itself off. He shifted his gaze to Post, who had restricted his conversation to a few polite phrases during dinner. His lieutenant remained silent, failing to murmur appreciatively at Saunders's yarns. Post finished the second bottle of wine before turning to the brandy.

Three

The Caribbean: An empty, brilliant blue sky is mirrored by an equally blue sea. The gunboat has left the rainy gloom of New Orleans behind her, pushing her hardened prow southeast into the Gulf under the power of her eleven-foot propeller at a steady ten knots. Diesel–electric engines provide the motive force for the propeller, giving her a throbbing, piston-driven heartbeat and sending sky-staining wisps of black carbon into the air from the central smokestack. Below the exhaust she leaves behind a trail of churned water over a mile long, flanked by the low waves of her wake.

The gray ship with her bleached white decks flies no flag, letting her armored bulk identify her, leaving the mouth of the Mississippi coasters and fishing ships scattered, parting like an antelope herd with a lion trotting through. The smaller boats fear an inspection shakedown or impressment of valuable crew. But once in the Gulf proper, only a two-mast schooner approached, and even that turned tail and put the wind to her quarter before binoculars and telescopes allowed positive identification.

The Kurian Masters of the Earth are not a sea-minded race. They avoid blue water and leave its security and commerce to their Quislings. There are few armed vessels anymore. The old navies of the world have been broken up for scrap and spare parts. The great tankers, merchant ships, and passenger vessels now lie in their last moorings, giant rolling stones come to barnacle-encrusted rest as the world fell apart. A few have been put to other uses: agricultural workers in what is left of Florida after the Great Wave that washed across it in 2022 go home from oyster beds, crab farms, and orange groves each night to cruise ships, living in cramped squalor under the last vestiges of the vessels' glitzy luxury of former days.

As the sea is out of reach of the Kurians and their Reapers, a loose Confederation of the Waves exists, nomadic oceangoing caravans of anything from a few sailing ships to hundreds, visiting land only in the most unoccupied areas for supplies. But the sea is a cruel provider. She takes her toll in lives, as well, probably more than the same number of people would suffer under the Kur. Some of these bands have turned pirate, raiding rather than trading for necessities the sea and isolated coastline cannot provide. When their depredations become too troublesome, an armed ship is sent to deal with the menace. While they have little use for it, the Kurians won't let a trifling thing like the sea stand between them and vengeance.

It was the third day out, and life on the plodding *Thunderbolt* had already turned into routine. The first light of dawn saw the Grogs hosing down and cleaning the decks. They devoured their morning fare with work-sharpened appetite. The cook, his mate, and the officers' steward then cleaned up the kitchen and prepared the meals for everyone else. The men tolerated the presence of the Grogs on the ship, especially since they took on so many of the petty labors, but drew the line at eating with them, or indeed sharing the same space. Grogs in tight quarters smell (even to noses not sharpened by the Lifeweavers) like a kennelful of mating ferrets, so they lived on deck in shelters rigged to the bulkheads of the forward well deck.

With their routine duties and weapons drill done, Ahn-Kha gave them leisure to fish. The rod-and-reel obsession began when a pair of flying fish broke the surface, leaving furrows in the calm ocean in their dash away from the ship. The Grogs hooted until Ahn-Kha reported that his team wanted to know if the "sea chickens" were good to eat and how they could catch them. Both Valentine and Ahn-Kha were strangers to deep-sea fishing, so he asked around the crew until one old bluewater man, less fastidious than the rest as to who he associated with, descended to the "Grog deck" to teach them how to use the ship's store of fishing poles and reels. Afterwards, the Grogs spent every spare moment fashioning lures, rods, and reels. Valentine prevailed on the captain to slow the ship to a crawl for an hour a day, when the garbage would be dumped overboard and the Grogs, wild with excitement foreign to human fishermen, pulled in all they could catch. It was just as well, for Grog appetites could tax the ship's stores on the three-month patrol.

Valentine's particular responsibility was the Coastal Marines. The Coastal Patrols looked on the marines as only one rung above the Grogs on the evolutionary ladder, and a short rung at that: gun-toting, useless ballast for most of the trip. Valentine put the rivalry to good use, organizing physical contests between them. Races around the deck, arm-wrestling matches, and boxing contests occurred each night, giving the two sides a chance to scream their lungs out supporting their contestant and abusing the opponent. Not all the diversions were physical; singing and musical entertainment were often a spontaneous part of the after-dinner leisure hours. As Valentine stood next to the Oerlikon on the aft gun deck, listening to the music produced by an improvising group of players and singers, he almost forgot these men were technically his sworn enemies. Under different circumstances, he might have been ordered to sneak aboard the ship and plant a bomb that would blow musician, wrestler, and fishing instructor to bloody shreds. All the while, a long line of stormclouds on his mental horizon, came the worries about what he had to do and how to go about doing it.

Valentine felt for the sailors. The captain believed himself an expert disciplinarian, when in fact his rules verged on pointless sadism. He had an elaborate system of uncomfortable punishments for the last man out of his bunk on a watch, the last man on deck for inspection, the last man in line at mess call. Since physics required someone to be last, Valentine thought the practice cruel: spending a watch-on-watch at the top of the old communications tower without food or water for being shoved out of the way coming up a hatchway improved no one. Of course, the captain's distemper was exacerbated by the ship's radio breaking down after leaving port. Valentine pointed out that their orders demanded radio silence until the pirates were dealt with, so the loss of communications made no difference, but Saunders just grumbled out his familiar "want of a nail" liturgy again.

The executive officer was even worse. Wishing to emulate his captain, thereby showing himself fit for command, Worthington out-Heroded Herod in his punishments.

Valentine and Post kept their marines busy, and as far from the eyes of Saunders and Worthington as the ship would allow.

Valentine felt nervous, bottled up. If he'd been on land, he would have quartered logs and chopped kindling, but there was no firewood to cut on a gunboat at sea. After they grabbed a quick dinner with the marines, they returned to the cabin and undressed. Valentine picked up one of his lieutenant's bottles and sniffed the mouth. It smelled like rubbing alcohol stored in an old boot. "Will, why do you do that to yourself?"

The two officers kept to first names when out of uniform.

"I'm still trying to figure out why you don't."

Valentine marked the tiny blue veins crisscrossing Post's nose and forehead. "Maybe I want to live a few more years. The way you're going, your liver will abandon ship or you'll get drummed out. Either way, you'll be finished."

"Hear hear," Post agreed, refilling his glass, his thick features under the salt-and-pepper hair taking on a red flush. "I figure you for the type to step into the shower, close the curtain, and blow your brains out with your service revolver. The system's rotten, and you know it same as I."

Post either trusted Valentine or did not care about being turned in. Either way, from their first days sharing a cabin, they began to tentatively express to each other unorthodox opinions about their Kurian masters. But neither had yet expressed it so directly.

"Did you lose someone, Will?"

"I was married once, yeah. Close to six years ago now. That's why I tried so hard for officer—it helped us get better housing. But it all went wrong." He took another gulp. "Not worth talking about. You're lucky, your wife gives you someone to live for. Not sure I even want to live for me anymore."

Valentine nerved himself for the plunge. "She's not my wife, Will. The license is forged."

Post looked up at him. "Yeah? What, you pretending for some reason? Might as well get married, that way you don't need false documents to get your allotments. If it goes wrong, just toss her, plenty other officers have done it, hasn't hurt their careers one bit."

Valentine opened the door briefly to check the corridor. He shut the door to their cabin again and sat down on the bed opposite Post. "Will, everything about me is faked. Her, my commission and service record from up north, even the name 'Rowan's not my own. My name is David Valentine."

Post turned over in his bunk, lying on his side. He put the bottle on the floor between them and took another sip from his glass. "Okay, you've got a false name. I don't get it. What is it then, an escape attempt?" Post asked, also lowering his voice. "Damn elaborate one. You'd better pick the right island—go to the wrong one, and the residents will eat you alive. I mean that literally."

"I need the *Thunderbolt*, and I'm going to take it," Valentine said. He let the words sink in for a moment. Post's face rippled from blank astonishment to incredulity, then back again to astonishment as the idea took hold.

"The original plan was to try with a small group of men I would bring on board," he continued. "That didn't work out, so I'm going to make do with what's already on the ship. The Chief is on our side, and so is Ahn-Kha, the Grog foreman."

"Our side? Whose side is that?" Post finally asked, his liquor-lubricated train of thought finally leaving the platform.

"Southern Command. I work for one of the Freeholds, the one in the Ozarks and Ouachitas. And I'd like you to join us, if you'll risk it."

Post reached for the bottle and took a drink, ignoring his glass. "The sun's gone to your head, Dave. What are you going to try to do, turn the crew? They didn't get this job by being unreliable. Plus they have families back home to think about."

"The families will be taken care of," Valentine countered. "It's in the works right now. In a few more days, they'll be on their way out of the KZ. One of our Cats is on the inside."

"Cats?"

Valentine's hypersensitive ears searched the adjoining rooms and corridor. Someone moved through the passageway, and he paused before continuing in his low monotone. "It's a nickname, I guess. It's a long story, but the Kur and the Grogs aren't the only ones here from Elsewhere. Earth is part of a larger war, and other worlds are involved. The Kurians are what you might call a faction of a people called the Lifeweavers.

"Their society split thousands and thousands of years ago when the Lifeweavers on a planet called Kur discovered how to become immortal through . . . I call it vampirism. They've been at war ever since. Way back then, the Kurians came here, and the Lifeweavers picked some people to hunt the things brought over from Kur. They explained to the primitive men that they were placing the spirit of Wolves or Bears or Lions or what have you into the warriors they chose. I still don't know what they do exactly or how. All I can compare it to is turning on something inside you, like a light going on once you close the circuit. There was a hiatus lasting about six thousand years when the Lifeweavers won and Kur's transportation network got closed down. We turned into a civilization in the gap. Then they came back, and the Lifeweavers appeared again to help us."

Valentine looked at Post. He wondered if his lieutenant thought him a lunatic, or simply an imaginative liar.

"I've heard rumors," Post finally whispered. "Weird stuff about men who can become invisible, or breathe water, or wrestle a Reaper to the ground. Is that what you can do?"

"None of those," Valentine said, smiling. "I can see and hear better, and they did something to quicken my reflexes. But that doesn't help me with this, at least now. The best hearing in the world isn't going to help me take this ship. But you could."

Valentine felt relieved for some reason. Something had felt wrong in keeping up the pretense in front of Post. Having a man he instinctively liked believing him a tool of the Kurians grated.

"I'm not the only discontented one, just the only one that shows it. But you tell most of the men what you just told me, they'll claim they're in with you and two minutes later go straight to the captain. Claim the Terrorist Bounty. It's big enough to live on for years, if you catch a real one."

"Post, in the KZ the 'rest of your life' is whatever the Kurian in charge wants it to be. In the Ozarks, you're not livestock, you're an individual. Part of a community. It's not Old World, at least not in material terms. But the old beliefs are there. Life has value."

"Some community," Post said thickly, his rotgut kicking in. "I've heard you folks are so hungry that when winter comes, you live off the dead."

This was not the first time Valentine had heard that grisly rumor. He was happy to gainsay it rather than cite invented facts to support it. "Not true. I will say we don't eat as well as a lot of folks in the KZ, but then we're not being fattened for the slaughter, either. I'm offering you a way out of all this, Will. A real escape—not like the bottle you're using now. More, a chance to fight back. You'll be with men and women working to smash the system."

Post picked up the nearly empty bottle and looked at the mouth in a sidelong way, as if it were playing some kind of tune only he could hear. He shut his eyes and opened them again, staring straight at Valentine.

He stood up, a little unsteadily, and extended his hand. "It ain't going to work, Dave. But maybe you won't die alone."

They shook on it.

A long moment passed, and Post sat back down in his bunk. He wiped his face, turning the gesture into a long, thoughtful pull at his chin.

Valentine slipped back into his pants and shoes and left the cabin for a moment, passed the word for the officer's steward to bring some sandwiches to his cabin. He stepped out onto the afterdeck, felt the engines through the rail. The Grogs were hurrying to finish up their duties, looking forward to an evening's rest, and off-duty marines and sailors lounged around the deck, playing games of card and dice, or sitting absorbed in wood carving, reading, or just talking. He smelled the men's dinners below, the sea air, and the oily smell of the diesels.

When he returned to the cabin, Post had his footlocker open and was unwrapping a burnished steel pistol from a terry-cloth rag. A matching gun lay on his bed.

"I wasn't planning on moving this minute," Valentine said, shutting the door behind him.

"Hope not. I'm too drunk to shoot straight. Thought you might want something to replace that .44 wheelgun you lost. Some mementos of my bright and shining youth."

He handed an automatic to Valentine. Its straightforward lines and large, businesslike grip made it instantly identifiable. "A Colt 1911 model?"

"One of the variants. Got a .45 shell that should stop just about anyone, good and permanent. Bought this pair fresh out of Officers' Training."

Valentine tested the slide. The weapon was in fine condition.

"Take one, Dave. It shoots faster than that revolver ever could."

"Happy to," Valentine said. Post also presented him with magazines of freshly loaded ammunition for the weapon. "Are the bullets reliable?"

"Better than most," Post said. "Not service issue—they come from a gunsmith in the old town. He's a good man, as long as you treat him right. I heard that a major went out one time, threw his weight around to get a free gun, and damned if his pistol didn't misfire just when he needed it."

The sandwiches arrived, accompanied by a gumbo soup made of the scraps of the fresh meats brought out of New Orleans. They pulled out a mini-desk between their bunks and ate in thoughtful silence, mopping up the remnants of the soup with the ship's fresh bread. For the first time since Valentine started eating with Post, his lieutenant did not wash down his meal with half the contents of one of the iodine-colored bottles.

"Can you tell me what you need the ship for?" Post asked.

Valentine had committed himself, and if he could trust Post with his life, he could trust him with the few details that he knew. Ahn-Kha would take over if he were killed, but if by chance both of them—

"I'm to find a stash of old weapons. I don't know what kind. Then I'm supposed to get them back, either going through Galveston or farther south by Mexico. That's the reason for the armed ship: it's supposed to help at the island, and then make sure nothing can challenge us on the way back. There's a man in Southern Texas who'll take it from there."

"Why don't they tell you what it is?"

"I think the danger is that if the Kurians found out about it, they'd either take it themselves or destroy it."

Valentine heard someone in the passageway outside, and held up his hand for silence.

"Where is it?" Post asked after Valentine had dropped his hand.

"Haiti."

"Haiti?" Post choked. "Jesus, I figured it was the old naval base at

Guantanamo. Sir, Haiti's hell's own greenhouse. It's pretty fuckin' big, and I've never heard of anyone getting inland out of range of the ship's guns and coming back to tell about it."

"I know roughly where on the island I'm supposed to go. There's some kind of traitor in the Kurian organization there who'll teach us about it. I know it will be bulky—that's why we need a ship and so many men for the job."

"There's an awful lot of *ifs* in your plan, if you don't mind me saying, sir."

"I know."

"I'm not asking you to follow me inland. I was counting on you to run things on the ship until I return."

"Sir, you want a weapon, think about this ship. She's well armored, carries a good-size gun, and you could put enough men on her to shut down water traffic from Louisiana to Florida."

"Any other time you'd be right, Will. But they tell me that whatever is waiting on Haiti is something that could really change the equation between us and the Kurians. Don't you think the risk is worth a chance to make a difference?"

"Some difference. Seems to me, the difference will be the one between being alive and being dead. Not that I really care," he added. To his credit, Valentine thought, he did not sound convinced of the last.

From that dinner on, Valentine did not see Post take another drink. His lieutenant suffered unvoiced agonies in silence, driving himself to keep up an appearance of stability in front of others, only to flee to the head or the cabin when the shaking in his hands got to be too much for him. Valentine never asked him to quit drinking; in fact, with the mental strain he was more than a little tempted to try the contents of the squared-off bottles himself after retiring at night. Valentine found a growing new respect for Post that replaced his previous feelings of pity. He admired his lieutenant for keeping the pretense of normality despite the torrents of sweat pouring out of him and God-knew-what other torments to his body.

The next evening Valentine arranged for a meeting in the arms locker with the Chief, Post, Ahn-Kha, and himself, purportedly to determine which weapons Ahn-Kha's Grogs would carry in their duties. The captain had suggested a brace of dusty shotguns, captured in some action long ago and forgotten. After viewing the weapons in question, Valentine asked that the Chief take a look at them and see if the ship's machine shop could bring them back to usability. Thus the conspirators were able to get a half-hour or so of privacy within the ship for a meeting of their group. Squeezing Ahn-Kha's bulk into the room proved to be only the first difficulty in a long line of challenges before them.

"We should make landfall off Jamaica tomorrow afternoon or early evening," Valentine began. "The captain plans to head straight into the harbor they are thought to use the next morning. God knows what might happen in the fight, so I think we have to move before then."

"How about we go into action and rig a shell to blow in the bridge during the fight?" the Chief suggested. "The crew will think the pirates just got a lucky shot, and Mr. Rowan assumes command. Looks legit."

"Who knows what damage the explosion would do?" Post asked, sweat running from his hairline under the hot work-lamp. The marine was balling his hands into fists and rubbing them against his thighs under the weapon-strewn table. "Maybe we go aground. So much for the *Thunderbolt*. I doubt the pirates would fix her up and take her to Haiti to oblige us."

"Yes, and we might not get both. The exec will probably be at the main armament. I think it's better if we do it before. Offer the men an alternative to the fight," Valentine said. "Freedom. That's a powerful persuader."

"Cut off the head, and the body will be yours," Ahn-Kha said, quoting a Grog proverb from his place, squeezed between the rifle racks filling up one whole end of the room. "We have much of the head of the ship here. We remove the captain and Worthington. Then we let the petty officers know who is in charge. They will do as they are told."

"Ahn-Kha is right as far as the captain and exec go," Valentine agreed. "But I want to give everyone else a real choice. We assemble the crew and give each man the option: join us, or be put off the ship in a boat with food, water, even weapons. They can take their chances on Jamaica or try to sail for the coast. All they have to do is go north—they'll hit Kurian territory soon enough."

"Will you tell them why you need the ship?" the Chief asked.

"Can't risk it until the captain and the exec disappear with the crew that want to follow them. I have no idea how long we would be on Haiti. The last thing we need is him trying to hunt us down."

Post shook his head. "You'll lose half of them. Maybe more. We might not be left with enough to keep this bucket moving."

"I think a lot of them signed on for sea service to get away from the Reapers. You can tell by their talk, their interests. They're free spirits, not conscripts."

They hashed out the rest of the plan while working on the shotguns. They decided they would let a few subordinates they felt could be trusted know about the plan at the last minute. Post felt that he knew two marines well enough to say they would follow him, and the Chief insisted that his engine-room crew would sign on to a man. Ahn-Kha said the Grogs would do as he ordered; few of the humans on board could even make themselves understood to the creatures beyond simple instructions.

They would take the ship in the dark after making landfall at Jamaica. The captain planned, as soon as he got his bearings, to move east along Jamaica's north coast and arrive at the pirate bay with the dawn. Around midnight, Ahn-Kha would go below and guard the arms locker with his Grogs, also controlling the nearby hatches to the engine room and generator room. The Chief would kill the power when this was accomplished. Post and the marines he hoped to recruit would go to the small store of "ready arms" on deck, and mount machine guns fore and aft covering the main decks from the gun platforms. It would be Valentine's job to take the bridge, doing whatever was necessary to keep Captain Saunders and Worthington from issuing any orders. With that accomplished, Valentine would assemble all hands on the deck and offer them their choice.

There was some dispute over what to do with the captain and the executive officer.

"You'll probably have to kill them, sir," Post predicted.

"I'd rather not. I'll get a pair of handcuffs on them and toss them in the motor launch. Or the lifeboat, depending on how many of the crew decide to go with them."

"It will come to killing," Ahn-Kha said. "They will turn the crew against you, if they can."

"Handcuffs and gags, then. I don't want their blood on our hands unless it is a matter of us or them."

Valentine spent the next day lost in his duties, so much so that he did not go up on deck as they caught their first sight of the blue Jamaican coast. In preparation for the next morning's activities, which he hoped would never be carried out, he and his NCOs attached reflective tape to the backs of their green-and-black camouflage battle-dress. Someone joked that Irish, a Coastal Marine corporal in their complement, should form his into the shape of a bull's-eye, since he'd managed to get himself shot four times in the course of his duties, and even Post laughed. At the midday meal, Ahn-Kha and the marines held an informal meeting in the crew's mess, where they went over the destruction the *Thunderbolt* was to visit on the pirates. Saunders hoped to reach the harbor before midnight.

His imagination continued to get the better of him as the afternoon wore on. It seemed the entire ship crackled with electricity, so tense were the men and their officers in anticipation of the fight tomorrow.

"I hope the Chief is doing better than I am," Post reported, joining Valentine at sunset at the ship's starboard rail. They watched the thickly forested slopes of Jamaica slide by like a rolling backdrop in a stage play. Post still trembled, and his shirt was soaked with sweat, but his face seemed more animated and his eyes brighter. "I tried sounding out a few of the men, but I chickened out at the last moment. I just couldn't bring myself to say what we're planning, the moment didn't seem right. I kept thinking about a Hood at my throat, got so as I could almost feel teeth. About all I was able to do was warn them to be ready for anything. Sorry, Dave."

Valentine shrugged. "Too late to worry. I talked to Ahn-Kha and the Chief—we're going to switch the time to twenty-two hundred. The men are supposed to be assembled an hour later, ready to climb into the boats for the landing. That way Ahn-Kha leading his Grogs to the arms locker won't seem so unusual—they're supposed to go ashore first anyway."

They forced themselves to act normally at dinner with the men. Valentine sat with one group he called his "deadeyes," the four best marksmen in the culled company. Post ate with the noncommissioned officers at the other long table in the galley. Though he had no appetite, Valentine forced himself to eat mouthful after mouthful of the traditional preaction steak and eggs. The beef was stringy and tough, but even the *Thunderbolt*'s indifferent cook's mate could not ruin the eggs. Valentine forced himself to have seconds on the latter, washing it down with glassfuls of faintly orange-tasting sweetened water that he guessed to be some concoction trying to pass as orange juice. He joked with the men, listening to service stories and telling a few of his own, like the time a supply officer fed an entire harem of young women in the loft of a marine warehouse, which grew into a thriving bordello over the years. When caught by a visiting inspector, he argued that pimping a whorehouse fell under his duties, since one of his official responsibilities was listed on his duty sheet as "recreation procurement officer."

With dinner finished, the marines broke off to leave the galley to the sailors, and Valentine retired to his shared cabin.

He looked around the close, bare room. A single locker held all his clothes, and a footlocker, the rest of his belongings. He spent an hour in a long shower and shave, and changed into his heavy cotton battle-dress. The combat fatigues, acquired from a tailor in Mobile when he first entered the Coastal Marines, were a tiger-stripe mix of black and dark green, spotted here and there with blotches of dark gray. Heavy pockets hung like saddlebags from the side of each thigh on the pants, but the short officers' tunic held only insignia and an expanding map pocket and a pencil-holder on one sleeve. He unlocked his chest and began to take out his equipment. He laced up his boots, traditional black service models, the leather softened and oiled by a year's wear and care. His final wardrobe item was a nylon equipment vest with heavy bullet-stopping pads slipped into the liner and compass, flares, first-aid kit, matches, and whistle distributed amongst the pockets. Post's .45 pistol went to his hip holster. He sank a machete into the sheath strapped across his back hanging over two canteens. Finally, he extracted the one item he brought out of the Ozarks, his old Soviet Russian PPD model submachine gun with the drum clip. It was a heavy-barreled, formidable-looking gun, restored by an old friend and given to him the summer he became a Cat three years ago.

Slinging the gun and drawing comfort from its familiar weight, he made a slow circuit of the *Thunderbolt*'s central superstructure. Ahn-Kha had the Grogs gathered on the well deck, talking to them. The Golden One looked up at Valentine and cocked his ears up and forward, giving his broad head the momentary aspect of a bull: his friend's equivalent of a thumbs-up. The gesture went to Valentine's nerves like a fast-acting sedative. He looked out at the nearly empty aft decks and turned the last corner on the rectangular walkway. Post stood at the foot of one of the stairways going up to the bridge deck, idling next to the arms locker holding the machine gun for the forward mount.

Valentine squeezed past and gave him a nod. "Ready?" Valentine asked.

"Getting there. Sure makes you feel alive, doesn't it. Like the whole world's been turned up. Sounds, smells, everything. I never noticed all the waves before. A million of them—"

"Just take it easy, Will. Wait for me to go up the stairs—then get the gun. You checked it, right?"

"Yes, it's fine."

"Just a few minutes longer. Ahn-Kha's still talking to his team. They haven't gone below yet."

Post gripped the rail, the tendons in his forearms rising up under his tan skin. "You know why my wife lit out, Rowan—er, Dave?"

"I might be able to guess. The system?"

"The system," Post said. "She and I had a difference of opinion about it. She left. I eventually came round to her side, but only after her stuff had two years' worth of dust on it."

Post looked out at the ocean and the sinking moon. Valentine thought he saw the man's lower lip tremble.

Valentine leaned over, knocked his shoulder against Post's. "One way or another, you'll be clear of it soon."

"First, got to get rid of this shit," Post said, tearing off his tunic. Buttons flew, clattering to the deck and falling with barely audible *plop*s into the ocean. Post stood in his stained undershirt for a moment, as if coming to a decision. He wadded up his uniform coat and fed it to the all-consuming sea.

"If I'm going to buy it, I don't want to go in their colors."

"I'll get you a different one when we get back to free soil, if you'd like," Valentine said. "Just try to live to claim it. I hope the exec doesn't come down those stairs and see you like that. He might have a few questions about your tunic."

"I'll pick him up and send him to look for it. He's a bottom-feeder if there ever was one.

"Could you do me a favor, Dave? If I don't make it, maybe you can look up Gail in the Free Territory. She would have headed that way— it's an easier trip than going across Texas. She's probably using her maiden name, Gail Stark. Tell her . . . just tell her about this."

"Can do, Will."

"Thanks, sir."

"See you at lights out."

"Good luck, Dave," Post said, offering his hand.

Valentine shook it and went forward to look down at the well deck. It was empty. Ahn-Kha and his Grogs were already on their way to the arms locker and engine room. A nervous thrill sparked up his spine, bristling the hair at the back of his neck.

He chambered the first round in his gun and lightly ascended the stairs to the open deck just behind the wheelhouse. As his head broke the level of the upper deck, he listened with "hard ears" to voices from the bridge.

"And when is this supposed to happen?" the captain said from somewhere on the bridge.

"Early in the morning, sir. The ship's power will be cut off, and that's when they'll take the ship," Valentine heard a high-pitched voice say.

"It makes no sense," Worthington's voice exclaimed. "They will be ashore by then, Grogs and marines, and Rowan will be with them."

"Can't argue it, there's something afoot, that's for certain," Saunders said. "Damn, there always was something about Rowan I didn't like. Haven't I said so time and again, Lieutenant?"

Worthington changed the subject. "I've already alerted the master-at-arms," he said. "I didn't know which marines to trust. Dortmund is bringing an armed guard up now, and he's—"

Valentine's worries cleared, as they always did when planning gave way to doing. All his questions were gone: it had become a matter of killing everyone on the bridge, and somehow holding the wheelhouse and upper deck through the coming confusion. The moon had disappeared below the horizon, leaving the ship lit only by the stars and its few running lights.

"Halt!" Valentine heard a voice boom from the bottom of the staircase. "Unsling your weapon, sir, and don't touch anything but the sling."

He turned to see Dortmund, three sailors lined up behind him, pistols pointed up at him. While he had been concentrating on the bridge, Dortmund had reached the bottom of the stairs without Valentine noticing. Valentine thanked God that Dortmund hadn't shot first and questioned later. He obeyed the instructions, going so far as to crouch to put the gun on the stair below his feet, and readied himself for a leap—

—when the loud, deadly rattle of a machine gun roared from behind the sailors, filling the night with noise. Dortmund's men fell forward, jerking spasmodically as if swept off their feet by an electrified broom. The hard plinking sound of bullets ricocheting off metal stairs and walls punctuated the sound of the slugs tearing through flesh, a noise that reminded some part of Valentine's mind of eggs thrown against a wall. The four-petal blossom of the machine-gun's muzzle flare lit Post's snarling features as he fired the support weapon from his hip, using a thick leather strap to help him wield it.

One sailor went overboard with a cry; the others fell at the bottom of the stairs.

Valentine retrieved his own gun before they hit the deck. Blood had been shed, and his hopes of a simple seizure of the ship were cut down as brutally as Dortmund and his henchmen. He peeked over the edge of the deck above, only to be met by a burst of bullets that zipped out to sea past his ear. Worthington was no fool; he had armed himself before going to the captain. Valentine had to get down to Ahn-Kha and his Grogs, so he would at least have a nucleus of armed men to command.

The lights died, and Valentine felt a change in the ship's motion. The Chief had level-headedly proceeded with the plan upon hearing the firing above.

Valentine backed down the stairs and joined Post, where his lieutenant covered the starboard side walkway from the base of the stairs.

"What the hell happened?" Post said. "Where did Dortmund come from?"

"One of the ship's boys overheard something and went to the exec. We've got to get to the Grogs."

The ship's public-address system squealed into static-filled life. "All hands, all hands, this is the captain speaking. . . ."

Valentine grabbed Post by the arm and pulled him into the stairwell leading into the bowels of the ship, almost jerking him out of his shoes with the force of his movement. Two shots rang out from the top of the stairway, cutting the air where they stood seconds ago, as Saunders's voice continued.

". . . Captain Rowan of the Marines, Lieutenant Post, the Grogs, and an unknown number of others are attempting to mutiny. They are to be shot on sight. All hands to the aft deck, all hands to the aft deck."

"Make a hole, damn it! Make a hole!" Valentine barked, exiting the stairway with Post in tow, waving his submachine gun to accentuate the threat as they pushed back sailors popping like magical rabbits into the narrow passageway. Somewhere around the T-junction corner ahead he heard Ahn-Kha's bellow, barking out orders in the Grog patois. The captain's voice continued to issue orders over the PA, including one to the dead Dortmund to report to the Oerlikon. An emergency light bathed the corridor in harsh shadows. Valentine turned a corner and caught sight of a knot of Grogs standing behind a small, bright spotlight pointed down the corridor. He shielded his eyes.

"Ahn-Kha, it's me and Post! Cut that light for a second."

The two men hustled toward the improvised barricade.

A pistol fired from the darkness behind them, and Post grunted. He sagged against Valentine, who turned and fired up the passageway. Ahn-Kha leapt forward with apish agility, blocked the floodlight with his bulk, and put his mammoth arm around Post's chest. The machine-gun clattered to the steel floor, but Post gripped the strap as Ahn-Kha dragged him backwards. Valentine backed down the corridor, but whoever fired stayed safely around the corner of the intersection at the end of the hall.

He reached the Grogs outside the arms locker. Ahn-Kha had improvised a barricade of mattresses and a wooden door, which the muscular Grogs still worked to construct as they shifted a beam to let them pass. Ahn-Kha carried Post into the arms locker and gently stretched him out onto the floor. Valentine knelt beside his lieutenant, who had blood staining the undershirt across his chest.

Post groaned and coughed. "I can taste blood," he said.

Valentine found the wound, high enough on his chest to nearly be at the shoulder. He grabbed a first-aid kit off the wall and found a compress within. He applied the dressing to the softly pulsing hole. Noticing blood on the floor, he gently lifted Post and found another hole opposite.

"Good news, Will. It went straight through."

"Watch . . . out. The captain'll have the marines on you in a minute."

"Most of them won't be armed. All they'll have are whatever guns are scattered in the ship."

"Stern. He'll send men down the hatches." Post was pale with pain, but still thinking clearly enough. His bravery gave Valentine heart.

"We've blocked everything off," Ahn-Kha said from the doorway. "The Chief is welding the access hatches shut."

A Grog hooted and fired toward the T-intersection forward. The shotgun blast sounded like a grenade explosion in the confined area of the metal passageway.

They heard a clatter around the shadowed corner of the T-intersection facing the barricade. Ahn-Kha knelt behind the mattress-shielded door, the pump-action in his hands looking like a child's toy.

"Mr. Rowan?" a voice called down the hall. "It's Partridge. I've got Went and Torres with me. What's happening, sir?"

Valentine exchanged a look with Ahn-Kha, and mouthed the word *marines.* "I don't have time for the whole story, Party. But everything the captain said over the intercom is true. Post is with me. We are trying to take the ship."

"What're you talking to him for?" a voice said from around the right-hand corner of the intersection.

"Shut up, See-Pee. It's our officer," Valentine heard Torres growl.

"You planning on going into the Blue, sir?" Partridge continued, ignoring the byplay.

"Something like that. It's a life away from the Reapers to any man who comes with me."

"You move, and I'll shoot you down," the unknown voice from the right side of the T-intersection threatened.

"Hey, what're—," Partridge began, but the sound of shots cut him off. Valentine heard four shots in rapid succession, and the three marines appeared in the corridor, Torres and Went holding the wounded Partridge between them. They squinted in the glare of the spotlight, holding up their free hands. Torres had a revolver in his, and Went a rifle.

"Bastards! You killed Delano!" someone yelled from around the corner as the marines approached the barricade.

Ahn-Kha plucked the wounded man over and bore him into the arms locker, and put him down next to Post. Valentine helped the other two. Torres followed Partridge, who had blood already soaking through the right side of his uniform.

"We're with you, Mr. Rowan," Went, one of Valentine's deadeyes, said once they were safely behind the mattresses again. "When we heard the announcement, Party, he said, 'Who'd you rather take orders from, Saunders or Mr. Rowan?' I grabbed my match rifle, and Torres got Corporal Grant's pistol, and came to see what was happening. That bastard Delano fired first, sir, and we shot back. Everything's dark and confused. I heard firing forward. I think everyone's shooting at each other."

"I'm glad you're here, Went. I want to be straight with you. This is not going as I planned. It's us, the Grogs, and the Chief and a few of his men. We're outnumbered about eight to one."

The corners of Went's mouth twitched back into something that, if not a smile, was at least a wry grimace. "Leastways the guns are here." He peered over the edge of the barricade. "They won't take me alive. I'm not going to get delivered in handcuffs to some Hood."

The hatch to the generator room at the bottom level of the ship opened, and the Chief's face looked up at the assembled Grogs and men. "Tight as a drum, they're going to have to blow a big hole in the ship to get at us from down here. Captain's going to have an interesting time commanding the ship without engines."

"Good work, Chief," Valentine said.

Valentine heard a commotion down the hall and sought out the location with hard ears. The captain was speaking to someone, demanding a report. Saunders did not care for the answers, he began to yell. "That's all? And you let men *join* them?"

"They shot Delano, sir, and he had the only gun right then."

"You've got a wrench in your hands—you should have bashed some skulls in with it. Out of my sight!"

After a moment, Valentine heard Saunders's voice raised again, this time projecting from somewhere along the starboard-side corridor.

"The attempt on the ship has failed, Rowan. You know it, and I'm sure it's starting to dawn on those deluded enough to follow you."

"We're ready to wreck the engines, Captain, if we come to believe that," Valentine called back.

"You're a dead man, Rowan, and so's your pet drunk. But I'm offering an amnesty to whoever turns you in. I'll hush all this up. Like it never happened, long as they frog-march you and Post out."

Valentine looked over his shoulder; Torres and Went were both looking at him. He read doubt in their expressions, but whether it was doubt in him or doubt in the captain's promise he could not say. He slowly placed his gun on the floor, butt end pointed at the marines. "Takers?" Valentine asked softly.

Went blanched, but Torres just smiled and shook his head. Partridge groaned something from his position on the floor of the arms locker.

"What was that?" Valentine asked Torres, who knelt beside the wounded man.

" 'Tell Captain Saunders to go fuck himself,' " Torres repeated for the wounded man.

Valentine picked up his gun. "We put it to a vote, Captain, and it's unanimous: Go fuck yourself."

"You'll all bleed, you renegade bastards," the captain swore.

"Tell me, sir," Valentine shouted back. "What happened to the last captain that failed in a mission because of a mutiny? I heard Kurians ordered—"

"By Kur, Rowan, I'll make it so hot for you, you'll wish you were in hell. I'll keelhaul you. You'll beg me to let you die, renegade!"

Torres disappeared into the arms locker and returned, scooting up toward Valentine with something in his hand. Valentine recognized the can-shaped object as one of the ship's grenades. "Play much pool, Mr. Rowan?" Torres asked, putting two fingers into the ring atop the explosive.

"Not my game, Torres," Valentine whispered back.

"Can I try a two-bumper shot?"

"Be my guest."

Torres pulled the pin and listened for the hiss. Valentine saw a thin wisp of smoke appear from the central fixture that held the fuse. The marine stood and, with a left-handed sidearm throw, sent the grenade spinning down the corridor, whirling like a gyroscope toward the voice of the captain. Valentine kept his head up long enough to see it bounce off the bullet-marked wall at the crossbar of the T-intersection and heard it hit again somewhere in the corridor corner leading to the starboard passageway.

There was just enough time before the explosion for cries of "Grenade!" and "Look out!" to be heard, before an orange flash lit up the corridor.

As the ringing noise faded from their ears, Valentine felt the sweat running down the skin over his spine.

"About time for the captain to try something really stupid," Valentine predicted grimly, hearing voices yell back and forth from both sides of the intersection. He hated the thought of what was coming.

The captain obliged him. The loyal sailors and marines of the *Thunderbolt* tried to take the barricade with a rush. One of the machine guns from the upper deck appeared around the portside corner and began firing blindly toward the barricade. Valentine and Torres knelt behind the mattress-reinforced door, while the others took cover in rooms off the main passageway. Valentine heard the bullets hitting the door with a chunking sound, but the mattresses slowed down even the large-caliber shells enough so they failed to do more than dig into the solid wood.

When the gun's belt ran out, the corridor filled with screaming attackers trying to rush the barricade under the cover of a few pistols in the front ranks. The spotlight lit them up with unearthly clarity, ghostly faces white and straining. Ahn-Kha lifted the machine gun Post had dragged with him, and firing from his shoulder swept the corridor, cutting down the attackers running at them two abreast. Valentine added short bursts from his own gun. They flung the men down into bloody heaps well before the hopeless attack reached the barricade. A pair of men dodged into the dark laundry room, only to be hurled out again by shotgun blasts from Ahn-Kha's Grogs waiting within.

The charge was bloody but brief, and when it was over, Valentine counted eleven dead and wounded heaped in the corridor, lying in a thin lake of spilled blood under spattered walls. Only their blood penetrated the barricade, seeping in under the mattresses and door, until its odor overwhelmed even the cordite in the air.

Valentine sank to his knees, reloading. "Last thing I wanted. This is not what I wanted," he heard himself saying over and over again, waltzing on the edge of hysteria.

Ahn-Kha placed a reassuring hand on his shoulder. "Steady now, my David," the huge Grog said. "Better them than us."

A figure arose from the bloody heap in the corridor, pushed up by an arm and his one good leg. The marine tried to take a step back toward the intersection when he slipped on the slick red liquid pooled on the floor, falling full on his injured leg with an agonized scream.

"Would you help Cal before he bleeds to death?" Valentine shouted down the corridor.

"You won't shoot?"

"No, for God's sake. Get him, would you?" Torres added.

The tacit truce allowed a pair of sailors to pull the wounded men away around the corridor. Ahn-Kha placed a new belt in his machine gun, closing the receiver with a determined slam.

"Partridge died," Went reported. "Sorry, Mr. Rowan. And I think Mr. Post is in shock."

Valentine crawled into the locker and felt Post's pulse. It was weak but steady, his breathing shallow.

A half-familiar burning smell tickled Valentine's nostrils. He looked up at the ceiling, where smoke began to flow from an air-supply vent. He moved to the hatch to the engine room. "Chief, looks like they're burning something in the ventilators, can you do anything about it?"

"Yeah, I noticed," the Chief called back. "I'm turning off the fans now. The access to the smokestack is welded shut—otherwise, I could shunt it out of there. It'll get smoky, especially if they burn something in the stairways, too."

"How about reversing the fans?"

"We'd have to rewire them. We're just going to have to cough for a while, I think."

The squawk box crackled to life. "Last chance, men," the captain's voice gloated. "We've got some fires going in the ventilators, and we'll be dropping bits of fender tire on for good measure. It's going to get unpleasant down there in a few minutes, if not lethal. Anyone who comes to their senses will get mercy. Too much has happened for it to get covered up now, but I'll do what I can."

"Why can't you shut him up, Chief?" Went yelled as Torres solemnly laid his tunic over Partridge's head.

"It's on an emergency battery up on the bridge. I could cut the wires, I suppose—"

Ahn-Kha wrinkled his nose. "Disgusting."

Valentine began to cough at the harsh smell of burning rubber filling the room, causing his eyes to water.

"Try this," the Chief said, passing Valentine a damp rag.

Valentine imitated the Chief and his men by tying the cloth over his mouth and nose. He did not notice a difference.

Eyes watering in the noxious burning-rubber smell, Valentine tried to come up with a plan. If all else failed, it was his duty to at least deprive the Kurians of the *Thunderbolt*. He could have the Chief open the scuttle to the ocean, and let the sea take the ship and his mission with her. Perhaps he and Ahn-Kha could even survive the swim to the Jamaican shore. . . .

Something hit the side of the ship with a resounding thump. A slight sideways motion rocked the *Thunderbolt*, barely enough to make a man unsteady on his feet. Had they run aground, or drifted into a reef? A second later, Valentine heard firing from above.

Valentine looked up at Ahn-Kha. The Grog's hornlike ears were twisting this way and that, listening to the confused clamour from above. Valentine recognized the sound of voices shouting, almost cheering together, intermixed with the gunfire. He and Ahn-Kha exchanged questioning looks.

"It has to be the pirates," Valentine said.

"Aww, shit, just what we need," Went said, his voice sounding strangely pitched owing to a set of improvised noseplugs.

Valentine hopped up to join Ahn-Kha. "You're exactly right, Went. It is just what we need. Men!" Valentine said, raising his voice and calling down to the Chief and his men below. "Let's make some noise. Yell for help, everyone!"

They all looked at him for a moment, uncomprehending. Valentine took a choking breath. *"Heeeeelp!"* he howled down the corridor.

Torres and Went began shouting, as well as the Chief and his men in the engine room. Valentine yelled until he saw spots in front of his eyes, taking unpleasantly deep breaths of smoke-tainted air. Ahn-Kha outdid all the men, bellowing loudly enough to rattle cups in the galley. Ahn-Kha's Grogs joined in, beating metal tools against the pipes and walls, adding a metallic clamor to their combined voices.

He held up a hand for silence. "Kill the spotlight," he ordered. Torres turned the switch at the back of the lamp, incautiously putting his hand on the light's housing and burning himself. Torres swore.

"Quiet there," Valentine said, listening to footsteps in the corridor. Two sailors came around one end of the intersection, a marine from the other, holding their hands up.

"Don't shoot Captain Rowan!" the marine, a corporal named Hurst, begged.

"Mr. Rowan, we're giving up to you here," a CP petty officer added.

"Okay, come forward. Keep your hands in view, men," Valentine said, nauseated from the burnt-tire smell. "What's happened up top?"

"Dunno for sure, sir," Hurst reported. "The exec had me watching the engine-room escape hatch, in case y'all came up that way. All of a sudden we got small-caliber fire. Sweeping bad, sir. There was a ship alongside, and a boat, too, come up in the dark while everyone was busy. Nilovitch got hit, couldn't do anything for him, so we came below. Had to jump over the smoke fire they had going, heard a lot of shouting and shooting behind me. Figured it was a good chance to throw in with y'all. Then we saw these two," he said, gesturing to the *Thunderbolt* sailors.

"My David," Ahn-Kha said, but Valentine was already reacting. Lights appeared from the T-intersection.

"Get over here, men," Valentine said, and he and Went helped them get over the barricade as Ahn-Kha pointed the machine gun down the passageway.

"In there," Valentine ordered, indicating the hallway behind the barricade leading to the aft storage lockers. "Torres, keep an eye on them."

He heard voices coming from the two joining corridors. "Musta been back here," one of the voices said. A few shots still sounded from forward.

"Hello?" Valentine called down the hall. "If you're looking for the people yelling for help, you found them."

The voices hushed. Valentine hardened his ears, searching where his eyes could not go.

"Mebbe a trap," someone muttered around the corner.

"If it is, you can tell the commodore you avenged me. Quiet now, I need to listen," a female voice said. "Hello back," the unknown woman added, a bit more loudly. "This ship is in the hands of the Commodore's Flotilla, of Jayport, Jamaica. I offer you a chance of surrender with fair treatment. Why were you calling for help?"

The owner of the voice stepped around the corner, and all that Valentine could make out in the smoke and darkness was that she was a tall woman. An equally tall man joined her, and at a motion from her hand he opened a kerosene lantern and held it up, revealing the two of them. They both wore loose cotton shirts, cut as pullovers with deep V-necks, dark culottes topped with a sash and gunbelts, and boat sandals. She had dark hair pulled back from her face and handsome, large-eyed features showing Latin blood in her golden complexion. The man behind her was ebony-hued, eyes narrowed suspiciously as he searched the men on the barricade, a revolver in his other hand.

Valentine thought it best to match her and hopped over the barricade, though he took care to land on his good leg. "Ahn-Kha, tell your pair in the laundry not to fire. It's over."

Ahn-Kha barked something out, answered by grunts from the darkness of the laundry room. Valentine moved forward to meet the two at the intersection. She looked at the bodies, and Valentine saw her reading the story in the carnage.

"Surrender might not be the right word, but we won't trouble you."

"You in a position to cause trouble?"

"Not if you play fair by us. My name is Valentine, out of Southern Command in the Ozarks. God knows how I could prove it to you, though. Our plan was to take the ship, but"—Valentine indicated the barricade behind him—"it went rather wrong. Help us, and you'll have my thanks, and my word that we will not harm you or the *Thunderbolt* further."

"You are a long way from Mountain Home, Valentine," she said, showing a better knowledge of his land than he would have guessed. "My name is Carrasca, First Leftenant of the *Rigel*."

"What's happened to the rest of my crew?" Valentine asked.

"A few were killed. Someone from the bridge fired a machine gun into us, and more were shot off the superstructure, but most surrendered. I see your men are better armed than the rest."

"We had the arms locker and engine room, about the only thing that went right tonight. You picked a good time to board."

"Lucky for both of us. Can you clear out that mess in the corridor? I need to send men down to watch the engine room."

"Nobody is going to sink her," Valentine said.

"It is my responsibility to make sure of that. I'm sure you can understand."

Valentine stepped aside as more of the *Rigel*'s men entered, nodding to Ahn-Kha. The Grog gripped the door of the barricade and lifted it aside. Carrasca gave orders, briefly and to the point. Valentine admired the way her men were in control, even in the confusion of a fight. Whoever these pirates were, they had a discipline different from, and superior to, the fear-inspired one that dominated the *Thunderbolt*.

The defenders from the barricade huddled in a silent little group in the arms locker, like children unsure of a new teacher.

Valentine decided a gesture was in order, if nothing else to preempt the orders that would soon be issued from their captors. "Can we get the fans on, Chief? Our friends here put the fires out. Let's get some air down here. Turn the power back on, and start the engines, if you please."

The Chief pushed his stunned men into their positions. "Sir, tell these islanders not to keep pointing their guns around, will you? The fingers on all these triggers are making me nervous."

Carrasca leaned over the hatch. "Bierd, have your men watch their weapons." She turned back to Valentine. "I'm sorry, but for the safety of your men, you'll be put under guard. Could you bring your men up on deck?"

The diesels coughed into life, and Valentine felt the roll of the ship change as the propellers began to bite.

"C'mon, men, up on deck. I've had enough of this air. Let's get these bodies up, too."

The sailors, marines, and Grogs started the grisly work of clearing up the corpses. Valentine picked past the remains of a burning pile of tires and rags, following Carrasca to the stairs.

The intercom buzzed to life again. "Congratulations, men," a deep voice with a singsong musical intonation announced. "Thees is Captain Utari. D' ship is ours. Fair shares all round."

As the pirates cheered, Valentine felt the rudder turn the *Thunderbolt*'s vital tonnage toward Jamaica.

Four

Jayport, Jamaica. February: Like Malta in the Mediterranean or Singapore on the Krai Peninsula, Jamaica is the key to the waterways around her. Dwarfed by larger neighbors—Cuba to the north and Haiti to the west—the mountainous little island of blinding white sand and lush green hills sits like a tollboth in the center of a network of water routes around her. North is the passage between Cuba and Haiti leading to the coast of Florida and the Bahamas, west is the Yucatán channel off the coast of Mexico, and to the south is the Latin America coast. Far to the east lay tiny island chains and cays that mark the boundary like a lattice curtain between the Caribbean and the Atlantic proper.

In the days of the great buccaneers Morgan, Blackbeard, and Captain Kidd, the legendary pirates of the Caribbean pillaged French and Spanish possessions in the New World, spending their loot in the sinful dens that the seventeenth-century Babylon, Port Royal, boasted. The latter-day freebooters of Jamaica are after no such glittering wealth. Their desired booty is limited to food, medical supplies, technology, and shipbuilding materials.

The latest ruler of Jamaica rests near the old center of Kingston around the great southern bay. But the Kurian's realm extends only to the foothills of the Blue Mountains. These peaks, named for their color as seen from the sea, give the island its serrated spine that resembles a sea serpent resting in the Caribbean. Outside the Kurian's land, isolated coastal communities live in the primitive conditions of the Arawaka Indians Columbus discovered, building huts of thick grasses and banana leaves, or of mud and thatch. A few are lucky or powerful enough to control one of the pre-2022 buildings still standing after the titanic wave that washed across the Caribbean, followed by foundation-shattering quakes and roof-ripping hurricanes.

In Montego Bay, a bloody-handed sea lord rules with a brutality that would curl Morgan's mustache, and among the central mountains, an unnamed band of killers, thought to be the remnants of some drug kingpin's gang, leave piles of severed heads along the jungle trails to warn trespassers away. But for the most part, the Jamaicans are a gentle people, taking the bounty nature sewed in the rich volcanic soil of the island and the surrounding sea and sharing what little they have with the generosity of people who have known hunger and misfortune between periods of plenty.

One bay to the north, however, is an exception to the rule in a number of ways. The pre-2022 buildings are in as good a repair as local materials can make them—though one wave-gutted, multistory hotel stands untouched in its beach-front location—and hundreds of white bungalows of wood and thatch show the best example of what can be created out of clay, leaves, and coconut coir. Two thick palisades of wood run for miles from the high hills to the west to a great oval bulge along the flatter ground south and east, bordered by fields of rice and corn with the jungle cut back from the walls.

Sailing ships now dot a broad concrete pier that at one time berthed cruise ships. At the end of the pier is a gray-and-rust ship, a relic of the Old World dominating the center of the bay like a castle's keep. She sits separated by thirty feet of water crossed by a floating bridge leading to a portal in her hull big enough to drive a truck into. She is a strange sort of ship, four decks of superstructure crowded over the bow, and perhaps a hundred yards of what used to be flight deck broken only by the housing for the ship's offset stack. At the top of her aerial stack, a white flag with a red cross alternately ripples and droops in the shifting noontime air.

Farther out in the shallow waters of the bay, on a calm day it is easy to see the outlines of sunken shipping, now encrusted with coral, forming an underwater, unbuoyed wall guarding the seaward approaches to the dock. At the south end of the great concrete pier, a gate stands beneath a guard tower, allowing passage of landward trade, as well.

This is Jayport, refuge of the Commodore's Flotilla. Its history, a story too long to be recounted here, goes back to the last days of 2022, when two ships of the Royal Navy and a liner full of refugees came here and established the floating hospital. But this flotsam and jetsam of the world-that-was eventually formed an alliance with a band of island mariners. Now their combined children roam the Caribbean from the Texas coast to Grenada, raiding off the Kurian Order just as their English forebears plagued the Spanish Main and French Colonies.

Standing on the *Thunderbolt*'s bridge, David Valentine watched as they approached the Jayport harbor. The ship threaded her way through the reefs, unmarked save for two points where the surf splashed up against the coral obstructions projecting just past the surface. A fishing trawler led the way, like a pilotfish swimming before the gray bulk of a shark, and behind came the graceful pyramid of wood and canvas, the three-masted clipper *Rigel*. She had shortened sail to keep position behind the plodding gunboat.

Valentine squinted his eyes against the glare of the sun. The light refracted off the armored glass of the bridge, glittering with spiderwebs of cracks from the bullets of last night's fight. Carrasca, the officer in charge of the prize crew, watched the *Thunderbolt*'s progress from the wing projecting out of the bridge deck over the ship's side, her black hair now untied and fluttering in the landward breeze like a pennant. She watched the course of the *Thunderbolt* as carefully as if she did not have a guide through the reefs protecting the port. The pirate at the wheel wore a sleeveless, cut-at-the-knees jumpsuit, his thick legs planted wide on the deck. The helmsman looked as if he spent time fighting tiller ropes, rather than the hydraulic rudder of the *Thunderbolt*.

"This reef is a bastard," the helmsman commented to Valentine. "The gap likes to silt up—many's the time I've heard a scrape going over it."

Valentine moved outside the enclosed wheelhouse and joined Carrasca on the starboard side. He looked down at the forward Grog deck, where the other surviving "loyal" hands of the *Thunderbolt* sat in an apathetic bunch under guard. They remained under the supervision of the chief petty officer, a frog-faced toady of the captain named Gilbert. The captain had never been found, dead or alive, and Worthington had been killed with the crew trying to load the main gun just below the bridge.

Valentine could still see the wine stain of his former wardroom mate's blood on the wooden planking. Somewhere to the rear, Ahn-Kha and the men who joined Valentine's fruitless attempt to take the ship were already scrubbing the decks clean after laying out the corpses in a neat row. By tradition they should be sewn up in their bedding, but the cloth was too valuable to waste in such a fashion. The fourteen men who had died last night would leave the world as naked as they came into it.

"Nice breeze," Valentine commented, watching Carrasca's wind-whipped hair. Had he reached out his arm, he could just have touched the longest strands.

"We call it the Doctor. It usually blows all day. Then there's the night wind off the island, it's called the Undertaker. It doesn't smell as good, but it'll keep you cool." Valentine enjoyed hearing her speak. There was something of the music of a Caribbean accent mixed with Hispanic pronunciation.

"Pretty view," Valentine said, applying it both to the woman and the island, though he kept his eyes on the bay. He was used to the coastlines of North America: flat expanses of beach, wood, and marsh. On Jamaica, the hills rose right out of the ocean like a green wall.

"Yes. You'll want a hat. The sun is strong, even this time of year."

"What's that big ship in the center?"

"She's the hospital. Once was the Royal Fleet Auxiliary *Argus*. She's been here my whole life; I was born in her. So were a lot of the men you see around here."

"How many people do you have?"

"A census isn't one of our priorities. There are the townspeople and plantation families proper. I'd guess around seven hundred or so. Then there are the ships' crews. You could add in the folks inland and along the coast, fishermen, and a few free spirits who come in with a hold full of grain or pork when it suits them. Oh, and the rum distillery. You might say that they're allies of ours, even if their product goes out on Kurian ships, as well. Maybe six thousand people could call Jay home."

"Jay? Does that refer to Commodore Jensen?"

She looked away from the ship's bow for the first time. "You've heard of him?"

"He's not the most popular man up north. They're starting to take Jayport seriously in the KZ."

"KZ?"

"Kurian Zone. My former employers."

"Ahh, I see. We call it Vampire Earth."

Valentine smiled, his first unforced smile in days. "Lurid."

"Saying the name is inaccurate?"

"I wish. Our maps show this island as Kurian controlled—Vampire Earth."

"Most of Jamaica is theirs—or his. We call him the Specter."

"Friendly terms?"

Her mouth writhed. "No. We're no lackeys of his. As long as we don't bother him, he leaves us alone. Better for us."

"Better for the Specter, too."

She crossed her arms, and looked him up and down. "Just like . . ." The sentiment trailed off. "Would you like to meet Commodore Jensen? I suppose he'll have to decide what to do with you and your men, in the end."

"I'd be grateful if you could arrange a meeting, if you think you can."

Her lips parted, revealing white teeth as she smiled. "I'm sure of it. I'm his granddaughter."

The ships docked and began to disembark wounded. Valentine said a quick good-bye to Post as attendants carried him and the other injured off and placed them on wheeled litters. The attendants then pushed the litters toward the hospital ship, which in proximity dwarfed even the bulky *Thunderbolt*.

Then the Jamaican soldiers, then prisoners, and finally sailors came down the gangway Valentine had last climbed a week ago in New Orleans.

Valentine, with nothing to do but wait, watched Jayport's inhabitants. They were for the most part black-skinned, long-limbed, and healthy looking. A messenger boy received a hollow wooden tube from an officer on the *Rigel* and sprinted off toward the shore like a runner in a relay race. He wondered which building held whatever passed for government headquarters among the low, whitewashed buildings clustered around the bay. Fishing shacks and a few hung nets dotted the beach.

Valentine felt the odd sensation of standing on a firm surface after days at sea. Some of the Grogs sat down hard, holding their heads in their hands at the motionless feel of terra firma. He enjoyed the brassy sunshine—the climatic changes still echoing from the cataclysm of 2022 that cut the amount of sunlight north of the tropics were not so noticeable in the central Caribbean. Farther down the dock, the "loyal" hands of the *Thunderbolt* squatted on the bare concrete surface, slapping at flies hardy enough to venture out this far from shore. Some glared in his direction, some looked to him plaintively, but most just contemplated their surroundings with a fatalism bred by a lifetime in the KZ.

Dockside idlers examined the *Thunderbolt* from behind a rope line that divided the captured ship's part of the dock from the landward extension, where a few armed men in white T-shirts and khaki shorts that looked more like school uniforms than police kept locals and new arrivals apart. Men bearing platters of fruit followed by graceful women with tall wooden tumblers of water were allowed past the line, and they began distributing the island's bounty to Valentine's men and prisoners alike.

"Enjoy, mon, enjoy!" said one, handing out bananas and halves of coconuts.

"No worries, mon! Spring water for now, maybe some rum later," added a woman, her voice bringing out the cadenced phrases more as if she were singing than speaking. She exchanged a few words and a smile with a dockhand, but Valentine could make no more out of it than he could Ahn-Kha's Grog patois.

One man leaned toward a guard's ear, pointed at Valentine, and spoke. A few others craned their necks, and Valentine wondered what sort of dockside rumors were already floating around about the fight on the *Thunderbolt*.

Valentine tasted his first fresh banana—he'd had banana bread and a pudding mix in New Orleans, and there was no comparison—and followed it with the meat and milk of a coconut. He strolled over to Ahn-Kha and the Grogs, who were learning to peel their fruit before eating it in imitation of the humans. A knot of the Chief's men crammed down the colorful fruit with Went and Torres.

"What do they have in mind for us, my David?" Ahn-Kha asked, scooping meat from his coconut shell with his strong, flexible lips.

"We're safe for now. It seems they give the royal treatment to prisoners. They'll try to recruit the captain's men, I suppose. They don't know which category we're in. We're not under guard, but I don't think those men at the rope gate will let us just wander into town."

"They left you your weapons. They locked the rest back up in the small-arms room. They are either very trusting or very confident," Ahn-Kha mused.

"Either suits me, for now. We're lucky to be alive, old horse."

"Your race needs to learn to greet every day with those thoughts."

"There's something kind of old-fashionedly formal about the way they've handled us. It's like we've stepped back three hundred years or so. Like letting me keep my guns: a captured officer used to be allowed to retain his sidearms in the days when wars were fought by gentlemen against other gentlemen. I'm half expecting an invitation to dinner, rather than an interrogation."

The invitation to dinner arrived two hours later, waking him from a shaded nap. Like humans, Grogs laugh to indicate amusement, so when a barefoot sprout of a boy in ragged white ducks and a straw hat arrived with a note from the commodore requesting Valentine's presence at the Governor's House for dinner, Ahn-Kha laughed loudly enough to send the flies fleeing in alarm. Carrasca arrived shortly thereafter with an escort, announcing that they were to be moved to more comfortable quarters. They formed up behind her, and the procession of visitors walked the pier toward town.

The wide pier reminded Valentine of an etching of London Bridge he'd seen long ago in a book. Crowded with buildings at the landward end, so much so that it resembled a narrow street for the last hundred yards before it reached the shore, the walkway was where goods from land and sea traded owners. Two-story buildings, making up in floors what they lacked in width and depth, overhung both the street to the inside and the water to the outside, creating a shaded corridor leading toward the town proper. Carrasca explained that the twentieth-century dock was one of the best-built foundations in the bay, an important consideration on an earthquake-prone island. Valentine's men and their baggage were placed in a series of rooms above a clothing-reclamation shop, next to an empty storage room that would accommodate Ahn-Kha's Grogs. The prisoners from the *Thunderbolt* were placed alongside the dock in a permanently moored ship, where Carrasca assured him they would be well looked after. Valentine asked to see the wounded who'd been taken to the hospital ship, and Carrasca wrote him a note that would get him on board. He and his men were free to move about the pier as they wished.

"But you might not want to be too visible," she warned. "A lot of characters come into port. We're sure we get spies sent by the Kurians now and then. Once a small fishing ship blew itself up at the pier— perhaps you noticed the big patched-up crack. We depend on trade too much to deny access to the pier to strangers. But even men such as you whom we assume to be friends are not allowed in town, and are searched before going on board the *Argus*."

Of all the choices Valentine had faced in the last twenty-four hours, the most unexpected was deciding what to wear to dinner at the Governor's House. With the message he had in mind to say to the commodore, he preferred looking like an ally rather than a castaway. Going in his full Coastal Marines uniform would be inappropriate—he no more represented the Kurian Order than the Zulu nation. Lacking anything else presentable, he wore his tailored uniform trousers and good boots, topping it with a simple white shirt. He washed and combed out his thick black hair and drew it back into a tight pigtail. Torres completed the ensemble with the loan of a short black jacket and a strange combination of sash and cummerbund, an item common to what passed for aristocracy in his native part of Texas. Valentine's long arms dangled from the sleeves of the jacket, but he at least looked properly dressed.

One of the ubiquitous messenger boys—this one had shoes on his feet—arrived at the rooms to escort him off the dock as the sun went down. The breeze had reversed itself with the cooling of the land. What had Carrasca called it? The Undertaker. It smelled of the decay on the seashore rather than the clean ocean.

The boy led him past another watchman's post on the dock and into the first of Jayport's streets. An open carriage rocked back and forth on a heavily patched turnaround at the base of the pier; a single horse shifted impatiently in the traces before an elderly driver. The old man's white hair and whiskers framed a round black face; he gave Valentine a look more like that of a suspicious police officer rather than a taxi driver.

Carrasca waited for him in the carriage, wearing a neat blue uniform tunic with her hair in a tight bun at the back of her head. Oddly, the uniform made her even more feminine, thanks to her wide, dark eyes and portrait-perfect face. The thought crossed his mind that perhaps Carrasca—or the commodore—wanted to make as good an impression on him, mirroring his own efforts in securing proper attire.

Valentine assumed the attitude of one who took her presence there, in a cushioned and polished carriage, as if it were the most natural thing in the world.

"Good evening, Lieutenant," he said with a perfunctory bow that seemed to suit the occasion. "Does this mean you are doing me the honor of being my escort to dinner tonight?"

"Thank you, Mr. Valentine. My duties on your former ship were such that I could be spared for an evening." She opened the tiny door to the carriage, and Valentine primly took the seat opposite her. The corner of her mouth flickered up, and he answered with a raised eyebrow that dissolved their playacting pretenses. She giggled and he snorted.

The driver called out a low "move on," and the carriage lurched into motion as the horse started off at a brisk walk, iron-rimmed tires squealing on the mix of cobblestone and tar.

"Actually, Valentine, your presence is a bit of a coup for me. For a people whose ships travel a thousand miles in every direction, you'd be surprised how cut off we feel out here. We get shortwave contact sometimes, but it's usually passive—we've been burned a couple times by talking over the radio. The only people we really trust now are the Dutchmen to the south."

He could smell her now, a mixture of soap, a coconut-scented lotion, and a hint of perfume blending with the warmer female scent escaping out the collar of her uniform. The animal in him wanted to tear open the tunic, pull her head aside, and let his lips explore her neck, his hands those round, high breasts beneath. . . .

Madness. He regained control of his thoughts, crated up his lust, nailed it down, and padlocked urges too long sublimated.

"Please call me David. We're both off duty, aren't we?"

Her pupils narrowed for a second, then widened again. "Maybe. You may call me Malia, if you like."

Valentine liked. "Gladly, Malia. So the commodore wants an inter-view?"

"He's always eager for news from the north. The people we pick up know less about the real story than we do."

"I might disappoint him," Valentine said. "I've been . . . I suppose you'd call it 'undercover' for about a year. My only current information is what the Kur are up to on the Coast between Florida and Texas. I'm sure it will be useful to him, but if he needs current news about events farther in than that, I'll be a dry well. Since I'm part of your triumph tonight, maybe you can tell me more about how you managed your am-bush so well."

She shrugged. "I had little to do with it. Your captain's mission wasn't a secret, though if you ask me, they sent out too small a force even if everything went right. This town has grown in the last few years, grown a lot. It's funny how word of a haven gets around—we have mari-ners showing up from all points of the compass looking for shelter. We've even started another settlement farther along the coast at Port Maria to help accommodate the newcomers."

"Jamaica can provide for you all?" He looked at the few wanderers on the main street. The Jamaicans made up for the drab streets and whitewashed buildings by dressing in brightly dyed colors: deep reds, brilliant yellows, and heavy purples.

"Rich soil and richer waters." She waved to a young couple out for a stroll. "But back to your ship. Your captain did not keep his mission a secret. We have a spy or two in most of the major ports on the Vampire Earth. They tell us when something worthwhile is shipping for the most part, but we heard about your—or *their,* I mean—plans while you were still outfitting. Just because the *Thunderbolt*'s gun could sink anything we have afloat didn't mean we couldn't do something about you at sea. One of our cutters kept watch at the mouth of the Mississippi, waiting for you to come out, and then it raised every sail when it saw you, and beat you here by two full days. A coastwatcher told us of your landfall by radio. We need to keep an eye on Montego Bay and the west end of the island all the time as it is.

"We knew you were moving up the coast, so we went out to meet you on it. I had a motorboat full of men, cut low, it would be hard to see. We were heading out for you from the time the moon went down. When we heard the shooting and saw the gun flashes, Captain Utari brought the *Rigel* out and put the extra men in the boats. Your captain was foolish to hug the coast like that."

"No one was expecting you to come after us. It turned out for the best. Or at least, I hope it will. I need the ship, Malia."

"I can't imagine what your Southern Command would do with a gunboat, other than sink it trying to get it back up the Mississippi. I promise you we will make better use of it. You have enough problems, judging from the shortwave we get."

"What's that?"

"Battles, shortages. It seems that nothing but bad news ever comes from the north."

"We're still standing. That's something. So you made for the *Thunderbolt* when the firing started?"

"Yes. We expected it to be a lot worse. We had an inflatable boat full of explosive we were going to use as a last resort. All the confusion you caused made the difference; otherwise, I expect it would have been a lot bloodier."

"It was bloody enough," Valentine said. "If it weren't for you and Captain Utari, I doubt I'd even be alive now. I'm in your debt."

Her voice turned colder than any winter Jamaica had ever seen. "Then pay us back by leaving us alone. We do not need more trouble from Vampire Earth. We have problems enough."

The carriage moved up a slope, clusters of white buildings giving way to trees and lush ferns. Valentine smelled the rich aroma of green growing things all around and felt newly invigorated in the cooler night air. "Aren't you afraid some cruiser is going to show up and get your town under its guns?"

"We're pretty sure they do not bother with big warships. Our worry has always been a strong landing force. We've also heard rumors about some kind of Grog that takes to the water—that's one of the reasons you saw armed men on the docks. It's well for us the vampires don't organize themselves properly."

"It's their weakness," Valentine agreed. "They're about as coopera-tive as a cave full of rabid rats. They can't see past the next infusion of aura."

"Aura?"

"Do you call it something else here? It's what the Kurian Lords live off. Kind of an energy created by sentient beings. No, strike that—it's generated by anything that lives, but it's just hundreds of times richer when it's created by an intelligent being."

"I thought they drank blood," she said, puzzled.

"Their Reapers do, but the Reapers are just puppets, walking and talking tools for the dirty work of killing. There's some kind of mental link between the Kurian Master and his Reapers. The Reaper feeds itself off the blood, yes, but its Lord gets the energy we call 'vital aura.' Either way, your calling it vampirism is correct, even if it sounds kind of . . . poetic."

"Not a pleasant subject for conversation on such a beautiful night, David. We're almost there."

There emerged out of the palms and night. The Governor's House turned out to be a substantial building constructed on a flat prominence jutting from the steep hill, or small mountain, just west of the town. Behind it, somewhere in the forest, the wooden wall wound down from a watchtower at the top of the hill. The building itself was fashioned of cut and whitewashed stone with a red clay roof, reminding Valentine of an old Spanish mission he'd seen on the Texas coast. The driver waved to a pair of white-shirted police at the entrance to a flowered courtyard and wheeled the carriage around a fountain in the center of the circular drive. The horse seemed to know the routine better than the driver, and it stopped before the door at the tiniest murmur.

"Thank you, Jason," Carrasca said, patting the driver on the shoulder. "We will be several hours, so be sure to have your dinner."

"I'll see to the horse first, but thank you, miss."

Valentine stepped out of the carriage, and held the door open for his escort. "Miss?" he asked, as the driver moved off.

"Jason taught me to ride and drive. I grew up here. He's as much of a fixture of the place as the commodore. His father saved my grandfather's life way back when. He's a bit of everything: bodyguard, driver, interpreter. He knocked together my first boat, a little clinker-built toy I learned to sail. He also made that," she said, pointing to a flag that fluttered from a corner bell tower on the building, built to cover the door as well as the road coming up the hillside from the sea. "It's dark so you can't see it. Our flag is half blue and half green, with a sun in the center, kind of like the old French sun-king design. Do flags mean anything anymore?"

"Flags? They're not much used up North. Maybe nobody in the Free Territory could figure out what color represents survival. I'll have to have a look when it's lighter."

Valentine's night vision could pick up the emblem, even if the colors were muted, but he said nothing. The physical gifts of the Life-weavers aroused suspicion in some people, as if he were no longer human. To this woman at least, he wanted to be a man rather than some kind of curiosity.

He sometimes wondered what exactly the Lifeweavers did to their human creations. The nearest thing he could compare it to in human experience was puberty, a sudden shift into an entirely new body type, complete with changed abilities and desires. Would any of it be passed on? His own father had been one of the Lifeweaver's elite, but apart from a remarkably healthy childhood—despite several bad falls, he had never broken a bone, nor could he remember a serious illness—he had not been the most athletic of the young men growing up around him. Only his ability to sense the presence of a Reaper, as a cold shadow appearing on the fringes of his consciousness, distinguished him from the others in the Lifeweavers' service.

"Mr. Valentine?" Carrasca said, calling him back to the present from his contemplation of Jamaica's night sky.

"Sorry, my mind wandered," he said, turning to the door she held open for him.

"That's the only way it ever finds anything," she said, following him into the wood-paneled entry hall.

A boy took them down the hall to another plant-filled courtyard. Valentine paused at the tile surrounding the door at the other side. Each piece had been painted with delicate tropical blossoms.

"Beautiful," he said.

Carrasca turned. Her eyes arced up and across the span of tiles around the portal. She looked oddly wistful. "You like them? That's my work. I spent a few years obsessively painting. When I was a teen."

"I was an obsessive reader. I was—"

He had started to talk about his parents, his brother and sister, but stopped himself. He needed to watch his mood tonight.

She took a step closer, lowered her voice. "Orphaned? I know."

"Same with you?"

"The same."

Valentine read the hurt as if he were looking in a mirror. He extended the crook of his elbow, and she took his arm. "What can you do?"

She gave him a gentle squeeze with her forearm. "Go to sea. That's what finally worked for me. But let's change the subject. Tonight's a state dinner."

And they passed down a hall to a dining room. The furniture in the Governor's House, richly covered and well carved, did not match—the collection was perhaps pieced together from various recovered antiques on the island.

The man standing in the dining room did not match the elegant furniture either: a stumpy, tanned man bristling with energy and heavy white sideburns. The latter first traveled down his jaw, then turned up to join his mustache. He was broadly, powerfully built, and stood with the ready stance of a judo sensei. Perhaps because of the thickness of his chest, his arms seemed stunted by comparison, dangling afterthoughts on his barrel frame like the forelegs on a *Tyrannosaurus rex*. He stood beside a sideboard, over which a hand-inked map of Jamaica hung in a gilded frame. Behind him, pairs of French doors opened out onto a balcony filled with fragrant white jasmines and red ixoras. According to Carrasca's account, her grandfather had served as an officer in the Old World's Royal Navy, which had to put him close to his seventies.

"Sixty-eight, my son, sixty-eight," he said, turning to the young people. He slapped his broad belly, the gesture cracking like a pistol shot in the enclosed room. The expanse of stomach, which hung out from a gaily colored shirt over suspendered canvas trousers, did not ripple from the impact, demonstrating still-firm muscle beneath. "Everyone always wonders that when they see me, but are too polite to bring it up. Thought I'd save you the trouble. Am I right, Leftenant?" he asked, buttoning his shirt to preserve some formality at the meeting.

"And they always guess 'not a day over fifty,' sir," she said, suddenly transformed into a young girl amused at her grandfather's antics.

"The next question, at least to any young man who sees the two of us together, is where did she get her height and her looks?" Jensen said, apparently reading Valentine's mind again. "Maria—my daughter—was even shorter than I was, may she rest in peace. It's her father's doing. Tall, handsome Cuban man he was, hair like yours—Mr., Mr.—"

"Valentine," Carrasca supplied.

"That's the problem with age, my son, and it's a real bugger. What happened thirty years ago is bright as the island's sun, but what you talked about just this morning disappears into a fog. But there was more to Eduardo than looks. As brave and as sharp as they come. Also dead, by the way. Should fair fortune be with you and you see long service, Valentine, you'll see too many of the best ones die."

Valentine's memory, always too ready to parade the faces of the women and men he had known and lost, rose to the occasion. Jensen gathered as much from the expression on his guest, and he changed the subject.

"Let's eat, the cold dishes are already served," the commodore said, moving to a chair. "Come down by me, you two, no sense shouting at each other over twelve feet of table. That American President Eisenhower used to take dignitaries out on his back porch and talk to them, said he 'got a better measure of the man' or some such. I do the same thing over the dinner table. Cook tells me the chicken turned out well, and no one does a glazed ham like he does. Cook!" Jensen bellowed through the wall. "We're ready when you are."

By the time they were seated, one of the picture-frame-like carved panels on the wall opened, and the sweating cook appeared with a tray. He began to arrange dishes before the three: chicken swimming in orange sauce, some kind of peppery-smelling stew, corn and potatoes surgically carved and neatly arranged. A second man followed, bearing a thick ham glazed with slices of pineapple and something that looked like black cherries.

The three began to help each other to servings from the varied dishes, as the cook poured wine into glass goblets, the only matching dinnerware on the table.

"Captain Utari doesn't know what he's missing. I invited him, but then he hates this sort of thing. There's no sailor like him, but he refuses to do anything with shoes on, or eat anything that can't be bitten off the tip of his knife. Or maybe he just has a superior sense for the ridiculous. But as I'm fond of saying, this Port wasn't just founded to preserve life, but to—"

"—preserve a way of life," Carrasca finished, reaching across the table to pat the commodore's hand.

Valentine sipped lightly from the wine.

"Don't like it? It's a bit harsh, I know, but I get tired of rum and brandy," Jensen apologized. "Jamaica's a second Eden as far as I'm concerned, except for the wine. Don't know enough about it to tell you why. Years ago we had some pretty fair stuff from the old hotels and resorts, but it's been used up over time."

"I wouldn't know. Haven't had many chances to drink it. What I've had has been from dandelions or blackberries. This is rather good—in comparison."

They spent a few minutes eating under the anxious eye of the cook. He hovered like a teacher watching his pupils take a make-or-break exam. Valentine, who usually disliked the feeling of having too much of anything: alcohol, food, or even leisure, ate heartily until he heard his innards groan in discomfort.

Valentine raised his glass. "May I offer a toast? To the bounty of Jamaica, my hosts, and especially to the author of the best dinner I've had in years," he said, dipping the goblet in the cook's direction.

"I second the motion," Carrasca said, eyes reflecting flickers of the candlelit room.

"Hear hear," added the commodore through a full mouth.

Fresh fruits and a sweet, milky pudding identified as flan finished the meal. The commodore enjoyed a private dessert, a toasted marrow bone. He went to work on the contents with a miniature fork, and Carrasca turned to him expectantly.

"Young man," Jensen began, sucking unabashedly at the bone, "my granddaughter tells me you tried to take the gunboat."

"Had matters taken a better turn, we would have gone straight to Haiti."

"Valentine, there's nothing on Hispaniola but death. Are you looking for allies in the islands? You wouldn't find any on Haiti who'll help you up north. They have miseries enough."

"Or here," Carrasca said, her eyes turning hard. "We had a group of you Freeholders arrive before, when I was sixteen. Marched them through town and everyone cheered. They gave us lots of talk about guerrilla cadres and hit-and-run raids. Uniting the different parts of the island to go after Kingston. All they managed to do was get some of our inland people killed and a lot of families on the other side of the Blue Mountains hanged. There wasn't any cheering when they left. If you think the people of Jayport—"

"Nothing like that," Valentine said, startled at her sudden turn in temper. "I'm looking for a weapon, not allies. I'm not asking you or anyone to fight Reapers."

"Malia," her grandfather said, "the reprisals weren't Mr. Valentine's fault any more than they were Major Hawthorne's.

"Forgive my granddaughter," Jensen added, turning to Valentine. "After the aborted uprising, they wiped out one of our settlements up in the mountains. That's where her mother died," he said, clamping his mouth firmly shut and looking at Carrasca. "My great mistake."

"Not yours, Granddad," she said. "You saw the uniforms, counted the guns, heard Hawthorne's promises. Believed in him. He knew the kind of words to use. Even on Mum. She was a widow, Mr. Valentine, and—"

"Let's not bore our guest with family business," Jensen said. He looked at his granddaughter for a moment, as if trying to summon her mother's features from Carrasca's shapely face, then turned back to Valentine. "You need that ship you were on, the gunboat, to get this weapon?"

"Get it and get it back to the mainland. We needed something big enough to carry it, a ship that could anchor off the coast long enough for me to find it and load it, then be able to go back unchallenged. The *Thunderbolt* is as large as they come in the Caribbean these days."

"You're wrong," Jensen said. "The Dutchmen down south have an old cruiser still working, God knows how. I think it used to be an American ship, too. It could blow the *Thunderbolt* in half, but the Dutchmen are on our side. In fact, I was planning on feeding your gunboat with their diesel fuel."

"Was?" Valentine said, sensing an opening.

"Mr. Valentine, I'm looking for a weapon, too. We are growing here. It's getting harder and harder to support the people we have. Always more coming in, not always the sort we need, but still mouths to feed. I've never been much good at turning needy people away. The best land, at least for planting, is on the south half of the island. It's not just my people I worry about; it's my ships, as well. This harbor is worthless in a real storm. But if I could get old Kingston, take it somehow from the Specter—that's what we call that trumped-up devil running things there—a lot of our problems would be solved. A real harbor with a real shipyard, though it's run to ruin like everything else, would mean a lot to us. Just that every time I've tried"—he nodded in his granddaughter's direction—"it's gone wrong."

Jensen stood and went to the map of Jamaica above the sideboard. He extended one of his short, thick arms and pointed to the coastline.

"The Specter has it pretty good. He's about as secure in his position as he could be. Lives on a sort of estate, in a castle, no less." Jensen pointed at a black square just off a crescent-shaped bay on the southern coast, west of Kingston. "They say he sometimes appears on the walls, to watch the women work his fields or see a new wagonload of the condemned come up the road, bound for the killing hole."

Just right for a Kurian, Valentine thought.

"He's jealous of his lands, always worried about another of his kind moving in. He has his Black Guard—that's those Reapers you call 'em—and he keeps a good-sized regiment of Asians to keep the rest of the Jamaicans down. Those are the Horsed Police. Then the Chinese and Indians in turn run the Public Police—more thugs, mostly a rabble, that organize the farms and labor using the hard end of a club. Same old game: elevate an ethnic minority to a position of privilege that said minority knows will disappear if the ruler does, then give a lot of brutes a little power. He's got informants everywhere . . . even within my palisade, I expect. Kind of reminds me of a web with a fat spider sitting in the center of it, sensitive to vibrations at the edges. We try to enter the web, we get stuck, there's just not enough of us to get to him, even with the guns we've been stealing and stockpiling. Years before

Major Hawthorne arrived, my son-in-law once tried to recruit some of the gangs in the mountains, but they killed Eduardo for his trouble. We can do what we want in the water around Jamaica, but that doesn't do much for us. He can get everything he needs from the land and the southern shoreline and the occasional armed trade ship. About all we've managed to do is keep his brothers and sisters from showing up to run other parts of the island, like maybe ours on the north coast or the Cockpit Country in the west."

"I suppose he never leaves that castle," Valentine said, looking at the scale of the map.

"We've never heard of it, if he has," Carrasca said.

"That's usual for a Kurian. Their Reapers act as eyes and ears. No need to risk venturing out," Valentine said. "They stay in their holes with just their servant or two ever seeing them. Immortality turns you into a recluse, evidently."

But this one likes to have a look around, now and then. Is he too secure for his own good?

Now that he knew more about the island's situation, he saw the chance of an answer. Maybe not even a chance, maybe more of a prayer. "Sir, I'll take your analogy about the web one step further." Valentine felt his skin flush, not from the wine, but from his quickening pulse.

"Don't let me stop you. I'm listening."

"His organization also has the weakness of a spider's web."

"What's that?"

"If you kill the spider, the web falls apart in a matter of days."

Even Cook paused and looked at Valentine.

"My son, I would say it is impossible," Jensen finally said. "The Specter lives in a bloody fortress, a real rock castle. It's about as old as the British flag on this island, and he's got it fixed up. Word is he stays in some cave beneath it. A dozen or so years ago, some of the Jamaicans on the other side got the same idea as you. Thirty of them swore a blood oath: they'd kill him or they'd die trying. They'd managed to get a key to a back door, thought they'd sneak in and do him in. They got together a few guns—the rest had fishing spears and machetes. Two of those Black Guard Reapers caught them on the approaches, and they died, to a man. Of course, the Special Police tried to round up their families, but I'll say this for the Jamaicans: they know how to keep a secret better than anyone I've ever heard of. Offers, bribes, even using torture they got only a name or two, and still there was enough of a delay for their children to head for the bush. Captain Utari lost his older brother in the attempt, by the way. That's how we ended up with him in our orphanage."

"Then what did you mean, you *would* say it is impossible?"

Jensen looked at Cook, suddenly uncomfortable. "This is going to sound like utter bollocks, Valentine, but I want to tell you, nevertheless. There's a woman living inland the Jamaicans go to for advice. Sort of a witch, she is, at least to them. They call her Obay. Over six feet tall, and they say she has four breasts. According to the stories, she once suckled four infants at once, her top two breasts thrown over her shoulders to two tied to her back, and then two to the front, and they grew up to be the four great headmen of the free inlanders. They really exist, by the way, they're known as the four Kernels, though I suspect what they really mean are Colonels. She holds festivals at the solstices and equinoxes, when they go to her for predictions. An oracle she may be, I'm thinking now," he paused, perhaps for dramatic effect, but more likely out of embarrassment. "At the last one in December, she said a man would come from the sea, a Crying Man. This man would rid the land of the Specter."

Valentine reached up to his face, and felt the old scar moving up from his chin to the level of his eye.

"I forget the rest," Jensen said. "How did it go, Cook?"

The cook cleared his throat. "The Crying Man would bring a storm in flesh, and a storm in metal. His eyes would see to the end of a long straight path, and at this path's end would come our salvation."

"What was your ship called, the *Thunderbolt*?" the commodore asked. "Thunderstorm? Thunder in metal?"

"Yes," Valentine said. "But the rest is a leap. I might be able to do it, but not because of an oracle. I have certain . . . abilities . . . that the Jamaicans who tried before lacked. To do the job, I'll need the ship back, on loan for a short cruise round the island. If I can get rid of the Specter, break his hold on the island, would you return the ship and crew to take me to Haiti and back to the coast? Afterwards you could keep her. I'm sure you'd find her useful."

"Valentine," Jensen said. "If you can do this, I'll give you the ship and a team of men who'd sail with you across hell's lava ocean in a powderhulk, no fear."

"That's what I'm counting on. No fear."

The party broke up after midnight. It turned out Jensen was a fan of mah-jongg, and he insisted on teaching Valentine. The driver from the carriage, now formally introduced as Jason Lisi, joined them to make the fourth. After the pieces were distributed, Jensen started telling Lisi Valentine's idea to oust the Specter. Valentine had to force his brain to do double duty as he explained his plan to Lisi while learning how to match up his tiles, when to call *kung,* and when a hand was over. Valentine asked about the depths in the waters off the southern coast of the island while keeping the ancient box-top from the mah-jongg set ready to remind himself what the bamboos and characters and flowers and so on were worth. He had a feeling that convincing the commodore to commit to his plan somehow rode on his ability to play the old Chinese game—easy enough to learn but difficult to play well.

He lost.

The experience left him drained. Jensen caught him rubbing his eyes and suggested that the party break up. "I'll think it over while I sleep," he promised Valentine. Valentine then accepted an invitation to stay in a guest bedroom.

The bedrooms all opened on the same balcony as the dining room. All had similar French doors open, inviting the soft night air. Valentine's room held the same cluttered hodgepodge of antiques—only the ticking on the mattress looked new. He found an old laminated "guest services menu" inside a nightstand drawer and relaxed, imagining the luxuries of a bygone age. Jasmine perfumed the air. What sort of assignations had transpired in the days when the Residence was just another luxurious rental property on Jamaica's sunny coast? He hung up his cumberbund and short jacket and tried to relax in bed, but his mind wouldn't let him sleep. He went out onto the balcony, barefoot on the cool concrete, and looked down at the moored hospital ship, the smaller *Thunderbolt,* and the town of Jayport.

Light still fell out the doorway from the dining room, though less than when they'd been shuffling tiles under the chandelier. Perhaps the commodore was an insomniac. Valentine walked softly to the edge of the light.

It was Carrasca, with her thick hair released from its confinement. She still had the mah-jongg tiles out, arranged in a three-tiered pile that looked like a Japanese castle. She tapped two of the tiles together as she stared at the arrangement, her lower lip thrust out in thought, a half-filled glass of wine on the table. Her wide-lapeled jacket hung on the back of her chair, and she'd partially unbuttoned her shirt. Valentine saw now that the shirt was far too big for her. Perhaps it had belonged to her father.

Valentine cleared his throat.

Carrasca glanced out the open doors. Then she jumped in her chair with a shocked gasp. Mah-jongg pieces skittered across the dinner table.

"Sorry to sneak up on you," Valentine said. He took a step into the light.

"Mother of— You frightened me."

Valentine noticed her arms were goose pimpled. "I'm sorry. Wrong of me to creep around my hosts' house."

"No, not that. Your eyes." She rattled out the words stacatto.

"My eyes?"

She shivered again. "They were—glowing."

Perfect. You're the wolfman to her now, Ghost. "Glowing?"

"Like an animal's at night, a cat's. Sort of orange yellow. I've never seen a man's eyes do that."

"Maybe they caught the light just right."

"Maybe. Maybe my imagination, too. Long day," she said, her words returning to their usual genteel pace.

"Sorry about your stack. What were you doing?"

"You can play mah-jongg solitare, too. You take the chips out of the bag and stack them in a certain way. The trick is to not look at the ones on the lower levels as you put it together. Then you pull them off in matching pairs."

"Didn't get enough after dinner?"

"I couldn't sleep. It relaxes me. My mind had too much to work on. This is like counting sheep."

"I'm sorry your parents came up in the conversation."

Some of the warmth that had been in her eyes earlier in the evening returned. "No. Oh, no, it wasn't that. You see, my grandfather talked to Captain Utari earlier. The commodore decided to let me captain the *Thunderbolt*. My first real command."

She led him out onto the balcony, and they looked down into the bay. The *Thunderbolt* looked like a toy ship.

"You're lucky Utari didn't want her."

She smiled. "He hates anything without a sail. Says there's no seamanship in engines."

"But you don't feel that way."

"You don't know sailors, David. My first real ship. My first command. I loved her even as we limped into the harbor." The light trickling out of the dining room played across her dusky features. "I can't wait to put her to sea again. She's the most beautiful thing I've ever seen."

Valentine could have said the same about the *Thunderbolt*'s new commander. He would have, if there hadn't been a hint of anxiety in her eyes as she met his gaze, wary against the return of that inhuman glow.

Five

The Specter's Lands: From the jagged course of Jamaica's Southern Shore to the spine of the Blue Mountains, the Specter's domain casts its invisible shadow over this sunny land. The Jamaicans somehow know when they walk within his borders; they grow nervous and sullen. No great wonder, for they have been returned to the slavery of three centuries ago. They work tiny plots of cultivated ground that form islands amongst the riotous growth of returned wild trees and grasslands. Viewed from a buzzard's eye high above, the topography resembles that of a tangle of grapevines, dollops of tended lands connected by one or two main roads. Smaller trails cut through patches of forest, with the vine's principal stalks growing out of what used to be Kingston. A few swaths cut in the red earth of the hills at the bauxite mines yield the makings of aluminum. This export is shipped north and west in return for the few technological necessities the Specter needs to maintain his control.

Slave labor, carried out at a dead slow pace, tends the fields in this, one of the most backwards and ill-governed of the multitude of Kurian Principalities. Organization is nil. Construction is moribund, maintenance haphazard. Technology, with the exception of the bauxite mines (under rust-streaked signs with the word JAMALCO *sometimes still visible) and the guns in the hands of the Specter's Chinese Quislings, has slipped back into a stage somewhere between the Neolithic implements of the Arakawa Indians and the eighteenth century. It is not unusual to see the land worked by stone tools, before the slaves go home to rude huts lit by charcoal fires. The Jamaicans have resorted to an atavistic belief system filled with good-luck charms, incantations, and totemism to keep the Reapers from the door. Rocks or coral painted with designs in chicken blood can be seen on some doorsteps, below patterned threads of beads that sway in every window. Some families never eat after noon, in the not unreasonable belief that an empty belly makes the body less visible to the Reapers' senses. The Reapers, in the manner of wild predators, usually pick off the aged, the sick, or the few who try to flee. The Specter's cloaked avatars often lurk on the beaches and borders, taking those who try to escape over the mountains or into the cockpit country of the Northwest.*

While the Reapers isolate and then kill individual troublemakers, any sort of mass disturbance is a matter for the Horsed Police and Public Police. With their intimidating combination of horses, dogs, guns, and clubs, the Specter uses them in one of the oldest tricks in the tyrant's playbook: that of keeping one race under control by using another. The Horsed Police are of mixed ethnicity: Chinese Jamaican and Indian Jamaican predominating. They control the more numerous but less disciplined members of the Public Police, little more than baton-waving bands of thugs, but effective enough in controlling the workers on their plantations. The great privilege of the Public Police is being allowed to use small boats to claim the cod, rock beauties, and parrotfish from the surrounding waters, though their better-fed families suffer nearly as much from the Reapers as the ordinary Jamaicans who work the crops and mines.

The Specter rests at the apex of this pyramid of power and fear, an engorged demigod swollen on the rich life aura of the island's fecund people. Cunning as a grave robber, for forty years he has jealously guarded his island paradise, turning down overtures of fellow Kurian Princes to join him on the island, and one attempt to wrest it from him by force. From a European-style castle overlooking a wide bay he feeds off one of the first discoveries of the New World as a maggot feeds off a corpse, decomposing anything he touches like a necroptic King Midas. With only the irritation of pirates to the north and a few scattered gangs in the mountains, hardly enough to threaten him even in the unlikely event that they united, one could wonder if he would have given the news that there was a Cat on the island much thought, so secure is he in his habits, behind his walls guarded by a thousand guns and the ferocious teeth of his Reapers.

It took all of three days for David Valentine to cross a 1,200-yard field. In fairness, the first day hardly counted: it had been spent survey-ing the estate's lands. The more rugged ground sloping down toward the bay turned into fields and orchards closer to the castle. A road servicing the Kurian's home wandered westward along the coast and eastward toward a settlement centered in the ruins of a beautiful Colonial Spanish square. The immediate lands beyond the castle's pebble-colored faces were filled with tobacco fields, stretching out from the walls like a green carpet. The distinctive odor tickled his sensitive nostrils as he allowed his nose a moment's play in the air from his perch in a palm. He had surveyed farms with staple crops, fruit trees, and livestock, but this was the first tobacco field he had seen since being dropped off by Utari's fast-sailing sloop.

The first order of business was to get a feel for the rhythms of the castle's lands, filling in gaps in the knowledge of local spies.

The Specter relied on his Reapers to guard the castle and the tobacco fields at night; Valentine had made sure of that after the second day's observation. Ordinary Jamaicans avoided the acres around the castle as if the air were toxic. Women dressed in neat cotton smocks or heavy black dresses worked the Specter's personal fields and orchards as their children played amongst the crops. Valentine guessed by the quality of their clothing and shoes that they were families of his Horsed Police. They worked in a curiously lackadaisical, though not disorganized, manner. Valentine had seen many fields where the people under the Kurian thumb worked with the maniacal intensity brought on by knowing that whoever turned in fewer bushels at the end of a season would go to the Reapers.

The Reapers, with their innate ability to sense human beings by the lifesign they projected, could spot anyone approaching the castle at night across the fields. Thus had the brave Jamaican band died the night they came to kill the Specter. The men might as well have approached the castle shooting off Roman candles. At night a cluster of humans could be marked miles away by a prowling Reaper. Even a lone man would show up in the empty fields as if a spotlight were shining on him from one of the four corner towers.

But Valentine was another matter. The Lifeweaver training of six years as a Hunter had taught him to shield his life-sign through mental discipline, a practice of shutting down parts of his mind until he became intent as a prowling cat, thinking only of the furtive scratching of the rat in the drainpipe ahead. Once in the proper mental state, it was as if a skeleton wearing his body were performing on a stage, marionetted by invisible strings from himself somewhere in a balcony above. Jamaica's tropical growth and abundant animal life generated its own form of lifesign, masked him from the prowling Reapers, and allowed him to remain at the edge of the fields in comparative safety.

He had another ability, equally useful but less explicable, even to the seemingly all-knowing Lifeweavers who had selected and trained him. Valentine could sense a nearby Reaper, mirroring its own ability to detect lifesign, though his own senses were far less precise than those of the vampiric Reapers. He once described the sensation to Alessa Duvalier as akin to "feeling where the sun is with your eyes shut." Though to be more accurate, it felt more like a cold presence in his mind, the creepy alarm that most people experience sometime in their lives when they wake up suddenly with the fear that someone is in their bedroom. The ability was unpredictable: sometimes he could sense a Reaper moving on a wooded slope a mile away, but other times walk over one sleeping in a basement below him with only a vague feeling of unease. In the absence of any authoritative opinion, he formed a theory that his ability had to do with the mental connection between the Reaper and its Master Kurian, but like most theories, it was probably half-right at best. Anecdotal evidence suggested there were others like him. Stories filtered in from elsewhere about other Hunters with the talent, but he had never met one and compared notes.

From the uncomfortable cradle of a palm tree, he spent the second night concentrating on lowering his lifesign and sensing the Reapers' movements. For what the sense was worth—and the more precise evidence of eyes, ears, and nose during his observation—he determined that the Specter loosed two Reapers to prowl his lands at night. One watched from the castle tower nearest the road. As would be expected, they retired with the dawn before the first women appeared on the road from the old colonial town.

He spent the third day in a long, agonizing crawl into the tobacco fields. Burdened by Ahn-Kha's oversize gun and decorated with some of the broad leaves cut from the crop, he inched through the fields at a speed a determined beetle could pace.

The crawl, punctuated by drowsy half-naps in the shadow of the tobacco stalks, gave him time to reflect on his plans. It was long past the point where he could change them, but his mind was nonetheless plagued with worries that he barred from his nighttime meditations.

What if the *Thunderbolt* was delayed in its journey? Her diesels were reliable but so ancient, a breakdown could not be discounted. How long could he stretch his two canteens, one now containing only a mouthful of water or two, in Jamaica's heat?

He might be able to hide his lifesign from Reapers, but he had seen lean brown dogs chasing and playing with the children as their families worked. Suppose one scented him and started barking? His cumbersome, single-shot Grog gun would be almost worthless in a running fight with the Horsed Police.

Could he get close enough to the castle so he could be sure of the leaf-sights on the rifle? Some unknown pirate of the commodore's command had looted the gun's telescopic lens, which would have allowed him to take advantage of its range. ("I'm sorry," Carrasca had said, "but any kind of optics are almost priceless here." A strict inquiry among the crew had yielded nothing but shrugs.)

He had spent two nights awake and taken only brief naps in the day. Suppose he fell asleep lying amongst the tobacco stalks on the most dangerous night of all? One vivid dream or a sudden awakening would reveal him to the patrolling Reapers, and that would be the end of him: even the toughest Bear would not challenge multiple Reapers alone at night.

Alone, with only fear to keep him company, he slithered beneath the tobacco leaves. He wished for the comfort of Ahn-Kha's presence. But Ahn-Kha was off to the east somewhere with his Grogs and some Jamaican friends of Captain Utari's, hiding from the comment their appearance would excite.

Post was resting in the old auxiliary hospital ship on the other side of the island, and the rest of his shipmates in the *Thunderbolt* were beyond the horizon. The Jamaicans could be trusted to keep secrets from the Police and the Specter's henchmen, but undoubtedly there were a few spies in the community. Suppose one should learn of their presence, and a hunt ensue?

Right now the Specter thought himself secure, but at the first word of a plot, he would retreat to his deepest hole guarded by the fury of a dozen Reapers, with his mounted men riding to his aid from every station for miles around. What then?

Valentine wanted to succeed, not just for the sake of regaining use of the *Thunderbolt*, but also for the aging commodore's hopes. There was more to his dream of a free Jamaica than space for his polyglot of buccaneers and refugees. A new freehold in the Caribbean in alliance with the Dutchmen to the south might mean much to the larger struggle.

His final plan had come to him only after hearing a description of the Specter's refuge.

"Some old British Empire mon build d' ting," Captain Utari explained, his cadence as rolling as the sea he traveled on, going on oral tradition and boyhood memory. "It 'twas like out of d' history book, high walls and towers at d' corner. For years 'twas empty, but de Specter, he brought it back and set it all up to his likin'. Dey say he do as much diggin' as buildin' an' it has basements an' catacombs beneath. You can see de ol' Devil at times, up on his balcony or the towers, watchin' us an' seein' to deem."

By *us* and *deem* the captain meant the Jamaicans and the Asian master caste the Specter had imposed upon them. On further inquiry, Valentine learned that the balcony faced the sea, looking out on a wide bay. The description transformed his vague idea into a plan. He talked it over, first with Ahn-Kha, and then with the Grog's refinements put a finished plan before the triumvirate of the commodore, Lisi, and Carrasca.

He stopped his crawl three-quarters of the way across the field. Any closer, and his view of the balcony would be disturbed. Captain Utari's description of the castle was accurate enough, though Valentine had always pictured medieval style castles as being much larger—he had seen pre-Kur houses nearly as big as this walled hold. But close up, he could see why the Specter chose this building for his lair. The towers, the narrow windows, the heavy stonework, even its grim, isolated location would appeal to a Kurian.

Nothing but the insects disturbed him during the long, drowsy day in the field. The sun sank, the stars emerged, and Valentine removed his mind from his body. Again the Reaper patrolled the edges of the fields as another stood in the tower, its head turning this way and that like a watchful owl. A curious fit of optics made the stars around the figure dimmer as Valentine stared, as if the thing were drawing the energy even from the twinkling star field. The Undertaker blew fitfully off the mountains, neither as strong nor as pleasant as its daytime sibling. An afternoon rain shower had left him cold and even more uncomfortable rather than refreshed, and the omnipresent flies and ants took their turns at disturbing his self-hypnosis.

Dawn approached, and a heavier rain set in, something Carrasca had assured him was almost unknown at this time of year. Valentine cursed the rain, the poor visibility, and Carrasca's meteorological acumen at dripping length. But with the sun, the clouds thinned and dissolved, fleeing in a burst of sky-flaming color.

The Reaper retreated with the growing light of dawn. Valentine, muscles aching, fought the urge to rise, to try to gain a view of the bay that would allow him to see if the *Thunderbolt* approached. Her blockish ugliness would be a comfort to him, and if things went badly—what the commodore called "tits up"—the gunboat's cannon could throw the coastline into enough confusion to allow him to escape.

The women on their way to their day's work in the fields saw her first. Valentine watched them point and chatter, suffusing a warm wave of relief through his clammy body. He pressed Ahn-Kha's gun to his shoulder and checked the slide of the sight for the umpteenth time.

The gun rested in an improvised bipod, a screwed-together contraption the Chief designed to help him with the weight of the gun. He had tied lengths of creeper to the barrel, careful not to obscure the foresight, over the dingy and green leather covering Ahn-Kha had sewn over the barrel. The gnarled, shillelagh-like stock was built for the Grog's larger frame, but Valentine padded the end with canvas stuffed with sawdust so it fit snugly into the crook of his arm. He opened the bolt and slid one of the .50-caliber bullets into the breech.

At this range, even firing upward, Ahn-Kha's shells would have a nearly flat trajectory. Valentine breathed slowly and deeply. He'd heard that the Kurians could sense lifesign as easily as their Reapers, but precise information was scanty. With the waxing dawn he knew that detection would grow even more difficult: sunlight interfered with whatever waves humans emitted. He tried not to wonder what was transpiring in the dark castle. No doubt some daytime sentry had alerted his officer, who would have a look, then perhaps pass the word of the *Thunderbolt*'s arrival to one of the Specter's retinue.

Valentine bet his life, so to speak, on the Kurian coming himself. The Specter would wonder what the *Thunderbolt*'s appearance portended. The Kur of New Orleans might have told him that their ship would be operating in his waters, but would he trust their word? She could mean the arrival of an ally in his on-again, off-again war with the pirates on the north coast, or an attempt by some other Kurian to supplant him and take the plentiful aura-fodder of the island.

By the plan, Carrasca was to bring the *Thunderbolt* into the bay and put troops into her boats. The Kurian would be eager to see, from his faraway vantage, whether the approaching men would behave as friends or foes.

The fortress came to life. Valentine watched two horsemen gallop out from behind the castle, one riding hard for the town, and the other turning on the road west. As the riders galloped away, hanging on to their mounts' manes, three torsos appeared on the tower. They changed from silhouettes to figures in the growing light. One held a box with a high antenna waving back and forth in the confused airs that preceded the Doctor's offshore breeze.

Valentine hardened his eyes as the figures went to the edge of the balcony. He sighted down the barrel with his own telescopic vision. The view sharpened, detail springing to life as his visual sense came at his will. The three figures became individual portraits. One was undoubtedly a Reaper, hood pulled well over its head to ward off the morning sun, another a rail-thin black figure, perhaps a Jamaican. Between those two, a fleshy, sagging form emerged. The first Kurian Valentine was to hunt reminded him of a Buddha in flesh instead of bronze. Though the Kurians, like their Lifeweaver brethren, could appear as

Eve's serpent or Abraham Lincoln if they wished. But this Kurian, for whatever reason, did not choose to put much effort into his human form. Hairless, with skin as gray as a corpse, it seemed to float to the balcony rather than walk. Valentine moved the rifle a fraction of an inch, putting the foresight squarely in the center of the Kurian's sagging chest. He placed his finger on the trigger and looked into the face of evil.

Valentine felt a shudder creep up his spine as their eyes met over the distance. The Kurian read him and his intent in a flash of thought. Valentine's mind clouded—he felt a rush of vertigo as if he were standing before an abyss. A kaleidoscope of color coalesced, filling his vision, a mental fog of chaos from which he would not return.

He squeezed the trigger as he felt his will fleeing. The recoil of the shot jarred his frame, startled him like a slap in the face, breaking the psychic link. As through a haze he saw a wound blossom at the Buddha statue's throat. The Specter's jaw dropped open in a silent, gaping scream even as the kick of the huge bullet flung it backwards, misting the back of the balcony with purplish fluid. But the disguise stayed. For a moment Valentine feared that even Ahn-Kha's bullet, big enough to drop an elephant, would not kill it, but then the head lolled. It sagged forward again, as if it were mounted on a rocking chair, and collapsed into something that looked like an umbrella with a bulbous octopus head at the top. Valentine heard a faint splat as it fell.

The Cat lay still, fighting the instinct to get up and flee. He knew his single shot would be hard to locate from any kind of distance. So he waited for the collapse he expected to begin.

The Kurian no longer animated the Reaper; the cloaked figure stalked the balcony to slay in animal panic. It seized the thin man by the throat, popping off the Jamaican's head even as its mouth sank against the neck. Blood fountained, sprinkling the Reaper, the rail, and the castle wall as the beast dragged its victim into the shadows.

While daylight lasted, Valentine had little to fear from the fiends now prowling the halls of the castle. With the link to the Kurian gone, the Reapers inside would mindlessly slay whoever remained behind the walls, and trouble no one until darkness came. Any Reapers wandering the lands of the Specter would probably do the same, grab a victim and retreat into a dark hole. Valentine felt a feral, id-tickling thrill at the thought of the fate of any of the Specter's Horsed Police sharing shelter with the vampires.

Eventually, and with proper organization, the masterless Reapers could be hunted and burned out of their holes. But that would have to come later.

He inched backwards among the tobacco plants. With chaos sitting in the Specter's throne, the Kurian's realm would totter and be ripe for the taking. It was time for him and Ahn-Kha to hasten its fall. As he crawled between the stalks, the freshly fed Reaper at the door to the balcony shielded its face from the morning sun and retreated into shadow.

"So this is the Crying Man."

If Obay was over six feet, it was by the width of an eyelash. Nor did she have four breasts. There was enough flesh beneath her woven robes—like Joseph's composed of many hues—on her to make it look as though she had an extra set. She had liver-spotted skin the color of milky tea and a crinkled forehead, with gray-black hair drawn back in tight braids. Obay walked with the help of two men—sons, Valentine soon learned—and a pair of canes.

The Specter had been dead for twenty-two hours, and his regime was melting away like ice in the Caribbean sun. Captain Utari had brought Valentine and Ahn-Kha to a trailside village with mountains blue green in the background, mottled by the shadows of clouds. Faint sounds of gunfire echoed from the direction of the main road to Kingston. Armed Jamaicans of every description, from a blue-eyed Scandinavian or two to glossy African, filled every piece of shade in the village. Most carried machetes and a smattering of old rifles. The smell of roasting pigs, horsemeat, and corn came from clay or brick ovens and oil drums used as barbecues. "Two of d' kernels bring d' men to Obay's call," Utari explained.

"Not enough. Not enough for the town I saw," Ahn-Kha said. He, the *Thunderbolt*'s Grogs, and Utari's men had been hidden on the outskirts of Kingston.

"More come every day. Don't forget our people, an' de city folks. We've waiteed for de day of liberation. When Obay make her promeese—"

"Her prediction, you mean?" Valentine cut in.

"A 'prediction' from Obay is a promeese, Cryin' Mon. You d' proof."

They went into a whitewashed brick house at the center of the village's only street, sixty or seventy feet of asphalt flanked by gravel roads. By the shaded windowlight Valentine met the Kernels under a brightly painted ceiling mural of crops and trees and birds and frogs. The owner of the house welcomed them with hugs before she and her family went back to bobbing before Obay. There was an oddly dressed retinue to either side of the oracle. One wore what looked to be the final remnants of a priest's vestments; the other had gold tassels and yellow braiding sewn to the shoulder of a sleeveless green dress army coat.

"Thank you, boys," Obay said, after recognizing Valentine. She extended a hand. Valentine shook it, touching a heavy ring on her fore-finger with a jewel the size of a pea.

He took another look, trying to read the script, as Ahn-Kha engulfed her hand in his long fingers.

"Yale. I would have been class of '23," Obay explained, sticking out her hand. The knuckles were enlarged with arthritis.

It was a pretty thing, but it looked like a man's. Valentine wasn't sure what to say, so he fell back on what his father used to ask the educated of the Old Order. "What did you study?"

"Pre-law. I buried the needle on my SATs."

"Essay T's?"

"S. A. Ts. Scholastic aptitude tests."

Valentine was flummoxed. "You had to do well on those to be allowed to learn? Sounds self-defeating."

"There's a long answer, but it's not important. Of course, it didn't hurt that my father was a vice president with General Mills. I started as a freshman with a major in Anthropology. Coddled rebellion. Then I got a taste of academics and college politics. I wised up by the end of my sophomore year. I switched to pre-law. With a history minor—I'd always enjoyed it, and you should take your share of fun those years."

"Never had the opportunity. Unless you count some classes at a shoestring war college. They didn't give out souvenirs."

Her sons helped her sit down on a bench. The assembly took their seats on chairs ringing the main room of the tiny house. Except for Ahn-Kha. The bench he tried let out such a groan that he shifted his buttocks forward to a comfortable squat with the bench as a backrest.

Obay looked down at her ring. "I was doing an internship in Boston when the Ravies hit. I ended up on a cleanup crew behind a guard unit. Loading bodies. Even martial law was breaking down—it didn't look like there'd be bar exams for a while. I saw the ring on a body—he had a suit worth a good three thousand dollars—and thought, what the hell."

"Boston's a long way from Jamaica."

"My father. Pulled every string with every man he'd ever known."

"Did he make it out with you?"

"He didn't even try. The airport was a nightmare. Gun battles between Boston Police and Massachusetts State Troopers and the National Guard. Nobody had orders. People crying, begging. I saw a man shoot himself right in front of his family."

She related her story without the shocked, vacant look that Valentine had seen on so many survivors of those days.

"I got flown down here with a bunch of children in a jet with enough fuel for a one-way trip. I guess there was a rumor that Jamaica was Ravies-free. A lot of the kids were sitting two and three to a seat. Babies crying. It was a frightening ride. The bombs were going off by then, and planes were dropping from the electromagnetic pulse. There was an army captain on board. Talked me and the kids through it. We ended up married just before I had my first boy."

She looked at the man in the vestments. Now that Valentine knew her face, he saw a hint of Obay around the son's eyes.

"Your visions are pretty accurate. A law firm could have used that, predicting a judge's decisions."

"Oh, that came later. Wasn't something I was born with. Given to me. I suspect you know a few Lifeweavers, too."

Valentine said nothing.

"One came to Jamaica. He had a small group of men—I suppose they were some kind of Special Forces. A mixture of Americans and British and Cuban soldiers, I think, going by the flags on the uniforms. The visit was brief; he was being chased."

The light broke through Valentine's doubts.

"I didn't understand much of what he had to say. I never even learned his name. Everyone called him 'the Brother.' It made him sound like a Mormon or an Amish or whoever that was that called each other that. Then I found out he was more like *The Brother from Another Planet.* He said I was going to be part of a new communications network. A biological one. They had me drink some kind of goop out of a tequila bottle, and I passed out for a few hours. When I came around, the Brother character was speaking in my head. Soon as he saw I was alive and getting his words without him using his mouth, he started glowing and told the rest 'Obey her.' Pointing at me, you see. Then he and the soldiers left. It made an impression on the kids. Everyone kept looking at me and repeating 'Obey.' Duane, my captain, had us go into a town in the mountains.

"Whatever he did to me, it didn't quite take, at least in the way you'd think telepathy should work. I get strange images now and then. Visions, pictures—sounds sometimes. Just had an audio last week with a lot of gunfire and explosions. The vision about you, it was a gray ship that seemed to be made of thunderclouds, and I saw your face, clear as I see it now. Your friend, Mr. Ahn-Kha, he was part of the clouds, too, with lightning in his eyes and fingertips."

"What do you see for the future?"

"Nothing from the Brother. But the men my sons lead will take care of their end, if your ships can help us with the garrison in Kingston."

"Dey come. Dey come tomorrow, Obay," Utari said.

"And then what?" Valentine asked.

Obay looked at the ceiling. The island's panoply absorbed her for a moment; then she returned her eyes to Valentine. "A new Jamaica. For all the factions, I hope and pray. With the Specter gone, even the Cockpit Country might see reason."

"And you?"

Obay played with her ring, twirling it on the shrunken digit between the enlarged knuckles. "Might end up using the old law studies before I die after all. What kind of constitution do you folks operate under there in the Ozarks?"

"They're landing now."

Valentine looked down from his perch on a rooftop water tower at Kingston in turmoil. Two days after the death of the Specter, the *Thunderbolt* and a pair of three-mast clippers sailed into the harbor as though in a naval show. All three ships were filled to overflowing with every willing man of the commodore's who could shoulder a rifle.

Faint booms came up from the docks. The *Thunderbolt*'s gun systematically blasted the harbor defenses. The posts were manned by the few troops still obeying orders under the Horsed Police officer. According to the Kernels, a Horsed Police officer named Colonel Hsei had tried to take control of the Specter's organization.

Valentine and Ahn-Kha, through their Kingston contacts, probably knew more about Hsei's struggle to assume the reins than the warlord himself. Formerly in charge of the city's garrison, the colonel managed to keep many of his troops together, even as the Public Police vanished into the countryside. Valentine had to admire Hsei's execution, if not his methods. A storeroom beside the regimental stables held the bodies of rivals and subordinates who failed to agree with his plan for Jamaica's future.

The same grapevine passed word to the inhabitants of Kingston that with the arrival of the ships, the north side of the island would finish the liberation of the south. The sons of Obay guided Valentine and Ahn-Kha to the city, and the Jamaicans filled rooms and streets with men and women eager to meet "the Crying Man" who had delivered them from the Specter. As they moved from village to city, time after time Valentine felt the touch of eager hands, as if physical contact with him somehow guaranteed their freedom.

Now buildings burned, and the clatter of hooves and echoing shots told the tale of the rising city. Ever since Valentine's arrival, machete and club had been matched against horse and gun, but without the Specter's organization and Reapers, Hsei's command had begun to crack. The booming arrival of the *Thunderbolt* and the commodore's flotilla turned confusion into collapse.

Valentine, Ahn-Kha, and a group of armed Jamaicans had occupied what in the late world had been a professional building of some kind. It was three stories of whitewashed brick, with broad balconies servicing the network of rooms inside. Until the Specter's death, it had been a barracks of the Public Police. Valentine chose it for its view of the city and of the main road north out of town. Equally useful for holding up reinforcements or Colonel Hsei's troops, its strategic location demanded occupation with what forces he could organize. The enthusiastic Jamaicans, led by men and women who had sprung seemingly from nowhere, had barricaded the highway before the building and lined the railings of the balconies with mattresses and furniture. Anyone trying to pass along the highway would hit the choke point and come under gunfire at a range that made skill superfluous.

Ahn-Kha looked out across the rooftops from beneath a straw hat and canvas parasol. Despite his fawn-colored fur and thick hide, he suffered from Jamaica's sun more than his bronze-skinned friend. They stood together on a tiny platform running around the edges of a rooftop watertower supplying the barracks.

"And the police, my David? How are they reacting?"

Valentine watched the *Thunderbolt* spit fire from her Oerlikon into a rusted crane, one of the harbor's few strong-points still fighting. A body, ant-size at the distance, plummeted from the tower.

"They're running. Looks like they have a dock secured. *Polaris* and *Vega* are being tied up to the docks—they didn't even have to send in boats. It's almost over."

"But not for us."

The Cat turned his gaze to the captain's compound. "It looks like Hsei has seen enough. Two trucks are being loaded up at headquarters. Horses too. Hell, they're firing into the mob again. Wait—yes, they are coming this way. The informants were right—he's going to run north toward the mountain stations. Better get your Grogs to the windows."

The Golden One picked up his long gun and moved to the roof-access ladder. Valentine watched the column for another minute, just to make certain of its direction. Hsei's men had perhaps been unnerved. The group leaving the barracks was as much of a mob as the Jamaicans hurling rocks from the alleys.

He swung down from the water tower and jumped to the gravel-covered roof, careful to land on his good leg. The work ahead would be bloody; he hoped it would be brief. Allowing Colonel Hsei to escape into the countryside with even a nucleus of armed men might mean trouble for the commodore and the Jamaicans in the days ahead; it would take weeks to organize an occupation of the various stations, forts, and barracks strung out across the Specter's lands. In the meantime, others might rally around the colonel.

Picking up his old Russian-made gun with its drum clip, he hurried down to the first floor. Grinning Jamaicans all around brandished their weapons and called out to him in their local patois. He understood only a phrase or two.

"D' dundus comin', mon?"

"We cut dey bakra asses now!"

Valentine nodded to their officer and went out to the front of the building. He and Ahn-Kha walked the balconies, cutting a serpentine trail down to the first floor, nodding and clapping the Jamaicans on the shoulder. "Keep down and wait for the horn!" he said, over and over again until it became as much of a singsong as their greetings.

He looked out at the barricade from the first floor, where Ahn-Kha's Grogs waited, covering the street from the windows and doors of the front of the building. What had been a parking lot sloped down to the highway. Carts and wreckage had been arranged to force any traffic moving up the road to negotiate a hairpin turn. Valentine wanted the obstacle to look to be the result of accident rather than design, so Hsei would stick his neck well into the trap before it snapped shut.

Valentine knelt behind the walkway barricade and searched southward with his hard ears. He picked up the sound of diesels and hooves. He nodded to Ahn-Kha, who had been walking back and forth in front of his Grogs, grunting out orders as he moved along the sidewalk fronting the shuttered windows. Ahn-Kha picked up a tarnished circular horn, an ancient foxhunting relic from Jamaica's colonial past. It had been gathering cobwebs on the wall of the barracks until one of the Grogs decided it would make an interesting headband.

The first horses reached the barricade, galloping pell-mell up the potholed road. Some fools fired from one of the upper levels, but neither the riders nor the horses took hit or heed. A horse vaulted over the frame of a broken sofa, unseating its rider. Valentine let the others pass and chambered a round in the PPD.

The first of the mass of riders trotted into view, coming up over a rise in the road like ships appearing over the horizon. Behind the clattering riders came the grinding gears of the two trucks and the higher pitched farting of a motorbike. Ahn-Kha barked something to his Grogs.

"Wait for the signal," Valentine said, loudly enough so it would carry to the balcony above him.

"Wait," he repeated.

The riders approached.

"Wait."

The Horsed Police slowed their horses to a walk as they saw the obstacles.

"Wait."

Now he could see the trucks: beds crammed with equipment, furnishings, and loot. Women and children, probably families of some of the Horsed Police, rode atop and among the cargo. Corrugated aluminum welded over the doors and windows protected the driver and passenger. A motorcycle with a sidecar puttered before the big diesels, but the sidecar held only a mound of possessions rather than a passenger ready to fire the machine gun mounted there. More soldiers jogged amongst the mob, already panting and casting aside their weapons in an effort to keep up with engines and horses. Strained, anxious faces in a dozen different skin tones looked warily at the partially blocked road and to the buildings at either side.

The vanguard of horsemen did not like what they saw and called to their fellows, drawing rifles and shotguns from saddle sheaths.

Valentine nodded at Ahn-Kha, who blew into the circular horn. Its wavering wail filled the air.

Wide-shouldered Grogs filled the windows and doors of the first floor of the barracks. Valentine heard shots crack from above. Horses screamed and plunged as their riders turned tail, fell out of the saddle, or dismounted by flinging themselves to the ground.

Valentine dropped two uniformed Jamaicans shouting orders. The PPD chattered out its harsh coda as he aimed short bursts into the crowd. Ahn-Kha methodically fired his rifle into the aluminum-covered cabins of the vehicles. The .50-caliber rounds blasted thumb-size holes in the plating and slumped the drivers within.

Cartridges fell like brassy hail from the balconies above as the Jamaicans emptied their weapons into the mob.

The motorcycle roared to life. Its uniformed rider gunned it, expertly swerved around dying horses and between the barricades. The cyclist threw his hips off the saddle to counterweight the tight slalom. The colorful insignia on the rider's uniform tipped Valentine to his identity: Hsei. He fired a burst but missed the racing figure.

"Ahn-Kha! The motorcycle!" he shouted.

Ahn-Kha stood and took a round from his mouth. In battle, the Grog kept cartridges in his lips, tucked into his flexible ears, and between his knuckles. He closed the breech of his gun, sighted, and fired. The bullet's impact threw the rider bodily into the motorcycle's handlebars. The bike spun sideways and crashed.

One truck, its driver dead, went nose-first into the ditch at the side of the highway. Riders and cargo tumbled forward and out. The truck behind halted, dead horses blocking its path.

Jamaicans flooded the street, wielding improvised weapons. Some grabbed the unwounded horses and ran off, leading their prizes. Others leapt into the trucks, looking for booty. But most of the mob concentrated their energies on the hated Horsed Police.

"Cease fire!" Valentine yelled, fearing any more firing would do more harm than good. At a word from Ahn-Kha, the Grogs put up their smoking guns.

Years of death and brutal treatment resulted in ugly scenes in the street. Whole and wounded Horsed Police, their hands raised in surrender, fell victim to the mob. A few Jamaicans flung themselves over the wounded and protected them from the clubs and knives with their own flesh, but the mob merely sought other targets. Valentine heard women's screams and saw some of the Horsed Police's children caught up in the mob's fury. A child fell under a club, skull opened and yellow-gray brains spilling to the pavement.

He shouldered his way into the crowd, stepping over bodies of the dead and dying, and jumped on the cab of the second truck. He fired his gun in the air.

"Enough!" he yelled, putting every decibel his body could produce into the bellow.

Ahn-Kha grabbed a horse, threw off its saddle, and mounted. He led his Grogs into the fray. The spectacle of the strange, apelike creatures distracted the mob enough for Valentine to get their attention. Eyes turned to Valentine and the Grogs.

"Enough!" he shouted, forcing a grin to his face. "The time of death is over!"

The mob turned from rage to celebration. Jamaicans joined Valentine atop the truck, waving their arms and calling out to their fellows.

"Free!" "Death is dead!" "Death is over!" came the cries.

Something gave way inside the exhausted Cat. He stood in the celebrating throng, shaking with exhaustion and emotion. He realized his head hurt; the sun struck his eyes like knives. He summoned a few Jamaicans and began to carry the surviving wounded into the shelter of the barracks. As his hands grew sticky with sweat and blood, he thought of the clean sea.

Six

Hispaniola, April: The largest island of the Caribbean has a record of woe. The rugged land remembers only moments of peace in its long history of strife and sorrow. Rule by colonial aristocrats, despots, corporations, or military dictatorships made no difference to the impoverished inhabitants. The new boss, as the twentieth-century song said, was much the same as the old one. The passage of the Kurians across their green island made the rest of their unhappy past a mere warm-up for the horrors to come.

The island's role as one of the first gateways of the Kur's invasion shrank the populace from the millions to the thousands. When the Kurians arrived, their Reapers hunted down the Hispaniolans in even the most remote villages on their way north, south, and west. The few slaughter-shocked inhabitants of the island remember these years in oral tradition as "La Fiesta de Diablos."

The beauty of the island stands in contrast to the ugliness of its history. Royal palms tower over empty towns, vanishing under a carpet of leafy vines. Nature left to itself covered the eroded scars left by charcoal gatherers in a dozen years. Cackling colonies of birds flit from enormous palm to enormous palm over an ocean of lesser trees and creepers. Gulls and sandpipers congregate on empty beaches, nesting in washed-up fishing boats. Further inland, wild dogs and pigs hunt and root through new and thriving forests.

What civilization there is exists on the east side of the island, where the Kurian families rule a retinue of Quislings from the gray ziggurat of the Columbus lighthouse. A few coastal communities dot the perimeter of the island, sending tribute to the Dark Lords in the east. Their combined Reapers hunt farther inland, or land here and there along the coast in search of auras. Perhaps something of the spirit of Columbus has entered the Santo Domingo Kurians, for they are some of the few who venture into the sea in ships in their predatory wanderings along Hispaniola's long coastline. The appearance of the Kurian "Drakkar" sends whole towns fleeing into the mountains.

It was not a bad storm; the Caribbean sees far worse during hurricane season. The spring storm lashing the channel in between Hispaniola and Cuba made up in bluster for what it lacked in size.

Valentine watched Captain Carrasca on the *Thunderbolt*'s bridge. A knotted rope and a stick, in a curious mix of hairstyle and seamanship, restricted her thick hair to the back of her head. She stood next to the wheel, bending first one knee and then the other as she rolled with the ship's motion like a slow metronome, owlish eyes watching the storm.

Since leaving Jamaica—gaps in the crew filled with the commodore's sailors—Carrasca had taught Valentine a good deal about the islands of the Caribbean: cays and atolls where some found refuge, larger islands such as Cuba and Cozumel, which fed the appetite of the Kurians. She knew winds and weather, currents and courses, radio procedure and sail setting; she spoke of them as easily as Valentine could describe his old platoons in the Wolves.

"How's the rudder?" she asked the steersman.

"Biting fine. She's a heavy ship. All that steel in this old ice-shover. Wouldn't care to ride this out in the *Guideon*. We'd have to heave-to."

"She's working. We're shipping more water than I'd like. The sea hasn't worked up much—I'd put it at three meters."

"Four sometimes, Cap," the steersman said.

"Any sign of the coast?" Valentine asked, trying to pierce the rain-filled darkness forward.

"By dead reckoning, it's there," Carrasca answered. "I don't dare get much closer. The best harbors are on the other side of the island, and we can't use them."

Cool and professional. The warm moment they shared that night on the balcony where she admitted her thrill at her command seemed like a childhood game of you-show-meyours-and-I'll-show-you-mine. Now she just watched him every now and then out of the corner of her eye, as though checking the professional wall between them for cracks.

"Your ships don't land here?"

"Nothing worth landing for, except fresh water or firewood. We hit richer lands. Now Cuba, there's good hunting there, especially on the north coast and in the stretch between it and the Florida peninsula."

"My work is on Hispaniola—the Haiti side."

"I'll get you there. Nothing's going to happen until this blows itself out, Valentine."

"I'll try and sleep. Have me woken if this clears, please."

Valentine descended from the bridge, weaving past a mix of the *Thunderbolt*'s old crew and new shipmates from Jamaica. He went to his cabin, formerly shared with Post, who now lay almost recovered in sick bay, thanks to the skilled teams of Jayport's aged hospital ship. Sea air and sun were speeding his recovery, but the former Coastal Marine was still not up and around for more than a few hours a day.

Ahn-Kha was on the cabin floor. The quarters smelled of Ahn-Kha's horsey odor and vomit, the contents of the Golden One's stomach having abandoned ship when the storm started.

"My David, take out your pistol and put an end to my suffering," Ahn-Kha groaned. He lay on his stomach, with four-fingered hands clasped over his pointed ears.

"Carrasca says it won't last long, old horse," Valentine replied. The motion stimulated Valentine, if anything, though he longed for surcease of the endless sounds of rain, wind, and the ship groaning in the weather.

"It's a new hell each hour."

"What's that?" Valentine asked, dropping into his bunk.

"My people . . . say there are four hells. The theosophists need to add one more, the Hell of Motion."

Valentine placed his boots on the floor, tucked them away from Ahn-Kha's head in case the Grog decided to bring up another ten gallons of digestive matter. Best to keep his friend's mind on something else. "They left out a hell?"

Ahn-Kha lay silent, as if gathering his words and putting them into English. "The Golden Ones believe that you must be purified by Hell before gaining Paradise. There is a Hell of Hunger and Thirst, a Hell of Pain, a Hell of Illness, and a Hell of Loneliness. If you suffer deeply of these in your life, you are spared them after death, and reach Paradise that much quicker."

"That's a lot of suffering to reach Heaven."

"By our creed, 'Only through suffering do you grow a soul capable of understanding others, and appreciating the'—what is it—the word for grace of gods?"

Valentine thought for a moment. "Beatitude?"

"I must look that up as soon as I can open my eyes again. I've never heard it. English has too many words for some things, and not enough for others. You take too long in the telling. Your words can never match the music of our proverb-verse."

"I'll work through a King James Bible with you. It'll change your opinion."

"Arrgh. Those tracts, most of them read like the family history of a group of nomad *pfump*-raisers. One of your theosophists tried to instill in me a belief in my own soul, and me having tasted only the bitter surface of the Hell of Loneliness and Hell of Pain in the time before we met. The fool. As if Paradise could be gained by affirming the divinity of some human. Bah!"

"I've always thought there was more to it than that, my friend."

"My David, if you wish to learn the true path to Paradise, you must read of the Golden Ones' *Rhapsodies*. Then you will be steeled to torments that must be overcome before a joyful afterlife."

" 'There are four and fifty ways of constructing tribal lays, and every single one of them are right,' " Valentine quoted.

"Then what is your opinion of your gods?"

"God? You mean Bud?"

"There is only one? I thought you had two or three."

"Depends who you talk to," Valentine said, sinking into his bunk. On his back, the ship's motion seemed to tilt him headdown first, then feetdown.

"I don't remember anyone calling your god Bub."

"Bud. It's from an old story the top sergeant from Zulu Company used to tell."

"Old stories are the best ones. The bad ones die young. Tell me about Bud."

Valentine sifted his memory. "The sergeant's name was Patel. He was built almost as broad as you, a helluva wrestler, too, and he always fought clean unless someone tried something. Then it was anything goes. But back to the story, before he was in the Wolves, he fought with the regulars, the Guards—"

"Yes, I've seen them," Ahn-Kha said from the noisy darkness. "Good guns, better uniforms, and the best food."

"They can fight when it comes to it. I think when Patel was with 'em they didn't have the nicest clothing. Especially where he was. He said it started while he was watching the ground south of Saint Louis. For a while there, it was trench warfare: the men and Grogs working for the Kurians were trying to blast them out of these hills with artillery. Got so there wasn't a tree standing, but the Guards just kept digging and digging. They'd build little caves of wood with tons of dirt overhead—they were called 'dugouts.' Anyway he was young, and he had this real nervous NCO running the dugout these twenty men were crammed into. The damn Grogs—sorry, old horse—the damn Kurian

Grogs started building these rockets they were launching off of railroad rails, and they had enough of a bang in them to collapse a dugout.

"When those babies landed, Patel said it felt like someone picked up the hill and dropped it again. The concussion outside was enough to stop your heart. Well, this corporal starts to lose it—they're in there and it's dark and cold and wet, with the noise and smell of burnt flesh, and as if that isn't bad enough, it seems like any minute they're going to get blown to hell.

"'Get friendly with God!' this corporal starts shouting. 'The time's coming, and you'd better know him! You gotta know God and be on a first-name basis with him to get into heaven. Hurry up, guys!'

"Of course, some of the men just tell him to shut up, but you've always got a joker or two who thinks a nervous breakdown is entertainment, so they start quizzing him.

"'Praise Jesus!' one hollers, trying to egg him on.

"'I'm talking about God, not Jesus!' the corporal says. He keeps looking at the ceiling of the dugout. 'Know him. Love him.'

"'Okay, what's God's name, then?'

"The corporal doesn't even think about it—he says *Bud* right away. Some of the guys think this is just too funny to let go.

"'Bud is my shepherd, I shall not want,' one starts to say. They start misquoting stuff like 'Praise Bud!' and 'Bud, bless this stewed rat, which I'm about to eat, and probably puke up again.'"

"Skip the food part," Ahn-Kha groaned.

"Well, after a couple minutes of humor like that, some old soldier yells, 'Shut your Bud-damned mouths, for Bud's frickin' sake.'

"The corporal loses it, says he's not going to stay in there with a bunch of blasphemers, and he heads out of the dugout with the shells and rockets still landing all over the hills. Patel thinks the corp is going to get killed, and so he goes out after him. Patel catches up to him thirty yards away and jumps on him, wrestles him to the ground in the trench, when one of those rail-rockets lands right on the dugout. Kills every man in there, either the blast or suffocation did them in. Patel and a bunch of others, even the corporal, tried to dig out the shelter to rescue them, but no luck. Sure enough, some of the bodies are blue, and this corporal starts pointing at the ones who suffocated and saying 'Bud's mark!' and things like that.

"Patel and this corporal get out of the trenches and are posted with a new unit in western Missouri in the bushwhack ground. This corporal seems sound enough most of the time, but now and then he points out the color blue and says 'the Hand of Bud,' or something like that. One day they're on patrol on a footpath and he just freezes, with his head cocked like a dog listening to a whistle. He says that 'Bud's whispering in my ear.' A couple of the guys pass him, maybe they thought he was taking a leak without bothering to use his fly, and go right into a tripwire that fires this harpoon through two men. Patel said he started to think that old expression about God looking out for drunks, children, and idiots might be true.

"After that, this corporal turned into the kind of NCO that stays behind to watch over the sick and the supplies. Until this one day, there's a beautiful blue sky. So he decides to climb a tree and look at Bud's handiwork. He falls asleep up there, no one knows where he is, they figure this time he's really flipped and run off into the woods. They don't even bother looking for him. Which is too bad, because if they had been dispersed, these three Reapers passing through the area wouldn't have caught all that lifesign in the camp. They went in and killed everyone but the corporal, maybe when he was in the tree talking to Bud, he didn't put out much more lifesign than a cuckoo clock. After that, the corporal pulled kitchen duty at an infantry training school by Mountain Home.

"Patel ended up joining some Wolves who were hunting the Reapers, he made himself useful when they caught up to the bastards, and ended up in Zulu Company.

"Funny thing is, every now and then in a tight situation, I'd catch Patel saying, 'Bud help me' or something like that. I don't think he really believed it, but Patel wasn't taking any chances."

The storm blew itself out overnight. Valentine arose and dressed around the slumbering Ahn-Kha. He checked Post, who slept with his familiar snore in the tiny sick bay.

The indefatigable Carrasca still stood on the bridge. She looked as fresh and alert as when Valentine had last seen her, rocking with the storm.

"That's Haiti, Valentine, dead ahead."

Valentine stepped out onto the wing of the bridge. Something loomed ahead, a heavy presence in the darkness. As the light grew, he could make out mountains coated in green.

"Why the white knuckles?" Carrasca asked, joining him in the open air.

Her words weren't in the cool captain's voice with its self-assured intonation. They tickled his ear like a playful finger.

Valentine looked down at the decorative wood top to the rail where his hands gripped the painted metal. He breathed out, half-laugh and half-sigh. "For over a year, I've been trying to get here in the right kind of ship."

"Worth it, I hope. The commodore thinks you're chasing a rumor.

Said it reminded him of the years after the Kurians first came, where ships and men were lost looking for remnants of the old society."

"That's what my father was doing when he ran into a Lifeweaver. This chase is something the Lifeweavers put me on."

She put binoculars to her eyes and searched the coast ahead. "How much do you know?"

"There's something on that island the Cause needs."

She frowned. "The Cause. You sound like Hawthorne of the hasty retreat."

Valentine involuntarily stiffened. Now a row of ghostly bodies lay between them, friends Valentine had lost, talents the world had lost, in the sake of "the Cause."

"I'm sorry," she said, looking away. "You've proved yourself to Jamaica."

"But not to you?" Valentine asked.

"It's the same thing."

Valentine stifled a laugh. He might have said those exact words. Jensen and Carrasca had proved themselves to the Cause by letting him use the ship, the same thing as proving themselves to him. He took his hands from the rail and rubbed life back into them.

Carrasca broke the silence: "Why is it nobody's thought to go get this whatever-it-is until now?"

"We didn't know it was there. It was put there hundreds of years ago by a Lifeweaver. He lived in secret among us, with a few followers. He guessed what the Kurians were planning, but he only knew about the one door. He and his people were ready for what was coming on Haiti, but something happened, they were betrayed, and I don't think anyone survived. One of the followers kept a journal of some kind, more as a record of that Lifeweaver's teachings, but in it was a section about this weapon against them.

"Like a lot of places, there's a resistance against the Kurians. These Haitians are fighting without really knowing what they're fighting. They just know it's evil, and they're doing what they can to protect their own people. They found a cache of weapons in a cave, along with this diary. They made sense of it and somehow word got passed to us. I never knew about it—I just got orders to join up with the Quislings on the Gulf Coast with fake papers and background. I think they chose me because I speak a little Spanish and French. My mother was from the French part of Canada, and I was raised by a priest from Puerto Rico. It took me a year, but I got into the Coastal Marines and managed to get myself posted to the right kind of ship to bring it back. It's a year I wouldn't care to repeat. Now it's like life in the Ozarks is something out of my childhood."

"Is there snow there?"

"Sometimes, in winter. The mountains aren't big enough to be snowcapped year-round. Why?"

"There's a story the people here tell. They think if you go somewhere there's snow all the time, like the north pole, the Kurians can't get you. It's all mixed up with stories about Christmas now, that there's this place everyone is safe from them with plenty of food and electronic toys and no fighting."

Valentine watched a frigate bird float above, drifting on the air currents with only the tiniest alterations to its wing.

"If only. I grew up almost in Canada. It gets colder in the winter than you can probably imagine, and the Reapers still made it up there. They don't come in winter, but we're still not out of it. You go much farther north from there, and the land can't support many people year-round away from the coasts. Just not enough to eat. And the old-timers say the climate is strange now, summers are longer and hotter, but somehow winter is even worse. God knows how the Kurians managed it. There's no safe place, or if there is, they're keeping it to themselves."

She nodded. "Cape Haitian is ahead. What is the plan?"

"The plan is to sail into the port as bold as if we have the proverbial balls of the brass monkey. We have a contact in town who'll get in touch with me. He's on the lookout for a ship from the north. Not sure what happens after that. Maybe we pull out and land somewhere nearby on the coast, and he gets us in touch with the resistance. They load us up, and back we go."

"Will it be that easy?"

Valentine found a smile. "Somehow I doubt it."

The *Thunderbolt* rounded Cape Haitian and turned her prow to the town, a cluster of white and gray snuggled into a stretch of flat land with mountains towering behind. The vivid colors of the Caribbean struck Valentine once more: deep blues of the ocean; brilliant blues and whites above; and behind stretches of white sand a green so lush, it hypnotized.

Fishing boats, hardly more than canoes, rocked in the gentle swell. Tall, lean black men threw nets into the water and gathered them again. If they noticed the *Thunderbolt*, they showed no sign of it. As the ship approached, Valentine observed that the fishermen were either naked or wearing stringy loincloths. Wiry muscle glistened under the sun.

A boat with four oarsmen put out from the docks. Its splashing approach scattered seabirds bobbing on the calm surface of the bay.

"Dead slow," Carrasca called into the bridge.

"Dead slow, aye aye," the junior officer there answered.

The bulky ship coasted to a crawl. The small boat cut across the prow, as if blocking the larger vessel's entry. A man in a simple gray uniform stood and put a speaking trumpet to his mouth.

"*Que bâteau?*" Valentine thought he heard.

"What did he say?"

"What ship is that?" Valentine translated.

"I thought they spoke Spanish here."

"Creole French, mostly. Or a form of it. But you can get along in Spanish, too."

Valentine inflated his lungs. "*Thunderbolt*, New Orleans. May we anchor here tonight? We will buy food," he bellowed, hoping his French would be understood.

"What do you do here?"

"We chase pirates. Have any sailing ships passed?"

"No, not close. Not since before the last hurricane season."

"May we drop anchor?"

The man lowered his speaking trumpet for a moment, then raised it again. "For now. Our officer will come. Do not lower your boat until then."

"Thank you!" Valentine yelled back.

The same four-oared boat brought out the "officer." Valentine watched him make the transition to the *Thunderbolt* with a fair amount of agility. He wore a similar uniform to his underling, though with gold buttons and a brilliant scarlet sash beneath his pistol belt.

Valentine went to greet him.

"Monsieur speaks French?" the man asked. His features were exaggerated: strong cheekbones, a pointed chin, knifelike nose, wide eyes, and handsome in a sensual, full-lipped way. Unlike most of the Hispaniolans Valentine had observed in the boats, who either had a full beard or were clean-shaved, he wore a mustache.

"And some Spanish," Valentine said, then realized, as visitor, it would be best if he began the introductions. "My captain is more comfortable in Spanish. I am Lieutenant Rowan, of the Coastal Marines," Valentine said, turning to introduce Carrasca. She wore a combination of her own Jamaican attire and a coat liberated from Captain Saunders's chest.

"*Sí, bueno. Muy encantado,*" he agreed, then touched his chest. "El Capitán Boul."

"I understand you wish to make use of our market?" Boul asked, seated in the captain's cabin. Even with a table fan blowing, the air settled wet and thick on the three people gathered in the small space. "We have only a few liters of diesel oil, I am sorry to say."

"My captain has ample fuel, but some fresh food and, of course, water would be most appreciated. We can barter or pay in gold."

"Ours is a poor market, unless you count fish. Though once word got around that you wished to buy, the people would bring in chickens, eggs, pigs, fresh fruit, and vegetables. It would take only a day or two more, and your ship would be fully provisioned."

Carrasca exchanged a look with Valentine and shook her head.

"I must be at sea again. The damned pirates have too long a lead even now."

"In our mutual interest, I will ask the fishermen as they come in. They see ships, especially in the waters between here and Cuba."

"If you hear any news between now and when we leave tomorrow, we would be most obliged. A few hours are all we need to replenish our fresh water supply."

Boul put up his hands placatingly. "My friends, if you choose to stay, I can guarantee most advantageous terms for your barter in the market. Our people would have little use for gold. But tools, trinkets, even pencils and paper will get you much good food."

Valentine leaned forward in his chair. "Captain, do you have some special reason to have us stay here?"

Boul drummed his fingers on the table, but stopped as soon as he looked down and realized what he was doing. "I will lay my cards down, as you New Orleans gamblers say. Though we pay tribute to the cursed ones on the other side of the island, we still suffer their torments. Even now one of their Drakkar, a wooden vessel known as the *Sharkfin*, approaches. On it are the Drinkers of Death, the robed ones who come in the dark. A ship such as yours in the harbor will make them think again about anchoring. I saw your gun—it would blow the *Sharkfin* into kindling. Our market is poor because even at the rumor of one of the Drakkar, the Dragon-ships, my people fly to the mountains."

"We can't stay here forever," Valentine said. "And were we to destroy the *Sharkfin*, New Orleans would hear about it, and it would be trouble for us."

"But you may save us this season. This would not hurt your patrol, perhaps three days here. And I do mean what I say about making inquiries among the fishermen. You may buy what you will, and each day you stay your men will feast on what my poor town can provide. We make a very good rum, vodka even from potatoes."

Carrasca nodded. "So be it. We shall stay a few days. We'll anchor so our gun can cover the sea. And your town, in case of treachery, Captain Boul."

"Thank you, Captain. You are helping my people a great deal. Though I cannot blame you for thinking it, do not fear treachery."

Valentine escorted Boul off the *Thunderbolt* and asked about springs flowing into town. Boul pointed out a beach and assured Valentine the water was good there. Nevertheless, Valentine made a mental note to remind the party about the water-purification tablets. He returned to the captain's cabin, knocked, and entered. They sat down and talked about the watering and market party.

"Fresh food and time. We lucked out," she said once they'd decided which men would do what.

"Unless this *Sharkfin* shows up. Much as it would be nice to blow it into flotsam, our cover story would suffer. Even worse, one of your own ships could sail in."

"Doubtful, nothing on this side of the island worth going after," she said.

"Well, with your permission, tomorrow I'll take a few men into town and have a look around. All I need to do is make it easy for this man to find me."

He stood up, as did she. As he turned sideways to get past her to go out the door, their chests touched. She glanced up into his eyes and then away, as if afraid of what she might find there.

The watering party left under the supervision of one of Carrasca's petty officers. They used the *Thunderbolt*'s two boats, the smaller motor launch and a lifeboat, heaped with plastic ten-gallon barrels. It wasn't the most efficient way to water the ship, which had been amply filled before leaving Jamaica anyway, but it gave the men something to do and added a touch of realism to the story.

Under further instructions from Carrasca, they also returned with planking torn from an old fishing boat. Some men fashioned it into a raft and attached a makeshift flag; then they towed the target out beyond the surf for gunnery practice. Carrasca made sure the distance was greater than that to the town, and she had her men lob a few shells at the target, to impress those ashore that the gun worked and they had shells to spare. She still didn't trust anyone on Hispaniola, no matter what promises came from below a handsome mustache.

Valentine was with Post when the gun began to fire. The healing lieutenant startled at the sound.

"Just gunnery training. I told you, remember?"

Post was red-faced. "Sorry, Val." He raised his arm on his wounded side. "Nerves might not be healed yet, but the shoulder's working great. Hardly a twinge." He flapped an elbow and smothered a wince.

Valentine went to the market the next day. Much of the town looked to be in rubble, victim to wave and war, storm or earthquake, and never rebuilt. What was still standing was gaily painted: blue-trimmed doorways looked out from whitewashed buildings, and elaborate designs like a child's drawing of men and animals decorated awnings and window sills. The widest street in Cape Haitian was crowded with straw-hatted food vendors, selling produce out of wooden carts. Valentine and his men would have been besieged by beggars and hustlers, except Captain Boul sent a set of navy-uniformed gunmen to act as escorts and intermediaries in the market. Which was just as well, because the Creole dialect of the streets was beyond Valentine's French. The acting-purser simply picked out items, and the strongmen passed out what looked like beaded ribbons to the people in the market.

Shouted offers for liquor, drugs, and even women tempted a few of the sailors, but Valentine and the petty officer kept them at work filling the cart.

"Hey Lieutenant, you want a good drink?" someone hallooed in English. "Wine, me got some wine. I have friends up North, and I know what you like, what you want."

Valentine spotted the man waving to him from the crowd, a dark bottle in his hand.

"Don't buy anything from that one, sailor sir," the sergeant of the escort said in a mixture of French and Spanish. "There's better wine to be found. Off, Dog-boy, or you'll be sorry."

He looked like a man to Valentine, and he didn't see any dogs. The man's eager eyes implored him across the sea of straw hats in the market, and he held out the bottle again. "Have a taste—you'll want more."

Valentine reached for the bottle, and one of the guards rewarded Dog-boy with a crack across the wrist with a baton. It dropped, but Valentine's reflexes saved it from crashing to the cobblestones.

"You don't want his piss, sailor sir."

Valentine sniffed the open mouth of the bottle. His ears picked up the sound of something clinking against the glass within. Dog-boy had disappeared into the crowd.

"Maybe I don't. I've got a drain that needs unclogging on board— I'll use it on that."

Valentine kept the bottle in his hand for the remainder of the session in the market, using it as a pointer. The purser and his men hauled their acquisitions back to the dock, yet another set of round trips were ahead for the motor launch.

Once back on board, past the Grogs hungrily eyeing the supplies coming alongside, he took his bottle down to the cabin and emptied it down the drain. Whatever was within refused to come out, so he smashed the bottle against the steel sink. A wooden tube, lacquered and stoppered, had been stuck inside. He examined it for a moment, then pulled out the cork, and extracted a rolled-up note from the tube:

> *To officer with black hair and scar—*
> *I will come to your ship tonight after midnight.*
> *I will swim to the anchor chain.*
> *Must keep clear of soldiers in boats.*
>
> *—Victo*

Valentine read the note twice, then got Ahn-Kha and took it up to Carrasca.

"Is he telling us there is danger from soldiers in boats? Or that he has to swim clear of them?" Ahn-Kha asked, after the note had been passed around in the cabin.

"The Oerlikon could sink any number of boats," Carrasca said. "I've looked around the harbor. They have a lot of those canoe fishing boats. I suppose they could put a couple hundred men in the water, but we'd sink them before they got halfway here. But we might want to shift anchorage, farther out."

Valentine shook his head. "He'll have a tough enough swim as it is. Let's wait until he's on board."

There was a rap at the door, and a teenager entered. "Captain, one of those rowboats dropped off a letter," he reported.

"Thank you, Lloyd," Carrasca said, opening it.

"Today is a day for notes," Ahn-Kha observed.

She handed it to Valentine. "An invitation to a dinner and beach party in our honor tomorrow night. However many officers and men as I choose to bring. I smell a rat with a nice mustache."

"We'll make some excuse tomorrow during the day," Valentine said. "A radio message. As long as this Victo is on board, we can take our leave of *El Capitán Boul*."

"You think he means to take hostages?" Carrasca asked. "Why didn't he do it today? There must have been ten or twelve men on shore at various times. He could have taken you and your party. That would have given him something to bargain with."

"He could be waiting for orders."

"*Huevos.* The man's a schemer—I could read his eyes," she said, touching the corner of her own. "He may be playing us false, but it's to his own purposes."

"I'm going to arm Ahn-Kha's Grogs and what's left of my marines. You might want to have the machine guns ready tonight."

"They'll be manned. I want everyone to have a chance at fresh food, though. There's an old tradition at sea to give your men a good feed before action." Her expression softened into that of the woman he'd played mah-jongg with in Jamaica. "Would you care to have dinner with me in the cabin?"

"Far be it from me to break with tradition," Valentine said.

The food tasted better in the cooler night air. Valentine put on a plain white shirt with his best pair of pants fresh from the laundry and went lightly up the stairs to Carrasca's cabin. Askin, her only lieutenant, answered the door. A handsome young Jamaican with hair cropped so short it made Valentine think of peach fuzz, Askin was dressed in a trim black uniform decorated with a heavy silver whistle on a thick chain. A linen covering added a formal note to the table in the wardroom. The *Thunderbolt*'s best plates and cutlery lay upon it.

"We really should have asked Post, as well," Carrasca said. She wore the same blue uniform Valentine remembered from the dinner at Commodore Jensen's, though now it bore an epaulette on the right shoulder.

"He's only just started walking," Valentine reported.

"The Chief doesn't care for formal meals, and Ahn-Kha—"

"Just wouldn't fit in," Valentine finished. "I don't mean with us, but in this cabin."

"It would be a bit like having a horse in here for dinner," Carrasca laughed. She sat, and the men followed suit.

Carrasca began uncovering dishes. "Askin, you did wonders with the birds."

"A sugar glaze from the beets on this island," the lieutenant explained. His diction held only a hint of Calypso.

She took another cover off. "The bean-and-rice dish is mine. Sweet potatoes. Crab cakes with goat-milk butter, and a fruit platter."

Valentine took a bite of a buttery crab cake, feeling guilty that he hadn't brought anything. He turned to Askin. "The captain tells me you've landed here before."

"Farther along the north coast, near the Samaná Peninsula," Askin said. "We were chasing some little trading ship. They beached it and waded through the surf to escape us. It took us forever to take off the cargo. Something must have scared some of them worse inland, because they came scampering back."

"Did they say what it was?" Valentine asked.

"I think they got a look at one of the mines. Bauxite, maybe. Those and the sugar plantations—they're hell on earth. Hispaniola is the worst island in the Carib."

"The Kurians have a knack for doing that."

"That old Specter by Kingston, he was a saint compared with the creatures running Santo Domingo. They don't even try to keep their people alive."

Unspoken agreement turned the three to their dishes, further conversation might spoil their appetites. Valentine had seen his share of cruelty in his years facing Kur, and worse, recently participated in it as part of his assumed role as a Coastal Marine.

The meal ended with fruit for dessert and a single glass of wine chilled into sangria. There were no toasts this time. Askin excused himself, carrying two green bananas out with him.

"He has the bridge as soon as it gets dark, even though we're at anchor," Carrasca explained. "I told him to be extra careful tonight. I warned the watch to keep an eye open for our swimmer. Now we wait, David."

Valentine sipped at his sangria, enjoying the sound of his name from her lips. "I have no complaints. I'm left alone with a beautiful woman."

Carrasca smiled, her teeth gleaming against her dusky skin. "Captain Valentine, I'm shocked. A breach of etiquette. But for God's sake, don't stop."

Valentine's innards warmed to the wine and the spark in her eyes. "I haven't had a woman to talk to in a long time, Malia. When all this is over, when we can both relax and take off our respective hats, so to speak, I'd like to spend some time with you. You're someone I can talk to."

"So that's what you'd do with me? Conversation?"

He met her gaze. "Yes, long, in-depth conversations. Late into the night."

"Really, David?" she asked. "How long has it been since your last good conversation with a woman?"

"Over a year. In New Orleans I was tempted to pay a woman to talk to me, but I resisted."

"It's better to wait for a decent conversationalist," she agreed.

"Yes."

"I'd like to talk to you, too. I'm sure you'd enjoy it. Women with any Cuban blood in them—well, they make great conversational partners. You'd be amazed at how many different topics I'm familiar with."

"I'm sure," Valentine said, smelling her femininity in the confines of the dining cabin.

"It's a shame, now that you've got me thinking about it, I've been lacking in decent conversation myself. The only problem is, we're both married to our duty. We can't have the men thinking anything else."

"Maybe if we whispered—"

"I tend to shout at the top of my lungs, when I'm really interested in the subject."

Valentine laughed. "We couldn't have that."

Carrasca bit her lower lip. "You speak French. Perhaps we could have a short—"

The ship's Klaxon went off. They froze. At the second screaming blast of the alarm, they hurried out of the cabin to the bridge, just a few steps away.

Carrasca killed the Klaxon and picked up the ship's squawk-mic. "Battle stations, battle stations." Aspin spoke to the engine room, asking for maximum revolutions.

Valentine stepped aside for men rushing to their stations. He looked to the shoreline from the wing of the bridge. Five great bonfires lit up the beach outside Cape Haitian. Wide fishing boats with double-banked oars approached like giant water beetles, men crammed inside. Pot shots from shore zipped through the air or *ting*ed harmlessly against the steel sides of the ship.

Why would they approach with the bonfires behind them, making them perfect silhouettes for . . .

He went to the opposite side of the bridge, heart in his throat, and searched the darkness. The stars went right to the horizon in the clear tropical night. No ship sailed out there; that much could be seen. He heard Carrasca shouting orders for the anchor cable to be cut. Valentine went to a searchlight and threw the switch. He began a slow sweep of the seaward approaches of the harbor, the searchlight's electric buzz filling his ears.

He probed the darkness with a knife of light. The beam fell across something small and gray, approaching like a sea monster with part of its snout showing. Orange light flashed, and a shell howled as it landed just in front of the ship. Water fountained into the air. But the cannon's flash told him what hunted the *Thunderbolt* from the sea.

It was not Boul's wooden Drakkar, but a submarine! The commodore had mentioned some old diesel ships in the hands of the Haitian Kur. It had a low profile like something from the Second World War. He hardened his ears in that direction even as the second shell approached and picked out the sound of churning engines.

He grudgingly congratulated Boul for a clever poker game. The thought stayed frozen in his mind as the second shell hit forward, beneath him. Time faded; the next thing he was aware of was a disembodied floating feeling.

David, I'm not going to hold you up anymore, his mother said. *You'll have to swim for yourself.*

Cool, slightly slimy Minnesota lake water engulfed him as she let go. Fear . . . He kicked hard and spun his arms like wheels until he broke the surface and felt air on his face again. The panic changed to triumph.

Swimming, Mom! By myself! Look! he sputtered.

His mother's bronze face split into a smile under its wet tangle of glossy black hair. *You're a regular motorboat.*

David Valentine spat out a mouthful of Caribbean as he came to his senses, disoriented. Distant and muted sounds echoed over a roaring in his brain.

He bobbed in the ocean, the waves adding to his sensation of drunkenness. Woolly-brained, he watched the *Thunderbolt* cut her cable and get under way. Someone had the presence of mind to turn the Oerlikon from the shore boats to the attacking ship. Red tracers crossed overhead, seeking the exposed figures on the bridge of the submarine. The deadly fireworks played across the deck of the submarine, tearing the conning tower's men and machinery to pieces. The submarine's gun fired again, and its shell detonated in the wake of the now-moving target. The Oerlikon's tracers shifted, and this time tore through the thin shield of the submarine's cannon. The thirty-millimeter shells blasted the gun's crew from the deck in a series of whipcrack explosions.

Valentine noted, rather dully, the *Thunderbolt* turning to escape the harbor—leaving him behind. She and the submarine traded machinegun fire; the bullets scrabbled against the respective port sides of the two ships. The ineffectual fire reminded Valentine of a pair of crabs battling with their oversize fighting claws, both too well armored to be damaged by the exchange.

Hard hands grabbed him by the shirt and hauled him into a boat. He looked around at a mass of black faces, eyes and teeth shining in the night. A few pointed their guns at him. He could make out voices now.

"Put those things down, you fools," Valentine barked in French. "I'm not going anywhere." He consoled himself with the sight of the *Thunderbolt*'s churning wake as she escaped the harbor.

They landed and trooped up the beach and past the wounded Haitians. The soldiers' screams and lamentations struck Valentine as surreal, with soft sand beneath his feet and a breeze licking his skin as though he were just back from a pleasure swim. A few of the women from the town tended to the men in a haphazard fashion, caring only for the faces known to them and ignoring others.

The soldiers moved him along with words and gestures rather than the blows he expected, especially after the brief, intense fight. They escorted him to the stoutest building off the market square, a cinder-block three-tiered structure with a collonade and a few friezes that reminded him of an elaborate wedding cake he'd once seen back in New Orleans. They brought him into the basement by way of an exterior stairway and metal door broken only by a narrow gun slit. A navy-uniformed warden led him to a cell. Its ten-by-ten concrete floor supported no furniture, and only a drain hole and dirty ring on the floor around it hinted that there had once been plumbing fixtures.

Cockroaches scuttled for the corners at their entry. What light there was came in through the face-size window in the door, where tiny shards of reinforced glass and wire still stood in the broken pane like the teeth circling a lamprey's mouth. He stood in the holding cell, wet and uncomfortable, while they searched him. Finding him weaponless, they took only his belt.

He waited what he thought to be an hour or so, and a familiar eye appeared in the circle of jagged, stained glass. It widened in surprise.

"My God! So it's true—the bargainer himself," Boul exclaimed in French.

"That sounds like the man who told me not to fear treachery."

A melodious chuckle came from the hall. "I know which side of the bread my butter rests on, my friend. Or in this case, on which side of this door I wish to be standing."

"Funny thing, buttered bread," Valentine said, emotion facilitating his command of his mother's tongue. He sat and rested his back against the wall. "If it is dropped, life always arranges for it to land butter side down."

"My bread is brought to me, so I wouldn't know. Listen, my friend. You'll have buttered bread, decent food, as long as you stay here if you'll tell them the whole truth. That through me your captain was convinced to stay."

"Are you sure you want to take credit for tonight's fiasco? Your prize got away."

"Your sailors were more alert than we thought, for all the illicit rum and tequila they bought today. But your ship was damaged, my friend, damaged. Whatever you sought to do here is at an end. The Lords of Santo Domingo still rule, and they know now that you play a false game."

"Thanks to those who would sell their countrymen's lives. For what? A uniform? Someone to bring you your buttered bread?"

"I must put an end to this pleasant exchange, though in the future we'll have freedom and leisure to talk. Well, just leisure in your case. But first a comrade of yours will join you. It seems he wished to see you again a great deal, so much that he risked his life to be in the harbor tonight. One moment please."

So they had Victo, too. Valentine waited, and rested. *So close, and you blew it at the end.* He closed his eyes and his mind and tried to reduce his lifesign. Not that it was necessary in this particular heart of darkness, but the mental discipline would calm him for whatever lay ahead.

A heavy tread outside the door, and a rattle of a key in the lock made him open his eyes again. He readied an apology for Victo, whose life had also been on the table in this mad gamble. Valentine felt a flash of resentment at the superiors, Lifeweaver and human, who pushed men to their deaths, sacrificed like pawns. But it wasn't Victo who stood in the doorway, glowering at him.

Captain Saunders.

"By Kur and the Catastrophes, I owe the devil his due. It *is* you," Saunders rasped. His skin was darker, his hair lighter, and the wattles on his neck more pronounced with weight loss. He wore loose butter-colored cotton clothes and rope sandals.

"Good morning, Captain," Valentine said.

"Stow it, renegade. Boul, put this man in shackles. He's slippery."

Boul yelled something to his men outside the door, who rushed to comply with the Haitian Creole. Valentine submitted to his boots being stripped off, and his wrists and ankles being clamped in steel. A second chain linked the upper and lower segments of the restraints.

"That's better," Saunders said, looking over the fittings with a careful eye. He snickered. "So young, so sure of himself. Plotting behind my back. I found you out still, clever man."

"Shouldn't you be getting back to the *Thunderbolt*, sir? It is your command, after all."

A paroxysm passed over Saunders's face, and he reached into his shirt. Valentine saw a sheathed knife under his arm. Saunders clutched the hilt with a trembling hand, then relaxed.

"You should be congratulated for being in the right place at the right time, Captain," Valentine admitted. "Was it dumb luck or evil fate?"

"It took some doing," Saunders said. "I got away from those bastards off Jamaica by only the thinnest margins. I jumped in a raft with Peatwo and my pistols while the fighting was still going on. We rowed for shore." Saunders still enjoyed talking about himself, and he began to pace the cell.

"Nobody noticed a missing raft. But we've been busy killing a Kurian," Valentine said.

"I rowed for shore, but it turned out there was a third ship there. Didn't know that, did you? A little fishing boat, just a wheelhouse and a deck really. From the other pirates in Montego Bay. The scoundrels on board were hoping one or both of the ships would be so damaged by the fight, they could get in on some salvage.

"Their sailing master, for he wasn't fit for the word *captain,* was a crafty one, lurking there. Pointed a bunch of guns at us, bobbing there in the raft. I saw him watching Peatwo with a look I'd seen before, so I took my pistol and put it to Peatwo's head. Promised to blow the boy's brains out if they didn't put down their guns, but I'd trade the boy for my life. The sailing master chuckled and brought me on board.

"He meant to murder me, of course, so as soon as I got on deck, I shot him and another who moved clean dead. I made the others throw their guns overboard, and between me and Peatwo, we got five into the raft. That just left us with three, enough to handle the ship but not too many to watch.

"I couldn't go back north, but I knew the only Kurians with ships nearby were here. We made for Santo Domingo. I ended up shooting another of those Montego dogs on the trip. I stayed awake two days at one stretch, promising myself with every breath that I'd see you again and avenge myself. I offered the Devil my soul for this moment."

"Not much of a bargain for either of you."

"Hold that tongue, or I'll cut it out—by Kur, I will. We got to this island, and I found the local Lords. I gave them the Jamaicans, and Peatwo for that matter, for the promise to let me serve them at sea. That came hard. Felt a bit like that guy in the Bible who had to sacrifice his own son. I couldn't have made it that week at sea without Peatwo. The Kurians didn't know what to make of me. But they had that submarine working; they used it at sea because it was almost unsinkable. The cannon's sights were wrecked. I fixed it up for them, and they gave me the command.

"We heard about what happened in Jamaica. At first I thought you had ideas about setting yourself up in style there. When the good Boul radioed Santo Domingo that you were seen off the coast, I knew the Devil had kept his part of the bargain. You'll rot here until I get the *Thunderbolt* back, and then what's left of you will go back to New Orleans for disposition. Dispossession, more like, of your traitorous hide. As slowly as I can make it last."

In a way, Valentine was relieved. He wouldn't be killed outright, and so far no one had bothered to wonder just what he was doing off the shore of Hispaniola.

"Better get that gun fixed, sir," Valentine suggested. "Otherwise the *Thunderbolt* will sink your pigboat under you."

"I intend to. The damage is repairable, within even the capabilities of the joke of a machine shop they have here in Haiti's wet asshole. But help is on the way."

Valentine feigned disinterest and said no more in the hope that Saunders would brag out further details. But his former captain turned to leave.

"Oh, Captain, one more thing," Valentine said. "Suppose you do get the *Thunderbolt* back. Are your new masters here just going to let you sail off in an armed ship that size? Our mutual friend Captain Boul, he may just have orders to shoot you in the back of the head once the *Thunderbolt*'s safely taken."

"A traitor judges all others by his traitorousness," Saunders sneered, as if he had hit upon an important point of philosophy. "Kur keeps her bargains with those useful to them."

"What about with those who are no longer useful to them? What happened to Peatwo when you didn't need a second set of eyes, Captain?"

"Boul, have him beaten!"

Saunders stormed out, letting his stomping feet do his cursing for him. Boul's lips curled into an uneven grin, and two heavyset Haitians entered, wooden clubs in hand.

An hour later, Valentine consoled himself with the knowledge that this pain would not be forever. Pain never was; the body either died or healed. In either case, the pain subsided.

But for now, he had an existence of seeping blood and throbbing pain. Blood stinging his eyeballs—the sting coursed up the side of his face like a hot circuit. Blood in his mouth, blood in his urine from the hammerlike blows to his kidneys, he fancied his toes were bleeding where one of the jailers had stood on them with thick-soled boots. And pain underneath, pain as deep as the Cayman abyssal. Vomit covered his shirt, and worse filth stained the inside of his pants.

He felt a callused yet gentle hand rock his head. Some kind of leaves went into his mouth, and the hand worked his jaw. He chewed with loosened teeth and swallowed; it seemed important to the hand.

"*Oui, oui,* my child. This will help, yes," a woman's voice said in Haitian Creole.

Valentine opened one blood-gummed eye and looked up into a

black face. Warm dark eyes looked down at him, a tenderness glowing there thanks to some inner light. He felt he must be resting in a lap—though the arrangement of her legs seemed wrong—but he only had a moment to enjoy the sensation before fading out.

When he awoke, he was in clean cotton ducks of the same kind he had seen under the straw hats in the Cape Haitian market. Something had woken him, and a sniff of fresher air made him turn to the door, which the breeze told him was open.

A figure slid in, moving mostly with its arms like a chimpanzee. It was the same woman who had cradled his head in her caressing hands. She was disfigured: two fleshy stumps were all she had left of her legs, and one arm ended in a leather-covered knob at her wrist. She had a wide nose, so wide it seemed to touch every other part of her face, below a cheerful yellow bandanna tied tight around her head. Swinging on her arms, like a cripple using two short crutches, she was at his side in two strides. She pivoted on the wrist-stump as neatly as a ballerina en pointe.

"Feeling better, child?"

"Yes. Whatever was in those leaves helped."

The door remained open. A lemon-sucking guard watched every move the woman made in the bare cell. Valentine noticed that she wore a man's wristwatch with a cracked crystal on her good arm.

"Food and water'll help more. I brought both. I'm Sissy. I tend to the poor souls in here."

"Sissy?"

"Short for Narcisse," she said, unrolling a bundle. A coconut and further food wrapped in bits of rag greeted him.

"Food doesn't sound that good, but that coconut—"

"As full of milk as a cow, child. You want me to hold it for you?" She sniffed at the air above his waist, like a mother wondering if a diaper needed changing.

"I think I can manage."

Valentine removed the coir plug and tipped the sweet, thin coconut milk down his throat. It tasted like pure honey.

"You're a good healer, child. I've seen men die from such a beating. Here you are with an appetite already."

"I'm grateful," he said, handing her the empty husk.

"You want the meat inside?"

"Maybe later."

"I understand, child. Been there myself."

"Sorry to hear that."

"Grateful *and* sorry." She chuckled. "That makes you two rungs up on every man in this town."

"Narcisse," Valentine said, not to his nurse, but to the ceiling of the cell. "That's a lovely name."

"Twenty years ago, I was a lovely girl."

"You still are. Nobody is more beautiful than someone who takes away pain."

She half snorted, half laughed. "Child, you're a charmer. Now you're three rungs up."

Valentine unwrapped a piece of cheese and nibbled at it with sore teeth. "Good of them to let you in here."

"Captain Boul's orders. I heard the men talking. They want you to live."

Valentine probed a loosened tooth with his tongue and refrained from comment.

"Ten minutes, and you'll need to pass water, bad," Sissy predicted. "I'll be back with a basin."

She swung herself to the door and glared up at the man blocking it. "Thank you," she said as he moved aside. Valentine almost felt the air chill at her tone.

Sissy helped him urinate at the end of the predicted ten-minute interval in such a matter-of-fact fashion, Valentine almost laughed at the procedure.

"Christ that burns," Valentine groaned.

"Pain means you're still breathing," she commiserated. "Told myself that before—and before that, too."

She put his head in her lap again and started to sponge blood clots out of his hair. "You're wondering, and you're too polite to ask. I'm like this from my own beatings, from trying to run away out of here. I started out in the sugar fields. Tried to get away once too often. I'd be dead, except I can cook better than anyone this side of the island. And they're afraid of my juju."

"Actually I was wondering about the watch. It doesn't fit you."

"Hmpf. Most people just see a woman with stumps. This belonged to my man, Robert," she said, pronouncing the name *Rowberr.* "He went to join the guerrillas, and I never seen him since. I think he's dead."

Valentine lay back, trying to fall asleep. There was no pain in sleep. "Do you ever think of running again?" he breathed, his voice hardly a whisper.

"Hard to run with no legs, child," she said, cradling his head again and bringing her face close to his so he could hear.

"When you bring me dinner . . . ," Valentine began.

Narcisse listened, gently stroking his head. But Valentine felt her body tremble with excitement as he spoke.

*   *   *

Valentine lay down, and tried to sleep away the afternoon. He'd gotten up and walked around the cell. There was one final wall of pain to get through as he did so, and then he felt his strength coming back to him as though a dam had burst. He put his back to the wall where the guard couldn't see him and squatted and stretched and tried a few push-ups. The exertion left him as limp as water. He tried to sleep. He told himself he would never be able to rest: there were gaping holes in his plan, beginning with the necessity of him staying in this cell for another meal. He tried to relax, worried that a change in mood could alter his lifesign signature. He hadn't seen any Reapers on Haiti yet, or felt their presence, but that didn't mean they would not come for him. And with all those worries, sleep still ambushed him.

He woke with a start at the sound of Sissy's voice outside the door. "What, you on hourly wages? Food's getting cold, boy. Get this thing open."

The door swung inward, and Valentine rolled over to see Narcisse. She had changed into heavier long-sleeved clothes, and the yellow bandanna had been replaced by a blue-green one.

Valentine rolled onto his side and knelt, as a hungry man looking forward to his meal. The guards looked in Narcisse's bag, poking through the contents.

"Awful lot in here."

"You know the cap'n's orders. He wants him well fed. He didn't eat much earlier owing to the beating—he'll be healing-hungry now. I'm going to give him a wash, too. That's what the water's for."

The jailers exchanged a look. One stepped aside so she could pass. She executed a neat hop over his foot, but her trailing culottes caught on his boot. Something fell from between her stumps and clattered to the floor.

The guards and Valentine looked down. It was a filleting knife—with a razor-sharp blade and a sturdy handle.

The guard outside the door reached for his rifle. The one inside bent to grasp at the knife. Valentine took his chance. Excitement overrode the stiffness in his body.

He sprang, bringing his fist forward. The defunct but heavy watch that once belonged to Narcisse's lover was wrapped around his hand in an improvised brass knuckle. The jailer turned his head at the blur of motion. What was left of the crystal shattered against the bridge of his nose, even as he tried to bring up the knife.

The other raised his rifle. To Valentine it seemed as though the guard moved in slow motion, and a rifle is an unwieldy weapon for a

close-quarters fight. Valentine whirled around the pain-blinded guard at
the door and stepped past the long barrel. He brought his watch-covered
fist against the second guard's jaw in a haymaker blow, trapping the gun
under his other arm. The gun fired; its bullet went into the cell, splitting
the air between Narcisse and the broken-nosed man at the door.

Sissy had the knife now, and stuck it up and under her opponent's
rib cage. Valentine grabbed his guard's head and pushed it as hard as
he could into the wall behind him. Two sickening, crunching thumps,
and he let the man drop.

"Get the keys," Valentine said, blood and cordite in his nose.

"They ain't good for the outer door," she said, slamming the door
to the interior staircase shut. "I got the captain's. Boul's asleep for the
rest of the day, and not much use to anyone for a while after that. His
chicken curry had a pinch of magic in it."

Valentine looked at both rifles and took the better of the two, an old
Ruger Model 77/44. There were no spare magazines, but one of the
guards had a handful of .44 cartridges in his pocket.

"Food and water?" Valentine asked. He took one of the guard's
sandals off and put them on his bare feet.

"Got it," she said, throwing the bag over her shoulder.

Valentine knelt. "Okay, get your arms around me. We're out."

Narcisse wrapped her arms around his neck, holding on to her mutilated forearm with her good hand. Valentine came to his feet easily;
she weighed no more than a loaded backpack. He went to the dead bolt
on the basement exterior door.

"It's the shiny steel one with the longest barrel," she said in his ear.

The door opened, and Valentine brought the rifle barrel up the
stairway.

"Most of the men that weren't wounded are behind sandbags in the
harbor. They expect your ship to come back for you. The white man
with the chicken neck wants to spring a trap once they land troops."

Valentine kept the rifle to his shoulder and ascended the stairs.
Where his eyes went, the iron sights of the rifle followed. He heard bang-
ing on the door Narcisse had locked back in the cells.

A trio of navy-uniformed men approached the stairway, rifles held
ready, hunched over as if trying to make themselves smaller. They
hugged the wall, all in a row, like the three blind mice. Valentine ducked
when he saw the rifle barrel come his way. The shot *ping*ed off the wall
behind his head.

He popped his head and gun back up and shot the front man as he
worked the bolt on his rifle. The other two dropped to the ground and
fired without aiming.

Valentine ran, popping off another shot from his hip as he crossed the street, trying to keep the other two soldiers hugging pavement. His opponents looked more interested in getting behind the twitching body of their leader than in shooting at him. He made it into an alley chased only by the sound of a gunshot from the roof.

"You okay?" Valentine asked.

"You'd be running a lot lighter if I wasn't," she said in his ear.

"I want to get away from the waterfront, if that's where the soldiers are. You wouldn't have a suggestion on how to get to the resistance, would you?"

"We'll get out of town and head west. Hope you're feeling better and some kind of athlete, child. These mountains'll kill you if the captain's men don't."

Sissy guided him out past the standing buildings and into a mass of rubbled buildings. A shanty town of sorts grew out of the ruins, homes created from rebuilt walls and roofed with everything from corrugated aluminum to old doors to woven palm fronds. Gaping locals got out of Valentine's path. He was running with gun ready and Narcisse clinging to his back like a baby monkey riding on its mother. He ran to the cane-brake beyond the rubble, then to the trees and momentary safety.

Valentine crossed the Plaine du Nord at a steady, loping run. Narcisse clung tightly to his back, Valentine's shirt tied around both their waists, to keep her from being bounced like a sack. They moved through the muted light of the forest, crossing old roads that were now only paths and the occasional overgrown foundation. During a break, he took a look to the south, at what looked like a tabletop mountain.

Narcisse panted: "How you run like that, child? Don't you tire?"

Valentine did not want to be reminded. "Oddly shaped mountain," he said.

"That's no mountain, that's the Citadelle. An old fortress. It took many years and many lives to build, they say. It belongs to him now."

"The local Kurian?"

She nodded.

"Why are we running toward it?" he asked.

"They wouldn't be expecting me to take you there. Once we come near the ruins of Sans Souci, we turn west into the mountains. Then you'll be among friends."

The dead air of midday enveloped them. Sweat poured off the pair and mingled as it ran down Valentine's back. Narcisse mopped his brow and eyes as he ran.

By nightfall they hit a grade that made Valentine slow to a walk. Evening birdcalls and air flowing like a slow stream seemed to whisper a promise of relief from the day's heat. Valentine found a heavy tree trunk and set Narcisse down between two roots. He passed her the water, and she spat out a beaded chain she had clenched between her teeth, and fingered the charm on it with her good hand.

"Those look like rosary beads," Valentine said as she drank.

"My favorite juju." She smiled, handing him the water. "They were blessed by the pope himself, in the long-ago, my mother told me. She got them from her mother."

"I thought you practiced voudou."

"Voudou's a bit of everything, child. Even the pope did it—he just didn't know he was."

Valentine emptied his gun and looked down the barrel. "Captain Boul's men take good care of their weapons."

"He dotes on that sort of thing. Every gun represents some piece of trading he did. He's just protecting his investment."

Valentine dried his chest with his shirt, eyes stinging with sweat. Even the thin cotton of his pants seemed to suffocate his skin.

"It's hot here. You'd think the shade would help." He bit into some kind of rice-flour bun from the sack of provisions.

"It is worse farther inland. The cool night is soon. Your name, Valent—Valenter?"

"Valentine."

"Oh, like the saint. And your first name?"

"David."

"Dav-eed," she said. "The king who danced. Your name is strong with magic."

"The only dancing I'll be doing is at the end of a rope, if we don't find the guerrillas." He looked east, where a long string of mountain feet ran down to the ocean. "Are you up to it?"

"There is a road along the coast. They will catch up soon on horses using it, once they know what direction we go. But perhaps they will not come this far. No man can run as you. This is a race for a story."

"Where is the finish line?"

"I cannot say for sure. They move. There are guerrillas to the west is all I know. Not many kilometers, I think. Their area begins at a place of good magic, and we are near it."

"So close to Captain Boul?"

"They have . . . an understanding, perhaps you would say. You do not know Haiti, David. The Kurian on this part of the island, he is more concerned with appearances than results."

"The one in the Citadel?"

"Yes."

"Do his . . ."—Valentine searched for a phrase—"'drinkers of death' visit Cape Haitian often, or use the road?"

"Monks of death? You mean the Whisperers? He does not use them much. Again, appearances."

Valentine thought for a moment, wondering if he was losing something between his barely adequate French and her Haitian Creole. A Kurian who did not use his Reapers much?

"I don't understand."

"Knowing that is the first step on the path to wisdom."

"Hope the path isn't as steep as this damn hill," Valentine said. He picked her up, retied his shirt, and carried her onward.

The next day, after a long mix of jogging and walking the rugged mountains of the coast, Valentine heard the sound of a hound's cry. It brought back memories from five years ago.

He was tired, hungry despite emptying Narcisse's store of food, and still sore from the beating in the Cape Haitian jail. Evening was well on its way; the sun had disappeared behind the mountainside. Picking a path through the tangled growth would become a blind, exhausting flight for a normal man. Valentine's gift of night vision would help, but he needed a modicum of light, and without some moonlight penetrating the clouds that gathered above the canopy, they were as good as lost among the lianas and creeping vines.

"We're being tracked."

"Yes, we are," Narcisse agreed. Her strong good hand still locked the ring of muscle and bone around his neck and shoulders that allowed him to bear her.

"You wouldn't have some hot pepper somewhere in that food bag, would you?"

"I wasn't planning on cooking, child."

Green *cotorras* screeched at them from the trees above. The noisy parrots mocked them.

"How did they catch you, when you ran before?" Valentine asked, pushing up yet another steep hill. Perhaps he could outlast the tracker, if not the dogs. Talking to Narcisse might get his mind off the pain in his legs and back. Exhaustion was an enemy that could not be beaten, but it could be delayed if he kept his mind from giving in to it.

"The first time was when I worked in the cane fields, in Santo Domingo. I hitched a ride on a taptap—"

"What's a taptap?"

"One of those painted trucks. They are still running after all these years. The only thing on them that isn't forty years old is the tires. The driver of this taptap turned me in at the first station we came to. There's a standing reward for runaways; he was a poor man.

"After that I met my lover; he was one of the guards who came for me. Kinder than the rest. After punishment, a whipping, he got me a job cooking at a waystation for the guards on one of the highways. They would stop, and I would cook and wash. I had time on my own when there were no soldiers to take care of. I went into the woods, and at a waterfall met a juju-man."

"A witch doctor, you mean?"

"Yes, Dav-eed. When I touched the stream to drink or bathe, he said I made writing in the water, which told him I could practice voudou."

Valentine set her down next to a great mahogany tree, looked downslope, and set the sights on his rifle. He worked the bolt and chambered a round.

"So he taught you?"

"People think voudou is all fear and hate, but there is love and healing in it, Dav-eed. There is a bad side—like anything, it can be used to destroy. Those who work their magic with both hands can cause much sadness. Have you ever heard of a zombie?"

"Yes."

"On the east side of the island, there are many zombies, slaves to the Evil Ones. They hardly need their Whisperers to feed from them. Such a sad thing, to have the *gros-bonange* taken, and the poor soul standing there, with no chance to even run."

"The 'great good angel'?"

"It is the spirit that enters you at conception. It animates you."

"I learned it was called the 'vital aura.' "

"One word or another—it is all the same. Didn't I tell you that already?"

"Yes. Seems different when it comes from a Lifeweaver."

"Still think there's nothing to voudou?"

"I never said that. I've seen enough to know not to laugh off anything."

Valentine settled down behind a thick tree root, stomach against the moist earth, with a good view of the slope. "Our *gros-bon-anges* may be packing for a trip. I'm going to see if I can't take out a couple of these dogs before the light fails. I smell a rain coming. That'll throw them off if they don't get here first."

"Wait for me to tell you to shoot," she said, sliding next to him for a better view down the hill. She removed her bandanna, and Valentine saw more scars going up the side of her head. They had a stretched-over, half-healed look to them: burns from long ago.

"Why, are you going to work a charm to make me aim better?" he asked, tearing himself away from the tales told by the scar tissue.

"Don't know one, or I would, Dav-eed."

The occasional barks and yips grew louder. Valentine tucked the rifle closer to his shoulder. He wished he had had more time to get familiar with the gun; it felt a little nose-heavy. Too late to fill the stock with lead weights now.

Slathered dogs came out of the gloom, towing a ragged black figure up the slope. Valentine listened for the hoof-beats of more men behind with hard ears. He heard nothing.

Valentine looked down the barrel and put the foresight square on the man's chest. He placed his finger on the trigger, then startled with recognition. He put up his gun.

"That's the man who sent me the message in the market."

She squinted. "Yes, I thought so when I heard the dogs. His name's Victo, but the captain's men call him Dog-boy. He hunts wild pigs with those things. He's a character. Come into town just to trade, though I've seen him around more lately."

"Monsieur Valentine," Victo hallooed up the hill in English, waving. "Have no fear." He held up a pair of boots. "Look, I have your shoes, sir."

Valentine stood slowly, his aching body fighting him. "Thank you, Victo. You know what a good pair of boots means." He put on cotton socks, another gift from Victo, and slipped the familiar boots back on his sore feet. The sandals had chafed his skin badly during the long run from Cape Haitian.

"I thought you'd be on the *Thunderbolt*," Valentine said.

Victo showed a healthy set of teeth. "No, soon as we knew you were missing, I put ashore."

"Where's the *Thunderbolt*?"

"Down the coast, off a little island. They won't be seen, unless another ship from the other side of the island comes looking. That's Roots land." Valentine took a good look at the man who rescued his boots: Victo was handsome, with coal-black skin stretched tight over lean muscle.

"Roots?"

"The guerrillas."

Narcisse interrupted in her Haitian Creole. "Men, we need to be moving now. Sun is going down, but that doesn't mean they can't follow us still. There's more dogs on this part of the coast than just yours, Victo."

"Yes, woman. He carry you all this way?"

"Like an empty sack. Up and down these hills, never knew a man could run like that. What do they feed you up north?"

"I'll tell you, if you'll tell the story of why the guerrillas are called Roots. Do you hide in tunnels?"

Victo laughed in the slow, easygoing manner of the Caribbean. "It's an old saying, *blanc*. When the old hero Louverture was taken from us, he said, 'Overthrowing me, they have cut down the trunk of the tree of black liberty. I will shoot up again through the roots, for they are numerous and deep.' We aren't numerous, my friend, but we are deep. Deep in the mountains, deep in the forests. Though for once, all men wear the same yoke."

Valentine took up his human backpack again, and swallowed a grateful mouthful of Victo's water. It seemed almost futile; the water left him as fast as he took it in. He thirsted as if the last time he had water was yesterday. "Never been so thirsty," he said.

Victo pulled a metal tin from his pocket, an old breath-mint logo in red and white still visible on the lid. He opened it. "Salt pills. Take two now. Two more later."

"There are springs soon. Don't worry, child," Narcisse said.

The Cat led the way, and the dogs circled as they hiked. It began to rain, one of the enervating downpours of the Caribbean summer. They made a queer procession, Valentine toting his human load, the rain-soaked dogs crisscrossing first in front, then behind, and Victo's long-legged tread at the rear.

They slogged through the night with an hour of fast walking along the hillsides, a ten-minute break, and then another hour of walking. By the time Valentine set Narcisse down again, he had lost the battle with exhaustion. His time in the KZ and life on the *Thunderbolt* had softened him from his years of run-walks with the Wolves and long treks with Ali Duvalier into the Great Plains. He had to take his mind off his legs, which felt like someone had shot them full of sulfuric acid.

"So you ran away from the station again?" he asked Narcisse. He put two more of Victo's salt pills on his tongue; they tasted almost sweet.

"Oh, yes. I heard you could get away if you reached the coast. There were boats, men who would take you across the waters to safety. But of course I was caught again. Brought to a coastal village, under a plantation owner. A terrible man, this one. He had four strong men hold me down, and he broke my legs with an iron rod. *Broke* is not a good enough word, he made it so the bones inside were nothing but splinters. You should have seen them—they looked like two run-over snakes. After that, there was nothing to do but take them off. The beast of a man gloated over me, said something about my not running anymore. He got his face too close. I tried to put out his eye. He chopped off my hand with a machete. For some reason, they let me live, perhaps as an example to others. For a while I went from plantation to plantation, and they would set me in the sun with a sign around my neck where the workers would walk by every day as a warning to others. Then Captain Boul found me. He had been a friend of Rowberr, in a manner, and he took me to his station on the cape."

"What ever happened to your lover?"

"He just vanished. I think that is the worst part of this time. You do not even know if people die. They just disappear. Perhaps they ran; perhaps they were killed. You don't know."

Valentine's legs no longer bothered him. He tried to imagine what it would feel like, to have the bones so broken they were nothing but pieces, and had to shift his mind to the trees towering overhead.

"My brothers and sisters, too. Just gone," Victo added.

"I'm sorry," Valentine said. It wasn't enough.

Victo nodded. "Let's sleep. It is safe—we are far enough into the Roots' lands that anyone after us will come slowly."

"Can you find them?" Valentine asked.

"They will find us."

Valentine would have slept through the dawn were it not for the birds. The parrots hollered back and forth between the trees like argumentative neighbors, while thousands more greeted the morning with song and call. Victo and the dogs slept in a snoring mass, and Narcisse lay with her back pressed up against his. He felt something disquieting in his crotch.

"Sissy," Valentine whispered.

"Yes, Dav-eed?" she yawned.

"I think a bug or something crawled up my leg."

"That is bad, especially if it is a centipede. Turn yourself so it rests in your trousers, rather than against your skin."

Valentine shifted, wondering if after all the hazards he faced he would finally be brought down by an insect. Whatever it was decided to cling to his thigh.

"It's still there."

"Take down your pants."

Victo woke up and looked at the operation. Valentine got into a position as if he were doing a push-up, and Narcisse helped him take down the loose cotton pants.

"It is a centipede," she said, smiling. Valentine looked down. It was long and black, with painful-looking pincers waving back and forth. Narcisse maneuvered her head and blew on the centipede. It didn't care for the breeze and began crawling down his leg. Still blowing, she herded it onto his lowered trousers, and from there used a stick to encourage it to return to the debris on the floor.

"They can kill, though for a man as healthy as you, it might just be very painful."

"The same thing happened to a friend of mine," Victo said. "It bit his sack—he said it swelled up like a mango. Oh, how he howled."

Valentine grimaced. "Thanks for waiting to tell me that."

Valentine heard the guerrillas first as he cast about that morning with his hard ears. The dog-led trio was following a game trail west up yet another hillside. Five or six men, keeping concealed, paralleled their track up the slope. He picked out their step from the cacophony of the Haitian forest: birdcalls, creaking trees, and wind in leaves.

He called a halt. The dogs startled at the sound of the guerrillas' approach down the hillside. Two came down to greet them; the rest observed from above. Valentine was relieved to hear glad words of greeting rather than a challenge when they caught sight of Victo. They were well fed if scantily dressed, with rifles tied across their shoulders and short wooden spears tipped with metal and thorn-bristled clubs. They embraced and descended into a bantering conversation Valentine couldn't begin to follow.

Victo turned to him with a smile. "They were sent to find us, Captain Valentine. Word of your escape reached the hills. They are also in contact with your ship. It is waiting off Labadee not far from here."

Valentine's growling stomach asked the next question. "Do they have food?"

"Soon, soon. Their company watches the road out of Limbe at the river. They have a camp there. It is a downhill walk."

"Thank God."

"But soon you will be climbing mountains again, my friend. You must see the keeper of the weapon against Kur."

"So you do know. What is it? Don't tell me I traveled a thousand miles for an old voudou curse."

"No. Papa Legba will tell you more. I do not know much about how it works. A very old magic, they say. But even the Whisperers fear to cross into this part of Haiti."

"Where do I find Papa Legba?"

Victo's eyes furrowed. "They did not tell you? You must go up to the Citadelle. To meet the Kurian there. We call him Papa Legba. He will show you the weapon."

Seven

La Citadelle, Haiti: A black revolutionary known as "the Tiger"—who earned his reputation by sawing people in half—dreamed of Haiti's Citadelle as one of a ring of forts to guard Hispaniola against a return of the white slaveholders. The work of two hundred thousand laborers, of whom twenty thousand perished and, according to island legend, had their blood used as mortar to cement the stones, reshaped the top of the mountain with battlements faintly resembling a giant ship. This grim monument looks out on eroded mountains, now being reclaimed by the lush forests of the days when Christopher Columbus viewed them.

Set in walls a hundred feet high and fully thirty feet thick at their base, gunports like shaded black eyes look out on the north coast of Haiti and the steep track leading to La Citadelle. It is exactly the kind of cyclopean monument the Kurians make their refuge as they order the affairs of men. Behind walls of cannonballs piled like banks of skulls, there are storerooms and cisterns enough to feed an army for a year, space for troops, and catacombs beneath ready for untold horrors. The Kurian Lord has perches aplenty to stand, brooding at an altitude of three thousand feet while the stars whirl overhead. He could contemplate his domain in security, knowing that even a United States infantry division of the twentieth century would have a tough time blasting his men from the mountaintop, but their like no longer exist on Vampire Earth.

Were the Citadelle's lord looking out from his sun-bleached battlements one bright April morning, he would have seen a strange column ascending the switchback trail to his door. A black man hikes in the lead, being helped up the hillside by his sniffing dogs. Behind him a muscular mass of apelike Grogs, using their arms as much as their legs to negotiate the slope, followed by a taller, fawn-colored relative carrying a gun with a six-foot barrel. Behind him a handsome, dark-haired man with a slight limp uses a staff to get help up the worst parts of the trail. Ragged black soldiers, all wary eyes and ready weapons, follow in single file. The Kurian might think it a strange, pathetic as-sortment to challenge the stronghold atop the Pic La Ferriere, *let alone the entire Kurian Order.*

David Valentine's second thoughts collided with third—and fourth—thoughts on the long climb. He had thrown the dice with his life lying on the table on more than one occasion, but never on such a strange gamble as this. Were it not for Ahn-Kha's steady presence be-side him, locking his long toes around tree roots and rocks as he helped him over washouts on the trail up the mountain, he would have re-turned to the *Thunderbolt* days ago and quitted his task. Despair had never struck him when the bullets were cracking all around, but waited to infiltrate once he had a full belly and a decent night's sleep.

He had rejoined the *Thunderbolt* after a morning with Victo spent following the Limbe River to the coast, and from there a short canoe trip to her anchorage off Labadee. Following a freshwater shower and a change of clothes, he held an open-air meeting on the stern, telling his story to the Jamaican pirates and New Orleans mutineers, and explain-ing what would happen over the next few days.

As sunset fell, the officers and men decided that Carrasca and Post would stay with the ship, and a few members of the crew would join Grogs and the Haitian guerrillas on the next step: making contact with the "Kurian ally" in his mountaintop fortress. This stirred the interest of the crew; they had more questions than he had answers. The *Thun-derbolt* would be safe enough. Her main armament had been repaired, and she was as ready to face a seaborn challenge as the day she sailed into Cape Haitian.

With that finished, the Grogs and men took their arms from the locker, and such provision as the NCOs could force them to carry. A beach party of sorts welcomed them to the mountains of Haiti, with comic sign language and a babble of English, French, and Spanish along with island patois the method of intercourse. Two mornings later, Val-entine found himself sweating up *La Ferriere*'s escarpment with his odd conglomeration, guided by Victo.

Two silent sentries in tiger-striped uniforms stood in the lot before the main gate to the fortress. A rusting wall of aged jeeps and trucks was the first, and least impressive defense of La Citadelle, blocking the last few feet of what was left of the road up the slope.

A circle of Haitians Valentine took to be porters lounged in the shade of the high point looking out over the path like the prow of a massive ship. Some slept, some talked, one or two eyed the visitors with interest when a pair of sailors lit cigarettes. Valentine thought of the thousands of their fore-fathers it must have taken to build this castle among the clouds.

The guards and Victo exchanged more singsong words in their Creole. Valentine caught "Papa Legba," and *"oui"* but little else. A man in a clean white uniform appeared at the main gate and led them to an inner courtyard. There did not seem to be many inhabitants in evidence, just a handful of sentries keeping watch on the approaches to the fortress. The faint cry of a baby came from a high, narrow window. Below it the sound of the visitors echoed between the courtyard's stone walls.

"Papa Legba awaits," Victo translated. He looked eager, like a child about to be taken to Santa Claus himself on Christmas Eve.

The majordomo in the white uniform had the rest wait, then led Valentine and Victo deeper into the fortress. The air inside the thick walls was cool and still. They went up stone staircases, past small galleys which once held cannon, and into some kind of common room. Shafts of light came in from openings in the roof to splash yellow on the high walls. A sizable fireplace dominated one wall, fronted by chairs and tables of mahogany, roughly finished as if the resident eschewed form for function. An old man sat before the fireplace. Nothing but dead ashes filled the hearth. He stood, his back still to them, and took a crutch from the wall.

"So they sent a Valentine to see me. My cousins to the north do have a sense of irony."

Victo fell to his knees, hands clasped under chin, and began to weave back and forth.

"I really am old. It's safe to say I'm the oldest sentient you shall ever converse with, unless you touch one of the minds encased in what you call a touchstone. But I hardly think they'd count."

Father Max used to talk about the touchstones, cryptically carven rocks containing a world's worth of information. Touching one caused what the old priest called a "revelation of sorts"—if it didn't drive you mad. Valentine had never heard of minds being encased in them.

Papa Legba turned around. He was a hunched-over, wizened figure, resembling a Haitian great-grandfather, right down to toothless gums. Weariness colored his every movement and expression.

"What's your game, Kurian?" Valentine asked.

"Show some respect," Victo interjected, his prayers over. "Papa's been protecting you since you came to this island. If you don't see that, you're a fool."

"You have no reason to love us, Valentine the younger. And I have even less reason to love you: I was once a Great One in the north. My mind-mates—what you would call a 'family'—are dead at your father's hand. From the perspective of my years, it hardly happened yesterday."

Valentine kept his face a mask, confusion and suspicion and interest all warring within.

"But that is war, and I hardly blame your race. I returned here to forget. Out of my sorrow came thinking, and from thinking came wisdom. After all, you've been supplanted out of your birthright, and you're being consumed even now. It is no wonder you struck back, though many said you'd be happy with Kur setting the parameters of your existence."

"Came to play god? I'm supposed to kneel before you and thank you for your divine intervention?"

The Kurian sighed. "One definition of man: a biped who is ungrateful."

He looked Valentine in the eyes. The Cat felt the same vertigo that he'd felt in Jamaica when he met the Specter's gaze across the sights of Ahn-Kha's rifle. He shifted his eyes away, feeling a little like a cowed dog.

The Kurian's toothless mouth turned up. "Let us turn from dark thoughts. Have a seat. Would you care for refreshment? No? Very well. To your duty, then."

"My duty is to bring back this weapon you claim to have. What is it?"

"A powerful one, a tool that can stop my brethren's avatars."

"What's it do? Shut down the connection between you and your Reapers, maybe? That would be handy."

"All in good time. You're an impatient race. Excuse me, I must sit. I tire easily," the Kurian said. "Valentine, surely you know that the first Door opened in the Western Hemisphere was right here on Haiti. There was a rich, rich harvesting of auras during the revolts against the colonial powers. I, and one or two others, encouraged some of the excesses. Papa Legba is the keeper of doors and gates, according to local legend. In this case, they were right. The door to the 'other world' was in my care. It is in my care now. The 'other world' just happened to be Kur."

Valentine bit his tongue. He envisioned what was beneath the mask the Kurian wore; a shriveled, blue-skinned batwinged octopus lurked behind the grandfatherly fakery. But to see one of the legendary doors—

"You'd like to see the gate, wouldn't you? I will show you. It's safe enough. This island isn't important anymore—my cousins do not use it. They have others, bigger and better located. Those hungry for their own principalities go through the newer ones on the larger continents. Asia is popular at the moment: they're much less troublesome than you North Americans. I'm 'just minding the store' as your kind used to say up North."

Valentine pushed at the old ashes in the fireplace with the toe of his boot. "You want to aid us against your 'cousins'?"

The Kurian shimmered for a moment in thought or emotion. "This is a beautiful world, with a gifted though primitive people living on it. I don't care to see it become a corpse, like Kur. Sad. Kur is a husk. The surface has been cleaned of all life save lichen. The same could happen here. That's why I stopped feeding on your kind."

"You aren't afraid of discovery?"

"I keep up appearances with the help of my scoundrel friend on the Cape, and a few others. Though it might be hard to say with whom the good Boul really sides, just as he does not know all my devices."

"I don't believe you," Valentine said in English, to prevent another outraged ejaculation from Victo. "How do you stay alive? I thought you needed to feed to live."

"I do feed, off vital aura, as you call it. Though you might say I just wet my lips, rather than drinking great drafts as my cousins do."

"You kill only once a month, I imagine. I'll write the Vatican and nominate you for sainthood."

"Your letter would be laughed at. There is still a powerful figure at Saint Peter's, true, but he comes from Kur, and his cardinals are to be feared. I will show you how I feed. No one dies. No one is hurt. I shall give you a tour, starting with the Door to Kur. Then you'll see me feed."

Valentine took his hands from his weapons. "You have me curious. 'Curiosity killed the cat' is another saying we have up North, though I hope it won't prove out today."

A pair of Haitian servants—"Voudou priests," Victo whispered in his ear—emerged at a wave of Papa Legba's hand. One had a small chair, like something a child might be carried in, on his back. The Kurian slid into it and crossed a seat belt across his chest.

"I have a litter for going outside, but this works better on some of the stairs, as you will see."

The priests led the way, through narrow corridors and down shoulder-width stairs. Valentine's sensitive nose noticed a change in the quality of the air, and he knew himself to be underground. The priests lit and took up oil lamps. They came to a wider corridor. A heavy door stood at the end, and Valentine startled when he saw two pinched-looking Reapers slumbering in alcoves to either side. The skin was stretched tight over their bony faces, and lips were rolled back from black pointed teeth.

"They sleep," the old Kurian said. "Have no fear."

Valentine found his heart beating in the vicinity of his Adam's apple as he passed the motionless robed figures. If they came around, they would make a quick end of him and Victo.

"I wake them once or twice a month, when sacrifices of goats and cattle are brought to Baron Samedi," Legba said in English, winking at Valentine. "I'm not the only one using that convenient charade. I would suspect there are a dozen or so Baron Samedis on the other side of the island, though the ceremonies may be a little more gruesome. Religion is useful. Don't think it applies just to ignorant Haitians. When we took your country in the days of your father and grandfathers, many of my cousins appeared as Jesus, and his supplicants were taken to Rapture in the embrace of the avatars. Dressed in white they look like tall, thin angels, and their serene eyes held many a Christian spellbound."

Beyond the doors was a well-room, less finished than the rest of the fortress, built around a pit, perhaps two and a half meters across. The stones lining the walls were not cut and shaped, but irregular, larger at the bottom and growing smaller as they neared the curved ceiling. The priests lit two more torches standing in brackets, and the room quickly filled with an oily reek. The Kurian slid off his chair-backpack. Thanks to the torchlight, Valentine could see that the wall stones formed a vaguely unsettling mosaic of light and dark rock, rather like tentacles reaching from the dark well.

"That leads to what is purportedly a cistern, Valentine. Care to climb down?"

Valentine looked down the granite-walled well. A series of metal rungs descended into the bottom. Only a single row of bricks acted as a warning of the depths beneath. Valentine's sharp eyes picked out a bottom lit by a dim red glow. He looked at Victo. The spy shrugged, wide-eyed—and kept clear of the pit.

Valentine felt a curious pull from the depths. "Why not? I've always wanted to see one of these Doors."

"If you hear anything on the way down, or while you are there, climb up quickly," Legba advised

"You can count on it."

Suppressing a shudder, Valentine clambered down the ancient metal rungs, testing each with a foot before resting his full weight on it. As he neared the bottom of the cistern, he felt it grow a good deal warmer. *Appropriate enough for a descent into hell.* The rungs gave way to handholds carved into the stone, placed closer together than the rungs on a regular ladder. Feeling for the holes with his feet, he descended until he stood inside the cistern.

Clammy sweat coursed down his back, but its source was not the heat. He loosened the machete in the sheath strapped to his thigh and touched the automatic at his hip. Three rings of characters resembling Chinese ideograms surrounded him, melted into the rock and lit from within. Curious, he probed one with his foot. His eyes adjusted, and he peered at the walls. Several tunnels, also circled with the ideograms, emptied into the room, the letters glowed red, like the heating coils on an electric burner. He walked over to one and looked more closely. It gave off no heat, and reminded him of an old present from the Lifeweaver who oversaw his training as a Cat. He walked back to the ladder and looked up.

"There are different doors down here. Do they all go to Kur?" he whispered up the shaft.

"In a way, Valentine. You're looking at me from Kur itself. The gate is in the middle of the well."

With two hands and two feet again on the ladder, Valentine looked around. "You must be joking. How can that be? I didn't feel anything when I descended. It just got warmer."

"The Doors work just like that. They are literally doors, joining one world to another. When you pass from a dining room to a kitchen, you do not feel anything save the heat of the stove. You haven't crossed thousands of light-years, you've just gone a few feet. I'm not a scientist who can explain it, but two pieces of space have been joined like a button joins two pieces of material in a garment."

Valentine sniffed the air, tasted it. It seemed drier than the air of Haiti, and it had a metallic tang like a blacksmith's shop when the forge is working. A whisper sounded from deep within one of the tunnels, and he heard a dry scrape like a snake shedding its skin on a rock. Valentine heard the shuffling gait grow nearer. He did not bother with a last look around, and shot up the ladder. A sudden, not-so-irrational fear of things reaching for him, grabbing him to pull him away from Earth forever spurred him in his climb. He sprang from the mouth of the well.

He was trembling.

"I thought I might skip the grand tour for now. Just out of curiosity, what does come up that ladder?"

"No one for thirty or more of your years, Valentine. And before that for a long march of years, much more disappeared down it than came back up. Remember, there were hungry minds on Kur for centuries before we seized your planet."

Valentine's imagination, always too eager to supply visions at the wrong moment, visited him with images of bound Haitians being thrown down the well to blood-smeared shapes below. The torchlight's dancing shadows turned to a magic-lantern show of human souls in torment.

Valentine's eyes met the Kurian's, and he felt that sinking sensation again, not unpleasant this time, for it calmed his pounding heart.

"You're a sensitive man, young Valentine," the Kurian observed. "What leaps your mind makes."

"I've seen enough," he said, sniffing at the substance clinging to his clothing. It smelled like flour. The procession capped the torches and took up lanterns and the aged Kurian and left the well-room. From his seat on the bearer's back, the Kurian smiled at Valentine's relief.

"We leave the Citadelle tomorrow morning, and I shall take you to my true home, the palace ruins. I invite you to share my hospitality under these austere roofs, but somehow I think you will prefer to sleep outside the walls tonight."

"You read my mind," Valentine said.

"What I could. Your father was—what is the expression—an 'open book.' You keep more of yourself under lock and key. Afraid of what's in there?"

Valentine backed out of the room before the Kurian could say more.

They strung mosquito netting between wrecked trucks. Valentine and Ahn-Kha bedded down inside a defunct tap-tap, still brightly painted where the encroaching rust had not yet touched. Faces, slogans, depictions of food, and animals adorned the old shell.

Ahn-Kha gnawed on the leg of something Valentine guessed to be a dog.

"My David, you saw a Door?"

"Yes."

"My father told me they were simple-looking things. Just an arch of stone, no different from the gate we used to go into the courtyard."

"This one was in a well. It couldn't have been one of the original

Doors of the Interworld Tree—those were supposed to be huge. They were built by the race that came before the Lifeweavers."

"I did not know this. I thought the Kurians built the network between worlds."

"Yes, but it's built on an older one, or they learned how to do it from an older race. Some kind of creatures made out of pure energy. The man who told me about it called them the Pre-Entities. They go back hundreds of millions of years. They were the original beings that existed on vital aura. They left behind their science when they finally died out, and the Lifeweavers found it. There was some kind of schism, and a bunch of Lifeweavers on a planet called Kur learned how to live off vital auras, becoming vampires, in effect."

"This word, *Lifeweavers*. In my tongue, they were called the 'prime movers,' I think it would be in English. Some of them use you, yes?"

"Help us."

"And the Gray Ones and other creatures who fight you, are they being 'helped' by the Kur?"

"Okay, use us. Change us even. You've heard people say they bred the Grogs. Maybe they did the same with us. Once a Lifeweaver told me that my species 'exceeded their expectations.' It makes me wonder. Lately I've felt like a pawn in a game of chess, but I can't see the rest of the board."

"Paw in chest?"

"A pawn. Chess—an old strategy game. Remember the Big Man's office in Omaha? You've seen the board. Eight squares by eight squares. The pieces are figures meant to represent different medieval icons. They move into an opposing piece's square, and it is removed from the game. The pieces are supposed to be kings and queens and knights and things. The pawns, well, they're the—"

"Cannon fodder," Ahn-Kha said, ears dancing, as they tended to do when he was pleased with himself.

"Yes. They tend to get taken off the board by the more powerful pieces."

Ahn-Kha crunched the bone between his teeth, like a ruminant with its cud. "Tell me, my David. In chess, can a pawn kill an enemy king?"

"Yes."

"Then be that pawn."

The next day, Valentine's party grew. A throng of voudou priests, porters, guerrillas, Grogs, and Valentine all shared a breakfast of rice porridge, ladled into wooden bowls from a larger pot. The unknown chef added texture by throwing in chunks of sweet potato, making three straight days he'd eaten it in one form or another. He had already grown tired of the endless parade of sweet potatoes and rice.

Papa Legba bobbed out the gate in a litter carried by four strong porter-priests. It reminded Valentine of pictures he had seen of Oriental monarchs being toted around in curtain-draped chairs. They left the walls of the massive Citadelle atop its mountain and made the descent northward on the landslide-broken road.

Valentine watched the sweating, straining back muscles of the porter-priests as they negotiated the trail. "You'd think a voodoo spirit could find a better way to get around," he muttered to Ahn-Kha.

On the way down, he had time to admire the view. Scattered clouds fled the coming sun. To the west, the Chaine de Belance and the Massif du Nord joined at the heart of the guerrilla country. To the north, partly hidden in morning mists, the old plantation plains stretched to Cape Haitian and the Caribbean, with further lower mountains to the east. New forests fought to make a comeback against soil weakened by erosion. He looked up at the fortress behind and above and tried to guess where the door to Kur was buried. *Odd to think that another world can be so close*, he thought. *As if you could climb the mountains to the moon by joining it at the horizon.*

Ahn-Kha glared at the sun, his ears drooping. "Too hot here, my David. It drains. The sun fixes itself to you like a leech."

"We won't be in it all day. They said it is only a few miles."

Valentine halted and let the men and Grogs walk by. The mixed forces had a sprightly step, though the Grogs panted in the heat. The new acquaintances, the feeling of being among friends—or in the Haitians' case, having allies off the island—formed a bond between the diverse groups.

The column plunged into new forest, vigorous young trees shooting upward, racing each other for the sun. As the land flattened out, they emerged into a field of palmetto, which in turn gave way to better-tended lands. Food crops and orchards surrounded them. In the distance, Valentine picked out the ruins of a mansionlike palace. A newer roof had been grafted onto old walls, though smaller wings of the old building still languished in disrepair.

Glorious gardens surrounded the hilltop half-ruin. Valentine had seen small decorative gardens before, but never anything on such a scale. Flowers representing each color of the spectrum stood in well-tended rows, clipped paths running around and between them, for a mile all around. A lake, shade trees, even a small fountain stood about the earthquake-ravaged walls.

Haitians in their eternal straw hats worked the fields and gardens. They had a sleek vitality to them: the healthy look that an ample diet and activity brings. Valentine had seen many farms and camps under Kurian rule, but never one where the occupants looked so hale.

Papa Legba, as Valentine was now willing to call him with grudging interest, descended from his litter. Valentine watched rib bones like oversize fingers spread and then close as the Kurian drank in the air.

"Come, come, Valentine, Victo. Walk with me in my gardens. Bring your giant guardian, if you wish. Francier, look to our guests, would you? Take them to a well, and let them pick their desire from the orchards."

Some of the sailors elbowed each other as they admired the lithe Haitian girls.

Valentine jerked his chin, and the gesture brought Torres forward. "Keep the men out of trouble," he said, before joining the Kurian. Ahn-Kha sang out a few orders to the Grogs and followed.

Legba made his way, slowly and painfully, to a bleached stone bench in the garden. Victo and Valentine each took an arm and helped him sit. Haitian girls, all muscle and gleaming smile, ran to his aid from the well, bringing water.

"Thank you, my children," the old Kurian said.

"You know what you are called up North?" Valentine asked.

"No. I'm sure my former cousins settled on something outrageous."

"The 'Once-ler.' It's from an old children's book by a man named Seuss."

Papa Legba shook his head. "I haven't heard of it. I don't read much human work. Some Dostoyevsky. A few lines of poetry, perhaps. I know a little Baudelaire."

Valentine watched it drink.

"So Kurians do live off of something other than fear and death," Valentine said.

"Yes, we eat. Though not as much as a human."

"The people here are so strong-looking. I was expecting a bunch of half-dead skeletons. I thought you were just taking their vital aura in doses rather than all at once."

"It is a hard thing to explain, Valentine. You know all life creates aura, even single-celled organisms. To a certain extent, this aura is also projected, just as your body gives off extra heat. The healthier a body is, the more it throws off. I'm able to live off this part of the aura, though only just. It is a bit like osmosis. I have to be careful when I sleep, however. I was napping in a grove some years back, and when I woke, the grass was dead all around, and I had killed the tree shading me.

"It has not been easy, no. And again no. Perhaps it can be compared to giving up a drug addiction. Except the body does not recover after healing itself of the need for the drug. I live with it, fight with it, every day. A real physical need, like starvation, not the psychological one so familiar to those who give up a habit. I can control myself while awake, but in my dreams, Valentine, in my dreams. When I sleep, it is six thousand years ago, or thirty, and I swill myself into a coma on the sweet screaming auras of your kind."

Legba's appearance flickered for a moment, and Valentine got a glimpse of multipupiled eyes, but the black face returned, licking its lips. "Why does evil have such strength? The thoughts, they grow on you in a way that virtuous deeds do not." Papa shut his eyes for a long moment, and his face became as false as a death mask. He opened his eyes again.

"My children, I've seen evil not just at its birth, but at conception. I was on the councils when we first began to learn from the *Anciens* about the secrets of aura. I spoke for scientific inquiry, for reason, for knowledge. What harm lay in facts?

"Harm, indeed. It had been so long since our race knew evil, it was as though we had regained the innocence of your Eden. Though the weight of the Opinion went against us, we did not fail in our resolve, so we met in secret. We pieced together what we could, supplemented the rest with our own formidable science that had researched aural energies. We called the others *Dau'weem*, which has no precise translation in French or English. The closest I can come is 'back-thinkers.' We were the *Dau'wa*, the 'forward-thinkers,' and held ourselves superior.

"It would be easier to lay the finger on one evil being. Say that this *Dau'wa* pushed us into what we became. But it was not so simple on Kur. We were scientists interested only in truth, and we were ready to subvert the Opinion even at the cost of our lives. The arrest of a *Dau'wa* galvanized us, and we began to plan against the day when there might be a more widespread persecution. We planned escape routes to other worlds, began to talk of weapons and plots. Sure enough, some of us, purely in the interest of science, tried out our theories on plants, animals, and finally a sentient. I remember the first time I fed on a sentient, some trembling wide-eyed creature from a long-nighted world of rock and ice. I consumed one and then another, and found that each aura was richer, as the terror in their pounding hearts mounted, knowing what was coming. I developed a taste for it.

"Some of them fought. We learned—what you would call the hard way—that it could be dangerous to drain the food ourselves, we turned to intermediaries, using our own DNA as well as others, to design the creatures you call Reapers. It took us ages to get the connections right, to get our animating guidance flowing out and the auric channels to us. In the midst of all this, we were unmasked. It was heresy on such a grand scale, I think the councils were unsure of how to handle it. They dithered, and we acted. Some fled to other worlds, including yours, and tried to carve out niches where we could live in hiding. A few recanted, but the rest of us used our avatars as weapons. We told ourselves lies, that it was us or them, justifying any tactics. They had forgotten war, but we took to it with a will, and our skill waxed.

"Kur was ours. During the battle, we made the most terrible discovery yet. A *Dau'weem* has the richest aura of all, like nothing we had experienced before. We began to openly boast of being connoisseurs of death, and we hunted our brothers up and down the tunnels of Kur.

"That proved to be a mistake. Had we pushed our advantage at that time, we could have owned every portal in the Interworld Tree. But we were like pirates who, having seized one ship in a convoy, immediately drink ourselves into insensibility on the contents of the wine chests, forgetting all the other fat prizes to be had. When the orgy of death ended, we found ourselves shut off from the rest of the worlds. The Doors were shut, permanently it seemed.

"The *Dau'weem*'s strategy would have worked. We *Dau'wa* might have stayed trapped on Kur, gnawing at it until the world lay lifeless, and then turning on each other at the last. But the *Dau'weem* forgot that Kur was the library of the *Anciens*. We learned to live off minimal supplies of aura in that long dark time, thousands of your years. I found, somehow, that growing gardens, thriving fish, and happy sentient life could give me enough to exist. I guarded my estate, for there was no honor among us *Dau'wa* where auric energies were concerned. I even killed for it. We despaired of ever opening another door when we discovered an intact portal from one part of Kur to another. It was like having both halves of an equation, we realized how to go about it, and we began to open doors. Not to worlds with many of the *Dau'weem*, but to worlds rich in sentient life. Like yours.

"I believe you are familiar with the rest of the story."

"So you kept living off the living, so to speak?" Valentine asked.

"No, I slipped into old habits, like an addict who tries just one more injection for memory's sake. We took life from your world, consumed it, and I joined in with the rest. When the time came to make the move here, I was in the vanguard, so hungry for a world of fresh auras, I forgot that I could do with less. But we did it right, we laid our groundwork well, found allies amongst your own people— imagine a bull offering some of his cows to the meatpacker—and when the time came, your dominion collapsed easier than we had hoped. Of course there was error. Our earthquakes sank islands and coasts we had meant to leave intact. The viruses we used to break down your social order were more lethal than we planned. But perhaps it was to our advantage, after all. In many cases we came as saviors, not as conquerors."

"It's been done before."

"Yes, from what I've read, your race is adept at exploitation."

"Can you tell me one thing about the *Dau'weem*?"

Papa Legba looked into his eyes, but Valentine avoided the stare. Locking eyes with the Kurian was too much like sharing his mind from the inside.

"Yes, young Valentine?"

"Did they make us? Humans, I mean."

"Made you? I doubt it. You're too flawed. Shaped you? Perhaps. They needed the equivalent of our Reapers, you must remember, something to do their fighting. Both the *Dau'weem* and the *Dau'wa* are too canny to fight through anything but proxies."

"I had been told you were just bad at it."

"Bad at it? Are we? Who owns your planet, young Valentine? Or more important, from your point of view, that is—who keeps the *Dau'wa* from controlling all of it?"

Valentine felt a hot flush come to his face. "As long as we're talking about weapons, you're supposed to have one. I've come a long way to get it. I trust it's not just smoke and mirrors."

"You've seen it already, from a distance, Valentine, though perhaps no one told you. But I'll show you the source."

Papa Legba walked down a grassy hill, into a stand of taller trees. Victo and Valentine helped him down the path. The trees stood in a ring around a hollow, a bowl-shape in the landscape. A spring trickled out of a rocky overhang and fell into a rill that emptied into a pool.

"There are many springs in this area. Some of them run beneath the floor of the great house, a natural cooling system. Though this climate is to my liking. I was always too cold when I ventured outside in the cooler lands."

They entered into a pine woods. The trees had the twisted, tortured look of timber that grows on a windy coast, and short needles, like those on a balsam fir. The wind-warped limbs of the tree extended in the direction of the prevailing airs like a woman's hair blown in the wind. Ahn-Kha ran his hand over the needles and grimaced.

"Strange sort of pine, my David. The needles are like thorns."

Valentine touched the bark; it was smoother than most pines, more skinlike. It made him think of the beeches of the north. The smaller branches had thorns growing on them.

"It isn't pine, Golden One. It is quickwood, to translate it into English," the Kurian said. "This is your weapon."

"Trees? You can't—," Valentine began, then fell into a stunned silence.

"This is what you came to find."

All the miles, all the risks, for a stand of timber. He stifled a hysterical laugh. "Quickwood? A tree is the new weapon against Kur? Okay, walking through a thick stand would be like walking through razor-wire, but that's not much of a weapon."

Papa Legba nodded. "You are almost right. The *Dau'weem* don't think like men, you must remember. They create organisms to do their work, not tools. Quickwood takes different forms, and there is a variant that grows into thorny hedges."

"A hedge? Do you know how big a hedge we would need to keep the Reapers out of the Ozarks?"

"Where is the famous Valentine patience? You've no doubt already fought the Reapers. Why are they so hard to kill?"

Valentine called up his ugly memories. "Well, they're strong and fast, for one. They're on you before you can bring your gun up. Even if you put a few rounds into them, those robes they wear slow the bullets, and if you do get flesh, that black fluid turns gummy when it hits the air, they never bleed to death. Then there's their skeleton—"

"That 'gummy fluid,' Valentine. Their circulatory fluid. They use it to transport oxygen as you do, though inside them it stays as liquefied as your blood. Quickwood has chemicals in it, in the sap and pockets in the thorns, to be precise, that act as a catalyst. To you it is an irritant that makes you itch. To one of the Reapers it produces an effect similar to that which happens when they are wounded and the blood is exposed to atmosphere. When it enters their bloodstream—"

Valentine made the mental leap. "Holy Christ!" he said in English.

"Yes, but it kills them much faster than the wooden cross killed your prophet. It is most effective if the wood is still living or recently cut, the results are nothing short of spectacular. But even wood that is older, as long as it has some residue that gets brought into contact with their 'blood,' will prove lethal."

"Why is it here? Why haven't the Lifewe—the *Dau'weem* planted this stuff everywhere?"

"That is a story that would be worth telling, if anyone were in possession of the whole tale. It was grown on another continent, long ago. Quickwood was used in the first incursion against us. By *us*, I mean Kur, of course. A few tens of generations after the victory, your people knew only to worship these trees, and in the intervening millennia, even that practice faded. I imagine the trees were turned into huts or firewood. Once harvested, it does burn exceedingly well and makes fine charcoal.

"The next part of the story takes place in the shadowy years as Kur again opened doors to Earth. A *Dau'weem* named Sen living on Earth, or I should say who was trapped on Earth, for the *Dau'weem* had closed all the doors and destroyed the connections as best they could. Sen learned of the new one that had been opened here in Haiti. He tried to reveal himself to certain authorities, but was branded a heretic and threatened with death. With a few of his followers, he searched throughout Central Asia, hunting not for treasure or lost cities but for this kind of tree. They found some survivors, and not without a great deal of difficulty managed to get it to this island, where they thought a great battle might one day be fought against Kur.

"They planted seeds and saplings, but were discovered by Kur's allies. Somehow the fact that they had brought quickwood to the island remained secret. I can't say for certain that they all died, but I know Sen was returned to Kur. I remember the triumph when they brought him back. A diary one of his men kept, in Turkish of all things, stayed in a cave they were using. It was discovered only a few years ago. Haiti's charcoal gatherers destroyed most of the stands of quickwood they planted, so even the fact that the secret was kept from Kur was almost turned to naught. I happened upon the diary and managed to translate it. I realized there were quickwood trees living on the national preserve around the old ruins here, and I began to experiment with it. I've resurrected the hedge version of quickwood. You are welcome to take samples of that back with you, as well. Both variants are hardy. They will grow anywhere more mundane pine can exist."

Valentine began counting tree trunks. "How much have you grown?"

"More than you can carry. You can take back saplings, seeds, even timber if you choose. I've seen to it that more groves exist in the mountains you see west of here. That is why the resistance thrives here on Haiti. The Reapers who go into the mountains do not return."

"I'd like to talk to the leader of the guerrillas, find out how he uses it in action."

"Victo here can arrange it for you. He's one of them."

The conference was held on the first night of May, under a new moon. Valentine, Ahn-Kha, Victo, and Post met in one of the spacious old rooms of the partially restored estate at Sans Souci. Papa Legba slumbered in a hammock chair on a veranda, with two of his attending priests squatting at the foot, ready to do his bidding should he awake. Narcisse was nearby, sitting on a cushion and cheerful in a red dress, watching the conference and Papa Legba.

Three great guerrilla warriors attended, arriving with ceremony they found appropriate. A praise-singer entered first, regaling the attendees with a litany of virtues and victories of their warlord to a Caribbean beat. Bayenne, the Rock of Thormonde (among other titles), was from the south, with a thousand soldiers and ten thousand subjects under him. Jacques Monte-Cristi had men, his "sacred knives" scattered to the west, blocking any drive from the other half of the island along the north coast. Victo served one of his lieutenants, in charge of the area immediately around Cape Haitian, nominally under the control of Kur. And finally there was Anton Uwenge, the Blue Devil of the Three Rivers, who commanded "three legions, one for each river of the north"—though the "legions" sounded like undersize regiments when Valentine pressed Victo for details.

Valentine, acting as host after an introduction by Papa Legba, began the conference at a long table in what had once been a magnificent dining room. "Thank you all for making the journey to Sans Souci. Please forgive my French—it is poor, and my understanding of your inflections even worse. I may have to use my friend and rescuer Narcisse as an interpreter at times.

"We've heard about the successes you've had on this island up north. We know you fight here with few resources but courage. We think you can help us, by teaching us how you use quickwood when you fight. I mean to take some back in a ship, so that we can do the same in the North."

The guerrilla leaders exchanged a few quiet words and gestures.

Bayenne rose to speak. "My men dig traps in the hills," Bayenne began. "Some big enough to swallow a bus, some only as large as your foot. We line the bottoms with stakes cut from the branches of the sacred trees. They wound the Haitian soldiers forced to fight us, and many times a man with a bad foot wound is no longer forced to fight. The others, the

Whisperers, they kill, as long as it is not a trap from last year. My men carry stabbing-daggers made of the sacred wood, as well."

Jacques Monte-Cristi spoke next. "Perhaps, *blanc,* you have seen the short spears some of my men carry? Except for the very tip, the blade is of wood, fashioned in such a way as to splinter and snap off in the wound. Sadly, it takes several men to get one of the cursed ones. They fight like demons. If you could get us better guns from the north, we would do more."

"We tried bows," Uwenge said, speaking in slow but clear English. "Blowguns, everything. Nothing will penetrate their robes. My men have wooden bayonets at the ends of their rifles now. But they still must get close. It takes a brave man to face one of the Whisperers. When they know a battle is coming, my men drug themselves with cocaine, sing songs, scream, anything to raise their courage. I never send out patrols of fewer than thirty men. If four or five come across a Whisperer, it is they who die. It is bad when they come from the sea in groups."

Valentine nodded. "It hasn't been for nothing. Your people are free."

Monte-Cristi nodded. "We sometimes think we are wearing them down. They do not raid into Haiti as they used to. But it grows harder and harder for us to go to Santo Domingo. They have established a chain of garrisons on the border in fortified posts, and they send out many patrols. Unless we use a small team, the garrisons send out columns. The men have to either scatter or fight as they retreat to Haiti. The columns corner them otherwise, it may end in brave battle, but they always win. Either way, we lose many men."

"That is the source of our guns," Uwenge added. "Without going into Santo Domingo, at least for me, there is no way to capture more. My men have wooden clubs and spears for reasons other than killing Whisperers. Boul in Cape Haitian smuggles a few to us, so we leave him alone, though he does terrible things to people trying to escape Domingo and then claims to be winning victories against us by pointing to the bodies. But he is useful to us, so we turn away and leave him to his games."

Post scratched the salt-and-pepper hair above his ear, extracted an insect, and dropped it to the floor, where he finished it with his foot. "We have a few extra guns on board, some ammunition."

"Anything would help," Uwenge said.

Valentine looked up from a map of Hispaniola. "Do you have friends, spies, anything beyond these garrisons?"

Bayenne nodded. "We have friends, through smugglers and traders. They pass us information."

"There are also the roadwatchers," Monte-Cristi said.

"Who are they?" Valentine asked.

"Spies. They watch the roads toward Haiti, let us know if many men go to one of the garrisons on the border. They also look out at the ocean from high points so we know when ships are coming."

"Do they have radios?"

"No, most rely on their children as runners."

"What about these garrisons?"

"We know that some have radio sets, the ones that are electrified. The rest use telephone lines."

"So most of their armed men are in the garrisons?"

Bayenne nodded. "Yes, or in the big cities on the coast."

Valentine thought for a moment, excitement building in him like a flywheel's electrical charge as it always did when he worked on a plan. "I'd like to see quickwood in action. I think we can help you get a new supply of weapons, but it would require men willing to go deep into Santo Domingo. I need to think this through with all of you. I can tell you this: We should be able to escape the pursuing columns. What do you say?"

"Tell us more, *blanc*," Uwenge said.

"First I need to know more about the interior of the island."

Eight

Santo Domingo, May: The Kurians outside the rebel territories of the Roots divide their subjects into a simple caste system. A young Santo Domingan is born into life as a peon, engineer, artisan, or soldier. The peons are the most numerous. They are the laborers who work the plantations, on the docks, in the fields, and within the mines. These establishments are known as stations, named for what they produce and for the man in charge. "Sugar Sanchez" would be a cane-sugar farm managed by a man (or infrequently a woman) named Sanchez. Peons are born, live, and die on the same plantation, though women are sometimes married off to other stations. The engineers are hardly worthy of the title—they are construction laborers responsible for maintenance of roads and buildings who enjoy a more varied life than the peons. Artisans can be found in the workshops doing tasks which take more expertise, enjoying enough comforts in exchange for their skill that they could be called "bourgeoisie" by the French-speaking Haitians. And finally, there are the soldiers, many of whom live in hope of distinguishing themselves in such a way that they are promoted to "Station Manager."

Being born into a class does not mean you stay there. An unenthusiastic soldier will find himself in a peon's barracks at a nickel mine if he makes an enemy of one of his officers. A young, vigorous peon may get into the soldier class through superior performance at the "trials," yearly contests held at some larger stations or towns by the Kurian Order's recruiters.

Geography plays a role in Santo Domingo's organization. The Kur control the island from the coastal cities, and as a traveler goes inland, the visitor will see less and less evidence of organization. The

Cordillera Central, the Caribbean's highest mountains, are comparatively uninhabited save for runaway peons and hunting Reapers. And the roadwatchers.

After the death of his parents and siblings, when Valentine filled the hours of youth in the Padre's library, he read a book about the space program. Though the astronauts were deservedly the heroes of the story, Mission Control back in Houston was the real nerve center of the operation.

As he stood at the roadside stop of La Miel at the unofficial border, a month's worth of planning came to a climax. He felt like the NASA flight director, receiving last-minute reports from the Haitians, the *Thunderbolt*'s crew, and even Santo Domingans before setting off.

He started off with Post, in charge of the core group of *Thunderbolt* marines and sailors who would use the machine guns brought off the ship.

"How are we doing with the ammunition for the belt-feds?" Valentine asked.

"I just finished checking it. The Haitians couldn't come up with any, or so they said. Leaving a supply on the ship, we've got a few thousand rounds, enough for one good fight unless we can pick some up."

"Let's have an 'alpha' gun and a 'beta' gun, then. Put the best gunner, by which I mean the least trigger-happy, on alpha. We'll just leave one belt with the beta team. The marines?"

"They're in good shape, plenty of rifle ammunition. I don't think anyone's got under sixty rounds—most have decided to carry over a hundred. About the same with the pack animals."

"Two canteens a man, at least, right?" Valentine asked.

"Yeah, some of the guys are carrying four."

"So far I haven't seen water being a problem, but we'll be moving fast. How are those pikes you came up with doing?"

Post shuffled his feet and looked down, but Valentine knew he was proud of his invention. Valentine had seen him working on them, and had a good idea of what Post was constructing, but he wanted his lieutenant to have his moment. Post waved a Coastal Marine over.

The man held an aluminum tube a good seven feet long. Valentine tested its heft.

"I wanted something light, of course. I found a bunch of aluminum pipe for electrical conduits in the machine shop. There was heaps of the stuff lying around in Kingston. It was easy to screw it together. Then we came up with the heads. It's that quickwood, threaded just like a pipe. Just a matter of screwing it in. It holds in well enough, but if we get a chance to stick it in a Reaper, it'll break off. Then you screw a new one."

He handed Valentine a sharpened cone of wood. It was perhaps sixteen inches long altogether, six inches of handle, threaded to go into the fitting at the end of the aluminum pole. The handle widened by an inch or so, before narrowing to a point capped with a sharp metal tip.

"I've seen those Reaper robes before. This'll penetrate," Post continued. "Material designed to stop a lead bullet doesn't do much good against a point like this. If things get dicey, you can grab a spare point by the handle and use it like a dagger. We've got an adapter for the rifles even, the men can put them on the end like a bayonet."

"The training with the Haitians?"

"We've got two pikemen to go with every rifleman. If it works like it is supposed to, the one with the shorter spear will stay in beside the rifleman. Then there's the man with the gun, and another with a long pike in back. Of course, that's only if we're up against a Reaper. Otherwise, the pikemen will be hugging dirt until they can get firearms."

"That's the whole point of this expedition."

Valentine met with Ahn-Kha next. The Grog held a mass of metal and wood the size of a ship's anchor in his arms.

"Practice with the crossbows?" Valentine asked.

"The new cords are holding better, my David."

"No shortage of nylon line on the *Thunderbolt*. Just a matter of weaving it together. We'll need Grogs for those. I don't think any of us are strong enough to cock a leaf-spring from a truck."

"Care to try?"

Valentine took the oversize crossbow. The wooden frame showed the usual Grog craftsmanship, from the reinforced trigger-housing to the heavy stock to balance the weighty span of metal at the front.

Valentine placed the crossbow on the ground, planted his feet against the reborn leaf-spring, and gripped the corded nylon. He heaved, and just managed to lock the cord over the trigger. He handed it back to Ahn-Kha, feeling sapped. Even a moment's exertion in Hispaniola's heat brought a fresh layer of sweat running over old accumulations of perspiration and dirt.

Ahn-Kha showed him one of the quarrels, also tipped with a metal point like Post's pikes. "See the wooden flutes? They will splinter in the wound. The quarrels are lacquered to keep the sap inside fresh."

"You're sure?"

"We shot a wild pig with one," Ahn-Kha said. "We dug inside, found half the shaft. The rest of the head shattered into splinters."

"How's it shoot?"

"Try."

Valentine lifted its weight with an effort. He tried to aim at a tree, but the weight of the crossbow defeated him.

Ahn-Kha snorted. "Try this." The Grog knelt into a three-point stance, and Valentine put the crossbow across his friend's back. Sighting on the tree was a good deal easier with a quarter ton of tripod. He tried the trigger.

The crossbow had more recoil than he'd thought, though it pulled forward rather than back into his shoulder. The quarrel spun oddly in flight; Valentine had only shot bows on occasion as a youth. The shaft buried itself into the tree trunk with a resounding *thwack*.

"We have four crossbows, and something even more interesting." Ahn-Kha threw a blanket off a lump on the ground, revealing something that looked like an old-fashioned cannon. Ahn-Kha unfolded a bipod at the nozzle, poured a measured amount of gunpowder in the muzzle, and tamped it down with a metal rod. Four wooden fins flared from the tip.

"It's a harpoon gun. Better range than the crossbows. The shaft might go clean through, but the fins will break off. We use loose-grain powder for this. The tight stuff launched it too fast—it didn't aim right."

"Seems a hell of a load to tote."

"The harpoon isn't the only thing it fires. We can load the head with explosives. It makes a good grenade thrower. I've designed one- and three-pound loads. We may find a use for them."

"We might at that," Valentine agreed.

He joined Jacques Monte-Cristi next. The guerrilla leader had an elongated face and deep hollows at his temples, as if a giant had grabbed his head as an infant and pulled his physiognomy into a new face. Gray frosted his shorn hair, and his eyes never rested. He had the lean, suspicious look that Valentine remembered from his years in the Wolves: that of a man who spent much of his time walking into danger.

"Have you heard from the others?" Valentine said. The French tripped off his tongue more easily with constant practice.

"My men reported that they are on the move. They will attack in the night the garrisons north and south of our route, and screen our movement into the central mountains."

"Rations?" Valentine had been asking the same questions for weeks, then offering advice until he got the answers he wanted. Now it was a matter of routine.

"Each man has two days, and we have a further two days on pack-horses."

"Let's take a walk."

Valentine took a turn through Monte-Cristi's campsite. Two hundred armed men, aided by thirty "pioneers" who carried extra supplies and tended to the pack animals, were gathered in chattering groups. Valentine expected more tension on this, the morning of the expedition. Instead he heard singing, joking, and laughter from the clustered men. There was little formal command structure to Monte-Cristi's "regiment"; some of the guerrilla leaders had eighty men under them— some commanded a dozen. Valentine knew the names of only the leaders, and the men under them were a nameless mass, though he knew many faces by now.

They looked at Valentine as he passed through, smiling and nodding. He caught a word in Creole and smiled as he silently translated it. Valentine had heard a few men call him "Scar," and it seemed that the moniker had become general.

"How did you become responsible for all this?" Valentine asked after they had passed through the men.

"My 'sacred knives'? Pure obstinacy, Captain. It is not well known, but I am Santo Domingan."

"Why shouldn't it be well known?"

"The two sides of the island have bitter feelings going back before the Kur."

"I see. How did you end up on this side of the line?"

Monte-Cristi walked him out of the village and up the hillside and found a shady tree. They sat on the ground side by side and looked down at the lounging soldiers in the village. War, as always, was endless stretches of waiting. Fingernail-sized wildflowers bloomed in the morning sun.

"I was in the Santo Domingo underground. And we were literally an underground. We lived in natural caves and tunnels. I was in the 'cadre,' which I suppose meant officers. Mostly we exhorted others to join, and our men to stay. Eventually they hunted us down to our caves and blocked us up. Two times they went in after us. None ever came out to tell how strong we were. So they turned to words. The National Guard promised us good treatment if we would come out, and we refused. They tried to smoke us out with burning tires. There is not much gasoline on this island, but they even used that. Some died choking. Have you ever seen a body of a man who is air-poisoned?"

Valentine shook his head.

"We began to go hungry, and the next time they sent a prisoner in with food and more promises, I gave my men a choice. They could leave with honor—they had already been asked to endure more than any man could be expected to survive and remain sane—but I would stay and die. I asked only that they leave me their knives, so I would have something to remember them by as I stayed in the cave."

"How many stayed?" Valentine asked.

"Very few, perhaps one in eight. And you know, I was glad. I felt that no man should have to die as we were, like some kind of vermin. Even if they marched them out to a firing squad, I thought that a better end.

"Those that remained . . . became ugly. We stayed alive in there seven months. No food but what we could catch, water that tasted like sulfur. They sealed the entrance and made the cave a tomb though we were not yet dead. We sickened and died. Some of the men took their own lives. We kept alive in ways that only one who has been through it before would understand. I kept up hope by looking for other exits, or seeing if we could enlarge the air holes to get out. We did find a cave with bats and we ate them, and I remember those days as you might remember one of the finest feasts of your life.

"So how am I alive and out, you are wondering? Some of the very men who left me their knives had slipped away, and came into the hills to get our bones. Our remains were to be relics in a secret monument to the resistance, you see. When they found us, I had to be pulled up and out. We were walking skeletons. Sadly, three more men sickened and died eating too much when we got out. But I still had their knives, and offered them back to their families. When I was well enough, we slipped into Haiti. My heart is weak and sometimes I think I am a little crazy, for all I dream of is those days in the darkness. I keep away the desire to return and die in that cave by fighting."

"So you became a leader because you refused to give up? That's as good a way as any to become a hero."

"But I do not deserve it. There are legends already about our ordeal. In Santo Domingo they say I turned my men into zombies, and ate them. Here in Haiti they say Baron Samedi came and brought us food from the other world, and anyone who has eaten it is never the same again. Both legends are part truth and part falsehood. Ever since then I have been Monte-Cristi, the one who lives for revenge for all those who died in the cave. I fear I will return to the cave, either in body or spirit. Both would mean the death of me."

"Narcisse told me that you were the kind of man to fight to the last drop of your blood. Sounds like you came closer to doing it than anyone I've ever heard of."

Monte-Cristi did not smile. He was the only Hispaniolan Valentine had met who did not smile at the slightest opportunity. "The men are interested in you, too. Your ship, the Grogs, the Jamaican pirates, they already say you are a white Toussaint-Louverture. A man of cunning alliances."

"They say too much," Valentine said. He thought of adding a platitude, like, 'We all do what we can,' but decided it would be trite. The man sitting next to him was beyond aphorisms.

"I think someone looks for you," Monte-Cristi said, pointing down the hill.

"Lieutenant Post. Thank you for the story . . . err . . . do you have a rank? Colonel, perhaps?"

"I am just Monte-Cristi. I would feel happier if I were Jacques to you."

"Then I will always be David to you, sir."

"Your other responsibilities await. I should get back to my men."

They walked back down the hill. Valentine noticed that Monte-Cristi breathed heavily.

Post trotted up to him, showing no sign of wound or alcohol. "That bandy-legged fellow's back, sir," Post said. "He's asking for you."

"That 'bandy-legged fellow' is going to keep us alive in the mountains, Post. His name is Cercado, and we're counting on him to get us to San José."

"No offense, of course. He's just funny-looking, whatever he's good at."

Valentine found the funny-looking man in question at the village well, drinking. He was short of stature, potbellied, and naked from the waist up and knees down. Tangled hair covered his head, shoulders, and even something of his face. He was a "roadwatcher," the one with the most extensive network in central Hispaniola.

"Good news?" Valentine asked. He had learned in previous conversations with the roadwatcher that most items in his brain were categorized as either "good news" or "bad news." This valley was "bad news," for there were troops under an active officer. Another mountainside was "good news," because there were strawberries to eat and many honeycombs.

"Good news," Cercado reported. "The soldiers in the garrisons think they are going to be attacked along the mountain roads. They've sent out many patrols where the Haitians have gathered. We could take elephants over the mountains, and it would not be known for days."

"How about food reserves?"

"There could be much more, if you could let me go outside my personal network. And this business about putting caches everywhere— both north and south of the peaks—much of the effort will go to waste."

"Tell them if it is not eaten in four days, they may have it back. We could be forced to turn aside, or even back, and I want that food available. Also, just in case word does get out and they find some of them, they might guess wrong about where we are going because of the supplies."

Valentine missed his days on the *Thunderbolt*. Being on a ship eliminated many of the problems of food and drinking water, thanks to her available tonnage of stores. He was back to the days of commanding Wolves in the mountains, constantly worrying about how and where he would feed his men.

"You've done all that I asked and more. Take a meal and sleep while you can. We'll be setting off this afternoon."

"I can sleep while walking. I shall find you on the south slope of the Nalga de Maco tonight. If you hear hollow-log drumming, that means bad news. Turn back."

"Yes, I remember."

"But you will hear no drums, I am sure. Our friends will cause too much trouble for that."

Valentine made a noncommittal grunt.

The column was already ascending the mountainside when they heard the shots. Some trick of acoustics among the clouds and hills brought the faint popping sound of small-arms fire and deeper explosions from the garrison to the south, where Bayenne was making as much noise as possible. His feint against the garrison guarding one of the valley passages into Santo Domingo was crucial to drawing away whatever patrols might be out north of the garrison.

The raiding column moved with Ahn-Kha and his Grogs in the vanguard. Valentine hoped their unexpected presence would frighten, or at least confuse, any patrols they ran into. The heavier weapons, along with the sailors and marines of the *Thunderbolt,* followed behind, with Post in charge of making sure the main body did not lose contact with the Grogs. The Haitians were next with the packhorses, accompanied by a mounted force of Monte-Cristi's men watching the front, flanks and rear.

Valentine, astride a Haitian roan with a white blaze across its face, walked the animal along the marching column of Monte-Cristi's men. A runner from the forward column sought him out.

"Bad news, sir. The forward van ran into a patrol. They shot at each other—no one was hurt."

Valentine said a prayer of thanks that the men Monte-Cristi chose for his runners spoke their Creole clearly enough for him to understand.

So the Santo Domingans were no fools. He had hoped their forces would pull in around the garrisons, fearing an all-out assault. Instead they were probing.

Hoofbeats behind announced the arrival of Monte-Cristi.

"We're found out already. The screening patrol Bayenne sent out missed them," Valentine said.

"Do we turn back?"

Valentine fought the urge to swear. "They're your men, no matter what we decided about the command. The risk is greater now, but I say no. I won't make it an order, however. We can go with less. Detach a good number of men, fifty or sixty, under a capable officer. Have them chase that patrol south and make it look like we're a flanking maneuver to cut off the garrison's road. If they do cut it, so much the better."

"And if they meet greater numbers in turn?"

"Then they run like hell for Bayenne or anywhere they think is safe. I want the Santo Domingans to do the bleeding, not us."

"Agreed. Papa Legba said you were a man to be followed, despite your years. We go on."

After a brief halt that allowed Monte-Cristi to organize the detachment, they got under way again. The column trudged steadily and slowly uphill. The sun vanished in a crimson explosion, then turned the sky over to the stars. With the night complicating matters, Post called frequent halts to allow the column to keep in a compact bunch. At every stop, the men ate some of their rations meant to last for two days, but Valentine left that to Monte-Cristi. He had been warned that the men preferred to carry their food in their stomachs instead of in their bags.

Cercado appeared out of the dark, with two skinny youths he introduced as nephews. The boys did not take after their uncle in grooming: their scalps were shorn like merinos in springtime.

"We had some trouble near the border. A patrol."

"I am sorry, Captain. Always in war is bad news. Always."

You just summed up war almost as concisely as Sherman, roadwatcher. "We're pressing on. You've got more of your family spread out up the mountain, and then down to San José?"

"Yes."

"How many are there?"

Cercado frowned. "Were it not for the accursed ones, there would be sixty-seven or more. My father had five sons and three daughters, and I am the second oldest. My father and my elder brother both died. Every year more die than are born. There are twenty-nine of us now. In ten years' time, the family of Cercado will cease to be, unless some of the infants survive. They hunt us up and down the mountains, and sometimes they find us."

"Why do you keep on?"

"Why do you?"

Valentine nodded at the feral-looking man, for a moment feeling an affinity for him stronger than his battle-tested friendship with Post. "I understand. I'm the last of my family."

"You are still young. Find a wife, have children, go far from them. There are other ways to beat them than killing."

"My father tried that. I'm still the last."

"I see. So you stick to killing." It was a statement, not a question.

Valentine looked back at the men. "How long until we can rest?"

Cercado took the question literally. "At the rate you go? A few more hours. Say five at most. Then you will be safe among the heights."

They reached the heights, grassy meadows on the rounded tops of the mountains that reminded Valentine of some of the weather-rounded peaks of the Ouachitas. They had come up far. Far higher than the mountain that held the Once-ler's Citadel. It was cool, even for Haiti in June, at this elevation.

Valentine walked his horse backwards down the column. He nodded at Monte-Cristi. "We'll rest until dawn," Monte-Cristi announced. The men groaned in relief as they sat.

There was Post to see, and Ahn-Kha. The Grogs were already sleeping in a heap of limbs and broad backs, like pigs seeking the comfort of each other's warmth in a cold sty.

"Rest, my David. I will keep watch," Ahn-Kha said.

"I'll join you. I can sleep in the saddle tomorrow."

"You are limping. You always do when you are tired. Stop pretending you're a ghost and rest," Ahn-Kha argued, sotto voce. Ahn-Kha's rubbery lips came to a point like an accusing finger.

"Wake me in two hours. Then you can sleep. Two hours, old horse, and that's all."

"Agreed."

Valentine unsaddled his mount and wiped the sweat from its back and muzzle. By the time he hobbled it, gave it a nosebag full of vegetables ground with sugar, and checked its hooves, half an hour of his two was gone. He looked at Ahn-Kha, standing atop a rock with the patience of a tree, as if the rock itself would succumb to fatigue before the Golden One would. Comforted, he slept beneath the statue-like shape.

"Up. You've been asleep two hours," Ahn-Kha said, prodding him in the back with one of his crossbow bolts.

Valentine snatched the bolt and rapped Ahn-Kha on the shin with it before the Golden One could react. "Thanks."

Ahn-Kha responded with a playful swipe of his long-toed foot that Valentine ducked under even as he rose. There was a hint of something in the air, the early purple of the predawn. He realized he was chilled. "You lie down. My blanket's warm."

Ahn-Kha grunted and wrapped what he could of himself in the blanket. "Thank you, my David. That scout, Sera—"

"Cercado."

"Cercado kept awake. He moves well. I've never seen a man who can vanish among the rocks like that. Only you are more silent. But he hides even his shadow in his pocket."

"Speaking of silence . . . ," Valentine said.

The Grog snorted and closed his eyes.

Valentine watched the mists revealed by the dawn, admiring the craftsmanship of the crossbow quarrel while waiting out the light. The quarrel had chiseled ridges running down the shaft, creating an artful, air-guiding line from tip to flange. The Grogs put artistry into everything they made, even something meant to be fired once into an enemy.

The pink-and-blue of first light revealed his column isolated as though on the shores of an island, surrounded by a calm gray sea of fog. Everything was reduced at this height: the trees, grasses, and flowers were all smaller, as if imitating the foreshortened landscape below. He woke Monte-Cristi, who in turn woke his other chieftains. The soldiers gathered at a spring Cercado pointed out. Their guide's discovery was hardly more than a seep, but the men lined up as though it were a tiled bath.

Valentine wished for a moment he were one of them, joking as they waited for a washup. His thoughts drifted back, as they did with unsettling frequency, to the months of Quisling service on the Gulf Coast. Ordinary soldiers weren't asked to put on the uniform of their bitterest enemy, salute men they despised, organize more thorough sweeps of coastal islands and bays to capture auras for the insatiable Kurians. At the time he told himself, told Duvalier, that he just followed orders, didn't kill anyone himself unless they were shooting at him. Usually in defense of their families. Maybe Duvalier believed him. Trouble lay in that he couldn't convince himself. He could still hear the squalling of terrified children as his men shoved them and their mothers into pens, ready to be shipped—

"The mists are a stroke of fortune," Cercado said from somewhere on the other side of the world. "If we move now, we can be back among the trees before they clear. It is downhill from here."

Valentine boxed up his terrible memories. For now. "Good. We'll get off this ridge while it lasts."

He endured a series of vexing delays while the men took up their arms and equipment. Only the packhorses were ready, happily cropping mouthfuls of mountain grass.

Post came up the slope from the head of the column as Valentine mounted his horse. "There's trouble with the Grogs."

Valentine rode off the ridge and came upon Ahn-Kha, arguing with his scouts. The Golden One used a combination of barks and gestures to encourage his reluctant charges.

"What's the matter?"

Ahn-Kha's ears were up and pointed forward. "Fools! They take the mists for poisoned air. They remember their grandfathers' tales of chemical weapons of fifty years ago, and they're frightened of descending into the fog."

"Post, keep the column moving, don't worry about the Grogs for now," Valentine said, using the quarrel to tap the horse's flank. It trotted down the grassy slope toward the fog.

"I'll ride in and come out alive," he hollered back. "Tell them I breathe just as they do." The mist closed in around him. The sun winked white on the horizon.

When he replayed the incident in his mind later, Valentine rebuked himself for forgetting everything old Everready had taught him about moving alone, his first year as a Wolf. He had failed to lower his lifesign and his anger at the delays kept his senses from knowing the Reaper was near until it leapt out of the mist.

It wanted him as a prisoner, not as a corpse, for it killed the horse with a kick that caved in the roan's skull. Man, beast, and Reaper crashed to the meadow grass. Man fell beneath beast; Reaper landed on its feet beside Valentine with feline poise. It turned, its bullet-stopping cape cracking the air like a whip.

Valentine reached for his holster, but the Reaper was faster. It planted a foot on him, and knocked away his automatic faster than his eyes could follow the motion.

His arm went numb. The Reaper reached behind him and removed his machete from its sheath across his back. Pinned as he was, he could no more grasp the machine gun strapped across his saddlebags than he could the mountaintop.

"Hel—," Valentine managed, before the Reaper's long-fingered hand closed over his face. Fingernails like steel talons dug into his cheek.

The Reaper dragged him out from under the horse by his head, its baleful yellow eyes staring into his from an unkempt tangle of thin black hair. Its mouth was open in a theater-mask grin, revealing pointed black teeth. It looked upslope at some motion Valentine caught out of the corner of his eye, and pulled its captive to its chest, putting the other arm under his knees, like a muscular hero taking up his lover. The Reaper turned to run.

Valentine struck. In pulling him free, the Reaper released his trapped hand holding the quarrel. He gripped the wood near the point and struck the Reaper in the pit of its stomach. The Reaper staggered, gripping him so tightly to its chest, he thought his back would break. Valentine fought the crushing embrace and lost. He could not draw breath.

Suddenly Post was in front of them, one of his pikes barring the way. Valentine looked up at the Reaper's face. Its mouth yawned open in a terrible grimace, fighting some inner seizure. It dropped him, and sank to its knees.

Valentine rolled downhill. He turned three full revolutions before stopping himself. Vision wavering from pain and dizziness, he looked up at the Reaper. Its eyes rolled up into its skull. Post stood frozen, staring at the thing in astonishment.

Ahn-Kha appeared in the mists, his crossbow cocked and ready. The Grog circled the Reaper, and saw the bolt protruding from the stomach, the wood swollen where it touched the avatar's flesh. Ahn-Kha came to Valentine's side, keeping the weapon ready but his attention on Valentine.

"My David. You are hurt?"

Valentine shook his head, cradling his right arm. "Not seriously. I think my hand . . . or my arm is banged up good." What he wanted to say was that it stung like a son of a bitch, but Ahn-Kha never complained of discomfort, so why should he?

"I heard your horse fall, and feared for you. I readied the crossbow, for only one of those would get the better of you, and came. Post, too."

"Stupid," Valentine grunted, flexing his fingers.

"For leaving the column?"

"No, stupid of me. My apologies, my friend, I put us in danger because I wasn't thinking."

"There can be no apologies between us. Come! Let us see how this quickwood kills."

The Grog pulled him to his feet with burly ease. They walked up the hill, Valentine feeling like a Sioux version of Richard III, limping along horseless and with paralyzed fingers. The head of the column appeared out of the mists, Grogs among the Haitians with weapons at the ready.

Valentine inspected the dead Reaper. Propped up on its knees, it seemed to be howling at the waxing sun rising from the Santo Domingo mountains.

"Tell your great friend that he hit it square," Monte-Cristi said. "A good shot, near enough the heart to kill it in a few seconds."

"No, that was me. I barely stabbed it. The wood went in an inch or two at most, that thing has muscle like armor plating."

Valentine thought back on those "few seconds," which seemed to his pained remembrance to be hours at least, and looked into the empty yellow eyes of the Reaper. He tried to imagine what it would feel like, having the heart harden into a solid mass. Did the Kurian at the other end feel the pain, as well? He found himself hoping so, before shrinking back from the sadistic speculations.

The men would waste the whole morning admiring the dead Reaper if he didn't move them along.

"Post, let's tighten the column up in this mist. Ahn-Kha, you and your Grogs will get a break for a while. Take a place at the rear."

As the various groups got themselves organized in four different tongues—counting Grog-speech as a language—Valentine retrieved his weapons and saddlebags. Monte-Cristi offered him his horse, but he declined. Penance for his foolishness would be being on foot for the rest of the long journey. A pair of Haitian pioneers retrieved the saddle and added it to the pack animals' burdens.

The Grogs looked at him, sniffing and pointing at the still-warm cadaver and muttering to each other. One licked its chops. Ahn-Kha growled something, and they turned abjectly away.

The Cat intervened: "Oh, belay that. They can dress and quarter it, as long as they do it quickly. But they have to share with any of the men who want a piece of horsemeat."

Valentine squatted in the hills looking down at the armory, which in turn stood in the hills above the dilapidated town of San Juan. Behind him, the serration crowned by Pico Duarte purpled the dawn's horizon.

His column had covered close to fifty mountainous miles in three nights and two days, and had once again been reduced when he detached Post to cut the valley road leading northwest out of San Juan to the garrison on Haiti's border. What was left of his command was hardly larger than the garrison inside the armory, if Cercado's estimation was to be believed.

Their march had been uncontested, if not uneventful, as they descended from the high mountains, following paths staked out by Cercado and his family. Until they ran into a trio of Santo Domingan soldiers on patrol.

Monte-Cristi's horsemen had finally run the scouts to earth this morning, and the hunt ended tragically, with the shooting of all three scouts when they came to bay among some rocks. Valentine seethed at the loss of vital information even as he congratulated Monte-Cristi's men for their coup.

He examined the armory from higher ground. It was built more to withstand thievery than assault, though inside a perimeter fence of barbed wire the buildings were linked by a series of walls and wooden towers. The whole edifice had the slapped-together look endemic to the Kurian Zone.

"The defenses are strongest to the town side," Monte-Cristi said, agreeing with Valentine's estimation. "If we can get through the wire before they know we are here—"

"See all the dog kennels?" Valentine said. "They'd start barking while we were still fifty feet outside the wire."

"So we turn around?"

The temptation was strong. He'd seen the quickwood work, up close and far sooner than he'd expected. Valentine had no desire to burn the lives of Monte-Cristi's soldiers, who had come so far so fast without letting fatigue wear down their spirits. Valentine couldn't take all the quickwood he could carry and then leave Hispaniola no better off than the day he arrived.

But there was more than duty and orders at stake.

If the Roots accomplished something to make the march worthwhile, won a victory, it might bring more numbers to their cause. A successful raid that didn't involve being ignominiously chased back across the border would hearten the Roots as much as it would dismay the Santo Domingan Kurians. But it had to start somewhere.

"No. We can't blow them out of there, and I can't ask your men for an assault. We'll have to do it another way."

"I cannot imagine how."

"With parley."

An hour later Valentine, Ahn-Kha, and Cercado walked out of the hills to the wire, a white flag in Ahn-Kha's hands. Again and again Valentine blew a small officer's whistle, drawing attention to their movements.

Behind them, Monte-Cristi's men and the Grogs flitted from tree to tree, appearing in as many places as possible. They appeared at the tops of rises, then sank into the long grass to show themselves again behind a tree. Even the bodies of the three Santo Domingan scouts were impressed into the action; they manned a wooden machine gun from the crotch of a branch while leaning behind a tree. Ahn-Kha's Grogs called to each other from a wide semicircle around the armory; their otherworldly voices echoed ominously between the hills.

The multicolored flag of Santo Domingo hung from the flagpole, its white cross visible now and then as the breeze took it. A small house stood before the flag. From it an officer with a braided hat emerged and observed them. Calling a few men around him, the officer strode up to the wire fence, looking toward his towers to see that he was properly covered. As he approached, hand on the pistol at his hip, Valentine took the safety off his drum-fed submachine gun.

"Translate for me, would you, Cercado? My Spanish may not be up to this."

Cercado nodded.

"What is it? Who are you men?" the officer called to them.

"We represent the free forces of Hispaniola," Valentine said, and waited for Cercado to translate. "We do not come to fight, but to find friends among those who would oppose Kur. Much of Haiti stands free of their menace, and we look to our brothers on this side of the island to join."

"Your men have been beaten in battle at the border. You are misguided. It would be best if you surrendered to me, not the other way around," the officer said.

"Do your generals always tell the truth?" Valentine asked through Cercado. "We give you an hour to decide. You do not have to join us, just leave us this place, intact, and you may go in peace. Though we would prefer for you and your men to join the movement which will see Hispaniola rid of them."

"Thank you for your terms. Here are mine. I will take your heads, or you will take mine. San Juan has many men, and others will come and drive you out of these mountains. The garrisons at the borders still stand. Two days ago they asked for more ammunition."

Valentine yelled in Spanish, as best he could: "Have you heard from the garrisons since then, my friend? And was the ammunition delivered? Or did it fall into our hands?"

The officer pursed his lips, but to his credit, he did not look doubtful.

"We shall use the hour given to make ready for you. Come at your peril. If I were you, I would leave. Remember what I said about your heads."

"You can be sure of it," Cercado called, not waiting for Valentine's answer.

Valentine had his group back up, still facing the fort, and the officer did likewise. The men said something even Valentine's ears could not catch, but their tones were anxious.

Valentine returned to the shadow of a battle line. He would be reluctant to attack the alerted garrison even if he had the men he was trying to feign that he had. Was the officer bluffing as much as he?

He paced for a moment or two, as Ahn-Kha stared down at the armory.

"If they are expecting battle, there is not much sign of it. I've seen the same men go in and out of the center building three times," Ahn-Kha said.

"They might have sent some of his men to the forward garrisons."

"Perhaps they need another push."

Valentine nodded. "He said he'd come for our heads, I believe. Give them a push . . . good idea, old horse. I think I know how to do it. Come with me."

He climbed up the grassy slope, crunching through strawlike growth burnt by the dry season's sun. Monte-Cristi was at the edge of a steep ravine cutting the side of the slope, urging his men to move the unburdened packhorses down at a noisy, jangling trot and then up again at a walk.

"The hoofbeats echo well, do they not, Captain?" Monte-Cristi asked.

"Very well. Jacques, I think I have a better use for those poor scouts we shot this morning. I need a tent spike out of the baggage. Is there a bellows with the farrier supplies?"

"No, no bellows. Nor an anvil. But we do have tent spikes." Monte-Cristi got one of his pioneers to retrieve a spike, and joined Valentine as the Cat and Ahn-Kha went up to the stand of trees with the dead bodies.

"Let's get out of sight. Get a good hot fire going," Valentine said. He looked at the dead bodies, faces peaceful in death. Rigor mortis would soon alter their attitudes.

A couple of the Haitians gathered, looking on with interest. Cercado joined the group. Once the fire had grown, Valentine thrust a tent spike in the center of the fire, and Ahn-Kha blew through one of the hollow pipes used as a haft for Post's pikes, handing it to Cercado when he could do no more. The Grog's capacious lungs aided by Cercado applied enough wind to get the spike hot enough, when held with a piece of leather, hot enough so that when Valentine spat on the point, the spittle jumped off the metal rather than make contact.

Sweating from the fire's heat, Valentine crossed over to the bodies and shoved the spike into the eye sockets of each corpse. He was rewarded with a gruesome sizzling sound and the smell of burning flesh.

Valentine heard the Haitians mutter to themselves when he, evidently not satisfied with the disfigurement, drew his knife and sliced the ears and lips from each skull. He then ordered Ahn-Kha to sever the heads with an ax. Three hearty chops from the Grog and some knife work left the marred objects grinning in the sun.

Still not satisfied, Valentine took up the knife and looked at the three heads for inspiration. The frightening thing was how easy all this was. He expected to feel revolted, but something akin to exultation coursed through his veins. He remembered some lines of Nietzsche about how easily man reverted to savagery. Inspired, he knelt and loosened the uniformed culottes.

"My David, are you sure?" Ahn-Kha asked quietly.

"If I'm going to do this, I'm going to do this all the way," Valentine said. He took up the first man's genitals in his fist, drawing them as tightly as he could from the bodies. He sawed through the skin under the scrotal sac and in a moment held the awful result in his hand. He returned to the head, and placed his bloody trophy in the dead lipless mouth.

Monte-Cristi looked sickened. One of the Haitians backed away, fingering a crucifix, but Cercado squatted and rubbed his hands in delight.

"We can't attack them where they are," Valentine growled. "This'll do one of two things. Enrage them so they come up after us, or send them running." Valentine continued his depredations. He finished by putting the three heads in a sack, and shouldered the bloody burden.

"Their hour has passed. Will anyone come with me?"

Ahn-Kha and Cercado, followed by a Haitian or two, walked down the hill, again covered by the white flag and blasts of Valentine's whistle. Valentine saw rifles pointed out of loopholes in the sides of the buildings, tracking them. Machine guns in the guard towers pointed ugly flared mouths in their direction, ready to spit fire. Valentine spoke into Cercado's greasy ear.

"Far enough!" the officer shouted. "If you seek death, you may come farther."

"You spoke of heads earlier, my friend. Here! These men served a

Whisperer, who now is dead on the mountainside. We will come tonight for the rest."

Ahn-Kha took the sack in his hands. The Golden One spun like a hammer-thrower and released the sack to fly up and over the wire wall. It landed with a knocking thump before the walls of the armory.

The emissaries scattered, followed by a shot, then a second, from the walls.

"So much for white flags," Valentine said to Cercado, as the pair took cover behind a hummock of earth. He searched for Ahn-Kha. The Grog lay concealed at the base of a tree.

"You fight as they do," Cercado said.

"Maybe," Valentine replied. "Actually, the whole reason I'm doing this is to prevent a fight. But if we have to face them, I want to do it with the advantage."

"Only two shots. Why not more?"

"Why not, indeed."

The skirmish line hit the wire after sunset. All through the afternoon and evening, Valentine rested and fed his weary men. He watched and waited. The town of San Juan, like most he had seen on Hispaniola through the eyes of his binoculars, was a patchwork of earthquake ruins, banana-leaf huts, and surviving architecture. A few women came to the gate, bearing baskets, but were turned away without admittance and wandered back down the six-mile trail into town.

The Haitians avoided his eyes as he moved among them, disturbed at his treatment of the corpses. Valentine tried to shrug it off as the natural uneasiness of superstitious men who had seen social taboos broken. The bodies had been beyond pain and as dead as Julius Caesar, whatever animating spirit they possessed was gone; their souls could be prowling the happy hunting grounds or barking in hell—he would never know. But their corpses might have saved some of the lives of the men now shifting their eyes whenever he looked at them. In a fit of ill-mood, he considered presenting Ahn-Kha's Grogs with the bodies as a feast—*that would give them something to mutter about!*—but discarded the idea.

With the moon still down and full dark upon the armory, Valentine hit the fence with Ahn-Kha and the Grogs. They threw hides over the wire, and bodily pulled up the posts of the nine-foot-high fence, tearing away a twenty-foot section. The Grogs covered the gap with shotgun and crossbow, and the Haitians poured through. Valentine signaled Ahn-Kha to let the Grogs start their howling. The Haitians screamed like demons as they crossed the compound and made for the buildings.

Not one shot was fired from the walls.

The Haitians poured up and over the stone battlements linking the buildings, using loopholes as footholds or boosting each other up by having two men launch the third over. There were a certain amount of mishaps to the attempt on the wall, but without bullets flying, the bumps and falls were comic rather than tragic. Axes and fence-post battering rams made short work of the wooden doors once the men made it inside the compound, as Valentine and Ahn-Kha's Grogs secured the perimeter and main gate, which gaped open. He heard shouting, splintering wood, and assorted whoops of victory from beyond the peaked roof of the main building.

Valentine was glad to see a corral with animals still in it, but judging from the way the gate was left ajar, only lame animals were left by the departing garrison. As he patted a dejected-looking mare nosing her empty grain bin, he heard the main doors to the armory swing wide. Monte-Cristi and two panting soldiers bowed elaborately.

"The Citadel of San Juan is ours, *mon capitaine,*" Monte-Cristi laughed. "Not a shot fired. Most of the garrison has evacuated. What is left is inside."

"Send a few men down the road, where they have a good overlook on the trail, but I want them still to be able to see these buildings. Get organized for a quick pullout, I'll blow my whistle, and loud, three times if I want us out of here. Is there electricity?"

"No, just fat lamps."

"Be sure no one goes looking in the dynamite shed with one, would you?"

Valentine left the gate to Ahn-Kha and passed the main gate into the compound. The hollow-eyed officer lay there, bound hand and foot, with two of his former subordinates holding on to lines tied to his limbs. An old charwoman sat on a step, smoking cigarettes rolled from newsprint as she watched events; a pair of Haitians clubbed the officer who had offered an exchange of heads with their rifle butts.

"Stop that!" Valentine yelled. Another guerrilla squatted before the officer, laughing and taunting the wretch.

"Stop that!" he yelled again, putting his hand on his pistol. The men stood and turned, and backed away, hiding behind each other like children caught at mischief.

"We join, we join, we fight the Capos, you see," one of the erstwhile Santo Domingan soldiers holding a rope said in French.

Valentine looked at his new recruits—they had probably been bad soldiers for the Santo Domingans, and would be bad soldiers in his

Cause, but he had to make do with what he had. Valentine tried to put words together in Spanish.

"Thank you . . . give him freedom," he managed.

The Santo Domingans looked at him blankly, either not able to understand why he would want to free an enemy or confused by his Spanish.

Valentine drew his knife and took a step toward them. They dropped the traces in alarm. He realized that he was snarling. He knelt by the officer.

"My eyes! For the love of God shoot me, but don't burn out my eyes," the man said.

"I won't hurt you," Valentine said, doing his best to soothe the man. "You won't be hurt at all. Have you left any surprises . . . booby traps?"

The man shook his head.

"You'll remain among these buildings until we've found out for sure. If you speak the truth, you'll be let go. Do you still say there are no booby traps?"

"No. No, sir."

Valentine turned to Monte-Cristi. "Jacques, put him under guard. Guard, not torture. God, I'm thirsty. Is there a well?"

"Between the barracks and that house your friend stayed in."

"See if you can find any carts, wheelbarrows, anything, to begin with. I saw a wagon by the corral. Start there. Then start loading, medical supplies and machine tools first, then hand tools, then good-quality guns, and finally ammunition. Put the best cart you can find outside the walls but inside the gate. Load any explosives on it. No nitroglycerin even if you find it—I don't want to mess with that stuff. Dynamite would be best, if it hasn't sweated. Nothing heavier than a grenade or a small mortar. We'll use bigger shells and any nitro to bring down this place later. Then we'll start looking for food."

Valentine climbed a ladder to look out over the walls on Ahn-Kha, and then moved to the well. After a generous water break, he moved inside the officers' house. He checked the radio first. It was smashed, and there were no notes on the clipboard hanging next to it.

He wondered how long Bayenne and the other Haitians would be able to keep up their facade of an attack on the border garrisons to the northwest. Even now the Kurians could be mobilizing. He took up one of the smelly tallow lamps and checked the bedrooms; he decided that three officers shared the quarters. Strange that only one was still present; no wonder the man looked harried and his troops were on edge.

Valentine broke open lockers with a crowbar until he found a supply of cigars. He heard someone else investigating the dining room and saw Cercado rooting through a liquor cabinet. Once the roadwatcher had satisfied himself that nothing alcoholic remained, Valentine asked him for his translation services. He walked out of the house and went to the officer, who was drinking a cup of water brought to him by the charwoman. He offered his prisoner a cigar and a light.

"Now things are easier between us that the ugliness is over," Valentine said through Cercado.

The man drew on his cigar and looked at Valentine through narrowed eyes.

"You have nothing to be ashamed of," Valentine said, and waited for Cercado to interpret. "With the troubles you've been having on the borders and elsewhere, we knew you would have only a handful of men."

"Men!" the officer said, his eyes filled with disgust. "If only. I was left with the stupid and the incompetent. I, I—whose father was at the storming of Monte Plata. Left with the imbeciles and cowards."

"I understand. It is the same on my side. These Haitians, they look formidable, but they are hardly better than animals. I would trust a horse to have more sense."

"Mine forgot what sense they had when they saw the leavings of those scouts."

"With your best men away, what could you do?"

"Yes, first they called up the militia for the assault on the island in Lago Enriquilo. It is time we took it back from the Kurians of Haiti. Some of my underofficers went with them. Then when your guerrillas started trouble at the border, our Capos ordered that every man be scraped up and sent to reinforce the garrisons. Otherwise, you would not be sitting here."

"Undoubtedly. The fortunes of war, sir. One moment while I find out if you keep your word about the booby traps, and then you'll see that I keep my word about letting you go. I suppose it is too much to hope for that you would join us."

"No. In the end, you will be hunted."

Valentine smiled. "We shall see." He jerked his chin at Cercado and had him follow. When they were safely out of earshot, he stopped the guide.

"This Lago Enriquilo—it's southeast of here in another valley, yes?"

"I do not know much about it. An island in the center of a lake that lies in the pass to Port-au-Prince. The Kurians here have feuded with the Kurians there before. This island is fortified, it has guns that command the roads in the valley."

Monte-Cristi moved about the courtyard, shouting orders to his men. He joined the two. "Not a great bounty, I fear. The tools yes, but few weapons. Some explosives, some ammunition."

"That's disappointing, but it will mean we can move faster," Valentine said. "Can we be out of here by dawn?"

"Even before. The men are looking for food now, but so far have little that is good for travel."

"If that's the worst luck we have on this trip, I'll take it," Valentine said. "We can raise some hell behind this Kurian's army on our way out."

Monte-Cristi nodded. He looked pale and weary. Valentine was about to tell him to get some rest when a call from the gate brought them to the walls.

A runner came in through the gate. "Engines, sir, coming up the road. Headlights, too."

Three trucks ground up the irregular road from San Juan, judging from the lights.

"Ahn-Kha," Valentine called, "get the Grogs out of sight." Then to Monte-Cristi: "Hell, we should have had someone put on a uniform. Where have our new 'recruits' gotten to?"

"Too late to find them now."

Valentine got a better look at the trucks. All were variants on the sturdy two-ton military model, the backbone of the world's former armies since the 1940s. So beat up were these that Valentine would have believed they had seen service with Patton's Red Ball Express. Metal panels had been replaced with bamboo and canvas, and instead of headlights, oil lamps hung from the front and sides like a nineteenth-century carriage. Each had a perfect set of off-road tires and spares, however, thanks to the abundant rubber trees on the island.

Valentine waved from the walls, hoping that he would just be a silhouette.

"Don't shoot, don't shoot," Valentine said to the men now gathering at the walls and main gate. "We'll need these trucks. Let everyone get off. Jacques, pass the word. Lower that gun!" he said, the last to a Haitian who was sighting on the driver's side "window," which consisted of corrugated aluminum with a triangular view-slit cut into it. "Nobody shoot until I do! Nobody shoot!"

The driver of the first truck dismounted, with not a few glances into the passenger cabin. He opened his mouth, as if summoning words, before ejaculating in Spanish and throwing himself to the ground, butt in the air and arms crossed over his head. Faces looked up from the beds of the trucks.

"I didn't catch that," Valentine said.

"'Shoot, shoot, it's the Haitians,' the fallen driver said." Monte-Cristi translated, raising his pistol.

"Wait," Valentine bellowed in French. "Don't fire!"

A familiar figure swung himself out of the cabin of the first truck. "I told you not to be a hero," he said, planting a boot in the upthrust Domingan's behind. "Don't tell me I'm late to the party again?" Lieutenant Post called up at the walls, a broad smile on his face.

Post looked as exhausted as Monte-Cristi, and Valentine was determined to allow everyone a couple hours' sleep in shifts while they loaded the trucks and assorted wagons. Monte-Cristi and his men looked after the few animals able to pull a load while Valentine spoke to Post.

"We found the road easily enough, sir," Post said. "Overgrown, deadfalls everywhere, mudslides . . . so picking a good ambush spot was simple, too. We let a rider or two pass before these trucks came running back from the border garrison. Full would have been better, but I figured you'd need either kind soon, so we hit these. There wasn't much of an escort, some men on horseback. The men went crazy with the machine guns—there wasn't an unwounded horse. I ended up pistoling three. Hated to do it. I don't know what's worse, screaming women or screaming horses. We got the dead and hurt off the road, bandaged up the wounded as best we could in the time it took to turn around the trucks and get things organized, and drove down here. I think we got into third gear once—it was mostly first and second. First in one of these is crawling, second is a quicker crawl. Only one checkpoint outside San Juan. I don't know if word that we were heading that way got out or what, but it was empty."

"Losses or wounded?"

"None, unless you count dysentery. Some of the men got gut-sick from eating the Santo Domingan's rations, I think. Or maybe it was from drinking lamp oil. That kid from Cercado's family, he knew every bend in the road, I'll give him that. You know, we could do worse than to give the road-watchers the weapons we find."

Valentine nodded. "We've both been lucky."

"From the stories the kid told me, there's a lot of discontent on the island. If some of the peasants here could just get their hands on enough guns and mortars—"

"That's the first thing I'm going to tell them when we make it back to Mountain Home, my friend. Get some rest: find a mattress and use it."

"Aye aye, sir," Post said, licking his dry lips as he eyed the well.

The rest of Valentine's evening/morning was an excursion into the curse of Babel. He found himself giving orders to work details in French, English, and Spanish, all of it reinforced with hand gestures and a constant struggle against exploding into profanity. He had to stop men from putting ammunition into weapons meant to be transported, and piling their own weapons in stacks to be carried on the trucks. Groups of men occupied themselves by removing food from one truck and placing it in another, and others, after having made three trips in and out of the armory, decided they had done enough and crawled under the carts and trucks to sleep. Men lit cigars by striking matches on the side of the explosives truck, tossing the matches into the sawdust used to cushion the cases of dynamite. Some of the *Thunderbolt*'s sailors and marines worked drunkenly, reeling and reeking from Haitian-soldier-supplied rum concealed in their canteens, before passing out from dehydration or dropping to their hands and knees to vomit. He caught the Santo Domingan deserters stuffing block after block of chocolate into their mouths, and briefly considered making an example of them. In the end, he put them under Ahn-Kha's supervision, and after they saw their new supervisor pick up a napping Grog by his ear, half-tearing it off so that blood ran down the side of the derelict's head, they took to their duties with a will. Valentine tried to comfort himself with the thought that he had been on more disorderly expeditions into the Kurian Zone.

Somehow, the sun found the armory above San Juan empty and the trucks and carts loaded. Behind a vanguard of cavalry was Post's "battle truck," piled with sandbags and fitted out with the *Thunderbolt*'s machine guns. Then came the other two trucks, towing carts filled with food and water. Behind that were horse-drawn carts and the pack-horses, hardly burdened now compared with the loads they had brought over the Cordillera Central. The engines gunned to diesel-fueled life. There was not room for everyone to ride, so the convoy would have to move at the pace of a walking soldier, though the walking men enjoyed the rare treat of moving with only their arms and a small amount of ammunition.

Valentine placed himself in the third truck, the one hauling the explosives, with the most experienced driver: one of the Chief's mechanics from the *Thunderbolt*. He was an aging, bald Asiatic, with the pulp-Western name of Handy Sixguns.

"Actually it's Hardy, and the family's real name is Chen," Sixguns explained when Valentine asked him his last name. He had always known the man as Handy, until he sat in the webbing that served as the passenger seat in the truck cabin. They made conversation while the vehicles inched forward out of the gate. "My father carried four pistols everywhere, he was a 'wheelgun man' he used to say, just like the old old cowboy books. Trucker in the old times with a Mobile–Birmingham run, jammed gears for the Kurians, too. I wanted more variety, so I went to sea. Ended up in the *Thunderbolt*, going from Galveston to the Florida coast line once a month or so."

"You know Galveston?" Valentine asked. "I've been there, but never had a chance to get off the ship."

"Spent some time there, the old *Darcy Arthur* got wrecked in a storm, and I was living on the streets there for a while. You grow up fast under *them*."

"What ever happened to the elder Sixguns?"

"I never found out. I went back once, when I was in my twenties. The house was just deserted. No note, no nothing. The neighbors couldn't or wouldn't tell me anything. Funny, I still look for his face everywhere I go. Bad not knowing."

Worse than knowing the worst? Valentine wondered. At least Sixguns could imagine a future for his father. Valentine had the sorrowful memory of a crow pecking at the hole in the back of his father's skull, his dead siblings, his mother's violated corpse.

A long mile down the road, the convoy halted. Post and two sailors trotted the road from the fort, where wisps of smoke could already be seen coming from the armory.

"When it hits that black powder . . ." Sixguns said.

Post trotted up to Valentine's truck. "We probably have another thirty minutes, sir," the lieutenant said. "I didn't want us to get caught in the explosion."

"Release the prisoner, not much he can do about it now," Valentine said. Post nodded and went over to the two Haitians escorting the captured officer. They cut the corded knots around his wrists and ankles. The officer looked back at his post, ashen-faced.

Valentine climbed down from his truck. "We're looking for good men, sir," he said in Spanish. Emotion gave him the eloquence to get through the semirehearsed speech. "I once served the Kurians, too. But now I'm with those who resist. It's not a lost cause, or a sure death." The part about serving the Kurians was not strictly true, Valentine acknowledged to himself, but he thought it might help the man.

"No, they have my oath. They have my sister in Santo Domingo. All I need from you is a pistol with one bullet."

"That's not the way—," Valentine began, but the man lunged at him.

Valentine sidestepped, stuck out a foot moving one way and a hand moving the other, and the officer went sprawling to the dirt. A Haitian raised his gun.

"No! Bind him again—he's coming with us," he said in French. Then in Spanish to the officer: "I'm sorry, I won't have you hurting yourself."

When they thought they were out of Valentine's hearing, some of the Haitians grumbled that a prisoner would ride while they would walk. Valentine shrugged it off. Soldiers that didn't grumble were thinking about something else, like their fears.

The trucks rattled into gear, and the men got to their feet, and the column was on its way.

The first stragglers appeared as they crossed a bridge south of San Juan. There had been some kind of skirmish at the bridge. Monte-Cristi's horsemen lit out after a few sentries who took shots at the column. After Post determined that it was safe to cross, Valentine ordered the men out of combat positions and back into the march order.

Valentine walked with the rear guard as the column headed south. He had heard riders somewhere to the east, and was not sure if they were some of Monte-Cristi's scouts or a Santo Domingan's. He saw six or seven ragged people, bundles over their shoulders or in woven baskets, following behind.

He found one of Monte-Cristi's subchiefs. "Who are they?"

The man shrugged. "Don't know. They attached themselves outside San Juan. There are two or three more now."

"Let me know if they try to catch up. I don't want one of them throwing a grenade into the explosives truck."

Monte-Cristi joined him at the rear of the column. "We ran into some soldiers from one of the sugar plantations. The riders treed one of them."

"Did they tell him the story and let him go?"

"Yes, *mon capitaine.* He is running even now, with the story that we are marching on Santo Domingo. But implying that we are stronger than we are—"

"We've got to play the role of . . . this reminds me of a lizard. I can't remember what it is called, but I know it lives in Australia. When it's threatened, these flaps of skin open up like an umbrella, and it opens its mouth and charges on its hind legs. It couldn't hurt anything larger than a bug if it tried, but the appearance of aggression makes a predator think twice," Valentine said. "Frilled lizard, that's what it's called," he added, his capacious memory coming to his aid. "We've got to look like we're charging, when we're really getting set to run."

"You are a man of strange interests," Monte-Cristi said.

"After I was orphaned, a teacher raised me," Valentine said. "I lived in his library. You were speaking of the militia. Where were the soldiers from?"

"A sugar plantation. From what I hear, it is a big one. It is on this road ahead, we will reach it soon."

"Good. I've heard of these plantations. I'd like to see one."

Valentine had seen many work camps in his years traveling in the Kurian Zone. Yet the worst the KZ offered in the lands familiar to him was only a shadow of what he found on the riverbank of the Yaque del Sur.

In the north, Kurian cruelty adhered to a certain logic. When it was time to kill, the Reapers usually performed the task in the dark of night, away from human eyes. Only certain auras were taken, and none wasted if possible, for infusions of vital aura were too valuable to whatever band of Kurians were in charge. Perhaps this green valley was only loosely controlled, or perhaps the island's people were fecund enough for auras to be in oversupply; whatever the reason, death worked overtime in this part of Santo Domingo.

Dead, leaf-stripped palm trees along the road presented the first horrors. Valentine saw bodies, some nothing but rotting corpses beneath a mask of flies, tied to the trunks. Above the tormented figures bleached skulls were tucked into nests of pepper trees, threaded onto smaller branches. On some, the branches had grown through or around the skulls, swallowing them behind bark and bursting them asunder.

Valentine locked eyes with one victim still alive, atop a magnificent body bleeding at the tight bonds around his chest; the man was crying, but had exhausted his tears. Flies clustered at the raw sores where the rope cut into him. Crows and vultures feasted on what was left of the man just to the left of him, and the one to the right had fallen apart, only the upper half of the skeletal structure remaining attached to the tree.

To their credit, the Haitians did not wait for orders. The trucks stopped and men left their places in the column and rushed, knives in hand, to cut those still living free. Valentine kicked a bloated vulture out of the way and walked up the turn-off leading to the station. The vulture squawked and dragged its distended body to the culvert beside the road. It paused in the shade of a white-painted sign reading AZUCÁR

D VARGAS. The Spanish word for "sugar" was peeling, but beneath the stenciled letters of Vargas's name were several layers of old primer.

Valentine looked down the cane-flanked lane.

A cluster of wooden buildings stood between two sets of high bamboo fence at the end of an unshaded gravel road. Valentine guessed them to be separate housing for the men and women of the plantation. Sugar cane stretched out to either side of the road, which was built up high enough to give a commanding view of the fields for miles. Cast aside at the gates of the establishment, like litter thrown along a highway, were more corpses long since rotted into a jumble of bones. Valentine saw a rat scuttle for cover among the bones.

Ahn-Kha appeared at his arm, showing his uncanny sense of knowing when he was wanted.

"I see a truck back there," Valentine said. "Get your Grogs together, and Post with his marines. Take whatever we need, animals, weapons, the truck if it will move, and some sugar. We're going to burn this place to the ground. Anyone carrying a gun or whip you shoot."

Valentine turned on his heel and went to Post's battle-truck. Post was helping carry one of the plantation hands to shade.

"Will, we're going to burn this place," Valentine said. He thought briefly of Duvalier and her various tales of arson in the KZ. She had been right. There were atrocities that only burning would cleanse. This was one of them. "I want it to look like it was never here, just a bare spot on the ground. Understand?"

Post pressed a canteen into the hands of the newly freed man. He stood, jaw set, stinking blood and pus from the peon spattered on his shirtfront. "Yes, sir."

Sailors and marines readied their weapons. Valentine chambered a round in his PPD and hopped up on the front bumper, holding on to the German logo on the grillework. The driver revved the engine, and turned from the line of torture-palms to the station road.

The truck roared down the lane, fast enough to kick up dust. A figure or two appeared in the doorway of the main building, rifles in their hands. The principal building of the plantation was a two-story brick house encircled by a wide shaded veranda. Post loosed a burst from a machine gun, and the men ran. Sharp rifle cracks brought them down, the fall of their bodies kicking up puffs of dust from the gravel surrounding the main house.

The truck braked before the house. Valentine released his grip, letting the final momentum of the aged Benz throw him forward. He landed nimbly and followed his gun barrel through the double doors. A man in a uniform similar to the ones he saw at San Juan stood at a glass-less window, gaping at the men dismounting from the truck. He threw his hands forward, palms out, as if hoping to halt the men by body language.

"Qué?" he managed to get off, before Valentine cut him down with a burst from the PPD. The old, awful thrill ran through his body as he smelled the gunsmoke and the man's blood.

Valentine walked into the kitchen and looked out the open back door. A woman in white rags ran, carrying a baby in her arms, a naked boy alongside her. He ignored her. He passed through an empty dining room and into an office. An electric fan whirred atop a paper-strewn desk. One window was shuttered and the other window stood open. Valentine looked around, a smashed gun cabinet showed an empty bracket between two shotguns. Whoever occupied the office hadn't had time to get the key. Or get his footwear, Valentine noted, seeing a set of high military-style boots by the door.

Valentine moved away from the window, not wanting to give a rifleman an easy target. Outside he heard Grogs hooting amidst the tearing crash of wood splintering. He returned to the front veranda.

Post had the *Thunderbolt*'s marines backing up the Grogs as they stormed the barracks. The Haitians were at the gates of the worker compounds, breaking bamboo posts with crowbars and axes. The *Thunderbolt*'s men stayed at the battle-truck, training their weapons on the unoccupied buildings. A rifle or two popped from the cane fields, but wherever the shots were aimed, they caused no damage.

"See if there are any animals in the stables," he told Post, the sight of uniformed bodies lying here and there turning his bloodlust into revulsion. At the Kurian system. At himself.

An hour later the plantation was in flames, and Valentine had almost a hundred more charges. Before burning it he had turned over the contents of the station house, barracks, and storerooms to them so they could carry off what they would. The problem was that they carried it off in the trail of his convoy.

By the time they camped, still on the banks of the river flowing out of the mountains of the Cordillera Central, Valentine guessed those following his trucks, wagons, and animals to number in the hundreds. Some of the refugees drove pigs and goats, or pulled donkeys along with children or the aged perched on blanketed backs. He found Cercado warming some beans and rice on the battle-truck's radiator.

"A good day," Cercado said, between spoonfuls.

"We've picked up a lot of stragglers, though."

"Who would blame them?"

"Please, go among them. Find out what their plans are. Tell them . . . tell them we are marching toward battle, and we need young men who would use machetes or guns."

"You can't be serious, Captain. I doubt if one among them knows one end of a rifle from another. They'd be safer using it as a club."

"Perhaps. If this keeps going on, by the time we get to Puerto Viejo, we'll have thousands of them. It would be—"

"Unfortunate," Cercado finished.

"Agreed. Go among them, talk to them, see what they plan to do."

Cercado spat. "That I can tell you already. They want to get away."

"Let them know that's not an option. If they want to be free of the Kurians, they'll have to do it themselves. I'm not Moses. I can't bring the multitudes out of Egypt."

The next day, the caravan crawling southwest along the old highway was outnumbered by those following it. The Santo Domingans never interfered with the soldiers, though Valentine expected that his men dropped back into their mass to distribute food and water, especially to the children. If they made it to the coast, it would be with an emptier belly and a tighter belt around it.

If there was a bright side, it was that from a distance, his column would be mistaken for an army moving down the road, occupying miles of trail. With Monte-Cristi's riders and the Grogs leaving the column on excursions to set fire to roadside police stations, gather weapons and ammunition, and cut down telephone wires, the Kurians farther east might be convinced their border garrisons had collapsed, and an invading host was pouring out of Haiti. In the intervening days, he might have a chance to slip away in the confusion without further battle.

Adding to this belief was the fact that the Kurians had already instituted a "scorched earth" policy as he moved east. They found fewer and fewer stations and plantations intact. Villages were burned and supplies destroyed or removed, adding to his logistics worries. They were beyond the zone where Cercado's roadwatching network had stashed food, and while water was plentiful grain was running out for the horses, and food became short for the men.

He reduced some of his problems by ordering the slaughter of a few broken-down pack animals when they camped that night, the second since leaving the armory at San Jose, sharing the ample meat out to the cooking pots of those trailing the convoy.

Cercado joined Valentine and Ahn-Kha at their cooking-fire, appearing as he always did with his mixture of good news and bad. Their guide smoked a cigar, sending satisfied puffs skyward with his back against a palm.

"The rumors you spread about an attack on Santo Domingo have come back to bite you, Captain Valentine," Cercado said. "Yes, it has scared the Kurians for now, but they are mustering forces west and east. These people have heard that the campaign against the island under Port-au-Prince has been called off, and their general is marching east to crush you. Even larger forces will come soon from the west."

"How soon?" Valentine asked, grateful that Cercado was keeping his voice down.

"Impossible to say. You must travel faster once you make the turn for the coast. They may move to anticipate you."

Valentine looked into the fire. There had been delays almost from the first minute—how many were due to his faulty planning? How many to bad execution? His quick raid into the Kurian Zone, to test the quickwood weapons and get more arms for the Haitians, had succeeded in the first task: he had seen how effective the wood was with his own eyes. The second, while not being a total failure, had come far short of expectations. And now it looked as if the column would be swallowed entirely.

"You've done all we asked superbly, Cercado. We're almost to the road to the sea. You and your family members should slip away now and go back to your mountains. Take whatever weapons you wish, even some of those from the *Thunderbolt*. It is the least we can do for you."

"Captain, Santo Domingo has not seen the like of this in many years. Such a rising will come to a bad end, or a good one. Either way, it will be the subject for tales and songs that the peons of this island will tell long after I die, even should God grant me a life a hundred years long. What man, if he is a man, would not want to be a part of it? Even now, the poor peons on the road call you Revenant. They say that a Reaper had you in its arms, but before it could bite you, you bit it, killing it. They say when you are wounded, you cut the body parts from your enemies and meld them with your own. Such tales are told of you—it curls the hair on my toes.

"I will tell you something else. The smokes you saw on the horizon today, they are not just Jacques's riders—they are the peons fighting on their own, or the Whisperers burning and saving us the trouble of doing it. The countryside has risen. They've borne evil after evil too long. The men are sending their women and children to you for safety while they take to the hills."

"I thought it odd that there were so many women among them, my David," Ahn-Kha said.

"This has been a long time coming," Cercado continued, scratching his hairy potbelly and puffing away on the cigar. "The Domingan rulers left a hollow egg when they called away so many to fight against Kurian Haiti. It only took your footsteps to break the shell. Who knows, maybe in other parts of the island, as they gather men to crush you, other peons can take their chances. At the very least, the trade in sugar and rubber to their brothers in the north will be reduced for some time. Both require many men. If the Kurians kill those who rise, who will take their place in the cane fields and tapping rubber trees?"

"We're already overdue at the coast," Valentine said. "We should have been there today. At this rate, we will be two more days on the road."

"Do we dare travel at night?" Ahn-Kha said. "A final sprint, tonight and tomorrow, and the devils get the hind end?"

"Devil take the hindmost is how we usually say it, old horse," Valentine corrected. He pictured the island in his mind, the various forces moving. "We'll get to the coast, all right."

He rose from the fire and went to find Post.

In the end, the Grogs' skill as pig-hunters saved the column. The stations along the road relied on pig flesh to feed their soldiers, and to a lesser extent the workers, and as Valentine's columns approached, they emptied their pigpens and drove the pigs into the brush. The Grogs had noses to rival Valentine's own, and they tracked the future chops and sidemeat to their hiding places. The dust-raising column developed a system in which the front end would take the meat and begin boiling it or roasting it, and by the time the tail of the column passed the fires, the meat was ready to be eaten at the next rest-halt by those hundreds upon hundreds bringing up the rear.

Men, some of them armed, began to join the column from east, west, and north, telling tales of horsemen closing on the column from the barren stretches in the more arid regions of the island neighboring the well-watered river valley. More formations followed, bearing artillery and armed vehicles according to some of the tales. Valentine put Monte-Cristi in charge of adding the best-armed and healthiest of them to his own units, though there wasn't time for anything other than teaching them the system of moving for an hour, and then resting for ten minutes. Valentine was grateful for the additions; Post had gone pell-mell to the coast with the *Thunderbolt*'s marines and sailors in the battle-truck to prepare for the column's arrival.

By midday they turned south for the coast, moving on a smaller, less-used road. Valentine hoped that the change in direction would throw off any designs for the column's destruction.

He managed to get his charges a few miles south of the old highway by moving on into the evening. When he finally called for a halt, the men dropped in their tracks under the bright Caribbean stars. Few of his soldiers rode; Valentine had turned space in the trucks over to the ill, weak, and pregnant of the column. Even so, there were those who turned off the road throughout the day to rest in the shade, and they would probably never catch up now. Smaller bands of Santo Domingan horsemen had appeared as it got dark atop the distant hilltops, marking his turn to the coast.

He found Monte-Cristi in the center of a circle of his chieftans.

"Ever fought a rear-guard action, Jacques?" Valentine asked.

Cristi's eyes lit up. "My men have performed many an ambush. We run all the better afterwards, knowing we've hurt them."

Valentine smelled the pork being roasted by Monte-Cristi's cook, his mouth watering, but he ignored his hunger. This was the final sprint, and there was too much to do.

"Just hit them fast, and keep moving for the coast. I'm afraid they've guessed we've changed direction, and they might try to cut us off from the bay. We have to beat them to it."

"We could, if we could empty the trucks of everything but the supplies. My men could march through the night."

Valentine looked out at the sea of Santo Domingans sheltering behind the pickets. "A lot of these people can't. They joined us out of belief in some stories we spread."

"You did not ask them to come. They must accept the fortunes of war. Not one in five of them will fit on your ship even if they do make it to the bay. They will be no worse off than if we had never come here. Otherwise, you will be asking my men to die for nothing."

"You've seen how things are run here, Jacques. They've thrown in with us. We're their only chance."

"They knew the risks when they ran away."

"But that's just it, they haven't run away. They've run toward something, the chance at a free life. I would no more leave them behind than you'd leave those men you were stuck in the cave with."

"I will tell you something, Captain. There were times—yes, there were many times, in that hole, after it was sealed, that I would have turned them all over to the Kurians for fresh air, sun, and a real meal. I . . . I prayed for the chance."

Valentine made a show of fishing around in his bag for a strip of dried beef, so that he would not see the tears on Monte-Cristi's face. "The important thing is that when you had a real chance to give up, you didn't. How many of the legends on this island had the same doubts? Louverture, Pablo Duarte, I'm certain they had their moments when they questioned themselves." Valentine did not add that he had learned long ago that the only way he could live with himself was if he acted according to conscience, rather than orders or even military necessity. Usually his conscience and his duty asked the same things from him, but on the few occasions where their needs had diverged, duty lost.

The moon rose, and the drivers loaded their vehicles once more with those who had to ride.

Monte-Cristi handed Valentine his horse's reins. "Ride today, Captain. I'll be afoot with my men in the rear. It will do everyone good to be able to see you. His name is Luc, and like me he is a defector from the Kurians; he is strong enough to bear even your oversize friend on these mountains. Take care of him should I . . . should I fall."

Valentine read the expression in Monte-Cristi's face, and nodded dumbly. He cinched the saddle on the speckled gray gelding. He slung his submachine gun, grabbed a handful of mane, and mounted. Luc heaved a sigh and pawed at the earth, eager to be off.

"Any sign of our pursuers?"

Monte-Cristi shook his head. "No. For now they just watch."

"Build up the fires as we go. I want them to burn for a few more hours at least. Take care of yourself. Dinner tonight with me on the ship?"

"I look forward to it."

"Let's get everyone moving. Quietly."

Valentine rode at the head of the column, just behind the rear guard. He had contracted the mass of soldiers and civilians as much as possible, but the troops at his disposal could hardly watch the front and flanks, let alone defend them with so many men detached for the rear guard.

They made good time despite the dark. When his sensitive nose picked up the smell of the sea, Valentine's heart leapt. He began to trot his horse up and down the column, urging the weary walkers on as best as he could.

Everyone seemed to sense that it was time for the last sprint. The Grogs at the head of the column scouted, and helped the pioneers with the worst parts of the road by cutting down trees into washouts so the trucks could cross. Valentine followed with a vanguard of armed men watching at all times as the others worked. He needed at least a small group of disciplined men to be ready for any emergency. Then came the overloaded trucks, the valves on the aged engines clattering in complaint. A few men traveled to either side of the road, visible through the scarcer vegetation in this more arid region of the island. Interspersed with the trucks, ready to give a shove, came the masses of Santo Domingans with their children and bundles in tow, hardly a goat remaining. Somewhere behind, more refugees followed, covered by Monte-Cristi's rear guard, composed of his most reliable men with the best weapons.

Valentine had enough on his mind, worrying about how he would find space, not to mention food, for perhaps two thousand extra mouths on the ride home without the Kurians intervening.

Which of course they did, just short of his goal.

A Grog shrieked a warning, and the dark of the road ahead burst into muzzle flashes. An automatic weapon swept the road, scattering both his men and the formation of pioneers. The Kurian soldiers were dispersed on the crest of a hill ahead.

Valentine could see the vast night out there, between the folds of the earth, and cursed. *Stopped!*

The Grogs came stumbling back, one wounded. Valentine got off Monte-Cristi's horse, led it into a gulley sheltering his soldiers.

"They must have just beaten us there, my David," Ahn-Kha said. "They are not dug in—they stand behind rocks and trees, or lie on the ground. It is just a screen, I think."

"But it's a well-placed screen, and we're the bugs."

"If the pioneers charge too—"

"There'll be that many more dead men. Any idea where their flank is?"

"No."

"Another hour, and I bet they have twice as many men. Give me your rifle. If we can at least get the automatic weapon . . ."

Ahn-Kha took his submachine gun. "Give the word, and we will go, my David."

Valentine's own men began shooting back at the soldiers ahead, and a slow, popping firefight took place and grew as both sides' soldiers gathered at the gunfire. Neither side seemed to have ammunition to waste; with no targets, the automatic weapon was silent.

"Ahn-Kha, I have a great favor to ask," Valentine said, adjusting the slide on the gun's rear sight.

"I know, my David. I will break for those rocks."

Ahn-Kha ran forward in the low, loping run of the Grogs, using his hands and feet. The machine gun fired, and Valentine's Cat eyes picked up the source. He placed the flange of the front sight on what he hoped was a head. He squeezed, and the heavy Grog-gun kicked out its .50-caliber shell. He slid back into the gulley.

"You got him," the Haitian at his right said, lifting his head.

"Keep—," Valentine began. Valentine saw the man's hair rustle as if a brush had been run upward through it, and he slumped. Valentine slid over to the corpse, and passed the rifle to a sheltering pioneer.

Valentine heard a whistling sound; then an explosion lit the night at the crest of the enemy hillside. He slid sideways for a better view and was rewarded by the sight of a second shell bursting on the crest, right in the middle of the road where the machine gun had been placed.

Naval gunfire, by God!

"My David, it's the *Thunderbolt*," Ahn-Kha shouted from his hiding place ahead. The sky began to turn orange, and somewhere in the distance, a rooster crowed. He heard shooting far behind; the rear guard was contesting the road with their pursuers.

Valentine took to his horse. They would not be ringed in.

"Over the hill and to the sea, men. To the sea!" he shouted. "*Sur la mer!*" the hills echoed. Valentine handed the Grog-gun to one of Ahn-Kha's warriors.

The Golden One let loose with a battle bellow, a blood-freezing sound. His Grogs answered, and went up and over the edge of the gully, their shotguns and rifles flaring in the half-light. There were no bayonets to glint in the rising sun, but the ivory in their oversize teeth shone.

The trucks gunned their engines and kicked up gravel from the road. Valentine passed Ahn-Kha. His friend sprayed the roadblock ahead with bullets from the PPD. The charging Grogs to either side made for an odd sight, going forward with two legs and an arm, almost like horses cantering. Valentine considered drawing his blade for effect, but the Haitians and Grogs needed no urging. He pulled his Colt automatic instead and briefly wondered how he would work the slide and keep atop of the galloping horse. . . .

The Santo Domingans did not wait to meet them. The sight and sound of charging Grogs amidst the *Thunderbolt*'s shell-fire proved too much for the thin line of riflemen. The cheering sight of knapsacks bobbing in the tall grass of the hillside as the Santo Domingans ran brought a victorious whoop from Valentine. The horse gathered itself to leap the roadblock, and Valentine gripped the mane. He saw dead men heaped by the machine gun as the horse jumped the felled tree.

Valentine heard shots from the fishing village at the base of the hill and saw the *Thunderbolt*'s marines deployed in a skirmish line advancing up the hill. Post, evidently trapped with his little contingent in the seaside fishing village, had heard the firing and acted.

The Santo Domingan soldiers surrendered or scattered, and the rout was complete.

Valentine swore to himself that he would see Post made into an officer in Southern Command if they ever made it back to the Free Territory.

As the column got moving again, Valentine reproached himself for jumping his horse into the most likely spot for another shell from the *Thunderbolt*. But in his later years that was forgotten when he remembered the pure glory of that moment, his first battlefield victory in eight years of soldiering.

Valentine saw boats drawn up on the beach, to either side of the village, under the guard of a sailor or two. Valentine had dispatched Post to the rendezvous with orders to gather every available craft, using the *Thunderbolt*'s forbidding bulk if necessary to confiscate a flotilla of fishing boats. Using all the *Thunderbolt*'s deck space, and a few large boats in tow, he hoped to get his charges along the coast.

It would be another long day while they loaded and supplied all the boats, but he had learned to expect nothing less.

By sunset, after an endless afternoon spent turning chaos into order, he stood on the *Thunderbolt*'s bridge in clean clothes with a hot meal inside him. The Santo Domingan refugees were crowded on board every seaworthy vessel. Monte-Cristi's rear guard had tumbled down from the hills into the *Thunderbolt*'s motorized boats, covered by cannon and Oerlikon. Last of all came Post's marines, setting fire to the huts of the village to add covering smoke to the debarkation.

But new worries replaced the old. Their cockleshell flotilla could fit the Haitian soldiers and Santo Domingans, just, but any kind of bad weather would lead to the possible loss of the boats, and perhaps the overcrowded *Thunderbolt*. The Kurians in Santo Domingo had a few ships, as well, mostly armed merchantmen that ran sugar and rubber and ore north. Any exchange of gunfire would be fatal to many of those crowding on the *Thunderbolt*'s decks. Waiting in the bay while they captured better vessels from other villages was out of the question. The Kurian forces had already gathered, lobbing mortar shells into the water as the *Thunderbolt* towed the boats out to sea.

Two single-masted fishing ships plodded alongside, reeking holds filled with mobs of huddled people. Dozens more stood forlornly on the shoreline.

He unburdened his concerns on the one who knew the waters best.

"Don't worry about the weather," Carrasca said, her hair blowing out in the fresh Caribbean breeze, just as it had that first morning taking the captured ship into Jamaica. The helmsman ignored them. "We have a few weeks left before worrying about real storms."

Valentine took the sea air into his nostrils like a drug. "We have to get farther off the coast. Two or three miles at least. They might have guns mounted."

"Let it go, David. We're at sea. My element, remember? Let me do the thinking for a while. You've done brilliantly. Maybe not what you set out to do, but it was the right choice in the end."

"I should—"

"Sleep. That's an order."

"Captain's word at sea is law," he said, turning up a corner of his mouth.

Her mock-serious attitude vanished. She glanced onto the bridge and stepped into his arms. He couldn't tell who started it, but they were kissing. "Sleep with me," she whispered. "Soon. When we get back to Jamaica. After we see this through." She broke off the embrace, leaving his body tingling. "Enough. You see, I take my duty as seriously as you. Tempting as the thought is," she added, looking at his crotch and then returning her eyes to his. She no longer watched him with that wary hint of fear that his pupils might be glowing.

Valentine, too aroused to feel embarrassed, saluted. "It's a date," he said, moving past her to leave the bridge. "I'll be in my cabin, if there's room to sleep between Post and Ahn-Kha, that is." He allowed his hand to trace the firm course of her buttock and thigh as he passed, puckishly wanting her to be as aroused as he.

Sure enough, Ahn-Kha lay on the floor, still smelling of gunsmoke. Post occupied his cot, having fallen into bed still in uniform. Post reeked of sweat and woodsmoke, blood and gun oil, tidewater and pig fat. Valentine did not even have to hypersensitize his nose to smell the story of his lieutenant's day. Valentine stepped over Ahn-Kha and managed to get his boots off before falling into a dreamless sleep.

A hand shook him awake. Valentine's nose told him it was Cercado before he was even partly awake.

"Captain, it is Monte-Cristi. Come, please."

Valentine rose out of bed, wide awake, but with the weighed-down feeling of a rushed awakening. Post and Ahn-Kha picked up on the alarm and stirred.

He followed Cercado out the door and down the short companionway to the officer's mess. Monte-Cristi sat up, held in the arms of one of his chieftans, some of his soldiers clustered in the doorway.

"Make a hole, dammit," Valentine growled, pushing into the compartment.

Monte-Cristi's breathing was labored.

"Jacques, what is it, a seizure?" Valentine asked.

Monte-Cristi looked up, wincing. "My heart, I think, David."

"He fainted away twice," the chieftan holding him elaborated. "We gave him some wine to ease the pain."

Valentine dashed back to his cabin, forcing his way past Ahn-Kha's companionway-filling bulk. He tore through his footlocker and came up with a bottle of white tablets. He rushed back to the mess.

"Water, someone," Valentine said, putting four white tablets into Monte-Cristi's mouth.

"It is ironic, David," Monte-Cristi said, after swallowing a drink of water to wash down the aspirin. "Hours of bullets flying around me, shells even. I've been on the run all day, and the moment I get to rest"—he shrugged, forcing a smile—"my heart chooses to kill me." He shut his eyes, and Valentine patted his hand until he opened them again. "We fooled them, going to sea like that."

"The Kurians forgot that the ocean is also a road."

"A good joke," Monte-Cristi managed.

"Yes, and we'll be laughing about it for weeks, over rum in your mountains."

"I—," Monte-Cristi began, but he simply faded. Valentine thought he had gone to sleep, but when he felt for a pulse there was nothing.

"Fuck!" Valentine said. He lowered Monte-Cristi to the deck. "It's a good heart, Jacques. It just needs some help. Ahn-Kha!" he shouted. "Get out of here, everyone, clear the floor," he yelled, forgetting to speak French, but his gestures served. Ahn-Kha entered. Valentine pounded on Monte-Cristi's chest and put an ear to his breast, listening for a beat. Nothing.

"Push on his chest, like this," Valentine said, demonstrating.

Ahn-Kha's thick shoulders went to work, the Grog's four-fingered hands on Monte-Cristi's breastbone. Valentine pinched off his nose and breathed as Ahn-Kha worked. A long, long minute went by, and Monte-Cristi heaved and gasped on his own.

". . . think . . . perhaps . . . ," Monte-Cristi said. His eyes fluttered, and he looked more alert. "Why am I on the floor?"

"Relax," Valentine said. "Don't try to talk."

The rest of the voyage, Monte-Cristi's health consumed Valentine's attention to the point where he actually forgot about the *Thunderbolt*, Carrasca, the Santo Domingans in their flimsy boats, and the weather.

He knew time passed only from the growth of his beard, and an occasional look out the window. He fed Monte-Cristi aspirin at each small meal and watched a little of his strength return.

"I feel . . . used up," Monte-Cristi confided, sitting in a canvas chair on the shady side of the deck as the coast slid by. "More so than before. But I will say this: Life is sweet now. It wasn't before. The past died the other day. Now I make my own future free of it."

"Your days carrying a rifle are over. Sit on a beach from now on, learn to fish," Valentine suggested.

"Why all this concern for a worn-out old man?" Monte-Cristi asked.

"Perhaps . . ." Valentine struggled for the right words, and would have struggled no matter what language he was using.

"Perhaps what?"

The man was beyond pretense, in himself or others. "Perhaps because I see you as one possible me in thirty years. Also, I didn't want an old enemy to lay his hands on you."

"Who? I thought you had not been to our land before."

"Death. The Grim Reaper, chief of all the others. When we got on board, I figured we left Death back on shore. Turned out He followed. The bastard's never satisfied. He wants more every chance he gets. So every chance I get, I kick him in the teeth. Sooner or later one of us is going to give up. It won't be me."

Nine

Free Haiti, July: It is easy to believe in spirits in the mountains of Haiti, when the misted woods press close all around. Groaning sounds that cannot be birds yet should not be trees echo through the night air. Even a trained ear finds them impossible to place. According to vou-douists, waterfalls and streams are favorite haunts of the spirits. When you come across a mountainside waterfall, cascading down a rocky cliff like a splashing staircase, you get the feeling of being the first to lay eyes on it since the forming of the world; it becomes easy to imag-ine it consecrated by apparitions dancing in the mists as the shafts of sunlight strike them. Then a dragonfly with a hand-size wingspan whirs by or a parade of ants crosses a root in a chitin stream, and the spell is broken. The forest is just a forest, and the water is just water again— until later, when the body is elsewhere and the beauty of the place weaves its magical spell, knitting memory and imagination.

The Roots rejoiced at the return of her warriors in sacred ceremony and profane revelry.

Valentine watched the sacred portion from a moss-hided rock, dew-dusted ferns brushing at his frame. Soldiers and civilians gathered at a waterfall in the forested hills, led in singing by their priests. Nar-cisse sat on a rock in the swirling waters at the base of the waterfall, like the statue of the little mermaid, calling the men to her one at a time to receive a cleansing dip in the river. Other voudouists escorted the supplicants into the water, or sang hosannas in the background. Part baptism, part absolution, and part bath, the ritual moved Valentine. There was none of the solemnity of Father Max's traditional Catholic ceremonies: the participants and audience laughed and encouraged each other through catcalls.

The Grogs sat high on the hillside, chewing fruit and watching the human performance below as if from balcony seating. Further above, Ahn-Kha stood sentinel with crossbow and gun, a watchful set of eyes allowing the humans to relax below.

Valentine, by nature an observer rather than a participant at this sort of display, sat on his rock with Carrasca resting on a patch of grass beside him, dappled sun setting her hair agleam. By nature scientifically minded, a few years ago he might have thought the whole performance silly animism; but he had seen too much of the inexplicable since beginning his journeys to laugh anything off. He applauded when Monte-Cristi waded into the stream. Narcisse took extra time over him, either through concern over his frailty or giving the spirits ample opportunity to work their magic. The aged hero was the last of the spiritual bathers. Some of the *Thunderbolt*'s sailors and marines shuffled forward, and finally Post went through the ceremony. He emerged from his dunking and beckoned Valentine to join him.

"C'mon, Val," his friend said. "It's cooler than the jungle."

Valentine and Carrasca exchanged shrugs, and he stripped to applause from all. A few pointed at the white pock left by the old bullet wound on his leg.

Narcisse laid her hands on him, reciting something that sounded like mixed French and Latin. He lowered himself at her command to hoots of approval.

"I knew you had a strong *ti-bon-ange*, my boy. Ogun himself told me so just now," Narcisse affirmed. Valentine felt refreshed, if not strengthened or healed. He waded back to the shore. He reached for his clothes, but Carrasca snatched them up.

"I don't think you're through yet. Do you see anyone else getting dressed?"

There were more singsong chants, and the returning warriors lined up to walk naked back to the village. Valentine joined in the lines. The Grogs scrambled down from their rocky balconies to follow.

"How'd you get the leg wound?" Carrasca asked, falling into step next to him.

"Up in Nebraska. Acting like a damn fool."

"A damn fool who saved my people," Ahn-Kha added from behind.

"Your people saved themselves," Valentine demurred. "But it was years ago. I'll take sea duty any time. Fewer forty-mile days."

"You'd cover forty miles in a day? On horseback?" Carrasca asked.

"On foot. It was common in the Wolves. We weren't so special. Two hundred years ago, Zulu armies in Africa could run fifty in a day. And they weren't even trained by the Lifeweavers."

They came to the village near the spirit-spot, a trailside cluster of shacks painted and decorated in bright colors. Dancing red figures, green snakes, blue birds, and less recognizable patterns wound around doorframes, roofs and windows in the Haitian style. Tables and barrels heaped with food and drink stood in the doorways and alleys; musicians drummed a tattoo on hollow logs and ancient plastic pails, calling all together. The spectators ate and drank with enthusiasm. Handsome Haitian women poured rum and juice into wooden tumblers, which were emptied as quickly as they could be filled.

Just outside the village a rivulet emptied into a field of clay-colored mud. A shaman brought them to the edge of the water. He began to shout imprecations to Haiti's enemies. Valentine understood just enough to know he called on the warriors to be armed and shielded in new spirit. Monte-Cristi yelled a response and belly-flopped into the mud; he rolled around until he was well coated. His men followed, eager as overheated elephants to go into a cool wallow.

"Go on, boy," Narcisse said. "Take on Ogun's armor."

Valentine bit off a response about Ogun's armor not doing pigs a hell of a lot of good. He stuck a foot in the mud; it did feel cool and inviting between the toes.

Post gave him a shove. Valentine fell into Napoleon's fifth element facefirst, rolled over, and let out a whoop.

"*Thunderbolt!*" he called.

The men shouted the name of their ship and dived in with the Haitians. Soon it was almost impossible to tell black skin from white—or Grog skin, for that matter, as all were covered in the grayish plaster.

Valentine, grinning behind a mask of mud, rose and advanced on Carrasca in a threatening crouch.

"Oh, no!" she said, backing away. "I'll never get it out of my—"

He vaulted out of the mud, landing beside her before she had time to turn. He clasped her around the chest and dragged her, shrieking and kicking, into the mud. He flopped into the morass, and she landed astride him.

"Bastard!" she laughed, flinging a wet handful of soil down at him. "At least you were undressed."

"I'll wash them myself."

Valentine watched her bind her partially despoiled hair up in a bandanna, and pull off her shirt with muddy fingers. Her shorts followed. She pinned him into the wallow with a knee, her eyes wide and hot. He felt her take his head in her hands and she kissed him, pressing against his body tightly enough to squeeze mud out from the join where their bodies met. When she came up for air, he saw her nipples hard beneath their gray coating.

Sailors, marines, and Haitians followed his example, grabbing women out of the hooting crowd and pulling them into the mud. A few ran or struggled, laughing all the time, but the only screams were ones of delight as the men planted muddy kisses on flushed cheeks, necks, and breasts.

Valentine rolled Carrasca over and kissed her, and then she returned the move. When their lips finally parted, she was on top again. She looked around at the muddy figures, dancing, playing, and making love.

"You've started an orgy, Captain," she said. "I don't know what I think about an officer that lets his men get out of hand like this."

Valentine cupped her buttocks. "I'll let them be, my hands are rather full of something else at the moment."

"Is that some kind of crack?"

He explored further with his fingers. "No, but this is."

She giggled an un-captainish giggle. "Another bad joke like that and a certain marine of my acquaintance won't get his brains fucked out momentarily."

"We'll talk some more in the bushes." Valentine picked himself up and offered a hand.

"Your tongue's going to be busy elsewhere."

He slapped her mud-covered buttock and followed her into the forest, first running and then walking, until they splashed across the stream and found a clearing, a field next to an abandoned hut, perhaps a former garden. Long grasses and palmettos had supplanted the rich soil's food crops. Valentine was in no mood to search for the perfect glade, especially with Carrasca exploring his hardness from behind, using it like a divining rod to find a spot to make love.

They sank to their knees, tongues exploring one another's mouths.

He found mudless patches of her body to kiss, and explored the rest of her coated skin with his hands. "Val . . . ," she began, and then trailed off into a Spanish–English murmur that grew more and more feral as he pressed her into his arms. She sank limp to the ground. He lay next to her, cradling her and running his hands up and down her body, lingering at her inner thighs. His mouth explored where his fingers left off, and she again took his head in her hands; she pressed her mons up to his mouth. The salty-sweet feminine musk hardened him beyond self-control, and he rose up from her sex and positioned himself between her legs.

He felt her open for him and he moved inside her, everything inside her warm and wet and magic. Her face grew contorted as he moved in her, ever deeper and faster as their passion waxed. She raked at his back with her nails, sending chips of dried mud flying like a sculptor working with ten tiny chisels. He shut his eyes, lost in his own sensations yet still aware of her. He felt an irresistible, toboggan-ride rush of pleasure, and the draining spasms came.

They drowsed away a few moments in each other's arms, tingling as if joined by a low voltage circuit.

"Another kick in the teeth," he mused, feeling the matted-down grass beneath his back.

"Huh?"

"For Death. There's more than one way to strike a blow for life."

She furrowed her brows, and then evidently gave up trying to figure out what he was talking about. Her hand explored him.

"Blow for life . . . and they say men don't come with instructions."

She moved downward, and took his limp penis in her mouth. Tongue and mouth, passionately applied, worked a resurrection.

"That's the spirit," she said, straddling him, coming up for more than air.

The Haitians showed their gratitude when it came time to fill the *Thunderbolt* with quickwood and provisions. Ahn-Kha and his Grogs supervised the cutting and milling of some of the trees into usable lengths. Smaller saplings were gently extracted by shovel, placed in clay cauldrons or wrapped in layers of dirt and burlap, and ported down to the beach one at a time. As a final gift during a visit to the beach, Papa Legba gave the entire ship's crew each a leather tobacco pouch with a handful of seeds for new quickwood trees.

"Kur is a dry place," the renegade said when Valentine asked about the seeds. "These will remain dormant for years if kept out of your sun, until placed in moist soil. They grow slowly, so have patience. Let the wood mature, and take only branches if you must."

"We'll see that they end up in the right hands," Valentine promised. "Perhaps someday you'll come north and see the groves yourself."

"No, I'll stay in the warmth and the growing gardens. In a cold climate, I doubt I could survive a winter without . . . a different means of support."

"Maybe cows would do, or pigs."

"You still do not understand, do you, Valentine? It is the sapient mind that gives us the kind of vital aura infusion that truly satisfies. Each aura has a different flavor: a man enduring hideous tortures, a woman desperate to save her offspring, a terrified child taken in the night all have a distinct feel when absorbed. The 'rush' as you might call it varies—an aura can be consumed in the time it takes to scream, or over the course of many painful hours. There were times when my—"

"Point taken," Valentine said, instinctively balling his fists.

"I forget my manners. Would one discuss cuts of meat or beef stew recipes with a group of cattle? Forgive me, son of mine enemy."

Valentine relaxed, but wanted to end the interview. "Perhaps when I'm old and the winters feel too long, I'll come back to the islands." He met Carrasca's eyes across the glare of the sand, and she cupped the leather pouch suggestively. "I'd like to hear more about Kur, and the other planets in the Interworld Tree."

"A strong mind is a blessing when the body grows frail," the Once-ler of many names agreed. "May fortune walk with you, for you'll walk into many lands bereft of it." He waved in his weary fashion and let his bearers carry him off. "The debt is paid," Valentine heard him say.

At the time the phrase was just one more curiosity from the enigmatic Kurian. It would be years before Valentine learned its significance.

He took his leave of Monte-Cristi, sitting at the edge of the beach in a hammock chair fanning himself.

"Did the river and mud cure take, Jacques?"

"Not as much as Narcisse's cooking. She's a gifted woman, something for the body, something for the *ange*. You were wise to offer her a trip north, it is something she has long dreamed of. I also have a message from our friend with the dogs at the Cape. They've fixed the holes in that old submarine. I wouldn't be surprised if your enemy comes looking for you. Though Boul is chafing, he may throw in with us in the end. The Santo Domingans have trouble keeping the last road along the north coast open, with these new guns the Roots have been shooting up their convoys. He senses a change in the wind."

"Then I won't worry about Haiti any more, Jacques. If my old friend Boul is thinking of throwing in with you, you must be sure to win."

"Some of our mechanics are making crossbows like those your apemen use—but smaller. Better against the Whisperers than spears." Valentine walked among Monte-Cristi's chieftans and soldiers, thanking them as best he could in Haitian Creole, before returning to Jacques. Their conversation moved on to military technicalities, smothering the good-bye in trivia.

Narcisse arrived with an assortment of potted dishes for the officer's mess, bags of provisions, and a chest full of Haitian spices. "Fried plaintains, fried pork, a bag of mushrooms—they're good on everything," she said, lifting lids and pointing with her mutilated arm. "Enough fruit to last a long while, fresh and dried. Now the spices—" She continued checking over the contents of her baggage like a marine preparing for a landing on a hostile shore.

"I'd have never left that cell if it weren't for you, Narcisse."

"And I'd still be getting stains out of Boul's underwear. We help each other, *blanc*."

He stepped on to one of the *Thunderbolt*'s launches, Narcisse once again riding in her place on his back, and as it left the beach Valentine felt sadness, and some relief. Relief at the fact that he found on Haiti what he spent over a year getting to, and sadness in saying good-bye to so many of those who risked everything to help him. He turned his body toward the ship, its outline changed by the potted trees lashed everywhere on the decks. The old *Thunderbolt* looked like a floating forest.

The launch hove alongside, and Valentine climbed aboard and reported himself present to the mate on watch. He and some sailors helped Narcisse to the galley, where she sniffed suspiciously at the Jamaican pepperpot the cook's mate was creating in celebration of leaving Hispaniola.

Valentine went up on deck and watched the preparations for departure. The motor launch was swung up, and a last few sailors and marines came out to the ship with the Haitians. There were friendly exchanges of cotton ducks for pigskin utility vests, earrings for copper bracelets, and so on over the side of the ship. There would have to be a strict search for smuggled alcohol, and the wearisome task of getting rid of lice and bedbugs which undoubtedly hitched a ride from the shore. But Valentine could leave those details to Carrasca and her mates. He and Post had to make sure the marines and Grogs were ready to fight if necessary.

The last lap. He needed to get the ship to the Texican coast. His superiors would handle the rest; he would be back to being a cog in a larger machine, rather than the axis driving the various cogs. Would he miss the taste of independent command he had been given? Being on his own was a banquet of endless servings of stress and headaches, but the freedom added spice to the dishes.

Thankfully, for this last voyage he would not have to turn into Captain Bligh on the *Bounty* and ask his crew to sacrifice for the cargo. The saplings were hardy enough to survive the short trip across the

Caribbean, assuming the *Thunderbolt*'s aged diesels held out, without taxing the ship's freshwater resources. After the challenges of the late months, Valentine was ready to spend a week supervising potted saplings.

Ahn-Kha again quartered his Grogs in the forward well deck, their old tentage replaced by a grove of quickwood plants, their crossbows and pikes stored below, shotguns and rifles cleaned and put away in the arms lockers. He wandered among the bunks of the marines. His complement was already displaying souvenirs acquired on the island, hung upon bunk and locker. Hispaniolan voudou charms wrought from wood and bead swung with the ship's gentle motion.

He returned to the deck for a last look at Haiti. The mountains, so green that the color deserved a richer word to describe it, stood out against the azure blue of the sky and the argent blue of the Caribbean waters below. It was an island of extremes: beauty and hideousness, laughter and despair, freedom and slavery. But from this island that had known an almost endless series of sorrows for the past six hundred years, a new world could spring.

Narcisse's dishes made a superb dinner, once the cook and his mate let her take over supervision of the meals. Valentine had the galley busy, and treated Post and the rest of the *Thunderbolt*'s marines to a feast. Good food and plentiful tobacco—all as night fell after an easy day's duties—made the men lively.

"How's life in the Ozarks?" a stout corporal with a stand of red hair asked. "I've heard the winters pass hard."

"Irish, I know a lot of stories get passed around the Kurian Zone about that," Valentine said. "There's enough to eat. Sometimes it isn't what you'd like as a first choice, or even a second, but we don't starve. You'll find out there's a lot of ways to cook chickpeas, and you'll get sick of dried fruit, I can promise you that."

"Women?" Hurst called, and the men snickered.

"That's one thing we're not short of. Fact is, there's so many, you'll find a few in uniform. There are a lot of lonely widows, too, which makes a man think, but if any of you have a mind to be a second husband, you'll have your pick. We've got schools, roads, there's a gambling boat, showboats, and I'm even *told* of a floating whorehouse or two on the Lake of the Ozarks. Being an officer and a gentleman, I wouldn't know details, naturally."

The men snickered and passed around comments under their breath, like kids in school, and Valentine heard Carrasca's name mentioned.

"Enough of that," Post growled.

A shout echoed from above. The collision Klaxon sounded. Something thumped against the ship's hull, a grinding jar that had everyone reaching for a table or a bunk brace to steady themselves.

"Vampir—," the squawk-box sounded, before falling silent. Valentine listened with hard ears, trying to shut out the bleating alarm, and heard the icy shrieks of Reapers.

"My God, they followed us!" Post said.

"Take arms, men—anything!" Valentine shouted. He didn't have so much as a knife on him.

"Quickwood, anyone have some?" Post asked.

The marines were already grabbing rifles and shotguns from the beckets in the wall of their quarters; a corporal coolly gave out bullets as the men took arms from the wall.

"Sir!" one marine shouted, running up to him with two of Post's screw-in pike-points. A scream, then a second, came from above— along with a smattering of gunfire.

"It'll have to do."

"Post, take Wilde and his team and get to the Oerlikon. Ignore anything else, I don't care if she's on fire, get that weapon manned. Irish, you and the rest of the men follow me! The forward stairs, we have to get to the bridge. Hand me that machete, Torres."

Post shoved a speedloader into a heavy .44 revolver with a trembling hand and gestured to his assigned men.

"Marines, you see a Reaper, shoot until it's down if you can. They'll have the advantage up close like this. Let me get in and get its head off, or stick it with the quickwood. If I catch it, get up to Post. Any more wood down here?"

"Here's a pike," another said.

"Take the tip off—it's too hard to use on the pole. Ignore any wounded, don't pay attention to anything, we go to the bridge. Now, with me!"

They moved at his order into the night's chaos. Valentine rushed out into the next compartment forward and gained the stairs leading up to the main deck. A marine caught his rifle going through the doorway and tripped, but the rest jumped over him and up the stairs in a steady stream.

The compartment above opened onto the deck from doors on either side of the ship, and Valentine led his men to the door opposite from the side of the grinding collision. If he could just get them out in the open as an organized team, rather than as frightened individuals, the ship might stand a chance. The deck door on the collision side swung open, and the men brought up their guns.

"Wait!" Valentine rasped, holding the flat of the blade of the machete against the man behind him. "It's Owens."

A sailor made it in and slammed the door shut behind. "They're everywhere—we have to get below," he said.

"You'll come with us," he said to the unstrung man. "Bellows and Gomez, Owens goes between you two. C'mon, the rest of you."

They burst onto the port side of the ship, running for the stairs to the bridge. Shots and piercing Reaper screams filled the night. As Valentine hit the first step, a caped figure appeared at the top of the stairs.

"Shoot it!" Valentine shouted, throwing himself down on the stairs so the men would have a clear view.

The Reaper lunged. Shotgun blasts flashed blue-white. Even the awesome strength in the Reaper's pounce was no match for buckshot at close range, and the wounded thing cried out as it was blown back. It recovered and vaulted over the rail to drop to the deck, but Torres swiveled the mouth of his shotgun and blew it into the darkness.

It splashed into the water, and Valentine ascended the stairs. He ducked without thinking, and heard the *whoof* of a Reaper's hand cut the air where his head had been. Valentine lashed back up, driving the quickwood pike-point in his hand up like a striking cobra. It caught the Reaper under the arm and drove through fabric built to stop bullets but not an old-fashioned point. Valentine felt sticky fluid hit his hand, and he got out from under the wound.

"Marines," he called down at the men and across the ship. His team was leaning over the rail to shoot at the Reaper that had blown into the sea; he had to keep them going to the bridge. He ran up the rest of the stairs. The wounded Reaper stood up, its jaws open in painful spasm as it clawed at the quickwood point buried in its armpit. It lost its balance and sagged against the upper deck rail.

Valentine paid it no more attention. Another Reaper, its back turned to him, tore away the metal door to the bridge, peeling it like a painter removing wallpaper.

"Aim for the face," Valentine said to the men who joined him on the upper deck. The Reaper whirled. Valentine heard screams and shooting from the stairs below. Torres, just behind him, fired at the Reaper at the door, throwing it against the bridge-cabin. Valentine circled as the others continued to shoot, pumping round after round into the thrashing creature.

He took a good grip on the machete and gathered himself.

The men stopped shooting, hurrying to reload. He dashed forward like a cricket-bowler, catching it in the throat with the heavy blade. The head did not come off, but he damaged the nerve trunks and vertebrae enough for it to go limp. It continued to snap at him with gleaming jaws, its yellow eyes dimming.

The wound closed over the blade.

Valentine left the machete wedged in its neck and went to the rail to look at the gangway below. The Kurian death machine at the back of his men had taken its toll in the seconds it took him to deal with the other. Twisted bodies and pieces of bodies lay on the deck. Three survivors fired pistols as it advanced. The Reaper used Owen's corpse as a shield. Valentine vaulted over the rail and landed behind it.

It ignored his presence, continuing forward toward the marines. Valentine lashed out with a foot, catching it in the small of the back, but he might as well have kicked the *Thunderbolt*. He took his other pike-point in both hands and drove it between the thing's shoulder blades.

The point struck near enough to the Reaper's heart to stiffen it instantly. The Reaper arched its back, its whole body bending like a bow, and hit the deck, still clutching Owen's bullet riddled body.

He was out of quickwood and had no time to look for the other pike-point among the bodies. "Everyone to the bridge," he said.

Irish hauled the Reaper out of the way of the damaged door. Valentine heard the welcome pounding of the Oerlikon from aft; Post must have gotten it into action. He went to the starboard rail and looked over the side. Kurian sailors were taking cover as the Oerlikon's fire moved up and down the deck of the submarine. Valentine saw a strange, thin smoke-stack at the rear of the ship. A snorkel on a submarine? Perhaps that was how it had crept up so close to the *Thunderbolt* without being seen. A quick rise to the surface, Reapers ready at the hatches, and all there would be to do was leap on board, an easy matter for the super-human avatars.

There was still fighting forward. Valentine heard the Grogs screaming and a gunshot or two from the rear. "Torres, take two men and cover the men at the Oerlikon from here. They'll go for that if they get organized. Who had the other pike-point?"

"Hurst, sir. He's dead below," Torres said. "I'll check—"

"No, everyone stay together up here."

The bridge door opened, and Carrasca stood at the portal, a shot-gun at her shoulder. "What is it?"

"Kurians, on the *Sharkfin*. They tried to board us. Too greedy. They could have just put a big limpet mine against the side and sunk us. But Saunders wants his ship back."

"What do we do about the Reapers still on board?" Carrasca said. "The Chief says there's some of them hammering at the engine room door. They'll get through."

"Tell the Chief to pour it on. Let's get to the wheel," Valentine said.

They went to the bridge, lit by a single red bulb over the map table. The instrument lights had long since gone out and never been replaced.

Valentine saw the sub making off, gathering speed as it ran. Post's Oerlikon bursts riddled the stern as it sought safety beneath the waves, explosions and smoke flying from the impact of the thirty-millimeter shells.

"We've got to get to the main gun. What a target! The Oerlikon is tearing it up," Carrasca said.

"He's just scratching its back—the real vitals are under water. We can still get them. The prow's reinforced, you know. Icebreaker."

"*Jesu*," Carrasca said. "If we get enough speed . . ." She went to the engine room squawk. "Chief, everything she's got. Maximum revolutions!"

"Aye aye, sir," the Chief crackled back. "Do something about those bastards on the other side of the bulkhead—they're tearing the rivets out."

"You want the wheel?" Carrasca said to Valentine.

"You're the better helmsman."

Carrasca took the ship into a gentle turn, letting her gain momentum.

"Ramming speed, Hortator," Valentine said.

A Grog lept up to the bridge window, howling in fear. A pale arm plucked it back down. Valentine heard a thud on the roof and more shots from outside.

"What's that?" the Chief said. "I—"

Carrasca hit the collision alarm again as the *Thunderbolt* knifed through the water. She aimed for the conning tower but didn't hit it square; at the last moment the submarine must have known what was coming and turned away. The impact threw Carrasca against the wheel. Valentine hung onto the instrument panel. The Reaper on the roof of the bridge fell forward into the cannon mount.

The *Thunderbolt* ran up and over the submarine, to the sound of tortured metal breaking up. Valentine saw the stern of the sub burst from the water like a breaching whale.

"*Madre de Dios*, snapped in two!" Carrasca said.

The Reaper on the gun deck jumped from the side of the ship, plummeting into the water by the crippled sub, perhaps summoned to the aid of its Master Kurian in its final need. Valentine had one more thing to do. He took Carrasca's shotgun and went to the door.

"Stay here, and keep the doors locked. The Reapers'll be

disoriented—they won't work together once their Masters are dead, but they're still dangerous. Wild animals in a trap: all confusion and pain."

Valentine glanced down to the Grog deck, but saw no sign of Ahn-Kha or his Grogs. Just bodies. Grogs, Jamaicans, and the *Thunderbolt*'s sailors were strewn in broken pieces everywhere on the deck like mannequins run over by a tractor-trailer, under blood-splashed quickwood branches. He ignored the gruesome tableau and went to the starboard arms locker, where he retrieved out one of the aged machine guns. He placed a belt into the receiver and hefted the weight. It was a more suitable weapon for Ahn-Kha, or a tripod, but it would have to do.

Another Reaper, its form misshapen by a missing leg, jumped from the stern into the water. Valentine moved forward, down to the Grog deck, and then up to the bow. He leaned over and winced at the damage to the front of the ship. Hopefully just her forward compartment was flooding. The ship could absorb this kind of damage and still proceed under her own power, were she fresh from the dockyard. Was she still sound enough to float?

The submarine was gone. All that remained of her on the surface was a fuel-oil slick, spreading across the water like a bloodstain at a murder site. And debris. And bodies. Swimming men struggled to stay afloat amidst the floating wreckage.

Valentine spotted one odd shape, a long thin tentacle with a heavy membrane attached. A Kurian, forgetting to disguise himself in his distress. Valentine loosed a burst into the struggling form. He swung the smoking barrel to the next swimmer, an oil-coated man in white, and killed him with another burst. A heavy form floated on a life preserver, perhaps dead, perhaps faking it. Valentine could not make out the features for certain, but the hair looked as though it might belong to Captain Saunders. He fired a burst into the body, which twitched at the impact of the bullets before disappearing under the oil. Another swimmer burst through the oil, taking a deep gasp of air, having miraculously escaped the sinking sub. Valentine shot him before he could draw his second breath.

The gun grew hot, and he had to slow his rate of fire. The brass casings dropped onto the deck, and hundreds lay at his feet when a hand touched his shoulder.

"It's over, my David," came a familiar bass.

"Oh, dear God," Post added, looking at the casings scattered on the deck. Valentine met his lieutenant's gaze, looking for understanding. Instead he saw disgust. Post could see only pitiful figures in the wreckage being murdered for no reason. Several Kurians had to have been on board the submarine for that many Reapers to attack at once, and it would be easy for one of them to pose as a sailor. As long as the Kurians lived, the Reapers that might still be on board the *Thunderbolt* could kill, plant a bomb, or otherwise sabotage the ship. He could no more risk a Kurian deciding to achieve a Pyrrhic victory by destroying the *Thunderbolt* that he could have let Alistar live back in New Orleans.

Valentine tossed the gun to the deck and left the bow. Ahn-Kha trailed him. Valentine was thankful for his comrade's silence. Ahn-Kha would listen and give his opinion sometime in the future, but now there was too much to do. He did not look over his shoulder to see Post, but he heard him unload the gun and pick it up.

"How many of your Grogs are left?" Valentine said.

"A hand-and-two." Ahn-Kha had forgotten himself in the crisis and used Golden One phraseology for six. "It was desperate, even with the crossbows and the quickwood. There were many of them. We hunted the last of them from the stern with the pikes. When we wounded one in the leg with a pike, it managed to tear its own limb off and escape. They've learned to fear wounds from these weapons."

"So the ship is clear? Will she be able to continue?" They descended to the Grog-deck.

"I do not know. That is for the captain and the Chief to say. I was thrown off my feet by the collision, but I was belowdecks and saw no water. She does not seem to sink."

"Mr. Post," Valentine said when Post joined them on the well deck. "We have to get the guns manned and ready while we're motionless. The submarine wasn't the only ship the Santo Domingans had. You'll be in charge of that. But leave me enough for a party to search the ship. Ahn-Kha with his crossbow, a couple of pike men, men with shotguns, four should do it. We'll look for any of our people who are wounded, of course, but we have to be ready for a fight. A Reaper or two may still be holed up somewhere on board. We'll check every corner big enough to hold a dog. Once we know the ship is safe, the Chief can go to work and see if she'll be able to move again.

"After that, we'll clean up the dead, and the ship. I don't want everyone walking over bloodstains for the rest of the trip. Any questions?"

Post shook his head. "No, sir. I think they already pulled up a sailor from the submarine portside, sir. Shall I shoot him, just in case?"

Valentine ignored the rebuke. "Let me talk to him."

The sailor was a Cuban by birth, but his mother had been taken to Santo Domingo when she and her family were captured in a raid. He sat by the entryway, trembling and wet from head to toe, with a blanket around his narrow shoulders. Valentine's Spanish wasn't up to the dialect, so Carrasca translated his story.

"I served on the *Sharkfin* four cruises, as a mechanic. I had just been called forward to get gas masks, because the damage from your gun was filling the engine room with smoke, when the collision came. Some of the men tried to get out through the old torpedo room, but those doors long since quit working. I made it out through the forward deck hatch—" Carrasca quit translating when the submariner howled in pain as Valentine grabbed his wrist and twisted it, dropping the wretch to his knees. The prisoner was human. A Kurian's disguise would have flickered.

"Val, stop!" Carrasca said. "He's just telling us what happened to him."

"I'm making sure he is who he says he is. Tell him I apologize. See if he'd like to join up with us—we could use him."

The Santo Domingan sailor seemed willing. Through Carrasca, he relayed why.

"The White Captain of the north, he was a madman. He convinced the Kur that if they got this ship, they could take over all the islands south of here. He promoted men he trusted, and to gain his trust they had to treat us badly. We worked like mad and were still punished. I had planned to swim away the first chance I could get, let the Haitians castrate me and use me as a slave in the fields. At least I would live."

"What about this last trip? Who was on board?"

"Seigneurs from the Samaná Peninsula. They had their eye on the lands west of Cape Haitian, and with this boat they could have ruled the coast. I had no love for them, I am glad they are dead."

Valentine silently commended the dead Saunders for his final throw of the dice. With the right men under him, he would have been able to snatch the *Thunderbolt* away from the Hispaniolan Kurians in the manner Valentine took it away from the rulers of New Orleans. A man of strange contradictions. Long ago he had quit asking himself why so many talented men chose to devote themselves to serving the enemies of their blood.

After the ship had been searched and re-searched, Valentine returned to his cabin, feeling an itchy burn from the Reaper-blood. He'd wiped it off quickly enough, but needed a thorough cleansing with pumice.

Post was rinsing his mouth out with baking soda in their cabin. Ahn-Kha had moved forward with the ship's remaining Grogs.

"Do you want to talk about it?" Valentine asked, scrubbing hard and working up a lather.

Post did him the courtesy of not playing dumb.

"Sir, you've pulled this whole thing, the ship, the quickwood, the Jamaicans and the Haitians together like a . . . like a magic trick, something out of nothing. I respect you for that. I'm not sure I can serve under you anymore. When we get to Texas, it's good-bye."

"It's what happened at the bow?"

Post nodded. "I can't stop thinking about the bodies in the water, sir. When you got those Santo Domingans away from their plantations, I thought that you pretty much walked on water. Woulda died for you then, if it meant accomplishing something you were trying to achieve. Never thought I'd want to die for anything or anyone. Maybe to get away from them, but not for anything."

It took Valentine a moment to regain his equilibrium. "You shouldn't have to die for anyone. Least of all me. Risking your life, weighing it against what you are trying to do—it's something any man does."

"Any man worth the iron in his blood."

"But you feel differently now."

Post waited a moment, but Valentine made no gesture to hurry him. The words would come when his lieutenant was ready.

"If your idea of the right thing to do is machine-gunning sailors who've had their ship sunk from under them, I want no part of it. You can cite precedents all you want, wrong is wrong."

"I had to make sure all the Kurians were dead. For all we knew, there was a Reaper squatting in the magazine with a hand grenade, just in case the *Thunderbolt* got the upper hand in the fight. If a Kurian has his puppet pull the pin and hug a couple of shells in its arms with the grenade under its chin, it's going to do it. Sometimes it is just as dangerous to beat the Kurians as it is to run from them. They'd rather destroy than let another own something that was theirs. The Reapers were clawing through to the Chief in the stern. I had to disorganize them, quickly, and that's the only way I had to do it.

"Remember, Post, they were serving the enemy. That's war."

Post shook his head. "I was serving the enemy. As soon as you gave me a chance, I switched. I bet a lot of those sailors would have done the same as that fellow we pulled out of the water. When you were shooting them, it was like you were shooting me."

"I understand. But I don't know how I'm going to get along without you. But go with my friendship. Shake on it?"

His lieutenant pursed his lips, then took his hand. "Could be you have what it takes for the kind of war this is and I don't. Sorry, Val, but

I can't see death like that again. I'm afraid I'd shoot you, or myself, or maybe both."

"Drop it, Will. Serving our side's different from working for the Kurians. I'll give you your choice, and wish you well when the *Thunderbolt* sails away. One thing, though: even if I did the wrong thing, the quickwood has a better chance of getting back to Southern Command if you come with it. Having it could turn things around, make a difference in a lot of innocent lives being saved. What happened at the bow was wrong, I'll grant you. But weigh it on the right scale. How wrong is it when a Reaper takes a six-year-old girl, because the Kurian running the show wants a different-flavored aura?"

Post shook his head. "That's a maybe. I'd rather deal in certainties, and those bodies floating in the diesel fuel were real, not supposition." He turned away.

"Will, if you're going to hate me, hate me for a good reason. Ask me sometime how I became a captain in the Coastal Marines."

Post would not, or could not, see that Valentine would have preferred to rescue the *Sharkfin*'s survivors. But the risk to the mission, to losing all their lives and even more time in the quest to get the quickwood into the hands of Southern Command required him to act as he did. Valentine had learned long ago not to second-guess himself where matters of life and death were concerned, or he would never be able to make a decision again. He had made right decisions and wrong decisions, and sometimes had to bury the bodies of those who died for no other reason than his bad judgment. Like Gabriella Cho, the night he left her alone and wounded in the confusion of a battle, or his old company's Master Sergeant Gator, lying in a hilltop grave in eastern Oklahoma.

Struggling with his own memories as much as he had with the Kurians, David Valentine went to bed.

Carrasca, Valentine, and the Chief decided the ship should be refitted before exploring a potentially hostile coastline, and two months in drydock at Jayport would allow the Chief to consummate a long-desired overhaul. There was the added incentive of replacing the losses from the encounter with the *Sharkfin,* so in the end Valentine agreed with yet another delay in his return to El Norte.

They returned to the harbor to a mixture of cheers and curiosity over their topiary. There were the inevitable problems with safely storing their precious cargo and finding living space for the crew during the refit, hampered by the occasional tropical storms and hurricanes brushing the island.

Valentine, Post, Narcisse, and Ahn-Kha were left with the leisure to recruit Jamaicans to join his marines, reduced to a bare handful in the fight against the Reapers. Valentine was shocked to see a soccer field filled with Jamaicans who wished to follow the Crying Man to sea, off their sunny island and into peril. In the end, he selected fifty for the short run to the coast; the *Thunderbolt* would be cramped, but it gave him a core of willing men to accompany him on the long trip back to the Ozarks.

There was also time with Carrasca as the Chief worked on the bow. Long rides into the countryside, talks with the locals, trips to sporting events and lunches made of market-square purchases filled the mornings. In the afternoon when the rains came, they talked or laughed or made love as the mood struck, and waited for the cool of the evening to walk back to the ship. Sometimes they spent the night at the commodore's house, joining him for mah-jongg or cribbage depending on the availability of players. The weeks passed like a dream. Valentine had never known so many idle days in all his years serving Southern Command. There was time to know another person, not as a comrade, superior, or underling, but as a friend and lover.

He learned her moods, and in turn she learned his. They pretended that the respite would never end by not discussing it, talking instead of the perfect hillock for a beach house or whether Valentine would make a better fisherman or planter. Valentine was more than half-willing to take these conversations at face value.

Reality intruded when the Chief refloated the ship, and they had to make ready for the last voyage. Then the idyll was over.

"You're a wanderer, too," she said as they lay together.

"What's that?" Sex always made him wool-brained.

"You wander. Is it so you don't have to put down roots?"

He rubbed his eyes. "I'm not blown around. It's more like a current."

"Even coconuts wash up, by and by. What keeps you at sea?"

"Same as you. Duty." He would have added something about his dreams of a better future, dreams made almost realistic-sounding thanks to the quickwood, but his lover sighed.

Valentine turned on his elbow. The whites of her eyes caught the night sky coming through the window. They looked wet.

"Are you saying I should wash up here?" He half hoped she'd say yes. He'd get the quickwood back to the Ozarks and return.

She didn't say anything for a moment, but her mouth twitched.

"What then?" he insisted.

"Nothing. Nothing important. Important as our duty."

Ten

The Texas Coast, October: South of Corpus Christi, the southernmost Kurian city in what had been the United States, the coastline is a collection of fishing villages hiding among ancient concrete resorts, suffering under the depredations of both the Kurian Alcaldes of Mexico and the Texas variety farther north and inland. The long stretches of the thin, sandy island running the coast of Texas provide a protected inland waterway that sees little commerce under Kur other than smuggling. Stopping this was one of the gunboat's principal duties in her cruises under Captain Saunders, when her crew spent years losing fugitives in the thornbushes and grassy hummocks of the half-mile-wide, seemingly endless coastal sandbar where once vacationing college students lost their underwear along with their virginity.

This part of Texas is typical of most of the state not under the direct eye of the Kurians: independent and isolated, asking nothing from the outside world and trusting no one.

The *Thunderbolt* followed her new prow into South Bay on a rainy dawn. A few open shrimp boats bobbed in the bay, and beyond them, some beach fisherman could be seen, their oversize rods hanging out over the lapping surf of the bay.

Valentine had never seen this part of Texas in his time on the *Thunderbolt*, though Torres had visited this coast on occasion in his days with the Corpus Christi Kur. Torres was the sole surviving crewman who knew Brownsville, so he stood on the bridge with Carrasca and Valentine.

Valentine fingered the leaves on a quickwood sapling; Carrasca had taken a fancy to one and installed it on the bridge. A few others had been planted near Kingsport, bordering the graves of the Jamaicans and Louisiana *Thunderbolt* crew who had died defending the ship from the Reapers. After explaining to the commodore the importance of the quickwood saplings, Valentine had placed further seeds in the dirt covering the bodies as they lay in their graves. He hoped one day trees would sprout and be used as weapons against the slayers of the sailors.

"Why no Kurians around here, Torres?" Valentine asked.

"Can't say. Seems that they never managed to get installed here. Not really free territory, so to speak, but there's a resistance here. I've heard of a Kurian or two coming to the area, but anyone going to work for them winds up with their throats slit pretty soon. Their Reapers can't travel much either, the resistance assembles and smokes them out of anywhere they hold up. Every now and then a bunch sweep up from Mexico, or down from San Antonio or Corpus Christi, but when they're gone, the resistance pops up again."

"What did the resistance think of the Coastal Patrol?"

"We never did much inshore except try to chase down smugglers so the resistance didn't object to us, I guess. But that's just what we heard when we came into the bay. There were only one or two safe places to visit, right up against the shore where the *Thunderbolt*'s guns could cover. The old hands told us to sleep on board if we knew what was good for us."

Valentine looked at the overgrown ruins. Palms stood up through roofs, bougainvillea sprouted everywhere, covering the ruins along the bay further.

"Looks like the work of hurricanes," Carrasca said, examining the coast through a pair of binoculars. While on Jamaica she'd dyed and recut one of Saunders's uniform coats, adding shoulder padding so she could fill it. The middle still hung a little loose thanks to the dead man's potbelly. "What now, Captain?"

"According to plan, I'm supposed to be contacted here, and failing that I need to go inland to Harland. Southern Command has a liaison officer here. He was supposed to stay around the bay, but I'm so overdue, he might have gone back to his base. That's where I need to get to if I'm not met here."

"Anything special we're supposed to do?"

"Act as if this were an ordinary patrol," Valentine said.

"Very well," Carrasca said, turning to the old hand. "Torres, what was the procedure? Do they have pilots?"

"No."

"So how would Saunders handle it?"

"Cruise the bay. Anything that looked oceangoing, we were to sink, unless we could board it and were satisfied it belonged to the Corpus Christi Kurians. Their signet was a crane over a sunrise, I think Asian-looking, only with Mexican colors. Stood out like a sore thumb in Texas. But if there was any doubt, we'd seize it and bring it back to New Orleans, and let the Kurians haggle it out."

"Then that's what we'll do. Helm, let's take a look at that inlet to starboard. After the check?"

"If the captain felt like it, he'd let us dock. There's a concrete wharf by the old Brownsville channel, and some of the harbor joints traded with us. Good place to pick up crabs, lice, and the drip from the whores. We were always under orders to go in groups of four at least, armed with rifles and sidearms. Don't try the chow—they give coasties rat meat."

"Shall we dine on board tonight, Captain Valentine?"

Valentine found himself smiling. "I've eaten rat any number of times. I'm sure Narcisse could spice it up into a state dinner, if she had to, Captain."

"Torres, what would the Captain do if he didn't want to give the men liberty in the port?"

"We'd raid a shrimp boat for food and leave, sir."

"It would be best if the captain decides to grant liberty. It can buy us some time."

They wasted the morning cruising the bay, but saw nothing larger than open fishing boats. Valentine was relieved. He didn't want to arrive at a strange port and start burning local shipping; especially when the success of his mission could depend on the aid, or at least noninterference, of the natives. With that out of the way, the *Thunderbolt* tied up at the pier near the stagnant channel. A few blocks of cracked concrete buildings leered out at them, garish—and misspelled—advertisements painted over doorways in a mixture of Spanish and English.

An afternoon rain soaked the men tying her up, and the gangway guard took shelter under the stairs to the top deck.

Carrasca, her new lieutenant, Valentine, and Post decided to dine one last time in the wardroom. With their combined coaxing, they got the Chief to join them. The Chief sat uncomfortably at the cramped table, awkward in his civilian clothes.

"They're the only ones that weren't oil stained," he explained.

They heard Narcisse's voice shout orders from the galley. With the crew now mostly Jamaican, the dishes reflected that island's preference for spiced chicken and pork dishes, leavened with rice, vegetables, and fresh fruits.

"Captain," Valentine began, as the eating slowed, "you, your officers, and the men have more than carried out your part of the bargain. I'm happy to leave the *Thunderbolt* in the Commodore's Flotilla. I know Mr. Post and the Chief will serve you ably."

Post elbowed the Chief. The Chief had met a woman in Jamaica, a beauty who could have appeared in one of the old tourism posters in her yellow two-piece bikini, and had decided to stay with the ship.

"Happily ever afters," Post said, lifting a glass of lemonade to the Chief.

Carrasca shifted in her seat and rearranged the rice on her plate.

Valentine's stomach did flip-flops as he looked at her. "Just see me and the cargo into the hands of my contacts here. You'll take my promise to do anything I can to help you in our common Cause. I'll never forget the *Thunderbolt* and her captain."

The object of his thoughts and memories smiled. "You'll always have a berth on any of our ships and a bed in Jayport."

Carrasca stared levelly into his eyes as she spoke, but he saw her jaw tighten after the last sentence. Valentine felt his throat go thick.

"Ah—thank you for the offer."

The table sensed a tension and covered it with technical talk about improvements in the ship since the overhaul. It lasted until the Chief and the two lieutenants excused themselves. Post closed the cabin door behind him.

Carrasca reached out and took Valentine's hand.

"Sorry," she said. "I've been preoccupied since we refloated. We've had no time alone."

"We're not the first couple sacrificed to the Cause."

"I'll miss the sound of your heartbeat." Her skin lost some of its usual glow.

"I wish we could say a proper good-bye."

"I know, and I agree. Discipline. It'll be lonely without you."

"You have your grandfather. The Caribbean, this ship."

"And you have your duty. We're both married, in a way, to both of them."

He lowered his voice. "It was a wonderful time, Malia."

"You'll always be a part of me, David."

Discipline or no, he kissed her, long and hard. It was agonizing to let her go, knowing that his lips might never meet hers again.

"Forgive me," he said, stepping away.

A full day passed, and no one from the shore tried to make contact with the *Thunderbolt*. A few idlers gathered to watch the sailors on the

Thunderbolt go about their daily duties, but no one requested permission to come on board, and the men who went in groups off the ship claimed no one spoke to them but bar touts.

"I'll have to go inland after all," Valentine decided at the end of the second day. Carrasca looked at him from beneath her black brows, pulling a wet bang out of her eye to do so. They both were plastered with sweat. Even with the windows wide open, the bridge was stifling in the windless harbor. The afternoon rain had succeeded only in dampening the heat.

"Have the Chief send some people in to look for a critical part," Valentine said. "Claim we have a breakdown. Maybe that won't incite too much comment. I don't like the idea of her sitting here, tied up to a dock, with the cargo on board. The people on shore have got to be wondering why the ship looks like a topiary."

"You're not leaving tonight."

"I have to. I've got a better chance moving at night."

"Alone? Can you pass as a native? From what Torres says, they don't like strangers poking around here. You don't want to be strung up in a tree by your own allies."

"They're only allies in the 'the enemy of my enemy is my friend' sense. Southern Command never had any luck getting Texas guerrillas to work with us, except right on the borderlands, where we could arm them—and shelter them if they had to run. Not that a Texan ever called it running."

She nodded. "Any orders while you're gone?"

"I hope to be back, or at least send word, in a couple days. If you don't hear from me in five, go back to Jamaica, plant the trees, and wait for the next Southern Command agent to head south."

"Somehow I don't think there are too many David Valentines to be found. Some woman needs to make more."

Valentine squeezed her arm as he passed out of the bridge and went to his cabin. He smelled the musty odor of wet Grog and found Ahn-Kha waiting, cleaning out his pointed ears with a delicate wooden implement that was part spoon and part chopstick.

"I needed a wash," Ahn-Kha said. "I've put out your things."

Valentine looked at his bunk. His dyed-to-black fatigue pants lay spread on the bed with matching moccasin boots (he'd made them last month of Jamaican calfskin) and topped by his combat vest and pistol. A canvas knapsack was already loaded with food and water flasks. A felt-brimmed hat with a beadwork band stood atop the pile.

"I don't wear hats," Valentine said. "Unless it's winter, and even then I like the stocking kind, or a coonskin."

"Start, my David. You'll blend in better. You want your drum-gun?"

"No, I'm going to travel light and fast."

"Then I cannot accompany you?"

"Sorry, old horse. I will take one of those pike-points though. Just in case."

Valentine went down the gangway with a group of sailors going to one of the wharf-side cantinas. He wore a rain poncho to conceal his lack of uniform, a borrowed gold earring pinching his ear and the hat rolled up in a pocket.

The men, under Carrasca's lieutenant, pushed two tables together and ordered the inevitable chicken, rice, bean, and tortilla meal. The cantina provided an outhouse for the comfort of its braver—or desperate—guests, and after a light meal and a lot of boiled water, Valentine excused himself. Feeling a bit like Superman from the old comic books, he exited the outhouse wearing a light leather vest, the knapsack, his weapons belt, and the hat. The poncho was in his knapsack and the sailor's earring in his pocket.

He hiked down what used to be a main street, walking just off the nearly worn away center line of the road and trying to look like he knew where he was going. Once clear of the harborside, he turned west out of town, coming to a line of shacks bordering the marshy flats, picturing a map of the Brownsville area in his head.

There were many palms above, some delicate limbed trees, and groves of thick kunai grasses and palmettos. His nose picked up the faint salt smell of the ocean, but the moist, just-overturned-rock smell of the marsh was far stronger. In the interest of speed, he stayed to the road, hoping that he would sense trouble before it found him. He fell into a steady jog. When his body warmed to the pace he fell into his old wolf lope, with hardly a twinge from his leg wound.

He stopped when he hit the old interstate, crawled into a thick stand of grass and napped after emptying one of his flasks and eating some dried fruit and fried bread. He took in the landscape as he rested. The sea had its beauty, but it was refreshing to be on land again with its confused breezes and variety of bird and animal life.

Valentine woke himself when the moon rose. He knew little about this area beyond the large scale map, and even Torres had been no help. According to his orders, the center of this part of Texas's guerrilla activity was supposedly near the old airport at Harlingen and somewhere called Rio Hondo.

The guerrillas saved him the trouble of finding them by finding him. As he trotted up the overgrown interstate running northwest, two men on horseback pulled up on a little rise above him. They had rifles pointed at the stars above out and on their hips, and reins in the other hand, ready to shoot him down or ride him down as circumstances warranted.

Valentine stopped and bent over, panting and rubbing his aching left leg.

"Yo down thar," a dry throat called. "You're the damnedest runner I ever saw. You'd think the devil himself was chasing you, but there's nothing behind you but empty."

"Keep your hands away from that gun, stranger," the other said. Like Valentine, he wore only a vest and had a gleaming Western tie at his throat.

Valentine was too tired for the good cop–bad cop routine. "I hope you're Texas Rangers."

"You do?" Dry Throat said. "Well, there's some that say that, and it turns out they hoped the opposite."

Valentine walked up the man-made hillside, hands above his head. "You'll find out if you give me a chance to talk. My name's Ghost, out of Southern Command in the Ouachitas. I'm looking for a place called 'the Academy,' and your colonel. I don't know his name, but I know the man I'm looking for, a friend of his. Patrick Fields."

"Seems to me if that were the case, you'd be well north of here, heading south."

"I came by sea."

"Haw!" Western Tie said.

"Handcuff me, hog-tie me, whatever, just bring me to either Fields or your CO."

"I'm Sergeant Ranson," Dry Throat said. "This is Corporal Colorado. Colorado, climb down and take his weapons, pad him down. We're on patrol, and we can't just quit whenever we feel like it. I'll send Colorado back for a guard, and they'll take you north." Valentine warmed to Ranson as a man who made up his mind quickly and correctly.

"Should I get out the irons, Gil?" Colorado asked as the young man unbuckled Valentine's weapon harness.

"No, man seems straight enough. If his story isn't true and he is a spy, he's going about this a mite odd."

Colorado rode off north. Ranson had Valentine walk ahead of him to an old roadside stop on the southbound side of the interstate. It seemed like any other decayed husk of the Old World, save for a ladder up to an empty platform where a gasoline sign once stood. Valentine decided it must give a commanding view, day or night—if the moon was out. He smelled water.

"Colorado will be back in a couple hours. Let me go up and take a look around. Do me a favor and walk my horse, would you? A few times around the building will be fine."

Valentine complied, as Ranson made a slow climb to the perch for a long look-round. When the Ranger returned Valentine handed the reins over.

"In the mood for some coffee, Sergeant?"

Ranson's lean face lit up. "You have coffee out of Mexico?"

"Better. Jamaican."

"Holy Moses, why didn't you say so? I ain't had coffee from anywhere east of Padre Island in years. There's a mortar and pestle we use for corn inside, and a coffeepot."

In three-quarters of an hour, they were sharing the coffee, the Jamaican beans campfire-toasted and stone-ground.

"Lord, that's good," Ranson said, sipping appreciatively. He was lean as a winter wolf and sat in an old wooden chair with long legs stretched across a pile of cordwood.

"You aren't worried I drugged it?"

"Naw. I'd kill you before it got me. Besides, you drank first, and I poured. So you've been to sea."

"Yes."

"I didn't want to say anything to Colorado, but a few of us have been told to keep an eye out for a stranger calling himself Ghost. Seems to me you're mighty overdue."

"It wasn't a pleasure cruise."

"Delays beyond your control. I know what you mean. I was on a patrol once on the Rio Grande. It was supposed to last a month. They ended up chasing us west—we didn't make it back till Christmas, five months overdue. My wife was collecting death pension already."

"So the Kurians have the river?" Valentine asked.

"The whole damned valley. Mexican Kurians, they call 'em the Alcaldes, like they was old aristocracy or something. Good farm land, some of the best in the world. The folks there smuggle us out what they can. How are things up north? We don't get news unless it comes roundabout."

"Hard, but Southern Command is holding out."

"And what were you out for? Intelligence?"

"I'll be happy to tell you if your colonel or Mr. Fields okays it."

Ranson winked with one whole side of his face. " 'Loose lips,' whatever that means. My dad used to say it when he was playing his cards close to the chest. Personally, I like a set of loose lips. 'Specially if they're attached to a genuine redhead."

Two more riders arrived with Colorado at the dawn. "Sergeant Hughes says we're supposed to cut our patrol short and see this man back to the Academy."

"Kind of him," Ranson said. "Switch to the relief horse. I expect they want him there pronto. Wish we had a spare for you, young man."

"I expect he can run some more," Colorado said. "He did pretty well there at the end on the road. I'd like to see that trick again."

While the sergeant passed on his report on the patrol, Colorado readied the horses, placing the saddlebags and rifle sheaths on the patient animals. Ranson mounted, still chewing on a snatched breakfast.

They set off, Colorado in the lead and moving his horse at a brisk walk, quickly enough so Valentine had to force himself to hurry at a pace just below a jog, which he found increasingly annoying.

"I'm going to run, it's easier than walking like this," he said, breaking into a trot.

Colorado kicked his horse to a trot, and Ranson followed. The sergeant smiled at some inner joke. Valentine set his jaw, and ran faster, passing the trotting horse at a steady lope.

"What the hell?" Colorado said. He touched his heels to the horse's flanks, and it broke into a canter.

Valentine had to pour it on to keep up with the cantering horse, but he did so. His whole body seemed suffused in warmth, a warmth that slowly grew uncomfortable. Even a Wolf couldn't move at this rate for long. His legs filled with a fiery ache, and his heart beat like a duck's wings. The sweating horse tired of the race, as well, and kept trying to break into a gallop.

"Cut it out, Colorado," Ranson yelled from the dust-trail. "You'll kill the damn horse or our friend."

Perspiration crusted with dust coated Valentine's face, but he kept pace until Colorado halted, fighting the urge to lean forward to catch his wind. He slowed back down to a walk matching the horse's, controlling his breath as best he could.

"Sheeet," Colorado said. "They shouldn'ta called you Ghost, it shoulda been Shanks. I never seen—hell, never heard of a man able to run like that."

Valentine concentrated on breathing.

"You done treating our ally like a bastard?" Ranson asked.

"Ally? We're taking him under guard, ain't we?"

"If them Reapers showed up, he'd be guarding us, not the other way around. Don't you know a Hunter when you meet one, you damned fool?"

"Ha! My pa used to say those Hunters were just good liars, is all. There's nothing to that story."

"Apple didn't fall far from the tree." Ranson said under his breath. But his eyes shared the joke with Valentine, knowing the Cat heard.

The Academy was easy to find. It bordered on a defunct airport whose runways now served as a rifle range. The airport's concourses and some of the hangars had been demolished, but the control tower still dominated the camp, reinforced with a pyramid of sandbags and timber all the way to the top. On the other side of the old military education campus there was a cemetery, graves arranged facing a giant statue that seemed familiar yet out of place to Valentine. "It's the model of the one that stood in Washington, Marines raising the flag at the top of Mount Surabachi on Iwo Jima," Ranson explained, and Valentine realized he had seen the photo it was based on. "It was a helluva fight in the Pacific in 1945. The men who finally got up there and planted that flag were from Texas."

Valentine remembered it differently, but he was in no mood to discuss military history minutiae at the moment. Ranson brought him through the rows of barracks, one lot vacant like a missing tooth, and took him to the brick headquarters. Like the control tower, it was layered in sandbags and barbed wire, with hard-points guarding both entrances.

"Don't worry about washing up," Colorado said as Valentine retied his hair when they moved through the door past a sentry. "The colonel likes to hear news first. Everything else waits, unless you're bleeding. Bleeding badly, that is."

Spurs clattering in the wood-floored hallway, they approached a reception desk. It was a beautifully carven piece of wood, like many of the items decorating the entrance hallway. Valentine got the impression every square foot of wall space was covered by a painted portrait or photograph. The only ones he recognized were Sam Houston and the Texas United States Presidents. The woman at the desk wore a cheerful Mexican print blouse and a ready smile, but Valentine saw a pistol lying right next to the phone.

"Courier for the colonel," Ranson said. "Tell him it's Longbow Resolution. The Ghost is finally haunting us."

Another Ranger walked down the hall and out the door, saddlebags hung over uniformed shoulders. Valentine found the contrast between the rough, tanned, mustachioed men and the ornate furnishings interesting.

"Map room, second floor," the receptionist drawled, looking at Valentine from under curled eyelashes.

"Colorado, you can go get yourself fed," Ranson said. "I'll see things through from here."

The younger man took the dismissal well. He hesitated only a moment before saying, "I'll see if I can snag us some bottles of beer for when you're finished, Sarge."

"You do that, Colorado. Thanks."

"Good luck with the colonel, Shanks," Colorado said, offering his hand. "Hope there's no hard feelings over our little race."

Valentine shook it and thanked him. Ranson lead him to a white-painted staircase, and they ascended past photographs of cities filled with pavement, glass, and steel.

Valentine loved maps, and the map room captivated him. A four-foot globe stood by one wall-spanning bookcase, but the other walls were covered with maps. A long library table dominated the center of the room, placed on an oriental rug spread on the polished wooden floor. Tall windows lighted the room. Chairs stood beneath the mounted maps on the walls. One of the maps, showing the Rio Grande region of Texas, was festooned with pins and colored ribbons. Valentine walked up to an older, glassed-in map of the state, which looked to date from Texas's earliest days.

A handsomely dressed Latino opened the door and held it open for the colonel. The Colonel of the Texas Rangers, Officer Commanding the Academy, had undoubtedly been a tall man in the days before his confinement to a wheelchair. Valentine guessed he must have stood close to six five at one time, judging from how high he sat in the wood-and-metal contraption he wheeled himself around in. He was gray haired and clear eyed, and gave the impression of lively vitality from the waist up, like an alert prairie dog whose hind legs are hidden in his burrow. He wore a bronze star enclosed by a circle, pinned over a frilly white-and-blue ribbon.

"Col. Steven Hibbert, Texas Rangers," the colonel said, extending his hand. "Glad to meet you."

The Texans were devoted hand-shakers. "Thank you for your hospitality, Colonel Hibbert. My name's Valentine, but I'd prefer if you just referred to me as Smith, or Ghost, in your paperwork, if I end up being mentioned."

"We generally call him 'the colonel,' " Ranson said.

"Whatever you're comfortable with, young man. This is my chief of staff, Major Zacharias."

After another handshake, the colonel moved on to business. They sat at one end of the long library table, so all eyes could be at the same level.

"Well, Ghost, your contact here went back north a month or so ago on a courier run. He didn't have much choice—he told us about you and asked for our assistance. Fields is a good man, about all he ever asked us for in the past was information about the state of things in Texas and on the Mexican border, and a couple of times he brought us warning of troop movements that saved lives. I'm willing to do whatever I can to help Southern Command. He said you'd have something needing to get north."

"Yes, sir," Valentine said, relieved at their accommodating attitude. "I'm to give you part of my cargo in exchange for your assistance. It's a weapon. Deadliest thing I've ever seen used on a Reaper." Valentine showed the colonel the quickwood pike point he'd brought, and explained the catalytic action the wood had in a Reaper's bloodstream.

The colonel and his chief of staff exchanged looks. "Well, now," Zacharias said. "That's good news. Some kind of silver bullet, huh?"

The colonel shifted his weight in his chair. "And you've seen this work with your own two eyes."

"Yes, Colonel."

"Because I've heard tales of big medicine against the Kurians before, and every one of them turned out about as effective as the bullet-proof vests made out of old sticks and beads the Indians wore."

"Not just me. Others, too—you don't have to wonder if I'm crazy. I'll leave you with what I can spare, some saplings you can plant and some lumber you can turn into weapons. We've found that crossbow bolts and spear-points work best."

"Our armorer will take a look at what you've done," the colonel said.

"It's a lot easier than trying to go in and behead them, that's for sure. Time is important, Colonel. Every day the ship waits in harbor—"

"Easy, now, son. South Bay isn't really our ground—not that it's Kurian. If we ride in armed for Reapers and offload you, someone will talk. If this stuff is important as you say it is, we might want to keep it as a surprise for the bloodsuckers. Major, let's put Harbormaster into effect."

Zacharias made a note on a clipboard as the colonel spun his wheels back to Valentine. "You get back to your ship and bring it across the bay to the entrance to the old intracoastal shipping channel. There's a white lighthouse there, manned by some of the Corpus Christi crew. We've got a spy there, and this sounds important enough for him to break his cover. He'll knock out their radio and make sure our Rangers grab the place. We'll make it look like a simple hit-'n'-loot. When you see two blue lights burning, one on top of the other, bring your ship in as close as the tide'll let you, and we'll start loading up your cargo. This will happen twenty-four hours after you get safely back to your vessel. Questions?"

"Two blue lights vertically." Valentine sagged into his chair in exhausted relief. The colonel's quick mind relieved him of his last few worries about getting his prize to the Rangers safely. He shook himself back to the present.

"No questions, Colonel. Some food and a few hours' sleep, and I'll be ready to go."

"You'll get more than that. There's still some things we have to organize. You'll have until dawn tomorrow to eat and rest up. That okay by you?"

"Better than okay."

"Major Zacharias, you'll have operational command. Put Flagstaff in charge of trains and logistics, use Three-Feather's reserve riders for the main force. I want plenty of scouts, too. Send two couriers now and get Harbormaster going. Ranson, you'll take our friend back to his ship and go onboard as liaison."

"Can I bring Colorado along, Colonel? 'Bout time he started working on a longer line."

"Sure, how often does a man get a chance to go to sea nowadays—even if it is just a ride across the harbor. Mr. Valentine, we'll meet again when your cargo is here, safe and sound."

Night on the harbor. The old lighthouse near the wrecked causeway had two lights burning.

Valentine watched from his familiar bridge-perch as the ship's boats, and a commandeered shrimp boat, moved quickwood, men, and material from ship to shore. There was nothing for him to do on shore, save hear Flagstaff give gruff orders to the Rangers and contingent of laborers he commanded. Oxen stood in their traces, and smaller horse-wagons held supplies for the two hundred riders Zacharias brought to guard the precious cargo. The eight-man garrison of the lighthouse was under lock and key, though five of them expressed an interest in moving inland with the Rangers. Valentine idly listened to the sound of waves lapping against the ship as he pulled his tiny collection of books from its railed shelf, lulled by the hint of motion as the *Thunderbolt* rocked at anchor. He felt melancholy. The *Thunderbolt* had become a home.

And it was time to leave.

He would miss the sound of the sailors talking as they washed down the decks in the morning, the smell of good coffee, the wide horizons of the sea. He thought of his father, and his description of the charm of naval service: "Duty at sea, especially when you were out months at a stretch, sounds like you're away from everything, that you'd be lonely and homesick, but you aren't. To a sailor, the ship is a home he takes with him. It's like traveling with your job and all your neighbors. There's nothing like it." His father had been right.

He also liked being able to hit the Kurians where he chose, instead of spending all his time parrying blows. Moving men, their food, and equipment was simplified by the tonnage a ship could carry. A real navy, well handled, could make the Kurian seaboard spend far more of its time garrisoning harbors and seaside towns, out of fear that a occupying force would appear over the horizon. The Free Zones in the Appalachians, the Ozarks, and the Rockies would be given breathing room. But he was just one officer, a spy-saboteur trained to work inside the Kurian Zone. Putting together real sea power would take combinations of time and resources the Kurians took pains to prevent. The great ports of the world were solidly in Kur's grip. But with quickwood—

"The quickwood beams are going now, Captain," Post reported. "These Texans are organized."

Valentine nodded. "They have to be. This pocket doesn't have any Lifeweavers. They're going up against the Reapers with small arms and guts, and a lot of people on farms and in towns slipping them news and supplies. They're smart, they don't fight over the Rio Valley or the coast, nothing that's important to the Kurians. Texas is a big place, they've got distance on their side as long as they stay mobile."

"I'd always heard they were just bushwackers in uniform."

Ranson, who'd approached and caught the tail end of the conversation, cut in to elaborate. He described how the Rangers would go into some one-horse village and relocate the residents. "Then a few Reapers and Quislings come riding in, lifesign reads normal, they think it's just another town. But it's a town armed to the teeth with men who know how to use their guns. We've got a heck of an intelligence network, most everyone between the Rio and San Antonio city limits knows what to do if they see a column coming into the area. We use a lot of heliographs, since the sun's almost always shining. The Kurians have been burned too many times—now they only roll through with big pacification raids. When that happens, the Rangers scatter."

"How much do you know about the quickwood?" Post asked. Farther back on the ship, proof of the efficacy of the weapon stood on the upper deck. A dead Reaper, frozen as a statue with skin hard as tree bark, stood gripping the ship's rail and canopy—though not truly lifeless, at least in the vegetable sense. The Reaper was beginning to sprout tiny green leaves.

"Everything," Valentine said. "I'll give another briefing to their weapons people. I'm going to leave them some lumber and saplings. Want to throw in your seed-pouch?"

"They'll need it more in the Ozarks."

"I'll carry it there for you, Will."

"You've got enough equipment, what with that ugly-assed gun you tote, Val, and there's still a lot of miles ahead of us. I'll bring it myself. You'll need somebody around to carry out your godawful plans anyway, won't you?"

Valentine felt his eyes moisten. "Why the change of mind?"

"More of a change of heart. When I was watching the Chief and his girl on Jamaica, and you and—well, I got lonely for a woman. The beach beauties were willing, but I want to find my wife. Tell her I was wrong and she was right."

"About the system?" Valentine asked, remembering their conversation before the mutiny.

"When we first got married, we didn't know each other that well. I was in uniform then, but it was for the food and the security. Gail was a sharp girl, and figured out I didn't really like *them*, or my job. We talked about us getting a posting way out on some frontier, and running for Arkansas. We used to talk like that a lot.

"Funny thing was, after I got married to her, all of a sudden I wanted to do better, have better housing and better food for us, or her really. I went officer, mustanged up from a sergeant to a junior lieutenant. Part of the process was indoctrination, of course. Lectures at the New Universal Church building—you know the routine. Then I had to spew the same stuff to my men: all about mankind poisoning and ruining the Earth, crime and overcrowding and starvation and homelessness. Then the shit that came down in '22 and how the Kurians came to restore 'natural order,' all that Darwin stuff they come up with about men needing control. Of course, the Kurians never admit that they probably started it all—they make it sound like they saved us from extinction. But anyway, I started to believe it. You probably can't understand—"

"But I do," Valentine said. "I've heard a few speakers for the Church. While they're talking, it seems reasonable enough. It takes the next drained body you see to set you straight again."

"Well, Gail and I grew more distant. She didn't like my talking about making captain, or joining the Coastal Marines to advance faster. I was drinking a little too much on days off with the others. But it was the baby that did it."

"Baby?" Valentine asked. "You never said anything about children."

"It would have been a baby, I guess," Post said. "Gail didn't want to have it, she 'couldn't bring a child into the world for *them*.' She aborted it—I hate to think how. I found out and said something stupid. I think I quoted the New Order's law on abortion like it was Scripture. She took off, I don't know where. Left me a note with her wedding ring: 'Maybe you can replace this with a brass one.' At first, I was actually glad to be rid of her. I thought her opinions might be preventing me from getting promoted." He ran his hands through his multitoned hair in frustration, gripping the locks at the back of his head as if trying to tear the memories out before continuing.

"I only realized later, after she was gone, that she was the thing that kept me going. All of a sudden I was ashamed every time I put on my uniform. I hated the job—I hated the people. Drinking helped me forget . . . let me go to sleep. Pretty soon it helped me make it through the day. Then wake up. Thanks to you, I got a part of my life back. I owe you that, whatever your methods. Now I want the rest of me."

Valentine stood on shore with his volunteers: a smattering of Jamaicans, many of the *Thunderbolt*'s remaining marines, and a few sailors who decided to go back to the Ozarks to look for their families. The group said their farewells to their comrades from the *Thunderbolt*. Narcisse sat atop a wagon, distributing voudou amulets and cheek-smacking kisses.

Captain Carrasca, dressed again in the looser pirate clothes Valentine had first seen her wearing, said good-bye to each of the men as they walked down the gangway. When she got to Ahn-Kha, she hugged him, her outspread hands making it just to the other side of his armpits. When that was over, she gave him a wooden tube that Valentine thought looked like a bamboo flute. Ahn-Kha bowed.

Valentine stood at the entry port last.

"I'm glad Will is going with you," Carrasca said. "I'd give almost anything to keep Narcisse in the galley. Won't be sorry to see the Grogs go. We can do without their unique odor. But the two of you will be missed."

"Torres will make you a fine officer of Marines."

"Yes, he's already polished those railroad tracks three times, and it's only been a day.

"One more thing." Carrasca stepped forward and embraced him in turn. Post tactfully drew the men away from the gangplank, and the pair stepped behind the lifeboat davit.

"If I ask you to do something for me, will you do it?"

"You shouldn't have to ask that question, my love. You're the best thing that's happened to me in years." He kissed her, softly and lingeringly.

"When you're back safe in your mountains, write me. We used to get courier pouches every now and then from Southern Command, years ago before the Kurians set up their intercoastal patrol chain. Now smugglers get newspapers and pamphlets to us through your logistics men. The commodore would like to see more, and so would I. Maybe you can set up a new mail run. From your stories, it sounds like you have the experience. Anything. Just let me know that you're okay."

"It's a promise. Write me, as well."

"I will."

They stood looking at each other, neither sure of what to say. She smiled.

"Almost forgot. I made you something." She reached into the baggy pants and pulled out another leather pouch. Stitched into the leather was the legend: *THUNDERBOLT* / JAMAICA-HAITI-TEXAS 2070 / CAPT. MALIA CARRASCA.

Valentine took the pouch. It felt as though it were full of a lot of coin-sized objects, only lighter. "Your quickwood seeds?"

"Look."

He opened it and extracted a handful of mah-jongg pieces. The bamboo pieces were delicately painted.

Valentine finally said, "Your work?"

"Of course. Should be rainproof, I lacquered them enough. You and Ahn-Kha and Post and Narcisse can play."

"Thanks, but . . . damn. I feel like I should send you away with something," Valentine said.

"You have," she said. "More than you know." Her eyes glistened with tears.

"How's that?"

"Hope. Someday we'll have ships going up the Mississippi to your Ozarks. I have a feeling . . . things are about to get better."

Valentine felt a pleasant thrill at the latest example of their minds following similar trails. If it weren't for the quickwood . . .

"Hope for someday, then."

" 'Someday.' That's all our generation has: hope." She raised her chin. "Texas is waiting. I don't wish the men to see me teary-eyed. Back to hard-nosed captain, Captain."

"Yes sir," Valentine said, saluting.

She returned the gesture, her emotions under control again. Valentine felt the old wall go up. It was as if they had never kissed. As if they were strangers. Inspiration came to him.

"I left that old Coastal Marine uniform coat in the closet in my room. You're welcome to that. It doesn't mean much to me, and won't do me any good where I'm going. All I'm keeping are the boots and the pants I dyed."

The wall vanished. "I'll make earrings out of the buttons," she said with a smile.

"Better and better." He caressed her cheek with the back of his hand. Carrasca . . . caress. He smiled to himself. "Good-bye, Malia."

"Adios, David. You can always find a home with us on Jamaica, you know that."

"I do." He hurried off the *Thunderbolt.* Valentine couldn't let his mind dwell on the idea.

Four days later, Valentine and Post sat in the Academy Map Room. A pair of electric fans fought a losing battle with the lingering summer heat. Ahn-Kha stood behind and in between them. His bulk wouldn't allow him to do anything but demolish the antiques in the room, and the Grog had declined the offer by one of the Rangers at the meeting to go seek out a piano bench.

"We've accomplished part one," the colonel said from the head of the library table, after hearing the reports from the various Rangers involved. "Now comes the hard part, getting those wagons up to the Ozarks. Zacharias, before my encounter with that piece of shrapnel, you used to be in charge of our northern areas. What's your suggestion?"

Zacharias's dark eyes studied the map, as if looking for something that would appear if he just stared long enough. "With the kind of men we'll need to guard the wagons, there's no question of slipping it through the San Antonio–Austin–Houston belt, though I bet we could get north of Corpus Christi. We're going to have to swing west of San Antonio. Not too far west, we can't be moving across the desert, either. The hill country could shield and water us."

"That means crossing the Ranch."

"The Ranch?" Valentine said. "What ranch?"

"You've never heard of the Ranch?"

Valentine began to shake his head, then stopped. "Wait, you mean what I think you mean? That's a legend in a lot of places. No one's ever proved it true."

"What's this?" Post asked. "I've never even heard the story."

"The Ranch," the colonel said, "is a real place. Maybe elsewhere sometimes it is and sometimes it's not, but I'll tell you it's true in Central Texas. We've seen it. The Ranch, Mr. Post, is kind of an experimental farm the Kurians run. According to our sources, they use it to come up with new life-forms. Biological servants. Even something other than humans to squeeze the juice outta. Intelligent, but easier to handle."

"There's a lot of strange sights to be seen in those hills," Zacharias said. "The Kurian settlements give it a wide berth, there's a huge stretch of empty ringing it. The Ranch gives us our best chance of getting up to the Dallas area and past it. Then it's into the pinewoods of East Texas, and you'll be home. Getting back will be easier with no cargo to guard. We can either break up and get home in small groups the direct way or trace our route back."

"It's your part of the country," Valentine said. "If that's what you want to do, I'll support it. Whatever gives us our best chance of getting through without fighting."

"Colonel, if we're going to try to get across the Ranch, I'd like to have Baltz along," Zacharias said.

"I'll send word."

"What's his specialty?" Valentine asked.

"Her specialty," Zacharias corrected. "Back in the cattle-drive days, they used to have one or two old bulls to lead all the other cattle, especially for things like river crossings. Baltz is kind of like that, except she ain't a bull. Bullheaded, oh yeah. She grew up in the Ranch, worked there. Not in the secret buildings, on the outside. She knows the land. We'll need her and her staff, sure as a hot summer sunset."

Eleven

The Ranch, Central Texas, November: Texas, at 266,000 square miles, is larger than any country of old Europe, and could fit a few Eastern states within her expanse. The same could almost be said of the lands around the Ranch, which stretch from the hill country west of San Antonio in the south to Abilene in the north, taking up the Edwards Plateau in the west and ending at the old I-35 in the east. Why the Kurians wanted such a vast expanse for their experiments can only be guessed at; perhaps the research stations they established on the Colorado River and the San Angelo area needed isolation.

The thorough depopulation of the area supported this theory. It is one of the few parts of the Kurian Zone run without the aid of Quisling forces. Its borders are watched by Grogs, either hardened to or oblivious of what goes on in the hinterland of the region.

It is one of the most beautiful parts of the Lone Star State, a land of limestone bluffs over twisted rivers, of rolling hills dotted with wildflowers and fragrant of sage. Longhorns, wearing no brand at all, roam the valleys alongside buffalo, with antelope watching from the hilltops and white-tailed deer sheltering in the cedar and oak forests. Cypress grows in the river valleys, and zone-tail hawks drift above the southern tip of the American Great Plains. If the wildlife could talk, they could tell of new, strange inhabitants wandering the hills.

David Valentine scratched the bristle on his chin in thought, raking his memory. Only one animal on earth looked like that, and they were called . . . "Zebras, by God."

"Yes, that's right, zebras," Amelia Baltz said.

She was a square-built woman, a thick, tough-skinned German as solid as a Gothic cathedral. She rode with Valentine and her staff at the front of the wagon train when she wasn't driving her buckboard or conferring with the Ranger-scouts on the best path for the column to take. Her "staff" consisted of a towheaded thirteen-year-old girl named Eve, a walking suntan who was all scrawny limbs under a face that twitched like a rabbit when she thought. There was also an assortment of animals ranging from riding and packhorses to dogs, cats, and the only chickens Valentine had ever known to lay eggs while traveling.

"The zebras, David, come from an old—I guess you'd call it a zoo—near Kerrville. It was home to ostriches, too, and they're thriving in the hill country. The damn things'll kick your head clean off if you startle them, so don't wander into the brush to take a shit without looking for something with a feathery white ass. Funny thing is, you come up on 'em head-on, they turn and run. You sneak up behind . . . *swish-whack*."

Baltz had a direct earthiness that came from better than forty years of life in the open. She wore bandannas over hair, mouth, and neck when the dust kicked up and settled on the broad brim of her hat, and an ancient pair of curving, head-wrapping sunglasses.

"Are we on the Ranch lands yet?"

"We're just skirting the edge. We've left the Grog-pickets behind. What they do if they cut our trail I don't know, they don't go into the Ranch proper, at least not anymore, even following an enemy. They ain't that dumb—no offense intended to your big-assed shadow there. The Ranch has its own security. One relief: the Hissers don't wander these hills, so we don't have to worry about lifesign."

"No offense understood," Ahn-Kha said. The Golden One walked alongside Valentine's horse, his long rifle protected from the dust by a soft leather sheath. "Perhaps the unusual animals are the reason people think this place is used by Kur for experiments."

"We don't think, we know. I worked their lands, when I was nearer your age, David, or even younger. I was an electrician; I handled the lines running between the stations. Being a specialist means you see some things they don't want you to tell about, so they made me live on the Ranch, with some of the other people they couldn't do without. About twelve years ago, they decided to clean house and bring in some new people. They showed up, and I didn't like the way they were rounding us up for a 'meeting.' I got Eve, jumped in a Hummer, and rode it till the oil ran out, then ran south on foot.

"I never saw much of what was going on inside the stations—I just worked the lines outside. When I had to work a box indoors, they blindfolded me until I got to the utility room. But even outside you saw things. Once I heard some kind of muttering in the underbrush and I looked down and these two pigs were nosing through some scrub. They weren't grunting, they were forming something like words, I just didn't understand.

"They've had a lot of trouble with breakouts. Keeping a pig in a pen and keeping a pig that thinks like you do is something else entire."

"I can imagine," Valentine said. He could imagine, too much. The hills felt as if they were waiting for him to turn his back. He would have almost preferred to hear that they were stiff with Reapers.

"Can you, boy? I wonder. There was a rumor that once something got out; they blasted a whole quarter of the place with nerve agents. Hold 'em up here a minute, me and the dogs are going to scout that tree line."

The wagon train always got under way before dawn. Each move was a two-segment effort. The mounted screen of ranger scouts moved a day ahead of the column under Zacharias's lieutenant, charting the course for the wagons and choosing the best spots for stream-crossings, resting places, and the next night's campsight. The convoy of fifteen wagons and the rest of the escort made up the second segment. The convoy spent only about six hours a day in motion. The oxen pulled better with frequent rest stops and out-spans, and those always meant at least a couple of hours of delay while teams were unhitched and then reorganized.

Valentine left much of the management of the column to the Texans, and he and Post worked at getting their men to patrol effectively alongside the rangers. With their baggage in the wagons, the mix of former marines and sailors had to carry only their arms and ready ammunition, and perhaps a canteen or walking stick. There was some grumbling about marching while all the Texans got to ride, and there was some comment by the Texans about having to guard and support "foreign mouths"—though there was no complaint about the quality of Narcisse's chuckwagon cooking. Ahn-Kha and his surviving Grogs stuck close to Valentine as he moved about, like children keeping close to their parent among strangers.

"If we run into anything, our men will be glad the horsemen gave them warning, and the Texans will be grateful for all our rifles," Valentine said to Post, when they talked over the men's adaption to the trail and their new allies. They both agreed that even after days in the wagons, sweeping wide around San Antonio, the column was still moving like a balky horse.

Steak on the hoof followed the wagon train, driven so as to muddle the wagon tracks and footprints. Regular barbecues in the evening gradually brought the two camps together, until Texans were teaching Jamaicans to play horseshoes and guitars, and the mariners were enthralling their hosts with stories and music, and dances and songs from the other side of the Gulf.

By the time they entered the lands Baltz identified as being on the Ranch proper, the column was as cohesive and cooperative as Valentine could have hoped, due to habit more than leadership or training. At rest halts, Valentine's soldiers took over the picket duty, fanning out to gather some of the seasonal crops growing wild: plentiful apples, squash, and pumpkins. Their foraging made a difference to the barbecues, and with the nights growing longer as October waned, the evening meals became more leisurely. Narcisse contributed her own ideas about cooking to the drive. Some of the Texans began to anticipate the nights when she cooked Creole dishes—the variety was welcome with night after night of slaughtered beef and preserved food.

It was at one peaceful camp, as Valentine walked the picket line with Post to make sure the sentries were under cover with good fields of vision, that a pair of the *Thunderbolt*'s sailors, one Jamaican and one former Coastal Patrolman, came running down from a grass-covered hill.

"Captain, there's some kinda big animals the other side of this hill. They're making a hell of a noise," the old New Orleans hand reported, moving from one foot to the other like a schoolkid asking for a trip to the toilet.

The Cat hardened his ears. It sounded like construction work, or logging. He thought he heard a tree being pushed over.

"Post," Valentine said, "find Baltz, please. Tell her to meet me on top of that hill. Let the camp know we've seen something, but I doubt there's immediate danger. They wouldn't be making so much noise if they meant to cause trouble. Take my horse back, would you?" Valentine dismounted and placed a drum in his submachine gun, and shouldered the weapon.

"Let's have a look," Valentine said to the men.

"Sir, that gun ain't gonna do much against what's on the other side of this hill."

"We can always outrun it."

"Two of us get away, then. The two fastest," the Jamaican predicted.

They filed back up the hill and began to crawl through the grass and brush when they reached the crest. Valentine looked back toward the camp and saw Baltz and Eve trotting toward their observation point.

"Losey, go back down a ways and show 'em where we are," Valentine said to the Jamaican, who nodded and crawled backwards out of sight.

Valentine heard the sound of another tree tipping and looked into the valley.

They were huge quadrapeds. More strange wildlife of Central Texas, he really couldn't—

"You've got to be kidding," Valentine said. "Those are elephants, but with two trunks. Or is it one trunk cut in two?"

"Can't see too well, sir. My eyes have been fadin' since I turned thirty. See how they're using tools?"

Valentine did see. The gray giants were using picks and shovels to dig in a clearing they had enlarged in a patch of woods. Other elephants used their foreheads to knock trees over, facing outward from the clearing.

"What did I tell you, boy?" Baltz said, creeping up on her haunches. The girl watched silently from behind. "Don't that beat all? Them 'fants, looks like three or four families down there, they're getting set for winter. They're making a windbreak, some of the trees they're leaving up will be pushed together to make sort of a roof. They don't like the cold. Don't use fire, though. They talk, and you can hear them a long way away, the dogs pick up stuff below our hearing frequency. I knew we'd run into some 'fants in the next day or two—the dogs signaled it."

"Why are they digging?" the sailor asked.

"Food storage. That's an old riverbed, and they're going to put stuff they gathered in the clay. They've figured out how to dry fruit. You'll see apples all over the place lying on stones."

"The Kurians thought they could feed off those? They look like they could stomp a Reaper."

"Nah, the Grogs hunt them with tranquilizers from horse-back, or vehicles. The 'fants haven't really worked out for them. I don't think they did much research on elephants, the wild things had a family loyalty they didn't count on. Upping the intelligence a couple of degrees was one of their dumber moves. We'd best get away from here soon though, if there are 'fants around, there might be hunters. Though the tracks I've seen today don't show it."

"You want us to move at night?" Valentine asked

"Just for a couple more hours."

"Light'll be gone soon—let's get moving, then. Eve, don't you ever say anything?"

"No sir," Eve said, eyes wide on the elephants.

"You'd better go pack up the menagerie," Baltz said to Eve. The girl took one long look, then scampered off. "C'mon boy, sightseeing's over. We should get away from here."

"Is she a relative?" Valentine said.

"She's been with me since she was a babe in arms. The Kurians had a research station in a crossroads town called Eden. I never found out what they were breeding. There was a fire, and they called in everyone with two arms and two legs to help fight it. Well, for some reason there were human babies at this station, most of 'em died account of the smoke, they dragged them out in this cart-cage contraption. Looked to be five, or maybe six infants in this cage. I saw her fingers moving and got her out. She started coughing up a storm, and even with all the noise she was making, I snuck her to my truck. I didn't know who to trust, so I started living out of my truck with her in it. Whenever I had to deal with anyone else, I put her in a tool case, with air holes, of course. She seemed to pick up on the danger, even though she was barely crawling—she'd keep quiet for hours until I opened it up again."

The next day it was Baltz who summoned Valentine. She sat her horse beneath a steel tower, a pair of power lines hanging from the arms.

"This is funny, Captain," she said. Valentine startled; it was the first time she had ever called him anything other than his first name, or boy.

"You don't mean funny 'ha-ha' I take it."

"No. Funny-scary. This is a main source line. It runs back up to an oil-burning plant in Abeline. It's dead, and I mean long dead. I haven't been this deep into the Ranch in years, but I'd say this hasn't carried current in two or three years, judging from bird and insect activity. I climbed the tower and had a close look."

"Maybe they found a new power source," Valentine said, but it sounded wrong even as a guess.

"You know the Kurians, son, they don't bother with something that's working. Civic improvements are the last thing on their mind. You're talking about a shutdown to at least half the Ranch, probably more, if this line is dead."

"Maybe they gave up on these experiments. Found them unproductive?"

"That might be. They have the patience of Job, though, which makes sense considering they don't die. What's wrong, guys?"

Her assorted mutts were whining worriedly and slinking around behind her horse. Valentine's horse began to toss its head. He dismounted and soothed the animal.

"It's coming from that brush over there," Baltz said, her horse under better control.

Valentine unlatched the flap on his .45's holster. He handed his reins to Baltz, and pulled his machete from its saddle.

"That's what I call a pig-sticker," Baltz said.

"A Grog would have shot by now. This isn't the right time of day for a Reaper, but I'm not taking any chances. Maybe he's got a motor-cycle helmet on."

Valentine cursed himself for not carrying one of Post's spearheads. He took a few cautious steps toward the brush, every nerve alert.

He heard grass move, and whatever was crawling through the brush changed course at his approach. Valentine made ready to leap forward or back, gun in his hand and machete held ready to swing.

A sound like fifty castanets came from the brush. It sounded famil-iar, only too loud; he hadn't turned up his ears that much. What kind of rattler would make that much noise?

He found out when the snake struck from cover. The king of all rattlers, its head as large as a melon, lashed out with mouth gaping and fangs pointed down and forward. It aimed for Valentine's thigh.

A blur of reflexes saved him from a strike moving faster than the eye could follow. He spun, pulling his leg out of the way as he brought the blade around and down as fast as a propeller. The fine steel edge severed the neck of the rattler two feet below the neck, and the head flopped to the grass, biting at nothing. The decapitated body thrashed back and forth, rattle still buzzing angrily.

"Jesus, that's a hell of a snake," Baltz said as the serpentine body slowed and stopped.

Valentine breathed until his heart slowed and the burning above his kidneys faded.

"You moved faster than the damn snake, boy. I didn't know what happened till it was over. You touched by God or something?"

"Or something," Valentine agreed. "Don't tell me the Kurians made smart, venomous reptiles."

"I don't think it was smart. Creeping up on all of us like that."

"If it wasn't smart, then why did they bother? Breed a few thou-sand of them and drop them on farmland in the Ozarks from planes?"

"I wouldn't put it past 'em. But they're new here. Dead lines, big snakes, no Grog patrols away from the borders. It adds up to some-thing. I'd say the Ranch is under new management."

"Anyone see a sign that said 'Animal Farm'?"

The reference was lost on Baltz.

*   *   *

That night Valentine worked with the snakeskin. He found something in it appealing and with Ahn-Kha's help he turned the hide into a bandolier. He didn't intend to be without a spearpoint or two in the future. After the camp trooped past the hide to whistle, gape, and ask the same questions over and over, he and Ahn-Kha went to work. They stretched lengths of snakeskin from wagonwheel to wagonwheel on one of the supply wagons, peeling off the remaining muscle and salting down the skin.

"The Gray Ones like snakemeat, my David. Even better than beef."

"They're welcome to it—there's enough to last them a week."

"This is good skin. Very light and strong. I think I will try layering it, so the scales go different directions. Make armor for the chest and shoulders. Better than sharkskin."

They ate and drank as they worked, with the other two Grogs squatting by the campfire, toasting snakemeat on sticks and watching their every move.

"Whatcha makin' boy?" the familiar voice of Baltz called in passing. She approached them with the rolling walk of someone constantly at sea or on horseback.

"A conversation piece, most likely," Valentine said. "There's some coffee left."

"No, really, looks like a big-assed belt. New clothes, Uncle?"

"It's for me," Valentine said. "Thought I'd keep a couple of spearpoints in a bandolier."

"Ah, yeah, your precious wood. Word around the campfire is that you've got some kind of weapon against the Hissers."

"Reapers, we call them."

"Hissers is more accurate."

"Depends on if you're describing what they do or what they sound like."

"So these spears kill 'em?" she asked, eyes narrowed.

"I've seen it more than once, more than twice. If the wood is fairly fresh, when it hits their bloodstream, it kills them. Fast."

Baltz laughed, a barking sound more suitable for one of her dogs. " 'Bout time we found something that did. Can I have one of your stickers?"

"Take a couple. It's the least we can do for your help. Help yourself to some seeds and a sapling while you're at it. When you get home, you can plant it. Maybe someday it'll be a liberty tree."

"A liberty tree?"

"Something old, so old it's forgotten. Has to do with the founding of the old United States. It's an idea I've been working on ever since I found out what I had to bring back. I picture these trees growing in all the freeholds."

"Pretty much everything worthwhile in life started out as somebody's dream, boy. This one's worth a chase."

An orange explosion of teeth and claws shot out from under Valentine's snakeskin-adorned wagon. Ahn-Kha dropped his blade in alarm, and Valentine jumped.

"That's Georgie, my cat. Wonder what spooked him?" Baltz said, squatting to look under the wagon.

"Shit!" she screamed, falling backwards in alarm.

Valentine knelt, hand on his machete and ready to jump, and looked under the wagon. A chimpanzee form hung under the wagon, glaring at him with red eyes and a rat face. But the oversized back legs were all wrong, and the tail . . .

"*Nusk!*" Ahn-Kha bellowed, and his Grogs grabbed cooking implements from the campfire.

"Hey, it's—," Valentine said as the creature dropped from its inverted hiding place, spun like a cat, and hit the ground running. The Grogs howled and ran around the other side of the wagon in pursuit. Valentine jumped up into the driver's seat of the wagon for a better look.

The oversize vermin shot like a brown bolt of lightning through the camp, startling and scattering men and animals. Someone managed to bring a shotgun up, but blasted only trampled-down grasses in the thing's wake. A flick of its cotton-tuft tail was the last Valentine saw of it, but his ears followed the scrambling claws through the darkness, northwest into the heart of the Ranch.

Valentine shook his head, wishing they were off the Ranch. He'd had enough of the Texas hills with creatures from an H. G. Wells novel popping out of the brush.

"Okay, so they made some cross of jackrabbit and rat the size of a raccoon," he said, turning to Baltz. "What else do we have to look forward to? Cockroaches built like armored personnel carriers?"

Baltz passed one of her assorted handkerchiefs across her face. "Boy, oh boy, I didn't know about those things. They must be new. Did you see those red eyes?"

Valentine sat down on the bench seat at the front of the wagon, rubbing the back of his neck under his black mane. "That might explain the rattlesnakes. To hunt loose rat-rabbits, whatever. Rodents. Snakes are the best rodent-killers on earth."

"My David, I think it is more than that," Ahn-Kha said.

"What's that?" Valentine asked.

"It was here to listen. Perhaps it understood us."

"Rats are smart, but English-speaking?"

"Smart at surviving, anyway," Zacharias said, coming out of the dark. "It got away. The pickets didn't even notice it."

Ahn-Kha pointed under the wagon. "It was here for some time. It got bored and started drawing, or gnawing."

Valentine looked at the scratchings. They looked like a cross between hieroglyphics and Indian cave paintings.

"Huh, an artist," a Texan crouching at the other side of the wagon remarked.

"My David, a hunted animal doesn't bother to doodle. I think the Kurians bred the creatures for their auras."

"I believe you've got it, old horse. Colonel Hibbert said something about that. Rodents breed like crazy, eat anything, and grow fast."

"True," Ahn-Kha rumbled. "The rat-things perhaps didn't like being eaten any better than you humans do. I think they fought back."

"Successfully," Valentine agreed.

Two days later, the Rangers riding screen for the convoy called up Zacharias and Valentine. They saw more of the "ratbit." The scouts had paused at the middle of a notch in the hills the wagon train would have to cross as they moved north. They were traveling through scattered trees, what in this part of Texas might be called a forest.

A smokehouse filled with cuts of meat Valentine guessed to be snake stood near a trampled out area that had the trodden-on look of a campsite. Tracks of wheeled vehicles, perhaps off-road bicycles, could be seen.

"The Grogs travel on four-wheelers and motorcycles sometimes," Baltz said. "Bicycles, too. Maybe this is a camp of theirs."

"Auntie Amy! Look over here," Eve called. They rode over and found a notch in the hillside filled with piles of apples, ears of corn, nuts, berries, and even alfalfa and hay for the animals.

"Hell, the Grogs didn't do this," Zacharias said.

"The ratbits?"

Eve gasped: "Look at the bark!"

Valentine saw a piece of bark tucked in the crotch of a sapling over the gathered supply.

TAK AND LEAV WOODS

"What is this, a bribe? They're afraid we're going to move in on them?" Zacharias said, after sounding out the words on the sign.

"Maybe they're trying to hurry us through. You think we're drawing something they're afraid of?"

"We don't know who wrote this," Valentine said. "It could be a bunch of well-read kangaroos." Valentine wouldn't have been surprised to meet Toad of Toad Hall after skirting the Ranch.

"Agreed," Zacharias said. "Nice gesture, to speed us on our way."

Valentine nodded, and turned his horse. "Something to tell your grandchildren about, Zacharias. The helpful ratbits of Central Texas."

Valentine heard the high, sputtering sounds of engines and reached for his binoculars. They were loaners from the Rangers. Carrasca hadn't been willing to part with any of the *Thunderbolt*'s optics. He brought up the lenses and searched the distant hillside.

A sharp-nosed head, no, two heads, were bobbing over the sun-dried grasses. The vehicle broke out of the tall grass and into the open. It looked something like a baby carriage with a single-bore piston-engine on the back. At the motorcycle-style steering controls was a ratbit, a second rider clung on behind, facing the engine. It appeared to be working some kind of lever. A throttle?

"Ingenious little fellers," Ranson said, pulling his horse up next to Valentine. Valentine passed him the glasses. "I wonder if they drill for their own oil and refine it."

"Easier to steal it, probably."

"They're paralleling us."

Valentine felt something was wrong with the picture. "It's plain enough to see that we're leaving. Are they making sure of it?"

The wagon train ground on to the squeal of wooden axles and the tramp of feet and hooves; the ratbits disappeared behind the hill.

"I think a tight picket line tonight is a good idea," Valentine said to Zacharias and Baltz as they began uncoupling the wagons and building the nightly laager around the oxen and cattle. "The ratbits have me worried."

"They seemed friendly enough," Baltz said, groaning and rubbing her back as she got off the horse. "Left us food, didn't they?"

"Nobody's dropped dead from poisoning," Zacharias agreed. "But it won't hurt to be in tight tonight. I figure on a brush with the Grogs when I set the pickets. I don't think we'll need eyes way out to buy us time to get set."

"Post," Valentine called.

"Sir?"

"New orders for tonight." Valentine stepped over and explained to Post what he wanted the sentries to do. Post made a circuit of the camp, passing on the instructions. He returned and idled next to Valentine, taking in the sky, until Valentine noticed his leg twitching.

"What is it, Will?"

"You okay?" He kept his voice down.

"Why shouldn't I be?"

"You look played out. I've never seen you this tired, even when we were crossing Santo Domingo."

"Tired of campfires and cold water, I think." Now that the journey was almost over, Valentine looked forward to turning over the quickwood and taking a leave. Saunders and the *Thunderbolt*, the Once-ler, Malia . . . He needed peace, a quiet room looking out over a lake, perhaps. He'd never work in the Kurian Zone again.

"You told me once to ask you about what you did to get your captaincy in the Coastal Marines," Post said, as though reading his mind. "You sounded unhappy about it. You said it would give me a real reason to hate you."

"Having second thoughts about not leaving with Carrasca?"

"No, it's not that. Val, if it troubles you, talk about it. If anyone's in a position to understand, it's me. I wasted half a life under the bastards. After talking to you about my wife that night back on the *Thunderbolt*, I felt better about myself than I had in years. Took the bottle right out of my hand."

Valentine felt uneasy. The Ranch was getting to him. Talking to Post was better than empty fretting. "Let's walk."

They walked, side by side, the summer-dried grass crunching under their feet as they circled the laager. At first, the words came slowly. He wasn't sure where to begin, exactly, and the events were vague as they came back to him, as disturbed mud obscures the features of a body being dredged from a lakebed.

He'd never even told Duvalier. So the story came hard at first.

"I came down from the north with fake papers saying I'd served on a cruiser on the Great Lakes. I talked right for the identity, and I'd been to some of the places in the background. They put me in this police boat on the Louisiana coast, looking for smugglers. There was a gunfight or two, but we had a pair of fifty-calibers on the patrol boat that settled most arguments when those opened up on the shoreline . . ."

The Coastal Marines had a tip about a big cargo going out of the west side of Lake Pontchartrain, in a red-painted barge. He and a squad of men took the barge easily. The tug captain tried to bargain his way out, offered Valentine and the troops money, liquor, tobacco.

Valentine had none of it. His job was to impress his superiors with his diligence and efficiency, not pluck tempting feathers for his nest.

Within the hearing of his sergeant and men, he turned down the bribe, made a show of moving the captain and his mates along with a pistol to the ringbolts.

Then he opened the cargo hatch.

Six families, in the dingy yellow overalls of Louisiana rural labor, were rousted from hiding spots among the more legitimate loads of cargo. There was resignation, not lamentation, as they were lined up, counted, and put in steel restraints.

He had no choice. A Reaper met the barge when it tied up at the Coastal Patrol dock.

". . . and you're thinking 'So what?' It goes back to my first time leading men into the Kurian Zone. My first real responsibility. I took five families out of Louisiana after a raid. It was a hard march—we even had Reapers on us.

"When we got back to the Free Territory at the fort, each and every one thanked me. Hugs, kisses, tears. I even met one of them a couple years later. Her name was Theresa Brugen. . . . She was a nurse-trainee at a hospital where they looked at my leg wound. She cried when she saw me again.

"I've always been proud of that trip. Those twenty-six lives, twenty-six lives changed, saved—it was the first time I really thought I'd made a difference. When I turned the families from the red barge over to the Reaper—it was like that evaporated."

Post shrugged. "What could you do?"

The faces appeared in the darkness, this time accusing. "I could have got them out. It would have blown my cover. Someone else would have had to go get the quickwood. Maybe in a year, maybe in a month. There are other Cats. Other ships."

"Ships with me?"

Valentine said, "What do you mean?"

"I'm not a philosopher, so this is going to come out wrong. Hope you'll understand anyway."

"Shoot."

"Well, Val, sometimes you'll try your damnedest and everything will go to shit. Other times you'll be drunk off your ass, trying your damnedest to kill yourself, and you'll find an answer to your prayers through a haze of gin. If I'd been as squared away as Worthington, would you have trusted me with your friendship?"

"Possibly. Depends on how I read you at the time."

"For all we know, Worthington was unorthodox as an upside-down cross, and just kept it hidden. Why let it worry you? Cause and effect is slippery stuff. Forget about the 'what-ifs.'"

"Easier said than done."

"Remember, I've got my own set of 'what-ifs.' Do what I do. Keep thinking about the 'what's-nexts.' "

Valentine heard engines in the distance when he hardened his ears as they passed out dinner. Some of the horses shifted restlessly as the wagon train settled in to camp. The sun was setting, and the moon wouldn't be up for hours. It was the time he'd attack, if he were the ratbits.

The ratbits were intelligent, no doubt about that. If they were hostile, why leave food? If they weren't hostile, why would they not communicate their good intentions in person or simply leave them alone?

He heard a familiar heavy tread behind him. "I will be glad when we are clear of this land," Ahn-Kha said. "I feel watchers."

"Did you hand out the shotguns?"

"Of course. My Gray Ones are armed, and Post is speaking to the other men who will be on picket duty now."

"What will you use, if it comes to that?"

"A shovel, my David. You remember the *skiops* the Golden Ones used. It is close enough. This will be a tough-and-rumble fight."

"Rough-and-*tumble* is the way you usually hear it. Shall we meet it at the pickets, or back at the wagons?"

"The pickets would be better, give your hearing a chance. The sun is touching the horizon now."

Valentine left Post in charge of the inner ring of sentries. Valentine had placed extra men at the wagons, reserves of weapons and ammunition ready just in case, and every bucket filled with sand or water. He wasn't about to have his cargo burned by ratbits, with a few hundred miles to go. He and Ahn-Kha, with the other two Grogs to either side, walked just behind the line of sentries.

"Excuse, sir. Where the sun swelled up. Hurts to look, but I think some of that grass might be moving," one of the Jamaican recruits said.

"Wind?" Ahn-Kha asked.

Valentine listened with hard ears. The brush and grassland were alive with the sound like bacon on a skillet.

"They're creeping up on us, right out of the sun," Valentine said. He had to admire the ratbits. The men brought up their guns.

"Don't shoot until you see them coming for you," he added, but worked the slide on his .45 and chambered a round just in case. "Maybe it's an embassy."

One of the Grogs hooted, and a Marine added, "Oh, my God."

A brown tide surged out of the heavier growth toward the strip of trees that marked the western pickets. The spaniel-size ratbits ran with little bounces, almost bounding as they approached, covering a yard of sun-dried Texas grass with every hop.

At least the ratbits weren't using guns. The pickets fired a few shots, making no more of a difference than they would if fired into one of the gulf's waves. The ratbits did not slow at the gunfire.

"Back to the wagons," Valentine yelled. "Just run!"

The men did not need the encouragement. There was something terrifying about the brown wave undulating across the Texas country-side like a carpet unrolling. A few threw away their weapons in mad flight. Valentine saw one marine catch his feet and fall. Before he could rise, the ratbits were up and over him.

"Gettayahiiii . . . ," the stricken man cried.

A few ratbits, farther ahead than the rest, were already beside Valentine, looking up at him as if to gauge whether he was worth jumping. Valentine leapt into one of the circled wagons. Ahn-Kha halted in a gap and stood behind interlaced trek-tows, swinging his shovel in warning.

All along the wagons, gunfire broke out, high rifle cracks, boom-ing shotguns, and the snapping sound of pistol shots. Wounded ratbits squealed as bullets tore through their small bodies. Valentine emptied his pistol into ratbits climbing the wagon wheels, then drew his blade. He cut air again and again as the ratbits jumped onto the wagon and jumped off just as quick as he swung his blade. He saw a ratbit fly back-wards, thrown by a blow from Ahn-Kha's shovel. The men caught on the ground did not last long—five or six ratbits would leap onto the unfortunate's limbs, slowing him so two or three others could jump on the back and bear their opponent down. He saw one man rise again, choking a ratbit with both hands, but another tore into his ear, bringing a scream of pain before he fell again. The air filled with high-pitched squeaks and squeals as the battle raged.

The ratbits drove the men from the wagons. Valentine could see them grabbing things and running off out of the corner of his eye. A trio of ratbits were making off with a sapling, grabbing it by the burlap that held the dirt and roots and—

He felt claws on his legs, and another rodent leapt on his arm. He punched at it, but it grabbed his wrist in wiry little claws and buried its sharp front teeth in the flesh between thumb and forefinger. He felt an-other running up his back. He dropped his sword to reach for the beast, desperate to stop the crawly feel on his body. A ratbit caught up the sword and waved it threateningly. But it did not slash at him.

A ratbit in the back of his wagon held up one of Post's spearpoints, and another made off with a quickwood quarrel. Something in his mind clicked. They were after the quickwood. *Quickwoods! Woods!*

"Cease firing!" he bellowed. "Cease fire! No shooting! They're not trying to kill us—they just want quickwood."

Already the ratbits were leaving. Valentine saw more saplings disappear, but the ratbits didn't seem to be taking any food, weapons, or other tools from the convoy. Nor were they stealing all the quickwood. They seemed mostly interested in the saplings, perhaps because that was the easiest thing to identify. While the ground was littered with dead ratbits, most of the men had just been held down and relieved of their weapons, to stand, as Valentine did, rubbing painful bites and watching the quickwood being taken. Even the first marine to fall came out of the tree line, holding his hands up, now avoided by the ratbits as he was no longer a threat. From beyond the tree line Valentine heard the sound of the small motors of the ratbits. He hopped out of the wagon and found a first-aid kit. With a cotton dressing pressed to his wound, he walked to the west, following the last few ratbits checking the bodies of their comrades and helping any who weren't beyond hope.

One wounded figure appeared to be of some concern, judging by the number of ratbits clustered around it. Valentine approached the circle of rodents, and a few turned, baring their teeth at him and reaching for small knives.

He held out his hands, hoping to make himself understood, and stopped. He pointed at his bandage, then at the prone ratbit. The teeth went away, but the ratbits gave no other sign that they understood. He tossed them the bandage. They jumped away as it landed, then returned, sniffing it and squeaking.

Valentine ran back to the circled wagons. "A medic! I need a medic!"

The closest thing he could find among the confused men was a pharmacist's mate from the *Thunderbolt* named Speere. He was young and awkward, but had performed his duties well enough on the ship. Valentine had him grab a first-aid kit and follow.

"What, are you kidding, Cap? There are hurt men back at the wagons," Speere objected when they came up on the ratbits.

"This fight wouldn't have happened at all if we'd made an attempt to communicate with them. I want to make amends."

"I'm not a vet, sir," Speere said, but stood up when he saw Valentine's face. "But I'll do what I can," he said.

The two humans slowly approached the ratbits. Fifteen or twenty were around their stricken comrade, squeaking and chittering. The ratbits made room, and Speere knelt beside the wounded ratbit. A ratbit was pressing a piece of cloth into a wound on the other ratbit's back. Judging from the gray around the eyes, ears, and mouth, this was an older specimen.

"Looks like a bullet across the back," Speere said, looking at the wound. "Might be some nerve damage, even if it didn't clip the spine. Doesn't look like he can move his back legs."

"Can you give it . . . him anything for the pain?"

"I dunno, a drop of laudanum might help. I don't think it would kill him, but you never know."

"Do it."

Valentine and the ratbits watched as Speere used an eyedropper to add medicine to a capful of water, then refilled the empty eyedropper with the mixture and shot it down the ratbit's throat. The ratbit seemed to understand oral medication, and after a minute's allowing it to take effect submitted to Speere, who was sprinkling antiseptic powder in the wound and then sewing up the tear in the skin. "Maybe it's worse than it looks," Speere said. "Didn't go too deep. Looks like this guy had some subcutaneous fat. It might have cushioned his spine."

"Let's get him back to the camp."

"You think they'll let us?"

"We'll find out," Valentine said, and turned his head back to the wagons. "Hey! We need a stretcher here."

The wagon train did not move on the next day. Valentine thought it would be best to let his wounded rest. Narcisse took over care of the gray-haired patient. She unrolled a sheet of leather; glass jars filled with powders and herbs stood in neat sewn-in pockets. She began to work her Haitian medicine and steamed something in a ceramic mug.

The next morning the old ratbit was doing better. It could move its legs, a sign that met with approval from the four other giant ratbits who accompanied it to the human camp. They all shared a thin soup cooked up by Narcisse.

A strange ratbit visitor came into camp with the dawn. Another oldster, this one with an eyepatch over its left eye, to match a torn-off ear on the other side. The wounds were from long ago, however. It bore a container over its shoulder. Valentine realized it was part of a rattler-tail. Its parcel clinked oddly as it moved.

It approached the other ratbit, and they chattered at each other. Ratbit-speech was a strange *yeek*ing sound, and whatever was said was over with quickly. The eyepatch ratbit dumped its sack on the ground, and Valentine smiled when he recognized Scrabble pieces.

"Can you understand us?" Valentine said.
The ratbit hunted with its eye in the pile.

Y E S

"We are sorry about the deaths. You should have tried this earlier."
The ratbit removed the three chips from the dirt and arranged more.

W E D I D S H O T B Y H O R S R Y D E R S

"We didn't understand what you meant when you said 'leave
woods.' "

N O M U C H S P E A K M E N

The ratbit removed that and started again.

N I E D W O O D F O R K I L M O N S T E R S

"The thing is, you took quite a few saplings. We need them. Understand?"

Y E S

"We can leave you a few, and some wood, and some seeds, to grow
more trees. Good enough?"
The ratbit did not rearrange the letters. It just pointed to YES again.
"Deal. Someday I'd like to hear about what happened. How did
you drive the Kurians out of this part of the land?"

W R E K T H E A L L S O W E N O T D I E

"Do your people have a name?"

B A T C H F I V E T E E N

The ratbits put on a feast that night, in the center of a wide half-
crescent of oaks and elms. Traces of a foundation stood in the yellowed
grass, smoke-darkened conduit pipes and junction boxes stood among
the wildflowers like scarecrows. Later Valentine learned that beneath
the soil there was a thriving town of tunnels and dens.
The humans only nibbled from the Batch Fifteen banquet. A

proper feast, to the hundreds of gathered ratbits, meant piling anything edible—to a ratbit—in a great heap in the center of the clearing
and then burrowing within the pile in a race for the choicest tidbits: a
bone with a bit of marrow, still-ripe fall fruits and melons, an ear of
corn still only partially eaten. It was a bit like dining from a restaurant
kitchen at the end of the night, fresh food, leftovers, and garbage all for
the taking.

The dinner looked to be a disaster, at least from the human point of
view, until the ratbits dragged a series of still-sealed cartons from a
clogged stairwell hidden in the grass. In them were candy bars and
chips and fruit-flavored drinks in shiny plastic packets, only a few years
old and therefore still edible. Valentine ate something called a Chocdelite
that was almost eye-crossing in its sweetness.

Zacharias joined him, and they sat on one of the wagons, next to
Baltz's orange tomcat, who was scrunched into a back-arched ball un-
der the seat as he watched the ratbits go to and fro. Zacharias offered
Valentine a taste of some orange-and-pineapple flavored drink.

"I'm thinking vending machines," Zacharias said, examining the
label. "Says it's from Florida."

"Nothing but the best for the scientists. Or the honored guests."

A faint sputtering from the sky made them both look up. An arrow
shape, like an oversize kite with an engine attached, flew overhead and
buzzed away a pair of circling buzzards. Another aerial visitor, a hawk,
flapped hard to gain altitude and avoided the airborne prowler. A ratbit
worked the controls from a tiny seat.

"I'll be—," Zacharias began. "Clever varmints."

"That they are."

"Did you have any schooling, Valentine?"

"Yes. About as good as I could get in the Minnesota backwoods.
An old Jesuit still ran a one-room schoolhouse. I lived in his library."

"I remember when I was learning maths from ol' Miss Gage. We
were studying multiplication, and she showed us how one pair of breeding rabbits could produce—well, I don't remember exactly, but it was
over a thousand—other rabbits once you counted their offspring . . . in
just a year. Makes you wonder."

Valentine nodded, troubled by the evidence on the Ranch that the
Kurians had gone to so much effort to find a replacement for the human
race.

Twelve

The Piney Woods, December of the forty-eighth year of the Kurian Order: East Texas is covered with timber, a wood-scape more extensive than all of New England. The pines stand as straight as Baptists on Easter Sunday, their evenly spaced branches ascending the trunk like ladder rungs.

Texas saw its first oil boom in this part of the state, but before that a timber boom brought white men to sculpt the land with its first roads and towns. After mankind's fall, the gently rolling landscape went fallow, and vigorous young forests have sprung up again from the old ranches and farms scattered around Lake Texoma to Sabine Lake in the Gulf.

The Texas Rangers are active here, as well, raising hell all along the informal border with the Kurian Zone that runs the length of the Neches River and along the road-and-rail "Sabine Corridor" the Kurians maintain from Shreveport to Dallas. The Lifeweavers are present to help the Texans in this part of the country. The Rangers have organized their own teams of Wolves, Cats, and Bears to hunt the Reapers, passing material and information to and from Southern Command through the network of Logistics Commandos.

The far north of the region, between the Red and Sulphur rivers, sees the least guerrilla activity. There is little human habitation to speak of. Southern Command proper patrols this area from its forward bases along the Red River. A few hunter-gatherer communities—usually Native American or Louisiana Creole—wander the area, pulling up stakes every few months to avoid the depredations of the Reapers and Quislings raiding out of the Dallas Paramountcy. With fall in its death throes and winter coming, a wet, muddy hush falls over the land. Snowstorms are not unknown to the Piney Woods, and man and animal both retire deep into the woods to wait out the cold.

The pines smelled like home. The crisp aroma in the chill breeze of an East Texas December tickled his nose and brought back memories of winter camps in the Ozarks and Ouachitas. It marked his first breath in the lands of the Ozark Free Territory in over two years.

Half his wagons ground along almost empty. The stores and supplies within had long since been eaten up, and with the ratbits of "Batch Fiveteen" having taken better than a wagonload of quickwood to fight their own war against the Kurians, the remaining wagons were traveling light.

Leaving the Ranch was not as easy as entering it. They had fought two nighttime skirmishes against the Grogs in the borderlands and hurried into the empty lands north of Dallas and Fort Worth. A team of rangers turned southeast to confuse the pursuit, and the Batch Fifteen rodents did their best to muddle the trail.

Valentine had some of the quickwood lumber turned into spearpoints and crossbow quarrels anticipating an attack from the Reapers, but the hunt never began. They broke into the cattle-drive routes running up from Texas and into the plains without incident. Valentine put a moratorium on further slaughter of the dwindling cattle, so from a distance they might look like another wagon train bringing beef and trade north to the railheads in Oklahoma and Kansas for shipment east. The Kurians in northern Texas, never thick to begin with this close to the Free Territory, seemed quiescent.

It was as though their enemies were hibernating out the winter: they did not send patrols or Reapers to trouble them. There was a nervous day at the Trinity River crossing when some riders observed them from a hilltop. They did not stay to identify themselves, but rode away before the Rangers on their worn-out horses could catch them. But as this area could be considered no-man's-land between the Free Territory and the Kurian Zone, they could have been anything from smugglers to robbers to scouts from some fearful community hiding in a river valley, wishing for nothing more than to be left alone.

"How are you planning to get back?" Valentine asked Zacharias as a team of Rangers went out to ride an old highway running northeast out of the ghost town of Paris, checking for signs of human habitation. Valentine hoped to find one of the Southern Command Guard garrisons or a Wolf patrol somewhere near the Red River.

"We'll head south. Hell with the wagons—there's plenty more where they came from. Ride slow down south until we hook up with the Eastern Rangers. They'll fix us up with remounts, and then we'll slip through somewhere between Houston and San Antonio. Won't be that hard this time of year. If the story of the Rangers in this century ever gets written, this'll make an interesting chapter. Bargaining with ratbits over magic trees."

"Don't forget the elephants with two trunks."

"The elephants we'll never forget."

Valentine laughed tiredly. It was good to be able to laugh again. *Just a few more days to tote the weary load*—the line from *Gone with the Wind* had been running through his mind of late. "I hope you know how much the help you've given and the risks you've run mean to the Ozark Free Territory."

"Well, young Captain," Zacharias said, from the vast age difference of five years, "you want my advice, the first thing you use the quickwood on is a campaign with us. You saddle up every man who can hold a gun and every cannon that's got a shell, and hit Dallas from the northeast. The East Texas Rangers come in from the southeast, and we'll hit 'em out of the Ranch, since the Kur no longer seem to be running things there. Once we've got Dallas cleaned up, the rest of Texas will be pieces just waiting to be picked up. Then we've got enough country to really live. Hell, old Kirby Smith held out against the whole damn Union that way, till the surrender. I expect we could do the same."

"I'm one of the squashed guys at the bottom of the totem pole, Major," Valentine said. "The idea sounds fine to me, but it's for men and women above my rank to decide."

They watched the wagon train go by. Narcisse waved to them from the back of her horse, and Valentine moved to put himself between the trail and a fallen tree trunk. A Texan admirer of Narcisse's cooking had rigged a saddle so she could put her stumps into a pair of cut-off rifle-sheaths, and Ahn-Kha fixed a quirt to her "short arm." Sissy had turned into an admirable neck-reiner in the last month, but had developed a taste for jumping—though often she ended up plummeting to the earth despite the horse mane gripped with her teeth. Valentine wanted her to arrive in the Free Territory with neck intact.

Zacharias stripped a handful of pine needles as he rode. "We gotta start winning somewhere. This is as good a place as any." He handed the needles to Valentine like a bouquet.

"Southern Command has grown into something that's like an egg. It can resist pressure as long as it's evenly distributed from all around. But if you rap it too hard in any one spot, it cracks. Your plan would mean all yolk and no shell for us in Missouri and Arkansas. I'll tell the brass—the Lifeweavers, even—everything I can about the state of things in Texas. I'll let them know you're ready. Napoléon once made a comment that you can't make an omelet without breaking eggs. Maybe they'll follow his advice."

"Yeah, I heard about that guy. Confederate general from out East, right? Rode under Bobby Lee?"

Valentine just chuckled again.

The scouts came back, signaling that the road was clear. The men of the convoy went about hooking up the oxen to the wagons one more time.

Valentine would always associate his return to the Free Territory with the old Shell Oil emblem. Three busted-up tankers were parked in a triangle blocking the road a few miles out from the Red River. The tankers had been turned into hollow forts, firing slits carved into the sides and sandbags mounted on the top. It was a typical forward post for Southern Command: easily created, transported, defended, and abandoned.

The watchpost stood on the reverse slope of a hill in the old highway. The road cut across the countryside; a long, straight ribbon placed over the hills and hollows as a testament to the days when engineers treated the topography as if it did not exist. The garrison must have thought them a column of Quislings, for they did not wait to greet them, but promptly retreated out, hustling down a culvert running along the road. Valentine watched five or six men run, with the bent-over stride of men keeping their heads down, appearing and then disappearing in gaps of the brush running along the road.

"So much for the valor of Southern Command," Valentine said dryly. Baltz coughed up something from deep in her chest and spat.

"If only the rest of our meetings were so simple," Zacharias said. "It would have been a faster trip. Perhaps your tall companion frightened them off. Shall I run them down?"

"No, spare the horses," Valentine decided. "They'll be off calling on higher authority. Suits us either way. But I'd better ride ahead from here with just one or two. I hope they don't shoot before trying to identify us. Interested in meeting some animals from Arkansas, Baltz? They're a unique brand of razorbacks."

"Sure, son. I've done my job: got you across most of Texas. If I catch a bullet, it's no loss."

"Ahn-Kha," Valentine said, "better take your Gray Ones and sit in the wagons. They might take a shot if they see you."

"Understood, my David. Be cautious, I am more worried about

you. Frightened soldiers do strange things. It would be ironic, but undesirable, to have all your efforts end with one of Southern Command's bullets."

The vanguard of the column reorganized itself. Valentine and Baltz, with Ranson a horse-length behind, holding a white flag, rode a half-mile ahead of the wagons. Groups of Texans rode before, interspersed with, and following the teams, with long files of Valentine's soldiers marching alongside the rattling wagon wheels, all moving at the patient pace of the plodding oxen.

Valentine looked at the rusting monument to the Texas oil industry. Weeds grew in the rotted tires; rust ran down the marred sides like red icicles. He smelled a fire smoldering inside the fort—they had caught the men at dinner, something even crackled in a pan—

"Ride. Ride like hell!" Valentine shouted, thumping his spurs into the horse's flanks. His horse leapt down the road, and the others caught its panic and joined in the flight.

A flash lit up the Texas countryside, followed by a boom that came up through the horses' legs and shivered him in his saddle. Valentine looked over his shoulder and saw one of the tankers rear up on its back axles, and another rolled forward into the ditch at the edge of the high-way. The base of the triangle, facing the rear of the fort, stood intact.

"They fired whatever they had in their arms locker," Valentine said.

"Must have been underground. Looks like most of the blast went up. Dynamite, I'll bet."

"Handy for engineering or sabotage. Just as well we weren't in the fort at the time," Valentine said. "That's not like the Wolves. Usually they're cleverer with booby traps."

"New standing orders, maybe," Ranson said. "Destroy whatever's going to fall in the enemy's hands."

They camped that night next to an old marker that indicated the state-line border was a mere two miles away. A chilling drizzle began just after sundown. Valentine sat underneath a tarp in front of the shielded cooking fire just off the road, part of the farthest-forward pickets with the convoy. He listened to the drops evaporate against the flaming wood. He felt drained, utterly and completely empty. Just a few more days, he told himself, and he could finally lay down his responsibilities and rest. His young body seemed as old and battered as the faded mile-marker.

"They are taking their time on the other side of the river," Ahn-Kha said. The Golden One had wrapped himself into a horse blanket. When wet, Ahn-Kha's fawn-colored hair matted down into a rain slicker, still keeping a precious layer of air in between the wet hair and his skin.

"They're watching us. There are two men with their horses about five hundred yards off, just east of here. I heard them come up once it got dark while I was circling the camp. Wind's blowing the other way, or you could smell them. I'll go out again with the white flag tomorrow—maybe they'll have worked up the nerve to talk."

The rain grew heavier. Valentine considered returning to the wagons, but it would be crowded enough under the beds. He had slept out in the wet before. It wouldn't hurt him to do so again. He threw a blanket over his head and did his best to ignore the rain.

He awoke with a sneeze. A Texas-size cold had come upon him in the night, and he blinked the gum out of his eyes. One of the pickets had a fire with a pot of hickory-nut coffee going under a piece of corrugated tin. The ranger handed him a cup without a word. Valentine drank, nodding gratefully and passing another cup to a second ranger on watch, and looked down the road. It was a sunless dawn. A sea-gray sky washed the landscape of its color.

Two men approached the picket line, keeping out in the open, guns across their shoulders like yokes. A few Texans recognized the attitude. In this part of the country, that meant parley. They wore charcoal-gray uniforms, mottled with streaks of pale yellow and brown, the winter camo of the Southern Command's Guards. One had a set of sergeant's stripes on his arm.

"You with Southern Command?" Valentine called when he felt they were close enough. His throat felt like it had a rough ball of twine lodged in it.

The sergeant narrowed his eyes. "You all smugglers?"

"No. Identify yourselves, and I'll do the same."

They exchanged looks. "Third East Texas Regiment, Noyes Brigade, out of Texarkana."

"I'm a Cat coming in with priority cargo."

"That so?"

"You call me *sir,* Sergeant."

Valentine cocked his head, and the man with the stripes added, "Sir."

"Code name's Ghost, requesting immediate radio or telegraph contact with Southern Command GHQ. Can you assist?"

"That'll be for Captain Murphy to say . . . sir. He's on the other side of the river. What's this cargo? Hadn't heard logistics were out on a raid hereabouts."

"I've got a dozen wagons back there that need guarding once we're over the Red. What's Captain Murphy's command?"

"We'll let him talk to you, sir, once your bona fides clear."

"Are there any Wolves around?"

"Not for us to say, sir. Even if we knew, asking your pardon."

"I hope you have more to say when your captain tells you to talk. Please inform him I need rations for a hundred eighty men when we get across the river. Thank you, Sergeant."

Valentine went back to the fire and let the Guards return to their command. He could get the wagon-train to the river, at least, and turn it over to Captain Murphy and his Guards. He had asked for a lot of supplies, but filling the Rangers' saddlebags was the least he could do before they parted. He took his shivering horse from its place beneath a pine tree and rode back to the wagon train, saddle-sore muscles protesting at the effort.

The crossing went slowly. Every bridge on the Red was down for miles, according to the Guards. Without a swing south to Texarkana that would eat precious days, they would have to cross at Two-Skunk ferry.

Valentine was sure there was an amusing story behind the ferry's name, but he was in no mood for fireside yarns. He wanted the psychological safety of the river behind him, and a warm drink in his belly. Then he would quit seeing Reapers moving between the trees at night and imagining converging columns of Quislings racing to cut his convoy off from the Ouachitas. The ferry was a small one pulled across by rope strung along the ruined pilings of an old bridge, and it could manage only one wagon and unhitched team at a time. At the rate the ferrymen—Guards doing labor they had little enthusiasm for—progressed, it would take all day to get the column across. He went over to Major Zacharias, who was sharing a cold meal with his men as they waited to push the next wagon onto the timber float.

"Zacharias, you've helped work a miracle. I can't ask you to do more, so feel free to go back south once we've crossed."

"Texas is as grateful to you as you are to her, Captain Valentine. Mission accomplished once you are across the river?"

"Yes. I'm told the captain of this company is finally arrived. Let me speak to him first, but I'm sure we don't need to bring you much farther. I'll arrange to have feed for the horses and rations for the men sent back on the ferry. There should be some supplies available here."

"Thank you, Valentine. I'd be grateful."

Valentine stood, idly scratching the ears of one of the oxen as the ferry pulled him across the Red River. The winter rains had raised its level.

"What kind of priority-one cargo is this, suh?" the ferryman asked, shifting his quid to a sagging cheek. "All's I sees is plants."

Valentine tightened his jaws in frustration. If a laboring ferryman knew there was important cargo in the wagons, then word would spread to every housewife and postman in thirty miles in a day or two.

"New kind of food crop. Like the heartroot."

"Heartroot?" The ferryman looked at one of the Guards.

"That mushroom stuff. Not too popular around here, sir," the Guard said.

Three years ago, Valentine and Ahn-Kha had brought the Grog-staple from Omaha, and Valentine was surprised Southern Command wasn't still distributing the mushroom-like growth. It grew a breadloaf-big hunk of protein, fats, and carbohydrates out of any wet garbage from a pile of leaves to a slop pail, and it preserved well if properly dried.

Valentine stepped onto the east bank, nursing a headache that spoiled what should be a feeling of triumph. He had done it. He was finally to the Free Territory with what he set out to get nearly two years ago. He looked around. A few Guards stood at their posts around the ferry, watching the teams get rehitched.

Ahn-Kha joined him. "My David, I made a promise to Captain Carrasca. When we were back in the Ozarks, I was to give you this." Ahn-Kha extracted the flute she had given him from between his football-size pectorals and untied the leather thong that kept it around his neck. He upended it and gave it two vigorous taps. A waxy envelope appeared. "It is a letter for you."

Valentine trembled at the memories brought by her handwriting.

Ahn-Kha withdrew and left him alone under a riverside sycamore. With rain running down the back of his neck and soaking his shirt, he could hear the creaks and groans of the ferry ropes in their wheels, the calls of the rivermen, and the wet pot-iron smell of the Red was in his nostrils. And he'd remember it all for the rest of his life.

He opened the seal and took out the sheet of Captain Saunders's stationery.

Dear David,

If you're reading this letter it means you're home and safe. I wish I were there to congratulate you. You have two things to congratulate yourself about, actually. The first is the

*success of your journey. The second I kept a secret so the first
would be completed. I'm sorry you have to find out about it
this way, but the fact of the matter is you're going to be a
father.*

*David, deep breath and keep your perspective. I'll be
fine. I'm not the first woman to have a baby, and I'm in a
better position than most. We have a wonderful hospital with
all the equipment, and what passes for trained doctors these
days. Jamaica will be a safe place for our child (and many
others) thanks to you. I hope it's a boy with your hair and
eyes, but I'll take whatever comes, knowing that he or she'll
be pointed out as the child of a brave man who helped my
harbor.*

*Right now, knowing you, you're thinking about how soon
you can get down here. Put this letter away and read the
above again when you've had a few days. It would be good
for me to have you here. It would also be very selfish. They
wouldn't have put you in charge of the quickwood if they
didn't think a lot of you, and I doubt your Southern
Command would be the better for you coming down here.
Someone like that loudmouthed fool Hawthorne would
probably replace you up there.*

*If the war ends, come. If you are badly hurt, come. If you
grow old, come, and we'll warm our bones together under the
palms. But don't come out of duty to me. We're alike enough
that I know you have a more important duty you must be true
to, or you will never be happy.*

Love,
Malia

Valentine swallowed. His cold disappeared in a flood of emotion.
He could leave the wagon train with Southern Command, take Post and
Ahn-Kha and his Jamaicans, and go south with the Rangers. A boat
wouldn't be that hard to get, they could sail with the prevailing winds—

A rider trotted past the ferry and turned toward the sycamore. A
Guard in an officer's uniform with captain's bars and MURPHY stitched
above his shirt pocket peered out from under the cowl of his rain
slicker and pulled back the hood. The rider had tight-curled brown hair
that reminded Valentine of a dog he had once known in Minnesota.
Eighty or so men on winter-fat, shaggy horses sat their mounts behind
him at the wagons. Valentine carefully tucked the letter back in the
envelope and thrust it in his shirt.

The rider dismounted. "You must be this Ghost," Murphy said, offering his hand instead of a salute. "I'm Alan Murphy. They said you had the blackest hair this side of hell. It's an honor—I don't get to meet many Cats. Do I salute you, or what?" Murphy eyed the new snakeskin bandolier with its three quickwood stabbing-points across Valentine's chest.

"In theory, I hold the rank of captain, but I don't use it much, Captain Murphy. I'm going to need escort either to Fort Smith or Arkadelphia, whichever works better for your men."

"My company is at your disposal, Captain—"

"Just *Ghost* will do, if you have to put anything on paper."

Murphy explained he had already been in touch with Southern Command. He was expecting a delay while other troops could be brought up to escort the convoy. Southern Command couldn't pull troops away from a river crossing, even if it was the time of year when they did not expect action. Valentine made arrangements to have the Texans resupplied, and he saw to it that bags of oats, sides of pork, and a generous quantity of beans returned to the south side of the Red with him on the ferry.

As he moved through the Texans, saying good-bye, trying to forget what he had just read, he felt a tug at his sleeve. He turned to find Eve behind him.

"Yes, Eve? Going to finally say something, are you?"

"Mr. Valentine, the man who works the lines on this side, he's bad."

Valentine groaned inside. He hoped the man hadn't done something reprehensible to the pubescent girl. "What did he do to you that's bad?"

Her face contorted in adolescent exasperation. "No, he didn't do anything to *me*. I said he's a bad man. Bad inside."

"How do you know a man can be bad inside?"

She shrugged. "I'm not sure. When I touch your hand, I know you're good. I can feel caring. That you do things to help people. I touched him while we were moving horses onto the ferry, and I knew he wasn't like you. He's done bad things to people."

"Sometimes soldiers have to do bad things. Sometimes they don't have a choice."

"Maybe," she said, as if turning the idea over in her mind. "But I do know I can tell who is good and who is bad in his secret heart. He's a bad man."

"Thanks for telling me, Eve. I'll watch myself. Just in case, take this," he said, reaching into the leather tobacco pouch he wore around his neck. "Here's a quickwood seed. You know what it can do, right? Plant your tree somewhere safe, where you can take care of it. Where only you know about it. Your people in Texas may need it. I need to talk to your aunt now before I go over the river again. Let's find her."

Baltz stood with Zacharias underneath a thick-limbed riverbank willow, eating plums from a jar of syrup. Valentine interrupted a conversation about the best route south.

"I'd feel better if we'd of run into some local Rangers. I don't want to be riding through the country blind," Zacharias was saying.

"They stay more to the south," Baltz said. "This patch is close enough to the Ozarks that they don't need to waste their time here."

"The wagons are getting across, slow but sure," Valentine said. "It's time for a last thank-you." He sneezed. Between the cold and Malia's letter—he was already desperate to reread it—he could barely stand to go about the formalities. He wanted the good-byes over with so he could think.

"Too bad all that rum's gone," Baltz said. "Sounds like you could use it."

"You have a supply of quickwood for the East Texans, right?" Valentine said, wiping his nose.

"Wish it were more," Zacharias said. "But this is good tree country. In twenty years, they'll have lots."

"Watch yourselves. None of the Free Territory boys are mixing with ours like they usually would. Maybe the Jamaican accents are making them skittish . . . but I get the feeling there's something wrong."

"Maybe Southern Command's had a setback," Zacharias said. "Or the Quislings have tried ambushes by posing as incoming Logistics Commandos."

"Wouldn't be the first time," Baltz said.

Valentine wiped his nose. "Losses in battle somewhere else, possibly. That might be why we didn't run into any Wolves. Without their patrols here, you're going to have to be careful. Could explain why these Guards were so quick to hightail it."

"You worry about yourself, Mr. Valentine," Baltz said. "We'll be fine."

Valentine shook hands all around. Texas style.

The sign outside town said BERN WOODS. Their destination stood in a farmland clearing a few miles from the river.

It was a widening-of-the-road town: two lines of buildings facing each other with a few houses scattered along the side streets. Like many old towns, the uninhabited buildings provided spare fixtures, glass, and shingles for the others. The outbuildings had a pulled-apart look where they had not been demolished entirely.

This close to the borderlands, the towns were walled, and Bern Woods was no exception. The plentiful pine provided makings for a tall stockade. Gaps between the brick buildings were filled with sharpened tree trunks and earth, with corrugated aluminum adding a fireproof layer to the outside. A tower stood at each end of town at the gates, looking out over scratch farmland and pasture.

Murphy waved to the guards in the tower, and the gate swung open. They passed one of the last outbuildings, a house with a faint piggy smell coming from it. Wire at the open doors and window showed that the old house was being used as barn.

Valentine hardened his ears and nose. His now-raging cold interfered with his sense of smell and hearing, but he could still tell an occupied pigpen from an abandoned one. This one was empty. It was hog-killing time, but why slaughter all the livestock? Did a family pull up and move? Were logistics punishing the town for hiding supplies?

He looked back at his men. Post, curious to see what Free Territory looked like, walked at the head of files of former Jamaicans and *Thunderbolt* marines, at least those who hadn't taken the Texas teamsters' places at the wagons, to either side of the transport. The men shivered in the winter wind. The men had a good chance of seeing their first snowfall that night if the temperature continued to drop.

The gates came to a rest with a thump.

A gallows. The sight of it froze him before his brain processed the structure. It stood in an open spot, like a broken tooth, between two buildings on the left side of the main street. Hangings were rare in the Free Territory, and only a few capital crimes merited them. Even Quisling officers faced the firing squad rather than the noose; the hangings that did take place went on in a prison, not a town square. The sight of a gallows was all too common in the Kurian Zone, however. Valentine's memory raced back to a story his first captain had told him, of a town secretly seized by the Kurians to trap the Wolves in his command.

"*Kenso,*" Valentine said to Ahn-Kha. The word for "danger" was one of the few in the Golden One's vocabulary that he knew. Ahn-Kha's ears shot up in surprise, then flattened against his bullet-head.

Valentine held up his right hand. "Ho," he called, keeping the horse moving to allow the wagon train to come to a stop without collisions, even as his feverish mind raced.

"What's the matter?" Murphy said. If it was an act, it was a superb one.

"We can't outspan in town. You want all these oxen milling around people's porches? Could get smelly," Valentine asked.

"I'm headquartered at this town. There's two corrals and a barn or two. They'll fit."

Post approached, ready as always for orders.

Valentine ignored Murphy. "Mr. Post, we'll circle the wagons in that clearing there, if you please. Downwind from the town, as a gesture to the civilians. Thank you." Post stiffened at the formal tone and elaborate pleasantries. "That is, if you have no objections, Captain Murphy?"

Murphy looked around at his men, then up the road to the town. "Well . . . no, of course not. Why would I?"

Valentine got off his horse and led it to Post. "Mr. Post, let's snap to it," he said, and then lowered his voice, tilting toward Post with his chin jutting out, as if upbraiding him privately. "I can't explain, but I don't like the look of this. Keep your gun handy, and alert the men. I hope it's nothing."

Post nodded and turned to give orders to the sergeants in the wagons. If the lieutenant looked upset to Murphy, he hoped that the feigned reprimand would explain the startled eyes and stiff backbone. Valentine turned on his heel and led his horse toward the clearing, Ahn-Kha falling in behind like an obedient dog. Ahn-Kha made as if to loosen the saddle on the horse and instead loosened Valentine's submachine gun in its sheath.

The wagon wheels resumed their noisy journey, squealing their axle-joints as the teams turned off the road and bumped to the clearing.

The captain came to some kind of decision. Murphy herded his men to the rear of the column. When he turned them one more time, to face the tired men bringing up the rear, he extracted a wide-mouthed pistol and pointed it at the center of the column. Across the distance, the Cat met the mounted man's eyes and read his fixed expression.

"To arms!" Valentine bellowed.

The hammer fell on Murphy's gun, and a flare arced out, sputtering through the sky in slow motion. The former *Thunderbolt* men threw themselves down from the wagons, pulling rifles and pistols. Post vaulted into the bed of the front wagon, where men were already loading a machine gun. Ahn-Kha brought up his long rifle, swinging the mouth toward Murphy, but the turncoat came off his saddle in a blur of horseflesh as his men dismounted and let their horses run.

The flare hit in the center of the column of wagons, and lay there, sparking. It spat out a chemical cough.

A wave of gunfire ripped across the convoy. Valentine saw heads appear at the walls of Bern Woods. The gate towers sprouted men as if someone had touched a wand to the platforms. He pulled out his PPD as a bullet smacked into the horse's flank. The wounded beast leapt sideways, knocking him to the ground even as it lurched, hind legs collapsing.

Smoke began to pour out of the flare, as if in landing it had opened some underground reservoir of purple steam.

The sound of shooting grew like the roar of an approaching wave. Machine guns added their deadly mechanical drum roll to the air-rending sound of gunfire. Panicked oxen bellowed and died. Other teams of horses ran from the explosions, throwing drivers from the runaway wagons.

Valentine smelled his horse's blood even as he tried to shut out the high, whinnying screams. Ahn-Kha swung the barrel, and his gun cracked. The Grog didn't shoot the horse; he dropped a figure in the gate tower firing an assault rifle. Valentine saw a Jamaican fall to earth, dying in a pose eerily like a Muslim praying.

The flare, after its brief fireworks, sputtered out.

Valentine sent a bullet into his wounded horse's head, then took cover behind the body. Ahn-Kha rolled to his side.

A hissing sound, and something exploded among the wagons. The blast threw a severed hand into the air, spinning it like a tossed daisy. Valentine squeezed off burst after burst into Murphy's men, emptying the drum on his gun. The turncoats were firing shotguns and lobbing grenades into the rear wagons; confused men got up to run, and died.

Another hiss and another explosion among the wagons. Pieces of a team flew as their wagon reared up on its back wheels, falling to pieces even as it overturned. Valentine saw something like a stovepipe pointing out from the stone roof of the town's tallest building. A recoilless rifle? More men poured from the gates at both sides of the town.

"Ahn-Kha!" he said, slapping his aiming friend on the shoulder. Valentine pointed. Heads appeared briefly over the barrel as the weapon was reloaded.

Ahn-Kha slid a finger-length bullet into the receiver. An ear twitched on the Grog as he brought the gun up and sighted with a rose-colored eye. Sighting in the time it took to draw a breath, the gun snapped and shot. Valentine saw a hat, or perhaps part of a head, torn away by the bullet.

The backblast of the recoilless flared in a gray cloud, and the shell exploded by Post's wagon. Old Handy Sixguns and the machine-gunners disappeared in the blast. Nothing but body parts remained. Valentine's marines were crawling out of the cross fire, or throwing away their weapons and sheltering among the stumps in the clearing.

The precious quickwood was burning. Two wagons flamed, putting oily smoke into the colorless sky. Valentine clenched his teeth until his jaws screamed in agony, reloading and firing his gun with tears in his eyes. He saw a Quisling rider grasp Narcisse by the hair and jerk her from her saddle, ignoring the blows from the quirt fixed to her arm. Post gone, his Jamaicans cut to pieces. Nothing mattered now.

"Away, David, away!" Ahn-Kha shouted, waving at the approaching troops.

"The quickwood," Valentine said.

"No choice! The smoke is blowing this way—it will cover us."

A bullet hit the limp horse, its impact causing still-warm muscles to twitch. Horses dragging a wagon came around the shattered front of the column. A Jamaican lay in the bed of the wagon, working the reins from the shelter of the bed. Ahn-Kha dropped his gun. The Grog pulled Valentine to his feet—grabbing him by the collar like a disobedient child—and ran in pursuit of the wagon.

Bullets zipped through the air all around: insects buzzing in their ears for a split second and then fleeing. Ahn-Kha caught the back of the wagon with one long arm as he hauled Valentine in tow with iron fingers. He swung up in an apish leap. A bullet caught the Grog at the apex of his jump. He dropped Valentine as he tumbled into the wagon. The wounding of his friend brought Valentine out of his mental maze.

Valentine felt something pull at his sleeve. The bullet that cut through his clothing hit the back of the wagon with a splintering *thwak*. He locked eyes with Ahn-Kha as the Grog's ear flaps fell limp. His friend toppled into the back of the wagon.

He ran. He jumped into the wagon just as one of the team was cut down by gunfire. Ahn-Kha lay groaning in his native tongue, hand pressed against his buttock.

"Sir! Sir!" the wounded Jamaican said, pushing a machine gun lying at the bottom of the wagon at Valentine with a bloody foot. "It's still got bullets."

Valentine took up the weapon. He rested it on the side of the wagon and turned it against Murphy's turncoats still burning and killing among the other wagons. The chatter of the weapon attracted bullets from all directions. Valentine waited for the inevitable impact. He would die with his mission, with the men he'd misled. Another flare landed by the wagon, spewing more purple mist. Mortar shells dropped, seeking his position.

Valentine heard hooves approach through the smoke, and turned the gun. Only a short length of bullets dangled from the belt.

"David!" Valentine heard a familiar voice call. "Captain Valentine! Men, find Captain Valentine."

Post came out of the purple haze, leading two horses. His clothes were in rags, and his eyes were bright in bruised sockets. Blood ran from a cut on his thigh. Another mortar shell exploded and the horses danced in terror, but Post dragged them on.

"Take Ahn-Kha with the other horse. He's hurt. I'm staying with the men."

"No use!" Post said, bringing the animals beside the wagon.

"Can't—," Valentine began, but Ahn-Kha's bloody fingers wrapped themselves around the snakeskin bandolier and pulled him bodily out of the wagon.

"My David, we go. I shall run. There's nothing else to do."

"No!"

The Grog hauled Valentine to a horse. He hopped on one leg, supporting himself with his other tree-trunk arm as though using a crutch. Post handed over the reins and helped the Jamaican into one of the saddles, then held the horse for Valentine to mount. Valentine saw blood running from Post's ear.

"No," Valentine said tightly, slinging his empty PPD and grabbing the horse by the throat latch. "You're hurt, you ride."

Post and the wounded Jamaican rode hard for the woods. A handful of others, including Ahn-Kha and Valentine, followed the two riders.

As they fled, a shell found the wagon. More oily smoke rose into the winter sky. Valentine ran with the rest, half-hoping his heart would burst from the effort. He ran from his enemies, from defeat, from his dead and wounded men. He wished he could run from his failure, but it stayed with him all the way to the trees and beyond.

Behind him, the quickwood burned.

Glossary

Aspirants: Teenagers, often sons and daughters of those in a particular caste, who travel with the Hunters and perform assorted camp functions.

Bears: Hunters and the most fearsome of the Lifeweavers' human weapons; warriors who go into a battle-fury resembling that of the berserks of old. The Bears are proud to take on anything the Kurians can design.

Cats: Trained by the Lifeweavers, these Hunters act as spies, saboteurs, and assassins in the Kurian Zone. Some work in disguises; others work openly.

Dau'wa: "Forward-thinkers"; the minority of Lifeweavers (mostly concentrated on the planet Kur), who used vital aura to become immortal, i.e., vampires.

Dau'weem: "Backwards-thinkers"; the majority of Life-weavers, who eschewed use of vital aura to become immortal.

Golden Ones: A Grog variant, more verbal and organized than the more common Gray Ones. Fawn-colored fur on their shoulders blends to white on their bellies.

Gray Ones: The most common kind of Grog, an apish humanoid with thick plates of gray skin. Marginally intelligent, though quick to adapt to human tools and weapons.

Grogs: Any of the multitude of creations the Kurians have designed or enhanced to help subjugate man. The term *grog* is in general use for introduced life-forms, but properly belongs just to the humanoid variants. Grogs come in many shapes and sizes; some are intelligent enough to use weapons.

Hunters: Human beings who have been enhanced by the techno-magic of the Lifeweavers to cope with the spawn of Kur.

Interworld Tree: An ancient network of portals between the stars, the doors of which allow instantaneous transportation across the light-years.

Kur: One of the nine planets of the Interworld Tree. A great storehouse of touchstones was found here; it was a center of Lifeweaver science and learning. Later it became a renegade world when the Kurian Lifeweavers began to use vital aura to extend their lives, touching off a civil war that has spilled over to Earth.

Kurians: Lifeweavers from the planet Kur who learned how to indefinitely lengthen their lives by absorbing vital aura. They are the true vampires of the New Order.

lifesign: Energy given off by any living thing in proportion to its size and sentience. The Reapers use it, in addition to their normal senses, to track their human prey.

Lifeweavers: The ancient race who discovered the old Pre-Entity Gates between the Nine Worlds.

Parang: A short, fat machete with a slight curve at the tip. Its three cutting edges can be used to skin game, chop down small tress, or even dig.

Pre-Entities: The Old Ones, a vampiric race that died out long before man walked the Earth. From their knowledge, the Kur learned how to become vampires by living off of vital aura.

Quislings: Humans who assist the Kurians in running the New Order.

Ravies: A virus the Kurians distributed to break up the social order of man, allowing them to take over more easily.

Reapers: The Praetorian Guard of the New Order, they are in fact avatars animated by their Master Vampire. They permit the reclusive Kurians to interact with humans and others, and more important, absorb the vital aura through a psychic connection with the avatar without physical risk. Reapers live off the blood of the victim, while the aura sustains the Master Kurian. Also known colloquially as Capos, Governors, Hoods, Rigs, Skulls, Scowls, Tongue-Tong, Creeps, Hooded Ones, and Vampires.

Touchstones: Record-keeping technology used by the Pre-Entities and discovered by the Lifeweavers. Touchstones hold anything from knowledge to memories; the data is accessible by a sentient being's touch. This can be dangerous for less-developed minds, such as humans'.

vital aura: An energy field created by a living creature. Sadly, humans are rich in it.

Wolves: The most numerous caste of the Hunters. Their patrols watch the no-man's-land between the Kurian Zone and the Free Territories, and they also act as guerrilla fighters, couriers, and scouts.

About the Author

E.E. Knight graduated from Northern Illinois University with a double major in history and political science, then made his way through a number of jobs that had nothing to do with history or political science. He resides in Chicago.